# The Tinker and the Gentleman

by Kathleen Burke

"The Tinker and the Gentleman," by Kathleen Burke ISBN 978-1-951985-32-5 (softcover); 978-1-951985-33-2 (eBook).

Published 2020 by Virtualbookworm.com Publishing Inc., P.O. Box 9949, College Station, TX 77842, US.

# Contents

Rodin on his famous sculpture of Balzac:

*One can find errors in my Balzac; the artist does not always attain his dream; but I believe in the truth of my principle... My principle is to imitate not only form but also life. I search in nature for this life and amplify it by exaggerating the hollows and lumps, to gain thereby more light, after which I search for a synthesis of the whole... I am now too old to defend my art, which has sincerity as its defense.*

# Prologue:
# October 28, 1980

THE HOUSE HUGGED ITS BACKDROP of trees and became smaller behind the woman. Humidity clung and high tides crashed as the hurricane's eye passed over. Reaching the walkway to the cliffs, she secured a scarf and headed towards the bodies.

No one could survive, let alone the two out there. Or perhaps decades ago they were doomed, and this night a termination to their meanderings.

She peered down the drop. They could never have one another in life. Had the storm brought them the freedom to touch, to finally claim one another, and the peace that had alluded them? Would there ever have been a way to achieve this joining outside of death's clutches?

Eyes stinging from the spray, she caught a glimpse of one. Bloodied and face up, the body slammed against a boulder, hair matted one instant, brushed aside the next, like seaweed. Retreating swells exposed another form, hugging the first in an embrace as real and alive as any could be, thwarting the force of nature in morbid unification.

Slippery rocks separated the woman from the scene below. A false move during descent could mean her own end. She could not, would not, attempt recovery. Her experience of New England storms told her the winds would soon shift from the north easterlies to less invasive ones. By then, help would arrive. The world would discover who had died.

The end had finally come. Its aftermath pinnacled in her mind. The dead would not soon be forgotten. The world would want to know why. She would face the torrent of inquiries from both sides of the Atlantic. After a while, the curious would disappear and her life would resume, this time so very different.

She turned towards the house. The boy, his silhouette against candle light, stood at the window. Already of regal composure, his gaze penetrated hers. Even from a distance, she knew he knew. He was waiting for her to tell him of the deaths.

For a moment she ushered herself to a private corner of her mind. She would, as best she knew how, introduce the child to the idea that he, of all others, benefited from tonight's event. He would take the reins of a powerful modern day empire—the wealth of so many, riches that tentacled to the core of major economies, the thrust of the coming decade.

She would tell him. He would react. Her job would be behind her. Yet even as she foresaw her own release she could not feel joy. She could only feel the presence of the child, the brush of the storm, the truth as it struck her consciousness like the waves, each time more profoundly. She and he, as though they were the only two on earth and the moment called for reverie, an appreciative nod to this pause, before the world would know.

She could spare him, could deny the reality, could take him in her arms and protect him. But no. To her own detriment, she had given for too long. Into the future, the young man would walk without her, to manage and grow into the adult he was destined to become. His years belied his abilities. Up to him now to prove he was capable and ready.

In this country, money demonstrated renown, the ability to transcend, the ownership of the four corners. It was the way, right or wrong. This boy would be ushered along a golden path crafted for him. All was his.

She would choose the road not the highway, opt for quiet rather than fanfare, calm over competition. At heart and through her own pain, she understood where her future lay. Embrace it she would, and release the child in the process.

One more look down. The face on the smaller one grinned, her upward curl genuine in an odd way, like the full moon one contemplates, its face bedecked with a smile that in reality is nothing but craters and barren land. A beautiful smile, one rarely expressed while alive. Perhaps, she had found her home at last. Perhaps she finally belonged. The smile, the livid sea, the man she embraced, the story they had written. Why not a smile?

The woman turned and made for the house. 3 AM in California, 11 in the United Kingdom, noon in France. She must get to those who must know. She shouldn't tarry. The boy waited.

♥ ♥ ♥

Clara tore at her hair and swore. The color was all wrong, too black, too old looking. She flipped on the television. Her hairdresser must squeeze her in today, for she had clients tonight, important ones, and they were in for a surprise. As a grin widened, she traced her breasts and thought of the lovely prospective employee she'd had the fortune to interview last night.

The sinewy legs, the long naturally auburn hair, the slight space between white and aligned teeth, Giselle was, simply put, an art form. An eighteen-year-old with a body like that and an accent from France was a sure hook into Clara's establishment, the most respected house in London. In short order, Giselle would be Clara's top lady.

The girl performed the most lascivious of acts right from the start, although she claimed to be inexperienced. Clara watched as the young woman snuggled out of her black skirt and revealed the skimpy underwear hinting at her treasures. Trying to suppress a wanton look in her own eyes, Clara watched the two men in the room who reveled in Giselle's movements. In physical fury, they reached for Giselle, her beckoning fingers, her soft skin, her swaying hips, demanding haven.

One man stripped and moved on top of her, inserting himself with the hard eagerness of his youth. Moaning slightly, she stroked the man's buttocks, whispered in his ear, and glanced suggestively at her onlookers. An ease and grace that bespoke a professional.

Oh, it had been the limit, especially when Giselle left him spent and breathless on the floor. Extending lacquer-tipped fingers, Giselle grasped Clara's wrist and pulled the older woman towards her. Gently she raised the silk gown overhead, ran hands down the behind and across the erect breasts of her intended employer. Contrary to typical business behavior, Clara let it happen, so enthralled with the performance, so titillated was she. Although approaching sixty, she was not about to refuse the come-on of so lovely a creature. In fact, she figured, the two combined—she with her maturity and experience, Giselle with her lusty freshness—would add to the array of sexual pleasures offered at Clara's.

After the customers left tonight, Clara thought, she would take Giselle aside and request a solo. She would ask her to strip, ask her to repeat the words, then demand an even more imaginative display of talent. The girl was already willing. After all, Clara was lonely at times, she too deserved the adventures her employees offered so many wealthy and worldly people. Why not the same for herself? It was time to sit back and relax. She'd worked hard her entire life, time to enjoy a sweet, soft body, the lithe movements, the caresses of a younger woman. It would be different and it would be fun. The delicious memory lingering, she decided to make Giselle her own right away.

The T.V. announcer detailed the horrors left in the wake of a hurricane along the northeast seaboard of the United States. In the state of Maine, the enclave of Glenrock was the hardest hit. Heart thumping, Clara turned up the volume and peeled eyes to the miles of damaged shoreline and downed structures. She pursed lips. This was the news she knew one day would reach her.

They were presumed dead the announcer said, as the location, the house, the shots of the two alive came and went. Clara neared the television and studied the photos, nodding slowly, understanding taking root. Then she turned off the television. Her head against the pillows of the settee, she stared out the window, hairdresser and last night's tryst forgotten.

It was finally over. Those two had seen it to the end, and would be remembered as one. They had transcended the world's dictates to pronounce themselves a unit, albeit in death, but a unit nonetheless. She grimaced. Too, they had succeeded in shaking up corporate America. How many, as the new day across the ocean commenced, would rush to their brokers and portfolio managers, concerned about the status of their bankrolls?

So many would worry, or go to extremes to try and predict the future, a future whose beginnings few could grasp as of this moment, and Clara was one of the few.

She tried to become introspective, feel something for the dead, but quickly shrugged away the tinge of regret. She always said whatever happened was meant to be. They ruined themselves and now it was over. She couldn't concern herself. Long ago, Clara had made a supreme effort to detach herself from them. She would not now welcome the memories easily, would not allow grief and mourning to rule the days to come. She had suffered enough.

In the still of the London morning, she nevertheless acknowledged one thing. She once adored them both and with the selfless gestures of one who gives all. But more important than those long ago days, she recovered from their inability to reciprocate. They were the non-givers, the selfish and egotistical ones. She overcame her pain, won a battle few choose to fight and regained her sense of self. Love had died a cruel death and now there was nothing, a blank. She lived each day, she derived pleasure, she stole moments of satisfaction. She lived empty but, she reminded herself, she survived. Gone emotion, gone feelings, forever dissolved the passions of a former time. She was released and free and it was, at best, a comfortable compromise.

A chuckle escaped at the renewed thought of the confusion surely ensuing stateside. Her faced paled as she thought of her own clients, most of whom reigned in the worlds of government and corporate finance. Some, many, would also be disturbed by this news. She frowned.

Standing, she reached for the phone to call friends in the City. They would know, would keep watch for her, and forewarn of the impact to the exchanges. She rang personal clients, two of London's top money men, and hung up satisfied.

What, she wondered, did the eighties hold for those who opted for love? How would they manage as the world eased its way towards the times destined now for sure? Shrugging, she picked up the phone. She was beyond all that. The eighties would be what they would be. Her destiny would coincide with the times. She was prepared.

That hairdresser must see her, he absolutely must. Especially now.

♥ ♥ ♥

Barbara de Roche placed the note on the counter, looked to the pool and the California sun having its way on the green-blue water. Tears surged again. Impossible. Her husband of all people, her new husband leaving her! Impossible!

She choked back sobs, shaking her head. How in the world could a man leave his wife the day after their wedding? What had she done? Last evening, hadn't he sworn devotion? How in the world could a late night phone call change all that?

Sadly, she knew him enough to know his note was not a cruel joke or a temporary diversion from his affections. Her fists slammed against the tabletop. Wrapped in the white silk robe she'd bought especially for him, she retreated to the chair, grabbing her head, overwhelmed by darting, delirious thoughts.

At eighteen, she was a product of her generation, a sweet woman ready to burst into the life of a good-looking, caring man. Innocent, attentive, and intelligent, she had everything a man could want without the usual simplistic self-centered airs of many her age. This was a nightmare, and it was happening to her, hours after her magical dream had come true.

She was so ready, so willing to be his wife forever. Her youth and ebullience had been the attraction initially, but he'd seen to her depth, he'd appreciated her mind as well. She was not a one-night stand nor was he the type for that. Why, then, why? She begged the morning skies for an answer. Yet, in the sparkling morning, the chirp of a bird washing itself in the pool was the lone reply.

She revisited the phone conversation, the soft tone coming from the other end. In spite of the news, Evan wore a familiar, eased expression. The caller shared a past with her husband. When his brow knit, he asked about the boy, then about the storm's course. He dressed and left. She'd been so tired, so accepting of his departure. After all, his job demanded such action at times. She drifted to sleep, as in love as always, as trusting as always.

But his note awakened her to the reality. She should have paid closer attention, should have scrutinized that perplexed yet assimilated look he wore. She reached again for the note.

> Barbara, I'm leaving. If you know what's good for you, you'll divorce me and take the house for yourself. It's over. I'm sorry. Evan

"Sorry! Sorry! Evan, how can sorry allow for this! There's no excuse, none!" She covered her face. This wasn't happening, it couldn't. Not Evan, not the man she loved till death.

# Part One: Summer Tears

*Where dips the rocky highland*
*Of Sleuth Wood in the lake,*
*There lies a leafy island*
*Where flapping herons wake*
*The drowsy water-rats.*
*There we've hid our fairy vats*
*Full of berries,*
*And of reddest stolen cherries.*
*Come away, O, human child!*
*To the woods and waters wild*
*With a fairy hand in hand,*
*For the world's more full of weeping than*
*you can understand*

The Stolen Child      by W. B. Yeats

# Chapter 1:
# June 1950

DINNER OVER AND THE CHILDREN settled in for the night, Alice Walsh exited the house, walked down the slope and over the cow rungs, settling on the stone wall that broke the waters of Galway Bay. Uncomfortable, she touched her belly and looked west.

The sun made its downward journey. She studied the surf as a bellowing cow reminded her of the next day's work. At dawn, the milking chores would wake the entire house here at their farm in the west of Ireland.

She hoped the baby wouldn't arrive early. There was too much work and Bob would be angered by the interruption. Plus, this being their eighth, he would no more take interest in it than the others, perhaps less. In his estimation, children were of no use until they could carry water or milk the animals anyway. Hadn't it taken him a year to take their first child Breeda in his arms? Even then the hug had only been for seconds. This arriving infant wouldn't change her husband's disposition towards children.

Eyes closed, the sun warming her lids, she imagined herself elsewhere, playing her solitary, guilt-inducing game. Her Catholic upbringing and rigid lifestyle left little time for dreams. However, Alice being Alice, from time to time defied the rigors of daily life to do as she was doing now.

Her mind did not roam freely. She chastised herself for the hundredth time for getting pregnant. This, of all things, was the worst possible scenario for a country wife. People would talk if the child did not resemble anyone. Worse, the child would also suffer, would forever be burdened with the unspoken condemnation of which locals were capable.

There was Bob to contend with, too. She recalled the night ten years prior when he approached her at a local dance. His tall angular body and washed brown hair had at first caused her to dismiss the inevitable—by marrying him she would be a farmer's wife, a woman with erased identity who would carry a great load but receive minimal reward for her efforts. She'd seen it too often to fool herself that she was not destined for the same with Bob Walsh. Her mother had settled, her aunts, too. No one left the village of Kinemmaera. All chose the associated, predicable, and limiting lifestyle of their predecessors.

She fell into his arms anyway, in spite of her good grades and excellent prospects for university, in spite of her desire to escape the town, in spite of her understanding of what marriage brought a woman who chose to remain. She did it because she was a romantic eighteen-year-old with wide hazel eyes and thick brown hair, a woman on whom many a young man had lingered his gaze. She enjoyed her budding beauty, loved the fun of garnering attention at the local dances, reveled in her emerging sensuality as she approached the age of majority.

Plus marriage meant release. She would no longer be attached to the O'Learys. She would be a Walsh and therefore of a different family. She could get away from the babysitting, the bickering sisters and brothers, the struggle for space. Her family was no better or worse than anyone else and therefore had to contend with the region's borderline poverty.

To his credit, Bob had built a house next door to his parents, tended herds of his own, and made steps towards independence. As important, Bob never took to the drink until the day's work was done. Never did one see Bob Walsh in the pub before nightfall and, those times he did make for a jar, he headed home before ten.

So, the night he asked her, she accepted, figuring the chance would only come along once and she had to decide in a hurry. Rushed to the back of her mind were thoughts of travel to Dublin for school, a job at the bank with a flat in Galway, or testing the waters with men outside her sphere of reference. She settled and her days, by and large, relaxed into the predictable.

Their farm overlooked the bay with a commanding view of the adjacent county. Around the corner and down the road, at the deepest inlet of Galway Bay, sat Kinemmaera town. A village of two hundred fifty, a single row of two-story whitewashed and color-coated buildings divided it in two. On one side, the quays, moored boats, and a smattering of homes. On the other, a handful of shops with bright blue or green shutters and bicycles parked at front doors. Beyond, farmlands and fields extended for miles and ended at the Cliffs of Moher and the outlands of northern county Clare. There were two pubs, a restaurant open in summer catering to English and Americans, O'Ryan's grocery, the post office, and Byrne's butcher. Where the road forked to the southwest, wild flowers and graves with stone Celtic crosses formed the setting for St. Michael's church and rectory. An ideal retreat for a Dublin writer or visiting American, it was a town where people struggled but where they maintained cheery dispositions in spite of the clouds and rains that arrived regularly from the Atlantic.

Her security a given, Alice Walsh nonetheless grew distracted. She dreamed of change, of moving on, but by then there was no way out. Bob stuck to a schedule of tilling fields and tending to cows all the while insuring the family had food on the table and was properly clothed. Four years following their wedding day, she had given birth to a daughter, twin boys, and a third boy. With the demands of motherhood, Alice's jaunty demeanor gave way to distracted expressions and mechanical gestures.

Bob was focused and directed, predictable and sturdy. The town murmured approval when the Walsh family appeared at mass each Sunday, what with the coiffed locks of the children, the pressed shirts, Alice in her tidy hat and gloves, and Bob with his tie. After service, they joined others at the pub, the women settling into the snug and gossiping about this and that, the men standing around the bar exchanging opinions about the races of the night before or the state of the ever-evolving government in Dublin.

Alice played by the rules until one day, in a spate of defiance, she left the town on holiday without Bob. It was five years into her marriage and she was pregnant with the fourth child. "I'm going to visit Patricia in Dublin. I'll take the children," she said.

Bob looked at her as if to a ghost. "You'll not, not when I need help. It's foolish."

She rolled her eyes. The haying was complete. She'd already figured his reaction, already planned for the best possible time. Still, she'd never seen his brows lower that way, never heard his voice crack with such disapproval. She trembled but stood her ground. "It's only for a little while. I'll be taking the train back

Monday week, I'm using the birthday money from Aunt Beattie."

Unable to support a woman with her own mind, Bob scowled, scuffed outside, and headed towards the fields.

Familiar with his darker side, she watched him go. He would hold a grudge long after her return, punish her in off-handed ways and when she was at her most vulnerable. She would have to suffer in silence, for they never confronted, never held discussions of any length. Like everyone, their lives followed a book of rules written long ago, men with the upper hand and women a necessary, sometimes bothersome, accouterment. If Alice went, she would suffer his wrath.

She went anyway and had the time of her life. Her friend Patricia showed her Dublin's rough-shod and frank beauty—the Liffey River at night, the stately Four Courts, Trinity and its yards, St. Stephen's Green. Alice basked in the pleasure of walks in the park, dinners with Patricia's friends, and drawn-out teatimes. Even with the children in tow, she managed to revel in the sights, the people, the window-shopping, and the mirth and music in some of Ireland's oldest pubs. When she returned to Kinemmaera, she vowed to maintain a yearly travel schedule.

Throughout the town, however, it was whispered that Bob couldn't control his wife and this emasculated him in the most humiliating way. Alice began to attract odd glances from ladies who would never dare set foot beyond the safe reaches of the west coast, let alone venture to places unknown.

The Walsh family was set aside. Still politely acknowledged in public, their presence nevertheless gave rise to rumination. No one let on aloud that the Walshs were about the closest thing to living in sin one could find but, in fact, most believed they were. If Bob couldn't put Alice in her rightful place, there was something odd about them.

What social life they had ended. Alice tended to mothering, Bob took care of the fields and they drifted as far apart as two people could while still living under one roof. Catholicism forbade divorce or even separation—except the one Bob chose to visit upon his wife.

He ignored her. She was less than the furniture, she was a maid and servant. He no longer looked into her eyes, no longer gave her the odd appreciative nod. Over was the affection—if one were to call it that—that Bob once bestowed, except in bed. When his urges took hold, he roughly pressed her to his body. She didn't dare say no, took his advances in stride and, once the grunting was over, tried to forget the escapade ever happened. During those moments, they were no more than dogs or pigs mating because the season had arrived.

Alice continued to bring children into the world, and acquiesced to Bob's advances, but never once did she capitulate on her yearly trips.

And so it was that eight months before, in the spirit of previous adventures, she'd taken a boat ride and train to London and enjoyed her week. Alone in the largest of cities, herself for company, she met the stranger with whom she shared her body and, as it happened, her entire being.

The man, his deep smile, his broad flat visage, the bluest eyes. Her nubile body and pale skin contrasted against brown hair and a nearly clairvoyant gaze, all bespoke a woman of the Celtic lands, an intriguing and beguiling beauty, a lure unique to itself. And, for the first time, she felt his desire evincing not only for her looks, but for her ringing laugh, her ease and ebullience. Almost instantly, they shared a calming space that required no words. She let him take her in his arms, she let him lead the way.

They made love into the small hours. She wanted him, and told him so, fell hungrily in love with his caressing voice, his sure grip, his fit body. Under him she felt no pain or shame. In the warmth of his penetration, she discerned the secret of genuine sharing, and wanted more and only more.

He had the savoir-faire of a man well-travelled and accustomed to having many women. She didn't care. Her wonder directed her actions, and she loved him in ways she never dared try before. In the fluid, contemplative aftermath of love-making, their exhaustion bespoke a completion of such immense proportion, that its contours could not be discerned.

Instead, when he whispered words suggesting forever affection, she delighted and collapsed, weak yet in happy accord with imagery that would prove illusory but that in the moment carried them both. She was in love.

It was at that interval, when they shared from the deepest part of themselves, that his seed was planted. For the rest of her life, she would know those seconds represented the totality of living for which she'd always yearned.

With the new day, like a perplexing yet charming dream, he was gone. She made for the train station and Ireland, renewed, pregnant for sure, but blissful and serene, fixing on a memory that would bestow upon her a cantankerous energy she would at once fight and embrace in the weeks and years to come.

Now she prepared her body and herself for the child who was not of Bob's tribe, who was of her but also of someone else, someone far away, someone this baby would never know. For Alice, in her Catholic way and with the resign of a prisoner, sensed the inevitable. The child would bear the sore mark of an illicit night of love. A string of predictable non-events would order her life on this edge of the earth.

As the purples and golds made a resplendent panorama over the bay, she prayed, "Virgin Mother of God, I beg forgiveness and ask you one thing, that the child resemble me. Oh, that this baby resemble myself!"

Night drew in shades of grey and black. Alice made the sign of the cross and set off for the house. A final look behind her and then upwards to the lone star that shone in the heavens.

♥ ♥ ♥

An ocean away in America, another child was born. Bundled in a hospital blanket and snuggled into her mother's arms, she studied her parents, an awareness of one with great wisdom.

"She looks like you," Régine Mallord said to her husband Nate.

"With those eyes, she could be you, too," he said, caressing his wife's arm. The motion said so much about his happiness and pride, yet also his devotion to the woman who brought their child into the world.

Régine smiled, tired but with gratitude. Their years of waiting had paid off with a gorgeous and healthy six-pound baby. "Laurence," she whispered to the child. "Your name is Laurence, ma petite. Tu vas avoir une vie, chérie!"

It always happened when Régine was thrilled beyond herself, the French inevitably spilled out. Although a four-year resident of the States, she still relied on her native tongue to express intimate feelings. And now, she'd reached a moment like no other. After trying so hard, a baby had graced their world. She looked into Nate's eyes and gave him her languorous, relaxed blink that had first taken his breath away one summer afternoon in France.

He responded with a kiss, for who could ignore the almond-eyed, sculpted face of his wife? It was, after all, what had drawn him to her in the first place. He, the down-to-earth man, the promising marine biologist chosen to join Jacques-Yves Cousteau on a trip to the depths of the ocean, had reached the limits of logic on seeing Régine for the first time.

During the war, Nate had excelled as an expert in oceanography and had been of value during submarine maneuvers in the Pacific. Once home, he continued to mine the sea's secrets and gained a grant through the U. S. government for joint ventures with France. He had journeyed there to arrange the year long trip with Monsieur Cousteau's team, and met Régine in the process.

She'd been prancing about with friends along one of Brittany's reclusive beaches, naked to the waist and oblivious to the curious regards sent her way by Nate and his associates. Her gaze met his in a coy, impish fashion. A devilish grin crossed her lips and she turned from him in a semi-embarrassed way that, rather than hold him at bay, forced him to seek her out. The tanned ingénue, her free-flowing hair, the girlish shrugs and giggles had him lingering at her side, following her as she collected shells into a bucket.

She led him to her parents and, during introductions, quickly covered her exposed body while waiting for the parental go-ahead.

Madame and Monsieur de Long had critically assessed the gentleman at their daughter's side, had asked the predictable questions—age, background, intentions. When they discovered Nate's affiliation with Cousteau as well as his elite education and American nationality, they broke into smiles and invited him to lunch.

A four-hour meal ensued that almost cost Nate his job as he'd later had to scurry back to his hotel and make apologies to work associates. But it had all been worth it. Although Régine was of a lineage that destined her to be of the greatest families in France, Monsieur de Long had allowed a single further adventure between this American and his daughter. The war was finally over. Why not allow this distraction for a time?

Nate and Régine commenced a long-distance romance that would terminate eighteen months later in a magnificent Paris wedding. The stunning heiress downplayed her name and all it represented, favoring instead the studious, dedicated American with dark eyes and hair. They made way for the States as soon as the honeymoon was over.

On outer Cape Cod in Massachusetts, Nate built a small grey-slated house facing the ocean and massive tumbling sand dunes. The wide and mostly deserted beaches ran for some thirty miles along the peninsula, giving them seclusion and a romantic setting. There, Régine adjusted while Nate proceeded with his study of marine biology at the Woods Hole Institute some miles up the shore.

Together they created a stir. Both with arresting looks, both intelligent and worldly, both striking a magical pose at any occasion. News travelled fast and, though Nate would have preferred to keep his wife on the Cape, they were more often than not called upon to be present at Franco-American affairs in Boston and New York. Régine, already a name in international circles, introduced her husband and proudly watched as he became as much of an attention gatherer as she. They stole the pages of gossip columnists and journalists and, everywhere along the Eastern seaboard, upper-crust society followed them.

In their own way regal, they basked in the renown one moment then disappeared to Cape Cod the next where Nate could pursue his work and Régine could attend to their home and hopefully produce the child they both wanted.

It was during lovemaking they created their most cherished memories, for Régine quickly dropped her virginal ways and fell into the habit of seducing Nate. Every day was a chance to try something new. She would order up panties from Paris with slits in ingenious places and, regardless of the gale-force wind and blowing sand, wore them to meet him at the door. Or, she'd feign sleep when he arrived late and wait until he crawled under the covers to snap on the light and reveal her body in studded beads and clinging silk that covered only her private parts. Following a dance across the bedsheets with an inviting pucker of her lips and a touch of her hand to her curves, she would peel off the rest and give herself to him in a luscious, unfolding act with the right dose of demureness. She rapidly learned the secrets of Nate's libido and revealed herself in ways he had only imagined in his most outlandish of dreams. She was a torrent of sensuality.

In their home by the sea, the couple engaged in their every whim when it came to sharing. In the dead of winter when the balmy Bermuda breezes eased up the coast, they walked naked along the sand, lowering their bodies and performing quick and impassioned love. In the still of a moon-lit night while the fire crackled or in the breeze of an autumn morn, they'd find one another and move towards the ever-real, ever-rich sharing they'd come to take for granted.

But a child never came. For all her efforts, the one thing Régine could not control was reproduction, and this caused growing concern. She took to reading on the subject, consulting with Boston's best doctors, even spending much money calling relatives in France for advice and comfort. Unsettling though it was, Nate reassured her that all would come in time. So, she tried to focus on what she had rather than what she did not.

Nevertheless, it would be two years before she conceived, a time Régine would try and rationalize as one during which she was deliriously happy. She dismissed those times she had slipped into an unfamiliar and nasty mood accompanied by the sense of abandonment she'd never experienced before in her life.

Her dark humors more frequent, she spent money foolishly. Once, when she made arrangements to attend a gala affair in New York at the St. Regis, Nate reminded her their budget was not the same as her father's. These eruptions forced her to contend with her situation in ways she was unaccustomed to—alone and without the accessibility of family.

But all was forgotten the day she learned of her pregnancy, a day they both celebrated with a bottle of champagne and dinner at a fine fish restaurant near Yarmouth. Once again the blissfully happy couple, they figured names, planned the child's bedroom, announced their news to everyone, and relegated their free evenings to staying at home so Régine could take care of herself and their new baby.

And so it was that Laurence came into the world, the child of a beautiful, cultured mother of means and a handsome, dedicated father who grew to love his daughter like no other.

As Régine fought sleep and the nurse entered to take the baby from her arms, Nate reached to the child and cradled her for the first time. He peered into the eyes, studied their depths, and blinked in surprise at the miracle he beheld. He could not suppress a boyish squeal of glee at the bond that obviously was extending at this moment.

"She knows me!" he laughed, touching her cheek and whispering into her face.

Régine smiled, and reached a hand towards her husband. So absorbed was he in the child, he didn't respond. She pressed fingers into his arm. He continued to focus on Laurence. Régine released her grasp and lay back, a knot tightening across her already spent body. Something hit her then, a notion that their story-book existence was threatened. At the same time, another call from within encouraged her to widen her embrace and become more inclusive, inviting, to share her man with another.

She forced eyes shut, tried to quell the growing sense that, for all the energy spent to bring this child about, for all her work to win love and attention from Nate, she was separate and apart from an emerging partnership this night— the love between a father and his daughter.

To herself, in the tiniest of whispers, and in French of course, she wished she'd had a boy.

Alice puffed out a plea to her sister Romney then lay back to let the contraction have its way. "I can't!" she screamed, her focus on the ceiling. She gripped the rough wool blanket and squeezed eyes shut, lips moving in prayer.

The baby was coming, several weeks early and in the middle of the night. Romney left to fetch Beth Flaherty who had some experience with premature births. Bob, in the adjoining room, continued his sleep with the children rather than witness the event. It had always been his way, to absent himself during these times, even more so now.

Nine-year-old Breeda appeared, extended a hand towards her mother's sweaty one and gripped as Alice succumbed to another contraction. "It's Okay, Mama, it's Okay. I've set the water..." The pale black-haired child watched as the woman on the bed calmed slightly.

"Thanks ever so much, lovie," Alice said, "It's ever so good of you, ever so good..."

Breeda's brow furrowed as Alice collected her forces to contend with another spasm that followed the previous by seconds. Breeda could tell this was not a good sign and went to the front of the house to see if help approached. Beyond the lace curtains, in the still July night, with the bay reflecting a midnight glow, a darkening line of clouds hovered over the horizon. Biting her lip, she returned to her mother.

On entering the stuffy room, her eyes widened in shock to see her mother's legs spread, the wet, bloody heaving place between them giving signs of a head coming through. Alice grunted and pushed as Breeda stood frozen in the doorway. Her mother's body pushed and thumped, wrestling with the life that made way into the world. Growing faint, she forced herself to her mother's side. But the blood, the cries, the base ways of her mother frightened her and she burst into sobs, running instead to her father.

Bob Walsh drew Breeda near. "Not to worry, not to worry," he said in a detached tone. "She'll make it, your mother. It's not to worry." Breeda clutched her father and tried to suppress sobs, but made no move towards the bedroom.

At the same time that footsteps pattered up the front walk, lamb-like cries rang throughout the cottage. Alice had given birth.

When Romney and Beth got to the room, the baby, squirming in a pool of blood, remained attached by the chord, naked and angry rose-pink.

"God love her," Beth whispered as she hurried to the kitchen for water and cloths. Romney grasped the child and held her as Alice peered between her legs. The sisters glanced at one another, then Alice lay back, unable to contain the tears.

"A girl," Romney whispered as Beth severed the chord.

A girl it was, with a round head, fully formed body, large hands and feet. The head was without hair, the eyes shut tight, and she cried still. In whispers and with deft movements, Romney and Beth washed Alice and the baby, tidied the room, and prepared the child for her mother's breast. Alice drifted to sleep.

Romney held the child and watched her sister for signs of waking. Romney O'Leary, Alice's daft sister, the woman who lived alone and who took to odd behavior like night walks and talking to herself, had always made a point of presiding over the births of her nieces and nephews. A reclusive spinster, Romney spoke Gaelic most often, wandered in her own bubble of disorientation, and had never quite made it as an accepted member of the community. At its periphery, she remained harmlessly aloof and distant to the town's affairs, opting instead for her one room chalet or treks along the jagged coast. Wild like the weather and unpredictable like the sea, Romney was left alone by others, which was best for her and best for everyone else.

Tonight, her steel grey eyes bore down on her sister who, for the first time in all the births she'd accomplished, had no interest in taking the baby in her arms. Romney looked down at the child, and understood why.

The resemblance was neither Walsh nor O'Leary. Inches from the baby's face, Romney scrutinized the new arrival. She patted the eyelids, traced the line of the little mouth, but refrained from further attention like cuddling or cooing.

A giggle escaped her lips as Alice came to. Extending the bundle, Romney studied her sister, as if trying to divine why this night differed from the previous first nights of birth. The baby, too, looked to her mother, towards the clean sheets and the hair splayed across the pillow, the white face.

The long term effects of what happened next were anyone's guess. Alice did not reach for the child, did not ask about fingers and toes, did not open her nightgown to give milk. She turned away from the child, and cried hard tears that bespoke regret, sadness, and remorse.

"The truth will be known, the truth will be known, one day, it will be known." As she mouthed the words, a picture of the baby was branded to Alice's mind. The child had the same nose, the same flat wide forehead, the same wondrously incomprehensible eyes of her father.

♥ ♥ ♥

In the four months that followed, Alice lived a hellish existence. The demands of an infant added to her burdens, and she found herself greatly weakened. From dawn until her head hit the pillow, an aching sensation overtook her body. Suffering a fever with no name, she sweat, shivered, and lost weight. Autumn's arrival didn't help, as the coast bore the brunt of the wettest weather and most severe winds, all of which made the cottage damp and uncomfortable. She had to force herself to move. The daily chores needed to be done—feeding the children and animals, tending to the peat fire, making due with the menu of potatoes, soup and occasional slab of ham. At twenty-eight, she looked double her age and the wrinkles that used to enhance her smile now dug deep into her opaque skin.

Bob didn't care. Already suspicious about the child, he stopped sleeping in the same room and chose instead the floor by the kitchen fire. They didn't speak, or spoke through the children, and Bob grew even more resentful. The dark days and foul weather didn't help.

The baptism of the child proved an unfortunate affair for what was usually a town-wide and joyous event. By then, the child—who would take the name Claire Mary—had sprouted a head of hair like no other, wiry blonde locks that sprung forth and felt like wool. As was the custom, the villagers gathered around the font inside St. Michael's baptistery as Father Flynn welcomed a new member into God's faith. But, as he poured water over the forehead and as Bob and Alice Walsh feigned pride, murmurs rose at the sight of the navy eyes and frizzed locks. How could it be? Both parents had the straight hair of their respective families and, through the years, not an O'Leary or Walsh had produced an offspring with such a head! No, this was strange, a debate for all forthcoming events, but out of Bob and Alice Walsh's earshot. Something was about with this child.

The priest continued his recitation, Breeda and an uncle John stood as godparents, and none too soon the ceremony was over. Whispers circulated about this brood living on the hill. There lurked about them a strangeness that meant they were to be avoided— politely of course, but avoided. Too, one could tell by the sinister look in Bob Walsh's eyes, that this was the last time one of his children would be baptized. There would be no further births into the family.

More unfortunate than the spell in church was later that night when Bob Walsh descended the cliffs near the house, Alice in tow. The sea frothed and the winds howled. Pounding his fist into her already hollowed face, he screeched.

"No child of mine, she isn't!" he screamed. He drew her up from the prostrate position he'd thrown her to and slammed a cold, rough hand into her already bloodied mouth. "You're full of sin, you whore, you damned cow, you wicked piece of shit!"

Alice let the blows take their toll on her already emaciated and defeated person. What Bob didn't know was that the physical pain was a mere distraction. Well before this night, sadness and hurt had corroded her heart and created in her a walking phantom who didn't care if she lived or died. As the sea swelled at their feet, she thought, "Let him kill me. It's over for me anyhow."

He left her, her back pinned to a sharp rock, her body maimed. He would have thrown her to sea, so bedeviled with shame and anger was he, except for the appearance of Romney at the hill's crest, who gave Bob a steely, chilling regard as she descended towards her sister.

A week passed and Romney tended to Alice, whose bruises mended as she regained her bearings. But Alice never went home. She slipped away, her departure time known only to Romney, her destination a guess to all. Alice Walsh left the town, left her children and the shame, for it was her only option. The people of Kinemmaera could be like the weather, unforgiving and relentless. She couldn't bear the guilt, had already served enough time, and didn't want her children to suffer. She would leave this spit of God's earth for another life, somewhere.

♥ ♥ ♥

As 1950 drew to a close, the world recovered from one war by moving towards other conflicts, and by forging economies that would redefine traditions and norms. An ocean apart, two baby girls progressed with distinctly different lives. Laurence, surrounded with bounty and joy, claimed her marine heritage from the outset. Claire, of what could only be called reckless beginnings, could stake no foundation, and knew struggle as her only certainty.

# Chapter 2:
# Summer 1958, Paris

GILES DE ROCHE RE-READ THE NEWS announcing the imminent return of de Gaulle to power. Relief cleansed his brow. De Gaulle was back, Algeria moved towards independence, and the French could now secure themselves alongside other world leaders. An industrialist and descendant of the family whose name he bore, Giles had been waiting for this moment since the end of the Second World War. France had taken her time adjusting. Indeed, she still delayed the inevitable rapprochement with the Germans on mutual coal interests. Entrenched in international disputes of no profitable consequence, the French slumped into fiscal disarray. His long-time friend de Gaulle would take the reins of the country and resume efforts he and others had started even before the war—grand economic and scientific advances befitting this country of energy and intellect.

Pauline de Roche walked in the room and embraced Giles. Reveling in the touch of his wife, he looked up from his desk, to the courtyard and gardens and, beyond, to the Eiffel Tower.

"Ma chérie, we've finally reached the best place of all!" he exclaimed, pointing to the paper and squeezing her hand. "Now, the de Roches can move beyond the corners of our Hexagon!"

Pauline nuzzled his cheek. His exquisite wife was already as happy as any woman could be. Of a well-established family herself, Pauline was content to be Giles's wife, living in the chic sixteenth arrondissement with its associated catered life.

A Bardot-beauty in her own day, Pauline still commanded attention when gracing any affair. Her blonde hair curled professionally about the top of her head, her limpid brown eyes, the slight yet sensuous body gave away nothing of her advancing years. Only the tiniest of laugh wrinkles lent a mature depth to her gaze. Pauline was forty-eight and didn't mind saying, for she knew she possessed the eternal qualities of a woman who cared for herself, of a woman who drank regularly from the cup of love. She believed love was all. Love made the old younger, the young more beautiful, the world a happier place. No one was happier than she, especially in the arms of her too serious but seductively handsome husband.

"We do alright!" she exclaimed, toying with Giles's thick black hair. "In fact, I know you'll call me a pest but I do want to discuss the vacation. The children and I go to the shore in less than a month and you and I have yet to decide when you'll be visiting! These things matter, too."

He smiled and turned to her, gazing at her double-breasted Chanel suit, to the lines of her hips and thighs, and drew her close. He planted a kiss then returned to the mound of papers on his desk. "We shall, Paul," he said, using her pet name, "I suggest you plan tomorrow night's dinner Chez Bernard, for the two of us. Then, we'll have time to talk at length." With that, he submerged himself in his work.

Pauline studied the line of his neck and the top of his head, then placed her hand on his shoulder, gently massaging the muscles under his suit. The newspaper stared back at her from one side of the desk. She scanned the headline story of de Gaulle's intended reorganization of the Assemblée, the pomp and flutter at the Élysée Palace and elsewhere about Paris. Settling into a chair, she flicked on the light and turned to the film notices. Those times he chose to occupy himself with business, movies replaced her passion for Giles.

Film had captivated everyone on Pauline's side of the family. Ahead of their time, the Duviviers ignored the bourgeois belief popular during the 1920s that cinema was solely for the working class and intellectuals. Her mother and father had seen to it the family took in any new film, both French and non-French, and encouraged their children to immerse themselves in themes, plots, and characterization. During Pauline's youth, she watched with awe the action-packed silent films of René Clair, Louis Feuillade, and Abel Gance as well as the quality expressionist works of the German studios and the feature films out of Russia.

Like her mother, Pauline displayed an early preference for the American films and spent hours viewing two and three times a Hollywood production. When, in 1927, the first sound film, *The Jazz Singer*, finally made its way from the U. S. to French shores, Pauline was hooked with the fever shared by movie fans around the world.

It had been why, during the desperate days of the late 1920s and early 1930s, when the world faced stock market failures, the Duviviers had invested in France's efforts to equip production studios with sound technology, so the French could enjoy French as well as English talkies. Joining with the Gaumont organization, her father modernized venues in an effort to outshine the Americans when it came to sound. But, because of the precarious state of the world economy and America's domination of the market, the efforts proved for naught. Much of the Duvivier fortune was lost to the American studio Paramount. That company bought up French properties and used them first as multi-lingual production facilities then, once dubbing grew in popularity, as places to churn out as many language versions of the same film as they could. This financial disappointment took its toll on Monsieur Duvivier who turned his attention from film to other, more familiar but less daunting, challenges within France.

Nevertheless, during the 1920s and because of the encouragement of her family, Pauline developed permanently star-struck eyes and took to joining her friends any chance she could for an afternoon at the movies. She dreamed of acting, listened eagerly to friends who knew this star or that movie magnate, read and re-read critical reviews and, above all, anything emanating from the States. Although empathizing with her father's woes, the die had been cast long before in the heart of Pauline. A lover of movies she would be no matter what. Her affair with film endured on a more secretive scale, into the early years of her marriage and long after her father relinquished interest in the field.

One time while still a schoolgirl, she visited a friend and chanced to be under the same roof as the woman who was to become one of the greats of French acting. Of similar age to Pauline, Danielle Darrieux walked into the salon to discuss her role in an upcoming production. Pauline was spellbound by the intensity, the dedication, the soulfulness of the exquisitely attractive Darrieux. With a nod to Pauline on introduction, the actress displayed the same detached yet effervescent qualities that would bring her to life on the wide screen and to millions of French people. Even then Pauline had seen the promise in the comédienne's eyes and, once Danielle grew in fame and popularity, Pauline would enthusiastically recall their brief encounter.

Pauline was never to become a famous actress nor even a middling one for that matter. Her background, supported by her father who now saw film as a debauchery and scam, was meant to prepare her for a partnership with a man of the business world, someone who revolved within sectors that excluded film. The Duviviers groomed her for the hand of Giles de Roche. When finally Giles obtained his degree from École Polytechnique and readied to take over the de Roche empire, he took Pauline for his wife.

She didn't protest for she loved the man. Her life was full and satisfying. How difficult to complain in post-World War I France with world-wide financial disaster looming, all the while she claimed membership in one of the oldest and wealthiest of French families! Pauline was not a fool. She was thankful for her position and, in time, her role as mother. Shortly after their marriage in 1931, she gave birth to a baby girl.

Pauline's days of movie madness mostly forgotten, no one took note when she suggested the child be called Danielle. After all, it was an acceptable name, a French name, a name with taste that went well with de Roche. But Pauline took private pleasure when pronouncing it for the simple and somewhat selfish reason she'd named her after the woman of her most cherished of memories—Danielle Darrieux.

At the sight of her twenty-seven-year-old daughter who entered the room, Pauline returned to the present. "I was just thinking about you, darling Danielle!" She leant her cheek to receive her daughter's kiss.

"Mama, we must talk!" Danielle said, quickly tapping her father's shoulder then sitting on the foot rest near Pauline. "It's about the vacation. You know father has me watching the coal processing works near Alsace. Well, it seems there might be renewed activity on the German side."

Giles de Roche turned his head towards the young woman. "They finally want to do business with us?" he asked.

"Yes, well, there's talk anyway," she said, outlining the recent efforts of German companies to better cooperate with the French along their respective borders and in industries they shared. "We've known it was coming, Papa, it was only a matter of time. I think, rather than go to Brittany with Mama and Evan, I should take a trip to the operations in the east, don't you?"

Pauline smiled. "I'll not stand in your way, chérie, if that's what you've determined to be best. Of course, you must go. You can meet us later, we'll be on the coast the entire summer. Your job matters, too. I understand."

Danielle then joined her father at his desk. The two weighed Danielle's strategy, developed during her stay in Alsace.

That was her daughter, thought Pauline, her father's child, the budding professional who had already made her mark on the de Roche affairs. In coincidence with her studious ways at school and her serious mannerisms about the house, Danielle had grown into the business person her father had always hoped for. Pauline, as a direct result of her exposure to the free-thinking, sometimes rash and always bold women of the screen, was a feminist well before the trend set in. She encouraged her daughter to help Giles, to learn the ropes, to become the next generation of successful magnates.

Danielle had not disappointed them. Her wide brow, piercing black eyes, straight evenly cropped hair, and no-nonsense movements conjured the words striking rather than pretty, male rather than female. At affairs of state and business functions and next to the classic good looks of her parents, she struck an unusual pose. Yet at the same time no one could deny her de Roche lineage. Most important, her misplaced appearance took a back seat once she settled in front of a slide rule and financial statements. The woman was a whiz at figuring key elements of any given operation and how things could be improved from a profitability, cash-flow, and operations point of view. Even as a child, Danielle had followed her father's work day and this had paid off by the time her formal education ended. Few women of her years could boast her grasp of the business. Like a sixth sense, she used her abilities to the max and it soon became evident she was destined to follow the path of her father.

At first, Giles hesitated, knowing well how the male-oriented community operated and how a woman, although not ignored in France, would be challenged circulating in the world of old money, contacts, and protocols. But Danielle had repeatedly proven herself. Each time a board meeting came up, she would devise an ingenious solution to the problem at hand, with numbers to back her theories and the suggestion she herself take the risk involved. Enough times the same scenario had repeated itself so that, in the few years after she became an employee of de Roche Frères, she was solidly immersed. She took her place rightfully and fully at her father's side and won respect and admiration all around.

Pauline had breathed a sigh of relief. Confident in her daughter and hoping Danielle would attain her wish to become a force within de Roche Frères, Pauline nevertheless had her own reasons for wanting to see Danielle succeed. First, the Depression had wreaked havoc on the French economy. It was time for fresh faces and new ideas, youth who would dare to bring France and her products into the arena of competition and advancement on a world-wide scale. Hardly an expert in international affairs, Pauline still read enough and heard enough to know one thing, her country men and women hesitated to go beyond the borders of 'La Belle France' to profit.

The French tended to keep to themselves, a strange and contrary habit Pauline had noticed even as a child. They projected a sense of superiority coupled with an undercurrent of suspicion about the rest of the world. In business, it was best to work with national concerns and keep a watchful yet wary eye on what transpired elsewhere in Europe and the United States. The international piece of the business puzzle was to be questioned, argued against and even dismissed.

Pauline had experienced this most viscerally in her father who, upon losing out to the American studios, developed a fiercely xenophobic attitude, especially towards the United States. This impacted his decisions and, in the end, was to cause his downfall. Pauline watched him turn from a man who believed in the future and wide-scale expansion, to one who mistrusted greatly, who held onto the simplest of things, like his pocket change, as if to say, "It's me, it's what I have. No one, no bank can better manage it!"

This particular attitude had no place in Pauline's psyche. How could the United States or any country for that matter be so bad? The people she saw in the American-produced films were like her, searching for life's answers, falling hopelessly in love, growing through their pain. Plus, these very countries had only recently joined in a superhuman effort to dismantle the Third Reich. How quickly we forget, she was want to say each time she and Giles entered this line of conversation.

*The Tinker and the Gentleman*

Giles claimed the U. S. had a cavalier and puerile approach to challenges, that they raced into things without thinking them through, that they wasted money on efforts like marketing and sales promotions rather than detailed studies of product specifications, market conditions, and profitability. Pauline could nevertheless rationalize all that. She, too, watched the States but from a different angle. Her sensibilities were more often directed to the human side of things, the emotional reasons behind motivation. As a young woman she watched the Germans rough up her own parents, kill one of her aunts, and destroy much of her country. She prayed her Giles would return from the army in one piece, and so had ideas about the Americans, too.

They had not seen war's devastation on their own turf for almost a century. They couldn't understand the sense of desperation and loss at the sight of troops marching in to claim one's land, the house you called home, indeed the people you loved. The French had suffered in ways no American of this generation could imagine. Let there be this caution, let there be this wariness, for the French had seen much and were tired. Better to be cautious than foolish, better to protect than share. Pauline understood.

Still more important, she was of France and embraced her country's assets. Well-traveled, she knew the French possessed unique and unsurpassed qualities—their ability to create sumptuous and unforgettable cuisine, their forging of technical ideas that led to revolutionary inventions, their artistic marks that promoted a view towards fresh sensitivities regarding light and motion. France had her troubles but she rightfully claimed her glories as well.

For all her thought, however, Pauline was no more about to interfere on a grand scale with her husband's business choices, nor her country's political path, than

29

the next person. She was who she was—a thoughtful sideliner and happily so. In Giles she sensed an intense interest coupled with this same hesitancy about overdoing things in the international arena.

Thanks to Danielle, whose attitude was more open, more accepting of change, more inclined towards merging with the global scene, Pauline foresaw positive days ahead for de Roche Frères. She prayed that endless success be bestowed upon her daughter. Since Danielle chose the business world, she should reap the rewards accordingly.

But the second reason went deeper than facts and rational thought, to the core of Pauline's belief system, indeed to the core of her being. The second reason was her son Evan.

Evan de Roche, her eight-year-old wonder, her late-in-life child had brought more happiness, more peace, more fulfillment than anyone could possibly imagine. Evan, with the dark hair of his father and his mother's light-filled eyes, the unusual turned up nose, the un-de Roche like quality of dreaming and leaning into heart-felt tendencies. Evan, the boy who differed from other de Roches, even his peers from school. Evan, the love of her life and the one she hoped might choose the career she had not pursued, the career that could formalize his already notable leanings towards feeling and emotion— the life of an actor.

Although unexpected, once the baby boy was presented to Pauline that summer eve in 1950, she knew she held in her arms a child of another dimension, a boy who was more than special, a child of the universe even as he lay quietly staring at her, even as he took the name de Roche.

From the very first, Evan had been wide-eyed and alert, had looked at her as if to say, "Here I am, I'm ready." Although exhausted from an ordeal most forty-year-olds would have bypassed, Pauline laughed and hugged him tight, so pleased was she of his bold, frank regard that would accompany him through life and add to his looks and charm.

He had been a model baby, cooperating as if an adult when it was time to eat, play, bathe, or sleep. He brought cheer to the household and no one regretted his presence, least of all Pauline. Evan was from the start both welcoming and welcomed, both giving and a gracious recipient of the efforts of those around him. Evan was from God, Pauline would say because, although not overly religious, she knew of no other way to describe his uniquely arresting qualities. He never flaunted what upper hand he may have been gifted with. Oh so casually did he go about winning over hearts, from their crotchety concierge to total strangers in the Métro. He was the child he was, special, and he was Pauline's.

Her life took a turn after his birth. While still responding to the social demands related to Giles's work, she rearranged her life. She attended the affairs of state, the dinners with visiting business associates, the lunches and balls for charity, but before and after she gave quality time to Evan. His nanny was only needed when Pauline went out with Giles. After, Pauline took over, took him everywhere she could from the kitchen where they enjoyed hours concocting extravagant desserts and tasty sauces to the museums, the parks and, of course, the cinema.

They were companions as well as parent and child, sharing secrets and laughing with zest—mischievous school children one moment then, in a blink, questioning philosophers searching for answers to some off-beat, pessimistic film. Evan already viewed a limitless horizon and, the best she knew how, Pauline encouraged his questioning, aided him to find answers, and followed his intellectual and physical growth with awe and pride.

Each night while drifting to sleep, she returned to the same thought. Her Evan was bound for greatness and, one day far and away too soon, she would have to let him go. For, contrary to the other de Roches, Evan's reach was boundless, beyond and towards visions that even she, the dreamer Pauline, could not fathom. One day the world would come to terms with this fact, once he was ready to direct himself towards its boundless, derelict embrace.

For now, as Danielle made plans with her father, Pauline basked in a warmth like no other. It would be she and Evan along the Breton coast, and for this she was overjoyed. Evan and she, together. She slipped from the room to find him and tell him the news.

# Chapter 3

*The fairies can have everything they want for wishing, poverty doesn't trouble them much and all their care is to seek out unfrequented nooks and places where it is not likely anyone will come to spoil their space.*
"The Priest's Supper" (an Irish legend)

MOST CALLED THEM THE GOOD PEOPLE, others used the terms wee folk or fairies. They inhabited knolls, fields and ruins along Ireland's west coast. With shrill laughs, miniature bodies, clothed in red or green, they pestered the locals' cows and upset rolled hay stacks. When threatened, they turned into red pigs, figured themselves into frightening dreams, and cast spells on humans given to trespassing their hideaways. But if you were their friend, they granted you endless hours of pleasure and fantasy by letting you in on their antics, by carrying you with them in a flight across the land, and even by heralding trouble for you to avoid.

Claire Walsh grew up using the self-appointed name of Klee ('clay'), this because early on she could not pronounce the Christian name. Her early years were colored by an innate sense of the wee folk plus a hankering for her Aunt Romney's bizarrely spun tales.

The summer Klee turned three, her raggedy aunt, head to toe in black and limping arthritically, led her to a grassy meadow a mile from the house. They sat on boulders and looked over the bay. Blue and violet evening clouds hovered at the western hills. Romney raised a finger to her lips and, with a playful wink, commanded Klee to silence. As the quiet bore down, Romney let out a low giggle. Behind a line of scraggly wind-bent bushes, the length of what Romney claimed was the fairy path to the sea, a rustling sound. Klee leaned forward, eyes fixed, and indeed noted the scurrying of pointy red hats above the brush. With the arrival of a breeze, they as quickly disappeared.

She pointed and squealed. "I saw, yes, I saw them!" She craned her neck for more but in no time the twilight stillness returned. Romney touched Klee's hand and they stood to go.

This first encounter with the wee people keeping her niece awake and full of questions, Romney broke her own rule and invited Klee to her chalet. The single-room thatched hut sat snug into the hillside. At a remove from people and troubles, the place was still close enough to facilitate errand-runs to the village. They sat by a peat fire as the tide swelled and gusts wailed. To the enchantment of her guest, Romney recited Celtic lore in the ancient tongue of the Gaeltacht.

Though Klee didn't understand each word, she sensed when Romney's stories switched from themes of luck and chance to revenge and mischief, when the fairies whisked away a country maid to care for a newly arrived fairy prince in need of mothering, or when the fairies punished a family through the mysterious disappearance of one of its members.

This latter point fascinated the little girl. Few reminders lingered of her mother save a photo of Alice with straight long black hair and a near grin that Klee focused on whenever she retrieved it from a bottom drawer.

"Where have you gone and why?" she'd ask, as though by asking enough times an answer would come.

But there was never a response, not from the photo, not from her siblings, and least of all from her distracted father who told her more than once to mind herself and her curiosity, for it would come to no good.

No matter how much Klee pestered her, even Romney would simply shake her head and return to tales of the fairies.

"Focus on that which you can fix, child, not that which you can't," was the predictable reply.

Klee tried to squelch this troubling sensation regarding her mother's disappearance, directing her energies towards the spark in Romney's eyes when the woman detailed revelries, like when fairies celebrated a marriage of one of their princesses or princes. Imparting tales of gold-filled pots, flying horses, humped men, nettle wars, screeching hags, and benevolent witches, Romney underscored the positive influence of the little folk and, she lectured, if you were kind and good and kept to your business, the fairies would see you were rewarded.

"Can I bring them to my house?" Klee asked.

"Not a chance. That house is not a place for them," Romney said with a dismissive shake of her head. "The devil lives there. The devil..."

Respectful of Romney's tone when she wished no further questions, Klee held her tongue. Romney stoked the peat as smoke rose from the hissing mound. Night was upon them. Klee wrapped her jumper about her and continued her vigil with a thorough stare that would become her trademark. The shared silence to which they'd become accustomed enhanced a closeness that others found disturbing. Klee placed her head against her aunt's chest. With an arm reaching around Romney's neck, she whispered, "Klee will learn Gaelic, too. I shall."

Romney only giggled. "Child, you have."

And so it was that Klee set out to befriend the fairies. Her days spent mostly at chores and menial activities, she maintained a watchful eye when she happened to pass by locations Romney declared as fairy forts. It was a child's dream to live where the fantastic transpired, where, if one concentrated and was still for long enough, several pint-size people would appear, traipsing along the distant cliffs one after the other or dancing to their own music atop some Norman tower. All became possible in the mind of the girl as she eagerly shared stories with Romney of how she happened upon a few lone fairies near a water well or by the roadside.

Not even the scoffs of her brothers and sister could sway Klee. The fairies were on her side, right or wrong, and she wouldn't betray allegiance. All was over if you gave up on the fairies.

As the years passed and she moved beyond the twinkling world of a child to her school years with their associated emotional hurdles, it took longer and longer to find the fairies. Most often, she was forced to wait until evening when, school work finished and dinner dishes washed, she would position herself on the stone seawall and watch as one or two sprites would scramble by and then only for seconds. Her sister Breeda would scold her for wasting time looking for "the devil himself and trouble for sure." Klee let it pass, like she let the comments of her brothers pass. They were bores anyway—reluctantly following their studies while avidly following the drink, local football events, and other goings-on in the community.

The lads, ranging in ages from ten to sixteen, had developed into clones of their father with the same black eyes and brown hair, the same slightly humped stance and predictable ways. Not a one stood out but as a result they all fit in, adapting better than Klee to the ways of Kinemmaera—this in spite of the Walsh family's reputation. As long as they did their chores and attended school regularly, Bob Walsh let them do as they pleased. So they grew, by and large ignoring Klee and paying attention to seventeen-year-old Breeda only when one of her girlfriends merited a second look.

From a rounded face, Klee's wide blue gaze became more penetrating and the black brows thickened. Her stare gripped onlookers, so much so that within moments of encountering her, most squirmed without knowing why, then hastened away. No sooner would she have put these fear-born reactions out of her mind, when someone who had not seen her in a while would pause, perplexed, as if trying to guess what thoughts hid behind such a regard. Klee was never free of the reminder that she rattled people.

In contrast to the dark straight locks of other village children, her blonde brittle hair grew up and out. She never bothered much about taming or cleaning it either. Most often, she let it have its way, proving to most town skeptics that she was indeed an oddity to be avoided. After all, insistence on the existence of fairies and an unswerving attachment to the retarded Romney were reasons enough to be wary of this young woman. Include her looks and, well, there's a lot of doubt, they said.

The sight of Klee waiting for the arrival of her elves gave rise to speculation from more normal folks, too, who tried to tolerate her but in the end shook heads and wondered. Perhaps, they would say, if she hadn't the misfortune to be born so wild looking, she might stand a chance. But really, she was doomed, now wasn't she? After all, they would whisper, her mother's reputation had not left *any* of the Walshes in good stead. If it weren't for the fact hers was one of the time-honored names in the village, one would guess her a tinker waiting for the next caravan to carry her along to another of the makeshift camps dotting Ireland.

For hundreds of years the tinkers roamed—landless, lawless, and sinister. Some said they were gypsies transplanted from the continent, others decried them as shiftless and lazy poor. Klee would watch a team of pipe-smoking men, the bejeweled women with creative headdresses, the brightly painted horse-drawn carriages, and wish to join them. With pitch-black eyes and vermillion hair, they would return her stare and she could feel their power, an inordinate pull shared by those who grip well the sense of base survival. Tinkers claimed no ownership and yet, Klee would nod to herself, they indeed possessed their space. Once the scuttle of dogs and noisy, shabbily-clad children passed, Klee would turn towards the village, trying not to envy their ability to journey and explore. She spent hours wondering how she could roam as they did.

All combined for a unique childhood. If not for Romney, Klee would have no friends. If not for the tinkers, she would never have cultivated notions of an existence beyond Kinemmaera. If not for the elves her mind might have slipped in the direction of most of the local people—towards the mundane concentrations of working the land and scrounging to make ends meet.

These unusual influences also allowed Klee to study and think for herself, the very trait inherited from the mother who had left Klee a child with no past. This she discovered by accident, when Romney let slip her mother's memory was without match in the town.

"She was a glutton for the books and master of detail, your mother," Romney said. "No blaming her for wishing herself beyond this land's end now, is there?"

"But where did she go?" Klee asked.

This time Romney gave her a long stare.

"She went with the tinkers and the fairies, to that place we all crave."

"What place is that?" Klee asked.

"To where no one spoils the space," Romney said.

Romney pressed fingertips to her middle forehead, and looked to the sea.

Following encounters like this with her aunt, Klee came to believe that what took place in the vast and forever reaches of one's mind had value and could be utilized. With Romney's help and that of a visiting priest who took pity on her solitary ways, she learned to read. By the time she reached school age, she was reading the level of a ten-year-old, having already mastered a good part of the Bible—one of few books in the Walsh house. Later, Romney was to collect books for her from the priest. When he was away, his tiny domain overlooking the bay was vacant and Romney knew where to sneak in order to reach his second floor library.

Klee learned Gaelic too, well before her classmates and, once in school, better than anyone. At first listening then repeating the tales she constantly demanded from Romney, she assumed the correct enunciation in no time and regularly recited stories to Romney.

Like her compatriots, Klee was not afraid to open her mouth and allow a tune or two to escape. She particularly enjoyed the special occasions when merriment prevailed—after haying and during Holy Days or wedding festivities. Anyone could huddle about the bar with a group and drink, dance, and sing rebel songs. Klee assisted at numerous occasions and, although her voice melded with others as the tunes spewed forth, she grew to discern the notes, the sonority of the Gaelic, the internal messages upon which the lyrics drew. She took to singing by herself while roaming the land.

The summer of her eighth year began as any other, with longer days that provided more wandering time. One day, Klee and Romney marched past the stony wall outlining one side of the Walsh property and made their way along a ledge that paralleled the shore. Wellington boots protecting their feet from cow dung and dampness, waterproof anoraks covering their bodies, they tramped in silence for over a mile before Klee broke out in song.

Absorbed by the sunshine and stillness particular to the region after downpours, her voice echoed across the bay and to the rocks below—a vibrant melody, one that carried in all directions the tale of a lover lost at sea, a song to which Klee had grown attached. Romney stopped, let the child advance, and listened to the voice as it became distant but no less distinct. Ringing off the landscape, the lyrics crossed the meadow and dipped to the sea, melded with the waves and created an unique movement. Her sounds undulated beyond the small town, beyond the waters, to stretches of the earth Klee had not yet figured how to physically attain.

Realizing she was without her companion, she stopped. Turning, the hood of her slicker fell and exposed her mop of hair. A questioning glance and beckon of her hand brought Romney again close by.

As Romney sniffed and in agitation brushed aside tears, she grasped Klee in her arms and hugged hard. "The song will free you. It will protect you for sure," she said.

Klee contemplated the mottled face and expressionless watery eyes of her aunt, and hugged her. As they weren't often given to physical expression, the two lingered together, a silhouette of raingear and boots, in one the gangly body, in the other the war-torn hair. Their image fell against the gorgeous blue day in a contrast like no other, a private moment wholly shared. Klee broke away first and snickered, peeking beyond Romney's shoulder.

"I see a fairy, Rom, over there."

Romney gazed into the blue eyes and tugged at the springy curls. "Aye, I do too, luv, I do too."

The wedding of Breeda Walsh took place the first Sunday in August, a time of year when twilight hit the bay in streams of pinks, oranges, lavenders, and navy blues. Evenings at the water's edge, farmers raked seaweed onto flat carts and hauled their load to barns for use as fodder should the supply run out in the dead of winter. Children enjoyed the dwindling hours of outdoor play before school started, families prayed for a lenient winter, and visitors journeyed home towards England or the continent. Summer passed in the west.

She was marrying Sean O'Faolain, quite a catch for a girl of the bay area, for he was originally from Galway and the son of a Dublin businessman. Earlier in the year while cycling through the town, Sean and his fellow riders took a break at a pub in Kinemmaera. He eyed Breeda and her friends as they made way to buy sweets at O'Ryan's market. The lads caught up with the girls and carried on with flirtations and banter found wherever the young, available, and energetic congregate.

Breeda and Sean hit it off, he with blonde hair and blue eyes and she with her darker coloring, demure mannerisms, and beguiling smile. More mature than most, the eldest Walsh child took early on to babysitting and mothering, knew what tending to the chickens and pigs entailed, and had to often forego fun with friends to help bring in the hay or drive home the cows. She was a good student, serious more often than not, and gifted with an even temper.

Their relationship bud forth into weekend visits from Sean that turned into prolonged stays during his school breaks. When he graduated, he asked Bob for Breeda's hand and the deed was as good as done.

Their mass was held at noon after which the wedding party and guests—including more than half the town—moved from St. Michael's church to the hall at the hotel down the road. Used most often for weddings or annual affairs, the spacious room housed several hundred people. White crepe paper decorated side rafters and potted palms stood at the head table to one end of the hall. Waitresses scurried about placing final touches on festively set dining tables. As soon as the majority of party-goers arrived, Tom Riordan's banjo and fiddle band struck up a tune.

Breeda in her creamy dress and veil and Sean in his dark suit made a fine couple and, from all present, received blessings and good-luck embraces.

Stand-offish and stiff in his new suit and tie, Bob Walsh would have preferred to stay at home by the fire or spend an hour or two at the pub but for his daughter, especially since she was marrying someone of decent means. Weddings reminded him too painfully of his own, when he'd been blinded by the beauty of Alice, by her innocent ways and eagerness to be with him. How often since her departure had he re-lived their life together, only to end up more soured by the thought of so many years down the drain? These days he didn't miss her, wished her dead or at least cursed with the devil. He tried not to think of her when he registered her twinkle built into one of the boys' eyes or the same sway of the hips when Breeda sauntered towards the house at the end of the day.

He never discussed his wife, indeed, never made moves to formally separate or talk with the priest. The hurt lingered in the back of his mind, unresolved and unattended to. His anger suppressed, his intentions on the present, he left her memory behind as best he could and, with rare exception, never thought about a replacement.

Wearing a borrowed pink A-line dress with black patent leather belt and matching shoes, Klee stood by her sister. A plastic barrette bunched the frizz off her forehead and she wore cotton gloves Romney had found. Throughout the ceremony, her feet itched from sprigs of hay caught between her toes. She resembled a cow rubbing its ankle in a fit of discomfort, and the entire congregation noticed.

Like Bob, Klee would have preferred to be elsewhere but not for the same reason. A Sunday afternoon was prime time for the wee folk. They did their work on Sundays and she had hoped to spend a few hours by the Norman keep on the lookout. Since discovering this enclave several Augusts back, she and Romney made a point to visit regularly. But, since Romney was also at the wedding, they instead conspired to sneak away during the after party to make the half mile trip to the keep.

She enjoyed the ceremony because she was in the process of learning Latin. Her Gaelic coming along, she decided Latin was next, for the simple reason mass was said in the language. She could also sneak Bob's missal from its place on the shelf in the kitchen, provided it was returned in time for him to reach for it when Sunday mass rolled around.

So, as the priest pronounced Breeda and Sean man and wife, Klee mouthed the Latin after him. The sonority was different from Gaelic, less throaty and easier on the jaws. Romney told her Latin was the basis of many other languages on the continent, that if she mastered Latin and Gaelic, she would have a step up on any other European language. So Klee proceeded readily with her tutoring, given by herself for herself for reasons even she didn't understand fully. She loved language—her own, her ancestors', that of Jesus. Which tongue didn't matter, but the discovery did. Therefore, the wedding having blotted out her plans for time with the fairies, she made do with the fact it was an opportunity to further her skills.

Like her other off-beat ways, this one caught some in town by surprise and gave rise to lowered eyebrows as Klee mouthed Latin in a not so discreet fashion all the while her sister, father, brothers and the rest of the Church sat motionless and teary-eyed. At one point her brother Stephen nudged her but Stephen was a bother so she ignored him, antagonizing him even more by reciting louder during the Gospel.

Bob never embraced Klee, never touched her, never directed more than monosyllables her way, contrary to other fathers, especially Moira Ahern's dad who brought his daughter to the fields, on errands, or simply for a walk. Other children were the same, even her own siblings. Every now and then Bob placed a comforting pat on Breeda's shoulder, and always the boys received a handshake or nod when they came in at the end of the day. Her father was not incapable of physical contact. Too, he did speak, though not much to her. Over a meal he could recount town events or regional news stories, could surmise about an approaching storm or winds, could tend to dinner if he had to and could thank Breeda when she managed to feed the lot of them. With Klee he was strained.

She grew to understand it was for reasons that, while not discussed, ran like a vein through Bob Walsh's person. Klee nonetheless tried to gain his attention and subsequent affections.

The Burren was terrain of biological renown that crossed through Kinemmaera and beyond to the hills of Clare. Scientists from all over the world visited, trying to divine why, under such circumstances of poor soil and inclement weather, rare tropical flowers and plants sprouted from beds of nearly solid rock.

After storms, they arrived in carpets of blues, pinks, and spurts of yellow. Klee would collect the wildflowers and present a fistful to Bob as he toiled in the fields. Her efforts went unrewarded. More often than not the man never looked twice. The buds would droop around her fist and she would study the creases and frown on her father's face, gathering that he didn't want to be bothered.

Klee stored away the experiences but tried not to dwell on them. Holidays or birthdays, gift-giving occasions of any sort, she had for a while concocted papier-mâché figures, painted landscapes, or clay bowls for him. Those too went unacknowledged. One day Breeda said, "Father doesn't fancy those things much." So Klee stopped.

The wedding night, Klee decided to take a chance. Usually, at some point the parents of the groom and bride connected with siblings and family in a slow dance. With others doubled up, Bob would need a partner. She made up her mind to be his and waited for the music to strike. As it happened, Romney pulled her aside just as the set began.

"The keep!" she whispered.

Not to be outdone by Romney who found the fairies more regularly than she, Klee joined her. They stood vigil, giggling and imagining which of the little people would appear and who would play tricks. But, their luck was not with them. As they were tiring of their watch, a gale drove in sheets of rain and they hurried back to the dance hall.

Wet, bedraggled and with drips forming at the tips of her strands, Klee caught her breath as Tim Riordan announced another slow song. "I give you 'My Special Angel' sung by a fellow named Bobby Helms. Right from America, one of the big ones of 1958 here in Eire!" Tim exclaimed.

Klee stepped past some adults to get a better look. In the center of the floor, Breeda shyly accepted her father's arms while Sean looked on. In stiff motions, Bob and Breeda danced the first few bars. Then Breeda joined hands with Sean and they folded themselves into their private, newly-wedded world.

Advancing, Klee called. "Daddy..."

> I know that you're an angel, heaven is in
> your eyes!

She looked Bob's way, got within feet, then stood to wait for his hand.

> You are my special angel, through
> eternity,
> The Lord shone down on me, and sent an
> Angel to love...

"Daddy...." she said again, louder.

With a glazed look, Bob looked right past the dripping and open arms of Klee. He called to his sons, "OK, lads, let's find us some ladies!" No sooner had he said that, then he reached for Mary O'Callaghan—a widow and distant cousin—and commenced an eased two-step.

Klee blinked, tried again, but Mary and Bob bumped her aside and kept right on going. She stepped into the shadows, trying to manage the lump in her throat.

> A smile from your lips brings the summer sunshine
> A tear from your eye brings the rain.
> I feel your touch, your warm embrace
> And I'm in heaven again...

This man dancing feet from her had no desire to love her, no interest in her livelihood, no inclination to even try. Klee ran from the hall, to the street and the fork for the road home from where, by the light of a half moon, she found her way.

Once there, she fell to the bed and cried. The harsh reality finally surfaced. "He doesn't love me. He never loved me."

In her life, she'd never cried so, never lost her composure to such an extent, and for so strange a reason, for so terrible a shock! For, the worst was not so much he'd ignored her, shunned her in front of the town. That she was used to. The worse thing was she still struggled with why.

Retrieving her mother's photo, she fought tears and focused, intent on extracting some revelation from this black and white face, anything to help her out of an isolation she claimed fully this night. But the shadowy regard returned nothing but the certainty that Klee inherited nothing of her mother—not that narrow chin, nor the dark eyes, not even that half smile.

She touched her bristly hair and pulled a curl to her mouth to suck on the strand, doubling over in a pain she christened her mother's sole offering. As she stroked her hair, a misted breeze landed on her forehead. She inhaled deeply then gripped her hair harder, pulling, screaming, then pulling some more.

"You must have cared! You left for other reasons than me! Yes you did!"

Fingers tangled in the locks, the perturbed disarray got worse as Klee crossed pieces of hair over one another in a fury of attempted braiding.

"There's nothing good about you! Not a thing! Nothing. This hair most of all!"

In that moment, a whisper filtered in from outside. Unsure of what she heard, she looked up, out the window to the night. A cloudy mass lifted through the room then disappeared beyond the brush to the shoreline, leaving a dampness encircling her bed, the house, the land.

She loosened her grip and fell against a pillow, eyes on the crack in the ceiling and breathed the moist air left in the wake of what she believed was a fairy visit. Her body felt light at the same time she lay clamped to the bed.

"My hair," she said in barely a whisper. "It belongs to me but not to Father, or to Breeda, or to the boys."

Romney appeared, a shadow against the bedroom window pane. Klee noted in the aging lady's eyes that which she'd come to discover for herself. Her companion beckoned her outside. She sniffed back her sorrow, brushed herself off, and left the cottage.

Romney spilled tears and embraced her niece with a fierceness Klee would recall for the remainder of her days as the single parcel of affection she received during her youth.

"Come with me, child, you'll not return there. I'll tell you why. You're ready now."

Klee followed her, down the path to the chalet, to listen to the reasons she had a father but didn't.

# Chapter 4:
# August, 1958

HER FATHER CLOSE BEHIND, Laurence raced down the dune. "I got here first!" she yelled. "You can't beat me!"

Nate caught up with his daughter, secured hands around her, and lifted her towards the sky. Gusts spiraled around them as waves broke in white billows at their feet. The day before, an early-season hurricane walloped the coast, leaving the entire peninsula debris-ridden. He lowered her and they walked along the break line.

"It's still wild," Nate said, looking to the horizon. "It will be a few days before things return to normal. Until then, we'll be camping inside the house!"

"I'm glad you made it home in time," Laurence said, referring to his ride from Woods Hole the night before. Fallen tree branches, live wires, and winds almost forced him to find shelter further up the coast.

"I'd make it through anything for my little one!" he said.

"Mama seemed distracted..."

Nate glanced at her. Tall already, her short brown hair whipped behind her, suntanned skin glistened with sea spray, and dark eyes shot sullen looks to sea. As of late, comments like that were not rare, and suggested a discomfort Nate could no longer deny.

He had hoped his wife's animosity would fade but, as Laurence came more into her own, Régine grew increasingly difficult. In Laurence, Nate found an eager companion to accompany him on his quests. By age three, as soon as she could swim, Laurence replaced Régine when it came to venturing into the deep and sometimes dangerous waters. Where Régine tolerated Nate's enthusiasm for swimming, fishing, and scuba diving, Laurence took to the activities with the same ease as walking. Her fresh, inquisitive mind left Nate pleased and amazed at her agility and grasp of the ways of the sea.

Régine allowed their play, opting instead for a sun bath on the shore or a day in town on the bay side where the sea was quieter and she could interact with other human beings. Their house on the Outer Cape was one of few and, especially off-season, seemed to possess a "No Trespassing" sign at the property's edge. Save the odd fisherman reeling in a catch or artist sketching along the shoreline, fall and winter months offered few distractions. None of this pleased Régine who complained about confinement, about her lazy daughter and inattentive husband.

Nate loved his job and, off-season, it provided him the solitude lacking during summer when vacationers took to boat, board, and sail. More inclined to stay on the Cape than attend affairs miles away in New York or Boston, he would reason with Régine that Laurence needed her parents, not the bombardment of humanity. The life of the sea was a child's paradise. She should be allowed to enjoy it while she could.

The distance between them grew, from as far back as when baby Laurence took to Daddy more than Mommy. And then, each time as a child of four and five she begged Nate to take her to Woods Hole where she could watch him work. And now, each time she sulked when Régine forced her to wear designer dresses or to drive the hours-long trip to Boston.

Amidst the dunes, the sandpipers, the gulls, and the waves, Laurence loved to swim. Bayside on summer evenings, she also took to canoeing with Nate and, during deep-sea expeditions, she reveled in being on board. When she turned eight, she donned scuba gear to marvel at what lay below the sea's surface. She would opt for a day by the sea, or in it, rather than errands, grocery shopping, visits with friends, or other forays in town.

As the years passed, Laurence and Régine grew distant. They didn't argue, didn't fuss over who was right or not. The few times they had spats of that nature, Nate intervened and made it clear he did not condone a home with that kind of tension. Not wishing to displease Nate, Régine was aloof during the increasing intervals when Laurence spent time with her Dad. She found interests of her own, not ones she would be able to support long-term, but at least ones with an element of satisfaction.

Her family in France received daily phone calls—expensive but necessary she would reason to Nate. If he wasn't going to allow her to journey more frequently to Boston or New York, he should at least let her interact with the outside world. She bought clothes, primped regularly at the beauty parlor and, during the summer, even organized a ladies' walking tour of the area with its bicycle paths, lobster traps piled in front yards, quaint shops, and galleries. It took her mind off the fact Laurence didn't need her anymore, and relieved her of thoughts of extended vacations in France or of leaving the scene altogether.

She hated the place, hated the dampness that seeped to the core of her bones in the dead of winter, the too-easily molded bedsheets and upholstery, the salt spray on her face. She felt as though her life were passing her by, that she would turn into one of the 'sea-hags' as she called them—those year-round, bone-thin, weathered women whose main preoccupations were scraping oysters and hobbling through town.

As each summer drew near, as the tourists arrived and crowds gathered shoreline to enjoy the outer reaches of what Régine considered the ends of the earth, she invented more deviant pastimes. Her jaunts about town with ladies on holiday included a new dimension—the men of those women. She tested the waters by letting on to the odd visiting male she was willing to forget her married status for a fling in the dunes.

An investment broker from New York first caught Régine's seductive glance and, early one afternoon as he and his wife stood in line for the walking tour, slipped Régine his phone number. None too soon they fell into one another's arms, away from responsibility and with eyes only for one another. She indulged in the man's yearnings, abandoned her fears of getting caught, let the time pass as if he were the best, the most alluring, the most virile of specimens. Her partner did not let her down.

He lay her on the ground and began kissing her scented body, top to toe, like a kid his first night with a woman. Régine let him do whatever he wanted—tickle her feet, bite her stomach, roll her over and press hard to her back. Abandoning herself to the passion, she grew even more charged, even more daring. She pushed him to her and held him, guided him to the place where he found succumbing warmth. They made a joint, muffled groan as their bodies met in a heat of unified pulsing explosion.

Afterwards, she found her dress, snuggled into it, and they returned to his car. An hour later, she was in bed with Nate who snored in deep slumber. That night, the powerful notion that she didn't need her husband kept her awake, and calculating.

She would not stop there. If the Mallord family was destined to remain at this seaside village, Régine could use her head plus other assets to obtain what she wanted from life. She enjoyed her partner's attentions, however he proved a mere tease.

The years accumulated and so did Régine's list of lovers. By the summer of Laurence's eighth year, Régine busily reunited with them at strategic and remote places along the bay and oceanside. She found Nate's lovemaking dreary and functional. He seemed satisfied with the occasional romp in the hay, which kept things predictable and opportune for Régine's other life.

Laurence could have him, Régine would reason. Laurence and her childish squealing ways as the two took off for a morning hike along the dunes or a foray amongst the low tidewaters, discovering all the crawly things the sea brought in.

Still, Régine couldn't fully admit to herself that her love for Nate had died. A part of her felt guilty about her errant actions and another part, deeper and more unsettling, wanted to return as the center of his world. No thanks to Laurence, Régine sensed that those days were gone. There was no way Régine could be the reason behind the wide smile Nate wore when Laurence returned from scuba lessons with tales of species of fish. No way Régine could outdo the thorough embrace Laurence gave her father each night to which he looked forward with eagerness he'd rarely displayed for his wife.

If he was aware of this distraction with his daughter, he never spoke of it. He seemed to have both women on two planes—Laurence incorporated into his professional life and leisure time, Régine accorded the pleasures of his body and the respect he readily gave her.

Nate would never leave the sea. Régine would never be a person of the sea.

She tried to find love with others, on isolated paths and deserted beaches, in the back seats of cars or in motel rooms, physically seeking outcomes that nevertheless escaped her during heated moments in the arms and body of another.

Most of all, it wasn't with Régine Nate talked of the future, it was with Laurence, and that day, when the two returned from scouting out the damaged shoreline, she knew her fate was sealed as an outsider.

"An ocean crossing!" she exclaimed, after Nate outlined a plan to journey across the Atlantic on an oversized DaySailer.

"Sure. It's been done before. We can even stop in Roscoff, my dear," he said, giving her a playful pat on the behind.

"It will take a number of weeks, depending on the stops," Laurence said, while spreading out nautical maps on the large wooden table.

"When are you two doing this?" Régine asked. "There is school to consider, you know."

"Oh, years from now. It will take us that long to plan," Nate said. "Still, it's something to look forward to, eh?" He joined Laurence at the maps.

Pouting, Régine left the room. Not only were the two spending each day together but, when Laurence finished high school, she was not bound for college. She would take off with her father, live in cramped quarters to travel the world, the two of them acting out the epitome of the secluded love scene. The two of them...

If asked, Régine would not have called herself a vengeful person. The reasons why she developed a distracted comportment, why Laurence seemed wary when in the same room with her, why Nate remained polite yet acutely distant had not so much to do with the obvious twosome against whom she was pitted as it had to do with another demon. That demon was time itself.

Time, in its way, wore away at her bright side. As the years progressed, an ornery throb reigned in a remote chamber of her heart. Its onset had been slight at first—the baby hands reaching to Nate's nose, the odd conspiratorial grin between father and daughter. Back then, Régine had suppressed any reaction. Because she felt so alone and far from her French family, she worked to dismiss the feeling as unfounded jealousy. But rationalizing only turned her inward. She shunned seeking help and, before she knew it, stronger, more negative energies emerged. Still, she had to keep chin up, had to re-arrange her feelings and call them something different, had to pretend she was fine. Somewhere inside she was still the girl of her youth, gazing at the tall American and falling in love, wanting his arms about her and his smile forever on her.

When the events of the afternoon in August unfolded, it was with a heart of stone Régine Mallord proceeded with an altogether new life, a life that fate left her, a life she would now embrace with the single-mindedness of a woman seeking revenge.

With plates and cups serving as weights, the maps were secured to the table. Nate looked closely at his daughter. "Something wrong between you and your mother?"

"No, she was...difficult...before you made it home."

"How so?"

"I can't really say. She yelling about no running water, about the phones being disconnected. I don't really get her sometimes, Dad."

"She misses France. I can understand," Nate said. "But, don't worry. When we sail to Europe, we'll take your mother to France."

"She hates sailing, Dad. How in the world will she stand it?"

Nate laughed, tugged at the strands of his daughter's hair and gave her the bear hug she loved.

"Let's get out there and swim!" Nate called.

Outside, he tugged off his t-shirt and headed for the waves.

Laurence hesitated, eyed the swells. It would be work getting over those monsters and what lay beyond was anyone's guess. Onshore winds strengthened the pull of the undertow. A full moon from the night before meant extreme tides.

Still, in this humidity, a quick, exhilarating swim was called for. Their house stood in the distance atop the dune. She turned to see her mother securing a window shutter. Nate was already beyond the swell line when Laurence stripped to her underwear and ran towards him, arms outstretched, screaming with delight as she made for his bobbing head.

She dove into an oncoming wave and emerged on the other side not ten feet from her father. But the ocean had become a blue-black force and she quickly realized she was out of her element.

"I'm going to shore!" she called as a swell drowned her voice and lifted her. She capitulated and let the next one ram her to the hard, sandy floor. When she stood, body shivering, she realized the length of one side of her was scraped. When the tingling diminished, she looked towards where she'd last seen Nate. He had disappeared.

"Dad!" She screamed, to no avail. A wave come towards her and she prayed he was body surfing beneath it, prayed his head would pop up somewhere nearby. But she saw only the grey sea, the burgeoning swells. She called again. His head appeared. She didn't need further warning. She yelled at the top of her voice, "Mama! Hurry! Help! HELP!"

High tide was bearing down. Unable to get past the waves this time, her forces waned. After three more tries, she finally conquered a less forbidding one. Further out, Nate's head appeared, then disappeared. She could tell he was falling victim to the rip tide. Diving in again, she made progress underwater by about ten feet. Emerging, she faced his panicked look a few feet away.

"Dad!" she screamed, an arm waving. He went under, his hands fighting every submersion with erratic splashing. No matter how hard Laurence tried, she couldn't narrow the distance from him. She weakened more. Another scream towards shore for her mother left her totally spent. Nate appeared.

"Turn back, Laurence, turn back!"

To leave him meant it was over. To disobey his command, she too would succumb. The undertow was too strong. He was being sucked in and, if she neared him, she would join him.

He was gone from sight. Laurence felt an ominous tug at her feet and sensed the tide pulling equally strongly at her own body. Nate's head reappeared but his eyes had gone blank.

Against every instinctive demand of every cell in her body, she turned from him. If not for his final words, she would have gone after him but Nate, ever conscious of his daughter's welfare when it came to the sea, commanded her to safety.

Hysterical, she scanned the shore, crying out his name, tears of desperation melding with the salty ones of the sea. No matter how hard she tried to glimpse something other than graying skies or the even grayer sea, she saw only water, water everywhere, and heard the thunderous pound of waves to shore. The undertow won. Her father had been swallowed by the sea.

She knew of its force; he taught her its unpredictable ways. Nate was an exceptional swimmer, never afraid, always in control. But his temperament didn't always allow for caution, especially with his ability to calculate risk and his insight.

Nature fooled them both. Her blue-ish fingertips clasped in front of her, her thin frame wracked with uncontrolled shivers, Laurence looked seaward, praying to see her Dad emerge, smiling. Yet, tragedy flickered in her gaze. Already taking root were the indelible images of her father foregoing his own fate to save her, his second love next to the sea.

Gone, now, was the well from which she drew her strength. Lost forever the many tomorrows filled with nautical plans and innovation, knowledge and its journey. The man the sea had taken was the hub of her life. Nate, although surpassing her in years and ever more experienced and wise, was still as vital to her as her limbs, indeed as her heart that pumped furiously as evening shadows grew and hope dwindled.

She turned, witnessing the second most chilling event of her life. As still as the bay waters in summer, as calm as a still pool, as prim and stately as always, Régine made no move to help, no move to reach her daughter, no effort to try one final time.

Although she would spend the rest of her life unsure of the truth, Laurence sensed that Régine witnessed the entire event with detachment, as if unwilling to challenge the gods, as if content, downright happy even, to see the events unfold as they did.

At that moment, as her mother's form became a silhouette against the clouds, Laurence wished she'd fallen to sea with her father. Even as she filled with grief and sorrow, a panoply of eerie feelings ran through her.

She made way towards the house, tackling sloping sands, panting and bleeding.

Steps from her mother she heaved, her head bent her eyes awash in tears. "Dad. He's gone," she said.

Régine made no sound, offered no comforting hand about Laurence's naked and wet form. There was only the flapping of Régine's skirt, the wind as it howled.

"Get inside," Régine said. "Your lover is gone now."

Laurence looked into the eyes of the woman who despised her even as they shared in the same loss, even as the life they both so cherished was snuffed. They stood, enemies and apart.

"And dress," she scoffed. "You can't seduce him anymore. *C'est fini, Laurence. Il est mort.*"

# Chapter 5:
# Summer, 1958

PAULINE WRAPPED A WHITE CHIFFON SCARF around her head and checked herself in the mirror. Save a touch of balm on her lips, she wore no makeup. In white cotton dress and tan espadrilles, she looked the picture of relaxation.

On the kitchen table of their summer home along Brittany's coast, Evan organized his maps. These days, he was intent on Africa. Each summer, he chose an activity that would absorb him through the season. At age five, he'd collected, categorized, and labeled regional shells. The next year it was birds, and not a day passed when he couldn't be found, binoculars at the ready, studying flight patterns, feathers, coloring, Latin names, and habitats.

With the maps surfaced questions about other European countries as well as the furthest reaches of the globe. Before long, Pauline surprised him with a world atlas and a detailed map of France, Spain, and the United Kingdom. Now Evan busily calculated how far away London was from Madrid, Madrid from Paris, Paris from Toulouse on into the night and then each morning after his croissant and chocolate drink.

"And so, Mama," he said, after announcing the distance between Edinburgh and Oslo, "Europe is still very big, but there are continents much larger—Africa, for instance, and others."

"We're not alone in the world, dear Evan," she said, sitting by his side with her café.

"I'd like to travel to these places—everywhere—one day."

"You may. Your father's business could extend to the four corners. You'll have the perfect chance then."

He peered out the window, reflecting, then flipped through pages in the atlas. "Due west is...is...America and let's see..."

The Ile de Batz was the place for an adventurous boy. At the northwest reaches of the island stood the de Roche estate, flanked on one side by inland roads, marshes, and brush, on the other by the rocky coast that slipped into the Atlantic. During the 1890s, great-grandfather de Roche had come upon a dilapidated farm cottage. Over the years, the simple stone masonry was added on to and embellished. Double doors and windows opened the rooms to the outdoors, wide-board oak floors added warmth, and a walkway the length of the top floor on the bay side offered a breathless view. Because it was a summer place, meant to be enjoyed by groups of people, walls were torn down on the first floor to allow for an open-plan living area with fieldstone fireplace and chef's kitchen. Three bedrooms with baths upstairs gave the de Roches privacy. A guest house added after the war accommodated the many visitors they welcomed during the three months the house was in use.

Pauline's touches created a veritable showplace, with Ancien Régime pieces, lace embroidered curtains, dried and fresh flower arrangements, pottery from the region, brass and iron cooking utensils on walls and hanging above cooking spaces. After the war, she had the grounds reworked. While the house and out buildings had suffered little damage, parts of the property had been bombed and craters still marked several spots along their private beach.

She was a lover of flowers and cultivated many; her rhododendrons, camellias, and azaleas were the most spectacular. Due to the mild Gulf Stream influence, she even managed rare strains of flowers from as far away as Africa and Asia. In one corner, she tended with pride a spread of *narcissus triondras*, or Angel's Tears, a species native to the region and seen most often on the south Breton islands of Glénan. Evenings when the winds were calm, the family would sit on the porch and point out the muted colors that stretched from their steps to the edges of the property. The floral esplanade was at first an added attraction but, as the years progressed, became like a member of the family. Each person had his or her favorite type of flower, everyone shared in the pruning, grooming, and feeding. Whenever pests cropped up, a concentrated effort was made to rapidly eradicate the offenders. The garden was a statement to Pauline's ingenuity, the de Roche ability to expand upon ideas, plus the Breton knack of using what one had to the maximum.

As Evan lingered over maps, Pauline stood in the doorway and studied him. At eight, he had the Mediterranean dark features of the de Roche side and grew each day to look more like his father. With his easy-going attitude and helpful ways, as well as his looks, she found she didn't miss Giles as much as she feared throughout this particular summer. With the exception of the Bastille Day break and a second long weekend earlier in August, Giles had decided to remain in Paris. It was a time of movement within the administration and Giles was a key contributor to business strategies, analyses, and estimates. Those closest to de Gaulle would decide France's economic direction and Giles was happy to comply. He and Danielle took the business reigns of the family fortune and cooperated with their government's move towards increased activity and profits. It was a good time for *les affaires* and each week Pauline received lengthy letters from her daughter and husband updating her on the goings-on in Paris.

Thrilling though these activities appeared from the letters, Pauline did not miss city life. With Evan, her gardens, and the sea, she thrived better than she ever could in Paris. Though she would have preferred Giles and Danielle visit more often, other family members kept her occupied with dinners, jaunts around the island, and car rides to the piers for arrivals and au revoirs. A splendid summer and, as it drew to a close, she found herself wistful.

One evening a few days later, Pauline insisted. "Evan, dearest," she said, "put away your tools. It's beautiful outside and we haven't walked yet. The sun will be setting soon and I thought we could go to the jetty and watch it pass over the Pont du Morans lighthouse!"

Evan looked up from his work and checked his watch. "Right," he said. "We have twenty minutes exactly. The weather reports said the sun will be setting at 20:34 tonight, three minutes earlier than last night."

Pauline giggled and embraced him, ruffling and inhaling the sea-salt aroma that had permeated her son's hair. "Let's go!"

He grabbed his cap and they left, making for the beach via the front porch. Two days before, Aunt Solange had departed and since then they'd had the house to themselves. As they ambled through the gardens, brass chimes Pauline bought summers before rapped against one another, as if to encourage their stroll.

"Let's go this way!" Pauline said, pointing left where a path cut a steep descent to the sand, the short-cut used by oyster fishermen to reach the bay during low tide. They picked their way past the occasional boulder and threw shoes aside, the still-warm sand between their toes.

Once on level ground, they made for the breakwater. As their imprints left a trail behind them, they walked the shore and began their 'movie game,' a trivial pursuit where Pauline thought of a movie and let Evan guess its name by answering yes or no to his questions.

"It's from the '30s," Evan said, a sly smile creasing to one side.

Pauline laughed. "Yes."

"It's always from the '30s, your favorite time. Let's see, the star was Charles Boyer."

"Yes."

"*The Mayerling!*" he returned.

"Oh, I can't fool you," she said, laughing and pinching his tanned cheek.

"You're easy to figure, Mama. Tell me the story again."

"I've told you hundreds of times, Evan."

"Again, please."

Pauline looked to the sea and, an arm relaxed across Evan's shoulders, began the tale of Rodolphe and Maria, two star-crossed lovers whose feelings overcame his royal background and her simpler one as they chose joint suicide rather than the option of living on earth without one another. It was a sad and true tale, a Romeo and Juliet story through and through, a story of the uncompromising ways the aristocracy seeks revenge against one of its own, even to the death. Because of his love, Rodolphe gave up his material possessions and ultimately his life for an interlude of love with the woman of his dreams.

"But there are so many others from the '30s, others with more cinematic detail and complex plot lines, Mama. I'm surprised you've chosen this as your favorite."

"There are many excellent films of the thirties but, mon cher, this one is a love story, pure and simple. It has no sub-plots, no superfluous motivations or extraneous supporting roles. It's about Maria and Rodolphe. It has the beautiful music—Strauss, Tchaikovsky, Weber. Music and love."

"And Danielle Darrieux in the role of Maria, of course," Evan said.

"Of course," Pauline smiled. "No one else could have portrayed Maria with so much energy."

They continued their trek until the outline of the lighthouse emerged from the mist. After helping one another over the jetty's slippery edges, they settled at the very tip to watch the red-orange late summer sun.

As they reflected in silence, approaching noises turned their attention towards a cluster of children playing tag. Four boys younger than Evan romped after one another, shouting and stopping only to inspect the odd shell or crab washed in by the tides. As they drew closer, it was clear one of the boys was deformed. With a larger than normal head and facial features pressed to one side, he wore a permanent frown and had one eye half shut. He had no hair and hobbled with one leg shorter than the other. Oblivious to Pauline's and Evan's regard, he stumbled along, doing his best to keep up with the others.

"Oh, he's so ugly!" Evan said, a giggle escaping. "Look, you can see the veins popping from his skull!"

A frown erased Pauline's bright countenance. "Evan de Roche, look here," she said, her fingers pulling his chin level with her face. "That child is like you or me. He has problems, true. But they are physical, no more. You have no idea what kind of a person he is, do you?"

Evan's expression grew troubled. "No, Mama, I'm sorry. It's just, he looks, well, a little bit frightening."

"Frightening to you, but not to him. He has obviously come to terms as best he can with his deformity. It is not acceptable at all, young man, for you to mock one who is less fortunate than yourself. Do you understand?"

He registered her stern regard. She was a woman with firm beliefs, and one of them had to do with kindness. He well knew her ways and had overstepped himself here. Pauline was never one to judge surface features, even though she and the de Roches were blessed with undeniable looks and charm.

Gaze downcast, he let the shame pour from his eyes. "I'm sorry, Mama. I never should have said that."

"It's alright, but remember, that little boy is one of God's children too and he has a bigger challenge than you ever will. He is not like others, he is different in body. It will be harder for him to compete. But with luck and without taunting comments from thoughtless people, he stands a chance. You, Evan de Roche, must understand it is your duty as one more blessed to give people like him that chance. Do you hear?"

"I hear." Evan said as he watched the boys. "I'm being unfair."

"Unfair and ignorant, if you'll forgive my strong words," she said. "You know, Evan, every person on earth has genius. Every one of us has something unique and special. It is our obligation to find that aspect of ourselves and use it."

"Like Danielle and her business talents?" he asked.

"Exactly. You don't know what that youngster might have about him that is special. But I'll tell you this, it is something he alone possesses, something if used

67

properly and to the fullest will allow him to live his life fully, in spite of his limitations."

"Genius," he said. "I never looked at it that way. I always thought genius was intelligence, like Descartes or Rousseau, rather than being something every man and woman on earth had."

"Every man and woman, my dear. We all have our genius."

"And you, Mama? What is yours?"

Pauline grew pensive. She smiled and hugged him for the hundredth time. As the breeze blew her hair and her eyes blazed at the darkening skies, she whispered, "I have taken advantage of my precious and perfect years with a man, a daughter, and a son. I have known and utilized love to the fullest. I have reached my goals, I am happy as a mother and a wife. I love my life. I have found my haven of eternal joy."

"It's so simple really. It's doing what one loves to do, no?"

"True. I love. I love you, and Danielle, and your father. I have all when I love. You see, it's why I love movies like *The Mayerling*. They're simple and to the point. And they treat life's basics the way they should be treated, thoroughly and with respect. Life is for love. I live that life."

He snuggled to her as the air became brisk. They counted the stars until the sky was full of them. Then, Pauline rose. "Come, time to get some sleep. Danielle arrives on the train tomorrow and I must wake early to fetch her."

"May I come with you?"

"I have made arrangements for you to stay here with cousin Thomas. He came in last night on the boat and is with the de Placides tonight. My journey will take all day and I must cross on the ferry to meet Danielle at

Roscoff. Her train doesn't get in until 3. It will be a boring day for you, dear, and Thomas is rather fun, no?"

The prospect of a day with Thomas, a teenager who always challenged him, met with no objection from Evan.

As they stepped across the cool sands, he looked at his mother's profile—her small nose, her smile, her eased way of walking. He also thought how much more than a simple nurturer and companion was the woman at his side. She was the very source from which the family drew its strength. His mother, Pauline de Roche, was a genius like no other. And he was glad for their time together, glad for her advice and admonitions, glad to share with a human being of so expansive a mentality.

He reached and gave her a quick peck on the cheek. "I love you, Mama."

Pauline blinked back tears.

As it turned out, this would be their final interaction. The next day, while waiting on the platform as Danielle's train approached, Pauline and twelve others became statistics in one of France's most tragic train wrecks. In a sudden malfunction, the train derailed at high speed, landing headlong into the station and killing all within yards. Pauline's death was instantaneous as she was hit head-on and decapitated. Danielle, too, died when she slammed through double glass windows on impact.

The confusion of the aftermath, the misleading details, left Evan at their estate and Giles in Paris unaware until late that night. When he heard the news, Giles made for the coast with strict instructions he would to be the one to tell Evan.

But Evan had already found out. That night, for lack of anything better to do and with no word from Roscoff, Evan and Thomas retired early. Evan took his radio to bed to listen to the 9 PM music show but the music never played. Instead, the boy heard details of the accident, the number feared dead, and finally the reference to members of the reputed de Roche family who were likely among the victims.

He silenced the radio and listened to the waves, tried to put the present at bay, and recalled the night before and his walk with his mother.

The hushing lull of the surf and the whispering winds were as if she spoke to him. "I'm alright, Evan, I am gone but you will carry on. Be strong for your father. For he is not as hardy as you, my love. Take care of all the de Roches, mon petit."

Her voice rose up time and again, throughout the night and before the news was officially given to him. His beloved mother was gone. He didn't cry until much later. That night was between him and her as she imparted her unconditional and plentiful love. He would carry forth with her ideas. He would help his father even though he, Evan, was without his anchor, his ever-vigilant and unselfish mother.

By the time Giles de Roche made it to the stone house, his wife's and daughter's mutilated bodies at a local morgue, Evan stood tall and met him at the door, saw the eternally unconsoled eyes and extended open arms to the man.

In Giles de Roche's hand, the white chiffon scarf, bloodied and torn. He stroked it as if pleading for the return of its owner, as if under a spell.

Evan took the scarf from his dazed father's hand, and raised it to his nose. No longer smelling of her, it exuded an ancient and unfamiliar scent—of death and finality.

It was then the first of what was to be a number of actions in a strange role reversal took place. Evan pocketed the scarf and embraced his father, let the older man lose himself in a wash of tears and sorrow, and led him to the couch where they mourned as one. Giles became the child, Evan the protector and consoler. Giles cried as one who would feel this loss as a fatal stab.

Quietly and like a man twenty years his senior, Evan said, "I will help you, Father."

As Giles succumbed to the misery that would mark him, Evan clung to a different perspective. So strong had been her ways, so perpetual her aura, so consistent and life-giving, Evan knew she lived within him still. He need only reach in his memory for her words, her laughter, her joy and he had her.

That night, in the arms of his grieving father and not completely apparent to even himself, Evan embarked upon the road towards his own genius.

# Chapter 6:
# 1959

FOLLOWING NATE'S DEATH, Régine sought out opportunities on both sides of the Atlantic. Acquaintances in New York proposed options that included hosting charity events and even acting and dancing. Boston, too, held possibilities on the educational front. Nate, a respected Harvard alum, had been a regular speaker at the science departments. As a result, a visiting assistantship was hers if she chose. Also, the French embassy in both cities had openings for native French speakers.

As she waited for Nate's twenty thousand dollar insurance policy, Régine toyed with her options. In addition to the freedom her widowhood granted, she would have the means to live the lifestyle of her choosing. She grew anxious and excited as the paperwork was processed and relatives sent condolences to the unfortunate widow and her daughter.

Still young at twenty-eight, she had grown overweight from hours spent munching in front of the television. She soon dropped the pounds and returned to her svelte figure. Her hair, dyed platinum out of boredom several years back, grew to its natural sand shade which softened her features and, when she smiled, made her look not much older than a high school student. These assets would help structure a lifestyle far from the dull one by the sea.

However, an event stalled her departure.

It happened quickly. She had gone to town one night during the Fourth of July festivities. A dance was in progress at the local hall. It was a time of plenty in the U. S., a time for friends and family, profits and risks, achieving wealth like never before. With Elvis leading the way, the continuing furor over rock-n-roll was poised to explode into new dimensions. As Régine swayed amongst revelers that night, she felt a need to join in with this younger generation.

A man who looked to be about eighteen caught her eye. He was slender and well-proportioned, had a wide grin with dimples and blonde-streaked hair. Régine recognized him as one of the many surfers who passed their days seeking out the perfect wave. He mildly protested Régine's advances as she enlaced an arm about him and veered towards a nearby hotdog stand. She let on she was alone, lonely, and available for fun of most any kind. His parents not far away, the young man hesitated and told her he might stop by her cottage the following afternoon.

But Régine was not about to accept his tentative promises. The next day, contrary to her habit of avoiding burning sun and powerful waves, she found the surfers. In a red bikini made in France, she prepared to spend hours if need be sunbathing nearby.

It wasn't long before she caught the attention of every surfer, and the youngster on whom she riveted her gaze was forced—through peer pressure and the sensation growing in his pelvis—to take note. He walked to her and sat down. It wasn't long before they arranged a date, this time in the privacy of Régine's home—dinner for two. She made arrangements with the mother of one of Laurence's school friends to accompany the girls to an exhibit at the nearby marine museum.

The young man, Eric, found himself with a woman he believed no older than twenty who lived alone and had boundless energies in the area of *amour*. An evening of wining and dining brought about his inebriated state. She looked even more beautiful then. As they took cognacs on the porch, his sunburned body became like hot coals as she drew him towards her own smoldering fires with gentle nudges, strategic caresses, the odd, suggestive joke, and her accent from a faraway place. By the time the sun set, she was in his lap, nibbling at his ears and causing him to forget they'd only recently met. He believed her as she spoke of love at first sight, of strong feelings, of her need to get to the depths of his soul.

That night, with Nate already a memory, she allowed Eric—the first man since her husband—under the sheets of her own bed. The hours passed, he with hesitant yet needy groping, she with the cool calculations of a woman who knew what she wanted when and how. In time Eric, too, lowered his guard and fell in line with the bohemian, seaside ways of this smoldering beauty who knew how to drive him mad for affections he never knew he craved.

Until Laurence's muffled noises broke their reveries, they basked in each other as if they'd never before made love, never before known the secrets of another human's body.

Régine presented Laurence as a relative staying for the summer, and waited until Laurence had fallen asleep before she, kissing and rubbing all the way, walked her lover to the door and said good-night. For both, it would be an evening to remember.

Normally, it would have been her first and last time with him. Excepting the wealthy professional men who felt no guilt paying her big bucks and who had the wherewithal to maintain discretion, Régine rarely took the same partner twice. But she could not easily dismiss Eric. His virile and firm body kept surfacing in her mind and, as the next day passed, she found herself glancing to the beach and strolling by the surfers. She waited for his call and drove to town to 'look around,' anxiety intensifying with each passing hour.

He came around that evening and they went out for dinner. Later, they made love on the beach and declared themselves hopelessly enamored of one another. The summer ended with Régine in a dream-like state over this new intrigue that had arrived in her life just as she thought the Cape was the last place she would find it.

With summer's end, however, came the disappointing news that Eric, being of a family whose tradition it was to attended Stanford University, made plans to head for the West Coast and a return to his life before Régine had charmed her way into it.

"You can't, mon cheer," she wailed one evening after a lengthy discussion of their options. "I'll not stand to see you go!"

"And I'll miss you, too," lamented Eric. "I wish tomorrow would never come and I could stay on like this with you."

To not follow in the footsteps of his family meant difficulties of a far-reaching kind and he had his professional goals to think of. He wanted to become a medical doctor, take over his father's lucrative Manhattan practice and continue the family's success. Régine did not hold the keys to his future as did a piece of paper from Stanford.

Régine was not about to let him forget her. Summer over, she packed Laurence and herself up and set out on the first of many trips to California.

It was a furious year. In the fall, Laurence stayed with Nate's relatives while the two spent Thanksgiving together. At Christmas, Eric took her skiing in Vail and Laurence again vacationed with others. By the New Year, Régine was ready to sell the house and make a home near the Stanford campus. In that way, her young man could continue to keep up with the pre-med program's demands yet still have her to come home to at the end of his day.

She was ready but Laurence was not, for she no more wanted to traipse about San Francisco with her mother and Eric than she wanted to continue this ridiculous coast-to-coast arrangement. The phone calls having multiplied and Régine having posted many a picture of the two of them together on the clip board in the kitchen, Laurence knew of the seriousness of her mother's affair.

One night after dinner, as her mother concluded a phone call with a realtor, Laurence said, "I think this is ridiculous. You're acting like people in those soap operas."

"What did you say?" Régine asked, gripping the handle of the phone, her back to Laurence.

"He's a kid. And I'm tired of moving."

Régine spun around and stepped closer. "Well, well, now, aren't we the big shot?" She dug fingernails into Laurence's shoulder.

Laurence's eyes widened. She shook her head. "I'm sorry, I didn't mean it. Please, please don't..."

"Come here, you!" Régine said, nudging Laurence. "Look at me and say that, you little creep. You and your angel bit that only worked for your father! Say it again, louder this time. I dare you!"

"I'm sorry, Mama.....

The slap hit Laurence's face hard, and a flash of heat ran from where it landed on her cheek all the way to her toes. "Stop! I didn't mean it," she mumbled, falling back over herself and onto the floor.

"Speak your mind, will you? Who in the hell are you? You little slut! I'll fix you!"

"No, Mama, no!" Laurence coiled into a ball, protecting her face with her hands, continuing to beg.

Régine kicked her, then pulled up the back of her sweater, stabbing Laurence's back with the pointed toe of her shoe, harder and harder again. "Give me grief, will you? Will you! You know better, better I say!" A final kick knocked the wind out of Laurence. "Stomach you, that's all I do is stomach you and your stubborn ways. When will you learn to shut up and get out of my life!"

Laurence lay on the floor as blood trickled from her nostril. Eyes closed, breathing labored, her silence drew only more anger from her mother, who dug her heel into her daughter's thigh.

"There! Happy? Don't you ever, the longest day you live, ever, give me trouble again, you little wench! I've had it with you to my eyeballs!" Régine raged. "No one is taking away my one and only love! No one, especially you! You've already done that once, you bitch! Do you hear? Do you hear?"

A gust of ocean air and the tick of a clock answered her. Laurence remained motionless.

# Chapter 7:
# December, 1965

THE TRAIN CAME TO A STOP at Dublin's O'Connell Station. From the interior of her compartment, Klee wiped the fogged window. Along the quay, workers in dark overalls and stringy hair joked as they rubbed their palms in order to stay warm. Women in short skirts, thick-heeled boots, and with bangs covering their eyes gripped handbags while keeping after running children. All headed in one direction, towards the exit that led to connections or to the city center.

She fought the urge to stay put and return with the train to Galway. After a long ride with many stops, she didn't feel the excitement of a new place, didn't hunger to discover the biggest conglomeration of activity, buildings, and cars in the whole of Ireland, didn't rush to make introductions—all things she had dreamed of doing the second Kinemmaera was out of sight.

But her ticket was no longer valid and she had no money. It was as she'd planned seven years back. As soon as she earned enough to pay for her exit out of the west, she wouldn't tarry. Now, after all that scrounging, she'd arrived at the threshold of her new life, a child at fifteen but a grown-up for all practical purposes.

She pulled her case from the overhead and it pounded to the floor. Scraping it along, she reached the exit and stepped down. Joining the other travelers, she took deep gulps of the frosty December air, tugged her scarf tighter about her neck, and tried to organize her thoughts. She must get shelter, must use her head. A sign pointed towards O'Connell Street and she followed it, burdened by her case but unable to part with it for it contained her only treasures: books. With the books, she hoped to somehow prove herself, either by tutoring children or helping out in a home for the elderly. She figured her age wouldn't matter, that a potential employer would sense her determination and give her a chance. It would have to be by someone's generosity she found work for she was still legally under age with no leaving certificate.

A couple of street workers eyed her, commented, then laughed. Unsure at first as to their source of humor, Klee studied them. Grudgingly, they resumed their tasks. She pressed her hair in place, fighting an urge to retaliate. Obviously they'd found her looks curious. No surprise, she thought, the story of her life. Since her departure from Kinemmaera, she'd not tended to her person at all. She imagined she looked a wreck but didn't care. Even those times she tried to tame her appearance, outsiders never seemed to notice.

Still a springy mass, her hair was blonder but no less errant. Bumps and mounds had multiplied on her face, the ugliest spots one could imagine, this at a time when her peers fixated on appearances and the opposite sex. She'd grown taller than anyone her age. Gangly, unkempt, and with that vigilant and penetrating gaze, she stood out not as a budding beauty but as an ill-favored child, a woeful error of some sort.

But the physical rarely preoccupied her. She had lived long enough with her features, had grappled with oncoming stares too many times to care what total strangers might think. She'd had to toughen when friends and relatives let slip the odd snide remark. At this point, a city dweller's comment was less than nothing.

She ambled through the throngs to the Liffey's banks where she stopped to catch her breath. The sight rejuvenated her. The skies were grey and the air brisk as petit waves lapped the stone embankment and the river coursed through the heart of the city. The monument of O'Connell stood across the street, near the General Post Office where some fifty years before the first steps towards independence were made. The edifices bespoke pride as well as triumph but, save the odd tourist taking a snapshot, went largely unnoticed by pedestrians. Voices from all around spoke of the new day, the value of a pint, the desperate cold, the errands waiting. Cars honked, people skittered across wide avenues, and in the distance youth headed for the iron gates of Trinity College. Dublin demonstrated a vastly different pace than the one she'd left a few hundred miles away. She gulped for more air.

In an alleyway, she scrutinized windows and doors for rooms to let. A first try introduced her to one of many harsh realities. The landlord was not interested in an inexperienced girl from the country.

"If you had some means, some way of making a pound here and there, I'd have a look," said one woman who answered Klee's knock. "Five pound a week, that's what I need right here!" She pointed to her palm, then closed the door in Klee's face.

She tried a few more places but encountered similar rejections. She found her way up Grafton Street to St. Stephen's Green where, on a bench, she stared at the greener than green grass and tried to gather courage.

A lawn mower made a disturbing hum and round beds displayed what remained of pink and white annuals. Children scampered ahead of their mothers. Students, businessmen, and tourists passed. Earlier, she'd been somewhat soothed to observe street people, tramps, and vagrants. In this manicured part of town, no one appeared to be in the same, itinerant state as she.

The sun peeked out and provided warmth. Taking advantage, she snoozed until afternoon shadows brought the return of chill to her bones and a reminder it would be dark soon. December was a month of short days and even shorter spells of sunshine. She made haste to find a bed for the night.

After enquiring at several shops, a butcher's wife agreed, in exchange for a day of work, to let her spend the night. The woman led Klee up a staircase at the back of the shop to a small three-room flat overlooking rooftops and a processing plant. In a room with fireplace, sofa, and two chairs she rolled out a mattress for Klee. As the woman prepared tea, they made brisk conversation. Klee told her she was from the country but didn't let on where. She gratefully drank two cups to the woman's admonitions about rising at the crack of dawn to help with the incoming slaughter.

Klee nodded, her eyes already lowering with a heaviness that gave away her exhaustion. The sounds of the odd trolley and passer-by beneath her window grew faint and she headed towards a long overdue sleep from which the devil himself could not have plucked her.

The next day, fresher and ready to repay her hosts, Klee made for the downstairs shortly after the wife nudged her to wake. Outside, it was as dark as the middle of the night, but brash ceiling lights showed the way. Wearing bloodied white aprons, the woman and her husband pointed to carcasses and knives, trays with wax paper for loins, chops, and breasts, and containers for livers, gizzards, hearts, and brains. While Klee took instructions, the blur of passers-by or the groaning engine of a bus provided distraction. Alternating between holding her breath and pinching her nose, she commenced fulfilling her obligation.

The morning dragged, dark and dreary until almost ten o'clock, all the while Klee learned the ropes. No stranger to animal parts, she still had to suppress the occasional surge in her belly at the sight of a decapitated pig whose feet were chopped off for eventual pickling and whose tongue was laid out for sale. The room smelled of intestines, body fluids, and death but Klee managed to work a ten-hour day with no complaints, little food, and an even temper. As a result, her landlord Mrs. Fahey, suggested she might want to spend a second night.

Once the final customer left and the 'Closed' sign was placed on the door, stained and sore, Klee trudged up the back steps. Mrs. Fahey showed her where the tea was made. She happily sipped the contents and studied steam rising from her cup while the Faheys washed and prepared bacon and potatoes. Her first full meal in days, Klee wolfed it down with appreciative glances. After, they gave her a sweet.

They agreed she could stay until the end of the week. At that time, she would perhaps want to look elsewhere. For now, the shop was short of help and Klee had demonstrated her reliability. Following a second cup of tea, all three said good-night.

Better adjusted and less sleepy, Klee lay on her mattress and listened to distant church bells, the rumble of trolleys and cars. The lull in her activity brought on a bombardment of emotions—the sadness of her past resurrecting only to be suppressed by the thrill of her situation, a hunger to belong in this environment mingled with her need for a chat in Gaelic with Romney.

She'd made up her mind long ago to leave Kinemmaera but, guarding the insecurity of a young girl, she wondered about her choice, feared the unknown, and tried to make sense of pieces she arranged in the puzzle called her new life.

The decision to go, made that August night of Breeda's wedding and born of shock and sorrow, grew into a need like no other to break away from a place she'd always sensed was never hers. Once Romney revealed Alice Walsh's dilemma, Klee knew what her instincts already told her—she was no more part of the west than her real father, whomever he may be and where ever he might live.

She recalled the tears, the sobs that spilled onto Romney's only dress, over her own pink frock that she herself had worked so hard to clean and press for the wedding. As was her aunt's way, Romney spoke in generalities. Because Klee was well familiar with Bob's disdain, she was able to infer that her mother had carried on with someone who she truly loved and, with Klee's arrival, was punished for that love. In a way, she could relate to her mother, could understand the desire to venture into the world and seek a better situation than that of being Bob Walsh's wife. She asked Romney where her mother went but Romney merely looked to sea.

"She's gone," she whispered.

"Where?" Klee asked.

"Perhaps the city, far away."

"Dublin?"

"Perhaps."

Klee cried, asked questions Romney couldn't answer, and eventually fell asleep on the floor of the chalet. She never returned to the Walsh home, and stayed with Romney until her exodus to Dublin. Neither Walsh nor villager, she was but a passing stranger, gifted and unusual, of a realm few grasp—a child of the wee folk, as Romney said.

Her happy memories of the west—her fairies, her Romney—would be cherished. The rest, Klee opted to disown and bury like a dead person. She was never Claire Walsh. She was Klee, simple and to the point. One name, her name.

Finally she was in Dublin, a place she would for a while call home, a place where she could establish herself and create a life of her choosing, without the sneers of disapproval, without the snubbing and the grudges against her. With luck, she might catch a glimpse of the woman she wished to know, the woman who once had a passionate affair with a stranger and who gave birth to Klee. For Klee dearly wanted to know her mother, wanted to hold her and tell her she understood why she left the bedeviled town of Kinemmaera, wanted to face her and let her see the product of her passion. Klee wanted to find the love she never had. She believed that love was somewhere out her window, in one of the rooms of a flat or hotel, around the corner perhaps or down the street. Dublin held secrets that she would uncover.

Christmas time brought snow squalls and frigid mornings, sleet-spattered roads with the associated car collisions, and school vacation. Students poured from the city to outlying towns in Ireland, back to England or the continent. Families gathered to shop and prepare for the days that brought businesses to a halt and created a general sense of well-being and benevolence throughout the city.

Well accustomed to Klee, the Faheys didn't flinch when making plans to include her in their simple yet festive celebration. She accompanied them to midnight mass on Christmas Eve, sang along with the choir, and enjoyed the sight of the 19th century St. Kevin's Church, adorned with lit candles and packed with everyone from the newest of babies to the oldest of Dublin residents.

The next day, she was warming herself by the fire when the Faheys handed her a package. Throwing the tissue aside, she exclaimed, "The hat!" She carefully removed a black felt fedora. It was the one she'd eyed for months in the display window of Brown Thomas department store.

"A little something to wish you well for the season," Mrs. Fahey said as she passed cakes around to the relatives who'd joined them for the day.

"Oh, it's broken you for sure," Klee said, shaking her head in disbelief. "I can't, I really can't."

In his brass Dublin voice tinged with mirth, Mr. Fahey said, "Sure it's broken us for sure. But, go on, try it on! It was meant for you, sure it was."

Klee pressed curls under the hat and, raising her shoulders in delight, felt the lush material atop her head.

"She's lovely, lovely," said an aged aunt.

"Sure," said Mrs. Fahey, straightening her white church blouse and indulging Klee with a smile.

Klee thanked them over and over, ran her hands across the wide rim and under to the silk lining. She'd never once thought she would have the fortune to wear an accessory so classy, and so unique! She'd first noted the hat after joining the Faheys at the Gresham Hotel for a Sunday tea. It was secured atop a mannequin wearing a red wool coat, and looked every bit the picture of continental flair. In the days following, Klee had eyes only for the hat. Each time she had the odd free moment, she scurried around the corner to Grafton Street and stood at the display window. She would imagine herself the hat's owner, dream of one day affording an ensemble like the one in the store. Those days they weren't too strapped with work, she would confide to Mrs. Fahey the hat in her possession would be her mark, her statement to the fashion world she was proud to be a 'black hat lady.' Mrs. Fahey laughed.

And so Klee sat, a rare bashful look reddening her face, while nervously adjusting the hat. The others commented positively, throwing out the odd joke about her standing out in the crowd. Klee could only nod.

Mr. Fahey of all people, a rugged and staid working man, noticed first how striking she was in the hat, and how she exuded a certain collectedness. That night in bed, he whispered to his wife, "She's a looker that one."

"She's different, you know, Danny."

"She'll have them racing after her in a while. Too soon, I'm afraid, too soon."

"We've come to own her in a way, haven't we?" Mrs. Fahey asked.

"The child's a good worker, no trouble, no trouble t'all," he said as they fell asleep.

Nearby, Klee clutched her gift. In the tiny space, she stood at the window and recited Latin and Gaelic to the empty streets, smiled at nothing, and stepped about.

She snuck to the toilet, a narrow room that faced a brick building. Not bothering to turn the switch, she grew accustomed to the faint outside light. Peering into the mirror above the sink, she studied her tallness, eyes ablaze, and the black hat propped on her head as if it belonged. Rather than the shyness that overcame her earlier, she oozed pride and confidence. Odd, she thought, how a hat could do so much. She stared some more.

The heater sputtered, the floor was ice. Into the smoked glass of the round mirror, she saw her future self. Her spots vanished, her hair remained tame under its stylish cover, and the black hat and even blacker brows gave her an unique allure; a face with an opaque quality, yet with skin so clear and pale, full lips and eyes that were beacons in the gray light. She felt in possession of a power to awe, the ability to command respect. The world her oyster, she was the lovely, uncultured, and exquisite gem at its center.

She closed her eyes and, in Gaelic, wished Romney a happy season. Shivering, she tip-toed across the floor boards to her mattress, placed the hat in its box, and lay down. The new year not far away, she looked forward to it, to the unknowns, to the person she was becoming.

♥ ♥ ♥

Days passed at a fast, predictable pace. The Faheys, content with Klee and her silent, directed ways, accepted her as part of their team. No one spoke of a departure but, come spring, Klee was growing restless.

It pleased her to be in central Dublin. There were book shops to browse in, university events to attend, people to watch, and tea salons where she could chat. She enjoyed the energy of the students, their colorful scarves, their youthful and positive attitudes, their different accents and ways. Not far away, world-famous Trinity was a welcome venue for visitors from China and the United States as well as from Rathmines and Wexford. When classes were in session, a permanent buzz livened Klee's section of town.

She would take breaks at restaurants frequented by students, would eavesdrop on their conversations, and carry on private talks with herself, comparing what she knew with what they were talking about. She found books to read at the Faheys, borrowed others from regular customers, and—inconspicuous at book shops— engrossed herself in passages from newly-released novels. The college kids had curriculums and focus, and

Klee found that what they discussed—from Kierkegaard to macroeconomics, from Latin to the Impressionists – jibed with her own perspectives. Should a topic arise with which she was unfamiliar, it became her next project, to find a book or article and update herself.

She particularly enjoyed being near the Celtic studies students. With an amused grin and oftentimes low giggle, she would listen to a pair grapple with the spelling and pronunciation of words she could spell in a wink and enunciate without flaw. Latin, too, she found she could outperform most. Yet, she discovered that most students were intent on languages she'd not yet mastered—German, French, Japanese. She made a promise to herself that, once her situation improved, she would start lessons. One required interaction with native speakers in order to make a language one's own.

When this concern grew into a constant and bothersome gnawing, she took to thinking about moving on. The Faheys, although kind and accommodating, had not paid her a penny and she therefore had no savings from which to draw should she choose to find her own flat. The work was tiring and left her mind dulled and unchallenged. Beginning at dawn, her spirits would gradually drop until 9 PM when the work was done. Then she was able to slip out for a walk. She didn't raise the issue but, as time wore on, the Faheys also sensed her restlessness. So, when she met Benny O'Hara one night at a pub and he asked her out later that week, Klee accepted partly from intrigue, partly from boredom.

They met on a Saturday in April, when the first hints of longer days gave those so inclined extra hours to wander the town in better light. As was their habit now, the Faheys had invited Klee for a glass at the Brazen Head, the oldest pub in Ireland.

While Danny and Mary walking briskly ahead, the breeze penetrated Klee's jumper and she had to struggle to keep the hat from blowing off. To the Liffey and down the along its banks, they arrived at the whitewashed Norman-style exterior just as others were lining up. Inside, with a pinkish glow to the lights, the snug and bar proper offered a cozy, welcome atmosphere. But it was the human warmth that made it especially enjoyable because, by 8 or 9, the patrons had packed in and, with smoke forming a thick haze, song invariably broke out.

Klee readily entered into conversation with students over politics, the trends of the Common Market, literature, and language. It was the chat she loved, the surprised look in the eyes of her interlocutors when she recited an Irish author in Gaelic or relayed some of her experience in the west. They would ask for more information but usually Klee would gaze off, imbued with thoughts she sensed these young people were incapable of entertaining.

That evening, Klee sat near two young men who were passing through on their Saturday pub rounds. They stood behind Klee at the bar, joked and sang with the group until their friend, Benny, arrived.

"Benny! Where in the divil have you been?" asked a tall, black-haired teenager wearing leather jacket and boots.

"Out and about, lads," Benny said, with a nod to the bartender for a pint.

Klee's back was to them as, sighing audibly, they soothed their throats with gulps of Guinness.

On noticing Klee, Benny exclaimed, "Will you look at that head will you!"

She turned. Into Benny's eyes she darted an annoyed look. "Sure but I'm lucky not to be burdened with the filth you have all over you!" she quipped.

"She's got a tongue, too, now, doesn't she, lads?" Benny returned, expressing a wide smile.

As the two stared one another down, his mates slurred out remarks. Benny contemplated her face and what he could see of her body, returning to the eyes as quickly as he'd averted them. He held his tongue. Mesmerized and amused, he reviewed again her thin crossed legs, her prim straight posture atop the stool, her coat elegantly draped about her shoulders.

"From the west are you?" he finally asked.

She turned away, leaving him staring at her back, the curls springing from under her hat. She felt a tug at one of them. "Get out!" she snapped, a hand to her hat to keep it from falling.

"They're real are they?" he asked. "Blonde hair black brows. A dye job, I reckon!"

Klee glared then stood, towering over most of them, which produced more comments and guffaws. She wove in and about people to distance herself.

At the other end of the bar, a group sang. Closing her eyes, she joined in, raising her voice above the others, eyes upward, fingers tightly locked.

"Good," she whispered, "I'll take my anger out on the Brits rather than those eejits across the bar." Standing and raising her fist at appropriate moments, leaning against total strangers in a camaraderie that slowly lifted her mood, she didn't notice Benny by her side until the tune was over.

Gingerly, he touched her shoulder. He didn't say anything but, again, they were eye-to-eye.

He was about as tall as she, under six feet but promising to be well over in due time. His face was the chiseled, hollowed one of a city youth who, out of the parents' house and surviving on his own, lived on meager sustenance. Eyes blue, pale complexion, a hint of a beard, his brown straight hair hung long over ears and neck. A slightly broad nose and thin lips bestowed upon him a suggestive, untamed demeanor.

His hand press into her shoulder. With sidelong glance, he said, "Sorry, I was out of line back there."

A grin pinched into her cheek, and she said, "Gowan, you were only up to having fun."

"Can I get yourself a glass?" he asked, making room for himself as the revelers broke into a boisterous tune. The Faheys nodded goodbye as she acquiesced to Benny's offer. He placed a glass of the dark brew in front of her and threw a few coins on the bar.

Klee was grateful for the noise, glad to have a moment to herself as this stranger stood by her side and relaxed in her presence. Normally, he would have received a cooler reception accompanied by more cryptic remarks. He was an ordinary Dublin lad, no different than the hundreds of teenagers she'd seen since her arrival. She already guessed that he'd squeaked by his schooling, that he worked in a mechanic shop or along the docks, and that he was anticipating the day when he could purchase his own motorcycle and have done with the need for the buses. No need to question, these things were discerned by his stance, by his gaze, by his way of nudging through the crowd. She knew he was common but couldn't bring herself to snub him.

It had been the touch, the hand on her shoulder, one she had never before felt from a man, warm, protective, and with prowess. At once, she sensed a need, a feeling growing for him that bewildered her on the one hand and held her transfixed on the other. She raised her hand to where he'd placed his and tried to relive the sensation of his touch, but it wasn't the same. It was her hand, not his, and the wool of her coat was already cool.

She grinned and he gave her a playful nudge. Again she felt the rise of emotion that frightened and held her moments before. A man at her side, touching her and, yes, flirting. It was a new experience, an overwhelming, enticing one. Flustered, she took the glass and sipped, wondering what was going to happen next, fighting an urge to touch back and see if he would repeat what she so wanted him to.

He began to sing. Klee sang too, half hoping he would disappear as she closed her eyes and offered solid, clear tones to the harmony of the crowd. If he left, she reasoned, it would be over and she would forget him. If he stayed, she sensed with a lurch in her stomach, she would want to dig deeper into what she sensed was altogether new territory.

The song over, the crowd resettled. Some left the pub, others scuttled to vacated seats, still others pressed closer to the bar. Sandwiched, Benny slung an arm around Klee. She studied his arm. He seemed baffled at the slender, confident figure she cut, the subtle regards beckoning him to come nearer, nearer still.

They strolled together, along the Liffey and to the gates of Trinity, winding towards Grafton and to the alleyways nearing the butcher's shop. He was of a long-standing Dublin family who held staunchly to the politics of home rule and a totally free Ireland. He understood Gaelic. He spoke with emotion and knowledge of the Troubles and his family's role over the years in the gradual move from dependence to agitation with the English. Unafraid to express his wrath and with the remembrance of one who saw torture with his own eyes, Benny surprised Klee with his facility for holding fast to an opinion and backing it up with fact.

It was not unusual to see anger and frustration in the eyes of most anyone on broaching this topic, but Benny's bitterness ran deeper. The Troubles were the Troubles, he claimed, and over the years many Irish had lost perspective on what the term meant exactly. He, on the other hand, could detail the years of Griffith's back-and-forth negotiations with the British, had first-hand knowledge of de Valéra as a spokesman for the republic as well as a personal friend of the family. It was with impassioned words and an eye for a future Ireland that Benny imparted his experiences.

But it was not so much his facility for history that impressed her, for she'd already met dozens of men with more prestigious backgrounds and even more hardened beliefs. It was Benny's body, his tough, rough hands, his bluest of eyes that, although not unusual for lads his age, invited Klee to a rapport of another, less intellectual kind. They didn't hold hands while walking, they rubbed shoulders only once or twice, but between them an electricity sparked. Klee found herself staring into his eyes, at his profile, enthralled by the flicker of a lid or a touch of his hand to his brow. He walked comfortably by her side, not forcing her into the pace of those in a hurry or those trying to keep the cold at bay. Her steps slowed the closer they got to Fahey's shop.

Pointing to the window, she said, "Here."

He pressed his lips inside his mouth and stared at the shop sign as she fumbled for the key. "It's dark inside."

"They're sleeping," she said, inserting and turning. The door opened and she stepped up.

"Can I see you again?" he asked, his body a silhouette against the night.

Her nod barely perceptible, she flicked on the light and backed into the hallway. She thought she saw him smile and then he was gone.

She pattered quickly through the shop and up the stairs, to the window with view to the street and watched as his lanky frame headed for the Green. After making herself a cup of tea, she sat in the darkness, hat still on, her coat thrown to the floor. When her breath became fog and her hands ice against the teacup, she tumbled to bed and let her dreams wash over her.

She would be seeing Bernard James O'Hara again. That was for sure.

# Chapter 8:
# Summer, 1966

THE NIGHT KLEE AND BENNY FIRST MADE LOVE, there was a fidgeting and fumbling that, save the intensity of the moment, would have been comical.

That summer, they rejoiced because Benny and his impromptu band managed to locate an abandoned warehouse for rehearsing. Benny played guitar with two others and the fourth member played drums. They dreamed of a future not unlike the Beatles and practiced endlessly. They made up for a lack of formal training and high-end equipment with their promising voices that did justice to rock and roll knock-offs. Benny debated quitting the dock job to devote all his time to music.

Book under arm, Klee would arrive at the warehouse after work, stumble over wire and boards, and embrace Benny. Then she would settle down to focus on the history of Romania or the 1066 Norman invasion, paying little attention to the group's sketchy and constantly interrupted tunes. Had she taken their music seriously, she would have been critical of their dangling style and off-tune chords. But she was smitten with Benny, happy to have the extended bright days, and glad to enjoy a moment of peace with her books. The band's noise was just that to her.

The group arranged Saturday night stints at area pubs. In the corner of crowded establishments, their tunes blared and the performance was rewarded with free glasses of Smithwicks. Typically, Klee joined the group at a place like Danigan's pub after promising the Faheys she would not be out after ten. The next day, to Danny Fahey's questioning nod, she showed up hungover and droopy-eyed. Nevertheless, she completed her work and caused no trouble. The Faheys tolerated her soirées because she had grown on them. They felt her the daughter they never had.

One such Saturday, and once inside Danigan's, Klee found a corner chair and began to read. She had quickly tired of the scene and now preferred to cloak herself in the shadows with a glass of Shandy and a book. Until the crowds grew unruly and the song was at its height, she sat absorbed in her own world.

That night, the group finished a round of "She Loves You" when Benny, as was his habit, thanked everyone and told them they would end the night with a medley of rebel songs. Klee closed her book and eased her way to the front of the crowd to where she could stand near Benny and sing along.

The song was of freedom, of past hatreds and getting even, and Klee's voice drowned out the others. She'd been reading of injustices laid on the Irish and, as the tune began, residual bile coursed through her system. With loud voice and soul-felt pride, she sang.

People at her side nudged one another, and stared. Bit by bit, others became aware of the sweet sounds emanating from the girl with the hat and hair. She sang and sang some more, absorbed in the lyrics of a people tired of war and ready for change. Then she closed her eyes and began another, softer folk song that in no time brought tears to the eyes of onlookers and a hush to the room.

Benny strummed. The other players stopped. Klee continued. With each verse, she demonstrated her range, her ability with notes, her understanding of the feelings in the hearts of those who listened. As the bartenders cleared glasses and the lights went from dim to bright, Klee sang.

She finally stopped and sought shelter in her corner while the group packed up. Patrons passed and, stared. She was ugly-pretty, young-old, mysterious-brazen. Unable to readily describe her performance, they only nodded, or smiled, absorbed in her magic, her song still alive as they stepped to the streets and headed home.

The last case locked and the pub empty, Benny took her in his arms and gave her a kiss. As always his was gentle and perfunctory. Klee expected no more because, in a shared yet silent understanding, she knew if his embraces were too strongly reciprocated, they would topple over an edge they had yet to come to terms with.

But this night was different. Klee exposed a facet of her being, a sharply different side than she'd ever let on to Benny, a hint at her mystery that compelled him to wish to uncover more.

They made for Fahey's and stood in the alleyway below the shop. He gave her another kiss. His tongue searched hers out, planting hunger and desire in the seat of her chest. She held him longer than normal.

Her blouse was blue cotton and her skirt was short. The night was still and cool, the sky bright. As Benny's embrace tightened, the sounds of footsteps slowed their growing desire.

"Let's go to the warehouse," he said, his breathing halted.

She let him lead the way, their hurried gait saying more than words, their needs clashing with the warnings with which they'd grown up. With harsh judgements and unyielding rules, the Catholic Church bore down on offenders. Though only sixteen, Klee had seen enough sheep, cattle, and horses give birth, knew why her classmates snickered when behind closed doors and out of reach of the nuns' hearing. 'Doing It' had to do with the body's private parts, with monthly periods, with babies and watching to make sure 'It' wasn't done at the wrong time, especially if you weren't married. Then, 'Doing It' was a mortal sin.

She knew all that but this night an irreversible forward movement had begun. They were as close as old friends. She knew his ways better, understood his moods, enjoyed and anticipated his attentions. Already she desired more of what lay beneath his soft shirts and leather jacket. The day he bought jeans, splurging a month's pay for the blue denim and tight look—she had gazed long at his thighs and let him see where her eyes wandered.

In order to sample more of her body, he often reached for her breasts, the thin barrier of her shirt keeping him guessing. He pasted his gaze to her long legs and to the sway of her pleated skirts as she walked ahead of him. Hers was an edgy comportment, but her body was most definitely a woman's and, that night as she sang, Benny decided one thing. He would share her voice with the rest of the crowd but her body would, and now, be his alone.

They found the makeshift stage and Benny arranged his jacket on the floor, lay her gently on it so her head fell into the folds. She reached for his neck and pulled him to her, her legs automatically spreading. Benny rubbed. His kisses mingled with low moans. He pulled at her blouse, popped a button as he found her bra and lifted the material. Her nipple hardened instantly and she drew in her breath. She pulled away, sat and curled her body from him.

"What is it, love?" Benny asked.

Brow furrowed, she extended her hand to his. She wanted to speak but the words wouldn't come, for she was unable to share with him that her body had never been touched by a man, never been an object of desire or caresses the likes of which he was bestowing.

Her pause had nothing to do with society or predictable human reactions to the first time making love. For Klee, it was a moment of stunning reality, a moment she would recall for the rest of her days. A man held her and wanted her, in the way of the most ardent lover, with the strokes of a person who cares, and deeply. She had to grasp for herself what someone like Benny had experienced first with his mother's hugs and then with the odd girlfriend later on. Klee had never. This night, Benny O'Hara's attention was the one thing she'd needed most many, many years ago, an arm about her shoulder, the touch that said 'I love you.'

She kissed him hard, let him press her against the jacket and remove her blouse, her skirt, her panties. In shadows and dampness, to the blare of a boat horn along the Liffey, as Dublin slept, Benny and Klee made love. He was careful not to hurt her, direct and expedient yet paced those times her breath quickened or she winced. His grunts of satisfaction came in waves. Her lower back ground against the cement. After, Klee lay in silence as Benny dressed. Relaxed and nonplussed about her nakedness, she let him take in the white of her skin, the dark patch of hair at her thighs, her wide, happy eyes. Her body was slightly sore, her mouth ached from stretching, but she was at ease.

"It's so familiar," she whispered.

"Huh?"

"Never mind," she said, snuggling against him.

Though she rarely shared thoughts with Benny, they had crystallized. A part of her former belief structure had been challenged, a belief that humans had no purpose but to experience pain, that humans could never as long as they breathed truly know what beauty was, for wicked and unavoidable hurt lurked always.

That night, she let a part of that tenet go, let it slip to her far mind and forgot for a while what she'd held so tightly to all these years. Benny and she, vulnerable and vaguely confused, had chipped away at a barrier that separated Klee from the rest of humanity. The complete crumbling of its hefty walls was a long way off but a crack had appeared. A man had loved her and, in doing so, had invited her into the world, a world around which she'd dabbled since her earliest days. How much she would continue to embrace that invitation was unknown. For now, with pleasure, she toyed with the offer.

They eventually took to the empty streets, and settled themselves alongside the Liffey where they waited for the first rays of sunshine to announce the new day.

# Chapter 9:
# 1968

ALICE WALSH RODE THE BUS to the north side and home. The day had not gone well. In addition to forfeiting hours at the bakery to a younger, more energetic woman, she'd spent good money on sealant to plug a leak in her rented room. She thought it a disgrace the landlord had not seen to the malfunctioning sink. Never mind, she argued to herself, if her latest plan took off, her worries would disappear.

Her thoughts turned to Claire, for today was her daughter's birthday. Why, when July rolled around, did the child still come to mind? Of all her children, she'd bonded the least with Claire, had every reason to let go of her forever. Yet days before and days after this date Alice speculated.

What did she look like? What was she doing? Was she safe, still in Kinemmaera? Or had she left town as well? Had the villagers maltreated her in any way? Did Bob ever share the truth? Her heart went out to the child. She knew the others would survive, for Bob would insure their security and basic necessities. But little Claire? It was not certain Bob would give her a fair shake.

Alice turned onto the alleyway that ended at a run-down brick building. Even in summer the stench of burning coal pervaded the area and, as she climbed to her third floor flat, she could tell the neighbors were cooking cabbage again.

"Awful smells. I'll never miss them," she whispered on entering her compact space.

She gazed around at her single bed covered with quilts and throws, a stove and fireplace. At the sink, she inspected the faulty plumbing joint, sighing as she realized she would have to buy a wrench. Everything was like this, always involved, always beyond reach, always at a cost.

She lay on the bed, lit a cigarette, and tried to ignore the three-day old puddle. The recently hired and too energetic shop worker came to mind. Alice's boss, Mrs. Flaherty, had kept the girl inactive long enough to tell Alice she would no longer be needed for the luncheon shift. Without a word, Alice had turned away and went about her duties. She hated the place—the smell of yeast that permeated her clothing, the heat of the ovens, the demands of customers. Three years ago, she'd felt it a job from which she could derive satisfaction. Like previous jobs, however, its demands proved overwhelming. Dublin was a tough town, tougher still if you didn't know the right people, and unbearable if you were from the country and unskilled.

Seventeen years before when she moved to the city, she had the confidence and pride of one starting out. Although her mind was still on the sin of leaving her children, she nevertheless viewed Dublin as a place where she could collect her senses and save some money. In time, she could reconnect. Her clueless ways and easily distracted personality, however, left her vulnerable to those who could read her better than she could read herself. The six week beautician's course was a waste. Not only didn't she learn the rudiments of hairdressing, she damaged her hair experimenting with dyes and perms. Her job at an ill-reputed salon only added to her disdain for chemicals, head after head of hair, and slippery-tongued customers.

Next, she sold gloves in a shop on Grafton Street, which required minimal ingenuity, a smile every now and then, and the willingness to plow through a mountain of leather and wool should one of a pair be missing. But after five years, her salary was no higher, her flat at the same desperate location on the edges of town, and her social life a miserable nil.

Although she'd tried to make friends, they were either too young and starry-eyed for her liking or too old and proper to accept Alice. She was an in-between thirty-five in those days, her beauty challenged, her past a forbidden secret, her eyes betraying her shame, and her distraction keeping meaningful work always at arm's length.

By the time she was forty, hope dwindled. With sullen spirits she stepped into a routine of long hours at whatever she could find and uneventful nights in her room or, weather permitting, a walk about town. Her hair streaked grey, her body thinned and with the hunched stance of a woman of many more years, she gave up on dreams of using Dublin as a springboard to something better, of finding a new partner, and of one day reuniting with her children. Circumstances had not met her expectations and now she was too resigned to care. She became one among thousands who mechanically performed survival-related tasks and rarely focused beyond the next meal or jar.

Even this latest idea she contemplated halfheartedly. True, it was bold, it would set her apart, but what of it? Too often, her tears and rumbling stomach reminded her that failure planted itself at her doorstep. At this point, one way pointed to freedom.

The men who found their way to her bed were fortunate. Anyone else with sense would have already begun to demand more money, would have taken referrals as a gesture of approval, and would have used them to her advantage. After all, sex was a means to an end. In her youth, the means had more to do with the stuff of fairy tales, of love, of feelings. Today, sex meant an extra pound or two, maybe three. It fed her, clothed her, gave her money for cigarettes, money she would not have otherwise.

Was that what Claire had become, she suddenly wondered? Had her daughter been ill-treated by Bob and left? It was possible, Alice thought with a shudder. Anything was possible. She touched her crooked jaw, the part most damaged when Bob Walsh had slammed her against the rocks. He had it in him. Claire was not his child.

She smiled. Something about Claire made Alice sense that fundamentally her daughter would survive. Claire was not like Breeda, the marriage of whom Alice had heard about, who was headed for the predictable pattern of husband and kids. No, thought Alice, her last sprite was different. Old Romney, who had right away made note, was not oft for declaring a child special. Claire had something, and Alice could feel her daughter's talent resonating even in her own bones.

As she dragged herself from the bed, she contemplated writing Claire, perhaps through Romney. Maybe her sister could reach Claire and tell her about her mother. No, Alice thought, shaking her head and facing the mirror, that would be breaking her new rules. Claire was who she was, dead or alive. Alice would not seek her out.

She traced the circles under her eyes and reached for the bottle of face make-up. After smearing the liquid on, she frowned at the results, went to the curtains, and closed them. Her first customer was due at eight. Maybe the dimmer light would spark his imagination.

"Foolish lady," she chided herself, reaching for her black skirt, "they don't come for a look at your face." She lit another cigarette, sat on the bed, and waited for her man.

♥ ♥ ♥

"I've the book upstairs, Mary! I'll only be a second," Klee said, flipping through the pages.

The Faheys recently purchased a phone and, proud of their possession, took care to insure its use was always for good reason. The book belonged downstairs and Klee was to list her calls so they could keep track.

She threw on her red, bead-studded singing dress and fluffed her hair. Before leaving the room, she re-opened the book to the Walsh name. Scanning the columns, she found no Alice. Odd, she thought, after two years they had never run into one another. She snapped the book shut and raced down the steps.

"Here it is," she said to Mary. "I'm up to ringing Benny I'll be late. He gets upset otherwise, you know."

"Still wearing that red thing are you?" Mary Fahey asked, her eyes wide. "If it weren't for Benny being with you at that pub in Dún Laoghaire, I'd worry as to who was grabbin' after it!"

Klee laughed and placed a kiss on Mary's cheek. "I'll be off for the weekend now. Benny's parents are taking us to the country for my birthday."

"Mind you not to be too late out there singing, Klee, now. Big name you're developing or not, I still see you as our Klee. Take care."

Klee paused. A familiar face in the club circuit, her talents coupled with Benny's band created a stir almost from the start. "Ah, it's fun, that's all, Mary. I'm looking forward to gettin' out to the country if you want the truth!"

She waved goodbye, stepped towards the bus stop, and breathed a sigh of relief Mary had not probed further. After the gig tonight, Klee and Benny were off for their first overnight in a hotel. He'd been begging her for months and had promised he would whisk her away on her birthday regardless of her hesitation. She agreed, up for adventure but more so because she had been a long time away from the country.

Along Grafton, she passed summer tourists, couples arm in arm, the odd dog on a leash. Brilliant blonde in brilliant red, no one could say she was less than stunning. The mere fact that long straight hair was in vogue and Klee ported her mop of curls gave anyone with eyes the message—here walks an independent woman, a lady who knows her assets and uses them regardless of trends.

As it had all her life, the hair grew natural. Her face remained free of make-up and, in spite of her height, her posture was erect. Her individualism paid off ever more handsomely now as, at eighteen, the spots had faded, her body boasted curves and moved in ways it never had at fifteen, and her hair only bespoke her naturalness. No matter how much an envious woman might scrutinize the black brows against the curls, there was no denying she was genuine from the word go. Klee had nothing to be ashamed of.

Still, she never became overly self-occupied. Benny was consistent with his compliments, she knew others' stares were no longer of disdain, and the Faheys' protectiveness could only be because, in addition to her youth, her looks could get her in trouble if she didn't watch out. It was all a very nice place to be, especially with the singing.

Her first voice lesson a year before was a present from Benny, regular sessions with an Italian man who taught at Trinity. Her range and the strength she'd built into her vocal chords held up well even in the most crowded and smoky of bars. It wasn't long before the music scene buzz had it that The Jades, Benny's group, boasted the hottest singer going. Since the first time at Danigan's, there wasn't a night that went by when, in her absence, someone in the audience didn't ask for her. Benny finally convinced her to sing Saturday nights.

Her reluctance wasn't so much because she didn't want to, for singing was proving lucrative as well as fun, but the resolution to further her studies had been made for two New Years' going and she'd not yet made good. Her priorities the day she descended from the train at O'Connell station had not changed—she wanted to teach or be part of the learning process. Possessed of intellect, she needed academic pursuits like she needed sleep and drink. Although self-taught and with an impressive knowledge base, Klee quickly learned from her acquaintances at Trinity the importance of sharing that knowledge, of partaking in exchanges with those whose abilities surpassed her own, and of receiving scholastic recognition. Klee had done none of that. She wanted a formal education more than the appreciative stares of strangers when she belted an octave out of sight, or the sweet smiles of the Faheys when they wished her good luck each Saturday. She wanted it more than even perhaps Benny.

In a relationship of fire and fun, they'd grown comfortable. Klee wasn't interested in widening her entourage of men. Benny was direct, present, and respectful. They loved one another and had said so many times. One day, Benny promised, he would marry her and they would settle. He held to his decision to make a good living in Ireland. Unlike many, he would remain rather than take to different shores to improve his lot. For her part, as long as she had her room at the Faheys and her solo walks and studies, it was Okay to discuss a future together. She cherished Benny and she cherished her solitude. At her age, it was difficult for her to tell which she preferred more. She had the best of both worlds.

When she arrived, the singing was in process so she made way to the stage, joined in the tunes, and quickly became the central focus. It was always that way—The Jades dressed in black leather with their guitars and drums, Klee in her red and blonde with her indescribable voice. She played into the crowd's demands, bowing to their requests, staying stage center, and joking with them. In reality, it was all about Klee. The Jades were an aside on Saturdays, but Benny only saw the pounds rolling in, their name in lights, and their future preserved. It was a grand time.

When Alice Walsh walked in, Danigan's was packed and smoke-filled. The only available seating was next to one of the amplifiers. Her companion, a retired English businessman living in Dún Laoghaire, followed rock and roll groups and had already heard The Jades many times. As he ordered a glass of vodka for Alice and a pint for himself, he continually praised them and outlined their success.

"Sure but she's the one, though," he said, pointing to Klee.

"I can barely see for all this haze," Alice said. She ruminated over the ten pound note in her pocket, of how undemanding, even generous, this customer was. It seemed that, more than physical contact, he wanted company. She had not been surprised when, after their interlude, he had offered to take her to dinner. But now she wanted to get home and sleep. She had to be at the bakery early. Sunday was a big day for bread and cakes.

She puffed at her cigarette and grew annoyed with the amplified sounds. The Beatles or no, she had little sympathy for young people who could afford a night on the town and whose only care was to insure they memorized every tune of every song on the charts. She sipped and squinted at Klee.

"What a lovely thing," Alice murmured.

"No doubt her voice is genuine," the man said. "She doesn't use the microphone like the others."

"He's in love with her, that young man beside her. I can tell," said Alice, with a drawn-out inhale. "Young love... They are sweet together, for sure."

Alice eyed her own companion, his worn suit and tie, his half-beard and dirty fingernails. She pressed her coat about her and tried to forget what they'd done a few hours before. This routine would be over soon and, she consoled, tonight she was ten pounds richer.

Then, Benny's voice boomed. "Now I'd like us all to sing a birthday song for Klee here."

"Here, here!" called the man beside Alice.

In no time, the entire place was singing 'Happy Birthday.' Klee, holding Benny's hand, with mouth slightly open, sought out the face of every patron, her gaze passing over each one, reaching to them for a split second, as she nodded with gratitude.

A charge gripped the base of Alice's spine. She studied, harder this time. It simply didn't make sense, could only be an odd coincidence...

But as Klee clutched Benny and fell into embarrassed pieces, Alice's eyes filled. Such a wondrous looking child! And already so accomplished. She shook, and hugged herself, in search of a strength that alluded her. Their proximity, and those eyes that reminded Alice of one man. She bent her head and placed her face in her hands.

When Klee finally looked her way, Alice was staring at the floor, and gave no signal of recognition. Even after all this time, it was too soon.

As the room went wild with clapping and cheers, Alice peeked again at her daughter and whispered, "Baby, someone's givin' you a happy day."

♥ ♥ ♥

"Benneeeeeee!" Klee screamed as they ran about the suite of a hotel overlooking the bay. "Stop it right now, I tell you, you're a bansheeeee!" She yelped again as Benny covered her with tickling fingers.

"I'll get you into those covers yet, Klee old girl!" he exclaimed, shoving her head under the sheets of the oversized bed.

He'd let the rest of the group pack up in order to speed away on his motorcycle with Klee. Too tired to drive down the coast, they settled for the outskirts. Once in the room, Benny stripped, cracked open a few bottles of Smithwicks, and promptly took to chasing Klee.

"I tell you, Benny, you're the devil, the devil!" Klee had one leg hanging out as Benny groped to find a sensitive area. "Stop it this minute or I'll never speak to you!"

He gave in then, pulled her out by the ringlets and planted a wet kiss. "I love Klee, I do," he murmured, reaching for the zipper of the dress he knew well how to remove. Klee settled against a mound of pillows, then untangled herself from him and went to the window.

They'd been awake all night and now summer's pale light emerged. The hints of a gray morning and the sea made a silhouette of Klee. She was ready. During the evening, they'd been sending wistful glances to one another, and now here they were. She returned to the bed and into his arms, reached for him and guided him inside her. In no time, a joint shiver overcame them. After, they lay still.

The moments following lovemaking were her favorite. Benny would doze and she would reflect, allow feelings to surface, time to try and figure this all out, all so strange-familiar, even after two years. To the cadence of the waves, she imagined herself a tinker travelling along a road of the west, breathing that wild cool air she still could recall. She leaned over and touched him, closed her eyes and envisioned the fairies blessing her with hay sprinkles and their chiming voices, for lovemaking was surely a thing of the fairies, as was the independence one sacrificed if not in charge of one's senses. When she opened her eyes, Benny was staring at her.

"I love you," he said.

She looked straight ahead to the window. It was coming. He was going to ask her. She would have to go carefully. As tough as he appeared, he was like everyone deep down. She didn't want to hurt him but also had herself to consider. A life in and around Dublin, a life of song night after night—no matter how much money or affection from him—was not in her cards. She must be honest.

"I've been looking at flats for us," he said softly. "We have the next four weeks booked so, I figured, not too much time. Around Delany Street...there's one for not too much the week."

She reached a hand to his. She couldn't bring herself to utter a thing. They would, as always during their most intense times, forego words. She would like to continue seeing him, but marriage would never do. She'd messaged him enough in the past months, in her refusal to window shop for a special piece of jewelry, in her choice to overnight at the Faheys without him, and most of all in her erudite affair with Trinity College. However he wanted to continue, if at all, she would agree. Except for marriage.

He waited. Grazing fingers across the hairs of her wrist and arm, he watched a band of gold expand over the water. An hour passed. The still, the quiet. He waited until the shadows disappeared and the sun's rays hit the island across the way, until he could see her face clearly.

Against her chest, he leaned a cheek with a lone tear that had already made a path to his chin, and hugged her hard.

She thought she would never see a man so handsome, so glorious in his masculinity as Benny that morning. In spite of the confusion, he was serene. He would never interrupt her silences. They knew one another that way.

When she stood to dress, she felt his eyes on her back, and a new tension between them. Moments later, he also dressed and readied himself.

At the door, he opened his arms, requesting with his eyes a final embrace. When her body fell against his, he held her tight. "You never told me your real name, my Klee," he whispered.

She curled a strand of his hair around her finger, stamping to her memory his smell, his penetrating grasp, his being. Into his eyes, she wished for an instant that time hadn't brought them to this place, and thought of her fairies. In Gaelic she quoted, "Be careful, and do not seek to know too much about us."

As if trying to see beyond the navy, to those depths she'd never revealed to him in their two years as one, with a closing conspiratorial grin he answered, "Yeats. 'The Celtic Twilight'."

# Chapter 10:
# 1968

AS ABRUPTLY AS IT BEGUN, Régine's affair with Eric ended. His father forbade his son to carry on with an older woman who, for all her charm, was interfering with Eric's scholastic efforts. Resigned, Régine fell into a routine of staying at home during the day and gallivanting at night. It wasn't long before her financial situation faltered and she was forced to take a part time job at the tourist bureau.

Soon after, she sold the house. In 1961, the state had declared a large part of their town National Seashore. The house Nate built was one of a handful that commanded a magnificent view on a location permitting no further construction. Rather than hold onto the property as guarantee of a comfortable retirement for herself and an education for Laurence, she took what profit she could and made plans to return to France.

She wanted her French family and more of the life she had left behind. The last year of high school, Laurence heard of nothing but Régine's need to leave the States and return to a decent, livable situation with family and old friends. Laurence's graduation behind them, they boarded a plane.

112

In the first class cabin, Régine chatted in French to Laurence and in halting English to the stewardesses. Wearing hot pants and with dyed blonde hair, she eyed the men. When one gave her an approving nod, she immediately responded with coy glances, shunning her daughter.

After the plane took off, she ordered champagne. "It will be mandatory for you to greet Tante Jilly," she said to Laurence, referring to an old aunt never before discussed. "She's intent on meeting you. We'll perhaps go to the seashore with friends, too. It's August after all. Then, you're free to do as you like."

"Free?" Laurence asked. Of all her mother's concessions, freedom was never one of them.

"Free. You can leave France, you can explore Europe, you can return to this God-forsaken country. I keep you in tow for a while, so the relatives see you. After that, you're a grown-up."

Laurence held her tongue. She didn't think it wise at all to voyage this distance only to turn around. Still, why would she want anything to do with the de Long side of the family? The U. S. was her home.

She looked out the window. Eleven years ago this month her father had died. How ironic to be leaving! How cold and insensitive of her mother to not let pass one word about Nate. Then again, she should not be surprised. Since that fated day, Régine had never so much as uttered Nate's name.

How Laurence missed him still! How many nights had she prayed to him, hoping he would hear of the horrible turn her life had taken, hoping he would come to her in a dream and suggest a way out. He had always found solutions for challenges. It was torture living with her mother and she had no idea how to better her situation. Young, under age, and so afraid of what Régine might do should she assert herself—Laurence's past eleven years in a nutshell. How in the world could she think for herself, now Régine was done with her? She closed her eyes, envisioned her father's smile, and tried to sleep.

They saw little of Paris, staying long enough for Régine to catch up on her sleep and shop. After, they headed for Brittany. Pursuant to May's student unrest, the de Long family had departed early for their Brittany retreat. Régine and Laurence would join them for the rest of the summer.

Aboard the train, Laurence tried to relax and take in scenery that reminded her of home. Once out of Paris, hills tumbled around Norman farms, church spirals marked the center of villages and, once they passed through the walled town of Dinan, the Atlantic peeked at them from beyond the Gulf of St. Malo. At Roscoff, they waited for the ferry to the Ile de Batz, the island visible from the mainland but separated by a deep channel.

The seaport intrigued Laurence, with its bustling commercial harbor and sturdy fishing boats that ventured as far away as Iceland. The church of Notre Dame de Croaz exemplified the town's architecture, flamboyant Gothic boasting a Renaissance belfry, carvings of ships, and even cannon embellishments. She toured the aquarium and museum, which was also part of the world-renown Roscoff marine biology center. Nate often mentioned the center and its affiliation with Woods Hole Oceanographic. While her mother primped at a café, Laurence grew endeared to the location and figured, if nothing else this summer, she could occupy herself in Roscoff.

She took a walk beyond the town limits and discovered the untamed and rocky coastline. There were shallows for fishing, beaches carved here and there, and fishermen loading seaweed onto carts.

For the first time in months she was on her own and able to commune with the sea. Once back in town, she sat on a granite wall and studied their island destination. The Gulf Stream drove in warm temperatures, the air was humid and comfortable. She fought the urge to remain immobile; she didn't really want to return to the ferry at all. Perhaps she could disappear into this pleasant community, study at the marine center, and in time journey back to the States. She'd been too young to remember her father's descriptions but she now understood why he chose to visit Roscoff. Too bad Régine had crossed his path in the process.

She felt her thigh, the bruise that had yet to heal from a recent lashing, and was grateful for the reprieve their stay in France represented. Weeks before, in anticipation of their journey, Régine stopped leaving facial reminders of her wrath. Since the break-up with Eric, her mother had found an outlet for her frustrations, unrealized dreams, and her misery. Now they were in the presence of family, how would Régine handle any upcoming bad humors?

Laurence rationalized that her guarded secret was inconsequential. At school she made little of the black and blue marks. They were a result of her own stupidity walking on the rocks, she would say, or her clumsiness about the house. No one wondered why her bruises never fully healed or expressed concern to speak of. Laurence grew even more secretive. It was the only way to cope. Masking her internal pain, she focused on her studies and the odd carefree moment at lunch.

As much as the abuse, she detested her mother's overnight visitors. Out-of-towners for the most part, men with tailored clothing and fancy cars embraced Régine and openly displayed their intentions the moment they arrived at the house, at which time Laurence was instructed to absent herself. Régine pounded it into her head many times. "You get out when my friends come. Stay on the porch or something, but don't bother us."

Fearing reprisals if she took off for a friend's, Laurence would make for the porch and, with the help of a gas lamp, read or listen to the waves. Even during winter she was often outside until after midnight, shivering in gale-force winds until Régine appeared and let her back in.

Calmed by the retreating tide, she whispered, "Free." Perhaps it was up to her to try and make haste to get free, to try and reach for another life. She was eighteen, and Régine had said to get lost.

The ferry horn blared and she made way for the crowd gathering along the docks. Already in line, Régine clamped a hand around Laurence's wrist, and dug red nails in deep.

"Please, it hurts," Laurence said.

"Ha! It hurts!" Régine hissed, shoving. "You weren't thinking of staying were you, Laurence? You'll see how lovely the island is. You won't want to leave."

Her mother's cloying, pretentious tone was the one used to impress but it made Laurence want to retch. Eyes downcast, she said nothing. All this was too familiar, a hackneyed game.

Twenty minutes later they arrived. Régine's mother Mémé greeted them. A petite, white-haired woman with eye-squinting smile and gentle demeanor, she embraced Régine and exclaimed, "We've been waiting anxiously for you, dear!"

"Oh, Mama, Mama! I've wanted to come back to France so badly. It's been too long..." Régine sobbed.

"So!" Mémé exclaimed to Laurence. "My grandchild, eh? Lovely, lovely..." She peered. "But, those are Nate's eyes! Oh, you are a beauty, child!"

"It's nice to meet you, Mémé," Laurence said in French.

"She speaks fine French! What did you mean in your letter, Régine, about the young Americans not caring about other cultures? Your own daughter already understands La France!" She hugged Laurence again.

"I'm not so good at it really," Laurence said, glancing awkwardly around.

Régine huffed. "Well, she won't have trouble mingling with the young people, will she, Mama? Come, let's get to the house." She put and arm about her mother and stepped towards the waiting car. Laurence followed.

♥ ♥ ♥

The next days proved a pace of another kind for Laurence. The de Longs were a tight-knit and large family. The estate-like summer 'cottage' sat at the edge of rocky cliffs on the north side of the Ile de Batz. Cousins, aunts, and uncles Laurence never even heard of invited her into their circle and treated her as one of them. She had her own room at the end of a corridor, a compact space with single bed, writing table, and bookcases filled with interesting material. Régine took a master suite next to Mémé.

Each day after a breakfast of croissants, brioches, jams and jellies, plus café au lait in oversized ceramic bowls, everyone would take to the outdoors for the odd diversion or two. Laurence joined Uncle Georges on a sailboat, fished with cousins, discovered the island on foot, and relaxed at the beach. No one forced her to do anything yet she helped about when she could, especially during meals.

Lunches and dinners were times of gatherings and long hours '*à table*.' From one until three in the afternoon, the de Longs sat outdoors by the cliffs or inside at a long wood table feasting on local foods and wines. They conversed about area and national politics, reveled in one another's stories of the day, and listened patiently and with interest to Régine update them on life in the States.

Laurence nearly let herself relax. She was better able to enjoy herself since, as the days progressed, Régine paid Laurence little attention and seemed to be making good on her words that her daughter was finally free.

One day when Uncle Georges went to Roscoff Laurence joined him. They spent the entire afternoon at the aquarium and about town. He brought her into a fish processing shop and they chatted with the Breton owner. The old gentleman, in blue overalls and beret, knew Georges well and was pleased to meet Laurence. As it turned out, the man remembered Nate.

"*Ah, oui, mais oui! L'Américain, oui bien sûr, je m'en souviens.* Nate...." His eyes twinkled as he noticed Laurence's face brighten. "You resemble your father, little one. He is in the States now?"

Laurence shook her head. "No, he died many years ago."

"Ah!" exclaimed the man, "The good ones go early, don't they?" He reached for her cheek and pinched. "You will follow the sea, eh? Like your father? He was a man of the waters, a smart one, too!"

Laurence's eyes misted. After they left, Georges asked her about her father. She detailed their idyllic existence on the stretch of land Nate claimed as his own, and hinted at her desperation now he was gone.

"Your mother is over him," Georges said. "She is looking for love again, I see."

Laurence studied the face of her handsome uncle and understood. With Mediterranean looks and deep tan, muscular body and charming personality, George was a catch. Laurence guessed her mother had already made advances. But Georges appeared wise to Regine's antics and his marriage to her aunt Chantel bore no signs of faltering.

"She is lonely," Laurence said as they waited at a corner crêpe stand for a snack.

"She is dangerous," Georges said, staring at Laurence with eyes that broke through her feigned impartiality.

"I don't know," Laurence said.

He reached for her wrist, studied. "What is this? You're sore, non?"

Laurence retracted her hand.

Georges offered the rolled sugared crêpe and smiled. "Here, petite, enjoy. I don't think your short life has been fun since your Papa is gone. I know Régine. I think she's not changed much. And," he said, giving her a warm hug, "I'm happy to meet Nate's child."

Laurence pressed her lips then bit into her snack. "Georges," she said thoughtfully chewing, "I wonder might I inquire about courses at the marine school?"

"I think that can be arranged..."

They headed to the pier from where the final ferry of the day was departing and drove back to the island as the sun set across the waters.

♥ ♥ ♥

With the summer's end came *La Rentrée*, France's en masse return from vacations and the commencement of school. In like manner, the de Longs said farewell and headed home in cars packed with their summer belongings and souvenirs of another memorable season.

Laurence and Régine remained, as Madame de Long preferred spending the month of September on the island. It was quiet and peaceful and, at seventy and with her husband gone, she was in no rush to rejoin the crowds in the city. Laurence would begin study at the research lab. Georges paid in advance for a marine biology course held once a week with labs two afternoons.

Vexed with the arrangement, Régine could do nothing about it without arousing suspicion. A number of times she had come close to displaying her true self. One of his final days on the island, Georges noticed definitively that all was not right. Régine pulled Laurence aside for a walk along the beach and returned without her. When Georges and Chantel went in search of the child, they found her dazed and with burn-like spots on her upper thighs and lower back. Laurence claimed it was her fault but Georges promptly questioned Régine about the incident and let on he was wise to her. She was to stay away from Laurence or he would reveal her actions to Mémé.

It was enough to keep Régine in line. The fear of facing Mémé—who all adored and respected— precluded any rash actions. Plus, she had finally received her mother's agreement they would visit Giles de Roche one afternoon. Régine was not about to let false moves get in the way of her next plan.

Familial telepathy and to-the-core devotion left others in the family sensing a problem in the Mallord mother-daughter relationship. One by one, they registered their feelings and left for Paris a bit wiser to Régine.

Unwittingly, Laurence played into their suspicions. Being the charming, helpful person only underscored

Régine's temperament and phony airs. Laurence enjoyed her stay with the de Longs and, after a while, told them as much. One thing Mémé approved of was a serious child. Already enamored of her granddaughter, she became more attached as the days passed. She was pleased when Laurence announced her intentions for study nearby and offered her own financial support.

Laurence began her studies and, no surprise, took to the course, the materials, her professor, and the setting. Each evening at dinner, she updated Mémé on her discoveries, relaying with enthusiasm the ideas taking shape in her mind for various ocean studies. It was clear she would do well. Was this the way to eventually free herself, she wondered?

Still, Régine remained, awaiting the weekend arrival of M. de Roche and stewing privately at her daughter's activities and successes. Laurence ignored her mother and immersed herself in work. Late at night the light burned on the study desk in her room. She read and re-read assignments, underlined and memorized key words, listed questions for the next day, and pieced together plans for the career she was meant for—the same one as her father.

Régine's hands were tied. Mémé was ever present. When Laurence wasn't at school, she was studying in her room. Plus, Georges called frequently to check on the promising student and to hint to Régine of his awareness of her ways. Régine and Laurence never spoke except at dinner when, haltingly, Régine would enquire about the day and, as hesitantly, Laurence would respond.

If Mémé comprehended any of this, she didn't show it. Her entire life had been spent in luxury, with a man who adored her, with every physical, emotional, and spiritual need attended to. Mémé preferred order and peace. Under her roof, there might be animated conversations when people disagreed—for debate was always encouraged—but never were acts of hatred or revenge tolerated. Her home a happy decent place, Mémé would stand for nothing less.

Laurence continued her studies, wondering when the next outburst would manifest.

# Chapter 11:
# Summer 1968

"BUT IT'S THE FUTURE, PAPA," Evan said one night while wrapping up the day. "Movies, cinema, all evolving, snowballs rolling into an avalanche!"

"I'll not deal with Americans influencing France, Evan," Giles said, taking a sip of cognac and leaning back in his leather chair. Spectacles low over his nose, a strand of salt and pepper hair strayed over one eye. He was most at home in this office where usually he closed out the day with Evan. "Now is not the time to invite foreigners. France is still recovering, still reaching to find herself. We must strengthen our own forces first, our own businesses and products, before we invite the outside. The Americans have already snuck in through back doors, what with their computers and subsidiary offices. You think I don't see the quantity of American movies showing along boulevard Montparnasse? My son, our French films are eclipsed by all the cowboys, comedies, and Brandos."

"But Papa, what if you invest in their distribution channels, for the films and the houses?" Evan asked. "In time, deals can be made, you say that yourself. First, distribution rights. Later, who knows?"

In dark suit and beige shirt, Evan was a throwback to the man's youthful self, complete with the fire and verve of the most assertive de Roche. Giles couldn't suppress a smile. "Evan, Evan, see here. I know you love the movies, have been following them for years like a fanatic. But, this is profit and loss we're talking about, not some game of chance. You don't remember your mother's father, Monsieur Duvivier, but he also had similar notions. He lost a fortune putting faith in the American production houses."

"I do recall, Papa, with all due respect. Mama told me, and I discussed this thoroughly with Uncle Marcel," Evan said.

"Marcel, Marcel," scoffed Giles. "He's a dreamer, always has been. Look, he hasn't even lived in Paris for over twenty years! How could he know the secrets to France's advancement!"

They were back to their perennial argument. While Giles based his decisions on the belief France must work from the inside out, Evan was receptive to international investment. It was mandatory France play the world-wide game, even if it meant losing a leadership position within certain markets. From banking to computers to movies to cuisine, it mattered most that France be involved, whatever the stakes. Evan felt at one with the Germans, the English, the Americans.

When the two men hit this impasse, Giles withheld comment, gazed off and sent his son a regard that bespoke his memories of war-torn France.

Evan pondered this aspect of his father, a man normally unafraid to risk. Versed in world politics, amenable to change when it made sense and spelled profit, Giles could nonetheless turn a blind eye to business of a different, and potentially more lucrative kind.

Giles never attempted speaking English. The few times he journeyed to London or New York, he returned saying the meetings had left him *fatigué*. Never once did he follow through on proposals introduced during those trips. It seemed Giles placed plugs in his ears and blinders over his eyes when he travelled for work. Once home, he delayed follow-up for one reason or another, and eventually the to-dos were forgotten.

Ironically, too, Giles verbally promoted international expansion, to a point. He often said a unified Europe was a logical notion and he was not opposed to setting up branch offices in Germany or Switzerland. But when it came to long term commitments beyond French borders, what the man truly felt was anyone's guess. A seasoned businessman, he could bluff with the best, and when it came to overseas affairs—especially American ones—Giles de Roche appeared less than honest about his true intentions.

Evan was forced to imagine for himself the reasons his father walked two distinct paths. So, when Evan proposed joint ventures with the Americans and Giles refused, Evan realized his father's distrust fronted a prejudice that prevented clear thought. For months, Evan tried to pretend he imagined it, but this side of his father gnawed at him, was reason to keep him up nights, inviting him to face some less than admirable facets of his father's personality. It grew into the silence that divided them during their nightly discussions.

Throughout his youth, Evan remained a model son, a sure bet for Giles's spot at the head of de Roche Frères. While striving to achieve the best marks at school, he also made headway with the employees of his father's concern. Summers he worked at numerous jobs within the company—carrying cargo to and from warehouses, painting, or doing the chores no one had time for, and even sitting in on a meeting or two. His low-key style and willingness to perform even menial tasks won him respect even from senior employees.

His youth, a potential excuse to limit responsibilities, only meant he would fare well for many more years to come. No one begrudged him his due and everyone remarked on his striking looks and associated nonchalance. Evan managed to balance his silver spoon heritage with a down-to-earth geniality that overcame barriers of jealously, competition, or strife.

He seemed to manage and accept with readiness the place carved for him years before. In many ways, it had been Danielle's professionalism and charm that made it easier for him to step onto the de Roche platform. Her impression lingered, like her picture that hung on the wall near her father's desk, a continual reminder of her energy. Because of their age difference, Evan never really knew her in life and now, as he walked the very halls she had, as he met people who sang her praises, he felt a closeness with his sister. Going to work at de Roche Frères brought her back and warmed him inside.

As important, he played the role of comforter to his father. Giles never fully got over the train tragedy. In a regard marked with permanent grief, a distinctly different view onto the world. The immediate aftermath found him distracted, taking walks away from the premises during lunch, spending hours in his office staring at the wall, wondering if and how the accident could have been avoided. If not for young Evan with his cheery smile and helping hand, Giles may never have resumed the demanding job he once performed with so much ease.

They worked together, relaxed together, and drew upon one another's strengths those times one or the other felt lost and vulnerable. A curious two-some, mirroring each another, destined to pull at the reigns of

France's future, and facing challenges never before encountered in the French work place.

Nonetheless, Evan had interests beyond the business world. He loved museums, expositions, books, and all the seasoned stage stars. Most of all, and always with his mother in mind, Evan loved the cinema.

He went religiously to movies and followed with enthusiasm the Nouvelle Vague of *cinéphiles* in France: Truffaut, Godard, and others. During lunchtime, Evan could often be found at his desk with *Les Cahiers du Cinéma*, the periodical written by and for cinema professionals. He was influenced by their mission to forge a heightened awareness of techniques and characterization, to encourage directors to dare innovative feats with the camera. He agreed with their efforts to take a second look at early French cinema, for it was a time of boldness and courage like never before. He analyzed the French and American films and hungrily took them in sometimes two and three times. Once inside the theater, Evan became part of the activity on screen, no longer an onlooker but a participant in the truest sense of the word.

Mornings following a particularly gripping film, he readied for work with difficulty. A part of him wanted to seek out the director—most of them lived in and about the city—to question, review, and challenge. Better yet, he wish to run into one of the stars and discuss process, technique, and feelings now the movie was distributed and he or she was on the big screen for millions to see. In his bones, he felt the French were on par or better than the Americans when it came to using visual techniques to express man's condition.

He was also again with his mother. A film over and with a look of concentration and thought, Evan would walk through the streets of the Left Bank in a private banter. It would have been she to accompany him all those times, it would have been she to review every aspect of the film as they walked arm-in-arm, it would have been she to instill a particular perspective. Alone, he felt her at his side, heard her laugh, saw the merry smile, and felt as though she'd never been gone.

So easy had it become to first lose himself inside the theater and then to reignite their closeness, and his trips to the movies took on another critical dimension. Not only was he in the pursuit of the latest and most talked-about film, he re-connected with a past of bliss and wonder and could again be the boy on the beach with a head full of dreams and a heart yearning to discover the world.

Business was acceptable, decent, and profitable. But Evan de Roche, slowly over time, felt a stronger pull emanating from his artistic side.

By the time May 1968 arrived and students spilled into Paris streets, protesting everything from the way faculties were run to the abuses of a consumption-oriented society, Evan was poised to embrace the unrest with a rebel's abandon and energy.

While a student at the Sorbonne, he heard rumors of the young Daniel Cohn-Bendit from the University of Nanterre who, along with others of the sociology department, had already interfered with the university's pace. The first ripples of trouble came on May 3rd, and Cohn-Bendit headed the pack when students moved towards the Sorbonne to organize a protest meeting.

In short order, the rebellion exploded. Barricades marred the once pristine boulevards and avenues of the capital. The pilfering of shops and other businesses, plus erratic public transportation, rendered law enforcement helpless. The unions forced their own agendas for improved work conditions and contracts. Agitation spread to the countryside. By the 13th, a nation-wide strike paralyzed France. De Gaulle and his government sat on a precarious ledge, facing the threats from a people no longer content to settle back and accept the status quo. The word of the day was aptly pronounced by Cohn-Bendit: "*Le pouvoir est dans la rue*—Power is in the street."

In the month that followed, de Gaulle held a referendum in an attempt to dispel the growing belief his government was ineffective. A surprise result of the general vote was the reemergence of the Gaullist party, this time in greater numbers. Apparently, de Gaulle was still in charge, but France was no longer the same. Students and workers alike participated in an effort that was to determine the direction of union negotiations and academic curricula. Some said it was the forging of an era that would carry France to a radical way of thinking, an order ruled by youth, with a revolutionary twist not unlike other countries when people demanded their due.

Evan loved it all—the traffic-free boulevards full of anger and outrage, pamphlets that criticized the bourgeoisie and lack of meaningful action within the government, and especially the popular phrases of the day. His favorite, "*Prenez vos désirs pour des réalités*— make your dreams reality—played on his lips even as he sat as the head of his father's meetings and tried to see beyond the roomful of wary businessmen to the issues at hand. He was torn—ever loyal to de Roche Frères yet an adherent of the emerging, heart-felt beliefs of his contemporaries.

De Roche Frères played an essentially conservative role in the events of '68. A division of the company comprised of coal workers was the scene of work stoppages, contract negotiations, and threats from the unions representing these workers. At a distance, Giles watched profits decline and employee absences rise. Like most Gaullists, he tried to maintain perspective, hoping that most of this would simply go away. In time, things did settle. There were some changes of contract regarding work hours and benefits but, in general, the employees of de Roche Frères were happy to return to work and earn what most considered a fair wage. The unions emerged stronger and companies like Giles's were forced to pay more attention to their demands.

An as pervasive but less tangible economic problem was to have more far-reaching consequences. Following the events, many investors withdrew their money from French institutions, preferring foreign markets with which to guarantee profits and growth. Unable to choose between austerity or expansion, the financial minister did nothing, thereby guaranteeing a major exodus of revenue sources. The franc was faced with devaluation, an inevitable result of fluctuations in the extreme.

This issue was a relatively new challenge for Giles, whose father before him had wisely invested prior to the Depression, leaving the de Roche family without monetary concerns during the 1930s. Yet now, to face a devalued franc and depleted capital reserves on a national scale would clearly spell doom for any enterprise, no matter how powerful or large. Nevertheless, Evan's innovative idea went unregistered by Giles.

Evan excused himself and left the office, promising Giles he would catch up with him later. In spite of the difficulties with his father, Evan also found time for fun, and tonight promised an adventure of a lifetime.

"Z," the controversial and political film about unrest in Greece, was in the final stages of production. Major portions had been shot in Algeria and interior shots remained which could be produced cheaper in and around Paris. Because Evan gathered regularly with students of the renowned cinema school, I. D. H. E. C., he was well aware of the storyline, the actors, and the film's progress. This was a pastime that allowed him to loosen his grip on everyday problems and to gain perspective.

At a café, he approached two students. "Salut, Albert, Étienne," he said.

Walls of the café still boasted posters and leaflets from the upheaval in May. Young women and men wore somber dress and, while sipping cafés and beer, discussed every aspect of film, from the promotion of the latest release to critiques of an up-and-coming director. Always with the opinions and essays of the members of the Nouvelle Vague in mind, they mulled over their mainstay next to food and drink. I. D. H. E. C. was the school of their idols—from Alain Resnais to Louis Malle—and they hoped to follow in such famous shoes.

"*Salut, mon vieux*," Albert said. A rangy, fair-haired youth, Albert was in his last year of school with every intention of producing his first film once formal studies were behind him. "We have news about "Z.""

"We can do it?" Evan asked.

"Yes. Her name is Patrice. She's returned from Algeria with her father who played a bit part."

"How? When? Now?" Evan asked, his voice high-pitched. This was the best news in months. Since he'd made these friends, they'd planned for Albert's new movie as well as tried to figure an 'in' to the setting of what promised to be France's next greatest film. All the while Costa-Gavras's team filmed in Algeria, they scouted production facilities outside Paris for any hint of when the film team would return for local work.

Evan did much of the footwork. He could, at varying times throughout the day, leave class or de Roche Frères and take his father's car to the outskirts. He would enquire and update the others on the planned dates for shoots, or any snags the production might have run into. With this information, they formulated action items for the next meeting. It was a heady, obsessive activity, inviting them all to think imaginatively and in the extreme.

Evan liked best the fact his comrades didn't know who he was, for he had never offered his last name. Although Albert often remarked on the style of dress and the fancy Peugeot, the upper class aura of the young man didn't get in the way of their friendship. While Evan was not like them and for some reason unable to attend the school he obviously showed talent for, they welcomed him and missed him in his absence.

They agreed to meet Saturday at the Porte de Gentilly where the train could take them south to the studios. Once there, Albert would locate Patrice and they would join her for a look at a film in progress.

"Z" coupled riveting action with provocative political ideas. Having read the book and after several sneak-peaks at the script, the young men surmised that its premise would formulate the basis of many action-packed silver screen stories to come. They relished its release as another way to re-live the crazed days of May when they first tasted the pleasure and felt the emotional charge of unrest and change.

Patrice Larchim, sitting on the steps of the entrance, embodied the myth of the exotic. Thick curly hair and brown eyes, black skin and long slender fingers bespoke her North African heritage. At their approach, she tucked *Cahiers* under her arm and stood.

Greetings were exchanged and all four entered the building, Patrice updating them on the crew's recent return and the concentrated efforts required in these final stages. Her father remained in Algeria and she, having applied to I. D. H. E. C., returned to France to wait for word. Her application was late and, if not for the personal intervention of Costa-Gavras, she may never have stood a chance. She spoke highly of the

Greek director and lent insight to the project Evan and his friends couldn't have hoped to become intimate with otherwise.

A few minutes with her, one easily saw she was meant for film. Her expressions told more than words, her voice murmured a sensuality that could carry a story, her body was arresting in its stance. Although a *pied noir*, one whose French family had long ago settled in Algeria, she seemed unconcerned about her nationality in spite of the prejudices of the day. She held her head high, flashed wide eyes, and had a way of placing one at ease in seconds. Evan had trouble averting his gaze.

Using only his first name, he introduced himself, joked, and gave her an appreciative shake of the hand for, without her, they would never have passed beyond the gates. Side by side they led the way and chatted about the desert heat and equipment problems, M. Gavras's style with the actors, the odd habits of Yves Montand, and the general outcome of the shoot in Algeria. Patrice was accommodating, cheerful, patient and watchful, even as they strayed from her to marvel at the set and seek out famous faces.

They spent the day watching, whispering, and commenting quietly as another charged filming day unraveled—the setting up, the make-up interruptions, the adjustments. Several supposed short takes took the longest due to the emotional message to be conveyed, a message the director believed should be done non-verbally. During those times, everyone was on the watch for that moment when the camera caught that which would force the boundaries of the medium.

During a break, as the young people made way for the outdoors, Yves Montand jaunted beside Costa-Gavras.

"He's an even bigger star with this," Patrice said, pointing to Montand with delight and tugging at Evan's arm.

"Hmmmm, not a bad looker," Evan joked. "After all, he's been long enough in France."

They laughed. Her hand slipped slowly from his arm, her gaze turned away. The hint of her sensuality dissolved as Albert caught up with them.

"It will sell, I know it!" he exclaimed. "We could go to Morocco, it's cheaper and the weather is predictable."

"Already on about the location!" Étienne said. "You've yet to show me a draft."

"But I've told you a million times. It will be about a fugitive from the law, why not have him run to Morocco?"

"Oh, now it's a fugitive! Last time it was a journalist!" Evan exclaimed. "You change with the days, Albert. Perhaps what we need is to jointly work on the script, get something concrete in our hands. Then we can see how much of it makes sense."

"And there's the equipment to consider. Did you see the size cameras they use in there? I'm overwhelmed by it all!" Albert said.

"Nonsense," said Evan, "Start small, think big. We can rent equipment from the school, no? It would be cheaper. Plus, I've already told you, I have a relative with a villa in the Midi. Once the summer has passed, we can use it for your location. It's outside Aix, we can film street scenes there."

"Mad car pursuits, guns in everyone's pockets, women in danger!" Albert went on.

"Cool, it, Albert. You want a film, you must stick to your original ideas," said Étienne. "Evan's right. Let's get something in writing."

They agreed to review scenes at their next rendez-vous.

The day too soon over, Patrice excused herself. They promised to keep in touch.

♥ ♥ ♥

By the time they drafted Albert's story, it was the end of June. School over and Evan's workload easing, they had more time, and so organized lunch meetings and wandered the parks. All the while, they crafted the film that would usher Albert into the limelight, or at least provide them with diversion during the warm months.

Early one Sunday morning in the Luxembourg Gardens, they attempted their first shoot. A rising mist promised non-stop heat. They planned to shoot some practice takes, develop them, then analyze the results. Patrice agreed to join them.

They slaved and fidgeted, moaned and complained over difficulties like securing, transporting, and trying not to break the finicky equipment. None of them wanted to be cameramen and it was an exhausting effort dividing up their talents to produce what during "Z" appeared to be a piece of cake.

Patrice was charming. In a blue one-piece cotton jump suit, she sat primly at the foot of one of the statues dotting the park, waiting, smiling as adjustments were made. Her lines memorized cold, she offered help where she could.

At one point, she was drawn to children playing with sailboats in the pond. Behind the lens, Evan followed her conversation with a boy holding a hand-carved wood sailboat. She clasped her hands with glee as the craft separated from the child's hands and glided to the middle of the pond. Adjusting the camera, Evan caught the contours of her body forming a silhouette against the nearby Senate building, then the boy's questioning look, and finally the joined hands as Patrice and the child edged along the pond to follow the boat. He used long shots then close ups, all the while nearing slowly so as not to disturb.

The boat retrieved, the boy secured the toy under his arm. He shook Patrice's hand and they kissed goodbye.

"Nice," Evan said, as she approached. "Very nice."

"You were filming!"

He called Albert to take over, and stood to one side. Rolling down the sleeves of his shirt he said, "You have a magic, I don't have to explain."

"I love being a part of this. It easy..." she said.

"You should follow your dreams. I hope they accept you at I. D. H. E. C," Evan said.

"And I. What about you? What about your dreams?"

He shrugged. "I have the means to enjoy lots of things. It is fun. Fun is what I'm after now."

In another hour, they finished and hurried to return the rental equipment in time. A few days later, all watched the test reel. When Albert and Étienne saw the boat scene, their mouths dropped. So simple yet so compelling, it displayed every innuendo of Patrice's persona, every twitch of the eye or giggle. So vivid the shots, so alive the motions, words were unnecessary. Evan, too, was transfixed with the results of his experimentation. They reviewed it again, agreeing repeatedly Patrice was meant for film.

Evan's ability to underscore the essential message of a scene was undeniable. Once the lights went on, Albert and Étienne exchanged glances in a shared communion, a quandary not anticipated when welcoming Evan into their circle.

To aggravate the situation, Evan, while beaming, revealed no hint of pride. He considered everything a joint effort with congratulations due all around, ignored the fact it was he who performed the artwork behind the camera.

Albert and Étienne began to speculate on their companion's touch with celluloid and with people. Evan had a gift. Would he ever use it seriously, they wondered? Could he ever? Their praises gradually diminished in favor of more pointed commentary about his background.

♥ ♥ ♥

Patrice and Evan, on the other hand, bonded easily and authentically over film, shared politics, and an attraction planted during their first encounter.

Finally accepted into the program, she gathered as many scripts as she could, memorized the female parts, and promoted herself as an available actress for any student effort. It wasn't long before her summer schedule was full and she spent hours at the school and in the company of her future comrades in film. By the end of July, she'd performed in three student productions and had tried out for a bit part in a German feature to be shot in Paris that fall.

Evan continued his work, profiting from the recent company reorganization to piece together plans that he, once the moment was right, could present to his father in the hopes Giles might consider an international '*politque*' within the company. His mind raced with ideas for cooperation with the Americans. Stubborn in his belief America was the way to go, he made friends with political science and medical students from that country and updated himself about economic strategies of U. S. concerns located in France.

Opportunities abounded for de Roche Frères. If Giles was prepared, they could forge joint ownership agreements for manufacturing and production facilities of two recently established U. S. computer companies. There were also inroads being made on the financial front with the stock markets, twenty-four hour exchanges, and communication capabilities linking data and voice over sophisticated electronic mediums. French territory must be crossed and the rights of doing so had yet to be agreed upon. Then, of course, there was Evan's preferred industry. He still believed that the distribution mechanics of French films abroad were lacking. It was only the big-budget ones that received any attention. He'd familiarized himself with the Avant-guard movements of New York and California, the university settings where French film was considered king, and felt that all French films deserved a fair shake, especially in the States. He foresaw a major financial backer—like de Roche Frères—joining with Hollywood and Paris studios to consolidate and streamline the effort.

To avoid push-back, alone he contacted heads of studios and distribution networks in the States. In halting yet methodical English he presented his family's portfolio and agreed to follow up with written proof the de Roches could back up ideas with money. One had to have money and lots of it. The U. S. operated in terms of dollars and cents. Too few dollars, not enough support, and a proposal was scratched without the slightest sidelong glance at any other, less tangible benefit.

Evan was proud of himself as he organized a report and prepared for his father's return one night. It was now or never. He would continue to help Giles but part of him wanted more of the excitement he'd recently experienced in London and New York, and with Albert and Étienne. France was awash in possibility, but Evan was finding that, beyond its borders, equally compelling opportunities awaited.

He confided in Patrice, who longed to travel abroad. Film and the love of it had no borders and both young people sensed that, in time, it would be a thread of long length and strong fibers capable of holding entire peoples together.

Giles called Evan a dreamer, an inexperienced wide-eyed child with little backup save the ideas he'd committed to paper and expectations that his father would do as he wished. "I can't believe you spent so much time on this!" he exclaimed. "You could be preparing for school in the fall—your grades were slipping last year as I recall. Honestly, Evan, since May and your age group took to turning mad on the world, if I didn't know you better I would think you were one of them!"

"I see the future through their eyes, Papa. It's a credible portrait, after all. My peers will run the world one day. Sure, some want to work more closely with the Soviets rather than the Americans or English. But, we all see the future as a global one! It's coming. It's here!"

"Evan, trust me. France has the power to handle that without risking current policies. If the Americans or English want to streamline film distribution, or create theaters to be financed and operated by one concern, let them show us how they do it in their own country! They can be as disorganized as us!" Giles, cigarette in hand, walked to the window of his study. He peered into the garden.

Evan studied his father's back. "I respect your choices."

"Good. I'm glad to hear it," Giles said.

"But...I disagree entirely with your hesitancy. Respectfully, I would like to see my ideas through."

Giles faced the courtyard and puffed on his cigarette.

Evan knew well this disapproving silence. At Batz years before, Danielle had asked to start work at de Roche Frères before attending École Polytechnique. So drawn to her father's world, she felt she could do without formal preparation. With a resounding pound, Giles had landed his fist on the table and said, "No!" Danielle choked back tears as the room filled with silence. If Pauline hadn't intervened, daughter and father may never have reconciled peaceably nor forged what was to become a great partnership.

Evan walked a slippery terrain. The confusion over his father's reluctance to listen began to take the form of a roiling in the pit of his stomach. There was no Pauline anymore, no calming voice for Giles to remind him he dealt with one of his children, no counter opinion to encourage Giles to tamp emotions. Over the years, Giles had lost perspective. Pauline's death created a man of less composure, a man who more readily took to envying those making greater headway than he, a man who was aging and facing senility without his beloved.

"You are stupid!" Giles yelled suddenly, catching on to Evan's threats. "No son of mine will go off and do ridiculous film work. How many times must I insist you keep your nose to your studies and your preposterous ideas to yourself! You're an impetuous fool at times!"

From the silence rose the smell of cigarette fumes and muffled voices on the street. Evan opened his mouth but no words came, for his entire body caved in at the insult, the anger behind the words. More than a simple disagreement, this was the culmination of pent-up feelings. By following his heart, Evan had triggered his father, who now questioned his son, and condemned without forethought. Evan, the only heir, would never leave de Roche Frères if Giles had his way.

Evan left the study.

♥ ♥ ♥

The old man's eyes watered. He focused on the rose bush that no longer bloomed in their garden below. In their love before the children, she had planted it with her own hands. Pauline had worn a straw hat and gloves, had pulled up her designer pants as if they were nothing special, and had dug and dug in order to position the bush in the center of her garden. Her smile had been wide and her face sooty, her arms wet from perspiration and her chest heaving. He'd told himself right then he would remember that moment, and today the shadow of her memory hung thick over his heart. How he hated to argue with Evan! How he wished that damn train had never derailed! However would he go on, was the question that obsessed him. His son's ideas Giles could never support, for they demanded too much of him in his declining years. He wanted only the continuation of de Roche as it had for generations. Evan couldn't see that one must have the long view, one must envision beyond temporary diversions the kind cinema presented. Oh, if she were only back in his arms, it would all go away! This night, this young man. If only, dear Pauline.

At the strangest times since her death, the puerile side of Giles took over, had the power of holding the man in a bubble that Evan would never pierce. He interlocked fingers and fought tears.

"If you could only know a woman as I knew your mother...," Giles murmured, eyes on her decaying artwork. "Dare I wish such happiness yet such sorrow on any man? Least of all, my son. My only son."

# Chapter 12:
# September 1968

THE LAST SATURDAY OF THE MONTH, the de Roche and de Long families met for dinner. They would be boarding up their respective homes and returning to Paris. The shortening days and rain portended a winter that would linger relentlessly along the coast of Brittany. As October arrived, with many services unavailable and phone connections erratic once the post office closed its doors, Batz grew desolate.

In the days leading up to the dinner, Régine was at her most unbearable. No one had adequately been able to explain to her why Giles never re-married. Mémé spoke highly of him, and often referred to the massive next door garden as a symbol of the couple's eternal love. The latter fact drew bland regards from Régine. Pauline was dead, a part of Monsieur de Roche's past. Love was hardly eternal.

The night of the dinner, her hair highlighted and her tan deep, she donned a short white dress, layered pearls at her neck, and made her eyes up with thick liner and dark shadows. Laurence joined them from Roscoff where she now resided in an apartment that Mémé had arranged. Visiting Batz when her studies permitted, Laurence knew this time was important. Since it would be goodbye to Mémé for a while, she wished to say so in person. In deference to her grandmother's request, she would also meet the illustrious head of the de Roche empire. A portion of de Roche investments was tied up in the marine institute and Mémé thought it a good idea for Laurence to update Monsieur de Roche on the curriculum.

Arm-in-arm, Laurence and Mémé walked across the lawn, through the flower garden, and up the steps to the de Roche home. Having scurried ahead of them, Régine was already inside when they passed through the doors and the welcoming smile of the maid, Betti. Decorated with dried flowers in oversized urns, the anteroom was cheery with a fire in the hearth and a tray of hors-d'oeuvres at their fingertips.

"Merci, Betti," Mémé said. "You see, Laurence, I told you Giles would go all out for us. Now aren't you glad you didn't wear those horrible jeans?"

Laurence laughed, "Yes, Mémé, yes." She wore a bright pink sweater and grey skirt. Her hair, drawn off her face with a gold barrette, placed delicate features in relief and complimented her wide eyes. A pair of tortoise-shell glasses bespoke her more studious side. She in her pink and Mémé in black were the picture of new and traditional France—the energetic youth, the retiring and peaceable matron.

Régine puffed impatiently on a cigarette and, ignorant of the ambiance, sipped on her apéritif and stole glances at the stairway. Periodically she inspected herself in front of a nearby mirror.

"I will be glad to get back to Paris, " she said. "The hairdressers will have to spend all day on this head!" There was no need to complain, for her blonde locks were perfectly coiffed and without a hint of dark roots. Whatever she referred to had nothing to do with flaw, for Régine spent her every waking moment focusing on her appearance, and had for the last two days spent every dime she possessed preparing for this evening.

When Giles entered the room, his gaze fell first on Régine. With an approving grin from under a white moustache, he held both hands to her and said, "Well, well, darling Régine, we meet again at last!"

Régine giggled, "But it's been ages, hasn't it? I must have been twelve, still a baby!"

"Nonsense," said Mémé, grasping Giles warmly and accepting his embrace. "You were seventeen, the year you left for America with Nate. How could you forget, Régine?"

"And this must be Laurence," Giles said. At arm's length, he studied her with a series of quick nods. "Ah, yes, I see Nate all over you! You walk in his shoes, I hear!"

"Yes, sir," Laurence said. "The institute."

They lingered over the appetizers then Giles, Régine on his arm, led them to the dining room where they settled to commence what would be a five hour affair.

More formal than the other rooms, a bay window opened up an entire wall and offered a splendid ocean view. Silver tray services stood on each of the side buffets, and a maroon and navy blue oriental rug spread across the wide-paneled wood floor. Betti guided them to their seats at the long mahogany table covered with Breton lace and dressed with rose and gold Limoges china. Hand-painted on a light olive wallpaper were extravagantly plumed ivory-colored peacocks peering from silver cages.

They started with fish soup and local white wine. Several times, Giles apologized to Mémé for breaking the long-standing tradition their families upheld to gather as one over the summer. But the troubles in the streets of Paris had led to a reorganization of the Assemblée and, although de Gaulle emerged victorious, many problems lingered with the unions and faculties. All would play into France's economic go-forward and Giles felt it important he and Evan be present for decisions.

"Ah, but it is only when I return to my beloved Ile de Batz that I see how much I have missed its serenity!" he said with a look out the windows. "And," he said to Régine, "had I known three beautiful women awaited at my doorsteps, well, Monsieur de Gaulle would have been the one left waiting!"

Laughing, Régine clasped her hand on Giles's arm and squeezed. With cool regard, Laurence took in the gesture. She sensed Giles de Roche was falling under the spell. He sent appreciative glances to Régine each time she reached for him with a smile or touch that, in turn, messaged his reactions.

To look at him, although his gait was as spirited as ever and his mind quicker than most half his age, one would think first of a union between him and Mémé. Their ages were closer, their histories shared, and their friendship permanent. Still, it was on Régine Giles focused his attention, listening politely, questioning her enthusiastically, and inviting her to join him in a tour of the many de Roche facilities once she returned to Paris.

Ever a man of manners and class, he by no means ignored the other women. To Laurence he asked questions about her work and the faculty. To Mémé he reserved the most deferential of attention. Mémé and he went back many years, even before their joint marriages and summer residences kept them in close proximity. Giles and Mémé had lived through the war and could recall the sorrow and sacrifice. Too, they shared the bittersweet memory of the lady who once was the central focus for Giles.

After finishing sole provençal with sprigs of carrots and beans, they rested with the remains of the wine while Betti arranged a dessert of strawberry cream on each plate.

"I adore this wallpaper," Laurence said.

"Pauline designed it," Giles said. "She created quite a stir at the Paris boutique where she requested such a pattern, a work that would be on display where the sea and salt air could wreak havoc! We finally had them agree to layer a protective coating on the paper—quite an innovative technique in those days." He stood and reached for the wall. "But that was the way she was, perfect and lovely, like this paper. Unfortunately, the paper outlived her."

Régine noisily scraped at the last of her strawberry cream.

"But, Giles," said Mémé finally, "although I loved her too and miss her still, how many times must I remind you, she lives in that boy of yours. Where is Evan by the way? I miss him, too! He could have shown Laurence such a time this summer!"

Giles sat. "Evan, Evan! He worked at more than de Roches Frères while in Paris this year! If you can believe it, he sided with the students during this whole affair."

"I would have thought him too busy, what with your efforts with the Germans now, and the Swiss I hear, no?" Mémé asked.

"You heard right." Giles updated the others on their successful ventures in the eastern part of the country where the Germans, Swiss, and French cooperated in mining efforts and in the Rhône valley where hydroelectric expansion was changing the landscape. "It is the next major industrial center for France," he said. "Evan helped, but always managed to return to Paris to continue to reorganize and better the world! I can't stop him now that he's eighteen."

They bantered over less charged topics like the upcoming season of fashion, and a rendez-vous once they were all back in Paris. Over cognac and coffee, they reminisced over the summer that slipped into the past, watched the sun set into the sea, and stoked the fire for warmth. Betti began packing and locking up and it was dark before Giles stood and apologized for his need to say good-night. He and Betti would be leaving soon. The next day promised to be a busy one and arriving in Paris during the night meant they wouldn't have to battle daytime traffic and congestion.

Régine tried to convince Giles to stay longer. Politely declining, he nonetheless offered to walk them home, reminding Régine they would meet soon in Paris.

Through the garden and down the path, the four strolled, accompanied by the brisk winds and whispering waves. They said good-night at the front door and Mémé and Laurence made for the inside. Régine stuck resolutely to Giles.

Laurence walked Mémé to her room and, after a prolonged embrace and words of love, left so that her grandmother could tend to her toilet. She tip-toed to her room, relishing the salt-sea smell of the covers as she took to her bed in the petit and cozy space that she'd made her own during summer. This evening would be added to the wonderful memories of her times on the island.

Hearing her mother's laughter, the shrill giggles and flirtations, she grit her teeth. Régine's heels clacked along the stones then stopped. Rising from the bed, Laurence peeked out the window and saw Giles and her mother in an embrace, a prolonged and suggestive one, one that bespoke their inebriated state. Laurence could well read the woman. Régine had advanced in her quest to seduce Monsieur de Roche.

She closed the curtains, lay in bed and tried to blot out the scene. At eighteen, she had already received attention from the opposite sex, indeed had refused requests to date a few engineers in her class. For Laurence, their interest conjured less welcoming imagery. She imagined these admirers reaching for her body, forcing themselves on her, devouring her with their mouths and words of love that would surely ring hollow the next day. Laurence had only the sexual antics of her mother from which to draw conclusions about affection, had never grasped her own ability to rise above the base and animalistic ways she believed had taken place behind closed doors of the Cape house. If that was what love was, she would pass, for she no more sought trespass of her body—the groping hands, the soured breaths—than she wanted to be close to her mother. Laurence Mallord was not to be fooled. On the physical front, men would be avoided.

Nevertheless and to her surprise, she did fall for a man. He was a student from Aquitaine whose high grades were on par with hers and with whom she shared the spot at the head of their class. She noticed him when he spoke one day of his diving abilities.

Pierre was a blonde with narrow gaze who spoke French faster than anyone alive. Laurence approached him to compare scuba experiences and to see if he knew of places to dive.

He invited her to join him and another student. The following Saturday afternoon, they made way for the bay in a borrowed boat. In wet suits and with tanks full, they dove into cold waters to discover the plant and animal life. With him, Laurence collected plant samples and later they came up with an idea for a term paper:

collecting and analyzing samples of local sea life. Marine biologists of the day already studied kelp and seaweed for their nutritional properties, and this was an expanding field. If her findings were of note, she might even get a research allowance to explore to her heart's content. Pierre suggested they work together. Laurence agreed.

That entire day he appeared as directed and serious as she. So the next week, when he asked her to the movies, she said yes, thinking he was after a break from study.

Not ten minutes into the film, however, he embraced her with charged emotion, whispered and nibbled at her ear, groped for her breasts.

She shrugged him away, kidding and smiling as if his gestures were something she could handle. Yet, when Pierre ran his tongue along her chin, she winced visibly. In no time, she returned to the shamed child, the pawn in her mother's vengeful game. To touch meant to hurt at all levels.

"Please," she whispered as his advances continued. "Stop."

"Chérie, you are more beautiful than you know. I love you," said Pierre, his eyes closed, his muscular body taut against her.

She looked straight at the screen. All feeling drained from her as he continued his discovery of her body, raising her blouse and finding her tiny firm breasts under the brassiere. He pinched and rubbed but his pressure went unacknowledged. As long as his hands groped, she remained still, in another place, far from the darkened theater and this man's caress.

"What is it with you?" he asked.

She heard the voice but did not respond, did not flinch, remained poised for what she believed to be an oncoming attack. Gone was the recall of their scuba diving adventure, gone the appreciation of his intelligence and charm. He was the devil she knew, a different face but the devil she knew.

He told her to ease up, claimed he wouldn't hurt her. Finally he let go of her and slumped in his seat. Until the movie was over she remained taut with wariness. Exiting the theater, she eased somewhat as people surrounded them. There was no possible way he could continue.

Still, because she sensed his frustration, terror seeped back. She headed towards the town center, aware of the dwindling crowd and the late night hour. Her apartment was steps from them but she struggled with how to say good-night.

He insisted on accompanying her. She pleaded with her eyes, hoped he would see her fear and be gone, simply disappear and leave her alone. He didn't, kept right on until they entered the narrow hall of the apartment building and, unnoticed by the dozing concierge, climbed the steps to her place. Her hands clammy, her breathing erratic, her heart pounded as he nudged her away from the *minuterie* and a source of light. He led her to an isolated part of the hallway. She knew then she should scream, or have broken away while on the street, but fear engendered her passivity.

In the dark, he resumed his advances, pinning her against the wall as he muttered incoherently and threw insults. "You'll understand what my love means," he said, ripping her shirt and biting her nipples.

"Please, no, please, no," she whispered. It was the best she could do, for she was already defeated, already violated. Whatever he did in the ensuing minutes would matter less than what pulsed though her veins—the helplessness, the capitulation, the lost dignity. It was over even as he began, as he pulled at her jeans, as he stripped and pulled her down, as he inserted his penis into her rigid form.

With a grunt, he finished and in seconds was dressed. "Putain," he snorted, spitting on her.

She lay on the cold floor as his steps grew faint, repeatedly rubbing hands as she sensed the seepage from between her legs. In this hall she shared with another family, currently in Paris, she felt as alone as could be, had no idea what to do, and no desire to move on or move out.

In time, she directed her thoughts to Uncle Georges and Aunt Chantel, to their laughter and praise. Good people, a twosome who shared in what many would know in their lives, but from which Laurence was excluded. She tried to feel beyond the throbbing pain, but failed.

She relived the futility of being in the waves that ate her father, saw the swirls pull at the man, saw her mother's directed fist, and wished herself dead. She felt as though she were going down, under a wave more powerful than she, unaided and ridiculed for attempting to find the equilibrium others seemed to claim. She'd been wrong to try and better herself in Roscoff. She was being punished now. As her mother insisted during the worst of assaults, as Laurence sensed at a bottomless place within, she was never meant for happiness. She was meant to be fodder for those who lived desperate lives, and one day, she would join them.

Her father had been released by the waves, Laurence had been left to deal with those with power to control. She was a sore on the face of humanity, never to breathe easy, never to revel in genuine love. She had overstepped her bounds.

Pierre would not be the last. She would kowtow to the devil, until one day the devil took her away, away to a place where she too would promote evil.

She stumbled to her room, unlocked the door, and fell into the foyer. Sleep alluded her as bleak imagery surrounded and drained her. Régine had been but the beginning, Pierre cracked the nut of her virginity with the same tools. There would be more, even with a focus on keeping them at a distance. But, at her core a growing certainty: one day she would capitulate.

She quit her studies and for weeks did nothing. A fog encircled her as she wandered unsure and unaware. Her next steps involved exit from Roscoff but she couldn't easily formulate plans. To leave without reimbursing Mémé would bother her too much, to live on in Roscoff without taking classes would be another form of the same thing. She had to find a way to get back to the States where, at least, she could try and begin a life of sorts without the influence of family, without Régine. Her only solution was to use Mémé's money to book a flight to Boston. She would reimburse her grandmother once she was stateside and working.

She couldn't face any of them in Paris with the truth, even Uncle Georges. This was too painful to think about let alone share. She didn't deserve the best life could offer. It was as simple and as complex as that. Though she'd come to know family who appeared to have faith in her, she would disappoint them in order to preserve what future she had left. It would be worse to open her mouth and speak, to do that would be reliving it all over again. She could not.

So, the day she encountered Evan de Roche, these thoughts influenced her decisions.

# Chapter 13

BY THE END OF AUGUST, Evan readied to turn the pages of his life. One evening before classes resumed, he set out to find his comrades. Étienne was still on the Côte d'Azur, having met a young woman whose companionship had become more important than Albert's film. Patrice recently returned from six weeks in Germany where she'd followed a film crew in the hopes of obtaining bit parts. Albert was somewhere about town. Evan wanted to brainstorm with them. He also wished to reveal his family background. They would welcome him, he thought, now he was preparing to commit more time to securing financial backing with distributors and producers. They could formalize, use the film as a step in the door, join forces on the business side as well as the creative front.

During the summer, the bulk of filming had fallen on Evan's and Albert's shoulders. They haggled over the right camera angle, the closeness of a shot, and the money required to bring the film to the screen.

Evan dismissed possible setbacks, insisting that he could handle those issues once they possessed decent footage with which to promote their project. He felt an independent producer would take the time to view and appreciate their work. Should that happen, money would be no object.

Albert didn't mind Evan's attitude half as much as he minded Evan's talent behind the camera. More often than not, Albert found himself on the sidelines as Evan coached an actor or went about scouting for settings at Métro stops and parks. He succeeded every time. Evan had a knack Albert could only yearn for and, as time wore on, it grated on him. Jesting comments too soon degraded into snide remarks. Albert often set about grumbling as soon as Evan, confidence emanating from his every pore, wrapped up a session.

"So, you did it again," Albert would say. He was tired of Evan's non-stop energy, his boundless capacity in the pursuit of one task or another, and his smile that never quit. Privately Albert maintained the film was his own idea. He challenged Evan's suggestions and couched insults during their more heated discussions, all the while claiming more work for himself than he could possibly handle.

Too excited with the unfolding of this their first attempt, Evan often accorded Albert the benefit of the doubt or even the implementation of an idea with which he himself disagreed. It was a slow process and, as the summer drew to a close and other commitments loomed, Evan felt relieved that their everyday encounters were numbered. Still, they both figured on following through, both hoped for the best.

In search of his friends one night, Evan canvased café hang-outs but saw nothing of Albert. They'd not met with Patrice since her return, so Evan decided to visit her. The day had gone poorly—problems with the equipment, and two actors hadn't shown. He felt the need for her impartiality, her positive attitude, and her smile.

As he headed down boulevard St. Michel, he mulled over another more recent but as negative interaction with his father. He again found himself edging away from adherence to the family tenets. His decision to go with film would be difficult to implement and might even mean he struggled without customary comforts. He would do it anyway, he reasoned. As he crossed an alleyway, he became invigorated with this his personal forging into the business world, a ticket he wrote of his own will.

Patrice roomed with a girlfriend on rue St. Jacques. Her window on the third floor was dark. Evan entered the building, pressed the *minuterie* and climbed the steps. His friend home or not, he would wait. Albert and Étienne, and now Patrice, practiced the open door policy of most students when it came to their friends. There was a key hidden under the rung on the landing. Evan could use it whenever he wished.

The stairway was narrow and steep and smelled of cigarette smoke. Muffled sounds came from behind a few closed doors as he marched to the corner apartment and turned the key.

Inside, a shout forced his eyes to the bed. Undercovers and in the dim light, two people lay. Evan squinted, his chest tightening, his grip on the doorknob damp.

"Evan," one whispered.

There was more rustling, a giggle, a hand dangling on the edge of the bed. The lamp flicked on. An outstretched arm was Albert's. Under him, facing the wall, Patrice.

"Vieux," Albert mumbled, trying to smile but fighting an embarrassed frown at the same time.

Evan froze. Of all their experiences, sex was an outside dimension. When the three men were alone, a light-hearted and playful joking broke out about women, including Patrice. Usually, it was Evan who silenced their repartees as soon as the topic veered to imagining sex with her. Although they all were interested, no one had the nerve to proclaim himself the one to make the first move. Plus, Patrice more often than not intimated a penchant for Evan.

What obviously transpired feet from him meant their status as friends was challenged. Evan made a move to leave.

"You wanted us?" Albert asked.

"Another time," Evan said, his gaze now on Patrice who stared past him. The sheets barely covered the mound of her breasts and Evan felt a surge in his groin. Her body a uniform tan, he felt her magical temptress stare even as she lay with another man. With vacuous stares, the two gripped one another as Evan closed the door.

He heard Albert say, "The one thing de Roche money can't buy, old friend."

Giggling recommenced and Evan made for the staircase. Outside, the night air hit him in a dizzying wall of heat. His knees knocked and his eyes smarted. The rushing of his heart, Albert's darting comment, the message within the message.

Albert meant for his comment to be heard. His friend's reveal bothered Evan, the soured expression, Albert's wry smile, a regard that bespoke contempt and conspiracy. Worse, too, was Patrice. She laughed along, offered snatches of her body in a feigned innocence at the same time she returned to Albert's arms, all the while Evan stood vulnerable and blistering. Friends? How had he fooled himself all these months? What did he overlook? Was he stupid or a fool, or both?

It wasn't as though sex was taboo or unheard of in his life. The de Roche men were reputed for their liaisons and indiscretions masked as temporary diversions from their business schedules. A woman squirreled away to a Spanish chateau or a country home in the Midi was accepted as part of a long chain of macho behavior that only Giles de Roche had shunned. As Evan grew into manhood, he was privy to male-only conversations about mistresses and clandestine rendezvous and took it all in with the distracted attention of his youth. A de Roche would, could, and often had to have a woman on the side. If Evan chose to do so, he would not be judged by his family for, although antiquated and often hurtful, adventures of this nature were routine.

Through his parents' love, Evan witnessed another perspective. Theirs had been a blooming that neither faded nor was replaced the entire time Pauline was alive and even after her death. Giles listened to cousins and uncles boast of their affairs but never indulged himself. Evan sensed that, as far as Giles was concerned, if his son were to choose this type of diversion, it was up to him. Giles would not interfere. Nevertheless, the young de Roche had grown up privy to what many called the perfect love and therefore was reluctant to take any particular avenue of short-term satisfaction.

Evan had no desire to cheat or traipse about behind the woman he would someday call his wife. And yet, as the years advanced and his looks drew even more suggestive nods from women, he found his principles teetering on a scale equal parts emotion and physical desire.

Many his age already experimented, indeed it was a time of 'free love,' a time to let it all go. Young people took to answering for themselves their physical callings. Some formed communes, some lived together, others married to enjoy what supposedly was heaven on earth. Evan knew he would join his friends one day, he simply didn't know when.

It wasn't something he discussed. Often, with a wink and grin, he side-stepped the scrutiny of his pals who, although naive themselves, enjoyed exaggerating their processes. Evan was smart enough to comprehend and also had the self-esteem not to feel he had to do something for which he wasn't prepared. Rather than collaborate with friends who grouped together and took the odd day in the country with a favored lady, or spend long weekends far from family and watchful eyes, Evan remained detached, his easygoing smile the only indication he was aware of what they spoke.

He could get away with it, too. A handsome de Roche could act as though he were experienced. It would be simplistic for others to think differently. Evan would be welcome into any woman's arms, even the most virginal.

Therefore, on finding two of his closest of friends in bed, the tremors in his body and blood rushing through his veins had nothing to do with the act in question. It had more to do with unknowns, with feelings with no name, rising emotions as yet unacknowledged. And all this forced reflection upon him.

He cared for Patrice, wondered about her love life, even dared imagine her body nude. Yet, at the same time, there was so much more to her. She was ethereal, sprite-like, so free, and such a joy to be with. Physical yearnings were often eclipsed by the intimacy of their conversations, by the depth of their insight for film, by their energy to bring a story to life. He wondered, but that was as far as it went.

Unlike other more brazen women, she remained aloof yet playfully engaged, equally enjoying all three men's company. When she was behind the camera and Evan controlled the machinery, they uniquely related. Yet, it was now common knowledge he could do that with most anyone, let alone Patrice.

Though he tried to push away the word, 'betrayal' played on his lips. Why did they turn on the light? Why did they leave the key within reach? Why had she stared in such a fashion?

More than the embarrassment of barging in on them, he felt a queasy uncertainty about where he stood in the circle. Was he outside now? Had this act marked some kind of denouement? Why? Why?

It was to a theater he took his troubles, for the answers wouldn't come and the confusion was as distasteful as a bad dream. "*Quai des Brumes,*" a film noir of the 1930s, played at an art house. He purchased a ticket and went inside.

It was a story from his mother's era, a statement about the unpleasant side of life. Out of a dreary existence and with passions laced with hatred and anger, the characters walked straight to their destructions. The hero, a deserter from the military, prepares to leave for America but is killed before his departure.

Evan left the theater less inclined to analyze for hours on end. The movie succeeded in drawing him into a state of discomfort he never before experienced. Coupled with the revelation on rue St. Jacques, the film exposed the side of life he rarely contemplated, the joylessness of despair, tampered emotions and hurt brought on through disregard.

A brilliant film, it had received praise of the highest order and was one Evan had seen many times. But tonight, it touched off a certain desperation. As he sipped beer in a café, he found himself sinking to a place that seemed to engulf him, promising no imminent exit.

What people do to one another, how the events of other lives entangle themselves in the lives of those in proximity.

He wanted his mother to speak to him. On the brink of breaking with his father, separate from his friends, a sordid story occupied his mind and he wished only for her smile, her encouragement, her energy.

But the bartender wiped the bar, a couple snuggled in a corner, and Paris retired into the wee hours of a Sunday morning. Evan was alone to decide if it meant so much, really, to step away from the de Roche fortune in order to follow his dreams, if it meant so much to take on the role of an outsider, if it meant so much to play the genial, positive Evan rather than opt for other ways to live.

Where would his choices take him? Was he as strong and capable as Pauline always said? Was he really special or was he believing words long ago pronounced by a woman who loved him too much to see other than his best side? Had Pauline really prepared him for life? Or did she shelter him from it? And was that what preserving the de Roche image really meant?

He thought to her favorite film, "The Mayerling." It too was of another era, a film about love in another time and place, a fantasy at best. He was now as informed, if not more, than she about the films of the thirties. The second half of that decade proved a time of harsh realism in film, when "*Quai des Brumes*" represented but the beginning of a series of noir pieces, when France faced war with blindfolds, hoping it wouldn't come but uncertain that her prayers would be answered.

"*Quai des Brumes,*" quay of the fogs. Evan sighed. At eighteen, his choices were many. Yet, as a de Roche, his destiny was ordained. Had she deliberately minimized the importance of that fact? Or, when she spoke of it, had he simply not listened?

Evan walked until the day came, thinking, thinking, asking his dead mother questions, then fumbling with his limited perceptions. His angel of answers, the force he believed always with him, was really gone, had been dead since he was eight. Pauline could no longer help him really.

# Chapter 14

PATRICE ADJUSTED HAIR IN THE MIRROR then checked her watch. Evan was late. She went to the window from where she could view his approach.

He might not show, but if he did, she would be honest. He would know of her foolishness. The night Evan walked in on them, she and Albert had made love but, on hearing Evan's voice, Albert switched to a game of hide and seek, a mean taunt of sorts she comprehended only once Evan had left. The look in Albert's eyes revealed his contempt.

Although displeased, she played along, but really wanted to get up from the bed, dress, hold onto her dignity. Albert constrained her, whispered his intention to inform Evan they knew he was a de Roche, a member of the richest family in Paris.

Albert had discovered this one day when Evan mentioned a dinner party he was going to at Tour d'Argent, a social affair the likes of which Paris saw once or twice a year—the marriage of a Turkish magnate's daughter. The newspapers had a field day, with pictures and gossip to last the rest of the year.

Albert recited the wedding attendees while Patrice stared at a picture of Evan beside an attractive Parisian socialite. Long before, Patrice had sensed Evan came from money. Those without often know better the width of the gap that separates them. She felt a tug of sadness, too. Evan was cute, a friend, and gave her input the others didn't, input she put to use on the stage. Why Albert chose to risk his tie with Evan by gloating over a detail such as this, she would never quite understand. If nothing else, didn't Albert see Evan as a conduit to further success?

Patrice was no fool. What Evan represented was more than bourgeois society. He was the very means to an end for a struggling actress. Contacts, spots on television, film debuts—the melding of Paris society with movie personalities was common and expected. Patrice stretched her imagination beyond petty class jealousies to envision a future associating with the de Roche family. She was ready to make amends in a hurry.

Since her arrival from North Africa, all three men helped her and she did her part to help them. If their friendship went on, she wished to continue in that vein.

Physical closeness was a natural consequence of days together, late nights at cafés, the odd meeting at her place or theirs. The fact Albert got to her first was of little import. One of them was bound to try. Though she would have preferred a fling to be with Evan, none of this mattered in the big scheme of things.

Only acting mattered, and therefore a rapprochement with Evan. He was the one who stood the greatest chance of becoming the next Truffaut. She wanted to let him know she was sorry, wanted her talented side to define her, rather than the interaction with Albert.

Since that night, Evan absented himself from rehearsals and dinners at their most frequented café. With Étienne's return, Patrice and Albert resumed the project but it appeared they would be doing it without Evan.

Progress slowed and, when they did attempt filming, they disagreed. Albert wanted one thing, Patrice and Étienne wanted another. Smitten with a girlfriend, Étienne wanted to include her in the action. Patrice was trying out for other parts or completing school assignments. The odd Saturday they got together, it took them most of the day to agree on how to move forward and, too soon, it was time to part.

She looked out her window and saw him. When he arrived at her foyer, apologizing for his lateness, he clasped her hand, and pecked at her cheeks. His face was flushed as he chatted about a recently viewed film. Beneath his surface, however, she sensed wariness. He eyed the bed with a lift of his shoulder, and sat on the chair near the window, unmoving.

"Evan, I want to apologize. My behavior the last time you were here was uncalled for."

Evan's gaze roved the room, to the ceiling and down. "You know my background."

"We saw the pictures from the Monthierry wedding. You thought you could hide it forever?"

"No," he said. "I was on my way to tell you that night as a matter of fact."

She paused, flung back a bunch of curls, fixed her eyes on his. "Oh."

Instantly, there was more between them than awkwardness. As she stared into his eyes, their hardness melted, and he became again her friend. She felt relief yet was unsure. Too sudden a dismissal was to not give the incident its fair discussion. Too quick a resumption of their friendship would cloud Evan's terms of a reconciliation. She stared, opting instead for the commanding pose that had become her trademark, like a tropical flower, an actress able to bewitch one second and crumble the next, a woman of exotic allure. If Patrice were to never achieve high financial status, she would always have her looks, looks that were in and of themselves tools to success. She sensed Evan saw through to her vulnerable yet alluring nature. These were qualities she'd not acknowledged for many years as a brown child of the ghetto, but ones she now utilized to obtain whatever she wished from people, from men. Patrice was in charge of herself.

He rose. "I've thought things over. It's not a good idea for me to continue the film. Albert is in control anyhow. It will do him good to accomplish this on his own."

"I'm not trying to convince you to return to the project. I only want to speak for myself. I'm sorry, Evan."

She coaxed him straight to the depths of her black irises, beyond to the soul of one who possesses the power to unmask. Hers were eyes that, via a wide questioning stare, could hold those of her onlookers, extract artfully disguised intentions and lay out the results. She read his look as one that suggested something more, another variation, an extreme. He reached for her and planted a kiss on her lips.

Hers were full and the kiss warm, the touch light yet hinting at other flavors of their togetherness. It was the Patrice of the park, with the boy and the sail, the woman who bent to take the child's hand, who kissed his cheek, who exuded a raw affection. But it was also a Patrice sending a piece of herself his way, an enchanting beckon, done with the slightest of motions, with no words at all. The use of charm to perform the magic of the ages. She touched his cheek. She wouldn't force, but should he be so inclined, she was prepared.

He closed his eyes. She studied the wonderful black brows, the sculpted mouth. She pressed fingers to the soft shaven skin slightly damp and supple. Her hand fell to his shirt, her nails skimmed the cloth, ran down the row of buttons. The shirt was tailored, and white, speaking once again to his background. How had they overlooked it so long? His chest was solid, a person in form, a young body. He was no longer the companion, he had become an object of her affections. She could feel herself warm, sensed her breasts thrust and retract so as not to endanger the moment. He was thinking it over, living a lifetime of decisions and debates. This was a man who did not engage easily, she thought. A man who struggled.

She should let him go, detach herself and thereby release him from his quandary. A second passed and she guessed the truth, for she was after all a detective of feelings, a seeker, a digger to the core. Indeed Evan helped her get there by praising her authenticity, her ability to incorporate gesture, thought, and memory into a stage-ready persona. Patrice was many people within herself, and she knew all kinds of men. What Evan represented was an experiment, another of a long line of experiments that drew her closer to her art, to the motivations of all beings. Evan had tipped her off that day in the Luxembourg Gardens—the acting path she'd chosen was for her the right one. With even more verve, she worked to better her talents and, one day, she would be on top.

It behooved her to ignore this opportunity and yet she couldn't conceal her surprise. She faced a man who had never crossed the line with a woman. Evan de Roche had never made love.

He answered her call with a hand to her arm, with opened eyes that fell again captive to her stare. She wanted to turn away one instant, for a piece of her preferred to leave him pure. He was already so chaste, agile, and innocent, a child in so many ways. Had she the right to be the one to help him step to the other side? The side that, once crossed, endeavors to mask all that is childish and genuine? Was she being mean or was she helping him?

"You are beautiful, Patrice," he said.

They kissed, his tongue worked through her, to her senses, killing what logic she toyed with. In seconds, urges kicked in. Experienced or not, he could rise to the occasion. Her toes slipped from her shoes, her leg slid between his. Her debate terminated. Evan would tumble now, too, if he let himself.

She drew him near, pressed her body to his. His return embrace let on where his thoughts drifted and she enjoyed the revelation of his new-found masculinity for she shared in it too, in every breath, in his every heightened awareness that her body was his for the doing.

They lay on the bed. She would go slow, would enjoy his pleasure as much as her own. He occupied another place that kept his eyes closed, his hands discovering her, first as she lay clothed, then with a titillating rush as she dropped the last curtain hiding her secrets. He sighed touching her skin, the bump of her nipples, the receptivity. He went over and over her body, and allowed her to remove his clothes. Then he adroitly lay her down. Meditating with his hands, his shyness diminished with each visit of her, with each of her joyous moans as she succumbed to his pressures and rubs, his searching of her deepest parts. Her slender body lay under him, patient and ready as he grappled with his own hardness and the sensation of their bodies molded together, of the skin of one acquiescing to the skin of the other, of the bones digging but not hurting, mouths locking a single destination in place.

Evan requested help, let her guide him to her, inserted himself into her, into the abandon that held them united and ecstatic, the boundless discovery of bodies shared. He thrust and observed at a remove, as his physical abilities took charge, forced, drew on a primal need to complete, to attain, to satisfy. He climaxed with a primal moan and dug fingers into her scalp, helplessly pushing through to the ends where he alone stood, a new man, a discovered person.

They lay quietly for a long time. A bus screeching to a halt, the chattering of children returning from school, the tap-tap of a lone pedestrian brought them periodically back to the room.

Spent yet wanting still, she held her hand over his sweating chest and imagined owning it, having him every night. Yet he was who he was and, although his hold on her was presently firm, his crossing into her territory a feat she could shout about, she knew too it was momentary.

As an uncomfortable rush took over her body, she debated in silence. A part of her was in love with Evan, indeed had always been. Now, after having ruled his senses, she felt her practiced ability to move on seriously challenged. It was never this way before, all the men—the few boys, the older students, all of them—none had loved her with a thoroughness that would not have been any more explicit had Evan stated it verbally.

She kissed him again, and he returned a tender hug, but he was already part of another space. She lay against the pillow and fought tears even with him close, committed even. It was natural for him to be absorbed with the sensations of the first time. She braced herself.

They could have met at a café and not risked what happened here, but she was only human and had fallen early on. It would be of no use to try and undo, try and pretend to could continue as before. He, with his future, she with her sensibilities. She couldn't let feelings interfere. To pine and wait, to hope and pray would not do. Though she loved him, she would end it now, for whenever the break might come, it would be she to hurt the longest and hardest. Understanding people was both a gift and a curse. She knew Evan.

The impression she had originally hoped to make, she reminded herself, was one that would endure solely through their professional interactions. But Evan's totality was too much to refuse.

They left the bed. As he dressed, he smiled, divining where her mind journeyed. Still digesting his physical prowess, which she doubted would come again in her lifetime, she was amazed that, rather than become the smitten first-time lover, Evan gathered himself. He donned his jacket, zipped. The sound was final.

"I will miss you, Evan," she said.

In his eyes, an inimitable sadness, a look that struck her more than their loving. Evan de Roche, a man of endless means and possibility. Although she doubted she would say no if he requested a subsequent visit, she knew too it would never happen. His sorrow fronted a deeper feeling, one not wrought from separation.

The despair of ambiguities, the contours of human limitation, the continual reminder that, for all its merit, there is in the aftermath of heights attained, a profound relinquishment.

Whatever they'd explored in her bed, Evan grasped its meaning for himself and in ways Patrice would struggle to integrate. He was truly a man of many facets, a stone so rare it had no name and, for a time, a gem she alone possessed.

# Chapter 15

KLEE SANG ONE MORE TIME with Benny's band. A previous commitment at Danigan's—and one over which a financial backer was to preside—compelled her to overlook the broken relationship and support the group.

Her days had resumed their original pace of work with the Faheys followed by a walk or a read at a tearoom. Although she missed Benny and at times wished she had a regular outlet for her singing, she knew too that if she stepped back into his life, it would ultimately bring pain. Benny had suffered enough.

He didn't bother her, but that in and of itself demonstrated how he carried his burden. Going forward, he would refrain from sharing his emotions, for Benny above all respected her wishes, even if it meant side-lining his own. She felt torn. But her practical side prevented procrastination. However much he might feel otherwise, Benny and she were not meant to be.

The agent, experienced in booking stints for local groups, was from England. Although Benny would have preferred an Irish backer, they had trouble finding one and this man offered his services without an attitude of superiority. Benny was hopeful their chance had come, and was ready to do the necessary to cut a single and thereby promote their talents to professionals.

He called Klee to make sure she planned on being at Danigan's. In a solemn voice, he thanked her. She told him a friend of hers owned a black dress, one that was better made for the stage than her red, that she would wear it for the special occasion. They nervously chuckled then hung up.

The dress was more than professional. Black sequined beads, short and with a single slit up one side, it enhanced every feature. A pert sashay to her step, the material would swish about as she moved. Slipping into silver pumps and wrapping a patent leather belt about her waist, she could have been a visiting Petula Clark or Dusty Springfield, anyone with experience and grace and for whom the limelight was but an aspect of her every day.

As she primped a final time, she conjugated French verbs. It had been two weeks reviewing present, imperfect, and past tenses. Now she was onto the irregular verbs, surprising demons that switched endings illogically and could only be mastered with memory.

"Je suis venu—'e' at the end if it's a woman speaking, no 'e' at the end if it's a man," she said. "I tell you, no wonder the English and French didn't get on. How could they?"

"What, luv?" Mrs. Fahey asked, peeking into the room they'd renovated into Klee's quarters.

"Only doin' French, Mary," she said, rubbing her lips redder.

"Where in the name did you get that outfit? You look a...well now, I can't say, really..." Mary's eyes were wide.

"I borrowed it, Mary, not to worry. It's a copy of some French designer."

"But, you and Benny..."

Mary's furrowed brow bespoke her pity for Benny and her empathy for Klee.

"It's only this last night, Mary. Benny's up to hoping they'll get a record contract out of this."

"And you don't think they'll want you back once the papers are signed and some fancy club in London's booked, now?"

"Can't say," Klee said, snapping shut her purse. "This is it for Klee, I told you, I take courses Monday week. I'll be a student from now on—with a butcher's knife in one hand, o'course!"

Mary smiled and shook her head. "Oh, but the Lord's given us a smart one to boot! What are we goin' to do with you! Klee's about a hundred things at once, she is!" A few admonitions about staying out late and Mary disappeared.

♥ ♥ ♥

Alice, too, was preparing for an evening at Danigan's. The days following the revelation culminated in her choice to see her daughter a final time. Final because Alice was off to London as the lady of her Englishman, Harry, who she'd come to know better and with whom she'd found an element of stability. He'd convinced her not to further her 'profession,' and promised her comfort of a basic, reliable kind—sharing his flat in London, joining him on trips, engaging in a slice of life one step up from her Dublin existence. She took him on with few questions.

Bags packed, Alice and Harry descended to the street and headed for Dún Laoghaire.

When they stepped into the pub this time, it was early. The band was setting up and a smattering of customers nursed drinks. Alice and Harry sat at the bar and ordered. Klee, on stage with the others but wearing a more serious expression, mouthed words to herself that elicited wry comments from them.

Alice tried not to stare. Instead, she watched the fellow Benny. Something told her he was still in love with Claire, and that same something told her he'd missed his chance. He tuned his guitar as he forced smiles in response to his friends' jesting. His gaze clouded when following the movement of Klee's legs. Alice felt for him even as her date sang Benny's praises and foresaw The Jades as a success. All Alice could sense was the bottomed-out heart and wondered when the break had come.

Claire was not as relaxed either. She fidgeted with her hair, ran a hand up and down the side of her arm, and calmed only once the lights dimmed and she could retreat to a corner with a book.

Alice had to laugh. She saw right through to the meaning of Klee's preference for the written word. It probably started with Romney, all those times little Claire would have been left to her own devices, and all those times Romney would have come to her aid. Early on, the books took on a special meaning and would continue to do so. Alice silently prayed thanks to Romney, without whose influence Claire might have resorted to other means to fight the abandonment and cruelty that surely characterized her life in the west.

"She's a reader," Harry said.

"Aye," inhaled Alice.

"I hear she'd not going to be with them after this. Tonight is a one night stand."

"Oh?" Alice asked.

"Yes, she has other interests apparently. God if I know what they are. How a young one with a voice like that could ignore this chance, I'll never know. She should have some of our experience under her belt, eh Alice?" He laughed and patted her thigh.

Alice lowered her lids. She would have thought the same thing but she knew what kind of child was Claire. In no way would the girl fall for the typical passions of her age group. Toy with these notions of grandeur for a time she might, but Alice was certain that Claire would ultimately follow an untrodden path. For now, as she stared at her daughter, she was happy the girl was alive and away from the Kinemmaera tragedy Alice had caused. Claire could do as she pleased.

"She's about other experiences, I believe," Alice returned finally.

"You speak as if you know her."

Alice looked at him, then took a sip. She couldn't let on, it wouldn't be fair. To face Claire now, in the presence of so many people, in a place the antithesis of her past, was as thoughtless as what she'd done to bring the child into the world in the first place. No, Alice would sit and watch, enjoy the sight of her own creation, and guard the memory within her. Tonight Alice was exactly that right now—the proudest of mothers watching her talented daughter move towards a life of promise. What mother wouldn't beam?

She blocked out Harry's babble, took another sip, and waited for the music. Not only was she with her daughter, she was with the memory of the man who helped bring the child into the world, again in his arms and tangled in love. Claire was a singer, a reader, a beauty God created, and Claire was the spitting image of her father, the love of Alice Walsh's life. She became again a young woman in London.

But it didn't turn out to be a simple reflective sit for Alice. Klee's power with song, cut through the rationale, and tore so at her mother's heart that Alice was weeping before she knew what happened.

When she looked at Klee, who faced the audience with a radiance born of raw talent, it was too much. She extended a hand, held it mid-air, then beckoned. She wanted to have her child in her arms, to press into the soft skin and have the deep-set eyes on her alone. She wanted to hug, only hug, and thank God for her child, for all her children, for she was above all the mother of her babies. Fronting for years as the working, unattached woman, she had all the while craved the challenge and demands of tending to her brood. Had she known how much she would miss her children, she might have withstood Bob Walsh's antics. She'd acted rashly and now, as she stared at her last born, she knew in her heart she'd done wrong, a wrong that could no longer be righted by going back to Kinemmaera. That would be suicide.

But there remained one option. She could reach out to one of them. She could tell Claire she hadn't meant to hurt her. Before she left Ireland for good, she could perhaps help mend what damage she'd caused for this child, this her last, but the one who, for reasons only guessed at, had left Kinemmaera too and materialized right in her mother's path. And she in Claire's.

In a barely audible plea, unheard even by her partner, she whispered, "Claire."

With an eased motion of her head, Klee's navy gaze met her mother's.

They were alone in the room, eyes on eyes, an outstretched hand speaking to their unchained relationship, and a mother who was finally, after years, offering up the role she had shunned.

Klee coughed, blinked. The lights prevented clear visibility. Ignoring Benny's call, she advanced and clasped her mother's hand.

In her dress and up close, she was breathtaking, a wide-eyed child with a regard that hinted at burgeoning promise. She was learned and mature, fragile yet unbending, a serious and awe-inspiring natural beauty. She did not take her eyes off Alice.

"Are ye well?" Alice asked, suddenly afraid of the piercing closeness.

"You look a bit like Breeda... Mum."

Their embrace ensued, of cries and sweet smells, of tears and unspoken relief. They hugged and separated, stared and hugged again, waves of reality marrying with a merry, bilious feeling.

The band struck up. "I must go," Klee said.

"Your voice is lovely," Alice said as she watched Klee's hand slip from hers.

"Where do you think it's from?" Klee asked.

Alice nodded, a smile. "I can only guess."

The group sang five songs, Klee in the lead, Benny on harmony. By the end of the night, Danigan's was its usual packed place and the agent smiled approval of The Jades.

A teary-eyed Alice watched, too. When the music was over, she told herself she would leave but she was unable to do so. The few words with Klee had been but a tease. Throughout the evening, she found herself wanting to know more, wanting to maintain their connection.

Klee had the same inclination. As she tried to break away from the agent's incessant questions, she nodded Alice's way.

Alice sat, ignoring Harry's curious stares and his questions. When he asked if she was her daughter, Alice nodded. Harry immediately babbled over the fortunate turn of events, how they could contract Klee to work in London. But Alice took no heed.

"I'd like a private moment with my daughter," she finally said once the lights were on. "I'll meet you at your place in an hour, how's that?" She left her friend and made for the stage.

They stood again facing one another, this time with the cachet of acquaintance and the shared will of discovery.

"Would you like to walk?" Alice asked.

"Yes," she said and turned to Benny, whispered in his ear. Benny looked to Alice and then nodded. Although the agent insisted he'd be interested in The Jades if Klee stayed on, Benny let her go. He watched the two women leave, eyeing Klee's back and her slender legs until he could no longer see her. Then he faced the agent.

Alice and Klee walked everywhere, downtown, to the Green, twice over the river, and as far west as Phoenix Park. They talked of everything, from Romney to the boys to Breeda's wedding to the various characters from Kinemmaera. The easy conversation broke the barrier of time and kept them off topics too difficult to face right away.

Klee focused on her stay in Dublin, sang the Faheys praises, and outlined her study plans. Alice talked of England and her new life. She said little of her years in Dublin and less of her encounter with the man who would take her to England and make her effectively a kept woman. They noted the fact each was on the verge of a new beginning.

"Sure but you've thought twice about going to England," Klee ventured. "I mean, it's England after all!"

"I know what you mean, luv, but I'm really not inclined to be too political, you know. It's a place I can better work, if you can understand."

"I can. It's just, after reading so much....well, never mind. I hope you'll write me."

"I will every week. You're staying with the Faheys then," Alice said.

"I am. I'd love to hear from you."

"And you'll keep up with the singing?" Alice asked.

Klee shrugged. "I doubt it. It's fun but I prefer my studies."

"Romney was good to ye."

"She was," Klee said. "I miss her."

"Oh, but don't you go worryin' about Romney now. You know well she's in the best place she could be!"

They reached the pub once again. Klee faced a strong breeze and looked to darkened buildings across the way. "What do you think of the tinkers?"

"Dirty."

"Wha?"

"Dirty," Alice said. She kicked a candy wrapper and hugged her coat about her.

"I marvel at the color red of their hair. Burned, it is."

"Yes, well..."

"And they travel, don't they?"

"Claire, have you ever been to London?"

"Why? Are there tinkers in London?"

Alice laughed. "Never. You see that's it. If you ever get out of this filthy Ireland, you'll never see a tinker again. Oh, and the city is grand! Big, with so much to see. Here is a damnable place. There, you can have a life."

They faced one another.

"I'll be off now," Klee said.

Alice reached and hugged tight, patted a hand on the curls. "You keep yourself warm now. And mind your studies."

With a measured grin, Klee said, "Take care, Mum."

"And you," Alice said. "You look...you look...so very...very lovely, Claire." She tapped a finger lightly on the nose, ran it down the broad cheek, and closed her eyes for a second. "Be a good girl."

Klee went in the direction of the Faheys as Alice went the opposite way.

♥ ♥ ♥

The evening would have ended fine if not for Benny standing on Klee's front porch when she returned. He had been drinking and wore a face so forlorn she knew exactly what was coming. Mechanically, he took her in his arms.

At first, she didn't protest, let him cry to her how he missed her, how he thought she was the most beautiful thing, how he would crumble if she didn't come back. The drink prodding him, words tumbled with his tears, his hands gripped for a hungering security, and his body was firm with want.

Gently, she pushed him from her and tried to explain, let him know he was special and always would be, that she appreciated him not coming around since their last talk. He fought her reasoning, and insisted on gazing at her hips and breasts.

"Benny," she said, "I'm sorry but I must go inside. It's been a long night, a big night."

"Your Mum it was?"

She nodded, a smile crossing her face.

"Oh, but you look so pretty, Klee baby. Can't I please have another chance?"

His begging drew on her compassion yet she couldn't break her promise. Benny would hurt even more in the morning. His broken heart aside, Klee had plans to stay up all night and think over the time with her mother. It was not a night to be with a man.

She managed to free herself. Inside, she stepped up to her room, her heart feeling for Benny and absorbed about meeting her Mother.

Contrary to her wishes, however, Benny's imprint would define the night. As she tip-toed to her room, a wave of nausea threw her to the bed and left her a ball of pain for excruciating minutes. She vomited suddenly, all over her sheets and her black dress, leaving particles in her hair and a mess of the room. Legs shaking, she limped to the toilet where she again retched. Her head ached but, feeling better, she thought that might be the end of it. She returned to her room to tidy a bit but was again forced to the bed.

She tried to remember what she'd had to drink but, save the inhaling of Guinness fumes as she and her mother passed the brewery at St. James, she'd only had water. No, it was something more.

On the bed she prayed for the pain to leave her at the same time she prayed this wasn't about what she feared.

Mrs. Fahey heard her noises and came. Turning on the light, she saw the mess, saw the ghostly pallor on Klee's normally rosy face, and knew right away the girl was with child.

Mary undressed Klee, took away the dirty sheets, remade the bed and placed Klee in it. She sought a wet cloth for Klee's forehead and made some tea. Placing it bedside, she made the Sign of the Cross and stood vigil beside Klee who had dozed off. As the night wore on, Klee woke twice, each time with the same nausea, each time with a worried look she sent Mary's way. But the woman could only hold the girl's hand and pray. This was the curse no woman ever wanted, and now under her roof there was one afflicted. In Ireland, there were few alternatives. You married and had the child or you went to England.

Mary Fahey was a decent, respected woman. She had come to love Klee more than perhaps Klee even knew. What began as an act of charity had turned into a most fulfilling undertaking, for Klee brought zest and humor, intelligence and love under the roof of Mary and Danny Fahey and they would have been the last people to cast her out.

But this was one of those things. An employee with protruding belly and no wedding ring was entirely out of the question. She could not permit Klee to stay.

Through tears, she fingered Klee's hair off her face and said, "And, child, didn't you have the world at your feet for a while, sure you did."

In the morning, this would be dealt with. For now, Mary rubbed the beads of her rosary and recited her prayers. From this point on, it was all she could do for the girl.

# Chapter 16:
# October 1968

EVAN SOUGHT OUT LAURENCE at her Roscoff address. Several attempts at visiting, and even tacking notes to her door, left him no closer to meeting this much-talked-about friend of the family.

He hired a fishing boat to get him to the island where he would be alone with the elements. During the ride, he joked with fishermen and caught up on developments in the town. The traversal behind him, he grabbed his sack of clothes, shook his transporters' hands, and made way for the opposite side of the island. As afternoon shadows lengthened, the air nipped and winds intensified. He quickened his pace and whistled a few movie tunes. Like his father, he was at peace on Batz, like his mother, his better side emerged in full. He gazed across the barren coast. On the jetty that gave a commanding view of his mother's favorite lighthouse, he saw her.

Seated Indian style and wearing jeans, she gazed over the water. Her hair was longer than he'd seen in photos. In the weakening light, she took on the shades of one of the boulders, pinkish red one second, blackest black another. She blended.

It could only be Laurence, he reasoned. With her family's house nearby and a village at the other end being the exception, there wasn't a soul on the island off season.

Harshening winds and cold did nothing to change her statuesque pose. He called to her but she remained motionless. He called again. Her head turned towards him. He waved, dropped his sack on the sand.

"I'm Evan," he yelled.

She watched him approach. Feet from her, he extended his hand. A gentle grip returned his greeting as he registered a sensation leftover from being with Patrice. Laurence slid to one side of the boulder to give him room. Her gaze rose towards two squawking gulls above them and her expression grew somber. Then she lowered her chin to again study the swirling water.

Normally he would have obliged this nonverbal request for solitude. She could easily look him up the next day if she chose. But this was where his mother's spirit reigned, where he too found the calm this young woman was part of, so he stayed put. Enticed as much by her indifference as by her beauty, he sensed that hers was a drama she would not readily share.

In time, he stood. "I'll leave you, Laurence. If you wish, join me at the house." Her imperceptible nod telegraphed a demure refusal.

As he lifted his bag and made for home, he sensed he'd not see her that night or the next, perhaps not during his entire stay.

After preparing a fire and meal, he settled by the gas lamp and tried to read. But she returned to him time and again—the silken hair, that poised yet impenetrable regard, her delicate, reddened hands. Like the sea's motion outside his door, her image expanded one minute, lessened the next. He longed to see her again. But she did not seek him out.

❤ ❤ ❤

It was time to lay his options on the table and so he did. Evan above all was a de Roche, a key contributor to the family's future. Father and son had not yet discussed at length this important fact. At sixty-one, Giles maintained his performance at all levels and with the same energy he had at twenty. Nevertheless, Evan had to prepare himself for his father's eventual stepping-down.

Evan assumed the delayed discussion about the future had to do with himself and not his father. Had he been in Giles's position, he too would question the seriousness of a son with eyes on Hollywood and foreign investment. Giles was of another generation. Evan was the future, but could only become the future of de Roche Frères if he put fantasies behind him and move in the traditional direction—increased profits from existing and stable industries like mining, fuel and fuel alternatives, plus intelligent management of assets.

Evan frowned. The franc was threatened and lately Giles took to protecting their losses in a most foolish way by withdrawing huge sums and placing them in the family safe. On discovering this, Evan had laughed out loud, but his father's stern regard and shrug had silenced what humor Evan found in the matter. Giles assured his son that one day they would again invest in other markets. Evan wondered about that, as well as his father's possible flirtation with senility.

Still, Evan wielded little power. As their heated arguments tempered to occasional quips about trivialities, Evan sensed he must either make his intentions known or Giles would decide for him. He therefore chose to let go of the cinema—at least for the time being. The strings of the family purse must be managed, and by an experienced member of the inner circle.

As he wandered the grey coast day after day, he convinced himself that this decision was the right one. He wished Danielle was still alive, wished for his mother's presence to reinforce his ideas, wished he could somehow combine all his talents into one happy pool of activity.

Try as he might to pretend otherwise, the road was paved for him, starting with the deaths of his mother and sister and followed by the consistent training and advice from Giles. Well before Evan took to the streets and unrest in May, his destiny was a fait accompli. What disaccord he voiced now would go unacknowledged.

Through his love-making with Patrice, he understood. Silently acquiescent and patient, expert in her ways, she remained ever cognizant of the reasons why they came together in the first place. He read between the lines of her apology and, even if he hadn't, he would have seen through her physical performance to the truth. Patrice chose to give of herself for two reasons. One, she cared. Two, he was a de Roche.

When the loving was over so too was the giving. To give of oneself in such a way implied giving one's all, but in this case their giving lasted only the moments their bodies were joined. To Evan that seemed most ridiculous, causing him much confusion. Patrice wordlessly signaled her happiness yet at the same time allowed him to slip away. Odd, he thought, how strong the body's yearnings, how they whip about a person's soul, confusing reality with illusion, and vice-versa.

As days passed, the intensity of recall diminished and the experience found its proper place in his psyche. He integrated within his heart Patrice's calculated plea for his forgiveness and acknowledged his own ambling, at times wanton, center of non-feeling—a trait that was indispensable in the business world, and one that, for all the family's gilded charm, fueled their success.

Like Patrice, his was born of the same insensitivity that could, given the proper channeling, strengthen throughout his adulthood. The supreme irony was that its birth had come from the act of love, an act that until then Evan had reserved for the most precious of encounters. The flip side of love was a multi-pronged fury. The positive was laced with negative and it would be Evan's challenge to discern how much or little he cared to embrace. A de Roche possessed the power to dish out as well as to live within the coils of this dilemma.

He returned to Roscoff and made arrangements to take the train to Paris. While waiting, he strolled the quays where the fishermen separated their catch— slicing filets, shucking oysters, and piling unusable parts. At the stand of his old friend, Jean Martins, he mingled with locals and bantered about his upcoming position within de Roche Frères. They already assumed he would one day take over and felt pride in his presence as he detailed corporate structure and business policy they could only hope to half understand. Still, because of his family's home on the island, he was one of them— a visiting Breton but a Breton nonetheless.

"Eh, you met up with the de Long beauty, friend?" Jean asked him.

Regaining the image of Laurence, Evan turned to Jean. "Briefly."

"Strange child, going back to America, like her Papa. Thought she might stay on at the school you know. Had the head for the sea—and the body, heh, heh!"

Evan allowed the jocularity to reign. Had it been he and Jean alone, he might have inquired further into Laurence's activities while at Roscoff. But now he would choose his words and actions carefully. From today, he was a bona fide representative of the family. When it came to women, in time, one would be pointed out as appropriate. Perhaps it would be Solange Lemuire, or Marie Pontivy—socialites from Paris with brains and beauty similar to his mother's.

An American with interest in the sea would not be approved of, no matter how gifted or worthy Evan might find her. He pressed lips and tried to shake her phantom-like hold. Wishing them all well, he made way for the train, preparing his speech with his father, looking forward to the man's content regard and open arms. They'd been estranged far too long.

# Chapter 17

PAOLO CAPIZZI RAISED HIS EYES to the ceiling and moaned. His best pupil quitting! Mother of God! Seven long years training one like her and now, for reasons unknown, she'd not shown for two weeks. Where was she?

He wrung his hands and stood by the window of his office overlooking Trinity's courtyard. The day was grey, the rain pelted. A handful of students raced across puddles and mud patches.

Time to return to Rome. Dublin had become a stranger once again. He thought he would find unique voices here, youth who were ready to challenge their vocal chords, who were ready to practice to perfection and utilize their song to partake in more than drunken choruses in area pubs. He'd thought....but he was fooled.

A priest visiting Rome had encouraged him to tutor the Irish. After making the long journey to Dublin and settling in at the College, he placed an ad in the paper and commenced giving lessons to a few local people and students. He first occupied himself with two young music majors who wished to round out their experience, yet who struggled with even the most basic notes. Later, he faced some hopefuls with the bad news that their voices were not meant for operatic solos. Still, his name familiar in classical music circles, he eventually managed to find the odd student or two with promise. Soon after that, they came more frequently, with more experience and talent. Finally, he nurtured a following, and from that came income to help him pay his bills and to address his own curiosity about Celtic singing prowess.

Paolo was nothing if not patient. In spite of the weather and the lack of musical outlets for his tastes, he persevered. Important for him was the search for at least one, maybe two great voices he could train and mold to sing arias or even complete operas. He had noticed a few Irish youth in Rome during papal ceremonies and in church choirs. There was truth to the saying they had range, and an unusual ability to echo a lonely chord that added unique dimension to choruses, prevailing in the background against even the strongest of sopranos. The quest for this type of singer occupied him, he or she existed he believed, and that the person needed to be sought out. It was like anything—the rare object of perfection required effort, as much to uncover as to nurture, then urging on, and always treating tenderly. With love.

His quest had to be for love because Paolo quickly grew disgusted with the food—the pasty potatoes, the overcooked meat, the greasy plates of chips. He loathed their habit of rushing through lunch, and missed his siestas as he missed his mother's tagliatelle. Worst of all, his porto was not sold in Ireland. As a result, the rare exception being Christmas when his mother mailed him a few bottles, he found little solace evenings at his flat. Without his porto, he struggled, listless, in his easy chair, trying to integrate the day and plan for the next. The country was backwards in so many ways and often he came close to leaving, but for his students. He enjoyed helping some, and loved working with one.

Her appearance had been the topping on the cake of an upbeat week for Paolo. From a cloudless sky, sun streamed into his office, a rare delight. Two new music teachers were due to arrive from the continent and, the following week the London Philharmonic was to perform a Mozart concert. All the excitement set Paolo in a pleasant buzz he'd not managed since leaving Rome. When she knocked on the door and stepped inside, he sensed right away there was something about her.

"You have a voice?" he asked, as he watched her remove a pert black hat. He blinked at the hair, suppressed a grin at her clown-like appearance, then—her gaze drawing him closer—squinted to better see.

"I have," she said. "I believe I have."

And he knew. The melody was untainted by her time in Dublin; she still held onto the airy accent of the country. He could work around that, better to start with her natural voice than to undo an acquired one anyway. And the whisper, well, they all whispered at times but hers had an intention, like some electrical charge taking hold. He reached for her hand and she placed long fingers into his, as if they belonged, as if she entrusted him with her life. Had he been in Italy, he would have hugged her but these people held closeness at bay—an odd habit given the cold and damp. Enthralled, he studied her as though observing a fine porcelain artifact, and pointed her to a chair. Her first brief words threw open a meadow of possibilities. At last, he found his candidate.

She was a worker! An adherent to their schedule, a reader of any and all books he chose to lend, a serious and focused student he could not have found from any of the visiting scholars at Trinity. A butcher's employee no less! But even that was marvelous for it coincided with his belief one had to overturn every stone, especially those discarded and lost under daily toils and distractions.

She sang from her soul. He didn't have to suggest it. Though she was only eighteen, he sensed her depth, those talents and skills that come not from books but that are handed down through the ages, that which can't be touched or even named.

"To your heritage, Klee," he said at one of their first sessions. "Reach for it."

Her nod, her eyes ever so serious and so lovely blue told him that she knew of what he spoke.

He could even speak Italian and she didn't complain, seemed to welcome his words as if they, too, were part of her musical experience.

She progressed fast, went from scales to ranges, from short pieces to longer ones. He proposed one by Verdi long before even his best students in Rome. She missed only a few notes, apologized the second she was off key, and resolutely continued—a soldier busy at battle. He loved Klee like no other student.

Now she was nowhere to be found. He allowed the first absence to pass, for she was reliable and not one to skip class, always offered to pay herself even though her mate Benny continued to write Paolo checks. If she missed once, she was sure to catch up with him and explain. Still, and for the first time ever for Paolo, he began to agitate for her. Her voice would have no price, no person with awareness could ever demand a no-show fee to such a God-given gift. So he waited.

By the second miss his fragile temper kicked in and he contacted Benny who was vague and uncooperative. Paolo sensed she was slipping away and this created urgency in his thoughts and the creeping realization that, in the derelict and wondrous ways of affection taking seed, his heart sang for her, too. For a fifty-year old confirmed bachelor, frumpy, bumpy, and balding, this proved a major occurrence in his life. His mother had long ago laid claim. Her Paolo was her Paolo and her doting was annoyingly problematic until the day he found music. Then, with his mother's approval, he'd taken on the profession with the verve of any newly smitten lover. Under her nose, he began an affair that was to carry him through life. Paolo had found his woman in music and so it went. Until now with this Irish singer turned runaway.

As he sputtered about his office and stole glances out the window, his jealousies and anger reared and he began to curse her and wish her ill. He'd given his all and wanted to see her off to a career that would grant her a rightful place in concert halls.

The silly Coleen differed little from the rest of them, interested for a time then distracted by some giddy thing or another like boys or hairstyles. She who could have been so revered, who could have broken all barriers, chose to be lumped within the walls of mediocrity.

And he'd worked so with her, with so much love.

He reached for the phone book to call Dublin airport. It was time to return to Rome. He missed his porto.

♥ ♥ ♥

The green and white Air Lingus plane approached the gate. In a cold, vinyl seat at the airport, Klee rubbed her legs against one another. Her ticket in hand, a passport gotten with her last penny, she adjusted her hat and bit her lower lip.

There was no way she would go to England. She'd read and heard enough. Even though Alice was there and might be of help, she was not interested. America was a vast unknown but she wasn't angry with America, and wasn't afraid to go there.

In her arm, a book her mother left on the Fahey's doorstep, an out of print anthology of Irish folk tales and ballads. "Darling Claire," she wrote on the inside flap, "This was your aunt Romney's. I took it before leaving Kinemmaera. With your interest in Gaelic, you'll put it to better use than myself. God be with you. Mum."

Klee flipped through the pages, her finger stuck at a place from where a page was torn. She'd read the book twice and had already committed many ballads to memory. She wondered about the missing page and figured she might contact the publisher. Her final days, however, were demanding and harried. She studied the milling crowd.

The announcer rattled off the destination, "Flight 762 Dublin to Boston now boarding..." She reached for her bag of books and made way for the queue. With luck, her stomach would keep still for the journey. If not, she'd ask a stewardess for help. She would not think about the baby right now, urgent that she maintain calm and try to plan her moves once stateside.

The ticket agent wrinkled his brow. "Are you feeling alright, Miss?"

Nodding, she passed him and made for the cabin, and a window seat. She would watch the clouds below and the green of the land she was leaving. She would listen to the piped-in music and eventually pull out a book to read. She was on her way, with her small folk, her books, and a few bars of song—what now remained of dear Paolo's hard work.

# Part Two
# Moving On

*Where the wave of moonlight glosses*
*The dim gray sands with light,*
*Far off by furthest Rosses*
*We foot it all the night,*
*Weaving olden dances*
*Mingling hands and mingling glances*
*Till the moon has taken flight;*
*To and fro we leap*
*And chase the frothy bubbles,*
*While the world is full of troubles*
*And anxious in its sleep.*
*Come away, O human child!*
*To the waters and the wild*
*With a faery, hand in hand,*
*For the world's more full of weeping than you can*
*understand.*

The Stolen Child     by W. B. Yeats

# Chapter 1:
# October, 1968

MÉMÉ FLIPPED THROUGH HER MAIL. "So, Régine, you say Laurence has let her school work go?"

Running fingertips down the front of her black Yves St. Laurent suit, Régine looked out the window of her mother's study. She threw back her head with a laugh. "Mama," she said, "now you see her for who she really is. All summer I watched you and the others fawn as if she were a godsend. Now you understand how it's been for me all these years. She's irresponsible, like her father."

Mémé pressed index and forefinger to her chin and studied her daughter. "She's gifted, like her father," she said. "You're hard on her."

"And you, Mama, if I may say so, are blind. She's trouble."

"Still, she had such promise...I hope she's alright."

Régine looked at her watch. "I'll be off to the salon. The show runs until three. Then Marie Ange and I will go to her place in Neuilly. She's decorated the kitchen with the Jacques Martel look. You know, the latest..."

Accepting Régine's kiss, Mémé nodded. "Fine, chérie, I'll see you tomorrow."

In a trail of Joy perfume, Régine left. Since returning to Paris, her days passed at fashion shows, luncheons, and dinners with friends or with Giles. Mémé hardly saw her except during breakfast when Régine offered clipped responses. Régine used her mother's name, check book, and reputation to make inroads at all the correct Parisian places. Mémé let it happen, first because she felt her daughter needed this support and then because she had little choice. Régine had commandeered the de Long residence and dictated a protocol that challenged Mémé's reserved style.

Mémé missed the coast already. She made an effort when Giles and Régine invited her to dine but, not want to begrudge her daughter her privacy, she eventually backed off and stayed home most often. The city scene was for the young and her entire clan, although omnipresent during summer, was occupied with their respective businesses and families. Paris was not the ends of the earth, of course. She had her garden and walks and found an element of peace knowing her family was nearby and healthy. Still, the days since summer's end had brought on change she'd not anticipated and, had it not been for Laurence's correspondence, she might have begun to believe her life had dwindling purpose.

The descriptive letters she received from Roscoff pleased her and when they stopped, she thought at first Laurence might be busy with exams. Now she wasn't sure. Plus, Régine's responses any time Mémé broached the topic of Laurence were peremptory, another cause for concern.

She pressed lips and looked down at her mail. On top, an envelope with Laurence's handwriting.

"Oh, child, I was so worried," Mémé whispered, ripping the edge. As she opened, franc notes spilled to the floor. "Nom de Dieu! What is this?"

In a few lines, Laurence apologized for her hasty departure and explained the francs were reimbursement for the loan. Mémé reread, then folded, studied the tan and blue notes strewn about.

What went on last summer? Had Georges been correct insinuating Régine had less than the most heartfelt intentions for Laurence? And what of those comments regarding bruises?

"Child, did I overlook a detail about you while we were all so very distracted this summer?" She reached for her black shawl and draped it over her shoulders.

The postmark was from somewhere in the States, Nantucket. Mémé made note and, for the time being, decided to say nothing to Régine.

Evan climbed the stairs to the résidence. As his steps echoed off the marble, he listened. All was silent. He turned the knob and looked down the long corridor towards the kitchen. No dinner smells. A glow from the study threw shadows into the hallway and adjoining rooms. Rather than go directly to his bedroom, he went to see if his father was still at work.

There, in the chair Giles alone had sat in since Evan could remember, a woman. Her hair was blonde and, in the latest Deneuve style, curved over one eye. Heavily made-up eyes studied something in her hands. She raised her head and immediately a smile creased into rouged cheeks.

In the soft light, she was an exquisite magazine model, a sophisticated twenty-something. The tapping of her nails on the side table made his eyes blink.

On closer inspection, this was someone much older, a woman hardly dainty, but feral and set. A beauty, but not. And she sat in his father's chair.

"Régine de Long Mallord," she said, a hand extended. "You must be Evan."

Her grasp was neither reassuring nor relinquishing. Wearing faultless attire and with steady gaze, she was ice, guile, and uncomfortably distracting.

"de Roche," he said before he knew it. He felt her dominance, her intention to be within these four walls.

She threw her head back, laughed. "But of course!"

The blonde locks swished to one side, an act of seduction or a mean joke, he wasn't sure. Her eyes were again on him and he tried to read through them but was unable to. They were soft brown one minute, bulbous and glowering the next.

Unabashed, she assessed his body, his dark eyes and exposed neck, his torso still exercised from the climb, his tight-fitting casual slacks, the suntan on his forearms and hands, the curiously pugged nose centering the otherwise chiseled look. She lingered, as if taking him in, as if she owned him already.

He shifted his weight, uneasy in what used to be for him the most relaxed of settings. Pauline and he used to talk movies long into the night. He and Giles had discussed more than business here. It was the family room as well as the study. The de Roche family room.

"Laurence's mother," he said.

He registered the flicker in her eyes as a wicked spark. He tried to find Laurence in her but was unable to. This creature had no resemblance to the ethereal woman on the rocks. Although their interaction on Batz had been fleeting and Laurence had not said a word, he felt he knew her better than most long-time friends, indeed had ruminated over her each day since their meeting. If this was her mother, then Laurence must look like her father. He guessed Régine to be the type to feel upstaged next to a daughter the likes of Laurence.

He was learning about woman. There were women who were content with a surface beauty, purchased at make-up counters and imitated from magazines. There were women who didn't much care about their looks which usually meant they couldn't afford to, for *comme il faut* (as required) meant money and not all were wealthy Parisians. Then there were the few natural ones—Patrice, Laurence—who faced the world each day with minimal effort in front of the mirror. They were complete to begin with. He guessed Régine to be the first type.

His throat constricted. The long journey from Batz over, he had hoped to tumble into bed but instead faced this stranger. Her in-charge mannerism distracted him. He hadn't caught on right away. This woman was dating his father. He grew rigid and a dryness persisted in his throat. He might have made a move to get something to drink if he hadn't noticed what it was Régine held—the silver-framed picture of his mother.

Her fingernails scratched, she smudged the glass. Her thumb hid a part of Pauline's face, a peek of his mother's smile, her wide eyes. Evan felt a rage like no other.

Noting where his gaze fell, she said, "She was...attractive in her way, your mother."

He opened his mouth to speak at the same time his father appeared. Régine rose, passed Evan and leaned into Giles.

After returning an embrace, he lowered Régine's hands and asked, "Son, the trip was agreeable?"

"Weather foul, but a restful time."

"I told you it would be," Giles said reaching for a glass and pouring sherry for Régine. "You two have met?"

"Yes," Evan said, moving to a chair.

"You must have seen Laurence?" Giles asked.

199

"Oh," Régine interrupted, "I was going to tell you, mon cher, the little cherub has disappeared! Imagine, after all Mémé did for her! I simply don't understand children these days, do you? Dear Evan, you will excuse me but I speak only of those like my irresponsible daughter. I'm sure...."

"She is lovely," Evan said.

"Then you did see her?" Giles asked.

"Briefly. Along the shore..."

"Ah, yes, always wandering and contemplating," Régine said, "Never serious or directed, ever. The child has some real growing up to do. Come, Giles dear, we're set for nine. I've told you, it took some effort to reserve this table. Hurry!" She returned to the desk and grabbed a leather purse with gold trim that matched her outfit. With a tap on his shoulder, she said, "Evan, dear, we'll meet again."

With that, they were gone, Giles laughing as Régine babbled on.

Betti's footsteps caught Evan by surprise. She placed a tray of *thé citron* and biscuits by his side. "Monsieur Evan, welcome back."

Evan smiled. "Betti," he murmured, "you always remember." The tea was customary for all family members returning from Batz at the end of the season. Usually by then fall winds sent a chill to the bones, signaling the end of mint drinks and lazy afternoon swims. He raised the cup to his lips and tasted. It soothed.

Betti tidied the study and made for the door, her apron still crisp and white, her simple black dress the attire she'd worn for over thirty years as maid in the de Roche house.

Evan reached for her hand. "Betti, Betti."

"Oui, Monsieur Evan?"

His eyes fell to the picture on his father's desk and the lines on his face deepened. "What is with Papa?"

Betti set her lips and stole a glance at Pauline's photo. She went to the desk and replaced it in its usual spot at the corner of Giles's blotter.

"Here," Evan said, beckoning, a hand outstretched.

He took it from her and rubbed, clearing the smudges to reveal again his mother's crystal eyes and iridescent persona.

"She is not what we might have wished for your father," Betti said.

He looked to Betti, reached again for her hand. "We know Mama can never be replaced, don't we?"

Betti nodded, her eyes smoldering. "True. But this, this person. I cannot guess what she's about, I dare not. Excuse me, Monsieur Evan. I will retire now. Drink your tea."

"Good night, Betti."

Like he had hundreds of times since her death, Evan tried to revive his mother. Yet, the night of the tragedy having been the exception, his mother was gone. Try as he might to invent conversations or fabricate adventures, he had difficulty, and grew frustrated with the fading recall of her once rich and textured life. She was tucked away somewhere, and when he most required her, she proved elusive.

He sipped his tea. When he finished, he took the picture, placed his sack over his arm, and walked to his room. No one would mar it again, least of all Régine, whatever became of she and his father.

# Chapter 2:
# October, 1968

DURING HER JOURNEY TO THE U.S., Laurence met a fifty-year-old film maker named Beatrice Magnell. Disembarking from the plane, Laurence had retrieved a roll of film that slipped from Beatrice's bag. They accompanied one another to baggage claim and, during the wait, chatted amiably.

Bea, as she preferred to be called, was slim and tall with short grey hair and blue eyes. In one ear, three pierced gold studs, in the other, a wide hoop. Casual slacks, white t-shirt, and deep tan spoke to her athletic style.

"It's a bother, the travel," Bea said. "But I tell you, the results are spectacular, once you come upon certain places. I doubt many Americans even know of that stretch along southern Corsica."

"You bring the films to producers in New York?" Laurence asked.

"Yes, the film is put to music and marketed as a documentary."

With her partner Sage, who composed the music, Bea edited then released her work through choice distribution channels. It was a lucrative niche that allowed the two women to pursue their artistic interests while living far from the 'crazy life,' as Bea put it.

Before Laurence could protest, Bea had convinced her that a few days on Nantucket would be the remedy for jet lag. After exiting the airport in Bea's Jeep, they headed south to Woods Hole where they caught the ferry. In less than five hours after landing in Boston, they pulled into the village of Madaket on the southwest tip of the island.

In the pre-winter chill, the only sign of life came from Bea's brightly-lit grey-shingled Cape tucked at the end of a sandy road. The interior comprised knotty pine walls, hardwood floors, and a fireplace. Crocheted oval carpets, a stuffed sailfish above the hearth, and draped netting bulging with multi-colored glass balls reminded Laurence of her former home.

Sage was somewhere out of sight, at the piano working through a few bars. The instant Bea called, she appeared. As trim and athletic as Bea, she wore her dark hair in a waist-length braid. Her face was rounder and she had the ruddy pink that comes from exposure to the elements without protection. Her black eyes sparkled and she smelled of soap and salt air when she reached to welcome Laurence with a bear hug. Then, she embraced Bea.

"So! You have found another hiding place that will no longer be as such!" Opening a silver cigarette case, she pulled a thin brown cigar from it. After lighting, she exhaled. Smoke made a cloud in front of her face.

"Oh, you should have seen it! Well, I suppose you will soon, won't you?" Bea asked, slipping out of her parka and dropping paraphernalia to the floor. She flailed her arms to dispel the smoke. "When are you going to quit, my dear?"

They were as one, bustling about the living room, setting water for tea, chatting to Laurence, to no one in particular, to each other. Over a snack of leek soup and fresh wheat bread, they held hands and shared intense regards. It was easy to see they'd been together a long time and soon Laurence understood they were lovers.

They chatted until Bea and Laurence struggled to keep eyes open whereupon Sage urged them off to bed while she cleaned up and finished her work.

As the days progressed, 'fortunate' was the word continually on Laurence's lips. The routine and the life by the sea tempered her anxieties such that, a few weeks into her stay, a day or two would pass and she didn't even think of Régine, Pierre, or Roscoff.

She readily adapted to the schedule. Mornings, Sage practiced. Her piano, the single piece of furniture in the third floor garret, stood by windows that gave view to expanses of water and sand. From that perspective, Sage explained, she drew her inspiration. At the crack of day until late morning, she reviewed basic chords, struggled with an emerging piece, and ended with a sonata by Mozart or Beethoven. Bea went to town to shop or to arrange with photographer friends, for she required dark room assistance and proper lighting to edit and perfect the work. Too, there were numerous phone calls. Bea often flew back and forth to New York. Laurence found a job at the drug store in town and arranged for a loan to pay back Mémé.

When possible, they convened at noon for a European-style lunch. Sage cooked for fun and to relax. Having spent years with Bea in France, she favored cream sauces, garlic, and wine to the more predictable dishes served on the island. So simple fish preparations, thin baguettes, and chilled rosés ruled. Until three or four, they shared updates of their work in progress or stories of past voyages and experiences outside the country. Almost as much as their professions, Bea and Sage thrived on international travel.

To Laurence, they accorded respect when she chose not to delve too much into her own time in France. That she was born in Massachusetts and had returned from a visit with relatives in Roscoff proved the totality of her revelations. Bea enjoyed speaking French with Laurence. During meals, they would tease Sage, speaking little English while coaching in pronunciation and slang. Sage was a sport and, although not overly engaged, played along and even surprised them once in a while with what she managed to retain.

The work done, the three took walks with their Great Dane, Pepper. It was time to refresh oneself, to return to nature, and to settle the soul. Laurence often entertained them by running into the icy waters, Pepper splashing along, emerging minutes later frozen yet exhilarated. They loved the solitude and spoke often of the peace and serenity too soon to be disturbed come spring when visitors would arrive to enjoy what the couple did year round.

Although Nantucket was fast changing from what used to be a summer-only resort into a late spring and early fall escape, Bea and Sage had no intention of leaving. The island was close enough to civilization to keep pace, had amenities and diversions, and was remote and stunningly wild which satisfied their artistic temperaments.

Their custom-built house was a fling they'd enjoyed following a particularly successful film Bea made in Africa. Nantucket was their preferred location because they'd first met on the island, had fallen in love there, and had already decided it would be their base of operations.

So, by the light of a full moon or sometimes to the accompaniment of howling winds and pounding surf, the three walked arm-in-arm, occasionally throwing a ball or stick to Pepper and expounding on one idea or another. They were philosophers when they took to their walks, free to say what they pleased, to comment and critique. Their return to the cottage included a sit atop the dunes in bright blue Adirondack chairs Bea had designed and built herself. Laurence took one chair, Sage sat on Bea's lap in the other. At such heights, they possessed the stars, and the sea was their entertainment.

Time passed and Laurence found she had no desire to leave. She helped around the house and Bea said they'd never seen the place shine so. In other ways, too, Laurence pulled her weight. The garbage went to the dump and the dog was fed before either Sage or Bea knew it. In addition, the fish and chicken stocks were boiled up the night before so that, in case Sage was running late mornings, she could dive into the cooking without bemoaning the prep work. Laurence swept, tidied, and arranged so much so the house became her private preoccupation, an activity that did not go without regular compliments from Bea and Sage.

All seemed idyllic until Bea and Sage had their first fight. It was one afternoon when they encountered difficulty editing the Corsica film. Sage disliked her score, Bea was not pleased either. It was too moody for the powerful scenes of cliffs and boulders, too strained for the quick-paced harmony of waves crashing to shore. Sage swore, Bea retreated into silences. Following hours of uncomfortable quiet, Sage abruptly took to smashing glass, ripping paper, and throwing at anything within arm's reach. Bea amplified the ruckus with caustic comments. It seemed the stand-off would never end.

Laurence slipped from the house and made for the dune chairs. A cup of hot coffee pressed to her lips, she watched the water and listened to the ebb and flow of the screaming inside.

"You're foolish!" Bea yelled. "How many times must I explain the mood to you before you get it!"

"Shut up!" Sage returned. "I wasn't there, I didn't see. You want music, you got music. I can't read your mind! You change with the tides, you!"

On and on it went until Laurence fully anticipated fist fighting and bloodshed. They screamed and ranted until, frightened, she nearly took the Jeep to town for help. But the cries died down, and Laurence sat on the chair hoping that the confrontation would not renew.

There was no dinner that afternoon and no one joined Laurence for the evening walk. Pepper ran only a few yards before turning back for the house where the two artists stewed privately, Sage in her studio, Bea in her room.

Laurence thought it was her fault, took another walk and began to think it was time to move on. Perhaps her presence had forced this unpleasant interaction. Perhaps they were being too kind and Laurence should take it upon herself to not outdo her welcome. After all, there had been no terms set down for the length of her stay and she paid no rent. She felt obliged to discuss the matter, to face facts about her own lagging goals and uncertain future. Lovely though the setting, she would eventually have to move on.

Ready to speak with Bea and Sage, she returned to the cottage to find a note.

> We're sorry you had to hear us. It's part
> of our process. Hope you understand.
> We're still in love. We still love you. Be
> back soon.          B & S

She re-read and blinked back tears. In the welcome stillness the waves breathed and the wall clock ticked. She looked up to the stuffed blue sailfish and laughed. "Oh, sometimes it's all too much for me, Mr. Fish!" she exclaimed.

She wandered to the garret from where she could climb the ladder to the outside widow's walk. On the roof, she saw the two ambling eastward towards a rocky cove. Arm in arm, Sage waved a cigarette and Bea laughed. Laurence went back inside and down the stairs. As she made way along the hall, she peeked into their bedroom.

It oozed cozy, with patchwork quilts, bright hand-painted shelves loaded with books, knitted scarves on hooks, and a wood-frame canopy bed. Antique dolls with ponytails and rouged faces wore lace-bordered velvet dresses. Dolls and dresses, attentiveness and affection.

Laurence picked one up and pressed it to her chest. Her friends were like children really—gifted, jovial, and sensitive. They played and worked hard then squabbled when things got to be too much. An arrangement new to Laurence, it nevertheless appeared healthier than what she'd experienced with Régine, and closer to Mémé's lifestyle on Batz. She understood that the fighting was not her doing and that Bea and Sage were human. Lovers and children. Sweet and vulnerable.

Once in her room, note placed on the beside, she retired for the night.

When Bea returned from Nova Scotia—a follow-up arrangement to conclude work begun the year before—Laurence held her breath. Their fighting exploded as virulently as the time before. Laurence retreated yet paid attention to the words that flew, to the crux of the matters being discussed.

She tried to comprehend what lay beyond the accusations. Bea tended to anticipate Sage's fury and therefore forged into prepared speeches. Sage was far and away too sensitive and proved a sitting duck for Bea's vengeance.

Laurence decided to intervene. Once the smoke cleared and the two went on their walk, she made way for the living area and sat on the couch opposite the door where Bea and Sage would see her. On their return, brown glasses perched on her nose, facing them, she stood and straightened her shoulders. "Ladies, let's have a talk," she said, a jean-clad yet serious contrast to the two adversaries.

She matter-of-factly listed contested issues, questioning the validity of each then suggested how to make good on constructive points. She thus was able to discard the waste material of the fight and focus on the essentials. After a slowly ramped up discussion, they were able to proceed with the project in a productive fashion.

Through her self-effacing comportment, Laurence became a key third participant in the production of the films. As a result, the next project went smoother and the finished product was formatted for test in record time.

For Bea's trip to New York, where she planned to discuss promotion and distribution, Laurence made necessary travel plans, scheduled meetings, and conversed by phone with artists and business people. She asked questions, updated herself on the unfamiliar, focused on the essentials, and became a near expert in the field.

At Thanksgiving, with the project largely complete, Bea returned to the island to join Sage and Laurence and to relax with nothing particular on the agenda. During dinner, the two women had a surprise for Laurence.

Bea started by explaining that they had a hobby, seeking out French films never before widely distributed throughout the States. The mechanisms of the French production process allowed for the author of a work, usually a novelist or screenwriter, to pass on production rights to a film director for a period of fifteen to twenty years. Once the window of time had passed, the rights reverted back to the author. Thus, there was no way for the film to be re-distributed unless the entire process was repeated. The film was usually forgotten and so lost to the public in and outside France.

During her many trips to there, Bea delighted in researching old films. Should she deem one noteworthy, she would scout out the creator or production company to see what could be done to reproduce or distribute the film. If successful, she saw to it the work was shown in New York or on university campuses, venues where a sensitivity to Nouvelle Vague and other French films prevailed.

Having once heard Laurence make reference to Jacques Cousteau and his underwater escapades, Bea arranged for a showing of his first film, "*Le Monde du Silence.*" Without giving details, she convinced Laurence to join them at the festival, where they might catch one or two of the rare ones.

"*Monde*" caught Laurence by surprise. As soon as the credits rolled—its original production in 1956—she was again with her father, for he had often spoken of the film. Indeed, Nate had collaborated with the young assistant director, Louis Malle, for underwater effects.

It was a beautiful film of fish and plant life, a visual voyage that brought her back to her youth. She touched on a time when she fed off the sea in the same way Cousteau did, with the same energy and rugged perseverance, mining secrets from the depths of what was to this day, in many respects, still a mystery.

When the lights went on and the room emptied, Laurence remained seated in the front row, studying the now blank screen, her eyes on a faraway place.

"It's time to go," Sage said, placing a hand on Laurence's shoulder.

Laurence let Sage take her by the arm and lead her to the car. In silence they drove to the Cape and caught the final ferry to the island.

It wasn't until the next day, after a return from a walk on the beach, Laurence spoke. She joined the others atop the widow's walk and sat on the ledge facing them. It was cold and snow flakes dampened their noses. She sipped coffee and studied her friends.

Sage held a Kleenex and rubbed her nose and, like a culpable child, periodically glanced at Laurence. Bea avoided Laurence's gaze, and tapped her fingertips repeatedly on Sage's thigh.

"I hope you don't think I was offended by the film," Laurence said.

"Oh, honey, one never knows with you," Bea blurted. "I never, ever meant to upset you..."

Laurence smiled. "You could never do that, Bea. Either of you..."

"Well, the way you looked so...I don't know, horrified yet pleased at the same time," said Sage. "It was rather spooky. And then not a word all the way home."

Laurence pulled out a photo and handed it to Sage. It was Nate, his scuba gear on, tanned and handsome grinning into the lens. Anyone could tell that whoever was taking the picture was the object of his eternal affection.

"It's you..." Sage's voice trailed.

"Father," Laurence said. "It's my father. I snapped it one day when he returned from a trip to Martha's Vineyard."

"But it's you," Sage said again handing the photo to Bea. "You're his image."

Laurence nodded. "He died when I was eight. The movie brought it back, all of it. You see, he worked with Cousteau. He was Nate Mallord. We spent hours at sea, at Woods Hole and elsewhere. I loved him so, still love him."

Bea handed the photo to Laurence who placed it in her pocket, pressed finger to her glasses, and looked to sea.

Bea and Sage studied the features that so resembled Nate's, the ones that had initiated their speculation. Nate Mallord was a folk hero to those who chose to discover the Cape and islands, an inspiration to all. Anyone who shared in his enthusiasm of local waters and who went back far enough, knew Nate Mallord was the one who had brought renown to the Woods Hole Institute and related oceanographic efforts.

Bea and Sage had spent hours trying to figure a way to tell Laurence of their adoration of Nate. The moment she displayed the same smile and willingness to try out new things with no complaint and an enviable dexterity, they knew that, in body and personality, she was Nate's child. They would have grown fond of her regardless, but this was an aspect of her to cherish and esteem. But, since Laurence never spoke of it, they feared invading her privacy, and chose to wait.

Now, the truth was out. Laurence seemed at peace. It was good, for they could move forward with their suggestion she stay on indefinitely, help them with their films, and become part of their off-beat family.

Bea broke into a gentle smile. "We loved him, too, chérie. And we also love his daughter."

# Chapter 3:
# January, 1969

BOSTON HAD NO FAHEYS, and Klee quickly discovered she was out of her element. Her first months proved a blur of jobs, terminated before they began, hunts for shelter, and nights at the YWCA with other vagrants and poor. If this was the promised land, one could easily be fooled. It did not welcome her, left her to fend for herself, and proposed little in terms of even the most elemental future. Not only was she expected to show proof of employment before renting an apartment, her alien status was in question due to her mannerisms and odd way of dress. Plus, no one understood her accent. She had to speak up and take on the harsh tones of those around her, this in spite of their accent that avoided pronunciation of the letter 'r' at the end of a word.

Eventually she found a garret in a triple-decker in Allston, a stone's throw from the trolley, facing the Charles River and traffic along Sorrow Drive. It was sizeable with several windows and her own bathroom, a luxury she'd never known. Because her first heating bill nearly broke her, she took to leaving the heat off or very low. She wore gloves inside, her coat too, and tried to keep bundled while sleeping. The cold aside, her place was adequate and high enough above the street to muffle sounds. She felt settled, at least. Had it not been for the generosity of a student, she might still be looking. They met at the Boston University library where Klee had been trying to keep up her reading.

On hearing the coed greet her, Klee had looked up, shocked at the sight of the first person in days who spoke in a friendly fashion.

"Are you Okay?" she asked. "My name is Tracy." She had short, auburn hair and glasses.

Klee nodded, pulled her coat closer. The hat had dirt spots on it and no longer held its shape. She wore the same outfit since leaving Ireland and her belly bulged.

"I don't think you should stay here. They close the place soon."

"I'm Okay," Klee finally said.

"You're Irish?" Her face brightened. "I went there last summer. I recognize..."

"Yes," Klee said, darting eyes about the room. She slid her hand to her belly.

"You really should get some sleep. If you don't mind my saying, you look sick."

The conversation started a companionship lasting from the beginning of December, when Tracy invited Klee to share her place, until Christmas when she returned to her home in the Midwest. Drawn to Klee's low-key style, Tracy informed the landlord of the new tenant and vouched for her. A box of Christmas cookies, money to cover two months' rent, and a well-wishing note were at Klee's door when Tracy departed.

During their time as roommates and due to their differing activities, they had exchanged no more than a handful of words. If Tracy knew of Klee's condition, she didn't let on nor did Klee venture forth with explanation. As far as Klee was concerned, Tracy was a little person who came to the rescue just in time. It was their way, the little people. After performing good deeds, the elfin Tracy had vanished.

Winter was frigid, unlike Ireland where humid Bermuda trade winds kept the air temperate and flowers blooming year-round. It was a cold that stiffened one's fingers, that chapped the cheeks, and found its way through layers of fur or wool. Klee had no protection, no double thickness parka like other students, not even a pair of slacks. She could barely afford the rent and therefore spent most of the time at her place of employment—India Garden—where she worked eighteen hours at a stretch, cleaning, cooking, taking orders, and trying to keep colds and flu at bay.

She didn't obsess over her condition. At first, while searching for work and spending nights at the YWCA, she scouted local libraries and updated herself on pregnancy. It wasn't a fearful thing, only an unknown, and her way of coping was to educate herself. The moral issues—whether or not she should be married, whether she should seek council, or whether she should go through with it at all did not concern her. She had only a sense of the life inside her.

Unburdened by Catholic guilt, she appreciated her time with Romney, and their hours of banter about Gaelic mores. Although the Irish had inherited a religion from Rome and a legal system from England, the authentic Celt had no qualms believing in gods, holding loosely to ancient ritualistic ceremony, and basically upholding a liberal sexuality. Klee didn't worry about saving face, giving the child a name, or dealing with the assured trials of raising a baby. She focused only on the stages of development, trying to understand what body part was forming or what physical function took hold. Had she not been strapped with basic survival issues, she would have been enthralled with the process. It was life and she was empowered to bring it forth. This alone fascinated her, dispelling what dilemmas might have befuddled other unmarried women.

She had seen lambs thrown to sea, had watched their dead staring eyes, their bodies float on the water's surface until the tides carried their carcasses away. The lambs were usually diseased, and drowning was deemed the most expedient way to be rid of them. Many evenings on the quay, watching the bobbing white wool, Klee swore that if she ever was in the position of determining the outcome of a sick animal, she would try and forestall life, however compromising that choice might prove in the long run.

This baby, too, would not be killed. What grew inside her was heading for a life in this world. She would not prevent birth, she would do what she could.

But she did worry about her size. Her breasts were large and tender and, even though for a while her height had helped disguise her condition, the baby was a mere three and a half months away. Her work apron no longer concealed her secret.

She moved slowly and often was under the watchful eye of the Indian man and his wife. They couldn't complain on the one hand, for Klee kept endless hours and was paid less than minimum wage. She never got out of line and offered help even when not required. She seemed to find strength from nowhere. Still, she sensed they knew she was pregnant and feared they might one day pull the rug out from under her. She worked harder and tried not to meet their stares. The job was her survival. Once her immediate concerns had passed, she would have to get creative.

Tracy informed her of student visas and suggested that Klee might want to apply to school. Once enrolled, she would be legal and then could take steps towards obtaining a green card. Klee filled applications and requested financial aid at three of the area's institutes of higher learning.

The students baffled and amused Klee. Some were attending school because their parents insisted. Others had ambitious goals, given the campuses of Harvard, Radcliffe, and MIT lining the banks of the Charles River. They spoke of leadership and corporate structure, of business and political convention, and challenged the current, war-driven economic policy. With ideas running the gamut from breaking down the oil cartels to targeting environmental priorities and attaining utopian ideals, they wore their student status with pride. Still others protested and marched, stopped traffic and cut classes to express their disgust over the Vietnam war, the government, and the establishment. It seemed unrest was the order of the day and most students were having one grand time.

She preferred quiet. Each night after twelve, she found her way out of Central Square and walked along the river bank until she crossed the bridge to her place. With minimal traffic and the trolleys stopped for the day, the city returned to a Colonial atmosphere with gas lamps aligning cobblestone walks and Federal-style brick buildings one aside the other. She would think of England and compose a letter to her mother, or wonder about the progress of Benny's band. To relax, she would read a French or German book and meditate herself to sleep, seeing bright colors in her mind as she thought about the child's hair color or felt the bump a kick produced. Anyone else would be torn with fright, weariness, or shame but Klee had well before faced those demons. They could not now pervade her person. She greeted each day the best she knew how and relied on her senses and sensibilities.

It snowed the night she experienced contractions. An engulfing pain filtered to her dreams and woke her with a start. She lay for a moment until another cramp threw her into a fetal position. To muffle cries, she buried her head in the pillow.

She calculated the weeks. Too soon, only twenty-five or six. It couldn't be the birth. Her room was a freezer. Icicles formed inside. Perhaps, she thought, the cold was affecting the baby. She rolled onto the floor, crawled to the heater, and pushed the dial to 'on.' In bed again, she listened to the crackle and pound of the heat coiling through wires as an orange glow lit the room. She felt good for a moment until she vomited. Shivers recommenced.

She stood but fell faint to the floor, her clothing offering little warmth as she struggled to get to her feet or at least return to the bedside. What to do? What to do? She bit her lip and tried to recall her pregnancy readings as another wracking pain developed.

It was the child, she was sure. However, not having seen one physician, having no inkling if the baby was healthy or bore some tragic disease, she couldn't determine the pain, let alone react to it, and was fast becoming too weak to do other than lie on her side and rock.

She watched the ice melt, drip to the floor, a steady, maddening noise. Her memory failed as she tried to recall the stage she was at and the potential false starts and complications. It was no use, she had no idea what was transpiring, except that it was grave and she required help beyond the printed word.

She grabbed clothes, stopping only to breathe deep when the pains came. She stumbled down the dark stairway, clinging to the banister, each step requiring effort as the tearing in her stomach took what reserve she possessed. She bit the side of her hand to prevent cries escaping, until she drew blood, then tasted the blood to try and blot out the other pain. She made it to the bottom and outside.

There was an inch of snow on the ground. A car rolled past. Quiet reigned as she looked both ways. Shuffling to the curb, she stuck her thumb out. This she'd already anticipated—that when the baby came she might have to find her own way. The hospital was less than a mile away. She could get there with blindfolds on. But for the debilitating pain.

When the next car appeared, she threw up her hand and yelled, pleading for the driver to stop. The large blue car floated past, unaware and gliding along the carpet of white.

"Please," she cried, to the disappearing rear lights. It was 2 AM, a dead time.

At the doors of Boston City, the nurse on emergency room duty found her limp form. Klee had passed out. Her hair was frozen in matted curls and her clothes torn like a peddler's.

"My God," said the nurse, reaching for Klee. "She's pregnant to boot!"

Aids dragged her in and even before they placed her on the table, they knew the contractions were dangerously close to precipitating a birth. Blood pressure, medications, rubbing of hands, belly, and legs became de rigueur as the resident on duty was called. A premature birth was on hand, to an unknown uninsured mother who looked as though she knocked on death's door.

There was no way they could save the child. In time, through uncontrolled thrusts brought on by drugs and encouraged by attending nurses' hands, the fetus was expelled. The bloody collection that spilled from Klee's body was a boy. His miniscule lungs had collapsed.

As Klee lay unconscious, her baby was taken from her. At the maternity ward, she was sedated and fed intravenously. It was now Klee's life to be watched for she, too, risked her own end.

♥ ♥ ♥

A day later, her awareness returned to congratulatory words about a newborn. At first, Klee thought they spoke to her, that she'd given birth to a girl. When she opened her eyes, she saw greys and whites and eventually the smiling face of the woman next to her— baby in arms, relatives at her side, all eyes on the swaddled baby girl.

Klee turned away and reached for her stomach. It wasn't as full as before nor entirely flat. For a moment she clung to the notion that the child was still within. But a void around her bed—the lack of baby paraphernalia, the absence of staff attending to her, the recall of what brought her here—discounted thoughts of life in her belly or life at all.

Rather than buzz for a nurse, she waited. Soon, someone would come and give details. She knew the essence of the report already, even commenced preparation for the coming days and weeks, what was to be a future without her child.

The nurse who admitted her, Pat Clancy, entered, fluffed the pillow, lifted Klee to a sitting position, and asked over and over how Klee felt. Grey curls bobbed about a face cleansed of emotion. She was trim in a white slack suit with name pin set above her breast pocket. Of Irish heritage, she expounded on her grandmother's accounts of turn-of-the-century Ireland. Klee tried to respond, but all she wanted was answers Pat avoided.

Later, a physician detailed the miscarriage to her. Klee let him speak, passing her regard first to the man then to Pat then to the man again. It had been routine, more or less, a premature birth for reasons they could only surmise. The child was not fully formed and, had he been born alive, his life most likely would have ended several days later. Lungs so small...

She mulled over the gender, and thought immediately of three male Celtic names. As the doctor's factual and unemotional words echoed hollow, she imagined a small version of Benny running about, crying laughing and playing. Brown hair and Benny's twinkle, a Dublin hooligan perhaps and an adventurous imp for sure.

The nurse retreated, the doctor too, perplexed at Klee's choice to refrain from questions or seek solace.

Klee was immersed in the life of the child as he might have been. Contrary to what the medical staff might think—that for an unwed woman in dire straits she might be pragmatic about the loss—she was not. She was as wrapped up in the child as if he were down the corridor with the other newborns, as fulfilled as if he were two days living and in need of his mother's milk.

To cross an ocean into a different culture, baby and all, and to explore the limits of her pregnancy represented formidable accomplishments. She would have preferred the child be in her arms, but the fact he died was not going to break her. It had not been she, to the best of her knowledge, who had terminated the life. It had been fate, something with which she chose not to tamper.

She'd done what she could and would now go on. A boy. Perhaps there would be others. Tomorrow, however, was for planning. She'd been thrown onto another course and would forge on.

A few days later, cotton between her legs and with instructions to take it easy, she left the hospital. Passing through the doors, she did not noticed Pat Clancy conversing with others in the emergency room.

"She didn't shed a tear that one," one nurse said as they watched Klee.

"Not one word, not one," Pat said, "I thought for a while she was mute."

"You know, Pat, what they say about those who don't show the pain. It only hides itself till later. That one, I'd say, has well disguised the hurt, but isn't rid of it yet. I'm not so sure she'll not experience it again."

Pat nodded. The night the baby was lost, she had already said a rosary for Klee, had felt it appropriate, as Klee was Irish and probably Catholic. Still, for all the types Pat had seen in her twenty-five years on the job, she had to admit, Klee was the oddest. "I'll never understand it. Not one word, not a one."

They returned to their work, to discussions about the upcoming staff meeting and the proposals for yearly bonuses. In time, too soon, another emergency would arrive.

# Chapter 4:
# London, February 10, 1969

Dear Claire,

Your last letter surprised me so! I thought you were readying for classes in Dublin and don't you up and leave for America! You're a brave girl, Claire. I hope you are well and taking care in Boston.

My flat is lovely ( two levels ), a sitting room and kitchen with fireplace downstairs, plus a garden out the back where I keep potted geraniums and where a rose bush might bloom for us in spring. Two bedrooms, bath, and toilet upstairs. I'm keeping well and have much to do during the day, although I've not yet begun work. The number 25 bus passes at the corner and takes me direct to Knightsbridge where all the smart shops are. Too expensive but fun to inspect from outside.

I don't know what else to say. Tell me all about America. I hear they're upset over the war. No surprise. I'd say the Americans are tired of war, like the English. Only a mile from here sits a hole from a bombing. It's still not filled in. People walk around and past it and I don't think they even see it any more. The War was such a while ago, wasn't it?

You looked pale when I saw you last. Don't go staying up late like you did all those nights singing in Dublin now. Tend to your studies and be a smart girl like I know you are.

Love, Mum

March 7, 1969
Dear Mum,

Thanks for the pounds. You didn't have to, what not working and all. I enrolled in two courses. The macroeconomics is dull and too general for my tastes but the professor studied with Milton Friedman ( a very smart man in economics ) all the way out in Chicago. I ask questions and he smiles sometimes so I think he finds me a bit strange. I don't care, I keep asking. My Italian course is easy, conversation like what I made with Paolo. Thank goodness for him. Still, I'm improving my accent and now have four languages under my belt.

There are peace demonstrations all the time. At Harvard across the river, a man named George Wald—Nobel prize in chemistry—speaks often. He talks of peace and gets the crowd going. The rallies assemble quickly and sometimes I'm too late for them but that's Okay because I rather prefer my studies. Still, when I get the chance, it's important for me to go and watch. They're so different from us, the American students.

I've been told St. Patrick's Day is a big thing. There is already talk on campus about nights at Liam's pub and other places with Irish names. Did we never have the same to-do over the holy day? I don't ever recall. It's funny, Boston. Some people resemble those back in Kinemmaera. The names are the same too—except no 'O' in front.

I'm taking care so don't worry and my color has returned. Mr. Kinnimurti at the restaurant feeds me a meal each day. I'm tired of curry but don't complain. It's getting a bit warmer, too. The Irish book of ballads is a great treasure and I read from it every night. There's a page torn out and I was wondering if you might remember what was on it?

Love, Claire

London, 29 March 1969

Dear Claire,

Don't go around getting yourself involved with those marches! I read about them and it seems the Americans take to disputes differently than us. In Chicago last year, there was trouble even during a campaign for president.

My friend tells me the Americans have a violent streak. Stay out of the messes.

I'm still not working but it's not a problem for the generosity of my friend. We took a trip to the country last banker's holiday. Out past Maidenhead, to a lovely town where we ate at a restored mill and had Dover sole like I've never tasted. I can still recall the dessert pudding!

You're so smart, Claire! Get your studies done and become one of those great scholars you've been talking about. It's still rainy and cold in London, and the Guinness is not as good here—it doesn't travel well. My friend and I returned to Dublin for a weekend and had a proper glass at Danigan's. The Jades play every Saturday and they look a bit more tidy. It's the brown suits they wear now instead of the leather. That must mean they're getting somewhere my friend tells me. I was glad to get back to London, even though it's cold.

Stay out of trouble and keep yourself covered good.

Love, Mum


23 April, 1969

Dear Mum,

Thanks again for the pounds. You really don't have to. I'm getting along now with the work and school. I'm putting money aside because I want to take a summer course. Imagine, they go to school year round here, even nights. Everyone is very busy, always on the go.

I went to Liam's pub for the 17th. Really, how they carry on during St. Patrick's Day! I don't think any of them even go to church or know it's a holy day in Ireland. They wear bright green, kelly green it's called. I had my brown jumper and black skirt and someone took to calling out to me for looking so Irish and yet not wearing green. I stuck my tongue out at him because he was well pissed and very rude.

They don't sing rebel songs but they try, and sing every song they can think of that has to do with Ireland, even songs I never heard before. Plus, when they crowd into the bars ( they never call them pubs ), the men are so big and tall, you can't see a thing that's going on. I went in the first place because some from the class were going out to Liam's. It's two trolley stops from my flat and not far to walk either.

Well, I couldn't resist not singing what with everyone having such a good time and myself receiving a grade 'A' ( the highest ) on my Italian exam. It was fun and someone even came up after to ask if I'd like to sing in his band. I said no and explained I was a student. He asked, 'Student becoming what?' That made me think. What will I become? Everyone here decides early on what to be. To me, it should be the other way around, you study then decide. I have so much to learn, how could I possibly know what I want to do later?

Never mind, I told him, I'm studying for greatness! He gave me a queer look but I held my tongue because all in all he was nice and made room for me to sing. My voice is in terrible shape, though, and I could do with a few lessons from Paolo. Not to worry, the singing is not what I'm after now, even though they clapped a lot and kept saying 'More, more!'

The dogwood trees and apple blossoms are gorgeous. All along Commonwealth Avenue ( the street names are very English ) they are and the sugary smell stays with me the entire day. I think, once the weather turns, the town will be a lovely place. It's not as dirty as Dublin but they are having troubles. The city finances are in desperate shape, as they are in New York, and people are talking recession and worse. It's the war that keeps going on and on.

Take care and thanks again for the pounds.

Love, Claire.

♥ ♥ ♥

"Studying for greatness!" Alice repeated, folding Claire's letter. "Imagine thinking like that, after all the child has been through."

She went to her room, donned hat, gloves, and jacket, thinking all the while how nice it was to chat with neighbors and even strangers about her very smart daughter in America. It brought her delight to see their faces. She knew they were envious, even though she herself looked the picture of plainness and lower class.

She frowned into the mirror, already fogged from the cool air seeping through the crack in the window. The place was chilly inside even though the forecast promised warmer temperatures. The bed was unmade and Harry's socks lay about. She grimaced. What a horror he was! Fortunately they only crossed paths once or twice in the week.

Harry continued to insist he was involved with the music scene. Since their return to London, Alice had made do with his stories about a future of wealth and fame that would follow once he discovered the perfect rock group. But nothing seemed to come of his promises and she had begun to suspect nothing ever would. Since the day she put forth the suggestion Benny's group be considered, she believed him full of lies.

"Why do I want a bunch of Irish running around London? I have me hands full with the kids in this city. Don't beat on me, woman," he said one night after dinner.

"I was only giving you an idea," she said.

"Don't forget, you stay here for my doing. You want to run the show, you pay the rent, too." He walked out the door to another supposed meeting.

That was the first of numerous confrontations. After that, Alice stopped asking. His pot belly, bald spot, and alcoholic breath were nothing compared to what she had put up with in the past. If he wanted to pretend to be something he wasn't, then fine. She would let it go. He let her stay in the flat, alone most of the time. She could watch television, listen to the radio, or read the dailys to her heart's content. Plus, they had plenty of food and the fire in the kitchen kept the place moderately warm—not such a bad arrangement for an unemployed woman who didn't have a pound to her name. He even handed her money every now and then, most of which went to Claire.

Whether he made it big or not, she had to admit her life had improved. To those in their East End neighborhood who bothered paying attention, she boasted she was the wife of a travelling businessman and that she had an intelligent daughter living in the States. She had quickly learned the proper clothing to wear and places to buy food and other necessities. She fit, as long as no one saw what went on inside the flat those times Harry chose to stay.

He was always drunk, getting drunk, or recovering from being drunk. He had money and she suspected it came from betting. His tickets were always spilling from his pockets and the times he called on the phone it was to the bookies. He was happy when he won, mad as a dog when he lost, and he often vented his anger on her.

Most of the time, she was able to make for the bedroom and lock the door. Other times he only wanted sex and, after, fell into a drunken black-out. The toughest were the beatings. Thankfully, they didn't occur often and, once finished, he was apologetic. She could also expect money as he made profuse claims to never harm her again. For that, a few bruises along the way didn't faze her.

Plus, she could go on. Each day was a question mark and when he handed her money or finally paid the often overdue rent, she knew another day or week was guaranteed. Far from the ideal life, it still had positive aspects.

She liked London. She could hide. She was an English person, a newcomer with an Irish accent and looks but a resident nonetheless. She could flash her cheque book about, purchase cosmetics at the nearby Marks & Spencer, and wear clothes that had appeared the week before in area store flyers.

She was older now and not interested in fantasy. This was the best she could hope for and it would have to do. If Harry left or got himself in trouble, she'd be stuck, but that thought was not one on which she dwelled. He cared in his odd way, otherwise he would have put her out. He cared about the sex, for he could never lure a woman half as decent as Alice.

She was still attractive in her way. Hair clipped stylishly around her face, she wore bright red lipstick which brought out the cream of her skin and the blue of her eyes. Slender and with grace that evinced when she walked around Knightsbridge wearing a new suit or coat, she caught the odd appreciative look of men her age or older. This attention sufficed. She wasn't washed out yet and, should old Harry give out, she might make do even so. London was a big place with lots of men and money.

Still, she had to be careful. When Harry made demands, she was prepared. It was the odd skimpy nightgown or black frills that caught his eye those nights he wanted only one thing. Her cunning paid off. He would loosen up and forget his temper long enough to fall into her arms rather than beat her to a pulp. She held sway with him in bed and, provided his state was not too far gone, could rally him around a less intense behavior pattern.

This was her secret weapon, not unlike the women she read about in cheap novels or the slick nudy magazines Harry brought home. They were smart in their own way, even if they indulged in too much off-color sex. Alice had to hand it to them for they were survivors like she—whores or widows with no money, young abandoned girls or aging matrons. She admired their fictitious antics, took to imitating with Harry some of their acts, and all in all found a respite from her fears. Sex had come to the rescue again. She meant to make use of it, until her body gave out.

She was not a whore, not a destitute street walker. She was Harry's 'respectable' lady with nothing to worry over except the state of her garden and the match of a blouse with a skirt.

She put much energy into keeping in contact with Claire, memorizing her daughter's every word. She wanted the best for her daughter, and wanted to keep receiving letters detailing accomplishments and abilities. Claire knew so much more than she, and had crossed so many thresholds. It was an exhilarating feeling knowing one's child was headed for greatness.

Alice could be content. Her own life, after all, had almost ended too many times. She found her happiness in Claire, and would do everything she could to hold the course.

One day she was bored and made a mistake. It was raining and, with Harry in Scotland for over a week, she couldn't stand one more minute inside the flat. A leak had sprung in the kitchen and the water heater gave out. Plumbing problems again. She figured a bus ride would do her good, and made for the corner stop.

The Knightsbridge bus wound north, terminating near Hempstead where she descended. Initially disoriented, the sight of a familiar restaurant and newsstand threw her to a time gone by.

At the entry door, she stood. It was the same menu, the same iron grillwork over the first floor windows, the same lace curtains inside. She tried the door and it opened to the sea blue decor with the same aquarium filled with black guppies and orange goldfish.

"Chez Claude," she whispered, reading the words on the menu, her fingers running along one side of the thick leather cover, her gaze finding the address at the bottom. "Cuisine de la Bretagne."

A blonde mustached man cleaned glasses behind the bar and looked up. "Yes?" he asked with a French accent.

Startled at first, she smiled. "The restaurant has been here a long time."

"Oui, Madame. Monsieur Claude is here since before the war."

"You weren't working here in 1949, I suppose," she asked. "'O course not, you're too young, aren't you?"

He smiled. "If you like, I can offer you a drink, Madame. We don't serve meals until six."

She looked around. Most of the tables were set for two. The candles were not lit like before, but similar elegant white ones bore hardened cascades of wax. Her eyes clouded. "If you please, would it be possible to sit for a while? I won't be any trouble."

The young man shrugged an Okay, then disappeared to the back.

She found the table by the window, peeked once from the curtain and peered out at the newsstand. It was the same, all of it. He'd bought his cigarettes across the street before they dined, had made a joke about the English cigarettes then purchased some anyway. His index finger was black and she asked why. He told her he'd slammed a hammer accidentally on it. She'd reached and kissed it.

He chose the duck *maigret de canard*, and she ordered sole. They enjoyed two bottles of red wine, something from the Rhône valley she could not pronounce. He had laughed. She told him he was full of it, that, had she an ear for languages, she'd speak as many or more than his six or seven.

In time, their hands had interlocked and she felt beautiful as never before, eternal, full of anticipation. He ordered a cognac and she had a taste of his. Remy. Strong and biting, lingering. The waiter left them to themselves, even long after the restaurant closed. The lights dim, the music a song of love, the air stuffy from cigarettes and humans, they whispered and laughed, shared intimacies never again to be revealed.

"If you promise not to tell a soul," he said, describing how he ruined a two thousand pound piece of stage equipment, accidentally knocking it over while working late one night. "I told them it must have been the dogs running about."

They both laughed, hard.

"And you?" he asked. "You must have a secret or two hidden behind those bluer than blue eyes."

"I do. You."

Alice returned to the present, lowered her head into her hands, and cried. If he hadn't been so utterly divine, so attentive, perhaps she would have forgotten him long before. Was he meant to reside in her forever? Was she wrong to have loved him so? Was it something that could have been prevented?

After all, he was lonely, too. They walked about the streets, on the rainy cobblestones and by the river, in the fog and even the pouring rain. How he'd held her close, her thin rain coat so poor an excuse for cover during those London days.

Claire, if I wasn't such a phony, such a coward and fool, I'd tell you about your father. For he was a man, he was! And learned, like you. He travelled and knew all the fine places, like this out of the way restaurant, like the hotel around the corner where you were conceived. If I wasn't so afraid, I'd tell you. It is your right after all. You might have it in you to try and find him, see for yourself how wonderful your father is, not like that idiot Bob Walsh. Your old Mum is nothing special, but your Dad! Oh, Claire luv, had I the courage!

She stood, nodded to the waiter, and left. Around the corner, the hotel had been demolished, replaced by an office building for estate agents and solicitors. On the ground level, a shop window displayed antique toys and furniture. She looked up to where the top floor used to be, from where she once scanned the rooftops of London. "The Charles Dickens place of chimney tops and smoke," he'd said, as they both stared out and before he pulled her to his chest.

The features, the resolve, the body and face—all Claire. The girl had inherited everything, and Alice was the only one who knew. The only one keeping her daughter from the knowledge, the only one guarding the secret so that one day, when she was gone, it would be gone too, never to rear, never to hurt or taint. She must keep it that way, for he was free now, untroubled by responsibility, the way he preferred. It was the one thing he clung to like religion, she remembered. He was his own man, would never settle or be settled.

She scuffed her feet as she walked, hurting for a return to their night. A single moment would do, to see him again. To look into his eyes and love back, innocent and with her entire being. It had been right to love him. It had been so very, very right.

Claire was about to become great, with her father's every feature and ability. His immortality was guaranteed. He would have eternity in his daughter, a wonderful thing, whether he ever knew it or not. Wasn't it he who said we must keep something for ourselves always? She recalled their most intimate talks, after they made love and when he shared his soul. Yes, even then he'd said he was keeping things from her. Even then she knew they would never meet again.

Hers was such a lovely secret. "To share it means I have nothing left. It's my only glory."

She found the bus stop. It had been folly to visit this place but, this once, she was glad she had. As the red double decker approach, she promised herself it wouldn't happen again.

# Chapter 5:
# March 12, 1969

> Behind the basic projects of the
> labor unions can be discerned
> concomitant signs of serious trouble in
> the French economic family. Salaried
> workers, peasants, storekeepers, and
> artisans are all discontent and, what is
> more, are worried—rightly or wrongly,
> this despite a satisfactory industrial
> output. Workers of every kind are prey
> to a latent pessimism, and in this they
> are joined by the owner class. The
> workers demand an immediate rise in
> pay, the shopkeepers want fiscal relief,
> the rich foresee the possibility of the
> devaluation of the franc. To shore up
> their fortunes, they buy gold,
> apartments, and furnished mansions.
>
> France-Soir

RÉGINE RE-READ THE ARTICLE. Energized, she tore it
out and hurried upstairs to wash and dress.

Soaking in a bubble-filled baignoire, she dismissed
the fact Mémé would have something to say about her

luxuriating in the middle of the day. Her wealthy mother was still frugal when it came to utilities, a French habit in force amongst the older generation. Years in the States had rendered Régine immune to the expense of electricity and water, a subject of incessant discussion at dinner functions presided over by Mémé's age group.

"Too bad," she smiled, sinking deeper into the lavender-smelling water, "I have an important engagement with Monsieur de Roche and must be at my best."

It was to the article in the paper she turned her thoughts as the warmth brought on a lustiness. She ran fingertips across her breasts and thought of the best way to broach her topic with Giles.

They would dine first, a late night Chez Julien, where the '30s decor and side-by-side seating would have him forget business issues and listen carefully to her idea. It would excite the old man, too. He was poised to bend at her whim, she'd seen to that. His smile told her she'd already won his heart.

Luring him in had taken longer than anticipated, no thanks to the mausoleum he called home, with every nook and cranny dedicated to his dead wife. From the start, she had felt Pauline's presence. Everything from the furniture to the garden to the aging maid Betti reeked of a former time, when Giles had eyes for only one.

Having educated herself, Régine understood Giles's disinterest in remarriage. Apparently Pauline was a goddess, a savior to all, including children, distant relatives, and of course Giles. More than one Parisian socialite extolled on Pauline's stateliness and gracious style. From Mémé to Giles, from strangers to cousins and aunts, all recounted the woman's bountiful nature and eternal beauty. There were no skeletons in Pauline's closet, a fact that grated on Régine.

Worse, when she set eyes on Evan, she saw beyond the handsome face to the boy-man. To his core, he was his mother. Should she ever succeed in ridding the house in the 16th of Pauline, she would not as easily disengage from Evan.

At first, she had toyed with vying for his heart, a potentially amusing dalliance but one she discarded after their first interaction. The boy was so layered with affection for his mother, there was little hope that any woman, let alone Régine, could fully claim his heart.

She would have to transfer her game plan to his father. At her age she stood a better chance with Giles, even though he too would be a challenge.

She sighed. Evan was desirable in ways she'd only dreamed of. More than Nate, his was an appeal that called out to a woman. Even during mundane exchanges, while in the middle of a business or vacation discussion, those dark eyes mesmerized, eroding all sensible notions, and driving one to the most basic of physical urges. Had he noticed her melting as they spoke? Had he seen beyond their tête-à-têtes to the fact she was laying herself out for him and, if he wished, could easily be led to his room and fold into his arms? Evan, Evan....

She shook her head, pulled herself from the water, and smiled. This article appeared at the right time. Mansions...that was the answer.

Old Giles was worried about his money. Though a topic discussed in generalities, its contours had surfaced enough for Régine to comprehend the man was concerned. The number one preoccupation of the wealthy in France: what would happen after de Gaulle? Who would carry on? Communism was on the rise. The de Roche labor force increasingly upheld leftist beliefs, most often those of the *Parti Communist Français*. An odd arrangement, given the de Roche fortune heralded from a time of business ventures attempted when the right was in power, when de Gaulle and others of his politics promoted the strategies Giles embraced.

His workers, and now his son Evan, invited the old man to consider the riskier directions of the business world. Régine could tell Giles feared the future. He'd already confided to her that he stored away money in his safe at home, and she found out he had other ideas for withdrawing his money should the franc take a tumble.

Régine reinforced his sense of doom, for she had an added advantage over Giles when it came to world policy. She knew the Americans were wary of the French, tired of de Gaulle's insistence on a French-centric view. Moreover, de Gaulle or no, the dollar supply dictated the health of most economies. The franc would devalue, gold would prove more investment-worthy, and Giles de Roche would be challenged with liquidity issues.

Giles could buy a mansion. Régine would help. He would then have a tangible sign that his money was safe, and she would gain his forever respect.

They would choose a desirable location, a warm climate where they could retreat at any time of the year. Not in Brittany, where the weather was uncertain. The interior Midi, she reasoned, rather than the splashy Côte d'Azur. A town in the back country perhaps, an hour or so by car from the Mediterranean, a village with one or two restaurants and Sunday market, at a remove but grand in its reclusive allure. She would decorate, her personal style that would astound Giles and remove any lingering thoughts of Pauline.

They would fall deeply in love, spend every free weekend and holidays there. The house would be theirs alone, a place where they could revel undisturbed in life's pleasures. She would make him love her and the past would be forgotten. Régine would be the new lady de Roche.

First, the Batz retreat had to go. Then, she would see to the renovation of the place in the 16$^{th}$. But she must tread slowly. Neither de Roche man would allow Pauline's memory to dissipate in one felled swoop. She would have to be patient. Cultivate her garden, as the French philosopher said.

She eyed herself in the mirror, pulled at the corner of one eye to eradicate the slight wrinkle. Her eyelids, clear of make-up and in the afternoon shadows, displayed a red tinge. Anger swelled as she thought of Laurence's clear alert gaze. It often happened when in front of the mirror, for Régine was always perplexed there wasn't a trace of herself in the girl. Nate had claimed Laurence from the very beginning, hadn't he?

If Laurence had had a touch of de Long, Régine wondered, might it have been different? Might not she have been more prone to embrace Laurence more genuinely?

Silly, she thought, reaching for make-up. What was meant to be was meant to be. Régine hadn't drowned Nate, he'd been the foolish one to dive into those waves. She snubbed Laurence for good reason—the child was out of control, overconfident and smug, flaunting her beauty. Too directed in her goals. A lady was not supposed to be so utterly single-minded. It was the child's own fault. Régine had been forced to put her in her place now and again. Thank God she was gone.

She touched the corner of her eye again. Perhaps it was time to seek out the attention of a plastic surgeon, catch those wily wrinkles before they deepened. She would discuss this with Marie-Ange, who although claiming to be thirty-five, Régine knew to be much older and well acquainted with the artisans of facial rejuvenation in Paris.

# Chapter 6:
# May, 1969

SPRINGTIME IN PARIS meant the return of puppet shows. In a corner of parc Montsouris in the 14th arrondissement, to the delight of neighborhood children, vibrantly hand-painted characters strut across the stage. Yelling at one another, joking, and addressing the audience, they fought with sticks, wept pretend tears, and concocted devious strategies. The children responded with giggles and claps, anticipating the antics, participating in the merriment and mayhem.

In time, the puppets exited the stage. Murmurs of excitement rose from the assemblage. The much anticipated moment had arrived when the head of Guignol popped up.

"*Bonjour, mes enfants!*" France's legendary and favorite marionette bowed to the screeches and pleas of the audience. His hat was red and pointed, his cheeks rosy, his face white. He waved white gloves and his permanent smile bore out his renowned personality. French children knew him as his or her special friend, a cultural pastime handed down from the last century, a national treasure.

"Shall we take a trip to the Midi today?" he asked, his hat bobbing up and down.

"Oui!" they screamed.

Marcel Duvivier edged closer, positioned his camera, and began shooting. Guignol was his favored entertainer, too, and the show was one of few occasions when he could study his preferred subjects—children— in their most unassuming poses. Expressions free of anxiety, they were lost in the puppet's antics. Several of them scratched their chins or tugged at clothing, mesmerized. Each followed Guignol's lead, what mischievous act he planned next, and whether or not the puppet would direct a question his or her way.

A girl with blonde pigtails and white pinafore, gaze fixed on the stage, a finger lost in the corner of her mouth, caught Marcel's eye. He raised the camera, adjusted depth of field, and snapped. She continued to look straight ahead, had no idea she'd been the center of his attention for a split second. He lowered the device and grinned.

"Perfection," he said.

He liked it that way. During puppet shows, in the streets with their parents, playing in the park, children photographed in ways he struggled to achieve with adults. He returned continually to the study of them, it being a way for him to gain perspective. Whatever film was in progress, whatever shooting assignment he took on meant stress and rigid time tables. The only way to seek a solution to the frequent and knotty problems was to temporarily get away. Most anywhere in France he could find a park, and thus partake in the world of children and Guignol.

This was why he lived in the south. It was warmer and Guignol's performances often extended into the winter months. Away from the city, he could better manage his distractions.

The show ended, he packed up and, grinning down at the occasional curious regard, herded along with the

243

children as parents led them from Montsouris to varied destinations and errands. The train ride to Paris had been long. His lids drooped and he blinked under the sun's brightness. As he strode along, some passers-by eyed his jeans and leather jacket; it was still rare to see so casual a look worn by most city men. Younger looking than his fifty-two years, his jaw was squared and he had the fair hair and easy smile of the Duviviers. He and his cousin Pauline had often been objects of similar note, with faces and bodies that seemed to keep the workings of time at arm's length.

For Marcel, youthfulness was maintained as a result of his work as photographer and film editor. Since leaving school early, much to the disapproval of Papa Duvivier, he'd taken up his passion, volunteering at various jobs with production houses and even aiding some of France's most well-known directors. Before Renoir left for the States, Marcel helped edit a few reels and more than once received the man's praise. During the thirties, he'd worked long hours at the Duvivier establishment near Gaumont, figuring the most efficient ways to release dubbed films to the public. Like Pauline, he remained permanently enamored of film and the film process. It had cost him his family's respect. But he had found his own source of joy and that was all that mattered. In time, his rebellious nature and indifference to social pressure had been conceded by his family. The errant child, he made for a life of his choosing, not one chosen for him.

That he'd had to scrounge for work and leave France during the war was of little concern. The film industry needed editors and assistants almost anywhere. He'd seen the world, too, more than he could say for most of the Duviviers and their cronies.

He sniffed the air. Paris had an allure in spring, even though now and again rain showers and chilly spells coopted the sun's warmth. Taking avenue René Coty towards central Paris, he relished the view of the city in which he grew up. In fact, the Duviviers had lived not far from here, in a large *hôtel particulier* near the Luxembourg Gardens. He passed the cemetery Montparnasse and studied the burial rows. He would not go in.

She was there, his cousin Pauline, her massacred and now decomposed remains the only earthly comment to the tragedy that ended her life. He closed his eyes. The memory already eleven years old, its resurgence still made a ring around the permanent wound of her loss. She'd been the only ray of hope in his otherwise confused and rebellious youth, the only one to side with his daring ideas and to encourage his daydreams.

As children, they'd raced around Montsouris together, engaged with the puppets and played at the pond. She kept up with him at most any sport, in most any game. Her glimmering ways placated the trials of facing his father with his decision to not follow in the family footsteps. She'd comforted him when he left Paris and kept her promise to write regularly. She sent pictures of Danielle as she grew, even more of Evan when he came along. She updated him on Giles's business and profit-making, and always sent a photo at Christmas.

When he received her season's greetings, he dwelled on her image the longest. To one side of the great Giles de Roche, her children taking front and center, she sat, demure and content to claim a retreating position. Her striking looks were embedded in the children, but her uniqueness she alone possessed, and it went beyond blonde hair and a saintly smile. Pauline kept him afloat, even from a distance. Magic to Marcel.

What had happened to de Roche Frères since? Marcel knew Giles was still in the money and in the know. Even though de Gaulle had stepped down, Gaullists like Giles remained in charge. Yet, from Evan's letters, he sensed a switch in focus at de Roche Frères, an edging away from the standard business practices of former generations. Pauline's attention to domestic and business affairs having died along with her, he wondered if the empire was thrown into an as-yet unnamed or unacknowledged frenzy.

Or was it the way of things? The world was changing. The year prior, even France's long-time scholastic traditions had been challenged. Could it be that much in this country was about to change? He shrugged, for the de Roche business was not why he had returned.

He'd finally agreed to meet with Evan and discuss his nephew's ideas to produce a film. Evan had been persistent with letters that kept Marcel abreast of the film's progress, had even gone so far as to call him in Aix once or twice, and then boldly mailed a test reel some months later. It was some story a friend, Albert, had come up with. In the end, he'd agreed to see Evan the next time he headed north. Marcel chuckled. Evan possessed the same dogged persistence as Pauline—an ability to see one thing through to the end, no matter what.

He would tell Evan the bad news first—that he hadn't liked the film. It was too loaded with emotional rambling, spoiled by plot lines that fizzled and tedious changes of camera angle. If Evan wanted to perfect it, the best he could do was hit the drawing boards again. The present version would go nowhere fast. Wasn't Evan paying attention to the New Wave movies? Couldn't he see that depth and intrigue could be developed without dialogue, and in the subtlety of a change of setting or a glance rather than wordy tirades and too many close-ups? The young man had a long way to go, thought Marcel.

On the other hand, the actress had been well chosen, had chiseled her style to build character into her role. Patrice should be involved in any future work Evan might undertake, for she was gifted and obviously a hard worker. And seductively beautiful, he mused with a grin.

He guessed she and Evan had already made love. Evan was most often manning the camera, and a good idea that was, for Patrice seemed to feed off the man behind the lens, seemed to speak to him with regards that enhanced her acting and drew out her finest qualities. Patrice was in love with Evan. How could Evan not profit from the attentions of so alluring a lady?

Marcel figured his nephew's age, nineteen, young enough to be unsure, old enough to understand his body's needs. Evan was handsome, of that Marcel was sure, even though he'd not seen him since the funeral. Evan had the style, too, that undeniable attraction of all de Roches. In bed or out, the women would flock. If, on the other hand, he was still a virgin, his days were numbered. If he continued filming with Patrice, she would grow weary of waiting. Even on film, she appeared eager.

He stood at the waters of the Seine. He should take a bus to the de Roche résidence, he was tired. But, he would walk. An occasional regard from a student or well-dressed lady would be welcome. It had been a long time for him. He might see about tending to his own needs while in Paris. One nice thing about the city—a man could get lost in it.

♥ ♥ ♥

Evan opened the door. His eyes widened and he threw himself at Marcel.

"Vieux," Marcel mumbled, moved by the tight embrace, the eagerness that was nothing if not Pauline's. They stood in the doorway.

"You should have told me, Marce," Evan said, brushing aside a tear.

"It was touch and go. You know I hate Paris."

"Liar," Evan said, nudging his uncle's shoulder.

Marcel followed him to the study. The entire house had Pauline's singular touch, the antique furniture, the custom curtains, the bouffant flower arrangements. "Some things never change," he said.

"Betti is still with us. Mama's choices remain."

They entered the study where a red-headed woman sat reading a magazine. She wore a navy suit trimmed in white with blouse to match. Her gold jewelry on wrist and neck emphasized the suit's buttons. She stood level with Evan when he went to her side.

"Solange Lemuire, this is my uncle Marcel," Evan said.

After handshakes and cordialities, they sat. Solange was a 'friend' which Marcel took to mean girlfriend. Carrying the groomed look of one raised in genteel Paris, she was a student at the Sorbonne and from a long line of Parisian banking men, firms Giles de Roche invested with. Marcel assumed the families were already hard at work settling the issue of marriage.

He took a cognac and Betti brought tea for Solange. The three made light conversation and he grew bored quickly. Evan was attentive to Solange. Yet they seemed ill at ease, attracted in an obtuse way. She watched Evan's every move and anticipated his comments, responding in a measured tone and with a dimpled smile.

Three swigs of his cognac and Marcel was more relaxed. In a low voice, with a tiny grin curling, he said, "Patrice."

Evan blinked. "Patrice, in the film?"

"The same," Marcel said.

For a second, Solange looked confused, then composed herself. Marcel began to enjoy the scene, for it was one to which he too had been subjected in the past. He guessed she'd arrived uninvited, that Evan was chomping at the bit to get her out, and on to discussing the film. Marcel hated formalities. He sought a second cognac, then slump into the easy chair, legs spread, boots tapping on the fine oriental rug.

"I think she's super—sexy, genuine, dark when she needs to be, bright other times. Use her, but ditch the film. It's history, Evan. That stuff went out years ago."

"Film?" asked Solange.

Evan gulped. "Something I dabbled in a while ago. I think we might discuss that over dinner, Marcel."

"Sorry," Marcel said with a wink at Solange who, startled, looked the other way.

Soon she made excuses to leave. Evan walked her to the door and agreed to see her again soon. Marcel moved about Giles's study, touching books, inspecting the desktop, standing by the window to view Pauline's garden.

"Remember the roses?" Evan asked.

Marcel turned to Evan. "It can't all be saved, I suppose. Listen, sorry about my behavior but I can't stand idle talk, you know. She's sweet and all, but, hey, I'd take that Patrice any day."

Evan laughed, reaching for his uncle's arm and moving towards the chair. "I'm so glad to see you, Marcel! Tell me all about Aix. I'm sorry we didn't get down to film last year—as you've probably guessed we ran into snags."

"Patrice is no snag," he said.

"No," Evan's voice softened. "She is no snag."

"Where is she?"

"I. D. H. E. C."

"Impressive. Pied noir and all, no?"

"Talented is the word, Marcel."

"You two get it on?"

Evan sniffed, looked down.

Marcel sensed the disturbance running through Evan, detected a familiar tinge of regret in his eyes. "Sorry, vieux, I guessed she might have made way to your heart, I didn't realize...."

"It's Okay," he said.

"Listen, let's go out. Mère St. Jacques still serves the garlic chicken I love. We can have a few glasses of *ordinaire* and talk, how's that?"

They left, making way for the north of town and the plentiful side-street cafés and bistrots often ignored by tourists but with the at-home charm and cuisine of grandmothers, recipes handed down strictly by word of mouth.

Over a meal of pumpkin soup and chicken, warm bread and carafes of red wine, they brought one another up to speed. Again Marcel made no bones about his dislike of the film, told Evan that if he were to become serious he had to take charge of a project, not let too many hands spoil the pot.

"It's about your passion. You must rear up and let everyone know what the point is you wish to make. This isn't the States, you know, where the production company has the final word. Once you become established, you, as director, are in charge. It's your baby, conception to birth. Love it or dump it, but don't nurture a malformed and doomed child."

Evan munched on his bread. "I have many things to do for father..."

"What? I thought you were filming."

"I've decided to put my energies where they belong."

Marcel took a long look at Evan. "You don't sound energized."

Evan pursed his lips.

"Why? What happened between all those letters and now? Why aren't you trying? The film is lacking, but that doesn't mean you quit! Not if you love to film. Do you?"

"I wouldn't say love."

"Like intensely. More than de Roche Frères, I venture."

"I did enjoy it. But I have an obligation to Papa, Marce. Please, I know you never took to the business, but I did, back when, and I made up my mind recently. It's Papa who needs me now. Perhaps, someday, I can toy with the film."

"Toy? If you toy you will never get there. You must take it seriously or not at all."

"I can do both, the film in my free time..."

Marcel sat back in his chair, lifted his chin, and looked at the ceiling. With a pound of his fist to the table, he returned, "How can you love two mistresses? Impossible! You either take one or the other, if not, eventually, the ignored one will stalk you!" His hand circled into the air and he continued to expound, raising his voice louder. Evan stared at him wide-eyed.

"I'm being too hard," Marcel said. "I understand your situation....It might have been so different, too, eh?"

"If we had not lost Danielle," Evan said. "But, Marce, I want to be a part of de Roche Frères, I do! There are many ways of combining my talents for film and responsibilities within de Roche..."

Marcel smiled, erased his hard look, and sipped. "I see," he said. "I guess I'm a simpler sort. I take one road at a time. You, on the other hand, are a driver to multiple destinations, no?"

Evan grinned. "How long are you here?"

"Till whenever. I had hoped to make a film with my nephew."

"You're serious?"

"Aha! There's the spark of Pauline I was waiting for!" Marcel exclaimed. "Now you're interested."

"Oh, I am damn it. But I must, you hear, must focus on de Roche, too."

"You'll stumble."

"I'll take my chances."

"You're insane," Marcel said. "Duvivier blood."

"Help me while you're here, Marce. A test cut, footage here and there. When I have time, I can build on it. It may take longer, but let's start something."

"You can't do it that way, Evan."

"I can."

Marcel wanted to dispute, for he grasped the problem better than Evan. But Evan was so eager and self-assured, ready to take on so much, he couldn't refuse. "I'll say maybe. We'll do some preliminary work, perhaps ask Patrice to ...."

Evan's gaze averted Marcel's. "Not Patrice. She's out of it. It's over."

In their silence, both men nursed drinks and concentrated on the murmur of other diners, the scraping of silverware on plates. After a time, Marcel asked, "She meant that much to you?"

Evan's brow knit, he studied his uncle, then lowered his eyes. "It's over. You understand..."

Marcel looked to the mirrors on the wall, the green bottles lining either side and along the ceiling rafters. But for the patrons' attire and his own jean-clad look, it could have been the thirties or forties. Those days in Paris were quite a time and he remembered well the women who crossed his path, starlets and prostitutes, all kinds. He had fallen like Evan. How could he be insensitive as Evan sat lost in the confusion he himself so well understood? It was always a woman who could churn your heart. Nothing else wound one so tightly, no other experience left such long wakes of recall. He should be more understanding. Pauline always came to his aid when he was trying to cope with an affair gone bad—even though she, too, unintentionally and before her marriage, had been a breaker of hearts. Evan had no one like that for support. He reached for his nephew's hand. "I'll help you, vieux. Just keep me out of the *les affaires amoureuses*!"

Evan smiled. "That won't be hard to do."

"Your Papa, where is he?"

"Batz. They've gone to open up."

"They?" Marcel asked.

"He's with Régine Mallord. You might have known her as Régine de Long."

The black of Marcel's irises grew. "Ah, the woman has returned has she? Is she still the same whiny thing she was as a child?"

"You knew her then?"

"I kept my distance when our families congregated on Batz. Yes, I remember. I thought the States had swallowed her, thought she'd left never to crimp the style of her family. The de Longs, always kind and decent. But she had a streak in her. A brat, a genuine brat, if I do say so."

"Papa is in love."

Marcel swallowed his wine. "Your Papa is getting old..."

He thought back to Batz, when Régine was a child. He'd been too many years her senior to pay much attention, but there were times when she forced her will with her parents, when she threw tantrums and had to be put to bed early. She was an only child, too, he recalled, cute and smart enough even then to use physical charm to her own ends.

"I remember Nate Mallord," chuckled Marcel. "I remember wanting to warn him. But, heh! We choose our partners, don't we?"

Evan gulped down the last of his wine. "Great meal, Marcel. Now, we walk about, eh? We can talk. It's Saturday midnight, early."

♥ ♥ ♥

Sunday morning, after attending church with her parents, Solange Lemuire excused herself from the noontime meal. Explaining she had studies, she left the résidence near parc Monceau and, crossing town to the Latin Quarter, arrived at the Sorbonne.

Students milled around the library doors. A harried-looking one with long hair and tennis shoes shoved a pamphlet at her. She glanced down to familiar jargon—the stuff of May '68. Students were still active, still trying to initiate change.

It had been a tough school year, with the unrest of previous semesters stalling the most basic scholastic endeavors. For an entire year, the faculty and students bickered over structure and form at the Sorbonne, a seat of France's educational system. Yet disruption dominated and Solange had more than once headed for a class only to find it had been cancelled or, once there, been exposed to discussions ranging far from the topic she'd chosen for her curriculum.

So many students were feeding off this recently achieved sense of liberty, this innovative approach to discovery. She found it distracting, didn't much care to have traditions dissolve. She had learned readily and well how to sit long hours and accept verbatim the words of a stodgy professor. She'd long ago stopped yawning and voicing displeasure over boring material and even more tedious homework assignments that were exercises in memorization rather than anything remotely thought-provoking.

Even though her budding beauty and girlish habits were typical of most eighteen-year-olds, Solange was of the established French class. She would prepare for her degree and then get married, the same as her mother, the same as all the Lemuire women. When in the company of female counterparts as they called for change and expounded on leftist theory, she remained nonplussed. All was incidental. She had her own notions about happiness and idealism and didn't require further influence.

A degree in mathematics would suit her, provided it was from the Sorbonne. She'd worked hard to be received into the Faculty and to maintain her grades. With graduation approaching, she was anxious to finish. Marriage and children held sway much more than books and campus disaccord.

Insuring no one saw her, she crumpled the pamphlet and shoved it in her pocket. Then, she asked a passing student the quickest way to the site presently in use by some I. D. H. E. C. students.

Her ponytail swished as she walked and she tried to settle the flutter in her stomach. Seeking out the source of her jealousies was a new experience. But the way Marcel had gone on, one would think Patrice Larchim the second Deneuve, or better. Solange had to see for herself.

Innocent in many ways, and very much saving herself for her future husband, Solange nevertheless was on guard. Like a hawk, she'd watched Evan's face that instant, as the two men exchanged comments about the

255

film. Evan's eyes had clouded. Patrice had been, or perhaps still was, a part of his love life.

Had it been any other man, Solange might have directed her attention towards other suitors. But from the moment she set eyes on Evan de Roche, she knew where her heart belonged.

Their first meeting had been over lunch, planned by her mother. Giles de Roche was a family friend and had worked closely with Monsieur Lemuire for years. As Solange's mother had explained, since the death of Pauline de Roche, Giles socialized little, making it clear to even the closest of friends he preferred to spend his days at work and then retire early.

The only reasons Papa Lemuire had proposed the dinner was because Giles himself had said he was concerned about fiscal policy and the outcome of recent moves that risked lowering the franc's value. Madame Lemuire had quickly arranged the meal, figuring she'd finally found a reason to bring the young de Roche face to face with her daughter. Solange's education almost behind her, Madame Lemuire was well aware there remained one final chore.

Over a meal lasting late into the day, the Lemuires and de Roches theorized and wondered about the future of France as Solange got to know Evan.

He was polite and engaging, according equal time to topics of business and pleasure. His bantering over mathematical theory demonstrated his expertise on the subject. He appeared interested with Solange's work at school and more than once complimented her on her good grades. The meal complete, the visit continued in the Lemuire's salon, where the couple chatted amiably.

His joking, offhanded humor, and twinkling eyes captured her then and there. She reveled in his playful grin and gestures, especially when he wrapped an arm casually on her shoulder and led her to the foyer by the hand, where they said good-night.

He was even more than her mother had promised. In bed, Solange remained sleepless, reliving their evening, longing for him.

The feeling did not dissipate. Through the winter months, she enjoyed a few more interactions but always in the company of family. Mémé de Long hosted a Christmas gathering, after which her daughter Régine managed to harness the de Roche clan for a celebration to ring in the New Year. To Solange's disappointment, Giles de Roche remained stubbornly reclusive, and therefore she saw little more of Evan.

She began to daydream in class, not hard to do given the radical topics dominating discussions. She wondered could she drop out and simply get married. Nothing else mattered but being with Evan and engaging in the same endearing meetings like the few they'd had to date.

She confided in her mother.

"Oh, yes, my love, Evan!" her mother said. "He's wonderful! We must continue with him now, mustn't we?" Her mother, a trim brunette with a year-round tan and sumptuous taste in clothes, pattered about the living area as if on a cloud. Affairs of the heart, especially her own daughter's, kept her perennially occupied.

"He was very attentive, Mama, and so kind. I really do hope we can get together again."

"Well, chérie," said Madame Lemuire, "you have already been formally introduced. There's nothing that says you can't contact him yourself. I understood you two debated mathematics. Let me suggest you try and continue on with that very noble French topic!" Her eyes became slits and she threw her daughter a suggestive smile.

But that day at the de Roche's had not been much fun. Marcel was bold, even brazen in his confidence. Solange had been ill at ease from the moment she crossed into the foyer. Evan, although pleased to see her, seemed preoccupied with film, an area of interest he'd not yet shared with Solange.

Then the talk of Patrice. Well, it was time to set things straight there. She would see for herself.

In the Sorbonne building pointed out to her, Solange found several studios, void of people yet filled with camera equipment. She was not surprised with the emptiness, it being Sunday, and wandered around until she heard voices. They came from a studio at the end of the hall—laughs, loud words followed by pauses.

She stepped to the doorway. Amidst several students and center-stage, a dark-haired woman was the only female.

"Patrice," whispered Solange.

A student looked up. "You, too?"

Solange reddened and mumbled, "No, no, I'm watching if it's Okay."

Patrice spoke. "Always good to have an audience!"

The group returned to their script and Solange stepped closer, keeping from all the lights yet inching forward for a better view of Patrice.

Not five minutes into the take, Patrice was wrapped in the arms of a male actor. He took off her blouse and lowered her to the floor. As they tangled themselves in one another, a sex scene appeared imminent.

Solange held her breath. Though she had often viewed nudity on beaches, she'd never been exposed to such antics. This was the act itself, or almost, and emotions stirred within that made her ill at ease yet unable to divert her gaze.

She imagined Patrice with Evan, the two locked together like this. Had Evan filmed similar scenes?

Were the two old hands at lovemaking simply because their 'work' had demanded it? Or worse, had Evan really fallen for Patrice?

Solange raised her nose. Patrice was *pied noir*. A de Roche would never spend too much time over someone like that.

Still, Solange listened to Patrice as she expertly conveyed feelings, handled herself with grace and was in total command of her faculties. This was an actress who would succeed, without contest, and at the highest echelons. Patrice's profession would come first, that too Solange understood.

What had the two done together? That was the question Solange debated as she left the studio and made for the streets. Patrice was lovely, she had to admit, background or not. Solange recalled that flicker of tenderness Evan had released at the mention of this budding actress.

In bed that night, Solange cried. She always imagined falling in love as an uniquely magical ride, held to fantasies of wearing white and being seduced by a man so loving and devoted he'd have no longing for another.

She loved Evan already, yet wondered about her ability to claim his heart. Respectful, gallant, and handsome, someone who, given her class and connections, was certainly attainable. At the same time, a feeling akin to terror rattled at the base of her as she began to understand a more insidious aspect of this potential union: in order to commandeer his emotions, she would have to change.

Solange had hoped a man more worldly than she would reveal the intricacies of love, would wrap her in his arms and sweep away the unknowns by taking the lead, and ridding her of adolescent uncertainties.

Yet, another age and time was upon her. Watching Patrice proved revelatory. Patrice was not a virgin like Solange. Her female colleagues were making love already, had well researched birth control, and had made choices Solange didn't confront.

She folded back her nightie and touched her breasts, then withdrew her hand. It was fear-provoking, discovering her body. She wanted someone else to do it for her. Now, she sensed, that if she were to get Evan de Roche, she might have to rid herself of those antiquated and idealistic musings like those of her mother.

Why was she a youth in the tumultuous sixties? She'd been so good, had done all the right things. Didn't she deserve the rewards for her efforts?

"Evan, Evan," she whispered, feeling again the force of desire, understanding it was time for drastic action.

# Chapter 7

IN NEARBY VITRY, Marcel connected with colleagues and took on the odd project or two. He shared his knowledge of film-making, as well as introduced his nephew to a close-knit, under-the-radar crowd made up of young and old, French and foreigners.

Evan soon became integral to the action and was often handed the camera to try out his luck. He appreciated the attention, adapted to the lingo, formalities, and sway. Marcel complimented when appropriate and critiqued when necessary. After a few months, Evan better grasped the drawbacks of Albert's film.

Marcel's was a lifestyle of the night. He slept until four or five in the afternoon then woke to meet with friends at a café. From there they would continue with the previous day's effort or commence another short. By midnight, having earlier enjoyed a drawn-out meal, they would have staked out a choice Parisian locale. In Marcel's estimation, late night and early morning were key times to collect footage of the people who made Paris unique—garbage collectors, ladies of the night, dignitaries arriving from various time zones, mannequins in storefronts staring at emptied boulevards.

261

They filmed a scene at Les Halles where they focused on butchers with carcasses balanced on their heads, couples exiting from the theaters, and foreigners sampling onion soup. They ambled through Montmartre, noting the facades of the homes of famous painters and interviewing an author or two. At Place de la Contrescarpe in the Latin Quarter, they more than once joined with onlookers for the performance of a hopeful actor, singer, or musician.

They wandered, cameras in tow, books under arms, until someone had an idea. Regardless of the hour or inconvenience to residents, they set up lights and focused their lens. At dawn, with the first rumblings of the Métro, they bid farewell.

Evan burned candles at both ends. De Roche Frères and his studies made demands on him from early morning until the dinner hour. Giles put Evan in charge of managing a significant budget and of the purchase of computer equipment. The effort exercised his engineering know-how and gave him a chance to work with professionals in French tech firms. Real-life challenges were often subjects of his school papers.

Although nights should have been a time for homework and rest, Evan sought relief from the day's toil with Marcel. No matter how probing a school issue or de Roche crisis, he met with his uncle. He derived more pleasure in reviewing footage from the previous night than he ever could from pouring over academic minutia. Like his uncle, late nights were his freedom.

Marcel took frequent trips, back to the south or to Switzerland, Germany, and Spain. He preferred conferring with his more worldly contacts rather than solely incorporating French methods. During his absences, Evan caught up with other work.

Begrudgingly, he managed to comply with Marcel's wish to refrain from drawing on the coffers of de Roche

Frères. Evan wanted to produce a film on a grand scale, the kind requiring sizeable financial backing, the backing he knew his father had the means to supply. When the topic arose, however, Marcel would shake his head. They were not to cross the line. Evan's dedication to de Roche and its policies thus avoided Giles's suspicions about his late night meandering.

Too, Giles was increasingly distracted by Régine. The couple dined out often and stayed out late wandering arm-in-arm along the river bank. More than a few times, Betti informed Evan that Giles would not dine at home. Given his own activities, Evan viewed this in a positive light.

♥ ♥ ♥

With summer came the usual exit to coastal retreats. By early August, Paris had emptied and Evan, ready for rest and fun, joined his compatriots. Giles, Betti, and he made for Batz. Roses, geraniums, and ivies were in full bloom, ferries ran regularly, and even more vacationers had discovered the island's allure.

Most of the first week, Evan relaxed in and around Roscoff. He saw movies, reviewed his studies, and kept in touch with Marcel via infrequent phone calls to Aix where his uncle enjoyed his own version of *les vacances*.

They would meet again in Paris but Marcel had suggested that he was tiring of the city. He indicated that he would do a few shorts, after which Evan was on his own. Marcel would continue to advise but, given Evan's progress, deemed a prolonged stay unnecessary.

As the summer advanced, Régine wore on Evan. Supposedly next door with Mémé, she spent every waking hour at the de Roche home. From early morning when she upstaged Betti by appearing with warm croissants until late at night when she cajoled Giles into a stroll on the beach, Régine staked her claim.

Mémé visited infrequently, preferring to welcome Giles or Evan at her place when they chanced by. She loved Evan and took time to feed him and ask questions about his studies and work at de Roche Frères. They also had a shared activity. Mornings the two would tend to the de Roche garden.

Wearing wide-brimmed straw hat and dark flowing skirts, Mémé carried a panier for clippings. Evan walked at her side, bending to cut and trim or pull at weeds. Along the way, they caught up.

"And you will graduate with honors, mon cher," Mémé said, her petit, bent form next to Evan's.

"I hope, Mémé. You know how hard 'X' will be," he said, referring to Polytechnique. "I must have superior grades to get accepted."

"You are France's future. You will do well," Mémé said in a tone that did not invite retort.

Evan arranged a bouquet, and placed it in Mémé's panier. They ambled through the swaying stalks and marveled at the resilience of certain perennials. Mémé evaluated with an eye for future growths and the memory of previous gardens. Periodically, she rested on one of several granite benches overlooking the water. When they paused, Evan wanted to ask her about Régine and his father but understood what topics Mémé allowed. Matters of love, her daughter, and Giles de Roche were ones she broached, not the other way around.

Yet, before they reached the end of the path and the border of their properties, Mémé requested they sit. She wiped her forehead and looked to sea. As if reading his mind, she fixed a black-eyed gaze on him and grinned. "So, your father is in love, eh?"

"Régine?"

Mémé nodded. "I can't put my finger on it but it doesn't sit well with me. You?"

"I can't say," he said with caution.

"Don't lie to me, Evan dear. I see you in Régine's presence. You are like a wary rabbit, stirring at her supposed dominance, stealing glances at the door for the opportunity to skedaddle away! Hey, hey, it's rather amusing to watch."

"I didn't realize..." Evan said.

She took his hand. "I am old now, Evan. These are not the summers of the fifties. We have lost our Pauline and Batz is different. True, the flowers are here but, as much as I am one to hold onto the happy times, the garden and your dear mother's memories are all that are left. Régine is back. Oh, she's a good girl, mind you. I think she had it tough in the States, frankly. Although one never knows...I enjoyed that daughter of hers. Anyway, Evan, we all must move forward, you understand? You have a life ahead of you, a great one! Imagine, to handle the de Roche future. It's impressive. Your mother would be proud!"

"I wonder."

"How so?" Mémé's gaze penetrated.

"I feel conflicted so often."

"Great men are conflicted! It's part of your destiny for you will juggle many options, a thousand at once. Has your father not told you a de Roche struggles even as he succeeds and attains great heights? It's the way, child. Get used to those feelings. You don't like Régine, your father is in love with her. You want to dally with your films yet you must calculate profit and loss. You love all women but will settle for only one. Your tugs-of-war are noble and good. Strength develops this way."

"Mémé, you're stronger than me. I often feel unable to stand up for the great de Roche name."

"Listen," she said, leaning on him to stand, "you need time, that's all. Take your holiday and use it for contemplation. Don't rush, but understand who you are. We're all watching, for yours is a mighty future. You won't disappoint, I know this!"

Evan eyed a jewel weed in the panier, its bright pink petals shivering as Mémé walked. He studied the sea for a second then grasped her hand, accompanied her home, and kissed her goodnight.

He returned to an empty house. The chimes clinked as he sat on the porch overlooking the garden. Mémé had always seemed an impartial party. Today, she'd voiced her opinion, another nod to his potential. It didn't make him feel happy, only lost. Once a source of solace, Mémé was at present a member of a camp whose ranks he wasn't sure he wanted to join.

How was it he felt he had no choice in the matter?

At Régine's insistence, the Lemuires visited for a week. Evan saw right through her plans. More than once in Paris, he noticed the two women speaking in hushed voices. Since May, the Lemuires had been frequent guests at their home in the 16th. Too, there were the Sunday dinners and evenings at the theater. Evan had not always been present but Solange had attended them all—another sign of each families' intentions.

He liked Solange, found her attentive and attractive, admired her clear skin and the freckles dotting her nose. Always dressed in crisp attire, her ponytail hung about her shoulders or down her back, a wide bow securing it in place. She was intelligent and worldly and her interest in film impressed.

But he didn't relish the camaraderie between Solange and Régine, visible from early on when Régine took to inviting Solange on shopping sprees and to fashion shows. Régine's ideas for the summer were obvious, too. At Roscoff, when Solange emerged from the ferry first, Régine urged Evan forward, trying to force an embrace.

A few days into their visit, Solange's aspirations to win Evan's heart were also evident. Constantly by his side, she discussed the latest film or some aspect of Truffaut's style. Mornings, she served croissants with Régine, the two decked out in striped designer shorts or sheer smocks over bikinis.

Summer was a time of relaxed morals. Woman sunbathed topless, children ran around nude, conversations veered every which way from the latest political scandal to the blatant affairs of close friends. Along with the warm weather and good food, needs of the flesh permeated the atmosphere.

From the gardens, Evan watched the two women on the beach, both topless, giggling and stealing glances to shore. They would meander back and forth, far enough distant to leave elements of their femininity to his imagination.

For a few days, he took it all in stride, feigning interest in their idle chatter. Régine more often than not, and only when Giles was absent, raised off-color topics like the film star they knew who took to having three women at once or the bordello tales of a famous writer. Solange was embarrassed yet attentive.

She and he went to a few movies together and shared less loaded conversations. Alone with her Evan was privy to a more serious, pleasant side and they relaxed more. He would invite her to bike ride or join him for shell collecting.

But, once Evan and Solange returned from an engagement, Régine was usually in the wings. Evan guessed Solange was being coached in the ways of love.

All this superficial behavior was water under the bridge for him. The beauty of Batz won out during the less than pleasant exchanges and Evan found himself growing more and more at ease.

The day before the Lemuires returned to Paris, however, Solange coyly convinced Evan that she'd not yet seen one side of the island and would very much like to round out her experience. Bayside along the less populated and rocky coast, they ate a picnic lunch and huddled together against brisk winds.

At first, Solange appeared content to watch the waves. While Evan lost himself in a book, she propped herself at his chest and dozed. In time, the sun shone stronger and she rose to take off her jacket. Underneath there was nothing and when she returned to her former position, Evan had a close-up view of her breasts, sunburned and with darkened tips pointing straight up.

He stared. She lay still, eyes closed, hands across her stomach. A slip of cloth covered her thighs as she rubbed one leg against the other. Then, she peeked at him and smiled. His body warned him that he would succumb. She placed her fingers to his chest and moved them up to the open 'V' of his shirt, suggestive digs reaching his already exposed senses.

She sat up and stared, the sun behind, hair whispering about her as she tugged at the bow and released strands to the breeze. He felt her cheek. She encouraged him with a soft moan, easing her body closer.

She was on him, pinning him against the blanket and kissing, a hurried, crazed movement, her lips against his, her tongue slippery and busy. She panted and let go light sobs as she tried to remove his shirt. She tugged at his belt, ran hands over his chest and thrust hips, all the while murmuring, "Mon amour, mon amour."

Her breasts, soft against his chest, rubbed one second then jiggled in the air another, leaving no time to intensify their pressure or beautify the moment. Ill at ease in her body, and even less comfortable with his, she introduced a situation that was neither simple nor without consequence. He finally lowered her hands and sat up.

"It's too fast," he whispered.

She pouted, panted, and tried again.

"We don't have to," he said, trying to settle her with a caress to her shoulder.

She bit her lip, drew his head to her chest. "Mon amour, mon amour."

"Solange. Stop." He raised his head and held her two hands.

She furrowed her brow, looked down at her naked body. "We must."

"Why?"

"It's expected. We're to be married after all, Evan. It's time."

"What?"

"Of course. It's planned. You know that, Evan."

He looked at the lowering sun.

She reached for him and kissed, this time slower, as if the first try had been enough for her to adapt to a better approach. She leaned into him and, tongue on his, drew his body near and forced him down once again.

She took his hand and placed it on her pubis, gently moving her body back and forth, her tension easing, as if she had one remaining chance to do good. Her hair fell about his face in a red-gold veil as she found his lower body. In seconds, she was massaging him, feeling his hardness and lowering her lips to his chest and stomach. He clenched her hair into his fists, let go an audible sigh. She came up again and met his eyes, this time with a triumphant glean that bathed him in her prowess and invited him, easy this time, to discover her.

They made love once, then again. Each time Solange breached a barrier, revealing her sensual powers and ability to lay claim on a man. Evan entangled himself within her embrace, for hers was a lusty and fragrant body, mingling with the salt and sea and driving him to the brink. What reserve he possessed, what understanding of her intentions he might have held were lost once she had him inside her.

He fell again as he had on rue St. Jacques, ushered to passageways, emerging at a clearing, an intimate belonging that drove away fear, focused on the instant, and made the world go away. A woman in his arms, peace was his.

"Evan, Evan," she screamed at climax. "My love, Evan!" She tugged at him for more and didn't release herself until it was clear he was exhausted. After, when they lay still, the brilliance in her eyes bespoke her awe, a look he'd seen before, a look he took pleasure in yet at the same time questioned.

Was it him or was it who he was?

Once they'd dressed and were headed home, he was silent, imbued with the heady experience. At his side stood a more assured woman, an evolved version of the girl who had arrived on Batz some days before.

Her hand firmly in his, her hair reflected the sun's brilliance, her gait was confident, with purpose. She spoke of everything from food to politics to amour to cinema. All the while, he walked by her side and listened. She asked questions and responded for herself. Loving had emancipated her. This new outlook, an embrace of her privilege, was worthy of herself and one and only one man—Evan de Roche.

# Chapter 8:
# 10 January 1970

Dear Mum,

I apologize for not writing. My job has changed. I work two nights a week at the restaurant and Thursday through Saturday at a nightclub named Johnny's. It's better money and the music is jazz which I enjoy. I sing two sets with whomever is playing. The variety allows for creativity with my tunes. I now have more time for study.

Americans categorize people. You must be 'doing' something, or in the process of preparing to 'do' something. When I say I'm studying for the fun of it, that doesn't sit well. People expect further explanation—like I'm studying to be a doctor or an economist. It makes me laugh. Once I told a rude fellow I was preparing to be one of the wee people. It shut him up.

I never heard from you on the missing page. It's a detail but I love the book and would like to find out what was on it. Was it ripped? Since the book was your favorite, I thought you might have a clue.

I'm keeping well. Don't worry and thanks for the pounds.

Love,
Claire

13 February 1970

Dear Claire,

I hope this night work is not getting you into trouble. You seem to have a habit of wise-cracking. Take care because some people don't enjoy that kind of discussion.

London is dreary and cold. It brings me down at times although I manage. My friend takes longer and longer journeys and I find myself alone much of the time. I've discovered the city and, during these outings, learn more about the English. It's an odd place but better than Ireland.

You should visit. There are lovely sections of London and the people are not all nasty to the Irish. Hempstead, north, is charming with wealthy, cultured people and many restaurants serving food continental style. It recalls a former time, a dreamy part of the city.

Don't go getting into trouble and mind your studies.

Love,
Mum

♥ ♥ ♥

Klee folded the letter and placed it with the others, in a shoe box under clothes organized in her closet. The money, too, she hid away, for she had no intention of spending a penny. Someday she would figure a gift for her mother. Right now, she would save.

She reached for her singing outfit, another short black dress but wool this time for warmth. Recently purchased red platform heels protected from the sleet and ice and she ignored the fact she stood above the crowd.

Singing, singing. In the manner she had at Danigan's, she became the favorite at Johnny's. The one-room club in central Cambridge was a corner stop for MIT students and city workers alike who, before catching the bus or trolley, could break for a drink and song.

Located next to the India Garden, Klee had stopped there one night and, predictably, had all eyes on her once she decided to open her mouth and sing. The owner was not two minutes evaluating her when he approached and proposed regular stints that would bring her more cash than she ever imagined.

Since the previous summer, she had proven reliable with her hours and gracious to the audience. Now, she was the singular Saturday night attraction regardless of the group.

She became more creative. To the music, she danced often and even contacted the group a day or two in advance for the planned songs. She would then invent skits in the privacy of her apartment. For her performances, she offered dances, jokes, and lyrics to accompany the songs and, as a result, usually brought the house down.

Too soon, however, she felt the pull of a familiar abyss. Her musical talents, passed on to others for their enjoyment and her profit, at the same time left her faced with commitment to that music. No sooner was she comfortable and established than people wanted her to do better, encouraged her to move along and take on more. Like in Ireland and with even more enthusiasm, America welcomed her song. Yet its beckon was of a seductive kind, a pressure she sensed coiling about her and squeezing her of breath. Didn't they see it was only a means to her ends? She loved her work yet could grow disgusted with it as well. This time joy for the crowd who loved her, the next, and in the privacy of her mind, a resurgence of mired memories and squelched tears.

Love and loneliness came together in song.

# Chapter 9

JOHNNY MEAR WAS A RETIRED RAILROAD WORKER in his late fifties. Because of a heart attack at forty-two, he'd stopped full time work and dabbled at odd jobs until he started the club four years back. It was an out-of-the-way place for locals, a pit stop for beer and friendly chatter. He didn't work too hard, took in a small salary, and kept an easy pace so as to maintain his weight and stabilize his blood pressure. The night job was a diversion from an otherwise uneventful life.

Klee had turned his place into a hot spot, this during a time when not many city clubs could boast regular, paying clientele. It used to be an effort for him to find bands interested in playing. Now they came to him, wondering if Klee might sing back-up or lead, and hoping to book the better nights like Fridays and Saturdays. In addition, he no longer sweated about last minute group cancellations because Klee could handle a show solo.

He enjoyed those times best for she sang Irish tunes or folk music that, although initially leaving the crowd unmoved, grew on them so as to enchant and capture even the most die-hard jazz enthusiast. Her voice alone was enough for Johnny. He happily cleared glasses, refilled drinks, joked with patrons and stole glances at the girl with the hair and tight dress. She sang with every part of her, dropping sweet regards, lowering her voice only to let go an almost piercing sound that rattled the crowd and left Johnny beaming. His angel of profit kept them coming.

He never worried about her for she kept to herself, drank little, and was as predictable as anyone. Off stage, she was serious and prone to extended silences as she read or waited for the band. She wore a complex regard that, when he least expected and in her absence, drove him to ponder her secrets.

Being one who cherished his own privacy, he never pried. Yet he often wondered about her. She never took guys home, never made reference to a boyfriend, and seemed to have a peculiar love affair going with her studies that included foreign languages.

She was strange looking but he'd long before gotten over her odd way of staring, the generous lips and layers of hair. In fact, what had initially appeared as sure losers on stage, had become for Johnny features as attractive as any flaunted by the loveliest of blonde Playmates. He found that, from a distance and hiding behind his gruff demeanor, he was growing increasingly fond of her.

She saw through that, he could tell. Her eyes sparkled when he handed her a check with a bonus or when she noticed him staring from across the crowded bar. Their connection went beyond employer-employee, to a level that brought Johnny to his days as a youth when he fell in love repeatedly and thought his looks would never fade. Klee was seeping into his heart, but he had to be careful. During these recessionary times he was a lucky man indeed.

Passion became a notion with new meaning. He wondered about her life outside work, and worried she was burning herself out. The few times he managed conversation, she detailed learning five languages, and described a place in Ireland that was hard to pronounce. He guessed she was trying to gain U. S. residency and planned to help her somehow, when the time was right. He wanted her to stay.

One night he decided to drive her home. It was early Sunday morning and snow had been falling all evening. She was packing up on stage.

"It's damned cold out tonight, Klee," he said, eyes on the bar. "I'll take you home." He'd worn a different shirt, blue, and with navy vest to match his jeans. He felt her gaze on him and wondered if she approved of his attire.

"Thanks, Johnny. I can walk," she said, humming as she wrapped her long black coat about her.

Her back to him, he watched her place the hat on her head, a lady soon to disappear from his sight for four long days. "I won't bite, you know," he joked. "C'mon, it's still snowing."

"I like the snow, kicking boots in the drifts."

"It's below zero! I won't take no. It's too cold and late."

She turned to him, acquiesced with a nod, then sat at the bar to wait.

He had a spacious brown Oldsmobile with rust along the bottom and yellow leather interior. She joked about it as they drove across the river towards Commonwealth Ave. She'd never been in so big a car. He proudly told her it was paid for and got decent mileage for city driving. Plus, it was such a junker, no one bothered to steal it. She questioned this practice of car-theft and he explained to her the propensity for youth to entertain themselves stealing cars for joy rides.

She peered at the dark clouds and tapped fingers on the dash, nodding every now and then as she perused the interior.

His desire felt wrapped in an urge to keep her safe. In her own bubble of contentment, she pointed the way, answered his questions about school, rent, or food with patience and the occasional observation about her new-found country.

She didn't want to stay forever, she said, only long enough to get a formal education. Important to earn her bachelor's degree which she was a year into, majoring in linguistics. She shared her planned courses and results of previous ones, delving into professors, their backgrounds, and levels of difficulty from one syllabus to another.

He had no idea what she spoke of, really. His studies having terminated with high school, she was the first person to illuminate him on the demands of higher education. He was impressed with her stamina and, when he asked about her residency status, she said she was hoping to continue using her student visa. If she were lucky, she might obtain employment and remain in the States, unless other options presented themselves.

Nonplussed by world affairs, she still followed the latest developments of the economy and Vietnam. Her eyes to the sky, she detailed White House policy and expounded on a different perspective about the upcoming peace talks. He was silenced by her knowledge, awed by her abilities, and feared her leaving. She was the kind of person he could have talked with all night.

Too soon, they were in front of her triplex. The car slowed, he put it in park and looked to her, expecting more on the state of affairs in Washington or the latest on a Harvard protest speech.

But her expression had changed. Her large eyes glowed a bluish haze and she wore a half grin. Her amusement sourced from within. He was charmed, and would have stayed for hours in the same position, watching and waiting.

With a wave, she opened the door. His heart jumped, though he thought he was under control. He didn't want her out of his sight, and asked too quickly if she didn't want to go for a coffee. She turned to him and seemed a thousand miles away as her incomprehensible stare forced him to blush. Her power was of another kind and he felt in the presence of an individual he couldn't categorize.

"Good night, Johnny," she said, pressing her hat to her head.

He nodded his farewell. She stepped from the car, made for the stoop and the inside. The light flicked on, her shadow appeared behind the lowered shade. She continued to stare out, a silhouette to his eyes—hair puffed, shoulders broad and set. He felt his heart pound. The light went off.

Another twenty minutes passed before he drove away. The need to remain, to protect, to hold. And yet, by all visible signs she took care of herself just fine.

It wasn't love as he had come to understand it, for he was old and she was young. He'd lived his years content with bachelorhood, the odd lady of the night. A few girly magazines for company. Needing a woman now was laughable. He therefore couldn't identify what he felt for Klee, and yet, he wanted her more than he ever wanted anything or anyone. He wanted to be with her and share with her. His life until now had been a half-life.

In bed he remained sleepless and distraught. He had fallen for a woman who could define his life to come and yet, because he'd never before known feelings of this kind, he debated and feared them, too.

Perhaps his life had not ended at forty-two, as he once figured it had.

# Chapter 10:
# April 1970

MARCEL PAID ATTENTION TO PATRICE LARCHIM. Throughout the winter months and from his home outside Aix-en-Province, he suggested to friends in Paris that they sign her on for bit parts. She was a prize. Yet Marcel was also aware that Evan bore wounds. Hesitant to proclaim her the next greatest film star while at the same time facilitating his nephew's goals, he nonetheless felt it his duty to help someone of her talents.

Underdogs were a lure. Faced with a promising actor who hailed from the aristocracy and an as-equally gifted orphan of the streets, he chose the latter. From the start Patrice intrigued him.

For all his qualms about returning to Paris the year before, it had been worthwhile in the end. He had met up with two promising individuals, one introduced to him by the other. That in and of itself was worth continuing with Evan who, although a breath of fresh air when compared to his family, nevertheless represented to Marcel the France of the *profondeurs*—those who upheld tradition and rarely challenged the status quo.

Evan had surprised him and Marcel was content to help him along, sensing his nephew would excel in the movie industry. Someday, Marcel hoped, the young man might disentangle himself from the corporate burdens of the de Roche clan.

At present, however, Evan's career choices were not Marcel's concern. His formal work with Evan through, he sought rest in the south, now that his nephew was better equipped with tools to succeed.

Next, Patrice. He called her and invited her to Aix. Aware of Marcel and his accomplishments, she accepted his offer to participate in the filming of a documentary around Marseille.

They instantly connected. Patrice was at ease with his style, open to his suggestions, and willing to put in the long hours so as to turn the film around quickly. He found her a pleasure from the start and opened up more than usual to her questions and inquiries. Over the span of a few weeks, they were like old friends, sharing each others' pasts and respective acquaintances with some of France's better known stars.

During meals and between takes—and like Evan before her—Patrice worked in a complimentary way with Marcel, neither cramping his style or bending to his sometimes childish whims. She possessed the composure of a true professional, with her own roadmap, a habit that quickly won her Marcel's admiration. They were a team—tough, hardworking, and fixated on their primary concern, film.

Marcel's word was respected within the business. What he said about whom to the right people could forge a career. Although he still spent much time mulling over Evan's future, he couldn't afford to lose time. Patrice waited in the wings, patient and lovely, and so he put thoughts of Evan aside as he groomed her for other, more visible roles once she returned to Paris.

In Marseille, their days flew by. It was business all the way, even though Marcel was careful to take note of the odd glimmer in her eyes. The more he worked with her and the more the film became a reality, he found himself figuring out how to promote her by himself. She was still raw in many ways and, once back in Paris, risked slipping into the slush pile of meandering talent. She was an outsider after all. It bothered him to think of her gifts going to waste for no good reason. One day he proposed becoming her agent.

"Agent?" she asked, her body limp against a chair in the hot sun of a Marseille afternoon. They'd just finished a take and she was preparing lines for the next day.

"It's the future. You hear of it all the time in the States," he said, his leg up on the table as he leaned back in his chair. He wore a cotton shirt with buttons opened to his chest.

Her eyes blazed interest with the mention of the States. "I see."

"Of course you see, lady," he joked, aware of her intentions to pursue international avenues.

They cracked open another bottle of wine and detailed plans. Marcel would remain in Aix, keeping in touch by phone and courier. He would seek out jobs for her in and around Paris, and arrange equitable fees from which he would extract a commission. She was free to take on other jobs as long as he was informed. They both agreed to pay attention to international spots as well, with Marcel indicating he'd contact associates in the U. S. and Canada.

Well aware of the connection with the illustrious de Roche family, Patrice forced the topic of Evan into the open. Marcel spoke in generalities, letting on Evan was busy with school and dabbling in film. Attentive but with contrived evasiveness, she inquired into his social life. By her downcast eyes, Marcel could tell she still cared, and he better understood Evan's sullen looks. The two young people were of the same ilk but, for reasons he could only guess at, had not deepened their connection.

"He should keep up with film," Patrice said, toying with her drink.

"He must decide for himself. Easier said than done when one is a de Roche," added Marcel with a wry smile.

"You extracted yourself from the familial web, I see," she said.

Marcel shrugged, looked to the tourists strolling along the promenade, La Canebière, and laughed. "When I have all this? All I could possibly want? The sun, the life of the south, my own mind to do with as I please? I beg you, think, girl. Would you pass it by?"

They shared a smile, the future in their eyes. It was a productive time, a successful film. Patrice returned to Paris, under the wings of one of the greatest, albeit low-key personages, in the history of French film.

# Chapter 11:
# September 1970

SUMMER OVER, EVAN THREW HIMSELF into his studies. One of the major *grandes écoles* in France, Polytechnique, accepted only the best qualified, most often those from privilege. Upon graduation, these students were poised for key administrative, industrial, and government positions. Indeed, even before entering Polytechnique, Evan and his classmates understood their career paths. De Roche Frères would claim Evan but, had he the choice, he could have targeted anything from Minister of Finance or Culture, even the presidency of the country. In fact, his status within de Roche Frères already guaranteed him the ear of the powers-that-be at the Élysée Palace.

When time permitted, Evan conferred with his father, in particular on the state of affairs at the coal and hydraulic facilities. Hydroelectric was a steadily growing field while coal suffered a decline, remaining solvent through interventions of the French government. Subsidies, wage hikes, and minimal lay-offs offered a shaky stability for those employees who had spent years in the industry. Executives within de Roche Frères shunned notions of a downturn, even though the signs abounded—cheaper labor and raw materials in third world countries plus antiquated French production methods.

At school Evan studied France's frazzled industrial web and a government reluctant to appropriately tackle the problem. He better understood the difficulties his father grappled with, yet also envisioned a way out. De Roche Frères could be better positioned by steering away from declining industries and moving towards burgeoning ones like computer technology, services, and aerospace.

Rather than side with Evan, Giles complied with the government. If the State was willing to subsidize, then there was reason to stay the course. He downplayed the decline in the coal sector and forbade Evan to entertain methods for winding down production with regional managers. However, he accorded Evan free reign over other innovative discussions, and even hinted at investing on the side. This pleased Evan who had every intention of pursuing that direction once school was behind him. If nothing else, he was of his age group, young and willing to risk. Dying industries offered no challenge.

At twenty, he was the image of Giles with a magnificent head of hair and a breezy style that enhanced his looks and bespoke his lineage. Informed and courteous, verbose when required yet unobtrusive most often, he was the epitome of de Roche grandeur for one with minimal experience in the professional world. Giles was anxious to welcome him on board.

When the time came, he gave Evan a corner office at headquarters, inside an elegant eighteenth century building on avenue Marceau near Étoile. With an ornately-carved desk, sitting area with leather chairs, and private quarters should he need to wash or rest, he could look beyond windows to cars racing around the Arc de Triomphe and below to the adorned passers-by and chic shop displays. Ever conscious of the tightrope he walked, Evan strove to master simultaneously his life of student and professional.

It was good for him, too, for he had arrived at an annoying and perplexing place in his personal diversions.

Solange was as attentive as ever. From their first sexual encounter the year before, their relationship continued at a predictable pace. She was occupied with her studies yet always in the wings. They were together weekends, for dinners in or on the town, and sometimes spent a day or two in the country. Journalists caught them at social events and newspapers ran pictures of the two arm-in-arm smiling into one another's eyes. The talk in Paris was they would marry soon.

Solange kept up with movies but, to Evan, her interest felt forced. More than once he caught her annoyed regard when he suggested taking in a film. She would nonetheless go along, as if the accumulation of a certain number of joint trips to the cinema was a guarantee of a future with him. She was too ready to comply, too eager to secure their relationship with the planned-for social affairs that would hopefully culminate in an engagement.

She spent an increasing amount of time at the de Roche home, even when Evan was away. The comradery between Solange and Régine was a given. Régine would lounge in her gowns, with aromas of Chanel perfume trailing in her wake while Solange, her outfits prim and with alert attitude, tread a more domestic stride by coopting Betti's chores, a move that did not go unnoticed by Evan.

Betti remained his one hold on more carefree times. With her, Evan could be a boy again, teasing or making funny remarks about anything he pleased, all to her loving regard. Or he could discuss business issues with her and, while she refrained from explicit commentary, he appreciated having someone in whom he could confide, someone with genuine concern and empathy for the impressive array of responsibilities he now bore. Her long white braid wound into a bun at the nape of her neck, and her gait had slowed. Yet her eyes shone for Evan, especially now with other admiring ladies prancing about the house.

It was kitchen work Betti most enjoyed, cooking sumptuous meals and cleaning the place until it gleamed. She had a flair for Norman cuisine, serving the splendid cream sauces atop a variety of meat preparations or fish selections, following with apple tarts lightly touched with Calvados. She would spend entire afternoons rolling dough for puff pastries and coordinating entrées. Come shopping time, she knew which merchant in their exclusive neighborhood offered the finest goods. She was of the country still, even though she had lived in Paris for over a generation.

# Chapter 11:

THE SATURDAY RÉGINE PROCLAIMED she would cook dinner, Betti quietly retreated to her room. That same day, Evan and Solange had taken in a movie. On their return, Evan relaxed with Giles while Solange disappeared to the kitchen.

The meal tasted different. Though more elaborate, and with each item from the best cut or containing the richest ingredients, there was an expediency built into the preparations that left Evan's mouth dry. He complimented sparingly and stole glances towards the kitchen. "I don't hear Betti," he finally said.

In low-cut purple dress and with her hair tumbling about her, Régine flashed her eyes. "Betti! Betti is not in the kitchen. I did all this, mon cher." She then launched into a discussion about the tricky sauce preparation.

As soon as dessert was over, Evan slipped from the group.

There were two staircases in the house. One, in the main entrance hall, led to guest bedrooms and a study. The other, a narrow back staircase, went from the kitchen to Betti's private quarters. Evan climbed to Betti's. The maid's domain, set apart from the rest of the residence, was of dated design yet one that suited the needs of the de Roches. Unlike some Parisians, they had not chosen to break down walls in order to create more space or to rent out apartments for income.

He knocked several times before she opened. Wearing a plain dress rather than her uniform, her face was drawn. "Oh, Monsieur Evan, I apologize..."

"No, Betti, it's me who should apologize. I didn't mean to bother you. Have you eaten?"

She shook her head. "I left Madame Mallord to the kitchen."

He smirked. "It wasn't as good as one of your meals."

Betti brightened for a second then grew doleful.

"Don't worry," he said. "Régine is not about to take over the kitchen. She gets bored too quickly with real work."

Betti struggled to speak. She and Evan had never talked about her problems and she was unaccustomed to the attention.

Evan pressed again. "Betti, you will never be replaced. Do you understand? Never!"

Betti looked into his eyes, then reached for his hands and kissed. "You're so kind, Monsieur, so kind!"

He left her. Stepping down the stairs, he heard voices coming from the kitchen.

"Evan is ever so handsome!" Régine said.

"I wonder when he'll ask me," Solange said.

"Soon. You've been doing all the right things. Remember what I told you, you have to be patient. He's twenty, has a while to go. Give him another year at least."

"It seems so far away! I want us to be happy and have a family."

"He does, too, dear," Régine said.

"Does he talk about me? I try to please, as you advised. It's not easy, you know, what with distractions like those horrid avant-guard movies."

Régine laughed. "He talks about you all the time, has confided in me he's in love!"

Evan shook his head. Régine was playing chess with his own life and, as he'd suspected, Solange was embracing suggestions on how to trap him. He sat on the step and listened as they detailed holiday plans that included a Christmas dine at the Lemuires. They giggled over when exactly he'd pop the question.

Solange said, "I feel at times that his heart is elsewhere. I told you about Patrice, didn't I?"

"Yes," said Régine. "I give you credit for spying on her like that! But don't even think two seconds about her. She's *pied noir*. He knows his bounds. You're associating with the next de Roche king! That is, after I sneak off to the south with my new husband Giles! After that, Evan is yours, chérie!"

They both laughed and tried to manage the dishes, but then decided to leave the work for Betti in the morning.

Evan drew in his breath. A part of him wanted to barge in on them. Another part was tired of it already. He better understood his discomfort about Solange, and felt cheated. Rather than join the women, he returned up the stairs and made for the second connecting level, descending to the study where Giles sipped a cognac.

"Son?" Giles asked.

Evan poured a drink for himself then sat, his dark eyes penetrating. "You and Régine are marrying?"

Giles chuckled. "That's a topic for another time." He resumed his pensive pose. "I was thinking about the business, Evan. Régine and I have had long talks and I want to bring you in on them."

Evan sat up. "Oh?"

"The years advance, I don't have to remind you. My age is getting in the way here and there and, quite frankly, I would like to slow down. I've been blessed with a clean bill of health yet the company is growing and changing at such a pace that, had I not the promise of your assistance, I'd have selected others like you for direct reports."

"We do alright at the moment, Papa. I don't understand..."

Giles laughed. "Of course you don't. You're young! You will understand better when you are my age! Anyway, I've been thinking seriously about your suggestion to decrease company emphasis on the mining. It makes sense but I've had trouble figuring how best to introduce the idea. Régine has a marvelous thought, one worthy of consideration."

"Régine!" Evan exclaimed.

"Mon amour, you've started without me!" Régine laughed, entering with Solange and sending Evan a perky smile. "Evan, you really must listen for this is the future."

"The future? Do tell," Evan said, as Solange grabbed his hand and cradled it in her lap.

"Yes. The factories and plants in Alsace. Well, Giles and I have decided it makes sense for me to become involved with them. As your sister before, I have significant experience in business affairs and...."

"What experience are you talking about?" Evan asked. With each grin she threw his way, he seethed. Similar to their first encounter, she commanded center stage as she slinked about, cognac glass in hand, and spoke in a breathy tone. Stopping at his side, she gave him a patronizing pat on the shoulder. Solange's clutch tightened around his arm.

"Now, the details of my education don't matter, dear. I lived in the States for ages, was present at many

Harvard affairs and was even an honorary member of the faculty because of my relationship to Nate. I go back years with solid business background, trust me."

Evan looked to Giles.

She spoke rapidly, as if to an empty room. Her gaze never met Evan's. At times, she gestured to Giles or caressed his shoulders. She talked of mergers, of restructuring at headquarters and regionally. She then hinted at her role in the company. "It will be part time at first, of course," she said.

"Doing what?" Evan asked. "You've talked for a half hour and I don't yet understand what it is you're on about."

Her laugh filled the room. "Ah, men! So confident in their business deals and with talk of compromise and five-year plans. But let a woman outshine for one second and they all of a sudden don't understand!" She moved to a chair.

"Forgive my ignorance," Evan said.

"Now, now, Evan," Giles said. "Clear away that tone and listen. I told you I'm interested in slowing down. Régine has long been a supporter of my retirement and I do feel it's a good idea to involve others—close family members and the like. You will run the company one day but I want to insure the best interests of de Roche Frères now."

"And you won't get that with me?" Evan asked.

"Of course I will. But you are in school, and I don't want company demands to distract you from studies. Again I must ask you to listen to Régine. Her ideas are worthy of note." He looked at Régine and clasped her hand in his. "Tell him!"

Régine grinned. "I'll be running the company with you from now on, Evan."

# Chapter 13:
# January, 1971

TO WELCOME RÉGINE into the family business, dignitaries, colleagues and government functionaries joined relatives and friends for a soirée at the de Roche residence.

Dressed in formal attire, Evan made the rounds. At his side, Solange wore a shocking-pink designer gown with hair in a tight French twist. Gold decorating her throat and ears, she beamed as the couple made pleasantries with guests.

Régine wore white. Her hair a mound atop her head, she was fresh out of a boutique, with eyes overly made up and swaying hips so as to catch the nod of all the gentlemen. She targeted the notable business people first, from the head of Cartier to the managing director of a division of the Poste. She gushed at their comments and insisted she was well trained, eclipsing any notion of the traditional business tycoon. Giles promised all present that he was in perfect health yet felt it best to not 'drop on his feet' either. He maintained Evan and Régine were a team with which to reckon and gave the impression he was more confident than ever.

Two journalists were invited, one from the *Figaro*, the other from *France-Soir*. The press was curious, this change in command being so far afield from expectations. Indeed, since Evan had taken on a part-time function, and with his know-how out of 'X', his future had already been the subject of published articles. A certain degree of change—reshuffling of management or focus on other areas—might prove the correct strategy. But to have a woman alongside him and for Giles to step down?

The reporters interviewed Giles and Régine who, without going into detail, assured them that profits would improve, even in the coal area—an issue the journalists did not neglect to bring up. More than once, the two expounded on the fact that there was not an inkling of anything outside a well-formulated restructuring behind the arrangement. After much questioning, the journalists had to admit the proposal had its merits, and gave every indication their articles would contain positive slants. The party in full swing, any initially doubtful onlookers fell in step with the festivities, a tacit concession to the reorganization about to take hold.

Evan, however, spoke only when addressed. He'd hoped Régine's fanciful idea would blow over. Instead, it had blown out of proportion. The first hints of irrevocableness came once she made a personal, uninvited visit to headquarters shortly after the September dinner.

Interrupting Evan's meeting, she had strolled in wearing a bright red Chanel suit, a wide-rimmed black hat, and hair bouncing at her shoulders like a school girl. Settling amongst the attendees, she listened for a while then began making suggestions. Evan had no option but to terminate the gathering and make excuses for Régine. Put out, she had complained to Giles who told Evan she was welcome at any meeting.

Evan began to suspect Giles was losing his faculties. A hard fact to face about one's father, it nevertheless was the only explanation why someone of Régine's limited abilities could make headway into Giles hallowed enterprise.

A few days following the party, he exploded to Giles.

"It's preposterous, Papa! She knows nothing, has never as much as glanced at a balance sheet let alone formulated one! We lost an entire afternoon last week while she lunched at Maxim's due to a birthday of one of the senior managers. It's out of hand already."

"Evan, lower your voice in this house. How many times must I tell you, Régine is worthy of a chance!"

"You're not there! You don't see she does nothing, except travel around the country spending the company's money! What they think of her in Alsace— all those macho miners and the like—I can imagine!"

"Here, Evan!" Giles retorted, his face red, his hands clutching the arms of his chair. "That's enough!"

The silence permitted a temporary settling of nerves. Betti pattered in and cleared coffee cups then left. Evan went to the window overlooking the garden.

Slowly, with less fire, he said, "I simply don't understand, Papa."

"Son, she holds a degree from Harvard. Although it's the States, it's still a reputable institution. I'm surprised at you! You who were once so eager to embrace American business practices. How can you ignore her talents, they're of the same strain as you've been proposing, no? Expansion, international cooperation, Common Market agendas?"

"But that's what I mean. Nothing of the sort is transpiring within de Roche Frères. In the weeks she's been around, progress has stalled!"

Giles moved to the window and placed an arm around his son. The two stared out. On the tip of Evan's tongue was one question: why didn't Giles marry the woman, for that was what she really wanted?

Giles returned to the chair behind his desk. His father cleared his throat and tapped fingers on the blotter. "Evan, my son, sit."

Evan pulled a chair up across from Giles.

"Do you really think I have forgotten your mother?" he asked. "I have not. Your mother was the finest partner a man could ever hope to have—and she chose me." Giles's eyes glimmered. "You didn't know how many men chased her, how many promised her much more than I ever could. Your mother had plenty of options!

"We lived a life, mon cher, a life of happiness few know. I can't impress my love of her on you, it goes beyond words. But, I'll tell you this, it has yet to die. I still love your mother."

Evan lowered his head. With a sad pleasure he listened to his father, for it had been a long time since the two spoke of Pauline.

"Régine has been wonderful for me—an old retiring man, with money. I know she is a contrast to your mother, Evan. I know this, for I too had to adjust to her in my life. After all these years? Do you think I have welcomed women easily? No! I've resisted them, dear son, and Régine has been patient for over two years.

"Try and see her as I do. She brightens my day. I have grown to appreciate her energy and her ability to adapt. Remember, she also experienced the pain of death. I knew Nate briefly, he was a treasure of his own kind. Imagine what she went through in some desolate place with a child to rear, unable to find someone with whom she could fully share her life. And now, she has come to Paris and turned her situation around. It hasn't been easy. I respect her.

"Perhaps this will all take time, this reorganization. I am not dead yet, Evan. I will prevail when you and she disagree. My input plays into any major decision. You are the future, and so is Régine. I have laid down my wishes and they shall remain. Do you understand?"

Evan nodded. "Yes."

"Good. Patience, my son. Change takes time, new faces are sometimes hard to welcome but often necessary. I myself have resisted change in the past, no? Hey, hey, you and I are made of the same stuff! Régine is a breath of fresh air, for me and for the company. We will take our time with her, welcome her. I cannot give her marriage, my son, but I can accommodate. I do love her for who she is..."

He took off his glasses and pulled out a handkerchief, rubbed and turned to face the garden.

"But your mother, no, your mother has no replacement. *Ma Pauline vit toujours au fond de mon coeur...*"

Evan fought tears. His frustration placated, he rose, went to his father, and leaned his head on his shoulder. The garden was brown and grey with patches of snow. Giles placed an arm around Evan, then returned to his chair.

"We understand one another?" he asked.

"Yes, Papa," Evan said.

"Good. It is time for me to prepare for Régine. We're dining with friends tonight."

Giles left and Evan sat in his father's chair, staring at the pens and paper, the ashtray and lamp.

The photo had never been mentioned or replaced. He wondered why Giles never asked for it, wondered if he should continue to guard it in his room. He opened a side drawer where a small lock box sat. It was Giles's spare change and Evan was free to dip into it if he needed to. It went back to the days when Giles initiated his son in the careful use of money. Evan smiled recollecting the times he'd sat on his father's lap and listened to how the box was to be opened with a special key, how only certain sums of money would be there, how Evan was supposed to ask before taking. All had been the first steps towards his future as the purveyor of the family fortune.

Years had passed since he even opened the drawer. He was about to close it when he caught sight of another object. In the back was the chiffon scarf Pauline wore on the day of her death. Torn and browned, it was wrapped in a plastic bag, air tight and neatly squared. He reached for it, unwrapped, and pressed the cloth to his cheek.

"Mama, Mama," he said, envisioning her gaze as it used to settle on him before he went to sleep as a child. "We're so lost without you."

It comforted him to know Giles still held to the souvenir, for it symbolized what Giles had said in so many words—that duplicating Pauline was an impossible task. He replaced the material in its wrap and nudged it to the far end of the drawer. Rising, he left the study.

# Chapter 14:
# London, 17 March 1971

Dear Claire,

I haven't heard from you in a while and I hope you're keeping well. Today is St. Patrick's Day and I remember you writing about singing at the pubs there. I hope you have fun and maybe you'll dress in green this time?

My address has changed as you can see. My friend has switched jobs and I'm in council housing (a lady friend lets me a room). The payment is cheaper but the heat is ever so dear. I'm glad spring is around the corner. I work at a clothing shop for older women. They're mostly on the dole and fret about spending a penny more than they have to. I wonder why they even bother sometimes. They leave without a word of thanks and often empty-handed. Life is tough at times, isn't it?

Love, Mum

London, 20 April 1971

Dear Claire,

Spring is here, it's not warm, still wet. I work all the time and have no fun except walks during my days off. Thanks be, I have my job. Many people are losing theirs. Of course, few would put up with what I do. Mrs. Gregory is a fright and as much of a miser as these customers. She tolerates me because I keep my mouth shut and work for near nothing.

You must be busy with school. I'm so proud of you and wish you'd write so I can keep up with your news. I do so enjoy your letters.

Take care.

Love, Mum

Alice pushed open the front door and looked to the mail on floor. In vain, her eyes scanned the envelopes for Claire's yellow stationary. She slammed the door and trudged upstairs to change.

The day had been long as usual, but this time, with the spring sales, she'd been on her feet the entire time. She changed into robe, dirty blue mules, and scuffed to the kitchen for tea and some left over chips. The kettle on, she rubbed her hands, and stoked the fire's embers in search of a spark.

In the corner, she wrapped a few pieces of coal into her robe then unraveled them into the fireplace. She lit a match and threw it in. Her stomach growled and her eyes burned from a cold she had been fighting. Her jaw tightened and her lips pursed as chills ran from her toes to her thighs.

Where was Claire and why hadn't she written? For months, Alice figured the lack of letters was due to her change of residence, that once Claire learned of the new address a stack would arrive. But, save a card at Christmas, none had shown.

She rubbed her shoulders. Could Claire know of all this? No, impossible. Unless her daughter journeyed to England, there was no one to tell her of her mother's desperate situation.

Having taken up with a woman years younger than Alice, Harry was long gone. He'd practically booted her out of the place last year, so enamored was he of his new tart. The two had barged in one evening while Alice sat in front of the television. Drunk and obviously in lust, they'd plopped themselves right in front of her and began kissing.

"And here I am waiting night after night for ye while all ye're up to is foolin' around with some cow!" she'd yelled after he followed her upstairs and hinted at the fact she was no longer welcome. "How in the world am I goin' to make do what with you hardly payin' me a penny and I've no work to speak of?"

Harry had shrugged, his mind elsewhere.

She'd packed and was gone in an hour. The first night she stayed with a neighbor but, not wishing to appear destitute, left the next day. It had taken a week to find living quarters she could afford and she was only able to sign a lease once she had employment.

Back to a Dublin existence once again—long days at a dull job, longer nights alone. Harry had disappeared, his promises with him, his security a thing of the past. She had no one to lean on, not even her boss or a friend down the street. It was a city where you were trusted if a long time resident or spoke in their accent. An aging Irish woman with no money who worked at a second-hand ladies store was lamentable, not worthy of a second glance.

She had to vent somehow, yet had felt bad begging Claire to write, and now wished she'd never posted the letter. But a part of her was anxious to see if her daughter would respond. And she hadn't. The holiday card contained a few Irish words that Alice couldn't understand and that was it.

If Claire missed her mother, she wasn't expressing it in words. Her next letter unanswered, Alice felt more anger than sorrow. There was Claire, off in America, making money and having the time of her life with other young people who had futures and lived in a place where they could succeed barely trying. Off singing and dancing she was, thought Alice, showing her pretty smile and leaving the lads drooling.

She probably had a man, like that Benny in Dublin, someone who really cared, unlike what Alice had known in her life. Claire was set, and she'd forgotten her mother. It made Alice want to throw things. But she stared at the lapping flames and absorbed the heat, for to waste energy was careless right now. She had to conserve her strength and get rest, take care the cold didn't worsen so she could make it through one more day, to the next paycheck and some food in her mouth. Angry thoughts could prove her undoing.

"Damn you, child," she whispered. She quickly covered her mouth. "Oh, Claire, baby, I'm so sorry, I don't mean to make little of all your work. It's so hard for me right now, so hard you could never understand. You're young now, aren't ye?"

# Chapter 15:
# April, 1971

THURSDAYS, KLEE SANG SOLO, a decision Johnny had made. Since the change, standing room only was typical.

As she sang, he would serve drinks, wearing his jeans and vest outfit, the one she said made him look like a cowboy. Most often, she wore the maroon outfit he had encouraged her to buy at a shop on Newbury Street. Though she'd balked at the price, she went in and tried it on as a favor to him. He reveled in the memory, a day they had spent together booking gigs.

The material shimmered, a one-piece pantsuit. The wide-lapel jacket had long sleeves with slits to the elbows, and opened so as to expose the curve of her breasts. She looked a child at the same time she was very much a woman. In the store mirrors she was a slim thing with an awkward regard. In the dimly-lit club, a brooding beauty. He'd been right to suggest she buy it.

Tingling at the thought of having her nearby for the entire evening, he poured whiskeys for customers. Earlier, she sent him a note, a just-for-fun back-and-forth in which they regularly indulged. It was written in Gaelic. With a wink, she challenged him to decipher its meaning, knowing full well he was incapable. Later, she translated for him. With her odd low chuckle and thick brows, she said, "It's from Yeats: *Be careful and do not seek to know too much about us.*"

He memorized the line. She had such a way when she spoke Gaelic, more engaged than her singing and much more seductive. From the very first, when she'd thrown out a "Sláinte" after sipping a cup of tea, he loved her sounds.

Since then, they had grown closer and jointly planned stints at his bar. She had solid ideas and a sixth sense about bands and their talents. There were those who were in it for the money and those who were gifted but required exposure. She preferred the latter profile and, having already shown herself capable of discerning between the two, Johnny often let her decide who would provide backup music.

She kept up with groups passing through town. Many a time she called him from campus with word of yet another band worthy of a look. He marveled at how she maintained her studies and sang into all hours of the night.

But, as much as she allowed him a peek at her nature, she thrived on her privacy. Once when he asked her out to dinner, she told him no because she was "not interested in love affairs." Her frankness surprised him but, after thinking it over, he appreciated her honesty. Many women he'd known, or heard about from friends, turned a guy down by lying. Johnny welcomed her up-front style and, because she'd been so gracious, didn't consider their friendship challenged.

He didn't overstep his bounds again and made do by driving her home during foul weather, meeting for an interview or two, and seeing her at the club. After their Sunday through Wednesday separation, she greeted him cheerily and updated him with school stories. Their game of quotations had come about when she suggested he take part-time courses. He said no, so she began teaching him a thing or two on her own. He loved the attention. In his mind, they were lovers, though he'd never dare let on to Klee.

At the club, he was on the lookout for any man who might show the slightest interest, which was often. Johnny fumed when they eyed her, even the most innocently enchanted ones. Klee's statement to him about disinterest in love affairs held for any other man too, but that didn't suppress his jealousy. Johnny couldn't resist shoving a too eager onlooker to one side and reminding him the lady was taken. When youngsters waited for her after hours, he would tell them she was going home with him, and secretly derive pleasure from their wounded looks.

She was easing into his heart and, in her presence, he had all he could do to keep his emotions under wrap. The dinner date refusal having been a nod to her preference for solitude, he knew she would quickly tire of an infatuated man begging her for time together. Klee was not to be tampered with.

Now he ruminated over her note and thought how much it fit with her personality and ways. No surprise there was a hidden message there. Whoever Yeats was, the man's words bespoke her own feelings. The note had been another playful and less hurtful way of telling him to keep away.

He sighed as he looked at her. He wanted to know her every secret, for there were many in her busy head, and she was holding onto them like life lines and for reasons unknown.

She'd have surely quit if she knew how much he thought of her. At home she was constantly on his mind. Lying on the couch or in bed and sleepless, he visited their interactions, a portrait of her black dress and curls the night they met solidly ingrained, her deep gaze transfixing. He wanted so badly to claim her. However, he knew well the very thing he wanted most would surely draw them the furthest apart.

How odd her ways, he thought many a time. He could understand her reluctance to date him. He was, after all, who he was. But the other young men, some handsome and better-educated, why didn't they rank a date or two? Hers was a singular life, one few twenty-year-olds would be proud of. And yet, she thrived, or seemed to.

Possessed of her and chained by her was Johnny. He loved the feeling, embraced the moments, and would cherish their tomorrows for as long as he had them.

She wasn't going to let anyone promote her. Johnny had made the mistake of suggesting cutting a record once and she let him have it. "No! Never, Johnny, that's my final word! I sing for you, I sing for the crowd here, but that's it."

"But Klee, baby, your voice is a winner. You know that don't you?"

"I sing for a living, I make a good living."

"You can make a better one..."

They stared one another down, a signal that barriers had been crossed.

"It's like I say, Johnny. No records. End of it!" She turned from the bar, threw coat over her shoulder, and nodded farewell.

"Klee, don't get upset. I was only asking..." he said, fretting her departure more than her anger.

She turned, tipped her hat. "It's Okay, Johnny. But heed my words."

"Okay, baby," he grinned sheepishly. "Do not seek to know too much about us. I hear ya, babe!"

"See you next week."

# Chapter 16:
# July, 1971

"Laurence," Don yelled, waving. "We're taking a break. Get in here!"

Stroking towards him, she grabbed the boat's step ladder and asked, "What's up?"

"It's getting late. We have enough footage for today. Plus, I've got to run these swimmers back to town."

"Okay," she said, flipping wet hair onto her back and easing aboard.

Don revved the engine. Two men and Laurence made up the team of photographers and swimmers in what was turning into a discovery of not only the waters around Nantucket but also the rudiments of film-making. Far from shore and onlookers, they shot footage of more unique varieties of fish. Laurence planned to edit the film with voice-over and music. She was adamant that they capture the commonplace fish as well as the more unusual types she'd observed during previous expeditions.

After weeks of planning, they took to the sea. Until the air in the tanks ran out, they worked—figuring equipment needs, attending to weather and boating dictates, calculating lighting requirements, all the while instructing volunteers.

This time, for cost reasons and because Don could only take one week off from work, they would do as much as possible in five days, then evaluate the results. If necessary, they could squeeze in a few weekends.

Having picked up photography basics from a friend of Bea, Laurence filmed the lion's portion. Her preferred method was diving in and trying techniques as opposed to planning above water. One couldn't stage the sea's secrets.

The first day, the results were adequate and gave them a sense of how to better capture certain species in a given light. The murky waters were a major issue. At a depth of more than twenty feet, it was dark enough to require assistance from artificial light. The initial results had revealed barely a trace of what Laurence shot. The next day, they had to re-shoot, but by then they'd acquired better lighting. Also, an underwater photographer who was summering on the island volunteered to help.

The third day proved a long one. The weather was perfect and the sea calm. They had guided the boat along the coast to the eastern shore then headed seaward until the island disappeared from sight. In no time, a school of dolphins greeted them, jumping high in the air, already portending a great sequence. Later, the crew spotted several sand sharks and the occasional sunfish, their black triangular fins twirling at the water's surface. They even filmed the passage of a few minke whales who, for a time, swam alongside the boat.

As they returned to the harbor, Don cracked open beers and passed them around. Exhausted, the crew soon slumped against the side boards, still in their life jackets, and snoozed. Not Laurence. She studied the approaching shoreline, eager to get going with editing, her lips already pursing into a game-day concentration. Tomorrow, she would waken Bea, scurry from the cottage, and make for the splicing table. As opposed to the others, who for the most part considered this a distraction, hers was a one-pointed focus. She wanted to make a living from film.

From the second she dove into the water during those Christmas holidays, her veins coursed with the sea. As she engaged with the currents, her land-bound concerns dissolved. Though Don and Pete had grasped her enthusiasm for scuba diving, neither could possibly have fathomed the extent of her joy. Since the debacle with Pierre, she had denied herself the one activity capable of reviving her and providing strength. The dive in, a split second underwater, and she was released. Home again.

"I can't wait to see the footage of the whales," Laurence said to Don.

At the pier, as they collected equipment, he studied her closely. "Hey, I've detected an accent. Are you French?"

"No," she said avoiding his gaze.

"I didn't think so. Mallord, well, that's not French from what I can tell."

"Huh?"

"Your name is Mallord, isn't it?'

She bit her lip. "How did you know?"

"I asked around. I hope you're not offended," he said.

Don had been more than helpful in the past months, a generous and kind friend. Laurence had trouble getting perturbed over his curiosity.

"I suppose it was a bit foolish to think it could stay a secret for long," she finally said.

"Why in the world keep it secret? Nate Mallord's daughter, and the way you work down there?" he asked pointing to the water. "It's something to brag about!"

"You know I'm Nate's daughter?"

"I put two and two together. Pete told me some months ago about a letter from France addressed to a Laurence Mallord. At the time, no one at the post office knew your last name and he and I didn't know you at all, except by sight. It sat in the dead pile for a while. Last week, Pete was clearing things away and saw it again. We got to speculating, what with Nate being from Woods Hole years back and you telling me you scuba'd as a child. Mallord is legend here. You take to the waters the same way. Anyhow, Pete told me he'd get the letter to you."

"A letter..."

"Sure. So, if you're not French, you have friends there, right?"

She nodded, her gaze scanning the bay. "Perhaps I'll get to Pete tomorrow."

"Do that. You Okay?"

"It's nothing, Don. Thanks."

"Pleasure. Always." They said good-night.

When the post office opened the next day, Laurence was at the door. The letter was from Mémé, from a full year prior. Although Laurence had placed no return address on her correspondence, Mémé was astute enough to send a response in care of the Nantucket post office.

The letter was brief and newsy. Mémé spelled out the previous summer's activities with Uncle Georges and Aunt Chantel, updated her on the gardens, and Evan who was good company. She sent her love.

Laurence folded the letter. Her thoughts had returned many times to Mémé, and she was glad to know her grandmother was keeping up. Mémé had not mentioned Régine. She hoped the woman was still in France, but wondered at the same time whose minds her mother was warping now—Giles? Mémé? Or had she made her way to Evan, that man who had been so polite on the rocks at Batz?

She walked towards the piers and another day of filming, the letter folded neatly in her pocket.

By week's end, the first cut was complete. They had over two hours of footage with plans to fine-tune and, if required, return to the sea for more. Friday night, the team dined at the cottage, a drawn-out affair prepared by Sage: sole, lobster, wine and fresh breads. After, they crowded around the living room couch as Don readied the camera and others sipped digestifs. Laurence stood by his side, watching with a nervous smile, her energies piquing.

Into the first ten minutes, there was no doubt they had done a good job. Numerous long shots of schools of fish were broken by the arrival of a larger, more ominous-looking part-fish, part-crustacean. They had captured many of the local species, and even had close-ups of area rock formations on the sea floor.

The dolphin and whale sequences added drama, the slinking eels and even one rough tail stingray enhanced the fluid magic and mystery, communicating that the island, though quaint and approachable during summer, was at other times a veritable force with which to be reckoned.

Hours later, they toasted their success and discussed the voice-over and music sequences to come. Laurence was adamant that they use one or several of Sage's piano scores. As it was still summer, Sage had little free time but promised to have a rough cut ready for Laurence by the end of September.

"She's got that one and only '*je ne sais quoi*' voice!" Don laughed, toasting her one more time as she stood to one side of the camera.

"Geez, Don," Laurence said. "Bea and Sage are as talented."

"Sage?" laughed Bea, patting her partner's back. "Not with her smoker's cough and crackly tone! She can compose but her voice, well..."

"Now, Bea," Sage said. "Enough. You take any opportunity to cajole at me for smoking..."

"Bad! It's death, my love!" Bea exclaimed.

Before their banter swelled into an argument, Laurence said, "Okay, Okay, I'll do it. It's better than listening to you two argue!"

"Good," said Don. "The best lady for the job. Lady Bea does her docs, lady Sage her music. Now let's get this other talent into the limelight!" He winked at Laurence.

By 2 AM most of the crew had left. The pound of the waves and the clang of wind chimes broke the stillness as Don and Laurence walked to his Jeep. "Thanks for everything, Don. Without you, this couldn't have been possible."

He threw a pile of papers in the back and hauled himself up. "You were the brains behind all this." His eyes fell on her and for the first time she returned a relaxed smile.

"That's what I like," he said, "When you unwrap yourself."

"What?"

"You're one of the most charming ladies I have ever met and yet you let so few people in."

Laurence's eyes were sad even as her smile remained.

"You, lady, you!" he said, winking once again and starting the engine. "I'm not trying to trespass, but now we're finished with the serious stuff, I had to say it. From now on, let's enjoy the process—contacting the world to help us market this thing, you doing the voice over, Sage the music. The essentials are recorded for all time." He leaned forward a bit. "Perhaps now you can ease up. Unwind. Like the rest of us. That's what Nantucket's all about—the grey lady—a place to let yourself go!"

She forced her smile wider. "I hear you, Don. And thanks. A million."

He tipped his baseball hat. "Can't convince you to have a beer with me tomorrow night, I'll bet?"

She shook her head.

His face broke into the same sympathetic smile he'd worn every day since they said hello at Porpus. "Can't blame a guy for trying!" With a toot of his horn and a flash of his lights, he drove away.

Pepper sniffed at her side. "You!" she exclaimed rubbing his ears. "You're happy they've all gone, I bet, old Pep! C'mon, let's walk."

After, she returned to the house. Wide awake, she sat at the kitchen table and stared at the centerpiece of fruit, wrapped cheeses, and a half-full bottle of wine. Mémé came to mind, the woman who had nudged her towards one of her dreams and who gave of herself so that Laurence might achieve. How many others since her departure from Roscoff had lent of themselves to help her along? And Bea and Sage most of all, the two to whom she owed her very spirit. A year before, it would have seemed preposterous to imagine doing what they'd completed. Now, the adventure was well underway.

Hearing the echo of her father's memory in the waves, she whispered, "Dad, you'd be proud! It's going to be a super film!" She found some writing paper and brought it to the table. Pen in hand, she began, "Dear Mémé, I have finally received your letter..."

313

# Chapter 17:
# August, 1971

EVAN HAD TWO THINGS TO ACCOMPLISH during summer holidays—a visit to Mémé on Batz, then a stay with his father. Giles had purchased an estate on the Côte d'Azur and, for the first summer in decades, the house on Batz remained closed. When Régine announced this to Evan, his initial shock had turned quickly to anger. Another conquest was hers.

For over a year, she'd been begging Giles to purchase. When he hesitated, she complained of the cool weather on Batz and pleaded over and over for a warmer retreat, but her efforts proved futile. Finally, she began scouting out properties on her own. Each month she left Paris for a long weekend, returning to announce several towns with spacious homes on hectares of land for prices that warranted attention. Giles listened half-interested, adhering to his belief that Batz was the retreat for him. Should Régine wish for warmth, they could vacation in the south every now and then.

But Régine persevered. During work hours, rather than attend to business, she engaged in lengthy phone conversations with estate agents and acquaintances from the southern towns of interest. In his nearby office, Evan could hear her, as she introduced herself as Madame de

314

Long and claimed a close association with Giles de Roche. She more than once gushed over a recently available property, supposedly owned by Italian or French royalty.

When coal production issues arose, she sought Evan's assistance. Numerous times he tried to explain the inevitable decline in the industry. In his estimation, it was more important that de Roche Frères cut losses rather than nurse the ailing business. Nevertheless she insisted on making a trip to Alsace where she met with union leaders who scoffed at any suggestion she made to encourage organizing.

She had a singular focus when it came to the company—keep revenue on the rise. The businesses in Alsace had yet to show losses so she planned to scrape off the profits and ignore any threat.

On his own, Evan put wheels in motion to sell off the unhealthy sectors. But as soon as Régine heard this, she complained to Giles. She felt they should wait for the government to issue a death knoll before de Roche Frères threw in the towel. Giles agreed.

Evan fumed as he drove through the streets of Roscoff. She was more in the way now than ever and he'd begun to dread going to de Roche Frères. To watch her flounce about, flirt, and crowd his space was a scant motivator. If not for Giles and his decision to step down, Evan might have left for Batz in late June, to get away from it all for the summer. But, to leave the company in her hands would be courting disaster.

At Batz, he exited from the ferry launch and headed to the other side of the island. He was not surprised to see the garden overgrown and the house as quiet as a tomb. But on noticing Mémé seated at the edge of one of the benches, her feet amidst entangled weeds, he couldn't suppress a sharp intake of breath.

The winds were off shore and she didn't hear him right away. He watched the lady in black sitting as if a statue—gaze on the water, head slightly bend, a hand on the cane she now carried everywhere.

How had it happened? So lovely a place, now so forlorn. On Batz he had always felt rejuvenated. The meticulous property, the exquisite gardens, the sea air easing its way through the windows and into the kitchen or dining room. How dismal now, even as the sun shone and light reflected off the waves.

"Mémé," he called, approaching.

She turned and waved. They embraced. Her cheeks grew rosier as she delved into details of the summer, how her nieces and nephews had come and gone with all their children, how longtime friends had stopped by as usual, how Betti—who had refused to go south—had been such a help. She and the maid walked regularly and Mémé was taking two naps a day. Her appetite was better and she found the fish tastier than in Paris.

"It's been a lovely summer. I only wish we had year-round neighbors!" She grinned at Evan.

"Me, too," he said, trying to be cheerful, but distracted by the weeds and dead buds, the geranium sprouts from the year before, the few that had managed to produce red and pink blooms.

"Now, Evan, you must remember time moves forward whether we want it to or not. Next year your father will return. He will always love Batz first. It isn't sold, he simply wanted time in the south."

"Régine wanted time in the south," he said. "Sorry."

Mémé chuckled. "Don't be. I know you've had trouble with Régine. I can tell she's being difficult." She pulled out an envelope, pink with red, white, and blue airmail stamps. "Here, this will cheer you."

Evan opened it and instantly he was transformed to Laurence's island, her work, and her life by the sea. Her film. A grin creased into one side of his mouth as he read her story of piecing the entire work together over the summer. Her elegant script and choice of words brought her back to him and he relived their interaction on Batz. He read and re-read, then handed it to Mémé.

"To complete a film in that amount of time is no small feat. She's fortunate and gifted."

Mémé nodded, placed the letter in her pocket. "You didn't pass time with her but, I assure you, our Laurence is going places. I'm glad to hear the States are treating her well. To hear Régine, one would think it a hell hole."

"Absolutely not!" Evan exclaimed. "There are many opportunities there. I've kept up with Americans living in Paris. It's a great place. Laurence was wise to return."

"She's a smart girl. I miss her. She could have stayed long enough to make good at the institute."

"She seems to have made good anyway."

"Yes, child. Come now, let's walk. The gardens are a disaster but the paths are still there. My legs need exercise."

They strolled then joined Betti for a meal. Until late they caught up, Evan sharing his thoughts on the government and the economy, Mémé listening and offering advice. Evan tried his best to be upbeat and to forget the negative force that was Régine.

After Mémé retired, Evan begged off Betti's invitation to stay the night and chose instead the house next door. Before settling in, he had to tear down protective, exterior boards. It was cool and damp inside, but he found blankets and opened a windows so he was comfortable enough. As he attempted sleep, thoughts of Laurence and her letter kept him awake and busy in his mind. Even on paper, she had a way. Odd, they'd never exchanged two words. He reminded himself to buy a map of the U. S. and research the island of Nantucket.

♥ ♥ ♥

A week later, he was in Cassis, the fashionable coastal town southeast of Marseille. Plush homes protruded off chalky cliffs that tumbled to the Mediterranean. The village proper boasted a main street with cafés, clanging moored boats and gift shops. A few kilometers from town, Giles and Régine lived in seclusion. Their chateau stood at the top of a hill that commanded a view of the sea and distant mountains. From the fourth floor, one saw straight to Africa, and the sound of larger swells crashing against the rocks rose to echo within.

An infinity pool, tennis and bocce courts, maids bustling, and an entryway worthy of the Ritz made the place a country club. Save the stone foundation and basic structure, the entire building had been renovated. The smell of fresh wood panels and painted walls pervaded and it was impossible to ignore the glitz of made-to-order marble pieces or the designer furniture. The Italian flair of the arcades and gallerias, the sumptuous spreads of regional cuisine, the hot sun—all in all a magazine-style Mediterranean abode.

Giles and Régine lounged poolside, she wearing practically nothing, Giles sporting white. "Oh, Evan, don't be silly!" Régine exclaimed on hearing he was only staying the night. "The Lemuires come tomorrow. You have to stay! Solange will be disappointed..."

"Someone has to manage the business," he said, ignoring her caressing hand as it slipped down his back.

Giles asked Régine if he couldn't have some time alone with his son. Régine huffed but exited.

Evan looked at his father, asked with his eyes the same question—why in the world he did such a thing as buy this ostentatious place rather than settle for Batz?

Giles was not interested in Evan's anger, only requested Evan hold his sharp tongue when in Régine's presence.

"But, Papa..."

"Son, how many times must we have this conversation? I'll not have you being unkind to her."

"She's incapable of running the business, Papa. And I cannot see to affairs properly if she continues. Nothing is getting accomplished."

"The company is doing well. I see the reports."

"For the time being, Papa. But I can't anticipate growth what with the situation in Alsace. A decision is necessary."

Giles studied the pool waters. "You speak a truth, Evan. But it's a tricky call. We must be patient."

"Papa..."

"Enough. We'll discuss when I return to Paris. For now, enjoy your vacation. You need the rest." Giles settled in his lounge chair and closed his eyes. "Tell me now, when are you proposing marriage to the Lemuire's daughter?"

Evan's brow furrowed. "I have no plans."

"You should think about it. I married your mother when not much older than you."

"It's different these days."

"Because young people take to sleeping around more? You think that changes families like the de Roches and the Lemuires?"

"I don't understand."

"Son, your father might be old but he's not stupid. I know how close you and Solange are."

Evan wrung his hands, knowing it could only be Régine's idle chatter that had Giles thinking Solange was the love of his life. He stood. "Papa, with respect, it's my choice. I have no intentions."

"Think about it. It's important for you to plan for a judicious and complimentary union."

Evan found his way upstairs, his head full of hostile words but his heart choosing to avoid confrontation. His father had fallen into a habit of not hearing when he didn't wish to. At the top of the stairs, Régine waited. She now wore a short black dress and espadrilles, her hair in a ponytail, her nails lacquered as usual.

"So, you've been with Mémé," she sneered. "I hope Betti doesn't miss us too much."

"She didn't speak of you," he said.

One thing she didn't have over him was insight into his own mind, and he knew at the moment it was his one armament. The longer he remained silent, the more it bothered her. In reality he had no defense, nor had he the slightest inclination to engage with her. She played dirty, drawing on Giles's weaknesses and her own apparent collectedness to create an image of control over anyone, including Evan. He had grown weary of this game but sensed she, having prevailed on the issue of Batz and the coal mining strategy, was even more motivated. She would continue to pester him, try to staunch his resiliency, sap him of willingness to cooperate, until he succumbed to her demands. Blow by subtle blow, she wore her enemies down. Not inclined to take on her kind, he sensed the contours of his own limitations, even as he fought to keep her guessing.

Still, he was not Giles. He would not comply readily. With her, he tread lightly, the two of them sniffing out which way a thought was heading, trying to outsmart the other in the quest for the upper hand. He was already entrenched in the coal and steel battle with her. Would he join her in others? Or would he lay down his arms?

He didn't know the answers but he possessed one trump card.

Mémé had broached the subject on Batz, wondering aloud to Evan how in the world Régine could possibly ignore Laurence for so long. Many times, Mémé told him, she had spoken of her granddaughter and as many times Régine had returned with an injurious remark. Laurence was a good for nothing, a user of people, masking behind a pretty face and causing ill for others— Régine's words against her own flesh and blood.

"I'm not sure what it is, Evan," Mémé had said, "But Uncle Georges was certain the two had a falling out. I can't imagine what the disagreement could be—they're mother and daughter after all."

As he looked into Régine's eyes now, he wanted to boast about Laurence's film.

Régine's eyes bore holes, trying equally to seduce and slay him. Two could play at her game. He was no stranger to it, only a disinterested observer of what families like his drew great pleasure in—tripping up those in their way, especially when financial security was threatened.

"Where is your daughter?" he asked.

She paused, turned until her back faced him. Placing a hand on her behind, slowly with her nails, she traced one side of her dress. She eased her head around, smirked. "Who?"

He raised his chin, eyes narrowing. "You should ask such a question."

She hid her face again. Her shoulders drooped slightly. Then, abruptly she turned and faced him with a plaintive stare. "Darling Laurence! How I miss her so!"

"Where is she then?"

"Oh, Evan dear, how I wish I knew...Excuse me, I must get a cigarette..." She made an effort to pass him. He pinched her elbow and drew her inches from his face.

"Do you?"

"You're hurting me."

"Do you want to know where she is?"

She turned away. "Really, Evan, dear, I would think it a detail to you, what with Solange and all. Anyway, I'm sure she's in the States..."

"So, you don't know."

"I didn't say that."

"Listen, you," she said, wrestling free. "I know for sure she's keeping busy with all her men friends. That's the way she is and..."

"Shut up! Liar!" Evan grit his teeth and would not let her pass. Nearing her face again he said, "One good thing is she's miles from you."

"Why, what do you mean?"

"You know what I mean."

He passed Régine and turned down another hall.

# Chapter 18:
# August 1971

ALL SUMMER, KLEE WORKED EXTRA HOURS at
Johnny's to save money for school. She knew which
ones provided the best fulltime curriculum and teachers
and, while there were many fine institutions across the
country, she focused on Boston. The University of
Massachusetts offered language courses and reputed
professors, and boasted a decent reputation. It was
affordable, especially for state residents. She applied to
a general studies program. Given her temporary
residency, she would require loans. It therefore made
sense to squirrel away every dime until she could cover
the first year. Should she be accepted, she would then
quit Johnny's and devote herself to her passion.

Impressed with her record, an advisor suggested she
make an appointment with the director of Celtic studies.
References made a big difference as to who was
accepted. In no time, the director—an elderly man of
Irish descent—grasped her expertise of Gaelic. He
received her warmly and they even bantered in Gaelic,
something Klee had not done since her days with
Romney. The director promised to put in a good word.

Johnny was happy to oblige her request for
additional hours and, nights without entertainment, he

323

put her on tables. She worked seven days a week—four singing, three as waitress. Though wearying of carting trays and taking orders, she kept her goal in mind and focused on loftier plans.

The club became her home away from home, with Johnny like a parent. Their camaraderie bloomed into a closeness she began to feel a need for those times he wasn't around, for together they kept one another's spirits up.

"Go for it," he often said, "you deserve the best."

She reveled in his words more than his longing stares. He had a way of taking her in that challenged what belief she might have that the relationship was platonic. He was taken by her and she knew it yet tried to downplay his advances, even once letting on she wasn't interested in a relationship. Over time, he relaxed his wanton look and handled himself more like a friend, or mentor.

His suggestion to cut a record was followed by her adamant refusal. Afterwards, they settled into a rhythm where each knew the rules, especially their boundaries.

She allowed him to drive her home nights, and helped out with band selections. She didn't care to promote herself in an over-arching way and he was not to push. He tried every now and then—by telling her he would like to record her voice for his personal benefit—but she glared back. He introduced her to some of his friends and asked if she would like to join them at a baseball game or boat ride around the harbor. She never went.

He kept trying and she kept refusing. It became a harmless game, Klee anticipating his requests and returning the odd quip or retort that kept him smiling, in spite of her negative response.

Though she sometimes wished to socialize more, her mind said no. It was not her way to stray about with people. Too much time had passed during which she'd had to focus on survival. It was now indispensable to do as she chose. Her life was finally of her own making and she wished to better mold it. Because of her penchant for languages, she bypassed even the briefest stretches of idleness. Unlike others, diversion meant an entirely different thing to Klee.

Study was her realm. She couldn't step beyond. An inexplicable void was filled when occupied with her studies.

Mornings, she drilled herself on work from the night before, taking self-prepared quizzes and reciting over and over those words, phrases, or declensions she'd missed. On her way to Johnny's, she carried slips of paper with lists of verbs. No matter what language, verbs kept her challenged. Nouns had modifiers but once the gender was learned, she could recall them with ease. Verbs, however, changed tense or form often and for no good reason. Verbs were tricky and she didn't fancy being baffled by them. To master them, therefore, would take all her free time—and if she had her way, her entire life.

Italian was sonorous, like her music with Paolo. Gaelic went to the depth of her soul, a personal, private song. It didn't hold her perplexed as much as the others, for it was the most ingrained, but she found that if she didn't practice, she quickly lost recall. And she liked to be quick, like a native. French was serious and explicit but once she got the hang of it, she felt the beauty of the words in the same way she did with Italian. Romance languages could bring her to tears. German and recently Russian were formal and stern, like businessmen. Her facial expression grew somber when she spoke these two languages. Her throat hurt after long sessions with German and she had yet to master Russian script. Nevertheless, like a mother with her children, she handled each language with a particular care and love, for each deserved the best from her.

Why were there so many different sounds and ways to say the same thing, she wondered? Why had the ancient and modern worlds advanced with so many tongues? Why had people chosen sounds and words that would bastardize, compromise, or completely overturn a given pronunciation or meaning? Languages had evolved for mysterious and wondrous reasons—to accommodate evolving technologies, to meld different cultures, or to dispel antiquated dogmas. As she studied, she speculated on why the world's people never joined in one common tongue, and why ancient and often outdated patterns and norms persisted.

She embraced the differences yet was perplexed. Through varied tongues, man had separated himself from other men. Would there ever be a merging?

Her time in the States solidified her determination, for here was the melting pot, the land of plenty and diversity. Here were joined races and creeds, beliefs, attitudes, and opinions representing all other countries. Here was the laboratory of Klee's dreams, a place she could perhaps uncover why people chose to remain different in some ways and come together in others. Linguistics was a step, she would take many. She would become a master of people, for her entire life so far had been a question mark about them—why they hurt, and why they loved.

Distance had separated her from her own direct experience with hurt and love but she was not beyond revisiting the pain. She'd lost a son—her one chance to impact another deeply, by living each day with a version of herself. Her life had been destitute until now. She wanted to bridge gaps. Her own lessons in pain had almost broken her, how many others shared the same hurt? And why in the world must this persist?

Some day she would find the answers, or die trying. It was her destiny.

In the meantime, she would sing, arrange finances, pay the rent, and kid around with Johnny. Little by little she would create for herself an environment of study and learning, where she could offer her best and find the peace that alluded. A book in hand, a verse on her lips, and above all quiet. Hers were simple requirements. And yet the world was so very complex.

♥ ♥ ♥

Johnny walked on dangerous turf yet kept going. The last weekend in August, he brought a tape recorder to the club.

Klee was on stage most of the evening, singing to the accompaniment of a woman on guitar and a man on saxophone. With the crush of students due to arrive the following week and many professionals on vacation, it was a slow night. Johnny gave free reign to Klee.

She joked with two men. Johnny had seen them before, had noticed how they managed to get front seats every time. Her eyes gleamed as she offered up lyrics and they complimented readily. It made Johnny's blood boil, for she had the body that forced one's mind to wander, legs that kept one transfixed, and those two were after her.

His mind on his own plans for the evening, he lowered the lights—a sign to Klee to switch to slower songs. She opened with a jazz tune. Clutching the microphone, fingers entwined in the wire, she lamented a love lost. The room filled with the silence Johnny had come to anticipate and revel in. No one else could transfix an audience like that. She was his maestro.

He switched on the recorder hidden under the bar. It would run for up to one hour and then he would have her.

This had started out as friendship, fast switched to infatuation, and now he was hooked. He'd even taken to driving by her apartment early mornings, simply to look up at the third floor and imagine her lying in bed.

All summer, the image of her face was a distraction. No longer could he sit at a baseball game engrossed in plays, calls, runs batted in, and averages. No sooner would he sit in his usual box seat and wait for the action than her face would appear, as if a huge Klee had descended onto the field. While his friends delved into the program, he daydreamed. Obsession seemed to be the only way around her refusals.

Though she would be angry if she found out about this recording, he had to do it. When she wasn't at the club, he wasn't living.

The tunes were light and sultry, sad but not depressing. Her voice manipulated lyrics about human pain, leaving upbeat imprints of even the most sorrow-filled partings. Should she choose, she could bring tears to the eyes of every on-looker. Tonight, she was doing both, all the while the little machine whirred and took in her sounds.

Her set finished, she thanked the audience and retreated. The room remained still until one or two people got up. Then, the normal buzz of talk, glasses, and stereo music resumed.

Sticking his head into the back room, he said, "You did good, kid."

"Thanks."

She was crouched in a corner, her coat for a seat, a book in hand. He stared at her mouth. A kiss would suit him just fine, to taste her lips on his, a forbidden delicious thought, one of many. He sighed.

"You sure you won't let me get you a contract? Could win you lots of time with all that saving you're trying to do."

"No."

"You know? I've been thinking. Don't you want to travel to those places you're learning about? How in the world are you going to get the real hang of them languages?"

Looking up, thoughtful, she said, "You have a point, Johnny. Maybe someday, maybe." She returned to her book.

How often he'd imagined the feel of her hair in his fingers, the skin against his. It was too much having her so close yet beyond reach. He stepped towards her. She looked up.

"Yes?" she asked.

The navy eyes were so large, so luscious and inviting. Yet her position, her tone, her perturbing curl of lip meant only one thing.

"Nothing, babe. Nothing."

He turned away, headed towards the bar. A bright spot on this evening was the recording. His treasure with which he could scurry home and pretend she was in the room with him, in the same bed. Together with Klee.

September was busy at the club and Johnny was more in love than ever. He'd duplicated copies of her music, in case one got lost. Nights after the club closed, he would lie in bed, play and replay. He even purchased a smarter machine that ran continually, so he could fall asleep with her. But after a while, it became difficult for him to enjoy her music at home. So in need of her physical presence, so aware of his love, he had to have her all.

It was during his toughest days, when he could barely put in a night's work, when all he knew was his desire and pounding heart, that he ran into an old friend. Roger Madden had left Boston after high school to live in New York. He and Johnny dated back to the days in Southie, their scruffy Irish neighborhood where they lit firecrackers under cars and soaped windows during holidays. When in Boston, Roger always visited.

They went for drinks one evening and Johnny spoke of Klee. On the fringes of certain New York recording circles, Roger asked to hear the music. Breaking his initial promise, Johnny took him to his place and played the tape.

Roger offered ideas right away—a small contract to begin with, perhaps a few bookings in New York. "If she squawks," he said, "I'll tell her how much these kids are making nowadays. Thirty grand when it hits the top ten! You mean your lady wouldn't consider that amount of change? She's interested in a fancy education, in bucks. Think about it, John."

Johnny's face paled. He ruminated as Roger detailed how rapidly a first demo could be cut, then Klee could return to her work if she wanted, without detracting from her present occupations. If things took off, she would never again worry over money.

"It's simple, John. You gotta explain to her how things work! I'm telling you, she's worth a gamble. Convince her!"

Johnny nodded. "I'd like to help her. She's the world to me."

Roger chucked, lit a cigarette and crossed his ankles atop the coffee table. "Love conquers all, pal. Try her out. She can only say no."

"She's already said no a million times."

"Let me talk with her then. I'll take in one of her shows, meet up with her after. Easy. Plus, then you get to manage her. You get to see her, you get to maybe have her, who knows?"

Johnny's gaze fell. "I guess."

Roger reached over and slapped his forearm. "Old buddy, you need to take charge. You're acting like she's some city boss rather than an illegal Irish chick with a voice and body that turn you on! What's with you anyway? What happened to the Johnny Mear who went after the ladies with his eyes closed?"

Johnny smiled. "I suppose."

"Don't suppose. Get her to buy into the idea. She'll come around. They all do. Dames like that love big bucks. Trust me."

Johnny's eyes darkened. "She's not a dame. She's Klee, Okay?"

"Okay, Okay, no offense, pal! Let's have a look at her tomorrow, heh?"

"We have to go easy," Johnny said. "If she says no, that's it. I can't have her quitting on me, it'll kill me."

"Sure, sure. Man, you've got it bad."

# Chapter 19:
# September 1971

MARCEL ROLLED OVER IN BED. Patrice slept by his side. Her breasts showed above the covers—dark aureoles, round exquisite mounds. He reached for her curls, rubbed the hair between his fingers, then ran a hand down her stomach and to her thighs. She stirred and took his hand in hers, asleep yet in control.

In control she had seduced him, led him to bed, and performed wonderful sex. She was a kitten and lioness, a voluptuous lady with one-pointed focus.

He had resisted for a time, rationalizing their business partnership. But she didn't care, didn't see sex as the barrier that would eventually separate them, a belief Marcel held about all relationships. The line crossed, women and men used the altered state often to devious ends. He saw it coming with her yet tried to delay the inevitable. In many ways, he had preferred the father-daughter amity of their work arrangement.

But she had other ideas. She was not in love, she told him, so he didn't have to worry. She wanted to share an experience, that was all. She respected his needs and wasn't going to cling or make homing motions. Plus, she was constantly with him—films, engagements, meetings. He had already slept with her in his mind. Why not?

Theirs was a poignant union. She was vulnerable, unafraid to seek out ways to please him, coaxing the maximum from each move. Tomorrow was for tomorrow, she said. Tonight, I am with you.

Her whispers had brought him to multiple climaxes and he now felt satiated and revitalized, and thought back to the last time he'd felt so good. Years.

Years ago, this was an almost nightly experience—one woman or another, her heart exposed, the temporary tenderness. He had grown accustomed to having a woman at his side, grown to delight in the night, and to release her the next day. Years ago, it seemed the pattern would never be curtailed.

Now, as he held this woman-child, he questioned the act, thought of sin and immorality. She was so young, even though she had been willing. And he was no longer a kid. His still-fit body sounded alarms he had never before registered. Taking her on had been trespassing in a sense, though he couldn't entirely figure out why. She the one more in charge, had left him with a heightened sense of limits, and of time. The sexual tension, the fluid moments, the tease of permanency departed even as they climaxed, even as she clung in the embrace he had once regaled in with so many other women. In spite of her eagerness, in spite of the lushness that communicated to his veins, he was aware of a fatigue, a tiredness and boredom. He had been in a loop, always the same refrain, over and over. New ground was off-limits. To have a woman forever was not his way. He had never let anyone in really.

Was this why the intervals between love making had increased over the years? All those he left, even some with promise, all those he never called again, all those whose memory he cherished after the fact, and those who disappeared of their own accord. Was each encounter a foray of lust and lust alone? Had he come face to face with resistant pieces of himself? And grown wary? What was transpiring to diminish this delightful supply of beguiling women, how had the years claimed his one escape? And what would he do to fill the void? He sighed, and buried fingers in her hair, trying to overcome the pressing ache, trying to thrust feelings aside one more time.

Plus, they had such good news—a trip to film a movie in the streets of New York. Patrice had contracted a bit part, and Marcel would join her. They figured it was an appropriate time for her to meet with American producers who Marcel knew and to make herself known on that side of the ocean.

Ecstatic and sleepless, they passed the previous night wide awake and wandering the streets of Aix. Thanks to Marcel, Patrice was already an up-and-coming actress in France, with hopes to extend her renown to other countries.

"You'll see," said Marcel, "it's different there. They talk about liberty—to them it's the pursuit of money. Money equals happiness."

"Our left-leaning friends would have something to say," Patrice said, snuggling into his arms.

"I have something to say about it. It's wrong, all wrong. But," he sighed, "we do it, too. We do it anyway."

"We do," she said, raising her chin and reaching for his lips. "I love you."

Eyes open, he kissed her lids as she searched for his mouth with her tongue. Her body pressed against his and he pulled her down, down under the sheets, undercover and enmeshed in her hair, her body, her all.

♥ ♥ ♥

New York City was on the brink of financial collapse. There was talk of federal assistance, increased taxes, layoffs of city employees. But along Fifth Avenue, designer boutiques, high-end department stores, and fine art establishments operated as if lucrative times prevailed.

Patrice and Marcel stayed in Brooklyn and each morning rode the subway to the West Side of Manhattan and the office of a friend of Marcel's. From there, they went with crew members to the designated location of the shoot. The script detailed the story of a young French boy who moves to New York with his parents. Orphaned shortly after his arrival, he lives the life of the streets and becomes acquainted with all sorts of characters. In time, he meets a young woman—played by Patrice—who encourages him to discover museums and the theater. He grows interested in the arts and eventually becomes a violinist.

Because Patrice was of French heritage but also grew up in disparate Algerian neighborhoods, she was able to give advice to the boy actor. Their days were long and it took a while to get accustomed to the American habit of rising before dawn and starting work at the ungodly hour of 6 AM. After non-stop work, their bodies and spirits were so drained, they could barely muster strength to take the subway home, rest, and prepare for the next day.

Work proceeded for three weeks when a dispute about funding and rights to the film halted production. Marcel and Patrice took advantage to discover the city.

They toured Greenwich Village, went to museums, took train and cab rides all over Manhattan and the boroughs. They bought American-made articles, especially clothing. At Army-Navy stores they purchased fatigues and t-shirts, high-top boots, and of course jeans. Patrice loved the feel of the material, was happy to wear the blue denim all the time and mix and match t-shirts and blouses each day.

Here, young people uniformly dressed in jeans. Largely frowned upon in France, jeans were a nod to American status and an inability to dress with chic. Patrice and Marcel didn't concern themselves about disapproving looks. They joked about it, predicting it wouldn't be long before French youth would take to jeans and a more casual style—at greater expense and with more panache. For now, they both felt unique and special, not slovenly or unworthy of respect.

One day, they passed a music store and decided to check out new arrivals and to compare prices.

Inside, a young man with shoulder-length hair sat behind the counter humming to Rolling Stones music rising from the store-wide stereo system. Row upon row of records reached to the back of the room and potential buyers lolled about the aisles.

"Look at all those, will you!" Marcel exclaimed, pulling Patrice close as they made for the jazz recordings. "Let's see what they have of Sarah Vaughan."

At the end of one aisle, they fingered through labels. No one forced them to move on, no one stood watching over them. All was relaxed and 'cool.'

Marcel purchased several jazz albums and Patrice chose a Beatles record. They were about to leave the store when they passed a room to one side of the cash register. It was sound-proof and two people with ear phones appeared to be jamming. On enquiring, they learned that, to sample music on a particular recording, one could make use of the acoustically correct room. Marcel asked to sit in on the current selection.

It was a woman's voice, jazz, a tune from the forties. A wail one minute, a tender cry another, hers was an impressive range with some scat thrown in for fun.

"Who is she?" Marcel asked the technician who adjusted the stereo.

"Klee. New."

"A single?"

"Yep," he said, "this isn't released yet. It's a test cut of a friend of mine. She's never recorded. Not bad, huh?"

Marcel sat on the bench and Patrice joined him. They listened to the song a second time. Another customer wanted to buy it but it wasn't for sale.

"You gotta get her recorded, man," still another said, his eyes bright. "She's heaven."

"My friend is looking into it," said the technician. "He promotes new singers. Seems she isn't ready to come out." They laughed.

Marcel leaned to Patrice and whispered something. She kissed him and stood, waved goodbye, promising to meet him later at their hotel. Then, he sat against the bench. "Do you mind if I listen one more time?" he asked.

The tech looked at Marcel then shrugged. "Sure. I see some folks out there with questions." He placed the record on the player, hit the automatic button controlling the needle arm, and moved to the door. "Later."

"Thank you," Marcel said.

He listened all the way through, then replayed the song. He closed his eyes and his senses absorbed into the melody. The voice wasn't American or English. Her range he'd never before heard, a rise in pitch followed by a descent that startled. Even without lyrics—those times she hummed or simply repeated a sound—she bespoke a tale. Interspersed throughout the notes, in the reaches of the silences, she embedded feeling. So complete, so uninhibited, natural yet nearly inhuman. Outer world. A sound so incredible, like nothing before.

He'd paid attention to all the greats for many years. This woman was a hit. Before leaving, he left his card asking to be notified if any of her music was ever released.

# Chapter 20

"WHAT IN THE DEVIL?" KLEE SCREAMED. "You go off and convince me to do this job for a friend o' yours and now you want more? Not on your life, Johnny Mear, not on your life I won't!"

"Klee, please. It was a great song, a beautiful one."

"Enough!" she said, her eyes ablaze. "I did you a favor, that's it. You want me around, don't ask me to record."

They were alone in the restaurant after a particularly busy Saturday. She plopped into a chair and threw back her head. Eyes closed she rubbed her temples.

"I'm sorry, babe," Johnny said. "I'm sorry."

She appeared to nod off, but her hand massaged slowly and her body was tense.

"Can I take you home?"

She slid a look his way, face pale, her mouth set. Shaking her head she bit her lower lip. "Yes, ye can."

He gave her a meek smile. "You always slip into a stronger accent when you're mad?"

"Yes," she said, "stark raving mad, as you say, stark raving..."

"Aw, don't go getting upset now, Klee. Old Johnny goofed. I'm sorry. Roger promised the demo tape would be the end of it. Now he keeps calling for more." He took keys from his pocket and tugged at the sack of money containing that night's receipts. They locked up and exited, greeting the humidity with deep intakes of breath. The air stagnated from the day's moisture and lowered clouds.

"That place is too small, Johnny," Klee said, as they rounded a corner towards the parking lot where Johnny's was the only car. "Those cigarettes, the smoke."

Inches taller than he, she strode ahead. He quickened his pace. "I'm fixing the ventilation, you know. Should make a difference. Got a deal from a friend of mine."

Once over the river at Klee's, he pulled over to the curb and shut off the engine. He reached in the back for a wrapped gift.

"I have something for you," he said. "Mind if I come up and give it to you?"

She squinted at the gift. The rectangular box was wrapped in red paper with silver trim and a white bow on top, a card attached. "I guess a cup of tea won't hurt."

They climbed the three flights and Klee let him into her garret. Beside a single bed stood a writing table and lamp. The window he'd many times looked up to was opened and the shade not yet drawn. To the left, a bathroom. The rest of the room had books—piled on cinder blocks, spilling from a suitcase, and a bean-bag chair holding several stacks.

"Man, I knew you read, but..." he said, scratching his head.

She went to the bean bag and cleared books. "Here, sit. Sorry it's all I have and the bed is for me."

He dutifully sat as she moved to a compact burner and put on the water. "You're tired, aren't you?"

"No. Usually after work Saturday nights, I read until morning. All night long there might be all of one or two cars going by. Sunday mornings are quiet. I like quiet." She handed him a mug with a tea bag in it and poured.

"All this time I thought you were entertaining men and now I see how wrong I was. There's no room for another here—these books win out, don't they?"

She sat on the floor near him and reached for one atop a nearby stack. "This is my German pile. Conversational German," she said, "only it doesn't work that way."

"How so?"

"You can't converse with a book. You need people. It's the one thing that frustrates me studying all these languages. I need time in the countries. That'll come later I guess."

"You could have it sooner than later," he said.

"Never mind," she said, quick to catch on. "May I?" She opened her hands to request the package.

He handed it to her. "Happy birthday."

"Birthday!" she exclaimed, easing fingers under the tape so as not to rip the paper.

"You won't tell me when it is so I figured I'd get you a gift anyway."

"Well, you're close." She opened the box. Inside, a pair of bell bottom jeans and a matching vest. "Johnny." Eyes wide, she lifted the clothing. "They're lovely, lovely."

"I know you like your Irish clothes there, haven't changed since you started working for me—not that you're grubby or anything. I saw these at the Jordan Marsh and, well, I thought of you."

She embraced the clothing, whispering, "Thanks, thanks a million."

"You'll wear them then?"

"I will." She checked the label. "I think they're my size."

"Try them," he said.

341

She disappeared to the bathroom.

At the window he studied his car, then turned into the room and looked at her bed, his gaze with the longing he knew she disdained. He went to her desk and ran a finger along the side, studying the pens and pencils, the block calendar set for Saturday, the notes to herself to do an errand or see some professor. Her writing was neat, curled, and spread across the page. He touched her notepaper. Another sheet caught his eyes, a bill from Boston City Hospital.

"$84.50 received 8/14/71. Final payment on bill # 39706. Klee Walsh for obstetric services $2987."

"Obstetric services," he whispered, whistling low. He reread the note then turned as the bathroom door opened.

She wore her white work blouse with the jeans and vest. Her hair bounced and she looked down at herself. "They're so comfortable!" she exclaimed, turning to face a wall mirror. "I'll wear them next Thursday, what do you think?"

He took in her behind and long legs as she primped, his gaze stalling on the curve of her hips and derriere, the slope of her shoulders. He couldn't speak.

They faced one another. "Thanks, Johnny. Thanks," she said.

He nodded, lowering his head.

"You Okay?" she asked getting closer.

"Me? Er, yes I'm fine."

"Don't lie," she said.

He took a deep breath, turned, and looked to the desk where the bill sat. "Klee, baby, why didn't you tell me you owed this kind of money?"

She darted a glance to the statement. Her look darkened. She went to the bean-bag chair, lay back, and studied the ceiling. A car rolled by. "It was when I first came here. I was expecting. The baby died. Six months old. A boy."

"Gee." He went to her but she didn't let him touch, sat straight and looked at him.

"It was meant to be. I tried to have him, but he died. The bill had to be paid. It's paid. I worked to pay it, you see?"

"You should have told me. I would have helped."

"No." She rubbed a hand on the new material.

"You know I care for you. I would have done anything."

She murmured something he didn't understand. Lying back again she closed her eyes, and talked about Ireland, about her home in Kinemmaera. Of the wee people and Romney, the times they hunted for periwinkles or sought out fairies, the times she danced and sang at pubs. She told him of how you never saw such vivid colors, the land as it changed—with an approaching storm—from blue to purple to grey, the cows as they stood, immobile and in wait. There were weddings, prolonged revelries unlike in the States, and merry gatherings for no particular reason. Families had many, many children, without heeding how they would care for them. She spoke of Dublin, too, of the energy and desperateness, of the Faheys and their gift. The hat she so loved.

"They gave it to me," she said. "But they gave me so much more. They let me peek into a future of possibility, for they were always like that—peaceable, accepting, and kind. I learned so much from their hard work, from their giving. It was a tiny place, like this, but I was never alone. Mary had tea and Danny had stories. And I was a part of them, you see."

"Why did you leave?"

"The baby. It would have been too much for the Faheys. And I was ready to go."

"Why the States?"

She looked at him and saw his troubled eyes, reached a hand to his cheek. "A toss of the coin, you might say. And it hasn't been so bad."

"You came here all alone and, and the baby, and oh, babe, how did you do it?"

She let him clasp a hand around hers. Raising a finger, she said, "Shhhh, be careful. And do not seek to know too much..."

"About us," he finished.

They sat for hours, until Sunday's morning light. It would be another sultry day in Boston.

Roger laughed. "Man, you gotta charm her, make her see she's worth a mil!" He shook his head at Johnny. "I tell you, a record contract will keep her with her books for the rest of her life! Think about it, you can be her manager. No more club, just you and she and all your money!"

Johnny stared into his beer. They had met at an area bar to discuss signing Klee onto a one-time contract. Roger was hot to get her to New York. In spite of Johnny's excuses, he anticipated her fortune and the fortunes of others—including himself.

"Rog, I hear you. But you don't know her like I do. She's not money hungry, and she's not used to people like you, or me even. I tell her she could retire and read for the rest of her life and she looks at me like I've lost my head."

"She's not yet up on how things work in this country."

"She's fine the way she is. I don't know that I'd want to be involved with changing her."

"Who says we're changing her?" Roger asked. "Look, we're offering her a way to get that fancy college degree. All she's got to do is cut a record. How difficult is that?"

"For her, it is."

"Why? Tell me why. One good reason," Roger said.

Johnny took a sip. "Look, I don't really know, but..."

"Then she must not have a reason. She must be confused, John! You gotta make her see, how many times do I have to say it! People need to be sold on things. Geez, I'm beginning to see why you stayed here instead of joining me in New York. That town would eat you up..."

"Don't start that," Johnny said.

"Convince her! Can't you do that? You said you two was tight."

Johnny looked away. "We are. I know a lot about her. But she's still a private person. Likes it that way, you know?"

"She likes hotshot degrees, clubs, men smiling at her blonde hair and blue eyes. I've seen her, remember? She hasn't had the taste yet, the incentive," he said, rubbing his index and thumb together.

"Huh?"

"Real success, the life of her own choosing." He kissed his two fingers. "Sweet!"

"True."

Roger finished his glass, put it down, and signaled for the check. The two men were opposites, he in his navy pin stripe suit and red tie, Johnny in his black cotton slacks and baseball jacket. If not for their shared conversation, one would have never figured them as associates.

"Listen," Roger said. "I'm going back to New York. I'll call you in a few days. That should be enough time to, you know, get it on with her?"

Johnny blinked and gave Roger a quick look.

"Hey, man, you've got the hots. Let her see what you're made of. She's after you. I've seen her giving you the eye. You might be older but she likes them that way. Why would she let you drive her home all those times? Go on, get it on! It'll take the steam out of her temper, give you time to convince her."

"Rog..."

Roger put his hat on and placed his wallet in his jacket. He slapped Johnny on the back. "Bye, Johnny. And remember, convince, cajole, close!"

As Roger exited, Johnny felt the rise of desire. Since the night with Klee, he'd held fast to the memory of her touching him, of her hand in his. She'd been tender and more open than ever, and she'd let him into her apartment.

Was she bit by bit falling? Or was he blinded? Was Roger's idea worth following, or was he simply another man mouthing off because Klee was attractive and talented?

As he mulled over his choices, he felt warmth rise into his face. Maybe he did stand a chance. And maybe, once she opened up more, maybe they would get to a point where he could have her in ways he'd only dreamed about so far.

His life had never been so full, and at the same time so riddled with anxiety. Through her camaraderie, he'd allowed a situation into his life that increasingly tormented him. For all his dreams, for all his smitten looks, they'd never come close—except once and then only as friends. He'd hoped the clothes might have suggested to her his feelings, but she'd been as distant as before.

He wondered if her hesitancy was what held him. Was this about conquest or true love?

He wished things were like before, before Klee walked into his out-of-the-way hangout. Time marching on was different for Johnny. She was young. He wanted a comfort zone, a guarantee in his advancing years. He wanted it with her.

# Chapter 21

"HER NAME IS KLEE," Marcel said to Evan.

"Like the artist?"

"Like."

"American?"

"Not sure," Marcel said. "She lives in Boston. That's why, my friend, I thought of you. If you're embarking on a trip there, you'll have time to look her up."

They were at his home in Aix. Marcel puffed on a cigarette and watched his gardener tugging at weeds. Statues of nymphs and figurines dotted the grounds. High stone walls promoted privacy, water splashed from the fountains, and greenery succumbed to the browns and maroons of late autumn in the south.

Evan's eyes widened. "It's a big place, Boston, and I'll be occupied most of the time." He was referring to his decision to take the executive seminar at Harvard which allowed working professionals the opportunity to study with some of the world's most noted business people. He'd found out about the program through friends and made arrangements to take temporary leave of Polytechnique.

He would finally visit the country he'd long felt possessed an enviable business environment. Because of his family background and record with

Polytechnique, he would not only be an observer but also a contributor to panel discussions and presentations regarding the Common Market. It was for this reason that Giles, initially opposed, had agreed to the arrangement. As Evan explained to his father, France must be among those countries represented. Giles had trouble with this interest of Evan's and questioned the so-called innovative techniques for managing large corporations. But he readily agreed that Evan, as a visiting executive, would be a positive addition to any forum.

He would stay for two months and Giles would run de Roche Frères with Régine. This, too, Evan figured could be advantageous, with day-to-day proof of her incompetence. The affection Giles had for Régine continued to expand, however, a fact that left Evan as perplexed as ever.

After much discussion, Evan received Giles's blessing coupled with warnings about taking too much at face value. Ever the conservative, Giles believed it important to research while maintaining a calculated distance.

Because of their shared interest in the States, Evan wanted Marcel's advice, too.

"I don't know Boston, but you'll get around. I got around New York and that's larger by far."

Evan looked away. "Patrice enjoyed herself?"

"She did. She worked hard, too. I must say she's a single-minded lady when it comes to her profession. And other things..."

"You are in love?" Evan asked.

Marcel chuckled, stood, and poured another glass of whiskey. "Love, my friend. Are we ever really in love? She's a superb woman, free and strong. I like them that way. But love? Don't ask your old uncle such things. Would you care for me to intrude on your affairs?"

349

Evan shrugged. "They're of no consequence at the moment."

"I hear you're about to wed." His gaze slid towards Evan.

"Paris has no secrets. There is talk, yes, but not from me."

"Régine, our great lady of de Roche Frères, then?"

Evan smirked. "Who else?"

"Well, you can simply tell her to fuck off!"

Evan burst out laughing. "How I'd enjoy it!"

"She deserves a boot in the derriere if I do say. I understand she quotes from the radical party now and again. Touts the fact Giles, and thereby de Roche Frères, is making room for women and therefore responding to that group's belief the present political system must better integrate genders. And I thought the last person to pay any attention to leftist interests would be your father, Monsieur Gaullist himself! Yet he does."

"She's shrewd," Evan said. "She even engages in debate with ministerial aides to better grasp the party platforms, all to impress Father and keep her position secure. It makes me want to retch."

"Not here, old friend, that chair cost me a day's work!" Marcel exclaimed. "Forget them. Go to the States, have a good time, open your eyes and discover. There is much that moves over there. Take some time off to see about Klee, she's nearby. The record store owner said she sings regularly at a place in Cambridge called Johnny's. Ask around."

"Perhaps."

"Do it. Or get out and about at least. You need to remove yourself from the mire you wade in! Remember you promised me you would keep up with film? What has happened to that? I've heard no word."

Evan shrugged. "Like Solange, it sits and waits for me to make up my mind."

"You were passionate when we last worked together."

Evan watched the gardener struggle to shut off the water of one fountain. "Klee. Like Paul Klee..."

"No relation. As I've told you, I don't know much about her, except she has a winning voice."

Evan took out a small notebook and jotted. After, he sat back and looked up at Marcel, his eyebrows knit. "Have you ever felt so uncertain you want to jump off the earth?"

Marcel smiled. "It's a state, isn't it?"

"Did you make the move or did you let things happen?"

It was Marcel's turn to contemplate. More solemn, he walked to the window and pressed hands atop the lower ledge, his brow on the cool glass. "I was a coward. I let things happen."

"And how did they turn out?"

Marcel waited long before answering. "I'll never know."

The words rang in Evan's ears. His uncle's words were signals that Marcel would share his wisdom but not the details. Evan let the silence envelope him. As evening lowered, they remained—one staring out the window the other staring at the dark.

♥ ♥ ♥

The next day Evan departed, Air France to London then across the Atlantic. In Boston, skies were overcast and he had tired of wait lines and delays. Right away, however, he loved the animation and tension of the place. Ushering Evan to a waiting limo, the driver exited the airport and followed the Charles River along a wide avenue jammed with cars that seemed oversized and overcharged. They crossed a bridge into Cambridge.

351

The architecture on campus made Evan think of England and he no sooner was settled into his dorm than he met up with several English—and French, Dutch, Iranian, Indian and more. The place was a beehive of erudite goings-on—demonstrations against the war right outside his window and the briskness of heels tapping on tiled, waxed floors as students made way to and from classes.

Current events, challenges and *politique* abounded. Students grappled with pie charts of anticipated corporate growth with the same verve as with details of Nixon's moves in southeast Asia. Most accepted Evan and inquired about his country's situation, his personal goals, his reasons for being. Although struggling with his lycée English, he managed, and found himself for the first time in months, energized and looking forward to each day.

The schedule called for twelve-hour marathons with minimal breaks. His routine of lingering over wine out of the question, he instead joined others in sandwiches at local diners or meat, potatoes, and milk at the student cafeteria. He shared a compact dormitory room with a Greek student. Both soon appreciated why the accommodations were so threadbare and austere—one spent little time in them. Sleep was not in the forefront of anyone's mind.

There were many youth who felt like he did. The world had to better come together, trade barriers had to be broken, the European Community had to have its day. Few revered the Gaullist regime he grew up with and even fewer understood his country. During breaks he would expound on the changing France at the same time he underscored France's habit of taking her time to realize these changes. Many wanted to hear his stories of May '68 and he was happy to recall the events. Radicals, leftists, innovators, all congregated here. And many of them were in the same program as he, business people like himself. It was as if, having dreamed of this situation, it had suddenly turned into reality.

Marcel needn't have suggested he open his eyes. One couldn't help but open. To close even for a second meant you risked missing engagement and everything was worthy of note. Evan had found a milieu like film, challenging and nurturing.

He didn't get to Johnny's until one Saturday night several weeks into his stay, when Christmas was around the corner. Cambridge and Boston were decked in oversized red bows, strings of white lights, and Santa-themed department store glitter. With two French students as company, he suggested Johnny's and they had no trouble getting directions. Johnny's was an 'in' place for those Harvard students who could spare a few hours of diversion.

The place was packed. Smoke prevented clear seeing but a cloud of even the darkest fumes could not have barred her from sight. She wore red, and a bow in her hair. They seated themselves at her feet, to one side of the stage where a couple had just left. She glanced their way, as if to assess something. Then, she signaled the piano player and the lights lowered.

Glasses clinked and a few onlookers whispered. Most were staring at her, expressions anticipatory. She accorded an unique nod, joking here, commenting there, chuckling to some secret merriment. To Evan's table, she gave the last flicker of a glance before her lids lowered and she sang.

Had it been any other song, Evan might not have become so quickly enthralled. But it was one he'd heard before in a Paris wine bar run by a British couple.

"I go around the world...still I can't get started with you..." The Cole Porter tune hit him in a wave of sentimentality. Klee hypnotized. She sang to the room yet, after a while, Evan sensed that she sang to someone or someplace removed from it, a place in her mind perhaps, or to a very special person.

Evan noted how readily the crowd related to her words, or perhaps they were relating to her as an individual. A few men were clearly eyeing her for one reason, others engaged with her voice and the gestures of her long fingers as she beckoned one minute, clenched the next. But somehow, what overruled attraction or curiosity was the way the audience was transported, to the same unknown and untouchable place where she herself drifted. Alone in song, she floated to a fanciful destination, carrying the audience with her and allowing for the duration of her tune, a dream of another order, beyond those of the night, reaching far and away.

She finished. The room exploded in applause. Evan stood with others. He noted another aspect of her, different from the singing lady of a few minutes before. She appeared amused by the attention, as if she didn't understand it really, almost as if she had wakened to a scene in which she did not participate. She blushed. Handing the microphone to a musician, she disappeared.

"She's shy," Evan thought. His friend tugged at his jacket, reminding him he was the only one still standing.

The evening flew. Klee sang whatever people requested then threw in some tunes of her own, jazz mixed with pop and some classic, too. Some were ballads. A woman sitting behind Evan whispered that Klee was Irish. He took an even closer look at the skin and the eyes, the rhythmic gestures. Many had spoken of the Irish beauty, the lady of the sea-bound land possessing a look not of a magazine, something rather plain on first glance but arresting at the same time. The true Celt was natural, and the colors of a sun shower—

misty grey, ruby dark, and with the pierce of a twinkling star. A rare breed, the kind one must seek out.

He marveled at his uncle for discerning her talent solely via the medium of sound, without ever having set eyes on her, without ever having an exchange with her or witnessing her song in person. Marcel was a talent scout of the highest order. Evan beheld one of his uncle's greatest discoveries.

She returned to the stage, responding to requests for more oldies. As she collected herself, she caught Evan's stare and accorded him a pensive few seconds. He felt in an instant she knew everything about him. He beheld more than a singer. Something put her out of reach yet he struggled to define what it was.

"It's a song from 1957," she said. "I was a girl then, it was popular where I grew up." Her gaze fixed to center audience, she began.

> You are my special angel sent from up above
> I'll have my special here to watch over me...
> Angel, angel, angel!!!

She looked up to the ceiling. Evan was riveted, for he first thought she sang to him, or to someone in the audience. In the same way as prior songs, she removed herself beyond the room.

"She's singing to herself. A song for her," he thought, as the piece ended and his friends clapped. "She needs to sing to herself."

After, he said goodbye to his friends and remained at the club. A few stragglers sat at the bar and the man who looked to be the owner cleared glasses and glared at Evan.

She emerged, a black hat on her head, a wool coat covering her bright red dress. The bow she'd worn during her act was now stretched around a book. She slid onto a stool and began reading. The owner made pleasantries and, from what Evan could detect, it was genial banter tinged with admiration and camaraderie.

As he stood to go, he took another glance her way. She was lost in her book. Before leaving, he checked the schedule for her next appearance.

♥ ♥ ♥

In the following weeks, Evan went to every performance, sometimes foregoing an important soirée or a visit from a Washington official. He found her different each time, yet always grounded in her singing. She sometimes mimicked other celebrities or danced along with the tunes in the style of old music halls. She commanded a wide range of scores and often allowed audience request to determine the outcome of an evening, warming the already relaxed ambience of the place. The final song sung, most patrons chose to linger, asking for more.

Evan tried to get to her but she was a butterfly, flitting off stage and out of sight as soon as her break came. Never did she dawdle with the audience and, her show over, always appeared at the bar in coat and hat, presumably to be escorted home by the owner. She noticed Evan many a time and took to looking for him in his regular seat but never prolonged her regard or spoke to him. Evan figured she must be used to the attention of admirers for he noticed other regulars. A following already, a voice of unusual caliber, with oddly appealing looks to boot, Evan held tight to Marcel's prediction and vowed to be the one to unveil Klee to the world.

If only he could get to her! Through the exercise of attending her shows, his own reserve manifested. He couldn't bring himself to intrude on the private space she so obviously cherished. And the boss kept his own version of a "No Trespassing" sign on her. Johnny was a hurdle to overcome and Evan more than once grasped the man's message that communicated possession and ownership. Evan dared guess the man was even in love with Klee.

He finally broke down and called Marcel, given international phone usage was considered an extravagance by most French. Marcel accepted the charges and listened.

"Make friends with her. Go slowly at first. She sounds the type to run if you get too pushy," Marcel said.

"But that's it. I can't get near her at all."

Marcel chuckled. "You'll find a way. Be patient. Your time is best utilized preparing. If she's Irish, find out about Ireland. Learn a few Gaelic words. I'm not surprised to hear that. There are many Irish in Boston. Read up on the music she sings—the composers, the history of jazz. She sounds smart, too. What books does she scurry around with? They must mean a lot if she overlooks you for the written page!"

Evan laughed. "You've already got me thinking."

"Give it your best shot. It thrills me you are faced with a challenge like her. It sounds like she's not money-hungry or even driven by fame—and those types are the best kind. Patience, vieux, patience."

When they hung up, Evan's mental wheels were rolling.

He went to the Celtic studies department, cutting classes to brush up on her country's history. He inquired about other jazz clubs in the area, and listened to groups and singers. In a few weeks, he was immersed in the local music scene and had all but given up on his business classes. Save the visiting French dignitary or panel discussion, Evan soon disappeared from campus. To seek out and find artistic talent, like Marcel had with

Patrice, like he too had on a minor scale, drew on his preferred inclinations.

At Johnny's he made friends with the regular customers, noted their observations about Klee, why they loved her voice, why they returned. There was an aura about her, they said, and a question mark in the eyes of her beholders, all of them. He loved the fact Ireland was remote, isolated in its surrounding seas. He wondered what part of the country she came from and was thankful one customer remarked her accent was softer than the Dublin one, that she was probably from the west or the south. He listened carefully when she talked, for then he caught the odd inflection or rise that revealed her origins, hence her depths.

One night, his chance came. Hurrying out to begin the second set, she dropped a book near the stage floor, a collection of short stories by Flaubert.

Returning to his chair, he watched her with renewed perspective. A woman living in the States, from another country, reading in his native tongue—she was truly an enigma. She kept right on singing, opening some hearts and tearing others apart. He was spellbound, and more determined than ever to carry her to a place of repute— a place she belonged.

He waited for the applause to die. Then, in the split second before she hurried off stage, he leaned forward and in French made a quick reference to her reading material.

She shot a glance his way. "Français?" she asked.

He nodded, gave her his widest grin. "Et après? Je peux?"

She nodded in the affirmative.

The evening ended, Klee spent several minutes at the bar in what turned into a heated discussion with her boss before she finally made for Evan. Shaken, she quickly shrugged off the exchange. A determined look crossed her face. "Nous parlons français, d'accord?"

He agreed, pleased to again converse in his native language. They exited.

She walked at a clipped pace beside him, books under her arm, eyes hidden by curls and the brim of the hat. She forced words, corrected them, then looked to him for approval. He had no trouble understanding her, and repeated what she said with minor changes. Excepting the briskness of everyday French and its associated slang, she had the language down pat.

They crossed the bridge to Boston and he offered her a coffee. She agreed and they found a late-night diner. Inside it was warm and the coffee plentiful.

He didn't mention her voice, didn't promote his ideas about her singing, didn't force her to talk about herself unless she wanted to. He offered help with French and jotted names of recent well-received novels, even a bookstore in New York she could send away for French editions. He gave her names of friends he'd met on campus and his own address in Paris. He also mentioned German speakers she could contact. Bowled over by her knowledge and unassuming ways, he soon realized her personal interests did not revolve around the club, only the paycheck the club provided. She spoke not at all of a singing career. Too, she said nothing of her past, mentioning only a brief stay in Dublin and affirming she originated from the west.

All night they talked, until the snowbanks at curbs were tinged with pink morning haze. They ordered breakfast and, after he walked her to her place, bid farewell at the front door.

"You wouldn't be interested in more French conversation sometime, would you?" he asked.

"Sure," she said, a strange chuckle escaping—a low almost moaning sound.

Even after a long night, her eyes scintillated. Hungry for knowledge, she stomped her feet from the cold and chattered, maintaining a wide-awake look.

"I have to commend you on your stamina," he finally said, at a loss but unwilling to terminate their night.

"We both learned of one another. And you gave much of yourself. I thank you, sir." She tipped the black hat and winked. Her hand extended and she shook his. "I'm going in to do some reading. You can stop 'round later if you want."

"You're not sleeping?"

"No. There's too much to do. I'll catch up later on sleep."

He looked up at the run down building. "Is your place adequate?"

"It's home." With that, she turned and inserted the key. "Later?"

"Later," he said, feeling the exhaustion drain from him, replacing itself by energy she seemed to transmit. "An hour or two?"

"D'accord!"

They met later that day as well as two more nights before Evan left for Nantucket. Both eased into a connection that kept Klee challenged and Evan on edge. He told her much about himself, and listened to her stories, but had yet to broach his primary intention.

Once Klee left Johnny's, her mind appeared to have been cleansed of musical inclinations. Still and at all times, he retained Marcel's advice about restraint. Even without his uncle's input, he gathered she didn't like people managing her life.

If he were to work with her, he would have to get smarter or she would have to change. He was doing all he could to encourage the mining of her musical talent. Yet she didn't catch on, or refused to, and was as absorbed in her world of study as ever.

At least they were friends now. He bought her a bottle of wine, wished her a happy holiday, and said he would call on her in the new year. It was all he could do.

# Chapter 22:
# December 1971

CHRISTMAS WOULD NOT BE JOYOUS THIS YEAR. An unadorned tree stood in the living room and the wind chimes portended a blustery forecast. Laurence had come to revel in winters on Nantucket, with snow showers one minute and penetrating sunshine the next, with navy white-capped waves crashing even as the violets and mauves of a setting sun calmed blowing sands.

Bea and Sage had grown unusually silent, and their productivity on the job had slowed. This was the tip-off to Laurence, as the last thing they'd abandon would be their very source of strength and vigor. What was most disturbing was that she couldn't discern the problem.

Laurence's role as peacemaker during disputes was a thing of the past; the two lovers rarely fought. Their conversations were open and frank, with the three women sharing most every detail of their lives. Appointments, visits to the vet's, ailments, finances, dinner recipes formed the daily grist to their mill. Laurence knew when Sage was struggling over a score and required solitude, or when Bea was stuck and required help. They had, so far, been in agreement with the post production of Laurence's film. Bea and Sage stepped back more often than as Laurence managed the lion's share. Their lives were in sync, effectively without secrets.

Nevertheless, Laurence sensed a cloud on the horizon. Bea and Sage took longer and longer walks, excusing themselves politely yet never inviting Laurence. The couple had also journeyed to Boston and even New York, a practice in which Sage had rarely indulged until now. It seemed they were closer than ever, but even this suggested something amiss to Laurence, for in the past they often spoke of requiring space from one another in order to enrich their union.

After a night of inventory at the store, Laurence retired early. Although physically spent, sleep alluded her. Three days before, Bea and Sage had left unexpectedly to Christmas shop in Boston. She tried not to begrudge them a trip off-island, but was anxious for their return. She felt uneasy, for she'd never have left for the mainland without first informing them. It was how they took care of one another.

Plus, Sage had yet to finish the music for the underwater film. The few times Laurence mentioned the delay, Sage immediately reassured, explaining that she was fine-tuning the piece, that Laurence would soon have the final product. But Sage rarely played, let alone composed. Her practice time was minimal—about an hour each day—after which she drifted into moody silences. Until Bea was at her side, she remained at a remove and shunned regular activities. She wanted to be with Bea, no one and nothing more would do.

A car drove up. Laurence went to the window and peeked out. It was them. "Home, finally," she whispered, shoving aside off-color thoughts. She was about to head down the stairs but heard Sage sobbing, and froze beside her bed.

In the past, Sage's tears resulted from temperamental eruptions related to her work or a misunderstanding with Bea. She rarely cried for long as she felt it a waste of time. Happy-go-lucky, she was the most upbeat of the three. As the two settled themselves, Sage sobbed and Bea murmured softly.

"Everything Okay?" Laurence asked, peering downstairs.

After a pause, Bea said, "Okay."

Laurence waited for an invitation to join them in a cup of tea, but no one called to her. She bit her lip, crawled into bed, and looked out the window. Below, the crying continued.

In the morning, Laurence found both women asleep on the couch. Entwined in one another, Bea snored. In response to Pepper's licks, Sage opened her eyes. Laurence made for the kitchen, put on the water, then let Pepper out. After making tea, she brought a cup to Sage.

"Good trip?" Laurence asked.

Sage had lost her normally youthful look. Dark circles spoke to many sleepless nights and she wore the same clothes as the week before. In her arms, one of the antique dolls. She caressed the hair and touched the eyes, nose, and mouth, ignoring the steaming drink Laurence placed nearby. Bea stirred yet soon fell back to sleep. As Sage shed tears anew, she caressed the doll's face.

"I'm ill, baby," she finally said. "Cancer."

"Sage..."

"It's my smoke-torn lungs. Surgical options, radiation, consults, so few answers and so many dilemmas—that's what my days have been. Hell."

Laurence fixed her gaze on Sage.

"Here," Sage said, handing Laurence the doll. The ivory silk dress splayed across Laurence's lap, the wide painted blue eyes staring. "Isn't she lovely?"

"There must be something..."

Sage wiped tears and tried to smile. "No. We've followed the hopeful path for a while now. That's behind us. I'm sorry you've had these months to yourself. We've not been ignoring you on purpose.

"I've come home to die. I've made my decision. Some days will be harder than others. You will have to put up with me, for I've never been patient with physical ailments. I don't want to live out my days in a hospital. I want to be here on the island with you and Bea. Can you understand that?"

"Of course."

"I haven't forgotten your music. Is it too late?"

"It's never too late," Laurence said.

Sage crooked her finger. "Sit with us. I've missed being with you." Laurence squeezed close and they embraced.

"I've missed you too, Sage, oh how I've missed you!"

"Our favorite time of year is upon us. We must try to be upbeat. Be strong, for I'll give out every now and then and become a monster. The pain is horrible and I hate the infirmity. But here with you and Bea, I'll be able to better manage."

Laurence squeezed Sage's arm, felt the bone, stroked her papery skin. "I'll do everything I can."

"You already have. You've made my life whole. You and Bea, and our place with Pepper."

Laurence lay her head in Sage's shoulder. "I love you, Sage. I love you so much."

Sage resumed her former schedule as best she could, breaking to take walks with Bea and Laurence, this to relieve tension and to inhale the fresh sea air. She kept up with medications, and there were trips to the mainland for doctor visits, and tests.

She shared the initial bars of a promising piece, one Laurence felt would complement the film. But there were many interruptions. Sage slept longer, access to care often took entire afternoons, and sometimes she was too weak to work. She fought lethargy, but soon realized that the only sane option was to comply with her struggling body. Sleep provided a temporary exit from suffering.

Bea held off on editing and took to caring for Sage and tending to the house. Rather than use Laurence as a sounding board for her frustration and fear, she lost herself in menial tasks that could be interrupted without consequence should Sage require attention. She honed over her lover, preparing nutritious meals, seeing to it medication was administered and, on low energy days, encouraging Sage to at least try to get up and about.

She took few phone calls and Laurence handled what responsibilities she could. Callers were told Sage was ill and that Bea was indisposed. Bea cancelled trips abroad, Laurence told friends they would be in touch, and no one entertained long term plans.

Soon it became clear Sage was incapable of finishing the composition. During lucid moments, Sage would apologize profusely, promising Laurence the next day would be better and she'd have her score. But time and again, Sage proved too weak to attempt the keys. Her hands could barely stand a minute of song at the piano that was her lifeline, her source. Bea and Laurence had to lift her from the keyboard; it was time to rest or eat, and downplay the fact Sage may never contribute as she once had.

Without Sage's tunes, the stillness was interrupted only by the sound of distant waves, and this left Laurence and Bea exchanging sorrow-filled glances, for each knew what the other was thinking. How will we go on without her? How will be bear the total loss, as the loss descends upon us even now?

December continued with windy, sunny days. Sage would sit in the Adirondack chair as Bea and Laurence crossed the sands, throwing sticks for Pepper, waving and laughing and flirting with the sea.

Bea gradually told others about Sage. In the days leading up to Christmas, a steady stream of well-wishers appeared at the door. Holiday jocularity filled the house all the while Sage dozed in Bea's lap. Most islanders stayed, for there was no more beautiful place to celebrate year-end. Neighbors shared their respective plans, and memories of past holiday seasons.

A few times, Don took Laurence to town for supplies and to get her out of the house. Laurence had no interest in completing the film, so he didn't insist. They reviewed the intense summer of work and made plans to do the same once the warm weather returned, but the future included the understanding Sage came first.

When Evan's letter arrived, full of anecdotes of Boston plus a request to visit, Laurence wasn't sure what to do. Vague memories of his manners and tall, assured form emerged and she had to admit, it might be fun to again enjoy pleasant conversation with a friend of the family. She'd written regularly to Mémé who always had words of praise for Evan. Laurence felt she knew him even though she herself had not made a connection.

"Why not invite him?" Bea asked one night. "If he's in the States for the holidays, it will be lonely for him. He can stay here, the couch pulls out."

"What about Sage?" asked Laurence. "She likes her privacy."

"Oh, a new face will do us all good and you've said before that he's nice. We can manage for a few days. Plus, if he's going to school, he'll have to head back after the new year anyway, won't he?"

"He's rather vague about his intentions," Laurence said.

"Well, never mind. Ask him. You've not once had friends for a visit and we've had so many guests invading your space! C'mon, I won't take no for an answer, neither will Sage!"

Laurence wrote back, giving Evan her phone number, address, and hours of the ferry. She welcomed him to spend as much time as he liked, warning him the place tended to be desolate in winter but serene.

The next day, as she posted the letter, she felt an odd, stabbing sensation in her chest, as if she had sustained a blow. For hours, it remained, a background throb sending waves of nausea one second, shivers the next. Imagery of her days in Roscoff persisted. She reviewed her time with the de Longs. Soon, she identified the source of her pain—that same demon suppressed by virtue of her choice to form a new life, by focusing on only what was good and positive rather than destructive.

Evan was Giles's son. Régine had become Giles's lover. That meant Evan knew her, likely saw her each day. They spoke, dined, and worked together. Régine was apparently a fixture at the de Roche home as well as a partner in the firm. Mémé never went into detail so Laurence had to fill in the blanks for herself. Conditioned by years with her mother, she could only conclude a tenuous relationship existed between Régine and Evan. She hoped Evan wasn't fooled by the woman's wiles. Whatever else Régine had become, Laurence was certain her mother had not changed. If anything she'd gotten worse.

Was Evan here to spy? Or was Evan, like she, on the receiving end of Régine's rage? Few, save Uncle Georges and Aunt Chantel, suspected what Laurence knew to be true. Had Evan insight or did he wear blinders like so many others?

Laurence had come to terms over certain issues about her mother. She better understood the jealousies, self-serving affairs, and grandiosity. Régine had disdained the closeness between Laurence and Nate. Still, it didn't clear away the scars. Régine's mark was indelible.

With time and distance, Laurence had regained some of her own fortitude, had even produced work of which she was proud and that hinted to a former, gentler time with her father. A victim who comes around, Laurence slowly rebuilt a healthier life. But there was always a threat about her tomorrows, the unbidden rearing of anguish. In the wings of the stage of her life, sorrow hovered.

For all the love she was capable of giving Bea and Sage, for all the peace of mind and happiness the island had brought forth, the devil tip-toed around her psyche. The pain worsened as Evan's arrival date drew near.

Two days before Christmas, she met him at the harbor as the car ferry pulled into the dock. Islanders and visitors filed down the boat's plank, protecting themselves against the chilling sea mist with ear muffs, wool coats, puffy anoraks, gloves, furry boots and hats. Cheery calls and shouting reigned as travelers reconnected with family and friends.

Laurence spotted him as he emerged and stood at the top of the exit plank. As if programmed for one another, their gazes locked.

He was tanned, with straight hair hanging over the collar of a wool navy sailor jacket. Even from a distance, he had the deepest-set brown eyes she'd ever seen. With long legs and confident stride, he made for her. He appeared unperturbed by the new place, at ease amidst people he couldn't possibly know well, as if ready to embrace this remote enclave without fanfare or introduction. At the bottom step, he looked beyond the people to the village houses hugging the water's edge, studying rows of Federal-style construction with American flags and white columns, the grey-slated fishermen abodes, the cobblestone streets that bespoke the age of the former whaling port.

"*Bienvenu*," Laurence said, as he put down his sack and embraced her. They made the traditional greeting of many kisses on each cheek, then he held her shoulders and stepped back.

"*Si jolie comme toujours*," he said.

It was a sign they would speak French and Laurence accommodated his wish with a demure smile.

They found a nearby diner for a snack to revitalize Evan, and to afford Laurence the chance to update him on the situation at Madaket. At a wooden table near the windows, they downed yogurt and fresh fruit with coffee, taking in the view of passers-by and the main street of gift shops closed for the winter. Their conversation was light and newsy, dominated by Evan's energetic take on the States.

He enjoyed Harvard and had made contact with other business people like himself. He opined about the war as well or better than any American, his musings colored with a French perspective, seeing as he was one whose country had left Vietnam prior to America's arrival. He spoke of protest rallies and agitation over the invasion of Cambodia, events Laurence had heard of but did not dwell upon. He expounded on the differences between youth in America and in France, using anecdotes related to the music scene to make his points. Laurence had heard of Johnny's but not the woman with the voice. Evan proclaimed her the next greatest singing star.

They strolled around town and Laurence shared historical perspective, and even local lore to which few vacationers were privy. During the half hour walk, they managed to encircle the compact downtown area several times, thereby prolonging their jaunt and, in an off-handed and casual way, one measured step at a time, gleaning insight to each other.

She was reserved at first, deferent and courteous, pointing out what she thought would be most of interest to someone so cultured and educated. Gradually, though, she relaxed as he explained that he was ready for vacation and fun.

She wore jeans and her hair hung loose. Her expression deepened into a mellowness that brought into relief a clear face with make-up-free shine. She periodically nudged her glasses and stole looks at him. As tall as he, they stood out, tracing and retracing steps.

In Bea's Jeep, they drove west along the shore route towards Porpus. Evan marveled at the custom-designed homes atop sweeping dunes and the private driveways leading to hideaways owned by corporate titans Evan knew to be of the same families he met while in Cambridge. Laurence wanted to show him the location from where she shot the film, so they stopped at that pier, parked the car, and walked to the edge. The island wound around this indent of the bay, giving view to the village and fishing vessels still anchored in icy waters.

"I see why you stay," he said, as they stood looking out.

"I love it."

"You must have enjoyed Batz then."

She nodded but her gaze avoided his. "How is Mémé?"

"Save a slight hobble, still in form. Her spirit is alive and well. She speaks often of you."

Laurence smiled. "And you."

"Ah, you two ladies keeping secrets?"

She turned, studied the angular chin and his grin. "No, Mémé writes of your schooling and work."

"And Régine, I'm sure. You keep up with your mother's activities?"

She drew in her breath. Staring at the lapping waves, she raised clasped hands to her mouth, blew into the palms.

Immediately, he took them, pressed them against the wool of his jacket. The warmth passed from his hands to hers. In a swift, easy move she snuggled closer.

Her scarf blew, exposing her skin below her neck. His eyes fell on a pink spot. "What happened there?" he asked.

She went to cover it but his hand was quicker. With one finger he made a circular trace around the sore. "I had a friend who was wounded during May of '68. He had burns and bruises over one third of his body. Some, the scars from blows he received, are permanent."

She closed her eyes, and allowed him to pull her to his chest.

"I won't pry," he whispered. "I think I know anyway, my little one, what this is all about."

With both hands he held her head, cradled one way then the next. He straightened her chin so she could see into his eyes. "You are so beautiful, so very, very gorgeous."

She lay her head on his chest. The wind blew about. Boat riggings clanged. She embraced him around his waist, clutched the folds of his jacket. They rocked, then she stood back from him.

372

"Let's go," she said, moving towards the Jeep.

Releasing herself, she took a few steps before turning to look at him.

"You look exactly as you did on Batz," he said.

They got into the Jeep and drove away.

# Chapter 23

"HOW IN THE WORLD?" Régine screamed. "It's the most asinine thing a child can do, abandon his family!" She stormed about the room, her face matching the vermillion of her snug ensemble.

Seated in her chair, Mémé's eyes narrowed. "He's a grown man," she said.

"He's most disrespectful. Of all the lowly things, what with Giles the age he is! The man may not even be around next year. What would Evan have to say about that?"

"Giles is strong and healthy. Régine, calm yourself. You're getting upset over nothing."

"I'm more than upset! I had plans for us all, plans that now must be cancelled because Evan has taken so much to the States. How in the world THAT has happened I can only guess. Why, it's..."

"Régine, sit!"

She swirled around and caught her mother's stern regard. Retreating to a chair, she harrumphed against the pillows, kicked off shoes and massaged her feet.

"Relax. We can have a perfectly respectable holiday even if Evan doesn't join us. Continue to make your plans. Betti can accommodate the changes, you know that. Really, I must say your behavior makes me cringe. Evan is a grown man."

"Mama, he should be with Giles, end of story!"

"How would you have liked it if, when you lived in America, I expected you to return to France every Christmas?"

"It's not the same."

"Why not?"

"I had a child and husband," she said. "Believe me, if it had been my choice, I would have returned regularly." She sniffed and pulled a handkerchief from her sleeve. "If not for Nate and his dreaming, I'd have led a life of travel, I assure you."

"Since you've been in Paris, I get much input from you indicating how wicked Nate was. I was not aware your marriage had been so unhealthy. It's not as I remember the man, and from what Laurence said about him..."

"That little twit has no idea.."

"Silence!" Mémé exclaimed. "I'll not have you talking about your daughter like that. You can't claim she's a 'twit', as you put it. I met her, got to know her. She's a child to be proud of. What in the world has gotten into you?"

Régine tried to compose herself. "Mama, dear, I've so much on my mind with the workload Evan left behind and my own responsibilities at de Roche Frères."

"Speaking of your work, I received an interesting piece of news from Giles the other day. He tells me you carry a degree from Harvard. I never knew."

"Oh, Mama, it goes back in time, to the days when Nate gave seminars there. I never told you? Silly me! Really, it doesn't even matter because..."

"Then I should like to see your diploma. What exactly did you major in?"

"Economics."

"Giles told me business."

"Business economics," Régine said, reaching to the silver canister for a cigarette. "And I don't want to discuss it now."

"I do."

Régine exhaled smoke and shook her head. "Mama, not now, please! Can't you see I'm distraught?"

"Yes, and I don't understand. Such a prestigious accomplishment. You never even told Evan, and he is there now. He could have looked up faculty and friends of yours."

"Oh, they're all long gone, or dead, who knows?"

"Régine, look at me."

Régine slid her gaze to her mother.

"Now," said Mémé, "something's been on my mind for a while. You're not to take offense or to retort. You are to listen. I have seen your behavior around Giles. I cannot say I approve of your liaison but I can no more change that than the course of the planets. What I object to is your absolute need to control everything you do with him, everything that goes on in that house. I had a long discussion with Betti this summer.."

"Betti! What does..."

"Hush. Betti is a friend as well as employee, and she tells me stories that make me, quite frankly, ashamed. Remember, Régine, you are no longer eighteen and the things you do you must account for. Running around Paris at all hours, dressing in the fashion of a younger woman, calling upon government associates of Giles for financial favors for the company! These things are not appropriate for a daughter of mine or any woman of standing in Paris for that matter. I may be a senior but I have my sight and my mind. You have to contain yourself when you deal with people, not rush about expecting overnight results.

"And, above all, Régine, you are to accord Betti and any person in our employ the same respect you give Giles. They are family and they are as deserving of proper manners as anyone, sometimes more in my estimation."

"You talk as though I've wronged you."

Mémé sighed. "I know you're still adjusting to Paris, even though it's been a while now since your return. This is not some beach community where life is defined and arranged according to whim! There is a protocol to life here, people of our stature are refined, respectful, and educated. Your behavior, especially where it concerns Evan, will not be tolerated."

"Oh, so now I've offended Evan! What did he tell you?"

"Evan never said an unkind word about you. He wouldn't. Evan is of his family—a decent individual. You could take a few lessons from him. It is an admirable initiative, going to the United States. His experience will be put to good use on his return. I guarantee he'll get results for de Roche Frères."

"He does nothing, I do all the work around there!"

"Never mind. He's the son and heir to the fortune. He is well qualified. I trust he does the best he can."

"You call the best running around Cambridge and Boston taking in music halls? You should read the letters he sends to Giles! Late nights, women, some singer he wants to promote in France! I don't call that serious work," Régine said, lighting a cigarette.

"Your first cigarette still burns," Mémé said pointing to the ashtray. "And I received a few letters myself."

"Oh?"

"Yes, the young man told me about his work and his play. He's entitled to both, as are you."

"What else did he write?"

Mémé adjusted herself in the chair, lowered her chin, and stared at Régine. Waiting until Régine sat still, she continued, "He's doing something I feel is long overdue from you."

"Oh, don't start that again. Laurence has been on her own for ages!"

"He's seeing her over the holidays."

"What!" Régine shot up from the chair. "That...."

"That, what?" Mémé asked.

"That, that figures," Régine said, rising and going to the window.

"I think it's wonderful. After all, how long has it been since you've seen your daughter?"

Régine shook her head, fast little shakes that spun her around. "I don't believe it, I don't believe it!" she screamed as she threw on her coat and raced out the door.

Mémé watched with blinking eyes. The roar of Régine's Peugeot rounding the corner came and went. When calm returned, she picked up the phone and dialed.

"Georges, *comment vas-tu?*" she asked her nephew. "I would like to talk with you at your convenience. Yes, yes...it's about what we discussed over the summer. You had a point that I wasn't ready to face. Tuesday will be fine."

She hung up the phone. She would have to keep an open mind from now on. Uncontrolled behavior was akin to mental instability to Mémé. Something was up with Régine. If what Georges hinted at was true, well, Mémé would not sit back and watch.

She sighed again. At her age, she should be surrounded by children and grandchildren, not spoiled babies.

♥ ♥ ♥

Régine took the Périphérique to the edges of the city, found the first autoroute she could, and bulleted down the fast lane. Her eyes squinted hatred and she swore as she drove up the stereo.

"Damn, fuckin' damn!"

The cityscape gave way to suburban fields and fewer cars. She drove faster, to over 200 kph.

"I hate you, fuckin' Laurence! I hate you!" she raged at the top of her lungs. "Christmas with Evan! You bitch! You whore! Why can't you stay out of my life. I can't stomach the sound of your fuckin' name!"

She bore down harder, clutched the rattling wheel. She didn't care about anything, only her hatred for the child she once—so very long ago—thought might bring her so much happiness.

"Too long ago, it was," she wailed. "Fuckin' too long ago. I hate you!"

Her stomach lurched. She grasped the fur of her coat around her waist, and slowed the car to the edge of the road. Onto the shoulder she vomited into the mud, spitting and swearing, cursing the child who was miles away and unaware of the extent of the hatred her mother harbored for her still.

Her retching finished, she rubbed make-up stained eyes and looked down at her soiled mink. Tugging it off, she threw it into a ditch and got back in the car. She continued on, heading west, to somewhere she didn't know, somewhere that maybe, just maybe...

♥ ♥ ♥

Evan ambled along the cobblestones of Nantucket's main street, eyeing storefront displays in search of a Christmas gift for Laurence. Since his arrival, the feeling he'd first had on Batz had blossomed into a

379

headiness that kept his eyes soft and voice merry. More enchanting than he'd dreamed, her hair was silken, the body lithe and fit. In addition, she was charm and poise itself, even as she muddied her boots and picked after sticks to throw for the dog. How he loved studying her when she wasn't aware of his gaze! When she fixed tea, or typed invoices, or sat on the chair overlooking the sea. He couldn't wait for morning, lost sleep as she lay in the room next to him, dreamt of her naked body; he fell in love over and over.

By now he was well aware of the pleasures found in a woman's body. Several other women had been in his arms, and his bed. To achieve physical completion with Laurence, however, was not his focus. Hers was another kind of draw. She had a power over him like no other, not even Patrice, who for months following their breakup had occupied his thoughts, had kept him wondering about lost love and its pain, an activity that risked turning him bitter. Now, he knew his amorous forays had been but preparatory work, stagings for the real thing. With Patrice, his youth, his naiveté, his virgin state were manipulated and forever changed. Laurence's power was of all the senses, and reached to his very soul. Still, he was not unaware of what she could do, and undo, where he was concerned. In spite of his desire, he would go slow.

He thought of jewels, a ruby around her neck, garnets in her ears. She was red to him—vibrant and primary. But jewels couldn't enhance what was already there. She was even more precious than stones. Was there even an item he could purchase that would enhance her being? The answer was too easily no. She didn't yearn after things, nor had she coveted goods displayed in shop windows, and seemed contained within herself, snug in jeans and wooly sweaters with those long arms and the neck open to reveal alabaster skin. Might she want a fancy meal at the best place in town? Or a boat ride chartered for the two of them? No, too extravagant. She was basic, unadorned, and precious. She had it all, any man-made item was a runner-up.

He placed a call to Betti, who greeted him with too-anxious queries about his return. He could tell she was stressed, and guessed the reason, but he was much too involved at the moment to care about what transpired in Paris. He asked for her advice, took notes, then hung up with greetings to all and best wishes for the holidays. He wasn't sure when he'd be home again.

Then he called Laurence. She said she would meet him at 2 PM to catch the ferry to the mainland, and didn't push when he requested she ask no questions.

Next, he scoured the shops. For the first time since he could remember, he was nervous, although many would chuckle at his fears of such an undertaking. Laurence was too right, too much the person who deserved something straight from his heart. With luck, he might get her to crack that outer layer, so he could see more of her landscape. He'd never fallen in love till now.

Later when she appeared, in leather jacket with evergreen scarf hugged about her neck, he laughed, half from the silliness of the situation, half with the jitters characterizing any first date.

"Hi," she said.

"Problems at home?" he asked. He knew Sage had worsened and there was every expectation of another trip to the mainland.

"Not for now. Where are we going?"

He grinned and wrapped an arm around her, walked toward the waiting ferry, and stood by several large cartons.

"Yours?" she asked with wide eyes.

He placed a finger to his lips. "Ssssh, no questions, remember?"

"I feel as though I'm being whisked away to a secret hideaway."

"Perceptive lady," he said. They boarded and sat side-by-side at a window seat. The trip lasted two hours and, by the time they landed, Christmas Eve was upon them. He rented a car and, with the aid of maps, drove from the port at Woods Hole to the highway east towards the Outer Cape. She was polite and spoke of her film, and didn't flinch when the signs pointed to the place where she grew up.

"If you're going to the end, you're Okay," she said. "There's basically one road."

"All roads lead to the end," he sang.

She shook her head and laughed. "This is too mysterious, Evan."

"A little bit longer."

They arrived at the tip of Cape Cod, a dune haven of sweeping sands, seaweed and blowing reeds. It was dark as they parked at Race Point on the edge of Provincetown. He unloaded the cartons, left her in the car until he was finished, then led her down the path to shore.

Distant lights their only company, he lit gas lamps, spread table clothes, and wrapped her in a heavy wool blanket. Protected by a barrier of heavy canvas, they were soon as warm and cozy as they could be inside any house. Facing a roaring fire, he produced a picnic basket. With a sly yet unsure grin said, "It's a holiday meal. I'm going to prepare it for you *à la française*."

She shook her head. "I can't believe you. Mémé said you had a mind of your own but this!"

He frowned. "You're disappointed?"

She laughed again. "Oh, no, Evan! Goodness, it's so imaginative!"

Relieved, he opened the case and found an apéritif bottle, poured the ruby liquid into crystal glasses, and offered one to her. "Ambassadeur. Difficult to find outside France. A secret." With a wink, they clinked glasses and sipped.

"Mmm," she said, "It's not sweet like most, has a bite."

"I thought you'd like it. I brought some over for people I would meet during the seminar, but I found someone more special."

She sipped again and looked up, smiling. "This is a dream."

"Big dream," he said. "Big. Think big, Laurence, always big."

As he spoke, he unraveled package after package of pâté de fois gras provençal, chicken, garlic, fresh thyme and basil, fennel, sorrel, fresh asparagus, home-made stock, more wine, Epoisses and Cantal cheeses direct from France, fruit, after-dinner drinks, rich expresso coffee beans. He had the pots and pans, the spoons, sifter, measuring cups, the glasses for different wines, cloth napkins to match the table cloth, even extra candles for the lamps.

The meal took hours to prepare. All the while, they talked of his past, of his father and mother. A long time on his mother. He detailed how he and Pauline walked the shore on a magical evening and the next day she was dead. He didn't cry but she could tell he'd already grieved many times over his mother's memory. He was chuckling one minute, sad the next, philosophical yet again. She listened patiently, and in awe, for he was as complex as he was handsome, as smart as he was habile, as wise as the old moon that finally snuck from behind a cloud, and more attentive than anyone she'd ever met.

They spoke little of her, for she didn't offer much. He returned multiple times to the subject of Mémé.

Laurence felt remiss for leaving the woman, and wished out loud she could have continued visiting her. Régine was noticeably absent from their talk.

The meal was a success, from the moist chicken in a butter cream sauce with carrots and baby green asparagus, to the bottle of Maucaillou Bordeaux to the cheese and coffee. They didn't eat much but relished everything. Their conversation mattered most, and their time together. Neither wanted to interrupt the flow of dining and relaxed conversation.

Cooking was a hobby for him, he explained, and one in which he rarely had a chance to indulge. Pauline had introduced him to the French ways of food preparation, which involved commitment and time, and love of the catered palette. He had never tried the recipe before and gave Betti her due, for she had passed on precious culinary secrets.

On the edges of the world, by the light of a cold holiday sky and with the moon smiling down, for the first time in years, Laurence began to foresee a future. At first, she'd been worried, had passed sleepless nights wondering about Evan and his ways. But emotions had taken hold as if by the force of a wind, and she had yet to alight somewhere concrete. In twenty-four hours, she'd been whisked to a shore she never envisioned. Evan had won her heart.

He rambled, and she listened. He held an arm around her and kept adjusting the blanket about her shoulders. "You're not too cold?"

She touched his cheek and ran a finger over the stubble.

He eased a hand to her neck, caressing the white skin. Inches from her, her breathe and the slow husky voice when she murmured, "So, very, sweet you are, Evan de Roche."

He kissed her. She reached for the strands of his hair and played with one then another as her lips pressed against his and her mouth opened. He lay her on the blanket and settled to one side of her, easing his body close, breathing into her ear and kissing her cool skin.

"Where have I been?" he asked. "Why did I not take you with me years ago?"

She fell on him, a hand sandwiched between her breast and his chest, and dug nails. He found her hand, and the smooth skin underneath her clothes. Deftly he touched her nipple, and she caught her breath, biting his ear and begging, too. The rigidness of her grasp lessened, and she undulated in sync with the waves as he moved fingers over her chest, her stomach, the lines of her jeans. She opened her legs, and straddled over one of his, her beating heart murmuring a burgeoning purpose.

He dimmed the light. There was nothing in the night except their shadows, the features hidden but already familiar, ingrained in embraces imprinting permanence.

She didn't move to kiss him, only stared at the blackness and the outline of his face. "You won't hurt me, will you?"

His hand stroked her hair. "Hurt? Chérie, mon amour. Je t'aime, je t'aime. No one will ever hurt you again."

Their kiss, intimate and long, staked a claim, a kiss that was least of all physical, more a joining of the highest order. The hold eclipsed their human state and brought forth the fever of dreams.

He rolled her sweater from her shoulders and she covered her breasts from the cold. Then, he took his shirt off, and blanketed them both. They eagerly found one another, removing what clothing had already been stripped in their minds. She opened herself to him, and cried softly as he brought her slowly to a climax that ended with the pleading of her open, unabashed, and gripping heart, for she would never let him go.

Existing rather than living, the nights spent in quandaries wrapped in dark imagery that, in truth, had been illusory. Artifacts of a journey now in her past, she placed them in an imaginary bucket and tossed it to the waves. Evan held her and slept while she watched the sea. It was Christmas Day.

# Chapter 24

AT WOODS HOLE EVAN SAW LAURENCE off on the ferry to Nantucket, then drove to Boston for several previous commitments. After, he planned to return to Paris and inform Giles of his plans.

Laurence could no more focus on anything else than pretend she wasn't a changed woman. She relived the beach dine, savoring the taste of the food, Evan's charm, and the feel of his arms around her. While helping Bea tend to Sage, his words returned afresh, his smile grew more deeply ingrained in her heart, and the memory of his body filled her with sexual energy in which she reveled.

Bea was quiet and watchful, grinning with the knowledge Evan had become Laurence's shining star. With Sage ailing, it was hard for Bea to act as if Laurence's news was yet another happy event.

Following an operation, Sage now had a wound in her back that required regular cleansing and bandaging. In bed or on the couch, she lay on her stomach and could no longer take walks. In the confusion of drugs, what lucidity remained arose when Bea was at her side holding her hand. Her hair had fallen out and she wore a bright purple scarf about her head. Wrapped in her baby blue robe, she was a tiny child staring wide-eyed at the world. Talk was no longer of hope, only of release. Sage was stricken, a body with the life seeping from her even as she drew in the vital salt air.

Laurence took to the outdoors when she could. Inside, where death hovered, was jarring. Rather than suggest coziness, the crackle of a fire portended disaster, the chimes rang with a mortal chill. The upstairs garret was as Sage had left it the last time she played—blank music sheets on the floor, one of Mendelssohn's "Songs without Words" left open at the ready, her timer to one side of the piano. A pale blue cushion covered her bench, holding the imprint of her sitting, as if she belonged and was not on her death bed.

For Laurence to walk the beach was lonely, for it wasn't the same without the other two. Still, she had Evan now. The couple had talked of her returning to Paris with him but decided against it for the time being. He had his responsibilities and she hers. In time, they would arrange something convenient for both, and Evan hinted at ideas of his own. Her only requirement, aside from spending the rest of her days with him, was to finish the film and market it.

The music was the final piece and Laurence explained to Evan that, out of respect for Sage, she wouldn't seek out another composer. To carry on meant everything right now. Even though the end was at hand, Bea and Sage attempted regular activities and trivial time-consuming commitments as they did the arrival of each new day. And Sage every now and then still voiced her intentions to help Laurence.

Evan called her twice daily. They planned to see one another as soon as he returned from Paris, though he wasn't yet sure when that would be. As he explained, Giles would require help, and time to adjust.

She wondered about that, thought it odd the son of a wealthy French businessman would even consider alternatives to the life that had been handed to him. But from their conversations, she also understood Evan to have grappled long over his career choices. Though conflicted, he remained under the safety of an umbrella that not only afforded him privilege but gave him the freedom to pursue his other interests. It was time to stand up for what he believed in. Doing so would free him but it would break his father's heart. He knew he must plan judiciously.

When Evan spoke of music and film, he grew more precious to her, for her dreams mirrored his own. Presently, each struggled over issues less self-nurturing. For Laurence, those things were of an internal nature. Evan's were hard realities—money, fortune, the rights inherent in his name. To hear him talk, none of it mattered, but Laurence knew well the results of breaking with convention. There could be a price to pay for his affair with film.

She admired him at the same time she feared for him. Giles seemed a kind man but was also the man behind the fortune. It took guts, decision-making, and unswerving single-mindedness to build what he had built. Like his industries, the man was solidly made, and could shut off emotions if need be. And he now had an ally. Régine, if given enough rope, would strangle Evan like a dead rat.

The thought made her shudder and so she did what she always did when Régine came to mind—she switched focus. Bending down, she twisted of a piece of drift wood from where it was lodged, hollered to Pepper and threw the stick into the frigid waters. The waves chilled and she laughed a laugh she hoped might reach Evan's ears.

♥ ♥ ♥

From the outside, the de Roche residence appeared unchanged. Inside, the aromas of Betti's cooking reined, low lighting in the study created an inviting glow, and smoke curled from the hearth and chimney to the Parisian night. The dinner over, all sat around the festively-organized table, each in private rumination. Suddenly, Giles's aspirations to kick-start the holiday season were displaced by a single statement from Evan.

"I am quitting de Roche."

After a long moment, Giles rose and made for his study. Régine followed and Betti cleared the dishes. Evan stared at his wine glass. This news, coupled with his claim he wanted no more of Polytechnique, was an offense no de Roche would tolerate, let alone pretend to comprehend. Evan had stepped beyond the bounds.

Régine found Giles in his desk chair, which he'd swiveled around to face the window. His hands shook and he muttered incoherently, pounding a fist one second, shaking his head the next. She went to his side and ran fingers from the base of his neck down his shoulders.

"Mon cher, try to understand. He must do what is right for him," she said. "It's not the end of the world."

Giles dismissed her with a wave of his hand that sent her back-pedaling towards the bookcases. "You can't possibly understand. This is totally unacceptable. He'll not get away with this as long as I live! Ever!"

Muffling a perturbed tone, she straightened herself and said, "But there are ways to work around this!"

He shook a finger at her. "No! Do you hear me? There are no ways, none! Evan de Roche is part of de Roche Frères or a dead man. You are not to get involved, this is between two men. Do you understand?"

Her mouth puckered into a frown. As she fussed over invisible spots on her silk blouse, she asked, "Giles, mon cher Giles, what kind of tone is that?"

He turned from her and returned to the window, looking out at the night and the city lights. "It's about life and death. And death I'll have no more of."

Régine sniffed and hiked up her skirt as she settled on the couch, crossing legs and fidgeting with hair.

He opened the drawer, pulled out the wrapped package containing Pauline's scarf, and brought it to his lips. Eyes closed he murmured to his dead wife, losing himself in the scent of her loss.

Régine bit her lip. "Now this is silly. I want to help. Giles, there are ways."

As he had been years before on Batz, Giles was unconsoled. He wanted Pauline, and eight-year-old Evan. He spoke of Danielle and how his daughter would never have done what Evan did. Tears falling, he covered his nose with the scarf.

Evan approached and stood in the doorway, noting the exposed legs of Régine as she tried everything she could to stir Giles from his concentration, a man buried in the past. The two locked eyes. He again tried to find Laurence in her, if for nothing else than to seek out the comfort of Laurence's memory. But there was nothing. He turned from her and headed for his room.

♥ ♥ ♥

She spread her legs and felt desire tinged with disdain, for Giles was an old man and would never truly entice her the way others had. Oh, she'd been so patient and it had been worth it! Evan was playing right into her hand. She must, absolutely must, get Giles to come around, get him away from that rag he clung to. Into bed.

She stared at the scarf, then at the man. The one thing she couldn't control—family ties—encapsulated in a filthy piece of cloth. "Pauline," she seethed under her breath.

She could handle men, for they had simple requirements, but intruding females drove her to the brink. That scarf, inanimate, its odor of human remains, might as well have been Pauline herself. It dug a chasm between Régine and Giles.

She stood and stepped towards him, eyeing the scarf as if a fire raging out of control. Had she worked so hard these two years to end up like this? Would she forever stand to one side when it concerned this man and his past? Didn't Giles see she could handle the business for him? Why was he so stuck on Evan remaining?

Later, after he'd finally fallen asleep in the chair, she rose, took the scarf, and was about to dispose of it when he stirred and woke. More contrite this time, he allowed her to sit on his lap and caress his thighs, his chest, the hardening place between his legs. As she unbuttoned his shirt and placed kisses in strategic spots, he grasped her with a firmness she'd not experienced. For an instant she thought he was at last offering more than lukewarm affection. The thought was blotted as he said, "*Pauline, mon amour, mon amour.*"

Unflinching, she steadied her gaze on a lamp and its pale glow. She slipped her blouse from her shoulders and let him take her breast, let him fondle and caress, and call out the other's name. She returned with murmurs and more directed moves. As she played along, a grin formed, for she loved pretend, and the sense of the absurd.

"I'm here, my love," she whispered. "I'm here. Pauline is here. I love you."

The old man would fall and, one day when he finally woke up, it wouldn't be Pauline in his bed and sharing his fortune, it would be Régine. And he would be too old or helpless to do anything about it. Let him enjoy this silly delusion.

Her strokes made him harder and he was again a young man, Evan's picture, and what Régine imagined a romp with his son might be like. Strengthened by the words he believed those of Pauline, the man was virile, conveying his affections with each touch.

He kissed her hands, each fingertip, sucked her nails. He clenched her hair and the discovery of her breasts brought forth moans. Drawing him to the couch, she undressed him, lay on top of him, and guided him inside. Each of his words felt genuine this time, so unlike previous awkward trysts. "Naturally", she thought as she stared at his white hair, "he's with Pauline."

She bit her lip and suppressed tears, for she didn't want pride to interfere, not now, not as long as all was within reach. Once he was hers, and she comfortable for life, she might then allow the chagrin.

Throughout, as he craved her, as he continued to act as though time had never stopped on Batz, Régine paid close attention. She folded into his needs and became more fully aware of what she attempted. The only way to get this man was to become someone else. As he addressed his dead wife again, she thought, "So be it. If this is what it takes, I'll do it. I don't feel anymore. I don't feel anymore."

They slept on the couch. When he awoke at dawn, his first look spoke volumes as he blinked and tried to put words to the experience of hours before. She placed a finger on his lips to quiet him and recommenced making love. She would not give him a moment to develop remorse. She would nurture his senses until the next time when she would be even better prepared. From now on, each time they lay together, she was Pauline de Roche. And he would come around to playing the same game. Easily.

❤ ❤ ❤

Evan didn't waste time. He drew up a legal document to Giles's attention, stating he was prepared to relinquish all rights to de Roche Frères and the family fortune. He tidied up his office and carried away boxes. He requested Giles allow him another few days at the residence. After, he planned to take a final trip to Batz before returning to the States.

New Year's Eve, packed and ready, Evan passed his father's study and found Giles there. He entered.

They sat, Giles busying himself with paperwork, Evan studying the man to whom he was saying goodbye. They were never so separate—Evan in his jeans and leather jacket, the black hair ruffled over his collar, and Giles in his lounger and tailored shirt.

Evan spoke first, his voice calm, his eyes clear with the future he had already mapped out. He spoke only of Laurence, of his love, and let the reason for the document be known. He had no intention of trying to obtain what might have one day become his.

Giles listened halfheartedly, cocking his head to one side at the mention of Laurence. Once Evan had finished, he cleared his throat and said, "I will never understand why you pass up all you have for the total unknown of a life in the States." He turned and, gaze deepening, took in his son. "If it's love you require, why can't you bring the girl to Paris?"

Evan shook his head. "I have my reasons, the same we have many times disagreed on. It has to do with my belief we must do what is right for us, to follow our dreams. Believe me, Father, if I thought my full realization could be had at de Roche, I would bring Laurence back."

Giles nodded, his eyes lowering. "I hope you choose wisely and well, for I cannot help you. I cannot say I forgive you, nor will I support you. You know fortunes are passed within family concerns such as mine, yet it doesn't make sense to give the fortune to a man who will take it to the United States."

"Papa, I will make my money."

Giles sighed. "Evan! You will marry her, the de Long girl?"

"Mallord. Yes. As soon as possible."

"Return to France, son. It will be good for her, too. Mémé has long spoken of how she misses the girl. I believe she is smart as well as beautiful."

"My life is with her. In the States."

Giles pulled his hair off his forehead. "Ah, the seventies! Would that I had never made it here! It is tougher as one grows old."

"You have built a new life, Papa.

"So to speak."

They stared and Giles reached for his son's hand. "I will miss you. I think that is what is hardest for me. The Evan of full potential. Lost."

There was nothing more to say. Evan was free to go. He stood, took a look at the desk, at the scarf that lay there. "Goodbye, Papa."

As he walked out, Giles stared out the window, his back to his only son.

The next day, Régine found out about Evan's intention to marry Laurence. So, the wench was back, as cute and respected, as admired and sought-after as ever. This time, Laurence would not make it to French shores. She would never take the hand of Evan de Roche. She would never cross her mother again.

Régine made arrangements for a flight to New York. A day or two would suffice, then she would return. No one would be the wiser.

# Chapter 25:
# December 28, 1971

PROMISING TO JOIN THEM THE FOLLOWING DAY in Boston, Laurence saw Bea and Sage off on the morning ferry. Tears formed as she returned to Madaket. Sage, on morphine and incoherent, faced her final battle. Everyone had hoped the end would come on Nantucket but, given her complications, doctors and hospital staff would know better how to manage the pain.

Laurence tidied up, brought Pepper to the kennel, and arranged for someone to periodically look in on the place. She packed her possessions and spent a melancholy afternoon stepping back in time. The film, the music, the life by the sea, offered to her by two women who presently suffered so. She would remain with Bea until the end, would help in any way, and try to comfort her friend in her loss.

Laurence had told Bea she was in love with Evan, that she planned to meet his flight from Paris New Year's Eve, and that she would stay with him. Bea understood and, although saddened, encouraged her to follow her heart. She insisted Laurence not forget the film, that Bea-Sage Productions would provide a means to an end.

Later, the phone rang. Sage died in her sleep, out of pain and presently moving towards a world where her body would no longer anchor her in infirmity. Bea cried as she spoke in whispers yet, for the first time in weeks, sounded at peace. In the last days, Sage was not the Sage of their love affair. Refusing to dwell, Bea set her eyes on the future, as her lover would have wished. She gave Laurence phone numbers and addresses of Sage's relatives in Boston. They agreed to meet the next evening to arrange the funeral.

Laurence retired. The sea was calm and the chimes made no noise. A dog bark from afar kept her awake as she traced recent interactions with Sage and recalled tunes that had once drifted from the upstairs garret.

A car made its way along the sandy road to the edge of the dunes. The engine stopped and the door opened then closed. She wondered who it might be. Save the sea gulls and sandpipers, the threesome shared Madaket with no one in winter.

"Perhaps two lovers," she smiled, warming at the thought of Evan and enfolding herself in the blankets. Silence returned and she dozed.

At first, the noise was imperceptible, a faint scratching and scraping interrupted by intervals of silence. Laurence was unsure if she had dreamed it or not. Perhaps it had been the refrigerator kicking on, or an animal. Silence. She let it go.

Again the noise. There was no mistake, it was inside the house. She sat up, eyes wide.

"Who's there?" she called.

Nothing. She stood and went to the door, then down the hall where she could glimpse into the living room. A familiar smell reached her. Although perfume, its effect on Laurence was of a venomous clutch. Chanel, she knew it anywhere. She bit her lips and closed her eyes. Her body froze, a conditioned response, a seizure of former times. She moaned, whispered a prayer. The dark form approached.

The hand was raised, a stick in it. The fur coat, the dress, the odor—all moving towards her with the stealth of revenge. Her feet became jelly and she faltered. As the first blow lowered over her skull, she coiled into a ball and covered her face.

Her head hit the floor. Heels kicked into her side, claws dug into her skin and tore it, a fist shoved into her mouth. Her hair was pulled back then tugged, she was dragged down the hall. She begged, pleaded for help, for kindness, but her words were met with the familiar, hollow laugh, the voice telling her she was no good, damned, and in the way. The warning was without ambiguity.

"Stay away from Evan de Roche or you're dead. You whore, you bitch. You nothing!"

Nauseous, she swallowed blood. A blow landed between her eyes. In the final moments, the nails scratched her stomach and the fist pummeled into her chest. Her eyes bulged as her mother spat in her face and pain released Laurence from consciousness.

# Chapter 26:
# January 31, 1971

At the airport, Evan searched the crowd for Laurence. The entire journey from Paris, he imagined their embrace. More than ever he needed her, for his was a clean slate, a life begun anew, with Laurence the major component. He could plan only so much before reaching the impasse of her absence. He wanted to run ideas by her, listen and incorporate her suggestions. It was scary insofar as she was not by his side. With her, he was infallible, and could create an environment for both that had all the elements of what he lacked in Paris.

He sat on a bench and waited, confirmed the time. She'd told him she would be there, promised.

Travelers rushed about and he was soon engrossed in the pace. Back in the States, he was free to seek answers to questions most of the de Roches would never have posed. The facade Giles proffered, so tinged with bitterness, convinced Evan even more that his was the right move. No longer interested in falsely proving himself, he wanted his own rewards and successes, and in the entertainment field.

Ever since May of '68, he had questioned his motives. Now, especially with Laurence's love and Klee's potential, he did not feel guilt, only contentment that he would join others who had been unafraid to attempt fundamental change.

He looked around once more then went to the information desk. The receptionist handed him a telegram.

Dear Evan,

To write you is difficult. I have decided to pursue another relationship, one that has much promise, one well worthy of my interest. I will remember the moments we shared. The memories give me strength. You are a special man and are headed for greatness, as Mémé always said.

Please be happy as I plan to be. I am leaving Nantucket, so you won't find me there.

Laurence

# Chapter 27

KLEE DOZED, A BOOK ON HER LAP, the light still on. After turning down Johnny's invitation to dinner, she had said good-night, and headed home to welcome the New Year alone. A soft rap woke her and she sat with a start.

"Who is it?"

"Evan."

"Right there," she said, throwing on jeans and sweater.

At the door, he fell limp against her. She pushed back. Noting the look on his face, she embraced him and led him inside. He sank into the chair. His hair was greasy, his boots muddied.

"I thought you were drunk for a minute," she said.

He barely nodded.

"Early return from Nantucket?" she asked.

At the mention of the place, his gaze fell. He shook his head. Calculating the time difference with Paris, she figured he'd been awake well over twenty-four hours.

"Sure you're Okay?" she asked.

Her last talk with him had been specific. He would spend New Year's Eve and the next day on the island, return to Boston, and finish up what work remained at Harvard. Then, he wanted Klee to meet his future wife.

His forlorn regard, the shaking head told her something had happened to upset his plans. She required only minutes more, time enough to read through to his soul.

Hers was a quick intuition, one that aided in the toughest of times, one on which she relied more than on any human. As her first friend since Romney looked into her eyes, she thought of one word, the word whose meaning she herself had once been forced to accept as truth. Rejection.

She thought back to Bob Walsh and his behavior, to her youth when she refused to see him for who he was, to the futile hours pursuing a man who reviled her. She called back the night of her sister's wedding, and the endless counting of days until she could flee Kinemmaera. She thought it was all behind her now that she'd rebuilt herself and her spirits. She stared through Evan and discerned the origin of his pain.

Gone the Evan of one week before, the man of myriad dreams and potential, the man of spark and light who was the first to intelligently challenge her abilities and compliment her efforts. He had selflessly given his time to help her practice French, to temporarily forget about Johnny's, to let her be. Evan, eternally questioning politics, society, beliefs, indeed life itself, had welcomed her into his world which she found as deep and mysterious, as enlightening and full of surprises as her own. The person who wanted nothing of her but her patient ear and a fist full of song had finally appeared. How thrilling to again partake in the enchanted world known to those who believed anything was possible, and much was beyond the realms of this world! For they had discussed, had shared secrets, and had embraced one another's uniqueness.

Following his trip to Nantucket, he had first spoken of his lady friend, and she was as happy for him as he had been for himself. She missed him when he left for Paris and hid a package for him in her closet—a book of Irish verse. She wanted to present it to the couple, so the two together could accept the gift.

But the woman would not be joining him this New Year. Klee knew this even as the details remained unspoken.

She often cursed her ability to sense what transpired in another's head, the words unsaid. Knowing without knowing. She wished right now she couldn't feel the screaming of Evan's heart.

Crying was something in which she rarely indulged, for it disrupted her for days and scratched the surface of a part she never again wished to expose—the same part that cried endlessly one night with Romney. Tears hinted at a devastation.

She returned to her bed and began to read. The night moved to day and he sat, without stretching or reclining, only staring and rubbing his hands as if trying to bring forth some answer he had yet to find the question for.

Later, she padded about the room, put the water on, and tidied around him. The whistle of the tea kettle sent steam into the air and she stood in front of its humid flow, the cleansing tingle on her skin. She dipped tea bags in cups and poured the water. Next to him, she withdrew his bag, and poured milk into both cups. Offering one to him, she waited until he accepted it.

Locking eyes, she nodded, "Happy New Year. It will be in time."

♥ ♥ ♥

Alice Walsh made it to the bank before it closed for the holidays. She changed the dollars into pounds and stuffed them in her purse. Humming a tune for the first time in months, she took the bus to her flat and re-read the note from Claire. It contained best wishes for the New Year, more apologies for not writing and, best of all, the entire sum Alice had sent her daughter over the years—with interest.

"Thank the Lord the child wasn't born selfish," Alice whispered as she folded the letter. "I can forgive her not writing her old Mum. After all, she hardly knows me. But, the money, well, the money's mine really, isn't it?"

She pulled a case from under the bed and packed her things, leaving the balance of the week's rent on the desk beside the window. The money's arrival couldn't have been timelier. No more Harry, she thought, and no more of his kind.

She was done with waiting for dreams to come true. She was wiser now, and it was a good thing, for she was less marketable. But she'd already thought that one through. Months at the ladies' clothing store had placed her in close proximity with women a generation her senior. She had time to observe their ways and decided she would not end up the same.

Grey streaks or not, poor style of dress or not, she possessed the equivalent of one year's rent from Claire. She could use it as she pleased and, indeed, would make good, for it was her final hurrah. Exposure to all livelihoods in London had nudged her creativity and she was excited about her new challenge.

A final time, she thanked her daughter and sent a silent wish for a happy New Year. She'd once thought Claire to be her way out of the doldrums, for Alice could concentrate on Claire's future, send words of encouragement and support, and live through her. She thought Claire would come around and lift her mother out of the mess she'd gotten herself into. But Claire had not responded and now it was too late. Her daughter had other plans that excluded a mother; she could stay in Boston and sing or study or do whatever she wished.

Alice wouldn't intrude. There would be no further letters to Claire. Like her other children, her daughter would remain motherless.

Anyway, they were all grown now. Plus, Alice had always gone it alone, had selected other roads and formulated her own agenda. In spite of her companionless status and meager lifestyle, she was proud of her ability to dig herself out of troubles. For once, she wasn't going to rely on anyone—not a single soul. This she believed to be the very reason she would succeed.

She'd once heard that many achieved great heights in their later years. She held to that train of thought, prayed nightly she'd be one of those mature success stories. But even to prayers she no longer assigned power. Having at last understood there was no one but herself, she found this state of mind an inviting place to be. Alice stood at a crossroad with many directions and, money in hand, chose the one with potential for return.

♥ ♥ ♥

New Year's Day in the de Roche home, Giles closed himself in his study with the excuse he had to plan for the coming week. Betti had left a few days before, to holiday with relatives in Auvergne. The sole boisterous occupant went ahead with plans for a sumptuous meal, broke out vintage wine, and heralded 1972 as the best one yet.

In black dress with seams of royal blue wavy stripes, Régine arranged flowers, tended to a simmering stock, and sipped apéritifs all the while singing to radio tunes. Solange arrived a few hours before three, to help prepare for the dinner her parents would also be attending.

Unlike Régine, however, she was grim, and grew even more morose after peeking into Evan's empty room.

"Never mind," Régine said. "He'll be back. I promise. The States will either gobble him up or he'll get smart and return before that happens. You have only to wait."

Solange did not respond.

"You don't trust me?" Régine asked, frowning. "I know him. We've lived under the same roof."

"He's gone," Solange said, fighting tears. "He never loved me."

"You have it all wrong, Chérie. He's simply having the final fling of his bachelor days."

"So far away?"

"Well, it's a bit drastic, but our Evan seems to prefer wandering onto limbs. I imagine it's his nature, the successful entrepreneur and all. Runs in the family."

With a peculiar crimp in her face, Solange studied Régine. The blonde woman flitting about, talking as if she were the expert on human affairs, had for a time bothered Solange. There was something sinister about Régine's smile, something scheming about her swaying hips. Fine lines cracked about her eyes and, when they crinkled into a smile, Solange held her response to a nod.

The last time she saw Evan alone there had been no ambiguity. During a brief return to Paris, he'd placed a call to the Lemuire résidence, asked Solange to lunch, and escorted her to a bistrot.

She had thought it was a new beginning, the moment when he'd proclaim his wish to start a life with her. Yet, even though his eyes shone and he looked better than in her most daring of daydreams, he wasn't at all the lover of those same dreams. Polite, cheery, and civil, he updated her on his stay in Boston, informed her of his choice to change careers.

During the meal, she ignored his comments about 'moving on with his life' or 'living for a time in the States.' She feigned ignorance when his eyes settled on an outside scene. There was a simple statement to his behavior, a line to his actions pointing to none other than the worse kind of nightmare for Solange. She would have to be blind and senseless to pretend she didn't understand the meaning of this rendez-vous, yet a part of her clung to the fact they were seated opposite one another and, for the duration, she was his.

But she couldn't deny the look, a look half-fulfilled, a look requiring another's gaze to make whole. He faced her at the same time he was lost in thought. Evan's preoccupations revolved around another. Rather than fully embrace the fact, she tried to impress him with her gaiety, her light touches to his wrist, her laughter. She reacted pleasantly to his every word and babbled about anything, to prolong the time and pretend this was the first of many more encounters.

He remained polite, politely distant. The last stubs of bread cleared and the wine bottle emptied, she fought disorientation as he paid the check and stood to go.

Whether her actions had capped the inevitable or she had forever ruined her chance with him, she would never know. She threw her arms about him and created a scene. Digging nails into his shirt and kissing him repeatedly, she begged him to marry her. Her voice rose, beseeching, crying, but he remained mute and peeled her fingers from him.

Evan settled and made little of it, but that was the end. Never would she see him, and worse, never would she feel his body against hers. She had been a fool.

The desire for him still pulsed. Envious, she watched Régine commandeer the kitchen and the entire residence, for Régine had won her de Roche.

Solange showing up this day was an error, but to prevent the hurt from growing worse, her only recourse was to pretend the scene with Evan didn't happened, to act as though Evan were around the corner and soon to reappear.

She wondered where he was and with whom. Who had he been preoccupied with in the restaurant, and had he found her across the ocean? Did the woman know that her insertion in his life had broken what hope Solange had for happiness? Did she know she was destroying what ability Solange had to see a future at all? Did that woman know how lucky she was? And would she have the power Solange hadn't been able to wield—to capture Evan de Roche's heart forever?

Jealousy would rule Solange's days, jealousy of an unknown face—the face mirrored in Evan's gaze that day he said farewell, a woman of another land and mind, a woman who, in Solange's estimation, had it all now she had Evan.

♥ ♥ ♥

Mac Ryan looked up from his newspaper to the wall clock. 12:01 January 2. "Already the first day down the drain," he said, returning to his read.

The last bus of the night pulled into Boston's Greyhound terminal. It was the 12:20 to Maine, an all-nighter stopping at every town along coastal Route 1. Mac nodded to the driver as two passengers descended and made for waiting friends.

For eighteen years, Mac had worked the graveyard shift and he often joked he could run the desk blindfolded. He knew every bus, its origin and its destination. Regulars looked forward to his greeting and some even returned from trips to New York or

Baltimore bearing gifts of bottles of whiskey or Mac's favorite cigars.

It wasn't demanding work either. A coffee or two to break up the evening, his paper, and any news coming from the travelers sufficed. Indeed, he felt the bus company was lucky to have him. In spite of his wide girth and weight—upwards of two-fifty—he hid a revolver in a side drawer. There had been no violence or robberies on his shift, a claim he proudly made each time an area train or air terminal had similar trouble. The job had provided him with funds to raise his three boys. He could now look forward to his own benefits which included full pension and an adequate social security check come time. No heavy lifting, a decent day's wage.

The dullness of the routine and the quiet did not faze him. He let the odd bum in to nap, even chatted with a few of the homeless who stopped on their way to various tunnels and hideaways. He chuckled privately at the wildly dressed young people with transistors growing out of their ears or at the runaways angry at the world. He worried for the mothers with babies who asked him for directions to a YWCA or shelter. He smirked at the couples on clandestine rendez-vous and didn't bat an eye at the ladies of the night who made use of the toilets. No one bothered him and their entrances and exits broke the monotony. In their way, all provided him with a bizarre form of entertainment.

But of all the unforgettable characters passing through, he would long remember the woman who crossed his path this night.

She struggled to open the door. A baseball cap masked her face and hair reached to her waist. A slender frame was hidden by jeans, a thick sweater, and pea jacket. He guessed her to be a teenager or young adult. Head bent, she glanced about the empty waiting room to the bus outside. She hobbled and was burdened by the few contents of a knapsack slung over her shoulder. Until she realized Mac was her only source of information, she kept her distance.

"Ma'am?" he asked, noting a patch across one eye— a hand-made job of cotton with blood stains.

She swallowed numerous times before rasping. "I would like a ticket."

"To where?"

She pointed to the bus.

"To Maine? Bar Harbor's the last stop. You get there at 8 AM."

She nodded.

"One way or round trip, Ma'am?"

"One way."

"$18.50," he said, tearing off a ticket and running it through the machine.

She fumbled with coins in a pouch and stopped to nurse a finger. Her hair fell forward. He'd seen many kids with unruly hair and jeans and didn't fuss over them as long as they remained orderly. However, he couldn't take his eyes from her body, the grace with which she struggled to carry herself in spite of the obvious pain in every joint. Gentle and contrite, like she was lost or alone and didn't want to trouble anyone, she took deep breaths, forced her gaze and hands steady.

He winced as she faced him, for the damage was obvious. The bloodied, exposed veins on one cheek, the bloodshot eye, the purple bruise on her lower arm, dried blood under her nails. He bit his lip, accepting a twenty and ringing up the register. She looked to the bus and her face was again hidden.

"Cold up there this time of year," Mac said.

She nodded.

Just then, Art Flaherty from the coffee shop next door came in. "Here you go, black with two sugars," he said, standing to one side as Mac returned change. Art's eyes widened as he, too, noticed the bruises. She mumbled a thanks and headed to the bus where she slowly climbed steps to the dark interior.

"Man, you see that?" Art asked.

Mac shook his head. "Damn if I understand things these days. Young one's been beat. I know them bruises, seen other women with 'em before."

"Askin' for trouble they are, these young girls," Art said. "Staying out late nights, taking buses to God knows where at all hours. No wonder she's been hit on."

Mac looked thoughtfully at the bus as it pulled away. "Imagine the maniac who did it. He should be taken out and shot. If I ever found out who it was, my gun would be out of that drawer faster than you could say Mac Ryan!"

Art nodded, heading for the door. "Gotta get back. See you at three!"

Its blinker flashing, the bus turned left out of the terminal. Mac uncovered his coffee and sipped. "Good luck, little lady," he whispered. "Sweet thing. Too bad."

# Part Three
# How Deep is the Ocean?

*Where the wandering water gushes*
*From the hills above Glen-Car,*
*In pools among the rushes*
*That scarce could bathe a star,*
*We seek for slumbering trout*
*And whispering in their ears*
*Give them unquiet dreams;*
*Leaning softly out*
*From ferns that drop their tears*
*Over the young streams.*
*Come away, O human child!*
*To the waters and the wild*
*With a faery, hand in hand,*
*For the world's more full of weeping than you*
*can understand.*
The Stolen Child by W. B. Yeats

# Chapter 1:
# January 2, 1975

AFTER WISHING KLEE A HAPPY NEW YEAR, Evan hung up the phone. "Still the same Klee," he said, grinning.

Beyond the doors of his Manhattan office at the Franco-American Chamber of Commerce, copy machines whirred and phones rang. Most calls at this hour were from Paris, this being the time when the counter organization in France was finishing up for the day. As he answered his private line, his secretary entered and handed him a wrapped deli sandwich.

Another three calls took up the next hour—Paris for immigration information, Paris again to schedule a twin city ceremony in February and, finally, the chief financial officer requesting a review of balance sheets.

As commercial attaché, Evan was responsible not only for encouraging and promoting French-American business, but also for locating start up offices at strategic U. S. sites. San Francisco had recently opened, and a dedication was scheduled for its satellite in Sacramento. Minneapolis, Boston, and New Orleans were slated to open in the coming year.

Initially, the Paris operation resisted decentralization. But Evan convinced the French that, if they wished to pursue business opportunities in the

413

States, operations must expand. There was no way New York could possibly aid a French concern to establish itself in Texas. A Houston or Dallas branch was required. Implementing these changes implied a hectic pace. Yet, in spite of sleepless nights and irregular schedules, Evan thrived.

He believed, that the Chamber's charter was based on sound logic. The benefit to increased international relations was fostered by a spirit of enterprise, especially the energy found in start-up ventures. Locating and organizing office space, providing leads to potential customers, even helping family members adjust to the challenges of relocation, all mattered. Many a French company had settled in the New York area not only because of the Chamber's strategic location to shipping docks, airports and the largest metropolitan area in the U. S., but also because of Evan de Roche and his singular way of steering, and often charming, decision-makers to his point of view.

Their favored opinion of him was an asset upon which he regularly drew. The de Roche name alone signified status and longevity, qualities all French businesses strove to maintain. If Evan couldn't do it for a French company, no one could.

From the moment he moved to New York in 1971, he broke through perceived barriers. Early on at the Chamber, his role was first as employee and jack of all trades, then as advisor. By late 1972, when the incumbent stepped down, the attaché position was offered to him. He accepted with enthusiasm and proceeded to make promises that had long since been kept.

It hadn't been easy at first. Paris quickly found out about his retreat from the family operation, and his father's long silence over the matter. There were no published reports to verify or deny the two had a falling out but most believed the rumors. Plus, Régine Mallord was already an irritant in the minds of many a *directeur général,* and it took moments to comprehend reasons why the younger de Roche might have called it quits. Nevertheless, before Evan could turn his own name around in French business circles, the truth had to come out—and from the mouth of the ever respected and revered Giles de Roche.

Rather than pine, Evan moved ahead with his plans for the Chamber, developing what contacts he could and managing to foster interest stateside. He personally saw to the program's every detail and even made trips to Paris at his own expense in order to meet with companies considering a U. S. branch.

When in Paris, he never barged in on his father, never requested to stay at the residence, and never tried to sneak around behind the man's back. But, no sooner had he arrived than the news made it to his father's ears. Still, Giles remained mute on the matter.

Not all of his reserve was due to misunderstanding. Increasingly, de Roche Frères struggled. The devaluation of the franc, the dollar off the gold standard, and the future impact of Eurodollars played into the de Roche concern as it did every other company with minimal international focus. The imminent downfall of de Roche was causing its once ebullient, resourceful helmsman to obsess.

He didn't want to beg Evan for help, nor support his son in what Giles still considered a risky venture. On the other hand, Régine was over her head and Giles found himself falling for the same inconclusive business practices that he had before handing the over the reins.

Evan made the first steps towards rapprochement. Via the intermediary of a distant relative, he floated a plan for Giles. Evan would start a small, independent concern stateside, a consulting arm of the Chamber, that would help relocating French companies with knotty issues such as obtaining visas for employees, education and support for family members, and planning for capital expenditures such as computer equipment or machinery. Remuneration for these services would go in part to the Chamber, in part to Evan. He would in turn forward a percentage of the proceeds to de Roche Frères, thereby propping up the ailing family business at the same time he moved ahead with his own ideas.

Giles resisted. However, after several months, Régine sent word that the proposal was accepted. In a terse yet professional letter, she bought into Evan's arguments, maintaining that the arrangement would not only preserve the family name and fortune but further the economic progress of France in general. A letter signed by both Régine and Giles made the deal official.

In 1973, de Roche USA was established. A major coup for Evan, the venture quickly gained momentum as increasingly more companies began setting up offices in the U. S. In time a steady stream of dollars wound up in the bank account of de Roche USA. The employees of de Roche Frères—specifically Giles and Régine—could breathe easy once again.

Evan was pleased to see results. Yet, with the exception of his own company, he had no close affiliation with what transpired within de Roche Frères. Plus, he and his father had not interacted. Their grudge was shelved for the time being. Evan was simply too occupied to address the past.

Not only had he plans for the subsidiary, he also wanted to expand that portion of the firm solely owned by him. In his estimation, real estate was the way to go. With the continued conflicts in Vietnam, the recession took over, slowing most construction. He paid attention to the Boston and New York markets. He kept his focus on a phenomenon he'd already seen in France during the late '60s—that in spite of the building slow-down, housing was and would continue to be a market factor to reckon with. The baby-boomers' time had come.

He didn't concentrate on New York City per se, but bought large areas of land outside Manhattan and in northern New Jersey. When the economy recovered, office space as well as single family homes would again be in high demand. Computer companies in the Northeast were growing steadily and boasting heftier profits than other industries. There would be a need for transport, warehousing, and office space. Evan would be one of several with foresight to offer accommodations.

At times his French citizenship was questioned. But by and large, no one took notice. This re-enforced his long-held belief that the U.S. was the best place for an opportunist. Still, he had to make use of all his assets and found himself relying as much if not more on his ability to charm and entertain as he did with his accounting and marketing know-how. His time at Harvard served him well and, though he walked a fine line when it came to judicious—and legal—investment of the proceeds from de Roche USA, he was quick to comply with regulations and soon boasted a reputation for ethical business practices.

New York was a tough sell and he never felt a part of the inner circle as he had in Paris. He was welcome in exclusive clubs, invited to social and political events, and spent his share of time promoting city candidates or issues. Still, he sensed he was kept at arm's length from the really hot deals and buzz. Once his profits soared, however, acceptance proved less problematic. His goal was not to become famous, his goal was to prove true what he always believed, that markets were made by people with dreams and the energy to see them through. It wasn't long before Evan de Roche proved exactly that.

As a result of his success and attachment to his adopted country, he soon made moves to naturalize as a U. S. citizen. He would guard his French citizenship, but it had been in the States where his heights had been attained, heights once mere wanderings of his over-active student imagination.

He wore tailored suits, owned an upper East Side townhouse, and drove an Audi. His looks matured, but he was no less dashing. Women sought him out, he had no need to court or woo. He was active socially and articles about him as the 'bachelor to get' appeared in several national publications—a title he accepted with a wave of his hand and childish grin.

The busy, handsome executive of old-world civility was proving his fancy degrees and titled name were not the only things he had to offer. Evan had drawn on other, more innate abilities to create an envious situation for himself in one of the major capitals of the world.

It was as he wished. The harder he worked, the more projects he took on. The more accomplishments he racked up, the more new ideas he generated. He lived for his work and thrived for the next deal.

Klee was his one friend. He often thought that if she knew how much he looked forward to their visits, she might end the relationship as she had with so many others. But he was skilled in his dealings with people and knowledgeable of their make-ups. He held firm to the belief that if their rapports stayed platonic she would remain his pal. There were times when he wished for more—at the end of an evening of too much wine and the intelligent, lively chats the two could engage in, or during a long walk on a North Shore beach after her Saturday night singing at Johnny's, but he restrained himself. Pursuant to those dangling moments, he ultimately understood that their closeness was not about her being the woman in his life as much as it was her presence those times he allowed thoughts of Laurence to rear.

Not even Klee knew how crushing the blow had been, how its pain permeated at the oddest times and hurt as much as it had that New Year's Eve he arrived in Boston. He never discussed it, never as much as gave away her name to a soul, though he suspected, at some level of Klee's incongruously perceptive nature, his Irish companion knew.

He tried to bury his feelings for Laurence but, when he least expected, she was reincarnated in his heart. Her eyes shone brighter than those full Nantucket sunrises. Her mouth puckered to his in many a dream turned sorrowful. Her soft ways and inclinations grabbed at his senses if he so much as took a walk in the park. That her memory would never leave him was a given, that her recall had the power to bend and even break him remained plausible far too often for his liking. She thrived in his heart, a pain more real than any cancer, a stab as deep as any fatal one.

He could find relief in work and he could find relief in Klee. The new year was always the toughest and he always made a point to break from work and visit.

This year would be a good one, too, for Klee agreed to work with him on her music. Throughout the past year when both had a spare day or two, they created rough cuts. Evan chipped away at her obstinacy, in particular by convincing her that a recording was her ticket to travel and sojourn in all the places she'd so thoroughly studied.

"How can you stay abreast if you don't make those countries your own?" he asked on more than one occasion. "Don't tell me you're going to become one of those scholars behind university walls who believes she doesn't need to live the real thing?"

"O course not," she would quip. "I'll be getting to that now, I will."

He loved to tease her because it charged her with emotion that made her navy eyes go black and her head shake so her curls bobbed every which way. She would deny his accusations at the same time he could almost hear the wheels of her brain set in motion.

"Well, you already know the de Roches, so when you get to Paris, you'll have a place," he would say. No sooner were they on the subject of Paris than they talked of the countryside and its secrets, the wine vineyards known by few, the family restaurants in the heart of nowhere. They would move on to other countries and soon Klee was figuring how she could swing a world-wide voyage for less than $1000.

He would laugh at her sense of what things cost and push further. "So, you cut an album, it sells, and you're off."

Her eyes would narrow as she mulled over the idea and she would once again refuse. But as she delved into her studies and mastered her languages, each refusal was delivered with less energy. To maintain her expertise, she would have to travel, a lot. Evan had a point. It took three years before she finally gave in and allowed him to hire a sound person to record her live at Johnny's.

Each Saturday night, a recording technician Even knew would fly to Boston and tape segments of her show. After returning to New York, he and Evan would select the best tune and merge it with the running track. In time, one song would be selected for her first single.

Often he himself had flown to Boston to insist she hear tapes of the results. Each week, once the latest song was incorporated, he called to remind her that her voice was the best, that she had only to give the nod and her ticket around the world would be had.

She allowed the initial steps but warned that she wanted no recording until her last year of school. She wanted no part of public appearances or anything that put her in the limelight. Anonymity was her unbending criterion. Evan promised to comply.

He stared out the window of his office and smiled. The release date was set for tomorrow. With Klee, he could perhaps begin to act as talent scout, a hobby he'd toyed with ever since Marcel spoke of Patrice, presently a screen star in France.

The year before he'd gone to the Cannes Film Festival to watch her compete for best supporting actress. While there, he better educated himself in the industry with its flagrant ways and superstars, with its opulence and decadence. Underneath it all, he sensed an opportunity, one he'd ignored since his filming days in Paris.

Back in New York, he went to plays, cabarets, and other performances. He knew every one of Manhattan's theaters on and off Broadway. He read local publications and went to readings where one could find an array of talent reciting well-known pieces to small audiences. Readings gave an actor time to develop skill and to network. He enjoyed the coffee house atmospheres, and more than once jotted the name of a performer for future reference.

There were many kinds of actors, levels of expertise, and talent. For some this meant an easy ride to the top, for others, a more prolonged journey. He could watch Patrice walk on stage and know she'd done her time. Yet there were others who worked the system differently, who sidled up to the directors for a given film and thereby squeezed into a role by virtue of their dogged persistence rather than their talent. Others, rarely seen on stage accepting awards, were on the fringe as they tried to perfect their voices and other means of

421

expression, memorizing lines and auditioning over and over in order to catch the eye of a potential backer.

They were usually young, inexperienced and wide-eyed, too often lacking in the physical attributes the camera supposedly enhanced. But Evan preferred these types. Sadly, they would approach agents or film executives only to be brushed aside for some platinum blonde with an exposed body or some big name who had merely to mention his or her interest in a role and the deal was consecrated.

Evan saw an untapped resource in the strugglers and determined, as he had with Klee, that they required special nurturing and attention. They were the very ones to get easily discouraged and give up or try until lack of funds forced them towards other, less compelling, careers. He thought it a shame so many slipped past the eyes of casting directors.

Too, it was these sideliners who gave rise in Evan's mind to the deformed child on the beach at Batz, and Pauline's insistence on not overlooking the handicapped. Vividly this scene would return to him, often as a hopeful auditioner recited lines or as an actor or actress stomached rejection. Through no fault of their own, too many people didn't stand a chance.

He wanted to help, to bring about a change, however small, in the way talent was perceived and utilized. With Klee, he had opened that door a bit wider. Her singular way, odd looks and the powerful voice combined into a force to clear the way. No one could listen to her and forget her song, no one could ignore that along with the too wide mouth, the wiry hair, the oblique character, went an unforgettable melody meriting attention. With Klee, Evan would finally undo his childish behavior on Batz. With luck, she would help him turn heads in more ways than one.

But, his other commitments had kept major focus in the entertainment industry at bay. Until Klee had agreed to record, he remained on the fence about delving into it wholeheartedly. Now, her first release imminent, he re-examined his priorities with growing excitement.

Her voice had deepened. Husky trembling suggested sex and release at the same time it brought forth an airy innocence and freedom.

Evan would stare at the night sky, thank God for his time in Boston, and rehearse a speech to Klee, convincing her she needed an agent. After all, he would need a lifetime of preoccupation to forget Laurence. This would help greatly. He picked up the phone and ordered a dozen long-stemmed roses for Klee.

# Chapter 2:
# January 15, 1975

ALICE UNFASTENED HER BLACK SEQUINED DRESS. The zipper curved past her buttocks and to her thighs. She arched to reach the end of the zipper's track. Wide-eyed on the bed, her companion eased his hand to his groin. Underneath, she wore black underwear and silk garters. She stepped from the dress and traced her breasts. At the side table, a bottle of Pol Roget cooled in a bucket of ice. She popped the cork and let the froth spill onto the rug. With the same grin of compliance and complicity that had caught his eye, she stared at the man.

Soft tunes drifted from the radio. Red lamps threw shadows from either side of her French provincial bed. The champagne hissed in glasses. She wiggled her toes in the white bear rug as she turned and, back to him, unhooked her bra. Her hands ran down either side and up again. She grabbed her hair and piled it atop her head, wiggling in an exaggerated fashion. The man grunted with desire and moved towards her.

"Not yet, Pookie." She winked and pointed for him to return to the bed. He backed off, towards the blue satin sheets.

She closed her eyes again and tried to block out the vision of his balding head, a lone wisp covering the forehead. Even from where she stood, she could smell the alcohol and tobacco on his clothing. But he'd been alone at Sydney's, one of the posh London restaurants, and she'd already done her homework. He was a shipping magnate cast aside by his family but flush with fortune. She knew of his three divorces, his illegitimate child in Scotland, and his estate in Sussex, the villa in Italy. An infrequent visitor to London but, when there, he sought out one thing. Weeks before, Alice had determined she would do the seeking the next time he chose London.

Plus, if he was the furthest thing from attractive, his Rolls with leather, fancy accouterments, and chauffeur were not. Stench aside, his suits were from the finest tailors, the shoes could only be had from the Regency shop. He drank Gevry-Chambertin, fancied *maigret de canard* and, at the end of a meal, relished Cuban cigars. She had yet to match her sexual talents to his preferences, but anticipated this night as the first of many in which she would simultaneously please and discover. And get him to return for more.

She whispered his name, went to her bureau drawer, and withdrew a small pair of scissors with pearl-encrusted handles. Breasts exposed and slightly bouncing as she neared him, she held the scissors to her lips to kiss. She traced her chin, then breasts, then navel and finally to the thin string at her hips that secured panties. Handing him the scissors, she turned to one side.

"Snip," she said.

His hand quivered and he poked her skin by mistake, apologizing in his properly English way that made her giggle. He cut the material and she slid the garment down a leg, turning quickly so he could bury himself in her nakedness. He threw his arms around her and down the contours of her thighs.

While he sniffed and growled, she grasped his head, thrust back and forth and pushed them onto the bed. With a finger to her red lip, she indicated he must be patient still. She undid his tie and draped it around her neck. Unbuttoning his shirt in slow movements, she watched as he moaned for her. Alice murmured, snuggled to one ear, whispered her love. She let him lick her breasts.

Reared on her knees, she threw back the covers, directed him to the center pillows and reached for his belt. Unbuckling, she first wrapped it around her hips then carried his shirt across the room to carefully fold it on the chair.

"Baby, I can't stand it!" he cried.

"But it's so much better when we take our time, so much more memorable, you know," she said.

He tugged at his pants and she went to his aid, kissing the hair-free chest and pot belly as she lowered her head to his underwear and pulled them down. She sucked hard on him. As he held her firm and dug fingers into her hair, he came in hot spurts. His climax passed and before he had a chance to regain himself, she nurtured his penis to another erection that brought tears to his eyes and more begging from his lips.

Then she guided his hands to the hot ready spot between her legs. Her perfume rose to his nostrils. He turned her on her back while he tasted between her thighs. It was his turn to do as he pleased. He came once again and as quickly as before, pumping her and begging for more and more until they were two rolling bodies filled with fire and losing themselves in skin, sweat, and release.

After, he fell asleep. She rose. A silver robe around her and gold clasps tying her hair up, she lit a cigarette and lounged in a chair, rubbing her legs and studying the view of Regent's Park.

In her Vuitton purse sat two hundred pounds, previously agreed on and transmitted to her palm before they stepped outside the restaurant. She hadn't been sure of the going rate and had been prepared to negotiate. Pleased he hadn't balked at her price, she nevertheless reminded herself to up it the next time. A little banter over terms would be expected by her clients.

From her strip act to his wild begging, tonight had been a splendid beginning. She would have to acquire more, much more, in order to meet her rental payments and dress the part. Her dates would be men like the one snoring on her bed and they must return regularly, so she would have a level of guarantee.

She went to the mirror and appraised herself in the dim light. The cigarette smoke created a haze between her and the glass. She reached for the flute of now warm champagne.

Sipping, she toasted, "To the days ahead, lady Alice."

# Chapter 3:
# January, 1975

JOHNNY STEPPED OVER PLANKS OF WOOD, nails, and sawdust. "Time to clear out, guys," he said. "It's Saturday. I have a show to put on tonight."

The business having long before paid for itself, the club was undergoing improvements. His a respected and talked-about venue, Johnny enjoyed the job more than ever. It was fun to be interviewed by local reporters and to have radio stations cover live performances. In the last months, his name had appeared in two New York entertainment publications which had drawn even more pleasure-seekers.

A trendy atmosphere with low lights, snug seating, and predominantly jazz tunes, Johnny's had been one of the first clubs to gain a reputation and hence was better established than most. No matter if the visitor was a New York stock broker or a Houston oil man, Johnny's was the first on the lips of any hotel manager when it came to making recommendations. His was a place where one could experience the new Boston.

A mere year or two ago, the cost of the renovations—over $500,000—would have made his eyes bulge. With the Saturday night show and lines out his doors, however, he could now foresee paying off the amount in no time.

He wished to preserve the intimate atmosphere, yet more space was indispensable. Saturdays, the waitresses were challenged to balance trays over their heads, move in semi-darkness, and take orders only during breaks in performance. They often complained.

Black-leather tables and chairs in a larger room with more aisles, red table lamps, and floor illumination would allow for easier movement. An additional arm of the bar gave quicker access to the kitchen and storage space for trays. He also ordered a few more sinks and wall mirrors for behind the bar. With mirrors, he could catch his favorite lady as she sang, even when he was busy serving.

Having handed over the other shifts to college kids and a few full-timers, he now worked the bar only on Saturdays. The other six days, he spent in the back room sorting bills or ordering liquor and food. He interviewed vendors, solidified his supply chain and was constantly juggling the schedules of his growing staff. He managed alone but, during inventory or on a particularly busy weekend, was happy to accept extra help from energetic kids.

Amongst his employees, he'd developed a reputation for being a man who offered flexible hours and fair wages. He never had to advertise for help because a waitress or bartender would always recommend friends. He encouraged his employees, too. He asked about their studies, their home towns, their interests outside school. Some needed help with loans and, if he or she had proven a solid worker, Johnny didn't bat an eye as he wrote out a check to tide the youth over. He embraced their energy, keeping them busy and out of trouble.

Their upbeat ways colored his days more than any other time of his life. To pass the hours at his club was to participate in many lives and he found he was more attached to the kids than to the hefty bankroll he accumulated. This was living at its finest.

There was, however, a cyclical tendency to his week. He was still in love with Klee and missed her regular appearances, having accepted with difficulty the fact she considered her job at Johnny's one of necessity. He well recalled the panic when, acceptance letter in hand, she talked about quitting. Had he not approached her with an offer to pay her more to continue singing Saturdays, she might have disappeared forever.

In spite of having gained another few months, it was tough. As early as Friday morning, his heart would pound at the thought of her. Saturday afternoons, he could often be found stewing at his desk with a forlorn regard and distracted tone to his voice. When she arrived, her presence transformed him into an obliging, humble servant who walked on tenterhooks while she moved on and off stage. He often had to ask for help behind the bar because his eyes refused to leave her.

Unfortunately for Johnny, from 5 PM until after her last song, she was absorbed in her own world. Polite greetings and humorous farewells aside, she was as removed from the club's activity as anyone could be. Her songs over, he sweat in the anticipation of a few minutes of private conversation like the old days, but she usually excused herself to walk home alone. Their drives had been curtailed at Klee's request.

His emotions would dip and it would take all his strength to remain calm. In truth, her departure was the renewal of a malaise he tried to pretend wasn't there but that only grew with each passing week. When she left him Saturdays, he died a million deaths.

He blamed Roger and the failed attempt to convince her to record. Many nights, he relived the times she had been open and receptive to his advances, before the test recording and during her wide-eyed days when her dreams bubbled on a back burner. Now, her dreams were reality and she spoke all those damned languages. She presently reviewed homework in her head rather than the notes of the songs she sang. All he could claim were her tunes and her voice, but not the bead-studded body.

He had learned his lesson, however. Should someone approach him about her voice, he quickly let it be known she was not for sale. Like a child awaiting the reward of a piece of candy, he professed to be her manager and told the inquiring party to get lost. She was a student of languages, a linguist by profession. Aware of his protection, Klee thanked him many times.

But over and above her lack of interest, another sour note rang. It was the handsome Frenchman who visited from New York. Something in the twinkle of his too-wide eyes brought a sparkle to Klee's face, something no other man had done. During her show, the two never exchanged words but Johnny could tell there was communication, a sharing. Then, a sound engineer showed up with, of all things, recording equipment, and Klee adamantly forbade Johnny to kick him out. She said the man was doing her a favor and that Johnny was to give him the best seat in the house.

How hard it was for Johnny! Her navy eyes staring into him said it all—allow him to record for me or I'm gone.

Johnny had no choice but to believe she'd finally given in to the advances of a good-looking man. There was no other explanation. To Johnny, it represented a transgression but his hands were tied—to let Klee go spelled his ruin, to keep her only prolonged the same thing. A truth still held, in his mind as well as in the minds of many. Her voice distributed on a national scale would pummel her into stardom quicker than she could mouth those incomprehensible Gaelic passages.

Still another event loomed. She was graduating in May. Where would she go? Would she remain loyal to Johnny or would she slip away with the Frenchman? He had to know.

But for his love, he might have sought out other up and coming singers and tried to promote another as he had Klee. But for his love, he might have long ago insisted Klee either record for him or get lost. But for his love, he might have foreseen her attachment to a type like the French guy and found himself a lover of his own. But for his love.

His love drove him to foolish things now. He followed the Frenchman one night, all the way to Klee's triple decker. He parked outside and watched the light flick on, imagined what they were doing, and cursed his compliance with her wishes to 'just be friends.'

He continued to follow them. Each time, the Frenchman never spent the night, choosing instead to depart in the wee hours, but Johnny figured Klee had already led him to her bed. How could two young people pass hours together in that tiny space without doing so? It wasn't the way these days.

If he was angry enough, he would direct his Oldsmobile all the way to the Frenchman's apartment near the Harvard campus. He would seethe at the thought that this youngster knew Klee's body as well as her mind, and swear his revenge somehow.

Johnny couldn't bear to lose her nor could he bear to support the constant reminder she would never be his. For all his spiraling thoughts, however, he couldn't bring himself to take action. He could only observe her behavior—and that of the Frenchman—and worry about becoming a memory on the fringes of Klee's burgeoning future.

Johnny Mear was a divided man. His employees loved him, his patrons were unswervingly loyal, even his competitors admired him. He wore a smile and accepted his lot with polite reserve and the modesty of a gentle person on whom Lady Luck shone. Yet, he was in turmoil, boiling and spewing, erupting in the privacy of his home and in the recesses of his soul. To want a woman, to know she was right for him, and to have to settle for a glimpse of her shadow every now and again was hard enough. But to watch as she became part of the life of another, another with means, youth and energy Johnny would never see, agitated his inner devil. Johnny walked along the divide with eyes open, but had no idea the side on which he would eventually land. He only knew it would be soon.

Soon came too soon. In she walked one night, rose tucked behind her ear, a statement of her secret life, and a beacon to Johnny. His eyes bore down on the bloom as she passed, his head dropped, and he drew in a breath he didn't release until his face was deep red.

If not for the dim lights, others might have noticed. It was, however, still too early. He could camouflaged in no time, and was soon his smiling self. But the divide had grown larger.

# Chapter 4:
# 2 February, 1975

RÉGINE STALKED HER *trois pieces* overlooking the Tuileries Gardens, trying to pull herself together. Tonight, a business dinner with Giles and another company head. Tonight, a chance to reconcile, for no other Parisian woman would ever have cheated on Giles de Roche. Régine had.

Splayed across the divan, her latest ensemble from Givenchy—a navy suit with red belt and hat. New Charles Jourdan pumps and her freshly touched platinum locks would complete the look she hoped might sway Giles to a more understanding frame of mind.

She scowled, for she'd not taken time to shop for jewelry at Fred's. Rummaging in her gold box, she found a diamond brooch—a gift from Giles. Bringing the dainty piece to her chest, she moaned, "Why is everything so hard?"

The beads hugged one another and glimmered even in the gray morning light. She pinched her face into a frown. These business meetings day in and day out had drained her of what intentions she might have had of running the company.

Giles had returned to his former ways of working hard. Initially she had thought he would quickly hand things over to her, or a heart attack would force him to do so. Like his son, however, the old man had the perseverance of a mule and the acumen of the greatest of business giants. Reluctant to recommence his corporate life, he nevertheless picked himself up and gradually recharged de Roche Frères. She had to play his foolish game, for it was she who had begun it in the first place.

Entrenched in the mundane of profit and loss, she had sought excitement outside the office. In the form of discreet calls to acquaintances stateside, she promised tours of the city, trips to chateau country, and wine tasting at selected houses. In no time, men who had known her on the Cape appeared, complimenting her on her beauty and eyeing her curves the same way they had years before.

The beaches and bike paths of old were replaced by parks and intimate dining spots around Paris. Her Rolls Royce took them to Barbizon and Samois, towns south of Paris where she was not known and where cozy *auberges* lined the banks of the Seine.

Most of them were younger and so enchanted with France that she had merely to wink an eye and they were hers.

She drove them wild with her scents and with her clothes. Leather bikini panties this time, nothing at all the next. For those who preferred the innocent look, she wore baby blue short nighties and ponytails. For others, she adorned herself in red and black. She did anything for them, taking no money and, for those executives known world-wide, promising secrecy. Hers was simply a beckon to the wild side, a sweet short time from wife and kids, a tasteful reminder of France.

She never got attached or fully engaged, and held barely a notion of the physicalness of anyone sharing her bed. All she wanted was the feel of someone next to her, in her arms, desperately seeking her out, and then for them to forget it all the next day.

It was all Giles's fault, she would say, for he had left her unfulfilled, and her plans thwarted. Having targeted and won the hearts of the best known industrialists in France, she was now no longer free to openly seek alternative amusement, unless of course she chose to relinquish what she already had. She could only escape from the prison she'd erected by calculated movements and planned rendez-vous far away from the watchful eye of all Paris.

She could no more leave Giles than accept Laurence with open arms. She could no more rely on Mémé's protection than speak openly with Evan. Succinctly and in her own way, she had closed all doors without opening the one she'd hoped to. Pickled in a jar of luxury and esteem, she stank of her own vile smells.

Although her dalliances brought respite, she eventually paid dearly, and the man with whom she was found returned to the States to face a divorce lawyer and diminished responsibility on the corporate scene.

Régine had booked them into a country hotel. They had been snuggling together sipping cognacs when a journalist for a weekly magazine entered and recognized her. It took but several hours for word to reach Giles.

Enraged, he'd announced through Betti that Régine was to find her own place to live. She was to finish any previous commitments to de Roche then take her leave. She had begged, denied any wrong doing and swore allegiance, yet Giles had prevailed. If Régine didn't get out of his house quickly, Mémé would be informed.

Régine found an apartment and took to days alone, pills, and the precarious comfort of alcohol. It was existence at its worse and she lived in fear of Mémé's discovery one minute and the loss of her possessions the next, for without Giles she was again in dire straits.

She had to pull herself together. Enough was enough after all and it was now or never. She would profit from this rendezvous to get Giles de Roche or she would succumb to the loss, but she would not remain in limbo. Random affairs aside, she must convince him now of her commitment, and regain her position inside his heart.

Renewed affairs had only brought home the pain of Nate's loss, and had built in her the conviction she must get what she deserved. Not on this earth did another Nate live. She must protect herself for the remainder of her days. With Giles, she believed she still stood a chance.

In the dining room of the de Long residence, Georges and Chantel sat across from Mémé. The windows were open and a warm evening breeze cleared away the dinner smells. Mémé finished her coffee before speaking. Her gaze downcast, she asked, "So?"

Georges cleared his throat and glanced at his wife. From his coat pocket, he removed a photo and held it in his hands.

"You are aware that I have watched Régine closely these past years. Well, our suspicions were not without merit. I warn you, Mémé, what I am about to say has shock value..."

With a wave of her hand, Mémé said, "Shocks I have lived through, dear Georges. Give me the photo."

He handed it to her. Mémé drew it near, studied it, then looked to Georges. "What animal did this? This is no longer my lovely granddaughter. Who could have maimed her so?"

"I took it from a distance," Georges said. "She boarded the ferry before we could approach her. If not for a chance walk along the harbor—and the fact the entire town is so compact—we might never have seen her. She was well covered, as you can see, but the bruises show anyway."

"Mon Dieu, mon Dieu. One cannot deny those welts. Régine was on the island at the same time?"

"She spent one night in a hotel in town and flew out by private plane the next morning. We only have conjecture to go on, Mémé. Régine did harm the girl years ago on Batz, of that I am sure. It's too coincidental—the short interval Régine stayed on Nantucket coupled with Laurence's hasty departure. I spoke with a few locals who knew her. They said she was happy with her surroundings. What other reason than the fear of her mother would force her to up and leave?

"I visited Nantucket one more time before our return to Paris. Beatrice—the woman she lived with—has since moved. The townsfolk were not forthcoming except to say that Beatrice resides in New York City. It's a rather insular place." He chuckled and grasped his wife's hand. "We understood better why our Laurence chose to live there."

"You were unable to trace Beatrice while in New York?"

"That's right. Her name was not in the phone book."

"What about Evan?"

Georges adjusted himself in the chair and cleared his throat. "Evan did not want to discuss Laurence."

The old woman stared at the ruffling lace curtains. Her eyes narrowed. "Why?"

Chantel answered, "Oh, he's so busy Mémé! You should see all he's up to!"

Georges shook his head and raised a hand. "It's not all one's work, Chantel. Mémé, I cannot forget the look that crossed Evan's face at the mention of Laurence, filled with aching, a regard of tremendous chagrin, too deep to be of no consequence. The man is in love with Laurence or my name is not Georges de Long."

"They why has he lost contact with her?" Mémé asked.

"My guess is that it's Laurence's wish, not Evan's," Georges said. He looked to his wife, then continued, "Forgive my presumptions, they may be all wrong."

"No, dear Georges," Mémé countered. "You discovered Régine made a trip to the island after Christmas 1970. It was also the last time I heard from her. This, this monstrous picture tells me there is a link."

Mémé drew in her breath and, with the help of her cane, stood. She paced the room and then sat down again. "These legs. Old age is well upon me. Georges, I want you to find my granddaughter, whatever it takes."

Georges looked startled. "It's a huge country."

"Yes, and she's small and innocent. I grant you it will take time. Use the best facilities. Be discreet and don't mention it to anyone, especially Régine." She glanced from them to her hands, rubbing pensively. "How I dislike this, my children."

"Perhaps Laurence will contact you. It took her a while after Roscoff to finally write."

"But," said Mémé, "she had my letters then. She has nothing now."

"She knows your address."

"I can't wait until she writes me. I've been ignorant, or blind, all these years. There was an exuberant thoughtful child on Batz years back. What has she become? I must know."

Georges nodded. "I will do what I can."

"Good," Mémé said reaching for him.

439

"You still want the rendez-vous at the lawyers?" Georges asked.

"Under the circumstances."

"I'll call you once it's arranged," he said.

"And remember, not a word," she said.

Once they had gone, Mémé sat at the table and looked out the window for a long time. "It's a terrible thing, what I must do," she whispered. "I pray to God it is for the best."

♥ ♥ ♥

Régine grasped Giles's arm. They were alone in the restaurant, the client having departed a short time before. "Darling," she said, "Monsieur Picard makes a lot of sense, don't you agree?"

Giles jotted notes, then placed pen and pad in his pocket and said, "He has ideas. I'll meet with him next week, once I've had a chance to confirm his claims of growth and profit within his own company. One must do homework first."

"He might be the way out of our financial woes."

"There are no financial woes," Giles said. "I must remind you to speak softly and without condemnation when you're in public. '*Les affaires*' are ours."

Régine pouted and drew an embroidered handkerchief from her purse, dabbing eyes and mouth. "I only want to help."

"You can help by staying out of trouble," Giles said. "Really, Régine, you manage to find diversion in the oddest ways."

"Darling Giles! After all we've shared!" She ran a hand up his shoulder but he returned it hand to the table.

"I'll say it one more time, I'll not tolerate what you've done."

"But that's all behind us."

Giles smirked. "All Paris buzzes with tales of you! I continually avert eyes of those who scrutinize and wonder why in the world I put up with you."

"It was a onetime error! I've apologized, Giles. A woman gets lonely."

"Nonsense," he said. "You are not alone or lonely! Not under my roof!"

"But I'm no longer under your roof. It's horrible and I miss you!"

Giles sighed, took off his glasses and placed them in a case. "Come. It's time to retire." He signaled to the waiter for a taxi.

As the driver wound the car around Place de la Concorde towards rue Royale, Régine snuggled next to him. She kissed his cheek, murmuring. "I don't want to go home alone. Will you come back with me?"

Giles studied the lines of trees and the closed doors of expensive boutiques.

"Giles?" She nudged him and placed a hand on his lap, feeling under his coat to his chest. "I've missed you so." She leaned against his shoulder, sending the Chanel scent his way, settling when he did not pull his hand from hers. The driver announced their arrival. Régine tugged, forcing him to look into her eyes. "Mon amour," she whispered, "Just one digestif. Then you can go."

They entered her courtyard and took the narrow elevator to the top floor. She kissed his hand as they walked down the hall. Inserting the key, she allowed him in first, then flicked on a light.

He nodded. "Elegant, very elegant."

She took his coat, pecking the back of his neck and arms. "Sit," she said, pointing to her white leather couch. "The cognac is in the crystal serving set. I'll be right back."

In her room, she tore at her evening dress, leaving it a pile on the floor. A soft yellow peignoir hung in the closet and she grinned. "Quite an imitation," she cooed.

Having rummaged through Giles's personal effects before leaving his house, she had found several photos, one of Pauline wearing a similar yellow gown one Christmas morning. Young Evan and Danielle sat around her opening presents.

Slipping into it, she frowned. "Much too soft." Shaking her head, she put on more lipstick then fluffed her hair, insuring the tendrils hung equally about her shoulders and down her back. In the bedroom, she lowered the light and lit white candles. Stuffing her discarded clothing into a closet, she found the bottle of perfume she bought earlier that day, the brand Betti said Pauline had worn. She sprayed lavishly.

More glances into the mirror and she was ready. Her body warming, her mind tuning to the woman she was to become, she placed a coy smile on her face and drew in her breath. It was time.

Turning off the lights as she entered, she faced him. With a beckon, she reached for him and drew him towards her, burying herself in his chest and whispering her love.

His reaction was instantaneous. He pulled Régine's face to his and studied her half-closed eyes, his own bright with remembrance, delight mixed with emotion. A smile broke through what walls he'd recently built between them. As he ran an arm down the soft material of her gown, he became once again a man enraptured in a dream. He inhaled deeply and moaned.

She waited for his kiss and, eyes closed, nudged her body closer, the air of Pauline folding them into a cloud of make-believe. He could do no more than acquiesce to the aroma, the softness of his one and only. This Giles was the man who loved at the same time he lusted, a man capable of any physical manifestation of feeling, a man of boundless resolution to reclaim his past.

For the interval of foreplay, while the two swayed and teased each other with kisses, she gave into a sense of fulfillment and played at her own game of pretend. So long had it been, the feeling of truly being desired. So long had it been, her own open display of the truth within herself. More of him she couldn't possibly know and yet as he lifted her into his arms and carried her to the bed, she didn't see his white hair and gaze full of tenderness, or hear his murmurs of desire. She no longer saw Giles de Roche.

She found Nate again. At the outset of their love, it had been the same, the same as Giles and Pauline. Untroubled, released, and intent on forever, she had given Nate the same as she now gave Giles and received in turn his affection.

This odd charade brought forth her own phantom, her own love, her own deepest needs. She felt renewed, felt herself a person capable of making good, of discarding her vices and having the courage to forbear the everyday challenges from which no human is free.

Giles undressed her, lay her beside him and treated her as his goddess. He stroked tenderly and long, bringing her to climax with all his concentration, not allowing his own pleasure until she was satisfied. He gave of himself in such a way as to demonstrate the depth of his emotions. Pretend or not, his was a love Régine had hungered for, the love lost at the birth of her daughter, an unadulterated piece of another that allowed her to be filled with purpose.

Whatever the results of this night, Régine presently clinched the unanticipated. Her plan a success, it ironically had exposed her own lost paradise. For the first time in years, she lay in a man's arms and felt peace, wished for nothing more than the moment, the lasting present, the space of his love.

# Chapter 5

FROM THEN ON RÉGINE HAD TO HAVE GILES. By his side, she helped in any way she could and even admitted to and tried to rectify her past errors on the job. She requested assistance from advisors within the company and fell into step with the instructions Giles proposed.

Craving his attention, she lived for the night, when they could again slip into a realm where both thrived. Neither voiced concern over the foolishness of their masquerade. It was appropriate and good to find release from daily tensions and to experience an about-face to their once floundering affair. Their secret helped them face challenges others might fear, going so far as aiding in their joint cooperation at work. Their false identities as fuel, they performed at the height of their capabilities both in and out of the bedroom.

She became less garish, spoke in whispery tones, and honed a demure countenance. They danced at places where Giles and Pauline had once danced, they drove to the country Sunday afternoons and even made two journeys to Batz in the middle of the frosty winter to re-enact years gone by. To pretend. No one, not even Giles's closest advisors, could figure the transformation.

At night, the parallel duplicity emerged in full, he concentrating on Pauline even while penetrating

Régine, she intent on Nate even as she beheld the eyes of another. It might have gone on indefinitely, had it not been for an event that drove them to face reality in all its harshness.

Mémé died. Her heart gave out one night. The next day, Betti found her. Paris wept, for Mémé was widely known and, like her husband, was long upheld as the staunch person of means who lived a life of generosity. Her well-attended funeral was one Paris saw infrequently, with lines of mourners forming outside the church on St. Germain and traffic congested for blocks as the funeral procession brought her to her final resting place.

Régine was in the limelight as the city relived details of her mother's bravery during the war, as the priest recited her parents' many awards and medals of honor. Most everyone agreed the de Long reputation was one of the most enduring and admirable. In black St. Laurent and with Giles at her side, the bereaved daughter marched to the graveside and placed a wreath atop the casket while the final words of blessing were bestowed. Accolades, well wishes, words of sympathy and sorrow, all were showered upon Régine as the sole direct survivor in one of France's greatest families.

Evan returned from the States and Marcel made the trip to Paris. Both had lived their childhood summers at Mémé's doorstep and cherished memories of her encouraging ways and placid style. Hard to believe, was what they muttered to one another in the days following. Mémé was life itself, she had seemed inoculated from death.

At a friend's vacated apartment near Etoile, the two men stayed. Late one night after the funeral, as Evan packed, Marcel talked of their plans.

"So, vieux, you return to the land of plenty?" Marcel asked with a chuckle. He wore jeans and leather jacket with sleeves rolled up. In spite of slight graying at his temples, he looked as virile as ever. As a result of having spent all summer in Aix, winter's harshness had yet to rid him of his tan. His semi-retired state had left him with much time to rest and relax, unlike his nephew. "You're not staying to read the will?"

Evan laughed. "Mémé took care of her own, you know that."

"But she and Régine had a falling out. All Paris talks of it."

A look of surprise was followed by a shrug and Evan continued packing. "Well, I can understand if Mémé left her nothing. She deserves less."

"Come now," Marcel said, "your father's favorite woman and you wish her ill?"

"I know you tease, dear uncle," he answered, "but I prefer not to concern myself with such things, even if they're true."

"You haven't noticed their little pantomime?" Marcel asked.

"What pantomime?"

"She pretends to be your mother."

Evan shot a suspicious glance at Marcel. "What?"

Marcel shrugged, went to the window, and lit a cigarette. He exhaled, taking in the view of the wide avenues converging at the Arc. "I have eyes for the actor in everyone. Your father and she are on stage permanently."

Evan sat down, his brows creasing. "I haven't paid attention. It's been a tiring few days."

"I know well the act of deceit," Marcel said. "When a man takes a woman in his arms and pretends she is another. It is often the only way to cope, of course, when we lose forever that special one. But what Régine and Giles do is of far-reaching consequences, for themselves as well as for those around them. I see her imitating your

447

mother and it sickens me to watch Giles slip under her spell. His love of Pauline has no equal, is not to be imitated."

"I don't follow you at all, Marce," Evan said.

Marcel turned his way. "Perhaps I'm being too blunt, especially at such a sad time."

"Go on."

Marcel puffed. "Can you remember how your mother laughed, what clothes she wore, her perfume? Can you recall her words and phrases?"

"Easily."

"Then watch Régine. The witch mimics Pauline."

"Why?"

"To get your father. Hell, he hasn't come around to asking her to marry him. The woman will stop at nothing."

Evan was troubled, his gaze circled the floor then went to Marcel.

Marcel said, "See for yourself. She needs a man for security, nothing more."

"You're certain?" Evan asked.

"Must I pry open your eyes? Must I spell it out? Look for yourself. Stay one more day and take it in. The woman controls fully your father's heart." He sighed. "Ah, but I can't say that I blame her in a way. Haven't we all contemplated at least the same once a love is lost? Haven't we embraced foolhardiness in order to regain one more night with the one and only?"

"Stop." Evan wrung his hands.

Marcel went to Evan. They embraced. Evan dug fingers into Marcel's back. "We've walked a similar path you and I," he said.

At the window again, he lit another cigarette and puffed. In a softer voice, he said, "I have often playacted as Régine does. But each day blazes another path. I move on."

448

Evan placed his head on his hands and wept, not stopping even when Marcel gripped his shoulders to comfort. They embraced again and this time Evan rocked in his uncle's arms.

"Cry, cry my son," Marcel whispered.

Hours passed and they sat. Light from outside revealed tear stains on Evan's face and clothing. In time Marcel pulled up a chair and asked, "You wish to talk about her? The one who lies behind those tears?"

Evan brushed his hair aside and cleared his throat. "I saw her for the first time on Batz…"

In the morning, Evan left for the airport. Alone in the apartment, Marcel stared out the window and chain smoked. He should help his nephew but he could not. To reach out to another had never been his strong point. Long ago resigned to this selfish aspect of himself, he couldn't bring himself to aid even his favored Evan, the only family member aside from Pauline with whom he'd achieved an element of closeness. To expose himself to this shared pain was out of the question. He was immune.

As a result of Evan's revelation, Marcel could foresee the unraveling of the once promising life of his nephew. Shaking his head, he sighed. Evan must fight his battle alone, this the one battle Marcel wouldn't wish on his worst enemy. True love lost could leave open wounds for years. The young man would touch it and, like a disease that hides itself one minute only to rear with intensity the next. He would succumb to its powers gradually, and weaken until there was little left.

Evan would arrive at the neutral place Marcel had and become like him, a stranger to all but himself, an unknown to the very people capable of extricating him from his misery. Self-preoccupation would rule and Evan would call that living.

"Unfortunate, this world we embrace," he said. "You and me, young one. You and me."

He threw his clothes in a case and left the apartment. The train to Aix left in an hour and he would be on it.

# Chapter 6

AT THE LAW FIRM OF Salès, Grayère, et Montard, Georges de Long and Régine faced Etienne Salès, Mémé's lawyer. "The will acknowledges one Madame Régine Mallord as the direct heir of Madame de Long," Salès said. "We have agreement on that. There has, however, been a recent change as Monsieur de Long will confirm."

"Yes, Maître," Georges nodded.

Wearing black Dior suit with leather trim and a wide feather hat, Régine puckered her lips and dug nails into her purse.

"Then we have only to update Madame Mallord on the changes before proceeding." Clearing his throat, Salès continued, "It is Madame de Long's wish for her daughter to obtain a portion of the estate."

"A portion?" Régine asked.

"Yes, Madame. The estate has been divided."

Régine cleared her throat, tucked an errant strand of hair under her hat, and resettled herself. "Go on," she said, blinking rapidly.

"Madame de Long wished for fair disbursement of the properties in Paris, the estate on Batz, and her significant investments. Pending appraisal of the properties, the total of her estate is yet to be calculated, but we can estimate the entire amount to be on the order of five hundred million new francs."

Régine pulled out a handkerchief and dabbed her nose. "The breakdown?"

"In time, Madame, in time. I must first run through preliminaries. It was Madame de Long's wish you both be present to hear and understand this most lengthy and detailed process of inheritance. There is a grandchild," he said. "Laurence Mallord."

"What has she got to do with this?" Régine asked.

"Much," Georges said. "Continue, please."

The lawyer took the final will and testament and read introductory paragraphs as well as the list of relatives Mémé wished to consider. "Evan de Roche is the only non-relative and was unfortunately unable to make this rendezvous. He received word after his return to New York and has declined to be present. Nevertheless, we have the authority to inform him of his disbursement, divide the estate, and give him his portion.

"Madame Mallord, your mother left specific instructions regarding your portion. I quote, 'To my daughter, Régine, I leave one percentage of the accrued interest in the account numbered LR4610-099.'" The lawyer looked up. "That is a savings account she opened several years ago. I continue, 'She is to withdraw funds only under the supervision and approval of the executor, Georges de Long, and with the facilitation of legal counsel. These earnings are to be disbursed ten years from the date of my death in increments of five thousand new francs per year."

The thud of Régine's purse on the carpet brought silence. On her feet, she raged, "Ten years! This is atrocious! There is some mistake! It can't possibly be! After all I've done, after all I've put up with? It's preposterous, insane! That's what she was, insane, out of her mind. Her faculties..."

"Hush, Régine!" Georges snapped. "If you can't contain yourself, get out."

For what seemed hours, Régine faced the tall windows overlooking rue du faubourg St. Honoré, her body quivering. She closed eyes, pinched her nose. Slowly she moved to the chair. In a hoarse voice and an octave deeper than usual, she whispered, "There must be some mistake."

"Everything is in order as I see it," Salès said. "She signed the document herself and even includes a statement from her lifelong physician that attests to her sound physical and mental state. That is a rare thing these days. Most people don't bother."

Salès detailed what was an impressive group of financial holdings, one of the largest in the country. A discovery to all present, the de Long family owned the entire island of Batz with the exception of the de Roche estate. Over the last sixty years they had leased the terrain to residents. The entire island was bequeathed to Evan.

Georges and Chantel received the apartment in Paris and a significant chunk of savings. Laurence received the rest—liquid assets and long term notes that would keep her comfortable for the remainder of her life.

Face ashen, her knuckles white from gripping the arm rest, Régine muttered incoherently. Then her arms went limp as she lay back on the chair, a crazed gaze on the ceiling.

Georges nodded to Salès. "Proceed."

The remaining documents outlined methods of disbursing payment and passing on ownership, plus an account of all holdings with addresses, numbers, and history of acquisition. Years before, Mémé and her husband had paid attention to their assets and, unlike many who chose to hold onto cash, the two had expanded their earnings by investing in instruments considered innovative at the time. Mémé was hardly the *vieille fille* she appeared.

"We have one problem," the lawyer said. "Laurence cannot be found. I have tried, as I understand Madame de Long tried before her death, to locate her. We have retained a service to seek her out and believe she is still in the United States. The authorities there have cooperated with us and indicated she has not left the country to their knowledge. Of course, it is easy to come and go from one's country, but we will for now restrict our search to the East Coast where she last resided. Should that attempt fail, we will expand our search."

Georges nodded. "It is important to find her, regardless of her fortune. I hope we hear soon."

"And I," said the lawyer. "These matters of inheritance do have statutes of limitations. Once reached, the stipulations of the Civil Code take over. However, I must say that Madame de Long took care to insure no other person—save a direct heir—receive Laurence's portion. It is clear she held this child in high regard."

For the first time that morning, Georges smiled. "If you met her, you would understand."

Régine glowered. In time the two gentlemen called a taxi, ushered her outside, and watched her drive out of sight.

Back inside, Georges said, "She reacted as expected."

Monsieur Salès nodded. "Hard to believe how Madame Mallord could do such a thing to her own child."

"You should have seen the old woman's face when she saw the photo of Laurence."

"Madame Mallord has no idea you checked up on her?"

"None."

"Well, all is as Mémé wished," Salès said. "May she rest in peace."

# Chapter 7

ROGER DURONIER WAITED IN THE LOBBY of Bea-Sage Productions, a compact, windowless room with three chairs and magazines stacked atop a corner table. Moments later, Bea appeared at her office door. She ushered the man inside and offered him a seat. From a window overlooking Riverside Drive, the gray day spread across adjacent buildings, adding meager light to the low wattage bulb shining on Bea's desk. New Yorkers spilled onto sidewalks and arteries for the lunch hour. The hum of the city rose to the twentieth floor.

Eyes bright blue, face clear of make-up, she wore overalls and, save gold studs in her ears, bore no material sign of the up and coming producer—a title recently bestowed upon her by several industry observers. On her desk, a picture of Sage and, covering the wall behind her, a poster of Nantucket's Main Street. She closed several manuscripts and shut off the light.

"So you continue to search, Monsieur Duronier."

"Yes," he said, pulling a dated photo of Laurence from the folder on his lap. "As representative of Salès, Grayière, et Montard law firm, I am in search of the young lady Laurence Mallord. As we discussed on the phone and during my previous visit, she lived at your home on Nantucket several years ago."

456

"Correct," Bea said, reclining in her chair and reading from the man's calling card.

He wore a tailored suit and gold pinkie ring with what appeared to be a family emblem on it. What hair he had formed a black ring around the nape of his neck. With a steady, dark-eyed gaze he smiled.

"It is my job to uncover her whereabouts and, as I have spent a month now seeking information with no luck, I return to you. Aside from Monsieur de Roche, you appear to be the last person who interacted with her over the Christmas season 1971."

"Correct again. That is also the last time I saw her. She disappeared while I was at Sage's funeral. Where she went I have no idea. I, too, would like to find her for she was a dear friend. I have been on my own now for three years."

"You sold your property on Nantucket."

"Yes, there was no longer a reason to call it home."

"I understand," he said. "Is there any place Laurence might have wished to live? Anywhere she voiced an opinion about?"

Bea glanced away. "No, not that I remember. That is the strangest part of all. Many a time she spoke of how happy she was on the island. You've been there yourself so I'm sure you can understand. It suited her."

"She never once mentioned leaving the States or returning to France?"

"Not at all. In fact she planned to take on more responsibility in my company. She was a hard worker, dedicated."

"She filmed?"

"A short, unfinished piece."

"What was it?"

"An underwater film. She must have taken it with her. There was no trace of it when I moved off the island."

457

"Might she have continued that work elsewhere?" he asked, jotting notes.

"Oh, yes, she could have gone to California or Florida, I suppose. Those are prime locations for underwater discovery."

"I see," he said.

They talked a bit longer and Duronier explained how, at the wishes of her deceased grandmother, Laurence was now the heiress of a large fortune. Bea was helpful with information but could only speculate with the man about Laurence's whereabouts. At the end of the discussion, Monsieur Duronier thanked her and Bea walked him to the door, promising to keep in touch should she hear anything from Laurence. After, Bea returned to her desk but did not open her manuscripts. She stared out at low clouds now blanketing the buildings.

Then she went to the outer office door and locked it. Returning to her private quarters, she locked that door as well. Camera equipment and wiring lay strewn in her path as she made for a corner file cabinet. From a bottom drawer, she drew out a cassette tape. Next, she unraveled one of her movie screens, inserted the reel into a player, and flicked the button to ON. Instantly, the room was transformed to scenes of the Nantucket coast—the summer sea, the fish and dolphins, a waving Don every now and again. Twenty minutes later, towards the end, Laurence herself appeared. Underwater and making expert use of the scuba gear on her back, she collected star fish and other clinging life forms and displayed them for the camera. Even from behind the goggles, her eyes were so large they shone and her hair resembled sea kelp as it floated to underwater rhythms.

"Baby," whispered Bea, "I wish you'd tell me what this is all about."

Contrary to what she'd said to Duronier, Bea knew exactly where Laurence resided, indeed most details of the young woman's life since 1971.

It had taken a good part of a year to locate Laurence, for the young woman had become a fugitive even from her friend Bea. Had it not been for the tip-off received one day while checking out the Boston Greyhound station, Bea might never have found her in Maine.

The village of Glenrock, some thirty miles north of the resort town of Bar Harbor, hugged a stretch of Maine's rocky coast and, save the rough beauty of a place far from humanity, offered little to a young, talented woman.

Months passed and, with them, the accumulation of unanswered letters and phone calls before Laurence agreed to a visit. When they finally reunited, inside a one-room place she rented from a farmer and his wife, she visibly shook as Bea made gentle approaches and requested she confide. Little progress ensued as a determined Bea stayed at a motel in town and made daily visits. Worse than Laurence's shyness were the welts and sores that had permanently bent Laurence's nose to one side and left an arm limp and slightly paralyzed.

The horror that crossed Laurence's face as she described her need to "get away and be alone forever" drove Bea to imagine the worst. She never questioned, for Laurence was evasive about the truth hiding behind her wounds, but Bea was certain there had been major physical and emotional reasons for the departure and a history of bad interactions with someone Laurence refused to discuss.

Bea was patient. In time, Laurence returned to a closer approximation of who she had been on Nantucket but with one major difference. She wanted absolutely and positively to be left alone, wanted her anonymity as much as her life and made Bea swear to never ever reveal her presence to a soul. This request Bea had granted for it was the only way she could guarantee future visits with Laurence.

As she packed away the film, Bea thought about Evan and wondered for the hundredth time if he had anything to do with this. The one time Bea had mentioned his name, Laurence's head shake and ever so soft, "No" told Bea that, if anything, Evan had been a source of great happiness, a happiness that for some reason Laurence denied herself.

With so little to go on, Bea stopped speculating and took to aiding Laurence regain what decency and routine she could to a life, Bea guessed, Laurence had too many times prepared to end.

It was tough going. Regardless of Bea's regular visits, Laurence was barely present. Solitary walks on the shore were her primary activity. Even those days she appeared somewhat livelier, she spoke in spurts, opting for conversations about the weather or area events. Bea tried to accommodate but was repeatedly witness to regards and silences that hinted at some nightmare Laurence continued to experience.

What had once motivated Laurence to become the involved person with film, at her job, or interacting with locals no longer seemed worth it. The straightforward life of walking and eating and dressing was her preferred mode and she showed no signs of changing.

Bea offered to pay for a run-down farmhouse next door, one that was closer to the shore, arguing Laurence would have privacy for her walks and a place to occupy herself. But Laurence wanted nothing from anybody, least of all charity.

As she tidied her office, Bea decided it was time for another visit to Glenrock. She canceled appointments for the next three days. At her apartment, she packed a few belongings and led Pepper to the car. As the evening rush hour bore down on the metropolis, she sped out of the city heading north towards New England.

The drive took over ten hours. By morning, she was sipping coffee at a diner in upstate Maine, twenty minutes from Glenrock.

She couldn't tell Laurence about the inheritance. She couldn't mention the fact people were searching for her. It had already taken months of convincing, promising, and proving herself good to her word for Laurence to even allow Bea to stay overnight. The news to which Bea was privy would surely make Laurence suspicious.

As she got into her car to continue the last leg, she thought of Sage. Just over three years before, they'd spent their final days together. She remembered her lover's look the night she died, the weak smile, the clutching hand. Even as death descended, Sage made melodies with her touch, her presence. How difficult these times had been without her, how much Bea missed her still.

There was a night shortly before Sage died, when an important conversation had come about as they discussed Bea's hopes that Laurence would join full time at Bea-Sage Productions. Sage had let slip her suspicions Laurence had been abused and delved for the hundredth time into her own abused past—the infrequently present father who took to physically expressing his frustrations on his wife and daughter Sage, the mother who tore at Sage's self-esteem in order to retain a minuscule portion of her own.

Sage knew all the signs, sensed Laurence's dilemma from the very start, but had never imposed her knowledge. The night before she died, she did however give Bea one grave warning.

"Take care you never betray her trust in you, Bea. You're all she has, you're her survival. Perhaps the young man Evan will work out. Perhaps he won't. You, my dear, are her friend. Take care of Laurence."

With those words, Sage signaled to Bea the gravity of Laurence's past, the demons the young woman constantly battled, and the need to try as best as any friend could to put a stop to the suffering. Whatever Laurence's reasons for remaining isolated, Bea would never force her to divulge. Her affection for Laurence went as deep as her love for Sage.

"My dear Sage," Bea whispered as she drew in a breath of sea air and prepared herself for the day.

# Chapter 8:
# March, 1975

KLEE'S SINGLE WENT UNNOTICED by the music community, this in spite of distribution in local chain stores and mom-and-pop record shops. Worse, due to Klee's newcomer status, radio stations didn't even play it.

Evan chastised himself for not foreseeing the need for a mass marketing effort, and in no time sprang into action. He encouraged New York disk jockeys to play her song, called in anonymously to as many stations as he could to request the song, and convinced vendors to add the recording to their stock. All this he did without telling Klee, who remained unmoved about what was to her a relative non-event.

Still, and to any up-and-coming singer's advantage, there was a phenomenon about jazz. Those starting out often attracted the attention of the vertical and randomly-dispersed community of enthusiasts. New was innovative, and jazz had its roots in the most unlikely foundations. Those who played or sang jazz, it was argued, often stood a chance of making it simply because of its popularity and pervasiveness, and an ever vigilant gaze by music jocks on more than the big names and favored tunes.

False starts aside, the copies Evan sold to record stores did eventually sell out. Soon an undeniable buzz rose up in places like the Blue Note and other spots in Greenwich Village. It was about the voice and its charged tone, about her range and clarity. It had been a time since one with her gifts came along. People began making demands on disc jockeys in New York and Chicago and, of course, Boston where her small loyal following proved itself once again.

Klee took the attention in stride, for she still harbored unpleasant memories of the lengthy recording session. The trip to New York had worn her out. In spite of Evan's hospitality, she was hurried from recording studio to offices back to the studio, signing contracts and hearing over and over again the sound of her own voice. Tired and angry because she had missed classes that day, she had finally excused herself for a walk along the Hudson River. Later, refusing Evan's request to stay the night, she caught the bus to Boston.

Before she left him, Evan had handed her the rough cut tape and suggested she ready herself for a road trip come summer. He figured it would take that long for the record to reach the multitudes and then it would be up to her to maintain the public's interest. She quickly put a stop to his musings about going on the road, reminding him of his promise and her need to travel the world in search of language expertise.

But he had a way of insisting! A way of seeing the world through rose-colored glasses and leaving her, albeit begrudgingly, thinking over his suggestions and even imagining what it might be like to be "on top."

Had it not been for Evan, she might not have recorded at all. She had sung for him in the same unabashed way she had accepted his roses. It was normal and right he should express his affection. Since then, another layer had formed in her psyche, a thought process incapable of eliminating Evan from her plans, a tenderness as yet unspoken.

She closely followed his work at the Chamber, advised where she could and sought help from her university's array of French professors and visitors. She reminded him not to forget Boston in his plans for expansion and played a key role placing ads that targeted local investors and aiding in preparations for the opening of Boston's Chamber.

He often brought up the Celtic link their countries shared, the same histories of resurgence against the English, the similarities of language and mannerisms and the fight that raged to this day, in Brittany and places in Ireland, for the preservation of language and independence.

Never did he mock her interest in seeking out the reasons for separateness brought on by languages or her ultimate goal of documenting the theory behind the world's myriad tongues. He encouraged and challenged her. She thrived on his intelligence and spirit. They grew even closer.

Close was dangerous but she tossed concern aside when it came to Evan, even though there was still one area they had yet to bring into the open. She knew he was hot property in the availability department, and he was well aware of her admirers, yet they side-stepped issues of romance and commitment. When they were together it was as if those things didn't matter. They had one another only at short intervals and focused instead on their shared time.

She divined his sorrow from the New Year's of five years prior and, more importantly, could relate. The woman who broke his heart had made Evan a half-person. She knew about half-people. Unlike Evan who could match a name and face with his thwarted dreams, she had only the diminishing recollection of her mother's sad eyes and Bob Walsh's fiery stare. Hers was a more insidious loss, one that went as deep as Evan's but pierced from a different angle. She might never know the man who stripped her of her other half.

March brought spring and occasional warm days. With school winding down, and for the first time in three years, Klee found herself with the odd free hour. All As to her credit, her files filled with recommendations for student teaching positions at a number of top schools, she had only to choose the road and it was hers. She took advantage of the time before graduation to read books and even splurge on a few popular best sellers. She also veered her attention to travel.

England and Ireland would be first. She wanted to see her mother and visit Dublin. Although she hadn't kept in touch with the Faheys, she guessed they would still be there. It would please Mrs. Fahey no end to catch up and Klee could get together with some Trinity professors who had visited her own campus and instructed her for a time. Her contacts now included some of the most prestigious linguists. Doors were opening as never before. She wouldn't ignore her new role as graduate and scholar. She had worked hard to get there.

But, as time passed, the more her recording took on a life of its own. Like a serpent slinking through the underground passages of clubs and music bars, it wound its way west to California and south to New Orleans. Jazz-only stations in Chicago and Baltimore researched her, and the recording studio where she cut the song regularly accepted interviews. As a result of call-in requests from people who were as yet unable to find her record in the stores, all-night radio broadcasters played her song two and three times. Evan phoned her daily to discuss the possibility of re-issuing the song in even greater numbers.

The once predictable pattern to her days already interrupted with trips to travel agencies and conferences on behalf of the Chamber, she found herself contending with a variety of phone calls. She had to show up at Johnny's earlier than 5 PM to take messages Johnny had been unable to attend to on her behalf. She soon had to carve out time to return calls on her own, so as to keep Johnny's crossed looks at a minimum. His place was becoming Klee central, as well as the spot some were already saying had made her famous.

She down-played the attention, especially in front of him. The dismal look on his face told her more than words, and their repartees had taken a bitter turn.

"You wanted to remain a nobody?" he asked. "You never should have cut that record. I told you years back if you did that you'd..."

"Okay, Okay," she answered, flipping through messages. "Geez, Baton Rouge and Houston. I've never even seen those places!"

"Get used to it, Klee, and don't bitch and moan when you make all the money you're sure to make. It's all part of it. I told you. I told you."

"John, now, I'm off to England in another few months. It'll all blow over then. All I have to do is say no, don't I?"

"Ha," he laughed. "You don't say no to fame and fortune in this country, little one. You take it for all you can. And then some. Only fools say no to what you're gonna get. Fools."

Pity surging, she realized how little attention she'd given him over the years, how much she owed this man, and how difficult their parting would be. But he was one with whom she simply couldn't share of herself. Johnny loved her man to woman. She could never touch that one. Ever.

He noticed her stare and said, "You haven't looked directly at me with those eyes in five years."

"John."

A shrug gave away his forced nonchalance, a rigidity replete with pent-up anger and unlabeled emotions.

"Johnny," she said, lips pursed. "You know we all move on now, don't you?"

"Don't start that Gaelic accent with me. Get to your messages and get ready for your act. They'll be pounding the door down tonight again, all right." He hung glasses in overhead racks.

"John, I never meant to hurt you. I had a job to do, like you."

"Listen, kid, I'm a big boy. I got my own life now and, thanks to you, I can do whatever I please. Don't think I don't have my own plans to 'move on' as you so philosophically put it. Don't think I'm hanging around forever. Don't, cuz I ain't. I got my own plans, I do."

A waitress came in and he complimented her on her hair and the way she always showed up early, following her to the back where they engaged in lively banter Klee could hear from where she sat.

She tapped fingers on the bar and looked around. Foregoing his initial choice of purple, he'd taken her suggestion and renovated in reds and blacks. He'd even placed a table behind the stage for her books, so she could sneak a read during breaks. Accumulated memorabilia of their years as a team.

Though permanence was never a thing worthy of envy, in her fury to achieve, in her quest for knowledge and the intelligence that could harbor her, she had created a place the very essence of herself. The club was as much she as it was Johnny. No wonder the man fought her now, for she was breezily indicating her imminent flight from him, he who had spent all his time insuring she would stay put.

She mustn't fall for his act, or let on she understood he was jealous, angry, and tortured. To comfort him with a pat or word of kindness forestalled the inevitable. She couldn't even state her wish to remain friends, for he might take it as something more. The Johnny moon was on the wane, and Klee had to find the courage to stick it out without falling for his manipulative gestures.

Clinging people wore her down. She preferred the wee people, those who flit in and then out of her life. Those who, like she, sang a merry tune as they worked then took to tiny crevices and caves to find peace.

She looked to the back of the room and said, "As Yeats said, Johnny, 'the nation of gay people, having no souls; nothing in their bright bodies but a mouthful of sweet air'."

His jesting with the waitress continued. Klee picked up the phone. "This will be all over soon anyway," she whispered, dialing. "I'll be gone in a bit, in a bit, Johnny Moon."

♥ ♥ ♥

On the phone with Evan the following week, she could hear the tapping of his fingers on the calculator as they talked.

"If another 10,000 copies are distributed and, say, 80% of them sell, you've got your first trip paid for. I figured you would want to stay at the grungy out of the way bed and breakfasts anyway."

"That easy, is it?"

"That easy. Remember, you're already in demand. Once you make up your mind about Johnny's, you can move to wherever you want on your return. That way, no one knows of your whereabouts."

"I can't leave Johnny's. Not yet."

"I thought you were well rid of the place."

"I need a little more time. Come summer, I'll make up my mind. After I return."

"You've told him you'll be traveling?"

"Not yet," she replied.

"What's the delay? The longer you stay, the more people get a look at you. You fry yourself then."

"Fry?"

"An expression," he said.

"Well, I suppose I can't go and do such a horrible thing to myself now, can I?" Fry myself."

"Gotta go. Catch up with you later. Call me when you've finalized plans for London. I have friends you'll want to visit."

"No, I won't want to."

"Okay, you won't. But call me anyway, promise?"

"I will."

Her last night, Johnny snuck to a chair to watch her sing. In the dim light and behind the heads of the young people who had given him the break of a lifetime, he watched and allowed her essence to erode his tough-guy exterior.

She was never more beautiful, white and red from head to toe, the hair wild and blonde, the eyes her centerpiece, her strong hands and voice anchors to her person. Not an onlooker was distracted, no one moved. She had them under her spell once more, for a final time at Johnny's.

He would live out his days in wonder at the scrawny thing she'd once been, and the more complete woman she became. He would single out those first months as bliss like no other, and relive their rides across the river and that one night in her garret as the affair of his life. There had been no sex, no kiss, and only a few touches.

Hers was an indirect love, a beam of light hovering over his head, full of her absence even as her person remained vividly painted in his mind.

The coming months would be hell, and he would have to live through them, for there was no changing what was to be. She was moving on as promised, taking herself to the places she always dreamed of, and leaving him with nothing but a hazy memory destined to dissipate into occasional dreams and even rarer recall. All was gone but her song and that would have to carry him.

Years before, when they had told him he could die of heart failure, he had wanted to live under any circumstance. But this had not been part of his wishes. To live a life without his Klee, for she was no one's if she was not his, was worse than the unknowns of death.

Johnny Mear was graced with physical strength and financial security, a following others envied and a lifestyle of ease beyond his wildest dreams. Yet, as she puckered those lips and let go her mournfully poignant tunes, he felt as though he was losing everything of meaning.

He better understood the expression about the best things in life. Free as the air, undaunted by man-made burdens, she had landed in his life and, for a time, gave of herself as she knew how. Basking in her talent and her drive, with those odd habits thrown in, he renewed himself. Klee perched atop his world, he required little more.

Now, the sore reality he could no longer deny. In so many ways, losing her should spell relief, but to him it was a paradox. Losing her was but recreating her deeper in his soul, in yet another form, but as alive and real as the lady on the stage.

It was too soon to cry, he was too empty. Love had many forms and too often was far, far removed from the physical. His spirit was filled with her now. And now was all he had.

"I love you," he whispered. "I'll always love you."

As if hearing, her eyes found his. A twinkle conveyed her gratitude. He sent her a quixotic smile, knowing she could never understand, knowing she was already gone.

# Chapter 9:
# 27 March 1975

AS FAR AS RÉGINE WAS CONCERNED, it was a rotten spring in Paris. No interesting shows, few tourists of note, and the hassles of the increasing workload she'd foolishly taken on to impress Giles. Worse, her options were dwindling.

She supposed she should be thankful for the job, for it meant her survival. Though she was still angry at her mother, she refused to dwell on the inheritance or lack thereof. To do so sent her into depressions that left her spent and unproductive. No, she had to come off the bad news with a chip on her shoulder but still standing. She would persevere in spite of her mother's foolish negligence.

It was up to Giles now, the sorry fellow. He owed her, and he would make good on his debt. She hadn't wasted hours at the office on rue Marceau for nothing. He would see to it she was better paid, and give her a position with decision-making powers. She would stay only if he complied with her wishes, nothing less would do. Then it would be time to make her move.

Between Régine and her goals stood time. And time's force would rule in the coming months.

He would marry her. He would have his second Pauline and she her home and security if it killed her. Enough of running around playing sweet lady of the night. She wanted all of what Pauline enjoyed, not just the sex or the odd wanton stare.

She would stop at nothing to re-establish her financial position. Her heart had frozen over from defeats. Her age was nothing to be impressed about, indeed a cause for concern—and reason for action. She required standing, position, respect and above all money to continue into her later years. It had been tough enough competing with the younger generation. She could only hope Giles was enough enamored with this 'Pauline' to fall one final time.

Her plan would succeed, there was no question. Time, however, dictated her pace. She must hurry.

# Chapter 10

As the plane took off, Klee read the note.

> Dearest Klee (the other famous Klee),
>
> Take these words of your namesake along with you: "Art does not reproduce the visible, it makes visible." You make visible, Klee. I will miss you. Think of me from time to time and try to get to Batz. You will enjoy it.
>
> Grosses bises, Evan

He was full of it! Yet she had to admit he colored her life so, she would miss his sense of humor, his upbeat attitude, his never-say-die ways. How he'd strengthened her in the past months and how they'd come to enjoy one another's company. If not for him, she would still be figuring a way to make this trip in the first place.

In a few hours, Europe. Her itinerary was vague, as she wished. In England, there was her mother to see, plus museums and sights. She would visit Marlow where Shelley once lived. Time permitting, she would walk some of the country footpaths along the Thames. She would try a local brew in a pub. Two students at

Oxford had already contacted her to encourage a visit. She would take in a play.

Of primary importance was a trip to Wales where she would for the first time experience the Welsh language. She could compare for herself the dialects and differences between Gaelic. Her last semester at school, she'd dabbled a bit in the rudiments of the language but found it as indecipherable and perplexing as Gaelic. Best to discover its secrets first hand.

There was Brittany, too. How generous of Evan to offer the estate, how challenging it would be to finally try out her French on French soil. She could take the ferry but it would have to be after her time in England.

In a bag at her feet, a present for Alice. They'd not communicated in years and, following a letter returned to Klee 'forwarding address unknown,' she figured she might have to devote all her time in London to finding her. Plus, once they met, Klee's lack of letter-writing would be discussed. She did not feel guilt over this. Her mother had her own dismissive style, so that particular issue would dissolve quickly.

The pilot announced they were passing over Shannon and soon would cross over the Dublin area before commencing the descent to London. She peered out the window into the night and thought of Romney somewhere down below.

"We had our times, we did," she said. "I hope you're well."

As they approached the London conglomeration and Heathrow airport, a thick fog lifted to reveal the daytime as well as terminals, cargo carriers, buses, and baggage carts. She disembarked and followed what seemed miles of corridors to passport control, customs, and baggage claim. Each pause brought lengthy waits which afforded her glimpses of other travelers—American business people, families on vacation, Arabs in gowns, and swaths of families from India. Behind the bustle and modern layout, she quickly discerned the provincial, rudimentary aspects of this gateway to Europe. Tired looking Englishmen wearing loose, poorly tailored suits smoked cigarettes and distractedly checked their watches. Workers with dark skin and hair and speaking languages other than English moved in and out of washrooms where they cleaned toilets or swept floors. Overcrowded waiting areas with worn plastic upholstery supported the stench and fatigue of travel. A dustiness and well-worn quality in the hallways and shop areas seemed even more dreary due to minimal lighting or brash wattage. It seemed England had emerged reluctantly from a long sleep to realize it had been taken over by multiple cultures and people. Rather than rise to the challenge, the country had decided to remain medicated in denial.

She tried not to mull over the hundreds of families making way for the first time to a new life here, as it brought back memories of her own trans-Atlantic voyage to a place where she had to start from scratch. Plus, in the same way as Kinemmaera, people took her in with odd regards as if she hailed from the moon. It had been a long time since she had been under such scrutiny. In the States, she was one of hundreds with unique hairstyle and clothes and had found her place in one corner of the country where people knew her and no longer found her an anomaly. Here again now, she was on display and a bad taste settled in her mouth.

Bags in hand, she changed money and headed towards the exits. Big airport or not, rude stares or not, the English were not going to intimidate her. She was on a mission, and this was a necessary and overdue stopover. With the entire day in front of her, she took a bus to the part of town she thought her mother might live. At the only address she had for Alice, she found a family of two children and their mother who had no clue as to who the former renter might have been. Other neighbors had the same response.

She walked to a corner to catch another bus that took her closer to central London. After wandering for hours, she found an appealing Bed and Breakfast along an avenue of row houses. The welcoming owner insured Klee could find no more reasonable place to stay as they climbed stairs to a compact room on the top floor with single bed, view onto a garden, and coals aglow in the fireplace. Encouraging the newcomer to get some sleep, the woman promised a snack of biscuits and tea later on.

London soon enveloped her in its intrigue. Easy to be anonymous here, she dissolved into its crowds and its pace. In museums she could wander and relive great historical events. At Leicester Square she took in a matinée. Along Knightsbridge, she meandered alongside the wealthy and backpacking tourists. She imagined being a buyer inspecting the latest designs along Regent Street. In the National Gallery, she daydreamed of herself as a Parisian curator inspecting England's masterpieces.

After a few days, she took British Rail to Henley, a village to the west of the city, one of many with remnants of an ancient age. While walking to Marlow, she noted pubs hugging roads with no sidewalks, cemeteries with graves dating to the year 1000, horses grazing in fields, and towns with names like those around Boston. At the oldest pub, she ate a ploughman's lunch of cheddar cheese, chutney, bread and butter while chatting with two local writers. The Thames split the city in two and swans glided under a regal white suspension bridge. It was romantic, Shakespearean, and gray. At night, she retired to an inn along the river and enjoyed the company of a family of ducks gliding to and fro outside her window.

In time, she made it to the rocky western shores of Wales, finding herself amongst a shy, reserved people who, while allowing her free access to their villages, remained aloof to her requests for information. She huddled in bookstores and bought historical and linguistic journals. These people were in their way like her, holding tight to themselves and asking nothing of strangers except to be left alone. She decided to do further research at Oxford. Before leaving, she walked the ragged coast. In the seaside town of Fishguard, she reveled in the isolation as ferries arrived from Irish shores through St George's Channel.

Should she return, she wondered? One more time, to see Romney, and scurry with the wee folk? One minute she felt tortured, the next she was at ease, for in the end she understood why she never fit in and why she left Ireland. Turning away from the horizon, she whispered that she would have to stay remote. Going back now might threaten the exterior she had taken pains to build, an armor of ability and focus that kept her fears and vulnerability locked inside.

At Oxford, she enjoyed a week with colleagues in an atmosphere similar to Boston. She audited classes, mingled with other linguists, and spoke Gaelic with experts. The walled town, its cobbled streets, the youthful pace spoke to her Boston frame of mind. Eventually she headed back to London where a phone book showed her the way to Alice.

Surprised to note her mother's address an upscale one in London proper, she dialed the phone number and immediately was in contact with Alice.

"This is such a bad time, Claire. The trip to Spain I'm planning and all…"

"Well, you can call me back if you like. I'm staying in the West End until I leave for France in a few days."

479

"France now! Well aren't we on the up and up!" Alice exclaimed.

"I've cut a record if you can believe it," said Klee. "It sold and I made a small profit."

"And you were so sure you would study your life away," Alice chuckled.

"Here's my number when you're able to…"

"I must run, Claire. So sorry."

The click of the phone signaled her mother had terminated the call. A nudge at Klee's subconscious at first made her feel that her mother's evasiveness was Klee's doing. Yet if her crime was not maintaining contact then the remedy eluded her, seeing as Alice had hung up. That in and of itself was a message similar to all those subtle messages of her youth: we're not going to tell you what's wrong but understand that something is.

Klee decided not to over-analyze. Her mother might be angry, or maybe not. Alice had plans and that was that.

She tried to forget, but two more days in London's congested foreignness brought about increased thoughts of Alice. Klee's last night she took a bus to her mother's with a gift in hand. It was a book about Boston's history that she would place on Alice's doorstep.

The flat was one of several in an elegant townhouse on a street parallel to Regent's Park. All was peaceful and refined. An owner eased his Jaguar to an underground garage. A nanny lifted a pram up steps. A well-dressed woman stepped into one of London's rotund black cabs. Inside, a doorman told her Alice was not home and agreed to pass on the package. Klee thanked the man and exited the building, down granite steps with white trim and wrought-iron banisters.

About to consult her guide to the underground, she saw her mother. A distance from the residence, Alice alighted from a Rolls, clutching the arm of an elderly well-dressed man. The chauffeur took instructions from the man and drove away as the two laughed and climbed the front steps. Alice kissed the man repeatedly. In shimmering gold jacket and matching heels, dyed red hair, and colored nails she was no longer the plain unobtrusive woman Klee remembered from Dublin.

The two disappeared inside. Klee snuck to a place where she could see the doorman greet them and hand Alice the package. After inspecting it perfunctorily, she placed it under her arm and returned her attention to the man at her side. While they waited at the lift, the man squeezed Alice's behind and they scurried inside.

Klee slumped onto the steps of the townhouse. There had been no trip abroad for her mother. Her decline of Klee's invitation to visit had to mean her mother did not want to see her. Another twenty minutes later, her mother's companion exited the building and drove off. Klee stood up, watching until the Rolls disappeared around a corner, and then took to the street herself to make way back to the B&B.

♥ ♥ ♥

The mind plays tricks on the traveler, she was want to say in the coming weeks. As she continued her voyage, touring Canterbury and the countryside, she found her sensibilities opening to attitudes and beliefs she'd never considered in the past. Her mother's actions that night in London had awakened Klee to the dark realities of making a living, worse than she herself had faced. Though initially in denial, after a time she was unable to pretend that her mother was other than a fashionable lady of the night. The clothes, the hair, the mannerisms all pointed to that. Those letters about being alone and miserable had preceded a decision to bargain with the seedy side of living. After receiving Klee's money Alice must have used it to craft this compromising path.

What drove a person to do such a thing, Klee wondered? Why not go for loftier changes like school or university? Was this an indication of how much she and her mother differed, and how they could never really know one another? Should she bother to keep in touch with Alice? Klee couldn't dismiss their few interactions as mere folly or fate, for she too had made specific moves to see her mother. Wasn't there something worth preserving in their connection? After that night in London, Klee was only able to ascertain that she had very much wanted to pursue her mother's attention and that was why she bought a gift, why she came to London. If she lost her mother, and the fading memories of what relationship they did have, what was left? After all, the other half had always been a mystery. She never even knew if her birth father was dead or alive.

Yet something about seeing Alice touched off the need in Klee to understand more completely where she came from. With adulthood and her accomplishments had come the creation of a life unique to her, one with a special texture because of others like Johnny and Evan who cared. Thanks to their encouragement, she sought more than singular accomplishment in and of itself.

Evan had triggered this need. In an odd way, her singing success was all the more magical because he had been involved—someone who truly cared for her as much as her success, like a brother one is close to, or a dear supportive aunt. Though it was Evan, he was family to her now, and that family notion had begun to touch on other needs Klee had not realized she had. The need to belong, the need to have someone to lean on, the need to understand her roots.

In London she faced a figurative maternal door slamming in her face and that hurt as much as Evan's attentions had uplifted. This passageway towards connection that had started with Evan also seemed to lead to her parents, and yet her mother had not really cared. Why stay, then? Why not leave? Klee normally could have shrugged and moved on, but she found herself unable to. She wondered had her intention to journey been linked at one level to her studies and at an even deeper level to a discovery of self through her relatives? Since passing over Ireland on the plane, she toyed with the idea of seeing Romney. Or was she asking for trouble? Was this recent discovery a hint that she was fool to tread where she never had before? Should she turn around before more disappointment came?

A simple way around this confusion would be to focus on the trip, to check off her list of things to do and execute them efficiently and without regard to whom she may meet, then eventually leave England. But her original distaste for the place had passed and she'd come to appreciate England as deserving of her time. The peaceable age-old country with its quirky habits, hot tea breaks and fogged-in villages all produced within a sense of serenity, a sense of respect for the millennia this country claimed.

As the days passed, she found it increasingly difficult to make her way to the Dover ferry for France. In the same way her initial impression of England had modified, her own internal focus underwent a manipulation born of thoughts that ranged from a steadfast determination to see and do everything she had planned interspersed with jolts of fear at a realization that she was facing more than foreign countries on this journey.

Languages were tenable. There were words and ways of working with those words. She could spend the rest of her days perfecting accents and uncovering new twists to literary classics and continue to be most productive. In that way, the study of languages was antiseptic and safe. Languages kept her occupied and distanced from the present day and the world that revolved outside her doorstep. Languages didn't challenge her to dig deeper than she dared, nor did they promote that warmth that had come when Evan hugged her after a successful recording session. Languages were her security blanket but they were not everything. This trip to England had opened her eyes. Sure, she used her language abilities as planned, but being here, near to Alice, Romney, and her past, had touched a place in her heart that long ago had gone to sleep. She wondered over this interior presence and grew pensive over its hold on her.

Eventually she decided to leave for Batz as she promised Evan. At least for a time it might have a settling effect and shake away these odd feelings. In a Dover pub she waited for the ferry boarding. A young couple embraced nearby. Outside large windows, the chalky cliffs contrasted light grey skies. She kept seeing her mother, the gold and red, the opulent surroundings. Why had she not asked Klee for help rather than demean herself like that? Why had she appeared in Klee's life and then as quickly disappeared? Why had she never told Klee about her real father?

The young couple cuddled and whispered as she looked out at the gray waters and realized she was helpless to conjure the man who had fathered her. She had no idea what he looked like, save her own face, hair, hands, parts that differed so from her mother and so might resemble his own. Why had there been no pictures saved? No memories recalled that could shed light on the man? Had Alice simply been desperate and ashamed of her new circumstances or had she simply not wanted to get too close to Klee in case tough questions arose about her father?

The couple moved to the juke box, slipped a coin in, and selected a tune. Klee's own voice rose into the empty waiting room, the song Evan helped her record. The jazzy moody music she made without much effort but that apparently had impressed enough people to make its way to these shores well before her. The sounds made her shiver.

But the shaking was more than recall of the potentially dizzying lifestyle that could be hers should she advance into the music circles as Evan hoped she would. Instead, a clearing away seemed to be taking place inside her, indeed had started evincing itself some time ago, exposing that raw core she had covered over as a little one in order to not be hurt. In contrast to her raspy assured voice that filled the room, a silent messenger knocked on her soul, speaking another language altogether, a barely decipherable call to direct her journey elsewhere than towards what she considered serious work but that now appeared to be a means to an end, a diversion until the real quest presented itself.

"What if I don't do this?" she asked herself. "What if I return to my books and Boston, leave these derisory thoughts here in Europe? Return to my contented life?"

She knew the answer even as she asked the question. She had already arrived at another, unique plateau, the view below a cloud-filled valley. To advance was to use all she had built until now for another purpose entirely. To go forward promised unknowns. Europe held the keys. Somewhere in a city of millions or a village of twenty lived a man she was meant to know. He must be found. He must be made visible.

She looked out over the cliffs and whispered, "What consequences await those who make visible, Evan?"

# Chapter 11:
# 10 June 1975

"DO AN ALBUM," MARCEL'S TELEX READ.

Evan tapped fingers on his desk. His thoughts exactly. Three months since the release and Klee's record advanced in the charts. As a result it had been easy for Evan to line up promotion and marketing.

"If I could only get her back," he said.

But in mind and body Klee was miles from recording studios. He could tell by reading her postcards. She stayed on Batz a month, long enough to take in its wonders but not enough to become entrenched in its allure. Now in Paris, she had no plans to leave. This could have been on Evan, since he gave her his friends' names and addresses. Her stay in Paris had also not gone without recognition from editors at a few Parisian music journals. He himself gave the nod to one reporter who contacted him to see if she would allow an interview. Under the circumstances of her warm reception, he should let her enjoy her stay, he reasoned.

He tried to focus on his immediate future. If he stayed at the Chamber, the demands of Klee's career could impede his ability to do both jobs well. Which did he prefer? Through this recording adventure, he realized he thrived on bringing talent to the fore and encouraging diamonds-in-the-rough to produce the best end product. Klee the obvious success story, his abilities were rooted in France when he led filming efforts and honed future stars like Patrice. This agent work was for him.

Chamber affairs progressed smoothly. His post of *chargé d'affaires* would soon be up for renewal. If he was sure about changing careers, he must move to recommend a replacement. He could offer to stay on as advisor, for it was crucial a de Roche remain in the picture. After all, his name and his father's reputation brought dignitaries to the U. S. and Evan's presence was key to the success of most gatherings. There was already scuttlebutt about him taking an ambassador slot. He was respected and sought-after; he needed to move swiftly but with caution.

Since the arrangement with de Roche Frères, hefty sums accumulated in the coffers of the French operation. Soon Giles's liquidity and security would be guaranteed. In the next five to seven years there was no reason to believe his father's business wouldn't be on top again. In addition, Evan's real estate investments had turned a profit and he used some of the gains to promote other singers and support actors in off Broadway productions. Step by step he'd found his way. The time had come for other pursuits.

Thoughts of music evaporated as Ricky Lincoln walked in the door. Blonde, radiant, and well-built, she blew Evan a kiss then sat down on the opposite side of his desk.

Giving an approving glance to her leather pants and white top he said, "You're early."

"I couldn't stay away," she beamed with sparkling teeth. "You talked up that part so much that I went home and memorized it. Do you have time to listen before we go?"

"Always," he said, moving towards his intercom and requesting no further calls. He removed his jacket, rolled up shirt sleeves, and accepted the script she handed him, an O'Neill play. Evan had been coaching her for a week and she was due to audition later that night. He watched her carefully as she assumed her role and recited well-rehearsed lines. At the end of the two minutes, he smiled.

"Ah, that smile I so rarely see," she said with a toss to her hair. Winking, she blushed.

"I must say you've captured the role," he said, eyes roving.

It wasn't often he indulged in the sight of a woman but Ricky was a refreshing departure from the ladies with whom he associated in the recent past. No less beautiful, she had the additional quality of ambition that exuded from her every cell, especially when she read her lines and made the motions of the characters she portrayed. Eyes a cool misty blue, complexion fair and clear, he recognized early on the talent behind her multiple layers and comprehended in her a woman determined to succeed.

From the first night he scooped her from a secretarial position at the Chamber, she gave her all memorizing lines from Shakespeare and studying acting publications and journals. He knew he'd found his next protégée.

They left the office and made for Broadway and 44th Street to the audition. Inside a cramped studio of over forty hopefuls and the director, a harried-looking woman with glasses and stretch pants took names and requested silence. Three roles were to be filled: two female and one male. Ricky had read about the audition in an industry publication and Evan encouraged her to try out. Broadway was tough and she had but a handful of commercials and a high school play to her credit. Yet she had moved to New York to make it big so was ready to experiment with most anything. The auditions began.

The first two female candidates lacked conviction and presence. The third, a buxom redhead with deep, modulating voice gave a commanding read. Scanning the woman's resume with a serious regard, the director requested she repeat the lines. A striking older woman came next and, while she read well, she did not appear to impress the director.

When Ricky got the nod, she eased into her lines with expert turns of phrases, her motions and gaze offering further insight into the character. After requesting a repeat, the director asked about her background. The would-be actress's professional, courteous and grateful style—behaviors Evan had encouraged—seemed to leave a positive impression. An hour later, and after the director debated with two assistants, Ricky and four others were asked to remain. Another round of readings brought the total hopefuls to two, but Ricky was not chosen.

As she and Evan exited, she pouted, "I don't understand. I thought I performed well."

"A rejection is one step closer to acceptance, remember," said Evan.

"I was better than that redhead!"

"You were! But you can't get into the mind of a director."

"I must have goofed. You said I was good, are you just saying that?"

"I never just say anything, Ricky," Evan said nudging her. "C'mon, I'll drive you home."

After a delay on the West Side Highway, they arrived at her place. Frazzled by their long day and longer evening, they collapsed on her couch. The night noises rose from the street—the hum of cars, distant boats and liners moving up the Hudson, nearby footsteps.

"New York never sleeps," he said.

"Tell me the truth. What was wrong?" she asked.

He shrugged. "Maybe what's wrong is your expectation. You can't live and die for these parts. Take each audition in stride. Nothing was wrong that I could tell."

"Maybe I was too anxious and that showed."

"I didn't notice."

She placed a hand absently on his thigh. "I don't know…"

Her nails tugged on his slacks, clear polish shining. Her lower arm was slight and freckled. She crossed her legs in an elegant pose, the role she confidently portrayed hours before forgotten, and in its place a dejected lady. Yet, in that chagrin he detected a poignant element, a sprout of helplessness ruling her regard.

"Look at me," he whispered.

"What?"

He closed his eyes and touched her forehead, her nose, her cheek. Skin soft, her voice innocent, he marveled at the feel of her. Her damp lips were smooth, and her chin a tiny crevice. She winced.

"You don't like me touching you?" he asked.

"I don't much like my chin."

"One can't simply read about characters then force oneself to become them, you know."

"Huh?"

"Feel your character's pain through every part of your body, exude anger or love to the very bone. Touch their souls by touching their sorrow. That's what we have to work on next, Ricky."

"I don't know what you're talking about."

Evan smiled and clasped her hand. "Look. O'Neill's characters are extreme—angry, vengeful, loving, endearing. There's no in-between. No spoken word that doesn't also carry a loaded meaning, and this meaning must shoot up from the actor's toes and target the audience's heart. "If it's about hate, you must hate! If it's about love, go there. All the way. Be ALL of what you speak!"

He grabbed the script and read lines about a daughter taking revenge against her mother.

"Do you really know what that is, Ricky? Did you ever feel like taking revenge on someone?"

"No."

He stood and beckoned her to her feet. "We're going to work on anger."

"Evan!" she protested, shying from him.

"Come here! I won't bite. Pretend I am the man you've wanted for years but I am married. You can't have me completely which is already painful. In addition, I am ambivalent about you. In fact, I'm having affairs right under your nose."

Ricky narrowed her gaze.

"Now, you meet up with me and it's your final chance to get me but I make fun of your...your...chin," he said pinching her chin.

"Stop!" she exclaimed.

He grinned. "That's it. We're getting somewhere now."

They worked the part another hour or so. Evan poked at Ricky's chin as she reared in annoyance that graduated to anger at his use of her fragility. Crying, she eventually raged at him without referring to the script, venomous words spilled. If her tirade surprised her, she hid it well. By the end of their session, she was a vengeful character.

Her mood was his delight. "See? I've killed off your reluctance to feel the part!"

He eventually gathered his things and headed for the door. Their session had gone long into the night. Ricky lay on the couch, spent.

"Evan. I'm still angry with you."

He returned to her and kissed her brow. "That's all part of it. It's all fun, no?"

She looked at him with veiled gaze, then tugged his hand. "All in fun? All?"

He watched her carefully. So far, sex had not entered their equation, though the idea had crossed his mind. Watching her on that couch following her improved performance, hair splayed across pillows, her shirt revealing her chest, he couldn't pretend she wasn't one of the loveliest women he'd known. An odd feeling took hold as she tugged his hand harder.

"Ricky," he said softly.

She drew him closer and he allowed the embrace. When her lips reached his, he allowed that too, closing his eyes and with them the door to his soul. He could tell that a part of her was trying to impress him and another part was simply desire directing her movements. She undressed, displaying her perfect proportions. She ran fingers across her chest, toyed with her nipples. In her gaze a gathering delight at the sign of his submission. Gently she pulled off his shirt and ran a hand down his chest, to his belt, surprising him with her deft movement to his hardened penis. He gave into the feel of her body pressing against his and allowed her to ease them both back onto the couch. Lying on top of him, she rubbed her body against his, knees bending, tongue lowering into his mouth. She danced light fingertips across his shoulder. Teacher role reversed, she commanded his body.

She mounted him and he entered her. In the ensuing excitement, she climaxed as quickly as he. After, they lay together and she fell asleep, her fingers entangled in his hair.

He stroked her arm, watching the New York sky turn from black to barely discernable gray. They were bound to get here, he reasoned. Tonight was as inevitable as the ticking of the clock on her mantle. Ricky was determined and so was he. Each used one another, each discovered through one another. And tonight was all part of it. He tried to sleep but was unable. These days, the moments following sex pumped a thickness into his veins, conveying a message he struggled to decipher.

After a while, he dressed and slipped away.

# Chapter 12:
## July 1975

"LAURENCE?" BEA ASKED, NUDGING HER COMPANION.

"I don't want the money," Laurence said.

"It's hard turning M. Duronier away and pretending I don't know where you are."

"No money."

"Laurence, what I'm suggesting isn't about the money. There is a way you can remain here in Glenrock AND allow me to protect your interests."

Bea stroked Laurence's hair then placed a hand on her shoulder. "You can't live like this forever, my little one. In so many ways, Glenrock is perfect for you. However, you live meagerly on your job at the grocery store. With your talents, there are other options."

"I'm content."

"Is content what you want for the rest of your life? You're only twenty-five! If you allow me to do as I suggest…"

Laurence raised her hand to stop the conversation.

"Listen to your old Bea for a minute. I know I sound a nag but trust me. I can comply with your wish to be alone. You can have all you need here in Glenrock but without living a barely sustainable life!"

Laurence shuffled to the window. In jeans and sweatshirt, her glasses lay low on her nose and tangled unkempt hair fell down her back.

A week prior, Bea had arrived to discover the cottage in disarray with unopened canned goods from a previous visit. A stray cat ruled the place that now boasted ruined upholstery and sour milk smells. A dead mouse lay curled in one corner.

The landlords told Bea they were concerned for Laurence due to her self-imposed isolation. The wife initially hoped that Laurence would be a companion, but from the outset the young woman preferred long walks alone and tending to animals, caring little about the goings-on in Glenrock.

Wednesday to Saturday, her job at Sam Ralsey's village market got her away from the farm for a full time schedule. Ralsey himself attempted to include her in town affairs like the weekly flea market and church gatherings but she declined. Most townsfolk wondered over this sweet, quiet girl who seemed to come from nowhere and have no particular goal in mind. Most young people from the area were anxious to get out of town, go to college or move to Boston to work. Why did she stay and what were her plans?

Ralsey eventually stopped inviting and, seeing as she wasn't harming anyone, left her to herself. But many continued to wonder and others invented unkind stories about the girl with a limp arm and skewed nose. Whoever she was, they said, she was odd and perhaps people should avoid her.

Laurence made tea while Bea turned up the radio. Her visit to Glenrock nearing an end, she had yet to sell Laurence on her plan to work through the issue of inheritance from Mémé. Loathe to detail the lawyer's persistence, Bea had nonetheless also grown increasingly annoyed by this invasion of her own privacy. Radio music played as Laurence poured milk into dingy mugs.

"Nice music," Bea said accepting the tea.

"It's a station out of Bar Harbor," Laurence said. "They broadcast in summer."

"Like WHYB in Nantucket, remember?"

Laurence smiled.

"You know, we never did something that Sage wanted. We never brought your film to market. It sits collecting dust in my office. Remember the party we had at the end of the shoot? How our pal Don there had the time of his life? Sage, too, before her world turned around."

Laurence stared out the window. "You know, a tune like this one—sort of prancing and light—was the kind of music I had in mind."

"Do you know the musicians?" Bea asked.

"No but they're local."

"Why don't we look them up? You know, I feel I owe this final edit to Sage."

Laurence turned to Bea. "You miss her, don't you?"

"Yes, but we had a good understanding about death. It's simply a displacement. Someday we meet again. If not," Bea said with a playful wink, "we'll have settled with other lovers. Anyway, enough of that."

"I've always wished the film had completed too," Laurence whispered.

"Then let's do it," Bea said.

They drove to Bar Harbor and spent the day inquiring about the band, eventually gathering at the band's summer cottage. Bea did all the talking. Phone numbers and addresses were exchanged before they said goodbye. In a few days, Laurence would meet up again to hear them play. In the meantime, Bea had Laurence's film sent from New York. They purchased the group's recordings and spent hours musing over their style. A rough cut of the interplay between sight and sound formed in their minds. When the film arrived, Mr. Ralsey arranged for a projector and screen. Mixing sounds to movements in the picture, they pieced together an initial score.

Using her rusting yet still agile talents, Laurence gradually adapted to this work schedule. She warmed readily to the sight of the sea and marine life and her gaze danced across the screen, especially during the amusing scenes with Don and Bea. To her own form undulating underwater she gave passing note. Bea sensed Laurence's love for the water remained and was as addictive in a good way as her sorrow was in a destructive way.

The band signed on for the project and Bea followed up with other arrangements that included meeting in the city to sort through technical issues. Everything seemed ready the day of Bea's departure when she woke to find an empty cottage. It was Sunday and Laurence was off instead of packing. Something was afoot.

Scouting around the barn and grounds she found nothing so made for a path that led to the water. Some hundred yards above a cliff, a scantily clad Laurence stared to sea as wind whipped her hair. Shuddering in the pre-dawn chill, Bea reached Laurence and offered her hand.

"What are you doing?"

With a look of horror, Laurence turned towards Bea then scurried down the rocky ledge, a treacherous path with few nooks for sure footing.

"Laurence! Come back!"

Bea slipped along, heading to where Laurence disappeared, a cave formed by rocks. She found the young woman sobbing in a corner.

"I can't do this!" Laurence screamed.

"Laurence, please, tell me what's wrong," she asked trying to steady herself and grasp Laurence.

"The reel. It's in the ocean. I threw it in!"

"No! Why?" Bea shouted over the sound of the waves.

Laurence squirmed from Bea's hold.

"Oh, no you don't!" Bea said. "You're coming with me."

But Laurence was quicker and ran from the cave.

Once outside, Bea peered over the ledge, trying to quell her own emotions as she thought of the ruined film. "Laurence Mallord, you are too much," she screamed. "We did so much work, so many hours! For what? So you could throw the tape in the ocean!"

She scurried up the rocks and caught up with Laurence who had not yet reached the clifftop. Catching Laurence, Bea held firm.

"You're not getting away this time!"

Laurence went limp and began moaning and rocking. "I can't. I can't."

Relaxing her hold, Bea pressed Laurence against her chest. "Jesus, baby, I'm so sorry. So sorry for you."

When Laurence had calmed, they made way to the cottage where Bea wrapped Laurence in blankets and made tea. When Laurence finally dozed off, Bea paced the room, her thoughts jumbled.

"Who in the world would ruin you, little one?" she asked, studying her friend. "If I knew, I could do something to help you. Mind you, if your father knew this he would do everything to uncover your secrets. He was like that."

For the rest of the afternoon until evening shadows, Bea contemplated Laurence's form and thought through the past—Laurence's arrival in the States, their happenstance encounter, their companionship and eventual close friendship, her work ethic, her enthusiasm for the sea, her glazed-over stare when she thought Bea or Sage wasn't watching. The girl needed professional help but Bea knew better than to bring that up. But there were still ways to help. How could anyone forget those few peeks at her joy when she was filming, those references to Mémé who she adored, the way father's memory reflected through her actions. Bea thought the filming would help and it had for a time. Still, she maintained, all was not lost. A tiny step had been made in the right direction, others could be, too. It was a question of pace, and patience, and Bea had insight into both when it came to Laurence. She would prevail and help her friend if it took all her time. If Bea didn't take charge, no one else would.

The next day, she nudged Laurence awake with a cup of tea.

"Laurence," she said. "I'm staying. I've decided to make my own film of the area to promote nature and the like. It's a hidden gem, overlooked for other more popular places in Maine. Perhaps you're not very concerned that I do this and that's fine. I was wondering, however, would you mind if I stay here for the time being? Until I find myself a place."

If Laurence felt relief at Bea's offer, she didn't show it but she gave a nod, and continued sipping her tea.

"Good, then. I stay, but not here with you."

Laurence looked up.

"I'll rent the next door house from the farmer and his wife. Once I get settled, I start filming right away. You're of course free to help out—I could use your help but I won't force you. After all, you have a job here already. But should you decide to, we can produce it together and claim it as our own work. If you would like contribute but not get credit, everything could be arranged through Bea-Sage Productions and no one would know you were involved. It's either way, as you wish."

Bea hesitated before continuing. "If it does well, it will also be a tribute to a part of the world your father admired—surely you know this from old National Geographic articles. He loved Maine but never got the chance to study the area. Provided we do this right as he would have, and of course with his same energy, an eventual film would be a tribute to him. Dedicated to Nate Mallord."

Laurence blinked back tears.

"All rights will be mine, unless you wish to share, of course. The most important thing to remember is that if we do this, or I do it, it will show that we appreciate all your father's efforts, begun but unfortunately never finished."

She reached and turned Laurence's face towards hers.

"I knew him, too, my dear, and Nate Mallord always finished what he started."

Laurence said, "It's...it's, well, it's good. Okay, Bea."

Bea excused herself to run a few errands. At the nearest large town, she purchased a scuba outfit as birthday present for Laurence. She wouldn't offer it right away but hopefully in time Laurence would be ready to commence an adventure she was meant to undertake. For her father and for herself. As for Bea, saving Laurence was no longer a matter of choice.

# Chapter 13:
# August 1975

PARIS AND KLEE FOLDED into one another like *mille-feuilles*, those magnificent layers that formed the base of puff pastries, eclairs and other ornate sugary goodies displayed in *boulangerie* windows and atop *patisserie* shelves. Using Evan's centrally-located apartment as base, she traveled entire blocks absorbed by the vibrancy and color. Groups of passing tourists occasionally interrupted and occupied her reveries and she noted the dearth of native French people, presumably gone for the vacation period. August in Paris meant many *fermé* signs on restaurants but Evan provided her with a list of places where she could dine and socialize so she would never be without options. Originally scheduled to stay a few weeks, early on she informed the concierge that she wished to stay the entire month, maybe longer.

She met people with whom she could practice not only French but Italian and even some Greek. Frequenting cafés filled with students and artists, she grew bold, more fluent, and wise to the subtleties of both language and gesture in this neverland of nuance. She fell into step with the late nights, the jazz bars, the pleasures that made the city eternal and full of light.

When Jacques Delange discovered her sitting at a café, she had so imbued herself to the lifestyle, his strong come-on and romantic overtones barely ruffled her.

Dark and with the same mystery Evan exuded, the stranger wooed her by complimenting her looks and her language facility. She, however, didn't take his bait easily or quickly.

"You must see Montmartre at midnight! Special, Mademoiselle, so special!"

"Been there," she quipped.

"Then Père Lachaise Cemetery is a must!"

"Three times."

"May I ask what you have yet to discover?"

"Nothing. No, no, and no! I am fine thank you. Please leave me."

"Ah, the faces she makes!" Jacques exclaimed. "Charming. Demonstrating your willfulness."

"Look, Monsieur Jacques whoever you are. I am busy."

However educated in the ways of the French she might have been, Klee remained ignorant of one thing. A blasé, disinterested woman only encouraged and piqued the interest of a smitten Frenchman. Jacques followed her when she left the café, sidling up to her as he teased and offered suggestions of what to do and see in Paris.

"The Panthéon! It's deserted at this hour. We can wander around and you will love its stone quiet, another place were Paris reveres her famous dead."

She rolled eyes and kept walking.

He placed fingers to her lips. "Shh. Say nothing, Chérie. Come anyway. For once, allow yourself to be led by someone other than yourself."

She grunted but followed, suspicious gazes passing to and from him as she scrutinized to digest this obtrusive personality.

Taller than she, his smile dug tiny lines around deep-set brown eyes full of mischief. His behavior led her to think the chase was of more interest than the end result and thus, she finally figured, her rude behavior only goaded him on.

"You take great pleasure in thwarting plans," she said.

"It's not entirely about pleasure, it's about what I know of you," he said, extending a hand to indicate a stone wall near the imposing domed edifice. Its walkways free of congestion in spite of a central Latin Quarter location, the monument basked in soft yellow light and staked its claim amongst residences and a few modest shops.

"Victor Hugo lies there," she said, staring at the columned façade.

"I suppose you know all there is to know about who lies buried there. I marvel at that. Truly." His voice had lost its churlish edge. He eyed her closely.

"I love to study other cultures," she said.

"You've come to the right place."

She nodded. "It talks almost, you know? Oozes a personality—strong, solid, and permanent."

"You and me will be long gone and there will be other couples to take our place, others for Panthéon to spy upon," he said, kissing her quickly.

"Hey!" she exclaimed.

"Can you blame me?" he asked.

Wiping her cheek, she stood. "Enough." She walked away.

"I was only trying to appreciate the person hidden away inside of you, under all that hair and audaciousness. The singer—where is she?"

Swirling around, she stared at him.

"You are the lady Klee, no?"

"How did you know?"

He laughed and swung himself off the bench. "Sing me a song. Please?"

He quickly kissed her cheek.

"You're mad," she screamed, loud enough to stop two passers-by.

His laugh reassured the on-lookers who moved along. "Good! YOU don't go mad enough!"

"You big bloke!" she screamed. "Mr. Smart-Nose arse! Get going now!" she exclaimed shoving him and moving away.

When she got to a corner, he cupped hands and yelled, "I go around the world, still I can't get started with you!"

She froze, turned, and stared.

"I only wanted to get to better know Evan's favorite protégée!"

"Evan de Roche?" she asked.

"The same."

"Why be such a bastard when you could have said so in the first place?" she asked.

"I'd still be a bastard."

They meandered a while longer then settled on a bench near a fountain. They compared notes about Evan and each other and even got to the point where they could laugh about their initial encounter. As night dwindled to dawn while they strolled along the Seine, she even sang a song. At first light, he escorted her to her place, kissed her hand, and bid adieu.

"When you are under the big lights, singing and breaking new hearts, when you are once again wound within your own tight orbit, think of the man in Paris who coddled you into loosening up for a while. Au revoir, ma Chère.

Tingling from the sweet satisfaction of song and interesting conversation, she rubbed her eyes and watched him jaunt down the street and turn the corner.

"I will," she whispered. "That I will."

# Chapter 14

KLEE STIRRED HER TEA as she took in the September Manhattan skyline from the Chamber offices. "As rude as could be, that man. Never mentioned your name until well into the evening."

"Don't tell me Jacques and his compliments disturbed you," Evan said.

"You know well what matters to me, and what doesn't," she said creasing her brow. "When do we start the singing?"

"Tonight. I'll take you to the studio after I finish here. We'll meet the folks and then you'll sing for them. They'll probably have suggestions for selections for the album."

"When can I return to Boston?"

"Next week, but, why Boston? I thought you might stay on in New York."

"The press comes down hard here. Do you know the morning I left Paris, two reporters for a New York-based rag stopped me outside my apartment? That's the doing of your so-called friend Jacques, you know."

"You'll have your privacy," he said, "but remember the big bucks you're getting. Big name, too. The world wants to know you."

"I hardly call twenty thousand dollars big bucks."

"That was your single. An album at the top of the charts will create a windfall. You'll have to travel hard and fast to avoid the curious. Goes with the territory."

"I won't record then."

He tapped fingers on his desk. Annoyed, she curled up in the chair and covered her ears.

"You love travel, Klee. It's written all over your face. The few disturbances from people like Jacques were flies in your ointment. I saw you alight from that plane. You've found your place in the sun in Europe, all of it, all those intriguing landscapes you can disappear into, relish the enchantment of all those famous writers, historians, and public figures you've read about all these years. They've grown as important to you as the air. In fact, your books have taken second place to them."

She looked away.

"I'm right, Klee. You won't easily stay put again. You live for all the nondescript yet poignant thrills of travel. This time, you came to terms with your sheltered Boston life and will never really be able to return there for good. But therein lies your dilemma, such a practical one yet not insignificant. To travel requires the green stuff. Mula, l'argent, money!"

"Stop."

"Performing's your ticket to that inner sanctum you cultivate when you seek out places unknown, where you try to relive history or recreate it or something I don't understand and don't want to. The world will adore your voice, and will want you handed over to be viewed at their beck and call and, yes, scrutiny. You won't like that but you don't mind singing. It's a means to an end. It gets you traveling. The singing displaces you. It gives rise to your gypsy spirit. Perhaps that stirring inside is what you really dislike."

"So, I've become that readable?"

"To me, yes." He stared at his fingers, stopped tapping. "Klee, you and I simply share a common ground, where others don't dare tread."

She stood, took a deep breath, steadied herself, then said, "Okay. I'm ready. Shall we?"

They walked out of the office.

# Chapter 15

RÉGINE SPLASHED WATER then buried her head in a towel, massaged temples and cheeks then gazed into the mirror. She pinched herself, pleased. The plastic surgeon performed miracles. Wrinkles around her eyes were gone and an extra tuck at her chin created a sweet dimple. Her eyes bulged in a molded look of surprise and, when she smiled, the forehead remained free of creases.

"Perfect," she cooed, reaching for her creams. She touched up makeup, spritzed cologne, and tightened the belt of her robe, then descended to Giles's study. He gave an approving nod to her silk ensemble and gold slippers.

"New hairstyle, dear?" he asked. "Or perhaps it's a month in the south that's revived you! Whatever, you look…beautiful as usual."

Flouncing her platinum locks, she stroked his hair then kneeled at his feet, reached for his face, and planted a kiss. He dropped paperwork and enclosed her in his arms. She prolonged the embrace long enough to sense his tension, then drew him up and led him to the bedroom. Lowering shades, she slipped from her robe and cupped her breasts as he lay against the pillows admiring her.

"They're so tender now, so in need of your touch," she said.

"I must have you," he said.

"Oh, darling, how I'd love to," she said, approaching but not lying next to him. "Go carefully, you understand."

He rubbed her belly. "The child, of course," he said.

The news of her pregnancy circulated in high society. Régine herself had contacted the newspapers but was eventually disappointed to read but a few lines in a Saturday issue and on an inside page. Giles himself had not received the news directly from her. An employee, assuming he already knew, congratulated him.

When Régine broke the news by explaining that she tried to prevent a pregnancy but, given its inevitability, their lives together must be destiny. When he voiced doubt, she offered that they would have a young person as company in their advancing years.

Although six months remained, her body had begun its adjustment to support the child, to her ever disdain each day when she studied her shape in the mirror. Yet, this gave her opportunity to purchase more designer labels and cover up at least until she no longer was able to. Fuller skirts were the rage, vests too, so she remained stylish. Important, for she had an agenda.

Giles had still not asked for her hand and she was losing faith he might ever. Her few remarks about giving the child a name provoked a mere pooh-pooh from Giles who already agreed the child would be a de Roche. She nonetheless wanted a marriage proposal, hoping a wedding would take place before she could no longer fit in the Givenchy gown she'd already purchased. Giles was not to be rushed. He no longer cared about ceremony. The reason why had everything to do with their continuing charade, which kept him attentive but not in the way Régine would have hoped.

The game was no longer fun, seeing as Pauline was the major theme. Régine had long before exhausted and grown bored with her initial wiles to trick him. But Giles thrived on their pantomimes.

"I'll take care of you, *mon amour*," he always said during their trysts. And provide everything for you, to you."

Régine seethed. It wasn't enough for her to have his quasi-promises of forever love. Claiming ownership to the title and social standing of the de Roche name mattered most. But Giles anticipated only his time with Pauline, the forays in bed with a woman who he would die loving. Their wedding had long before taken place. No more weddings.

She undressed him and tried to ready for the act but the sight of his sagging body and tired expression gave her pause. However distinguished in suit and tie, this man was physically in ruin. Yet she persevered with the motions of sexual desire, the predicted murmuring, the words he instructed her to say that recalled Pauline.

She had to give him credit. Two could play this game and Giles performed equally. He even came up with his own rules of engagement. Régine squirmed as the copulation advanced to its climax.

"Ah, Pauline," he moaned. "I love you."

"*Mon amour, mon amour*," she replied.

He drifted to sleep with her head cradled in the crook of his arm. As the lace curtains fluttered, her stomach rumbled, a reminder of her volatile condition that would rob her—the bulging stomach, the swollen ankles, thinning hair, bad teeth.

Panic struck as she wondered over the child's looks. What if it were a girl? Another Laurence? What if in her hurry to possess his fortune, Régine had created the very means to her end? A child, under the code of law as it existed, inherited most of a fortune, especially when the natural mother was not married to the father. How in the world could she force this marriage? She must find a way!

Her eyes smarted as she dug a hand into her belly, uncaring as to its effect on the fetus. In so many ways, she wished to destroy what she'd brought on and this thought process was taking precedence over her desire for Giles and what he represented materially. But this baby's growth was beyond her control.

Laurence. What if? She cringed at the thought. This romance with Giles could founder after the child's birth. Evan might intervene and talk sense to his father. Laurence might re-appear.

"At least," she thought, "that is one thing that's been taken care of."

The baby stirred. She rolled out of bed and dressed, stood in the window and watched a delivery truck unload cartons. Did Giles himself have devious plans in mind? Plans Evan had concocted? Once Evan found out about the baby, he'd take action, snatch the fortune for himself. He would research his past, Giles's past, Régine's past. And he would discover Laurence.

She lit a cigarette and continued to stare onto the street. Who to blame for this mess? Surely Mémé hadn't helped, the old coot, dividing assets so as to literally strike her only daughter from the will. Then Giles and his ridiculous behavior like a few moments before. In his way, he also kept Régine restricted from enjoying life. So many others who got in the way, not least of all Nate and their child.

Not caring whether or not Giles heard her, she moaned, "Oh, why did that child come along, Nate? Why did things go so terribly wrong?"

# Chapter 16

BEA WORKED WITH LAURENCE and by mid-September they'd formed a relationship of another kind, one that placed more stress on Bea and one with which Laurence initially struggled. In short, Bea made a pest of herself.

At the dilapidated farm she'd offered to buy for Laurence, she set up house. The two-story century-old structure hinted at a more manicured past with hardwood floors throughout, two fieldstone fireplaces, and a kitchen boasting an oversized cast-iron stove. Divided by a wide mahogany staircase, high-ceiling hallways interconnected a study, living area and, in back, the kitchen from where a back staircase wound up to three bedrooms with dramatically sloping eaves.

Patches of dead grass and unkempt plantings took liberties with the yard and the barn's roof had long ago caved in. Over twenty acres of fields bordered by trees guaranteed privacy. Hidden amongst the brush, a narrow overgrown path alongside rocky cliffs led to the open Atlantic. In fair weather, one could enjoy a private beach and mooring area for a boat or two.

Mornings, Bea had only to peek out and find the sun rising between a dip in the ledges. On chilly days, they stoked a fire and ran electric heaters. A working phone proved one of few amenities. She would have preferred staying with Laurence but, for practical business reasons, she chose living here. Although reluctant to embrace a constant companionship at Bea's farm, Laurence did take to joining her friend for tea each day.

Bea would share details of her film. Laurence listened but without the least offer to engage in the project. This daily visit helped Bea understand better the depth of Laurence's depression and also shed light on the fact that Bea's previous trips had done little to help the young woman get better. Someone needed to stay on with Laurence. Though they did not hire professional help, Bea did maintain contact with a therapist she'd consulted during Sage's illness. Key, the doctor said, was regaining trust and never trying to force the past from Laurence. By Bea's gentle and patient presence, Laurence might stir from her prison of fear and wariness.

Some days Laurence's removal from reality grated on Bea's nerves. Other days she sympathized and cheered at the slightest sign of improvement—a smile, a question about the film, a decision to try another flavor of tea. Sometimes, Laurence even peered at the notes and scripts strewn across Bea's desk.

One afternoon when Laurence joined her after work, Bea announced she was going to visit a producer in Bar Harbor. Laurence asked to go along. Since Laurence had taken to visiting Bea after her job at the market, Bea didn't overly react to this choice, but she was pleased.

Traversing back roads, Laurence even took the wheel of the Jeep for a time through muddy ways she knew well from running errands for the market. Once at their destination, however, she insisted on staying in the Jeep while Bea talked with the director. Afterwards, they made for home and ate dinner together. Periodically, Bea noted the change in Laurence's expression from her usual haunted look to one of placid contemplation.

"What about the music, Bea?" she asked as they worked on their soup.

"Well, I'll need my full time crew to continue," Bea said. "The band has a workable score but it will need editing and refining I'm sure."

"And the credits?"

"You know that comes last. We haven't gotten to that yet."

"I would like this movie dedicated to my father," she said.

Bea looked up from her bowl. Laurence gazed at her, her hand poised over her own meal, lips slightly pursed. She wore a look Bea hadn't seen in what seemed an eternity, a look of peaceful determination.

"We can do that," she said, keeping her response measured so as not to shake Laurence from her mood.

"The film needs to be finished. Expertly and well, as I know you can do, Bea."

"You don't care to help with the final touches?" Bea asked.

Laurence lay back on the chair. For a second, Bea thought the girl might return to her private world but, after a while, she said, "I trust you to do what is best. You know what I want."

"Laurence, we need money. A documentary like this appeals to a narrow market. It's difficult to get financial backing. I can, of course, dip into my own funds, but only to a point…"

"No," Laurence said. I have money coming to me, no?"

"I thought…"

Laurence leaned towards Bea. "My inheritance can take care of financial details, can it not?"

"I imagine so. I'd have to look into it."

"Will you?"

Bea bit her lower lip. "If that's what you want. Of course."

"This movie is for my father. Let's do everything possible to make it a success."

Laurence got up, cleared the table, and eased onto the couch where she laid down with a sigh, as though a weight had been lifted. In no time, her breathing was steady.

Bea began working on details in her head, with a growing sense that Bea-Sage Productions was about to witness its finest hour.

# Chapter 17:
# October, 1975

SHINY MAROON UPHOLSTERY, tasseled wool curtains and balcony box seats in the retro theater offered a perfect venue for lesser-known independent works. Long-haired youth sat elbow-to-elbow, speaking softly while waiting for the show to begin. Evan hearkened back to his energetic film days in Paris, yet he also felt at a remove. These people represented an authenticity he could not. In three-piece suit, he could have been mistaken for someone who'd lost his way and landed here by accident. He tried not to envy their breezy conversations, their apparent lack of regard about tomorrow, but he could not. He had yet to make his move one way or the other, the call of his artistic temperament or family demands? The two clashed; he had been straddling both lifestyles for years. He wearied of forcing issues.

A young woman glanced his way and smiled. He returned the smile and then thought of Ricky, presently in Los Angeles auditioning for a TV role he helped her obtain. On her own, she'd lined up more try-outs and had appointments with several agents. She would succeed as Klee had done. Talent coupled with marketing skill, a sure bet.

He had others, too, a young blues singer and a man accomplished in Shakespearean theater. Coaching them along the way to stardom helped Evan.

However, not every arrangement turned out as he'd imagined. Ricky, for instance, had fallen in love. Their evenings of practice had progressed from casual affection to lovemaking until he determined it was best to curtail the physical in favor of business. In spite of her pleading, and with a bluntness that had not come easily, he begged off. He wasn't in love and didn't want to hurt her. This of course hurt her more. The day she left for California, he waved goodbye to the teary-eyed starlet, alerted to a feeling of detachment, if not outright indifference.

As his personal quandary advanced, so did a facility to alienate. When engaged with a woman in business, he dangled his sexuality in such a way as to convey mixed messages. A more sensitive man would have been ashamed but Evan compartmentalized his life, another habit honed over the years since Laurence. What would happen to him? When he aged and could not as easily charm or seduce? How then would he carry on? As lights dimmed in the theater, he shrugged away the thought.

The woman looked over once again. He winked at her, recalling Marcel's words that one must never leave a stone unturned. He would catch her afterwards.

The screen lit up to a watery beginning, the intricacy and beauty of the sea around Nantucket Island. He felt his throat go dry as he whispered the credits: "Bea-Sage Productions."

From one scene to another, the visuals progressed— schools of silvery guppies, a lone sand shark, a family of minke whales—imagery narrated by the soft voice he recognized instantly. With a long shot of an abandoned ship, his knees weakened. Swimming around the damaged portholes and debris, her sleek body, intent on discovery, eyes from time to time visible behind her mask—the same deep-set, absorbing gaze from years before. Fin-tipped long legs paddled, her arms formed gracious ballet arcs and circles, and her hair floated in opposing undulation; she was one with the water. He swallowed and fought tears in order to stay fixed on the unraveling scenes.

A final time she appeared, as the crew pulled in lines and equipment and others settled on board the motorboat. In diminishing daylight, she leaned on a cushion and stroked an arm with a towel, her focus on a lowering sun that reflected back her captivating mystique. One with nature, one with herself.

And yet, this cohesion did not hide a sorrow, undeniable even in the presence of the sunset and jocular crew. A sadness without a specific label.

The credits rolled to upbeat and fiery music and, as he scrutinized every name and made note of the New York address of Bea-Sage Productions, hers did not appear. The final line froze Evan in his seat: "This film is dedicated to Nate Mallord and the sea he loved."

A murmur arose from the audience as others noted the man's name. After the lights went on, Nate scanned the theater, not for the flirtatious female but in search of Bea or someone who might have been part of the film, to no avail. As the place emptied, he stared at the blank screen, willing her face to appear one more time.

"Laurence," he said.

He'd not spoken her name in years. The word crossing his lips brought forth the impulse he'd been struggling to find. The desire to see her again, to look into her eyes whatever she may do in return. He understood the road, a path he'd so long resisted following, the way of his heart. He made for the nearest phone booth.

♥ ♥ ♥

It took another week for Bea to return his calls and two additional days to meet with her. She appeared more evasive than he remembered.

"I produced the movie," she said. "The actual filming was done some time ago. There really is nothing more to discuss."

"Surely you know where Laurence is and how she's doing."

"I'm afraid I can't help you," Bea said. "The film belongs to me. Ms. Mallord relinquished all rights."

"She had nothing to do with its release?"

Bea gave him a sympathetic smile. "You knew her, Evan. Her behavior should not surprise you."

He had no choice but to leave with no answers. The next day, he revisited the avant-garde theater to see the film again and again. He memorized lines, faces, and names should he need to use them in his further quest; he was not giving up. That night, foregoing a charity event, he withdrew to his place to mull things over. The film received minimal mention in the dailies and movie reviews, and this irked him. Had it been marketed differently, or handled by an established public relations firm, there would have been a greater push to the general public as well as within the smaller, vertical market of independent films. Laurence deserved better, to say nothing of her father in whose memory the film was made, something no one had done pursuant to the seaman's untimely death.

Into the wee hours of the next day he planned, all the while confronting a quivering that took to his shoulders, a chill wielding its way up his spine, especially when he closed his eyes and saw her face, her slender, flexible body, her dedicated underwater motions. The film was in need of more, but how could he do that without Bea's support? The rights were hers, the music spoken for. A sequel would require legal intervention and, of course, the Okay of its owner. Unable to figure a way to overcome these barriers, he finally called Marcel.

"I have a sticky problem, Marce," he said.

"I don't believe in sticky problems," said his uncle. "Speak."

The trans-Atlantic lines buzzed and, when Evan replaced the receiver, he wore a grin of gratitude.

"The dedication, of course!" he exclaimed. "Marcel's right! Someone wanted that film dedicated in a big way. Push the dedication thing. Find other backers of Nate Mallord's work. Go to Cousteau myself if need be!" How could he have forgotten the long-time friendship between Nate Mallord and Jacques Cousteau?

As Manhattan rumbled towards a new day, he stared out the window and watched a jogger hurry along the avenue. "Cousteau! Of course!"

Canceling appointments at the Chamber, he reset his course.

# Chapter 18

"LAURENCE, YOU'LL NEVER GUESS WHO CALLED!" Bea exclaimed running to the kitchen to find Laurence. "You there?"

"I heard you," Laurence said as she organized dishes in cabinets.

"Jacques Cousteau."

Laurence carefully placed a pile of plates on a shelf then turned around.

"Dad helped Cousteau film *Monde du Silence*."

"Right! I know! He wants to get together with us, with you!"

Returning to her task, she said, "You can meet him, can't you?"

"He wants to see you, Laurence."

"We discussed how inquiries would be handled once the film was released, Bea, remember?"

"But, this is Jacques Cousteau, Laurence."

"I trust you to do the right thing. You know well, a meeting with him is out of the question."

Crestfallen, Bea left the room before saying something she'd regret. Later, she dialed Cousteau's secretary and setup an appointment for his next visit to New York. Cousteau or not, she could not challenge Laurence's fragility.

♥ ♥ ♥

Evan booked Klee on a flight to New York from Boston, where Klee had returned for a language seminar.

"What gives you the right?" Klee asked.

"This is important. You HAVE to come down!"

"You need my voice again."

"Simply put, yes, my lady," he said.

"Publicity?"

"No, I promise."

"Liar."

"Klee!!!"

"Okay, Okay, I'll come down. But if one camera flashes I exit, you hear?"

In his excitement, Evan hung up without signing off. The wheels were in motion.

# Chapter 19:
# October 12, 1975

HER ALBUM WAS CALLED "MOOD," selections chosen by Klee that included jazz from the 1940s, and an emerging form soon to be called New Age. The cover was red, gold, and black—a design of her choosing.

The night of its release, she stayed with Evan and concocted a scheme. Rather than promote via record outlets and radio stations as was typical, they handed the track to two disc-jockeys Klee knew who worked the night shift at a local station. The men agreed to introduce the album following a brief description of Klee and her hit single.

Midnight came and went. She sipped her tea, cozied up against the window wall. Wearing jeans bought by Johnny, a white blouse with black trim, and hair knotted atop her head, she appeared the collected Klee of old. Yet, her hand trembled as she raised cup to her lips.

"You can't be nervous," Evan said, pouring himself a cognac.

"This city, a sea of lights and mortar, isn't it?"

"What are you afraid of?" he persisted.

"I'm not afraid."

"Me thinks she doth protest too much," Evan said, chuckling. "Hey, Johnny called a while ago wishing you luck."

The announcer said her name. She drew in a breath and closed her eyes. Evan came to her side, placed a hand on her shoulder, and whispered, "How do they say good-luck in Irish?"

The familiar tunes followed. They'd played the test cut dozens of times. Yet to hear her voice as it drifted through the room and made its way to thousands of homes in the listening area proved a different experience altogether.

Holding Evan's hand she sang along. It was a way to cope, for otherwise thought would have intervened. She might falter into smugness or even self-praise, behavior against which she riled. On the other hand, to withhold from listeners their choice of music was in itself prideful and selfish, wasn't it?

The two lingered at the window. There was no doubting that Klee would find freedom and Evan even more fame and notoriety. Were they ready?

Had the question been asked months before, both might have glibly responded that these problems were the kinds one would welcome, that of course they were ready. What transpired fed their dreams and so why not make them real?

Yet, the moment upon them, they could only stand, she adrift in her lyrics, he studying the talent he'd molded. It wasn't pride but closeness, a kinship interwoven with indebtedness. Having shared one another's struggles, they bonded in wonder.

Unlike his other women, she didn't require commitment when he only wanted sex. She didn't need him physically at all, for hers was a playground inside her mind's outer reaches. The tangible quickly bored her.

Evan had become the comfort zone Romney once offered. He cared without possessiveness and, though he owned many things and controlled many people, he sought out a depth in others that he himself spurned. And that was what charmed her. She engaged with his brown eyes insofar as to take in their sincerity. The sorrow behind them, she didn't question. Had Evan requested she share her thoughts, she'd have told him she knew of what he suffered.

Loss had coagulated around distraction. The arrival of some so-called priority—song, sex, mistaken identity—and they boomeranged into a quandary with no resolution.

As options presented themselves this night, a hesitancy lingered. The rich man with the moribund heart and the singer with the unfinished song.

The next day, as promised, Evan drove her to the airport without fanfare, press, or photographers. Blowing a kiss, she boarded the plane with her case and a package containing three albums to offer as gifts, one for the Faheys, the other for her mother, and a third—at Evan's request—for his uncle Marcel Duvivier. Her plans open-ended, he'd setup accounts at banks in London and Paris so as to transfer the proceeds from her record sales. The plane taxied towards the runway. She studied Evan's form growing smaller and smaller in the distance.

# Chapter 20

"INSANITY," KLEE READ. "A deranged state of the mind usually occurring as a specific disorder (as schizophrenia) and usually excluding such states as mental deficiency, a psychoneurosis, and various character disorders."

She placed the dictionary on her side table and stretched in front of the window at Dublin's Shelbourne Hotel. Elegance abounded—a view of St. Stephen's Green, fuzzy carpets, a king-sized bed with handstitched linens and covers. In her private bath, plush towels, expensive accessories, and even a wall telephone. "A disgrace," she'd said to the bellhop.

Nonetheless, travel fatigue regulated her attitude and she took to the accommodations. For two days she stayed in her room, reading books, sleeping, and regenerating. Her every need was attended to, be it dining service, a book purchase, or daily fresh-cut flowers. When, her first day, she told the maid that she'd already made up the bed, the managing director himself contacted her to object, so she stopped upending the cleaning schedule, and tolerated distractions like morning deliveries of newspapers and flyers about what to see and do in the Dublin area.

The ring of 'insanity' persisted, for it was the only way to describe the world in which she moved—the attention to her every whim, the sums of money in her bank accounts, the way people stared. This notion of madness also harkened to that familiar feeling from her childhood and that had journeyed with her to Boston, even when her head was clear and her mind on her studies.

Most people may have been equally mad but they managed to accept their lot and persist, regardless. Why then did she struggle? Should she seek help? Rationalizing her state as madness when things no longer seemed comprehensible was one thing but sharing these feelings was quite another. No, she couldn't ask for assistance.

The dictionary also described 'character disorders' and 'neurosis,' so she reasoned she may not be completely mad but simply stricken with a lesser condition. This helped her whenever the odd feelings in her stomach surged, like when some agent called to meet her for dinner or when she lacked desire to walk in the rain, an activity she usually enjoyed. She would tell herself it was her tiny disorder and not to worry.

♥ ♥ ♥

Though the city was more crowded than she remembered, once she made her way to Grafton Street she noted that not much had changed. At Brown T's department store, she took the escalator to women's coats and hats. An attendant helped her choose a tailored red wool coat and a replacement black hat as her cherished felt one had seen better days. The new one with its broad brim would better hide her face. After selecting a skirt to match, she was on her way.

Pedestrians in navy or black suit jackets and skirts veered wide around her, and some turned their heads. She made way through to the Trinity end of the street, turned left to follow the park and finally arrived at Fahey's butcher shop.

The once-humble, compact establishment occupied the entire floor of the building. Saturday morning shoppers stood two rows thick to purchase their meats for the Sunday meal. They hustled in and out amidst greetings, gossip, and arguing the prices of daily specials. Easing to a corner, she took in the raw meat smells and watched her former employers.

Mary hadn't changed a bit and seemed even sunnier than before as she bustled to and fro. Red-faced and with stained white apron tied around a plumper middle, Danny pounded away at a side of beef and confirmed orders back to Mary. Two young women wrapped packages and worked the registers. Klee waited until Mary caught her eye.

"Jesus, Mary, and Joseph!" Mary exclaimed cupping her mouth with both hands. "Danny, come see now! Our Klee is back!"

Danny's pounding stopped at the same time a hush fell over the store.

"Here now," Mary said finishing with an order and winding around the counter. "I can't very well hug you, me with my dirty hands all over that gorgeous coat!"

Klee threw her arms around the woman. "Mary, Mary," she whispered nuzzling her cheeks.

Danny, too, ignored his stinking outfit and embraced her as if reuniting with a beloved daughter.

Klee let them fuss then insisted they return to the growing group of customers who, while intrigued and amused, were also intent on completing their purchases. To move things along, Klee got behind the counter, threw her coat to a chair, and helped with orders. The hours passed thus and they were all so busy that the day ended with them barely sharing a few updates here and there. Klee rang up the last customer, gave the Faheys a hug, and promised to return for a more prolonged visit.

Danny and Mary watched Klee turn the corner.

"Ah, she's the black hat lady still. With the red coat to boot. You think she's really that big singing star they talk about, Danny?"

Fighting tears, Danny answered, "She is indeed, Mary. She is indeed."

Later that evening, the three sat around the fireplace above the shop. Upstairs remained unchanged save Klee's bedroom that now served as a study. No renter had replaced her. They reminisced.

"Wait till I see now," Mary said. "You wouldn't remember Molly Ahearn, now you wouldn't. I was about to tell you she was up to having twins but you two never met. No, Molly was here after you, sure she was."

Klee watched the flames and wiggled toes under a blanket Mary wrapped at her feet. In time, she pulled out the album from her case and offered it to them. Touched, the couple ran fingers across the unopened cover, voices cracking as they repeated the writing on the card, "To Mary and Dan Fahey, you will always find shelter in my heart. Klee"

That night, Klee abandoned the notion of returning to an empty room at the Shelbourne and slept by the fire with her friends. Before she left the next day, Mary drew her aside.

"They were looking for you up there they were. A Breeda and Sean O'Faolain. Your sister, is she?"

Klee's brow creased as she nodded slowly.

"Lovely girl, Klee, now she is. With four children. I had no idea you was off to America, you see, so…"

"What did they want?"

"Well, let me see," Mary said, glancing over her shoulder and lowering her voice. "I tell you it was about your aunt. Can't remember her name." She placed a finger to her forehead. "Wait till I see now…"

"Romney."

"That's the one. Bless her. Didn't she up and die right after you were off to America. To the day as I recall," Mary said, searching Klee's face. "I remember Breeda saying you and Romney were close. She did."

"How did she die?" Klee asked.

"I can't say, dear. Breeda was only up to stopping by, said they heard about you in a club and was up to wondering if it was you the same as their sister Claire."

"I'm going for a walk, Mary," Klee said, kissing her friend goodbye.

Mary called after her. "Klee, are you alright?" But she received no response.

For hours, Klee walked along the Liffey before finding her way back to the hotel. As the sun peeked from fast-moving clouds, she sat at the writing table staring onto the Green.

She'd never planned on returning to Kinemmaera. She could have ignored Mary's words but, having finally traveled to Dublin and having breached the gap that separated her from her past, she sensed the urge to make the circle complete, to arrive at the place from which she departed and to close, once and for all, the book on her dismal youth. Romney's death was reason enough but there were others, too, even though she'd tried to deny them. She would get to Kinemmaera and her aunt's shack to see for herself whether Romney was really gone.

Klee knew better than most about Romney, and could still hear the echo of her aunt's voice. Dead in body perhaps but the woman was never meant to leave the western shores. Romney's purpose was eternal and

Klee would find her spirit yet. She couldn't explain that to Mary or anybody. She could joke to herself all she wanted about insanity but to open up about her crazed aunt invited speculation by others, and that could lead to ruminations over her own state of mind. No, Romney's offbeat secrets they shared would remain with Klee. The wee person would find her happy fairy and insure they kept in touch.

Hiring a car meant showing up at the airport where she risked more notice, so she decided to take the train. Once in the West, she transferred to a bus, that wound along the Shannon Road towards Galway where eventually roads diverged. At the one leading to Kinemmaera, she descended and hiked the familiar four miles. Thankfully, evening had arrived, for she wished to remain unobserved—a tricky maneuver in the village. Before reaching the center, she passed the dirt road leading to the Walsh farm. A blue hand pump on a concrete platform had been constructed atop the well where they used to dip buckets. This addition aside, nothing appeared to have changed. She went first to the graveyard.

Romney's stone stood beside the one for Klee's grandfather Walsh. The date on her tomb was the exact day in 1968 when Klee left for the States. Brushing twigs aside, she kneeled.

"Were you sick, Rom?"

From the scraggly brush, a murmur rose up and drifted towards the bay, leaving a stillness in its wake.

She walked towards the village, keeping to back streets that lined the quays. Passing the priest's house, she noticed lights and wondered was Father O'Mally in residence. She rang at the front door.

A young woman wearing glasses asked in a soft British accent, "Yes?"

"I was wondering about Father O'Mally," Klee said.

"Of course. Father O'Mally is in Dublin. I'm leasing the house. Can I tell him who called?"

Klee noted the volume of Irish poems the woman clutched. "You like the book?"

"Yeats. My favorite."

Klee nodded. "I'll ring Father O'Mally in Dublin."

With the moon hidden, the sea shone brighter than the land as she wandered a byway that got her wet to her ankles. She neared the dirt path and cow rungs leading to the Walsh property. The front façade was lit up but she did not approach, and headed instead towards the rising slope that led to Romney's chalet.

Inside, a rat scurried past her foot. Dampness had ruined Romney's few possessions: a quilt, magazines, novels and Gaelic poems. She sat on a wobbly wooden chair and inhaled the peat smells.

"Rom," she said. "You were right about my song saving me."

Fingering fragile pages of a book, she recalled listening to Romney's recitations. How she would commit those passages to memory, and how the simplistic work of repetition nourished her mind and imagination. She pressed the humid leather book jacket with both hands then opened to a random page.

Eyes adapting to the dying light, she read aloud. Her voice fell into rhythm with the lines until she could no longer see the type. After a while, she stood, hands icy, face numb. The porous walls conceded to the wind, producing a soft whistle that synced to the movement of the waves. Still nothing from Romney. She collected as many books as she could, bent to clear the doorway and trundled along the path.

As she walked, an imperceptible rustle rose up from somewhere in the brush. She chided herself; it was the sea, or critters settling down. But her deeper self was on alert. The same low chuckle, the guttural tones could not be mistaken. They were, to Klee, no different than a caress, a nod to their shared times. Pausing, she let the sensation pass through and over her and understood instantly the message.

There were no more fairies in these parts. They'd long ago abandoned Kinemmaera town and, since Klee's departure, one by one the fairies of the fields had also exited. Few if any remained. The spread of humanity would obliterate the huts and the keeps and the knolls and the paths. They sought another place. Klee was to guard them in her heart for they would never ignore one who in former times had left them in peace. The wee people remembered kindness. She stood still, bowing her head to the books and whispering, "I hear you, Rom."

At the priest's house, she hugged the bundle of books then lowered them to the doorstep.

"Please be someone who carries the fairies safely from here," she whispered. She rang the bell and disappeared before the woman opened the door. Skirting a back wall to the main road, she registered unnoticed at a Bed & Breakfast along the Shannon road. In the morning she was gone.

♥ ♥ ♥

The next day, the renter talked excitedly about the visitor with the hair and the navy eyes. It didn't take long for locals to piece together who it might be. Claire Walsh had made it back and was likely this very morning heading to the farm she grew up on.

A local operator who worked the telephones out of O'Ryan's Market had all she could to handle requests coming from Galway wondering could she confirm that the famous singer Klee had returned. But nothing came of the excitement and, in spite of gossip in the pubs, no one could honestly say they'd seen her. They shook heads and agreed that it might have been someone who resembled her, some daft soul full of tall tales. Why in the world, they asked, would she bother with us now that she's become a big star in America?

There were others however who snorted and continued their chores with no comment. They knew well Claire Walsh was never coming back no matter how famous or how homesick. The physical proof of her mother's dismal ways, the child was doomed long ago. No, they thought privately, she'll never return to this place.

But no one suspected the truth that Klee took back to Dublin, about wee people and the seaside village of Kinemmaera.

# Chapter 21:
# November 1975

IN A STATE SINCE HE HEARD KLEE'S SINGLE, Johnny stewed. She was working with another to accomplish the very thing he'd suggested years before, the very thing she'd resisted.

His club was inundated with reporters intent to understand this most unusual star. Word was she was tall and fair and from Ireland, currently vacationing in Europe. Other than what her singing conveyed—which was up to speculation— the "Mood" lady remained shrouded in mystery. A woman making it solely on her voice with no help from shows or concerts, resorting not at all to her youth and looks was hot copy. Now that her album hovered at the top of the charts, this detail was even more glaring. She must be made visible, for admirers expected as much. Time for Klee to give her fair share.

Although inclined to agree Klee owed her fans, Johnny refused to offer clues. Discretion was her preferred style and, in spite of his irritation with her, he did not overstep the bounds.

But some who remembered her gave descriptions to the press. Others remarked on her outfits and color choices. Still others recalled how she read books. Soon her college degree was revealed. Not long after, an artist put ink to paper and a drawing of her likeness appeared in "Rolling Stone."

An employee showed the picture to Johnny one night. "It doesn't really look like her, does it, John?"

Shaking his head, he said, "She's not easily reproduced."

After the employee left, he grew somber. The picture was Klee but that was not what bothered him. As if they had insight simply because she was in the public arena, people acted as though they knew her. He disliked the casual way men dropped her name, or the way waitresses acted as though she were a close friend. It wasn't fair. He'd respected her need for anonymity. Had he been a fool or blind, or both?

He tried to suppress this irritation, until one night when Evan walked into the club accompanied by his New York entourage.

Women hovered and a press agent joined them at a table. Other patrons were drawn to the scene. In leather jacket and turtleneck sweater, Evan praised Klee's musical talent and, to more probing questions, offered convivial yet vague replies. Johnny keyed in on Evan's reserve, surely agreed upon between the young man and Klee.

"She's private, really," he heard Evan say. "Not the type to bother with publicity." And other comments like, "If I knew where she was, I'd let you know."

So, she had finally allowed someone in. Johnny should be happy for her, but he wasn't. He should be glad she was no longer a closed book, but wasn't. He should have let his needs go, but he could not. As much as he tried to put her out of his thoughts, she remained. His one love and, in a cruel maneuver that guaranteed Evan what Johnny had yearned for, she'd left him. He exited the club with the excuse he wasn't feeling well.

He took days at a time off, drank at increasing intervals, and even visited former haunts in South Boston. His reputation served him well and bar owners were happy to extend his tab, even offer him free drinks, and this exacerbated Johnny's behavior. It was weeks before people began to talk but talk they did. The man who showed up at noon and never left the club before the last table was cleared was absent for nights on end. He managed to pay bills and collect the daily receipts for deposit but, increasingly, responsibility was assumed by workers he'd taught the very qualities he now eschewed. Johnny dipped into a ruinous lifestyle and, when asked if he was Okay, he would mumble incoherently.

One night in a bar, he spoke with too much bravado to an attentive reporter and eventually embellished his night of wonder in Klee's apartment such that the reporter asked him to repeat his tale into a recorder. Buffered by non-feeling that masked a sorrow he called betrayal, he revealed her pregnancy and unique life in the west of Ireland as well as her tendency to steer clear of intimate relationships. He slandered her, even categorized her voice as a dime a dozen, hardly worth the public's time.

After, he went home and crashed, inoculated from the damage he'd done to the one lady he loved with all his heart. Still.

# Chapter 22:
# November 1975

KLEE TOURED GERMANY FIRST, then spent a week on a remote Greek island before journeying through northern Italy. Following a night in Aosta on the Alpine border with France, she rented a car and drove through the mountains, down to the Riviera, then inland to Provence where she planned to visit Marcel Duvivier.

With shortening days, she had less time to sightsee and often took to her hotel room by mid-afternoon. For the most part she stayed at family-run places where she could converse with the owners and partake in a meal. She jotted down regional recipes, helped to clean up afterwards and sometimes even joined other guests around a blazing fire. Equipped with books and comfortable quarters, she relished her privacy most of all.

She found Aix to be a pleasant town. Marcel's home was in a nearby village so she decided to walk. Along the way, she reveled in the lavender scrub, the way oak trees formed a canopy over her head, and the chatter of cicadas. The Roman-era enclave that Marcel called home was a smattering of white and beige stone abodes, most of them fronted by iron gates or low walls. As dusk approached, she pushed open the grillwork fence at the address Evan had given her.

"Hardly a hideaway," she whispered, staring at the classic two-story house. Olive-colored shutters contrasted with the façade's pale quarried stone. To one side of a circular drive, a bubbling fountain, to the other a turnaround for a car. Save lingering lavender spikes, barren flower beds outlined the front walks to the front entrance. She pictured the bursts of floral come summer. As guitar music drifted from the neighbor's, she sauntered to the front door.

After ringing to no response, she wandered towards the back, inhaling the scents of rosemary, sorrel, and thyme mingling with the ever-present lavender. A path headed towards a clump of bushes that opened to a field and brook, a gravel walkway leading to the water. Boules for playing *pelote* lay helter-skelter amidst iron lawn chairs arranged in a semi-circle, as if one party had ended and another was about to begin. She sat in one of the chairs and rubbed sore feet.

The muted colorscape contributed to a penetrating pleasure she had trouble placing. The house was not out of the ordinary for this part of France. Predictably, the gardens contrasted with more opulent English ones, and even the manicured beds of Parisian parks. Too, the lazy feel generated by the provençal heat was not unexpected. Nonetheless, she sensed an uniqueness. A seeping vapor, like the evening damp, something tangled in the weeds, run down due to season, yet emitting recall of a primal time, festive summer days that blended into night, the fluidity of life in the south, the owner and his wishes.

She guessed Marcel to be the influence behind many of Evan's choices. In his eyes, the glimmer of appreciation each time the man's name was mentioned.

Of course, she also knew that Marcel was from Pauline's side of the family.

She stared at the package on her lap and felt presumptuous. Offering her first album to one of the greats in French film? If Evan was correct, the man was bound to hear of her anyway. Why had she come so far to hand-carry it?

She retraced steps and headed towards the gate but stopped at the sound of the front door opening. A man stood and stared, startled. He muttered something she could not hear. Compact and casually dressed, he appeared well into his seventies with white hair and a cap partially concealing gray eyes. Across his forearm hung a netted shopping bag used for short errands.

"I'm looking for Marcel Duvivier," she said, embarrassed.

"Monsieur is in Paris, I regret," the man said. "Can I help you?"

Raising the package, she explained the reason for her presence. He smiled then beckoned.

"Ah, you see, Mademoiselle, we had no idea when you were coming! You should have let us know. Monsieur Marcel would have made a point of being here! Well, enough. Come in!"

His name was Jean and he'd tended to the house for over twenty years, keeping it up during Marcel's absences and organizing get-togethers when the director was in town.

After leading her down the hallway, they entered a living room.

"Here in the salon, you can relax while I make you something. Tea? Coffee? Apéritif?"

She asked for tea and he disappeared. Original paintings hung on high walls. In upholstered patterns of red and orange, couches and chairs were offset by pale oriental carpets and chiseled stone tiles. Italian lace curtains showcased massive arched windows. She guessed that a remodeled Louis XVI easy chair with tiger skin throw was Marcel's favorite. Ashtrays, magazines, and books lay about.

She wandered into the adjoining room, a narrow space with writing table and chair. A thick maroon floor-to-ceiling curtain covered a window. She reached to the pulleys to let more light in. The sun set behind trees, its rays intensifying a rusty glow from leaves and branches, the purple silhouettes of bushes.

Then she spied the imp, a two-foot high granite piece facing her some yards beyond the patio and forming the centerpiece to the backyard fountain. Offering up an urn, his curly hair and vacant sculpted eyes threw attention to a smile fronting a thousand secrets. Given its center stage view from his work room, she guessed it to be a family heirloom or one to which Marcel was attached, like some prized *objet d'art*. A prolonged giggle forced her to cup a hand over her mouth.

She thought of her own west coast Irish fairies. Her days of lightness and gaiety, so remote. How had she misplaced that insouciance? When was the last time she laughed? How had she allowed spontaneity to fizzle? Somewhere along the way, as she engaged with song and flirted at fortune's threshold, her merrier side grew dormant. Until tonight.

Jean's footsteps came to a halt. "Like Marcel, you study the gardens," he said.

He placed a tray on a table, arranged silverware, and poured.

"I'm going to fetch goods at the market before it closes, Mademoiselle. Then I shall return."

She swirled around. "I want to go with you. I won't get in the way, I promise."

He hesitated but she stepped towards him, locking her arm in his.

"Please. Should I leave France without that experience?"

He grinned apologetically. "*Mais non, Mademoiselle, absolument pas!*"

She took quick sips of the tea as Jean closed curtains and lowered lights.

They made for the market, and he outlined his daily routine when Marcel was out of town, and then the hectic one it turned into when he was in residence. To every question, he lingered thoughtfully and even threw in anecdotes as he saw fit. At the *marché*, cartons were angled on tables, their contents bulging with produce—avocados, zucchinis, broccoli and beans as well as bright orange melons and tangerines, green and yellow apples and bundled ivory-colored asparagus. They bought strings of garlic, fresh butter, and bottles of local wine. Jean adjusted dinner plans to a veal dish that would be ample enough for two. They debated cheeses and purchased baguettes, one for the meal and one for the next day. She delighted in the energy around choices, his attentions, his banter with the *commerçants* and especially the way he introduced her as a colleague of Evan de Roche.

She tried helping out in the kitchen but eventually settled with a glass of wine, out of Jean's way. As he cut and chopped, sniffed and discarded, arranged and sprinkled, he shared with her his own life story growing up in the south of France.

They indulged in a meal and conversation that Jean said was a sample of "the best of life." By the time they wiped up traces of sauce and bread, they were friends. He cleared the table then prepared coffee for them to take in the sitting room. In front of a fire, they closed out the day. Klee lapsed into silence and Jean, too, took to private thoughts. This nonchalance, this embracing style was surely Marcel's as well, she mused, enticing newcomers and return guests alike to the intractable call of Provence. This stopover was one she'd not have traded for dozens of gold and platinum albums.

They decided to turn in, and Jean directed her to an upstairs corner guest room. A down quilt of pink and pale green covered a canopy bed and a writing table sat at an open window and balcony. A side lamp glowed. Stretching out on the bed, she inhaled the garden scents and listened as Jean pattered around the kitchen arranging cleaned pots and pans. A bottle of aged Armagnac at her bedside invited tasting and so she did. The fiery sensation jostled her. She grew wider awake. The garlic, wine, and braised meat smells lingered and, when she ventured to the balcony, their aroma intensified.

The desire to stay bombarded, invading her every fiber, and winding its way to her heart, an unsettling yet tender feel. In the hours since her arrival, she'd been transformed by milieu, food, and companionship. The notion of permanence struck, weeks on end living idyllically, tending to her higher needs for variety, flavor, and yes, laughter.

"Your owner would disapprove seeing as he doesn't even know me," she said to the imp. With sleep and the morning, she told herself, her head would be straight again. Yet that was tomorrow and there were still hours in this night. She sipped her drink, closed eyes, and synched with the lethargy.

Who was Marcel? Re-thinking conversations with Evan, she imagined the man returning from an extended trip. Imagined him wandering the back yard as she had, trying his luck at *boules*, or lounging in a chair with a cigarette and reviewing recent interactions in Paris, Rome, or London. He would plan soirées with Jean. He'd retreat to his space, eye the imp, then settle with letters and paperwork for a while. Did he entertain much or were his adventures more clandestine? His entire place was sumptuous, appointed. Save the office, few items spoke to his success, his movies, or his fans. Yet, she sensed Marcel in every room, observing her through the imp, covering her hand with his like Jean had during dinner when he told a joke. Marcel inhabited this house in spite of his absence. Yet he eluded.

This shook her, for it touched on her own reserve and how she too baffled so many, even those who cared like Johnny, the Faheys, even Benny. If not for Evan, who peeled away at some of her surface, she would have long before accepted her clam-like nature as immutable. If not for Evan.

He challenged her, and in doing so her singing had formalized, the album became a reality. She didn't do it for herself, nor for surface rewards, like this journey. She sang because Evan asked her to, and so his magic had brought her here, where she faced herself on nights like this, especially nights like this, when she felt so nearly happy she almost said the word.

"I wish you were here to sort this out with me, Evan. You have your own cloud-covered terrain," she whispered.

She contemplated her forays to pleasant hotels and inns, her dinners with gracious and generous souls. Their tidy bedrooms, prepared snacks, and benevolent regards had everything to do with the receptive nature of her own heart as it did with them. But this fact frightened her. The world was full of decent people, she need not fear them, but something about that fact terrified.

Jean, as well, exemplified these experiences. This totality of a view, the amalgam of nature outside her window. What next? No place could be called home. She'd been a visitor, a traveler, someone on her way to somewhere, directed yet deprived.

A sorrow pierced. Why, she asked? Why this delicate bloom handed to me that I crush? Where is my even keel that permits rest, and calm, for more than minutes? I am scattered everywhere, scattering melodies, my heart across these villages and towns. To what end? Sharing splinters me. Giving demands an energy I struggle to reciprocate. I remain untethered.

She cursed Evan, his challenge to her reluctance. Having opened the door to her sensibilities, her vulnerabilities surfaced as well.

Before the song, she'd found comfort in the predictable, her studies, her schooling, her books. Now, even as she leaned into this forward motion, she nursed a sense of futility. Years tolerating a world that in the end wasn't all bad. But how to embrace it authentically?

She didn't crave the limelight. Large amounts of money bored her. Yet, there was more to this lifestyle. Sharing, projecting her voice in song, proved paradoxical. Like this trip, with its built-in exposure of self. To give—or to travel or to sing—meant to embrace more than lyrics, melodies, agendas, and appointments.

Her mother came to mind. Alice giving birth to her, and a youth that remained a puzzle. A child buttressed by fairy dreams. And drastic events never underscored as such. Difficult to finger and say, "Those are the reasons I suffer in my head!"

She looked at the imp. "You too are of the wee people, aren't ye? A nation of gay creatures, having no souls; nothing in their bright bodies but a mouthful of sweet air."

The imp's smile touched off her own. In time, she sang to the evening, a tune absorbing itself into the night.

♥ ♥ ♥

In another room, Jean listened to singing that bespoke a dangling, quiescent tale, a melody that grafted pieces of her to his soul—the gaze, the wide mouth, her gracious discomfort. The phantom sprite, whose energy had defined his evening.

"Monsieur Marcel," he would say, "the girl with the album came and went."

Before closing the shutters, and without fully understanding why, he said a prayer for the visitor.

# Chapter 23

EVAN PEEKED OUT THE WINDOW of the record distributor's office. "Photographers and reporters, damn it. Is there a back door?"

The man smirked. "Even if there were one, I wouldn't tell you. Those guys have been here for a week. This is your can of worms!"

"I can't discuss her, you know that."

The distributor folded hands behind his head and leaned back in the chair. "Rule number one: stars have no sacred cows. She's hit the top of the charts, her life's an open book from now on."

"No. This time it can't be like that."

"Suit yourself, man. Learn the hard way. No back doors."

Outside, Evan pushed his way past the reporters.

"Is it true she lives a double life?" one asked.

"We understand she's in Europe," another said.

Evan glared. "Let me pass…"

"When is she due back? Is she in London?"

"We understand she's got bank accounts all over Europe."

Evan swirled around, facing the man who spoke. "That's a lie!"

"We have proof from a source at Chase Manhattan," the man said.

Evan swallowed his surprise and pushed towards a cab. "No comment."

"Abortions, too. To cover illicit affairs?" one yelled.

Evan grabbed the reporter's writing pad and threw it to the ground before hopping into the cab.

Later that day, Klee called, detailing her itinerary. First, she planned to stay in London indefinitely.

"'Mood' is number one," he said, hiding his disconsolation. He didn't discourage her decision to remain in London, though the notion sat at the bottom of his stomach like indigestion. Instead he encouraged her to stay on if that was what she wanted.

As soon as she hung up, another call came in from a fellow Chamber member on stopover in London who said, "Hey, Evan, she's big over here, too. Heard her music at Piccadilly. Apparently, they like her enough to publish an article about her in one of the dailies, too."

Evan chewed on a fingernail. "And?"

"Says she's living the fast life somewhere in London. Where did all this about her sex life come from anyway?"

Evan closed his eyes. "If I only knew. Listen, mail me that article, would you?"

"Sure, but is it true?"

"Give me a break," Evan said, hanging up.

With Klee in London it was only a matter of time before she heard all this. She would retaliate against him for sure. Instead of savoring her success, she'd be miserable and alone. He must get to her first. He dialed Marcel's number. There had to be a way to stop this illicit and lewd forward motion. She wasn't simply a client, she was Klee. And he'd made a promise to her.

# Chapter 24

TO ACCOMMODATE KLEE, Alice cancelled two engagements. At the agreed-upon hour, they met in the foyer of Alice's home.

"Mum," Klee said, extending a hand.

"Hello there," Alice said, returning the handshake. "In London for a while are you?" The late morning chill made her shiver. Alice noted how Klee's gaze fell for an instant too long on her wrinkled forehead, the gray roots of her copper hair, and smudged makeup. She yawned. "Step inside away from this cold. Where are ye staying?"

"At the Brandish Arms for now."

"Brandish Arms? Posh. You've made some money with that album of yours, I take it."

"Number one in the States."

Alice stole glances at her watch.

"Can I take ye for lunch somewhere, Mum? Say, in the shopping district?"

Alice prettied up and they made for Regent's Street, settling at a pub populated with tourists. Seated at the window, they ordered the plate of the day. Outside, passers-by represented all corners of the world such that, red double-deckers being the exception, one would have been hard-pressed to guess their location. Distracted by the view and the hour, Alice made stiff conversation and picked at her sandwich. Save the brogue, her former mannerisms had disappeared.

Topics including weather, clothes, and Boston came and went, as Klee attempted conversation that quickly went flat. Finally, she handed Alice the brown paper wrapped gift.

Alice opened it with hesitation, looking around as she did. "Mood," she said reading the album cover. "And you're doing real well from what the papers say, aren't ye?"

"What papers?"

"Now, Klee, don't go telling me you don't read. I know better. You're all over the dailies here. Must be worse in New York."

Klee bowed her head.

"You haven't seen then," Alice whispered, tracing the glossy cover with a lacquered finger.

"About me?"

"About you. Lord, I would have guessed you to be with a publicity agent instead of allowing all these rumors…"

"Let's go," Klee said.

Alice sipped the last of her tea. "Never mind what they say. They haven't a wink about the truth those papers. You know that."

Klee paid the bill while asking the waitress where she might find the nearest newspaper agent. Around a corner from the pub, they found a stand and Alice watched as Klee studied a doctored, garish photo claiming to be of her. 'Newest singing sensation from America lives life of seduction and deception' the headline read. Subtitles went on. 'Love child aborted. Klee sings the blues.'

She crumpled the pages as Alice looked on. "Ye need to pay for it, Darling."

But Klee didn't move so Alice paid the cashier who studied them quizzically. Alice then guided Klee onto the street to hail a cab.

"Hear me, Klee. Them papers are all alike. Forget them. Go back to your Brandish Arms and relax. I have an appointment to tend to, so I'll let you take this cab and say goodbye."

She opened the door, explaining to the driver her daughter wasn't feeling well and needed to get back to the Brandish Arms.

Before the door closed, Klee asked, "Was it you?"

Alice gasped. "The cheek of ye! Accuse me of what you want, but not of selling out to gossip! Damn if I said a word!" But instead of slamming the door on her daughter, her conscious took hold. She lowered herself into the cab and they both sped off. During the ride, her daughter's look gave rise to pity.

"Ah, come home now. I'll get ye a hot bath and some tea. Don't worry."

At Alice's, Klee took her mother's advice and settled in front of the small fireplace with tea as Alice cancelled what plans she had for the afternoon.

"Look, Klee. Ease up a bit, you know? Life's tough no matter where you are. Let it go and forget it. Work with that Evan and mind your new life. You're not hurting, so."

Alice puttered around, anxious. When it got dark, she returned to the living room and lit a cigarette.

"Well, I have things to see to now, I do. Can ye find it to the Arms Okay?"

Klee barely nodded.

"I'll call a cab. I'm late. Someone's coming as a matter of fact."

"And you don't want them to meet your daughter?"

Surprised, Alice stubbed out her cigarette. "See here. I can't very well go about introducing my daughter now, can I? What with this news of ye being all over town. It would only get worse for ye. And me."

"You've told no one I'm your daughter?"

"Why in the world would I here? People barely know me!"

"You're ashamed of me."

Alice stuttered, "Don't go churning my words, Claire. I don't tell anyone for your own privacy, so there! Come along now." She stood.

"You were never proud of me."

Alice relaxed her shoulders, rubbed her forehead. She sunk into the chair and crossed her dressing gown over her knees. Voice softening, she said, "I was always proud of ye, proud of all of ye I was. You can't know what it was like." The clock struck 6. "Listen, Claire, it's time for ye to go."

"Who is he?"

"Who?"

"My father."

Alice's brow crinkled. Gripping her robe, she said, "I don't know him anymore."

"I don't care if you don't know him. I want to know who he is."

"Now look, Claire, this is all the past. And it's not worth talking over. You've gotten yourself this far without him, haven't ye?"

"It's about knowing my father."

"It's a long time ago, child."

The phone rang. It was the lobby calling to announce a visitor. Alice said, "You really have to go." She found Klee's coat and offered it to her. I'll get the lobby to ring you a cab."

"Cancel your plans," Klee said.

"Cancel? Like that you decide what it is I'm to do? I've been all day canceling plans to be with you! When I took all that time and those letters years ago to reach you and you didn't respond? What are you trying to pull here with your 'getting to know the old man' routine at this stage of your life? Who do ye think ye are, Claire?"

She gave her mother a long regard. "I'm an orphan."

Alice sputtered then threw the coat to the floor, calling the lobby to have her guest wait another few minutes. "I don't have to listen to this. Not after all these years." She made for her bedroom where she got herself ready to go out.

"Right to know. Ye talk about rights! Ha! I'll tell you about rights, Claire! There's no such thing. We all have to fight for what little we have. It's got nothing to do with rights. Human decency, eh? Rights? You'd do well to keep to your success story because it won't last forever. The past is over and forgotten. Rights…tell me about rights." She put coat on. "I thank ye for the album and wish ye well. Mind the latch on your way out."

Fumbling with keys, she took a final look at Klee. "It's the way of things, Claire. Perhaps yer too young but it's the way. Move on. Forget me. You're rich. What else matters?"

♥ ♥ ♥

In the coming weeks, those words from Alice would haunt Klee, as she lived an increasingly droll existence, crossing and re-crossing London streets, wandering parks and feeding pigeons. Though she could have spent a fortune in boutiques and designer shops, she didn't, nor did she hob-nob with London's in-crowd. She relived the afternoon with Alice—the look of surprise on her mother's face, the denouncements, the humiliation of her mother's dismissal. She tried to contact Evan without success, and concluded that it was he who had revealed her private information. This only drove her to the same pattern of wandering. Like a fly to tar paper, she stuck to London's misty scene breaking only to eat and sometimes sleep. Nightmarish thoughts exacerbated her moodiness. She began to plan next moves, for she was on to these people she'd clung to for too long—her mother, Evan, all of them. They cared only for her money anyway. They never cared about her. She should use her earnings for purposes other than singing for the masses.

# Chapter 25

New York Times Arts and
Entertainment Section
Sunday November 30, 1975

Last night, the renowned explorer Jacques Cousteau joined New York magnate Evan de Roche at the Lincoln Center premier of the documentary "Silence."

In a refreshing take on the maritime world around the island of Nantucket, this cinematic rendition departs from what is often straightforward narration. To tunes sung by the Celtic sensation Klee, one perceives the depths not only in a panoply of movement and color, but also from a perspective that appeals to more than the visual. In doing so, "Silence" articulates a vital theme—that the sea remains a precious but limited resource.

Simultaneous premiers in Los Angeles and Chicago also resulted in positive reviews for the independent concern, Bea-Sage Productions. A spokesperson said the company is presently inundated with requests for more. Could this be the first of many uplifting and thought-provoking portrayals of Nature at her finest? In this writer's opinion we could do with many more.

EVAN PLACED THE NEWSPAPER ASIDE and rolled out of bed. Even on his day off, his mind raced and his frustration grew over Klee's lack of response. She likely remained at the Arms, seeing as her withdrawals took place at a nearby bank, but she could have been anywhere in the city.

Her wrath would be upon him now that he'd allowed her music to accompany "Silence" without her written permission. Plus, with speculations of her past having filled British gossip columns, she was sure to hold him responsible, regardless of who sourced the details.

Two production houses in Los Angeles hankered for the rights to her album. The phones rang daily with requests to book her at top clubs and interview her on radio stations. Moreover, Cousteau agreed to merge his talents with Klee's in another documentary come time. There were already rumors of an Academy Award nomination. How could she ignore that?

By fine-tuning her involvement, he could promote while allowing her privacy. The big thing was to get her to agree to hand over the rights to her music. This way, she could guard anonymity while still making music and money. Title rights would grant him perpetual discretion over the use of her works.

Too, and seeing as she dismissed her own power, someone untrustworthy could intervene. For his part, if he had Klee to manage, a plethora of opportunities opened up, and he'd have no further reason to take on undesirable work. He could narrow his scope while enlarging his vision. Why let her fame die on the vine simply because she wasn't directed or focused? He could be her eyes and muscle, her force that kept things in the black and on the rise.

He could step away gracefully from the Chamber, where they already, and amicably, discussed his replacement. The de Roche empire was solvent and cash rich now, to the tune of $8.5 million. French businesses had begun to renew or invest in the States and that portended well for both sides of the Atlantic. No better time to move on.

He was 'on top' as was said, and there he wished to stay. But for Klee. His damnably stubborn and wily cohort seemed as elusive as ever and his one chore this Sunday was to reach out to her.

All day he rang places in London, called in favors of British friends, and contacted posh hotels and nightclubs to request they keep an eye out. The Brandish Arms would not reveal their client list but, the voice of the receptionist sounded so flat and disinterested, Evan had to assume Klee was no longer there.

Finally, a friend at a British newspaper said she would ask a reporter friend. Her favor, of course, was not without recompense. Evan promised her a night on the town during his next stopover in London, to which she added a requirement for a night at her place. These days the women in his life drove hard bargains.

The woman returned with details. Johnny Mear, a bar fly in Boston, had been a source. This she could backup with proof if Evan needed it.

The name Johnny Mear did not spill from Evan's lips without distaste. The man Klee thought was her pal was none other than the man who slandered her. Evan wanted to choke Mear. How could Klee have overseen this? She must have been desperate in those days. The way the man had operated, taking her in only to profit from her success, the way he'd tightened his hold on her so no other man could get near, and especially how he disliked Evan, all stunk of Johnny's low class and unhealthy propensities for Klee. That afternoon, Evan boarded a flight to Boston.

He found Johnny slouched at the bar, drunk already, unshaven and unresponsive. Evan settled at a stool and studied Johnny until the man sent him a glazed look of recognition. Then he lunged forward, grabbing the man at his collar.

"You know that stuff was lies about her! All lies!" Evan exclaimed. "Why did you do it?"

Johnny let out a slow grin, coughed and pushed Evan away. "I didn't do nothing. What're you bugging me for? That one gets what she deserves. Like us all, pal."

"No," Evan yelled, "not like us all. Who told you those lies? Who?"

"She did! They weren't lies. She had a baby." He stared off and away from Evan. "Lost the kid she told me. I dunno what those damn papers said. They all exaggerate anyhow." He lit a cigarette.

"Then she didn't have an abortion," Evan said, feeling weak as he grasped for a thought less daunting than that of Klee going after some illicit abortion in a dark alley.

"See for yourself at the city clerk's if you don't believe me. Damn reporters…"

"Why did you talk?" Evan asked.

Johnny picked up his glass and toasted. Chuckling, he said, "You love her. You know. You know what love does. Me? I'm through with love."

He got up and shuffled to the back room.

# Chapter 26

KLEE HIRED LOU BAXTER, a middle-aged private eye with a reputation as distinct as his angular features. From his earlier days as a school dropout in London, curiosity and street smarts honed sharp sensibilities. His sleuth-for-hire profession began years before during a stint as mechanic when he happened to run into a woman friend who was keen on outing her cheating husband. This Lou did in record time, was recompensed aptly and, from then on, never looked back.

The day Klee called, he was busy with two cases. No stranger to the newspapers, however, he heard the rustling of big bucks when the singer announced herself and so listened to her story. Her measured yet urgent tone caught his attention. This 'mystery woman' as the papers called her might also end up being beholden to him, and for profit.

Her demand struck him as straightforward, something he could accomplish while time-slicing with other clients. Shortly thereafter, he set out for Kinemmaera, to start—as he explained to Klee—where it all started. He met locals, listened to tales of the area and its families, and more than once heard of the antics of Alice Walsh. Though he tried to visit the Walsh farm, no one answered his call. One ornery man on a tractor, a brother of Klee's he assumed, threatened him with trouble if he ever returned. He left Ireland assured that what Klee had told him was true and that she deserved his time, for there was indeed some mystery surrounding her birth father.

She took his report in with a set face, unblinking eyes and tucked chin. At first she made light of what he conveyed to her, all the characters whose names she knew by heart, their predicted wary responses when it came to discussing the Walshs, especially Klee. Gradually her face waxed gray as the realization sunk in that so many knew of her origins while she was living there as a little girl, yet no one knew the whole truth.

"To think they were privileged to news that I had no clue of," she whispered.

On the lookout for capitulation or dismissal, Lou studied the curls, the wide eyes, and was baffled by her poker face.

"We're on the right track searching here," he said. "The word about your mother was all over Kinemmaera once she returned from London those several months before your birth. There's a good chance the answer you seek is right under our noses."

"My mother won't talk," she said.

"How about I try to get to her? After all, she takes men in, doesn't she?"

Klee glared.

"I've seen more than one woman let slip secrets after a drink too many."

"Do what you have to. She's the only one who knows."

"There is one other person."

Klee nodded. "She may never have contacted him after I was conceived."

"Well," said Lou. "Let's leave that out there as a possibility."

♥ ♥ ♥

After dinner, Klee went for a walk and found Evan standing outside the Brandish Arms.

"You!" she exclaimed, trying to pass him.

He blocked her. "I, too, can be difficult."

"Get out of my way!"

He grabbed her arm. "Don't do this, Klee. I've done nothing wrong. We need to talk."

"Talk about the next record that will make you richer? Talk about my personal life so you can blab to the press?"

"You've got it all wrong, Klee."

"No, I've got the truth now." She shook off his grip and made for the door.

He shouted, "Johnny spilled the story."

She stopped and turned.

"Mear," Evan said. "I confronted him in Boston. Years ago, you had him to your place. Told him of a baby." He took a step towards her. "Klee, don't look away. This is me, Evan. I never said anything to the press. I promise. I'm here to help."

"There were other lies in print…"

"Editorial license, no doubt. The media is crafty, the epitome of self-serving ends. I've been its victim, too."

"Lies, they were lies."

He settled on a stone wall and patted the place beside him. "Come here. You're not alone, you know. Famous people struggle with this. You can't let it get in your way. Remember, no one really knows what you look like so you still have privacy. It's not the end."

"It is the end, Evan. The singing is over."

He hooked an arm in hers. "Let's walk. I want to talk with you. You don't have to record again, but listen to me. There are other things you must be aware of."

They returned to the hotel lobby where they settled into a corner and reconnected.

Alone in bed that night, she cried for the second time in as many weeks. Since Aix, she'd been on a roller coaster fueled by emotions she could neither reason with nor argue against. The toll of years without answers had descended and drained her. To have come this far and yet feel so out of control. Better if she never sought the help of Lou, better if she had never given into Evan, better still if she had never opened her mouth that night to Johnny. She'd revealed herself for honorable reasons, she rationalized, to further her education and secure freedom, but at what price? What amount of money could equate with the simple, uncluttered, reclusive life she'd led in Dublin? Before the world held out its options for her, and before people offered of themselves? What price, and was it freedom after all?

In a maze of her own design, she no longer knew how to reach the exit. Caught between the past she could no longer claim and a future of distasteful choices, she couldn't waver indefinitely either. Song was the culprit after all. Had she not her voice, had she not been heard time and again, had she not been so smug to think she could control the output of her person, all might have been different. But she'd been led to this prison and cuffed herself with its clamps, simultaneously opening her mouth to sing sweet tunes as the grip tightened. Now, the song was her sole means. Few alternatives remained.

Dawn crept into her room, she sat up in bed and tucked arms over bent knees. Though her heart was heavy, her mind was alert. She saw into the future, down to the very facial expressions, hand movements, and words that, once ingrained, would signal her reinvented self. She had no other option. The road had already been mapped out. It was her own reluctance and denial that had disallowed forward motion. She wouldn't fight it any longer. She would take the road and become the one who was to be filled, the one who makes visible.

A call to Evan's room brought him sleepy-eyed to her. She outlined her intentions.

He would accommodate her wish to make use of the song, he would manage her title rights, he would pummel her to greater fame. She would be heard around the world, in every village, at every venue. No one would miss her song for it would be sung readily, hard, and at all hours. Up to her now to creatively force her father into the open by using her siren's call that had been born of him. Her voice would reach him and pull him towards her. The voice would make visible and hence free her. The greatest singer to come around in an age would make good on her promise and, one day, the man who owed her would come forth.

Her physical voyage neared an end, she could feel it in her limbs and disconcerted ways. The inner journey commenced, and she could handle this more easily, for she traveled light in spirit, and her song was always snug in her pocket. Her true weapon was not something of steel or iron, nor of the things money could buy.

♥ ♥ ♥

When she explained she no longer required his services, Lou took the news in stride. He accepted her check that represented the agreed-upon amount.

For a time after he left the Brandish Arms, he tried to forget her but was not able to. Klee had made her mark, as he guessed she had on everyone she met. Plus, her search tickled his imagination and the poignancy rooted at the core of her story tugged at his heart, for he was not the disconnected soul most people imagined.

567

Her loneliness coupled with that enchanting odd regard convinced him she was more than singer with youthful, awkward charm. The driven attitude and quips would stay with him, as would her preoccupied regard when she passed him the check, bidding farewell as she insisted she no longer wished to hear of her father.

Having taken on this now-unreciprocated camaraderie, Lou decided he would continue to seek out her father. This was the challenge he had been waiting for his entire life, something that drew upon all his experience and talent, something that seemed impossible yet demonstrated a means to an end. She couldn't take it away from him now.

# Chapter 27

ALICE PLACED THREE SETS OF BLACK LINGERIE and three nighties on her bed. Choosing one yellow teddy, she pressed it against her chest and examined herself in the mirror. The first client would get this one. Though the color did nothing for her face, Mister Banes was a pastel kind of customer, into little more than a few caresses and her spread legs. His was a quick £ 300, for he was as full of guilt as one could be.

When he and Alice first crossed paths while she was in the company of another client, his wife Milly was present. A prim overprotective type, it was her side of the family that provided the opulent lifestyle that Banes enjoyed. Their first night together, Banes made it clear that Milly was the jealous type and he was a destitute if not dead man if she ever discovered his trysts. When he sweat during sex, it wasn't only from exertion.

Alice was glad he was her first of the night, because he ranked among her most loyal and best-paying. His paunch and cigar breathe aside, he tiptoed so lightly around her she had barely to nod and he was ready. An easy lay, as the saying went, Banes would come and go by 4 and then her evening would grow more interesting.

For Chet Smith, a twenty-five year-old newcomer, she would wear light green, for he seemed puerile and chaste and she didn't want to scare him off. Another female in the business told Alice that his were eclectic fantasies, so her time with him held promise. Plus he insisted on simple one-on-one encounters which Alice preferred, too.

Increasingly her job involved multiples, not that she ever refused for it always meant more money and references from other women. Competing with younger and younger women, however, had begun to wear on her. She often found herself waiting out the foreplay while her client romped playfully with two or three others with firmer breasts and flatter bellies. Unlike other fads, this multiple thing was likely to stick.

She fantasized herself as the central focus of whomever she was with, that a man desired her fully and forever. What brought her to climax and kept her booking tricks was the notion that she was the man's universe. She preferred traditional positions in bed as opposed to strategic and physically demanding poses on cold floors and in bathrooms.

She frowned as she tried on the green, for it drew down her face and made her hair look brassy. Time for a dye job. Perhaps she would try a lighter shade next appointment.

She should be content, she sighed. It wasn't as though no one came knocking. Some men did prefer her straightforward act. Nonetheless, she sensed she would have to adjust to the times, and relinquish some of her preferences. The only alternative was to find more accommodating customers, but that wasn't the name of the game. Still, many clients were in their fifties and sixties and had no desire to curtail their relationship with Alice. These were the men who controlled the biggest purse strings in London, too. The younger, more demanding men had a way to go before they could tender her offers the likes of which she already accepted from lords and ministers of Parliament. She must be thankful for that.

She rummaged in her drawer while warning herself not to get complacent. This was a decent life compared to what she'd known, and far too lucrative to upset at her age. She would wait a while longer before settling into her preferred place in this crazy business. Anyhow, once she had thousands of pounds in her bank account, she could tolerate the needs of a few young faces.

She tugged at her red and black satin nightie. This would suit her final client. Nothing brought back her youthful attitude than black and nothing gave her that spark of witchery like red. She could forever try on dainty pinks and lavenders in chiffons and silks, but the black and red lent an odd serenity that complimented her actions.

Wiggling her derriere, she giggled. Those underage ingénues couldn't hold a candle to her when she donned black and red. Alice had the regal act down pat and the color scheme enhanced her tricks. All her men said it. Alice and black and red.

"*Rouge et noir*," she whispered thinking of Claire.

Where was her daughter? Still seeking out her roots? If so, Alice wanted nothing to do with that. She'd moved to another townhouse in an even more posh district from where Claire had last visited. She unlisted her phone number, specifically to be harder to track down next time Claire decided to build upon the family tree.

"I hope she gives up for it's to no useful purpose."

She paused and looked out the window while sitting on the edge of her bed. Why couldn't she get the child out of her mind? Since their visit, her daughter's gaze prevailed, so clear, so blue, so very like her father's. One that caught Alice's heartbeat and changed her breathing, blending the years into the present. Claire had no idea how much she resembled the man, and how her gestures, her husky voice, her disregard for protocol so distinctly set her aside as the child of the man. How uncanny, thought Alice! How without ever knowing that man, his daughter became him, right down to the line of work.

Was it this resemblance that so jarred Alice that she could no longer even face her own daughter? Had the hurt run so deep that she completely rejected the physical results of that night with him? She'd never really taken time to contemplate these things, until now. Damn the child. She should not do this to her old mother. Young people had no idea how they incited pain with their questions, their seeking, their sense of entitlement. The man was nowhere to be found, of that Alice was sure. He would always keep that part—that part Alice alone believed she understood—for himself. Daughter notwithstanding.

Claire would have to struggle through her own private hells if she kept this quest up. Alice had already been there. The man was off limits.

She reached to slip on her red and black. Her newcomer would get this one. His name was Roger Petrie and she liked the sexy tone in his voice when he called her. Her sixth sense told her he would be fun, especially since he got her giggling over the phone. They were to have dinner first—always a promising way to start the evening. She would be hungry by then, too. They could chat together before sex, almost like a real date. She did follow politics and local news, and was good at keeping up conversation about soccer and the like, too. Rare a man who catered to her other needs and this one seemed to peripherally focus on sex.

Time to check him out first, she thought, reaching for the phone. She always vetted her clients, to insure they were on the up and up and not cops or undercover agents. Her network of associates would help her figure this Petrie out in time for his arrival. Once she'd done that, she reserved a table at an upscale place. As she flipped through her address book she smiled.

"Perhaps we could go to Chez Claude," she whispered.

Risky it was, to join with another in her private world. This she knew, but what of it? A tiny dalliance, an innocent ploy of no consequence to Petrie. She had a right to dream from time to time, didn't she? Yes, Chez Claude it would be.

Lou Baxter tapped fingers on the steering wheel of his Fiat as he wound through London streets on his way home. After changing clothes, it would take the better part of an hour to get from his East Side flat to the address of the woman. He carefully reviewed his plan, and how he'd be into a role he'd only played a few times in his career. An alter personality was key at times to successfully uncovering the truth and Lou's alter, Roger Petrie, had held him in good stead before. He'd better double-check that the personal history and details were in place before heading out, though.

"Really," he said, "it's being an actor, that's all."

# Chapter 28:
# December 1975

IN THE STUDY OF EVAN'S TOWNHOUSE, Klee threw the newspaper into the fire. "Damn them thinking I'm a rebel!" she exclaimed watching the flames devour the news.

The follow-up recording to Klee's successful debut, a rebel song from Ireland, had apparently lent more credence to the picture already concocted of her past. Now, not only was hers an enigmatic one, but she also possessed a contrary, even violent side, a side her compatriots of the revolutionary persuasion understood. Klee had a link, the papers claimed, to the IRA. She was a singer with a purpose.

She rubbed her forehead to try and rid herself of the headache that pounded. "Stop, please stop!"

At the window, she leaned her forehead against cold glass in search of relief to no avail. The traffic lights below blended into a river of light.

"Papa, 'Irish Lady' is the name of my album," she said. "You enjoyed it? Do you wonder about me? My looks? I don't resemble Mother. What do you have to say, so?"

She knocked her head slowly against the glass, trying to level the pain by inflicting more.

"Ich spreche ziemlisch gut Deutsch, und verstehen fast alles, aber manchmal is est schwer freundlich zu bleiben."

"Ils ne me comprennent pas et j'en ai assez, Papa. Est-ce tu me comprends? Ma chanson au moins?"

Her fist pounded the glass. It cracked, creating wavy forms from the street activity. She smiled. "Now you're all muddled, no more lights one after the other in orderly fashion. No more buildings tall and reaching. You're cracked."

The clock on Evan's writing desk ticked. An hour remained before she collected him at the airport. She ran bloody fingers through her hair. She reached for pills the doctor had prescribed and took more than she should have. Tears fell.

"Big star, big star. Why am I a big star? Who gave me this? What did this to me?"

Back at the window, she leaned her forehead into the cracks, rubbed so that her skin broke. Blood tricked to her nose and onto her blouse. She licked what spilled across her lips, and continued to press her forehead as the throbbing intensified.

Backing away, she stared at the sight, and wiped her forehead. The blood was coming fast and she slapped her face again, smearing herself with red. She fell to her knees.

"I know you hear me, Papa. You listen all the time to me. Every day. I haunt you. There is nowhere inside you I haven't reached."

Crumpled on the floor, she dug nails into the rug and watched a stain grow larger. She gasped. "What a guest I am, Evan! Oh, God, so sorry! You never complain do you? You put up with me. Oh, you can never understand how the banshees take over from time to time. You could never. You are not made of this, as I am."

She fought sobs and forced laughter that rang shrill and pierced her ears. She clutched her stomach and fought nausea.

"Stay away, banshees. I don't want to cry anymore. Let me be."

Covering her face, she cried harder.

The phone rang and she ignored it. It stopped but shortly thereafter the ringing returned. She crawled to the receiver.

"Yes?"

The crackling of international connection and the sobbing Parisian voice on the other end brought Klee to her feet.

"Yes, I'm here," she whispered, leaning against a table.

In French, the hysterical woman announced that Giles de Roche was dead.

♥ ♥ ♥

At the airport, wearing hat and dark glasses, she hugged her coat about her. The flight from California had been delayed. When Evan alighted he appeared frazzled but beaming.

"Klee, baby! California bursts with energy. You must go there!"

He placed bags down and reached to lift her into a hug when he registered her solemnity. "What?" he asked.

She lowered her glasses. Pausing, his gaze fell on her black and blue forehead. He opened his mouth to speak but she placed a finger on his lips.

"Evan," she said, fighting tears and biting the insides of her mouth.

"Oui?" he asked.

"Ton papa, mon cher. Il est mort."

At home, he called Betti. Her coat and hat on, Klee stood looking out the broken window, biting nails and wrestling with the drugs and pain that wracked her still.

"What is on the floor?" he asked once he'd hung up.

"A mess."

He sighed and went to the couch where she eventually joined him. Placing her head in his lap, she hugged his knees.

"Heart attack. He never knew what hit him," he said.

She lifted herself, gulped, allowed him to study her face, however her disarray was not enough to hold his attention. Instead, he contemplated the flooring and broken glass while he stroked her shoulder, the ticking of the clock and distant traffic the only sounds.

Then he touched her hair, stroked her chin, moved her face towards his and took her in, every line, every crease, every crust of blood. His finger traced one side of her face as he drew inward and inward still. She turned away in shame for her own selfish moves, but he pulled her near and hugged her while rocking.

"Ma chérie, we both hurt. We do," he said.

She pulled his head to her chest and gently ran fingers through his dark locks, staring at the damaged window. Softly at first, she sang:

> I'm a free born man of the traveling people
> Got no fixed abode with no maps I have wandered
> Country lanes and byways were always my ways
> I never fancied being yonder.
>
> Oh we knew the roads and the resting places
> And the small horse sang when winter days were over
> And we'd pack our load and be on the road
> Those were good old days for a rover.
>
> There was open ground where a man could linger
> For a week or two for time was not our master

Then away you'd jump with your horse and dog
Nice and easy no need to go faster.

Now I've known life hard and I've known it easy
And I've cursed the life when winter's days were dawning
But I've laughed and sung through the whole night long
Seen the summer sun rise in the morning.

All you free born men of the traveling people
Every tinker, rolling stone, and gypsy rover
Winds of change are blowing; old ways are going
Your traveling days will soon be over...

When she stopped, he looked up at her.

"A song by the Clancy Brothers about tinkers," she whispered.

"What's a tinker?"

"You call them gypsies on the Continent. Wanderers." She chuckled. "Ah, the expression is now more of a joke, an insult if you will. You're a tinker if you're dirty, a low-life you call them here."

"That song did not mock them," Evan said.

"Where I came from, I was considered odd, like a tinker."

He kissed her. "The world needs more tinkers then."

He tightened his fingers about hers. Head bent he buried head in her chest and cried while she clung to him.

In Gaelic and with an even softer voice, she told him of her wee people, going over and over Romney's tales until he'd calmed again.

"Continue, Chérie," he said.

She revealed their tricks and described their homes, their chores as well as their spirited parties, the night flights across the land, and the pots of gold that many mortals sought. She wound a hand around his and tightened her embrace, all the while whispering the lore that many said had died long ago but to which she brought vivid recall.

"They seek those who are of them and I had the privilege. I am of them, Evan. I hold the keys to their secrets. It's the song, you see, the Gaelic. The treasure of many centuries. They gave it to me one day in the fields and I have it forever," she said covering her heart. "Listen, for they murmur. You must pay attention, for soon they are gone."

He touched her breast and she covered his hand with hers. Wide-eyed, he passed into her navy eyes and marveled at what seemed to be coming from them, a dimension beyond the day to day.

"Tu ne m'en as jamais parlé," he said.

"Shhh," she said. "Do not seek to know too much about us."

Suddenly he asked, "Where is your father, Klee?"

She leaned against the couch. "I have already lost mine. Time and again, over and over, forever into tomorrow."

A tear fell and she hugged him. He kissed her hard and reached for her shoulders to draw her even closer. He unbuttoned her bloodied blouse and let it fall, studying her paleness that glowed in the dim room.

"So beautifully crafted," he said.

She pressed hands harder against his back, her touch begging him on. His entire body was warm and damp. She clenched fingers into his shirt. He sought her mouth over and over.

"So long it's been for me," she whispered, shaking.

She caressed his cheek, his stubbly beard. In the darkness, they stared at one another. She could tell he was far away and when he reached again it was more a withdrawal. She understood they were never meant to make love.

"Odd our togetherness, Evan."

"Intertwined, somehow wickedly." He moved away and picked her shirt off the floor, gently replaced it over her head.

She traced the outline of his face then loosened her grasp. She lay against him and grew still as they dozed.

A few hours later, as the city rumbled to a new day, the clock ticked towards their eventual parting, Klee made tea while Evan took calls and arranged flights.

December made her think of Dublin and her exit from its scene. She recalled Benny's sense of humor and the pounding of meat cleavers at Fahey's. She tidied the townhouse as she'd tidied her room in Dublin and drank of the city's noises and sounds. She swept and listened to the news.

He emerged from his room shaven and wearing fresh clothes, a bag slung over his shoulder. She promised to watch over the house and wait for his return.

The brown of his eyes had deepened though he didn't penetrate her gaze with a playful twinkle or try and tease her into laughter. He touched her shoulder and pressed hard, imparting a silent *au revoir*.

With a nod, she took his hand. "*A bientôt*."

Then he was gone.

# Chapter 29:
# December 18, 1975

RÉGINE WAS LIVID. Not only was she excluded from the funeral preparations, Evan did not request she sit beside him at the church. Her repeated demands went unanswered. Unwilling to take his non-response sitting down, she vowed to show him. In fact, she would show all of them.

Struggling with her brassiere, she lamented her swollen state and a tent-style black frock, a similar style of the *vieilles filles* in the congregation. How, in her condition, could she withstand an hours-long service plus the frigid cold at the cemetery? How could Giles have died at such a time!

She had two weeks to go. Had the father of her child lived, well, wouldn't she be the happiest woman alive? Not only was she nearing the end of the nine months but she would also cradle a bundle representing her deserved financial reward. Finally.

This child would inherit a fortune, for she had done her homework and insured that, married or not, because she remained part owner, she claimed a portion of de Roche Frères. Plus, once the baby arrived, Giles would have no choice but to provide for it. Then she could relax. Eventually the baby's fortune would end up in her pockets.

She figured that she would outlive Giles, but hadn't counting on him passing so soon. His chest pains a frequent topic, they'd agreed to keep its frequency and severity to themselves. Giles never wanted to make a fuss.

Throwing personal culpability out the window, she reasoned that she was not his mother. Up to him to decide when to visit the doctor, not her problem if he neglected his own person. Besides, she had her own worries physically what with veins popping out on her calves and her stretched belly. Would she ever get back in shape so she could traipse across the sands this summer in her usual racy numbers?

This death was indeed ill-timed. Worse, Evan was back and she had to cooperate with him, adapt to a mode of mourning, and pretend she was still in love with his father. Awful stuff, this commitment business.

All of Paris watched and she would eventually have to answer to more than Evan. If he returned to the States, who would help her along as Giles had, to his likely physical demise? Using the excuse she was with child, she'd grown increasingly removed from the day-to-day affairs of the business. Giles let it happen, so he was partly to blame.

Fussing with her oversized garment, she huffed and tried to compose herself as she realized that, at least until the will was read, she had to be nice to Evan.

"I despise nice," she said, plastering a smile and descending to the guests.

♥ ♥ ♥

The funeral behind them, those closest to the de Roches congregated at the residence. Marcel had flown in from Spain and lodged nearby at the studio of a friend, but bypassed this particular gathering. Others from the Duvivier side crowded into the mansion to organize food and attend to chores alongside Betti. Georges and Chantel de Long updated Evan on all the recent goings-on in Paris. Younger nieces and nephews filed in, some of whom Evan had never met. They were overjoyed to meet the uncle from the States.

In the days following, French political factions enquired discretely as to Evan's plans and he found himself meeting with heads of state he'd only read about. Not only was there interest in de Roche Frères but they also paid close attention to stories out of Washington and New York, comparing notes to see if the young de Roche had the same sense as they—that he was prime for the recently vacated ambassador spot.

Evan used the distractions to his advantage, making himself available for any opportunity whether he desired it or not. This way, he kept focus away from his father's death and his own issues that had lately proven more difficult to dismiss. When it all became too much, he and Marcel snuck from the 16th arrondissement to the night spots of Place Clichy and Pigalle.

When the will was read, the die was cast and Evan was placed once again in a position to rearrange priorities, but this time with one difference. The option to adhere to Giles's wishes was his alone.

He received de Roche Frères in its entirety as well as the home on the Ile de Batz. In a generous offering that surprised everyone, Régine was left with a lump sum that, if managed properly, would keep her comfortable for many years. Without handing her the reins of the company as some feared, Giles established a trust fund for the child from which Régine could draw each month and that would be fed from a master fund shared by other family members. In addition, the house in the south was hers.

In no time, the word spread that Evan was back in Paris for good, not only as the head of de Roche Frères but also in charge of multiple international enterprises. Paris welcomed back its favorite and most available bachelor and speculation commenced not only as to when the President of the Republic would assign him the slot of ambassador to the U. S., but also when he'd select a wife. As the country approached the holiday season and a new year, Evan swirled at its charmed center as the envy of *tout Paris*.

Régine immediately packed for a week in the south, flaunting her new checkbook and spending lavish sums at all the name boutiques. There was the baby to think about, she claimed, and her own health to attend to. She needed rest and warmth, clothing to profit from both activities, and time to herself. And it all cost money, which was in easy reach now. She would kiss Paris goodbye, brown eyes shaded green and full-sized body bedecked in jewels.

When she readied to pass through the threshold of the de Roche home for what she figured was her final time, Evan caught her eye. In the uncanny way he gazed—had gazed at her from the start—he sent a signal that chilled her. Those unblinking eyes burned holes and he didn't flinch at her practiced, habitual glare. He studied her as she said goodbye to others, returning neither nod nor wave when she raised a hand in adieu.

She told herself to be careful, to keep her distance from him as she had from Georges when Mémé died. No one was going to ruin things now. No one.

# Chapter 30

WITH WEALTH CAME REPUTATION, and limitation. Régine soon discovered she was not as free as she imagined. France knew Giles de Roche's woman. This made for difficult days once she headed south to seek reprieve from all that had proven training grounds for her unique practices of bait and switch.

In Cassis, where the locals interacted with Giles at a more organic level, he was mourned with great passion. A stream of visitors arrived at Regine's house carrying food, preserves, and advice for the baby's arrival. The mailman left bags of letters and cards at her door and those who couldn't stop by phoned. These local well-wishers were not what Régine had in mind for sympathy. Their presence only detracted from her would-be position of standing. She'd always disliked the way Giles mingled with these types, drinking apéritifs at unremarkable cafés and playing boules with everyday folk. Two harried days into her stay and she was planning her escape. This kind of attention she could do without, to say nothing of the fact she was at her least presentable.

Though she criticized the locals, she did not miss the watchful regards of some of the gentlemen with broad shoulders and thick Mediterranean smiles. She would have preferred meeting them once her pregnancy was behind her, though. After all, in time she would be lonely for company. No sense enjoying all this money by herself.

Her doctor warned her to stay in Paris for the birth but she couldn't stand one more curious stare or Evan's surveillance which was sure to increase once he took a closer look at the company's books and realized her negligence. Had Giles left her sole owner, she'd planned to liquidate the assets and sell off. Evan would likely do the same, or perhaps make a go of it. Either way, he'd see how poorly she'd managed and that he would not keep secret. She would be mortified right out of the city. Regardless of health, she had to make for faraway places.

This baby proved problematic, too. With her windfall, she really had no further need for a child. The daunting prospect of motherhood at her age had her thinking long before Giles's death. She could hire a permanent nanny and have done with the daily exertions of parenting. Adoption was a delicate issue, but not one she'd overruled now the father was gone. With her new-found fortune, scenarios abounded as long as she was discrete, not an easy chore seeing as she'd spent recent months boasting of her condition.

A part of her was certain the child was a girl. It was her luck to have girls and they ran in the family. A boy may have proved a consolation, but a girl would only be a tortuous venture. She needed to rid herself of the child.

During this time, Laurence emerged in Régine's consciousness. Why not pay her daughter a visit? The little rat would love to see her half-sister, wouldn't she? Plus, Laurence may have been wanting a child for some time now but, unable to meet a man who could stomach her whimsical ways that so resembled her father Nate's, she'd remained without child. The ingrate might even come around to appreciate her mother once she left her with this little bundle of joy. Wouldn't she? Laurence was stupid and reclusive enough not to argue or fight back. The girl no longer possessed strength to push back, nor would she care to ever deal with her mother's wrath a subsequent time. Indeed, Laurence could prove the answer to this tricky situation separating Régine once and for all from true independence and happiness.

She booked a flight to New York.

# Chapter 31

AT EVAN'S DESK, KLEE RUBBED A TEACUP STAIN and studied her reflection in the porcelain.

"You are a toad," she said. "Wait until the world sees you."

Cleaning the townhouse fed her compulsiveness. Every time she readied to sing or compose, a dust ball flew by, or her hair required barrettes, or the laundry needed doing. Noise, the television, and her own crumbs after a snack gave rise to a sense of urgency, feverish cleaning that monopolized her focus. When she returned to her music, she found herself immobile except when a dirt spot was discovered on the sofa or the windows appeared drab. This pummeled her to the laundry closet for utensils to fix up the mess. Ammonia and sponges became her companions.

Deeper feelings coursed through her veins and they were, she knew, about Evan. Each time they surfaced, she fought the stomach pang and the throbbing head, opting instead for frenetic movement where she swirled in busy-ness that helped pass the time and helped diminish her thinking. They'd touched that night, come together in sorrow, but she hadn't felt sexual at all. His strong arms and hands bespoke benevolence, preventing a collapse under confusion that had peaked for both of them with the announcement of Giles's death. But it went no further than that. Evan wasn't for lovemaking. Perhaps lovemaking was over for her.

He called every day to check in and she told him that she progressed with her singing and that he'd be satisfied with the results. He suggested she add the gypsy song to her repertoire, but she was evasive on that score. As it was, he'd be upset enough to know she'd not done a bit of singing since his departure.

Standing at the windows, once again staring down on the city that had become overwhelming, she noted the reporters milling as usual. How could she sing about the tinkers? She couldn't even sing right now. The idea of exposing her background through celebration of the west coast of Eire was out of the question. It would never happen, nor would her descent to those creatures below who would excoriate her.

Still, out there was the man, she reminded herself as she gripped a mop. If you don't accommodate these newspaper types, you'll never get your story out. You've promised yourself to find him, to stare him in the face and ask the question you've wanted to ask your entire life. You must move beyond these obstacles.

"Pretend those people below are nobodies which they are. You are the one they want to see. You have something they want. You can use it to your advantage." Her breath made a cloud on the glass and she drew a circle.

One reporter looked up and she almost backed away but changed her mind and remained immobile. Others gathered around to peer at her.

"Ah, you're only little people in your way, aren't ye?" she asked, drumming her fingers on the pane. She gave a tentative wave and another reporter waved back.

"Ah, gowan, Klee. They don't bite," she said, retreating.

But her legs were jelly as she dropped the mop and padded across the floor. She sat on the couch, forcing a giggle, working on her stamina. The imagery of what her father's eyes might look like came to her. Blue like hers, penetrating and powerful. He'd smile at her their first meeting. Perhaps he'd even take her in his arms. But he wasn't going to do that if she stayed inside this prison. For sure he wasn't.

"Just this once. Run if they scare ye."

In her bedroom, she threw open the closet, grabbed coat and hat then left quickly.

Covered by her outer garments, no one noticed her as she emerged. Indeed she walked right past the milling reporters and crossed the street without a one calling out. This made her laugh. For all their preparation and staying on the lookout, they'd ignored her walking inches from them! She ducked into a nearby market and purchased a few items then headed back. Still unaware, the reporters talked among themselves.

"Okay, so, here it is, Klee," she whispered. "You make it or not right this instant."

At the entrance she stopped to fumble for keys and a reporter approached.

"You live here?" he asked.

"I do."

When he heard her, his eyes widened. "You Irish?"

"I am."

Two reporters shared surprised glances. "Klee?" they asked in unison.

"I am," she said.

After that, it was all she could do to maintain a protective distance. While one person busied himself with camera, others crowded around.

She took questions one by one, repeating to herself that the first step had been taken.

♥ ♥ ♥

The second step was not so easy. In a few days, three national magazines carried the photos accompanied by accounts of her affair with Evan, about how she'd been hiding in his Manhattan place. Most seedy of all, the reporters gave themselves all the credit for persisting in their quest to uncover her. Her photos were less than flattering and not one showed her smiling. Her mannish hat and coat drew shadows to her facial expression and made her look angry.

Refusing to surface a second time, she hired a service to shop for necessities while she took to scouring and vacuuming with a vengeance, chiding herself for even going out that day. At the same time, she pondered the reach of the magazines. Would she have to keep doing such a trying thing as appear in front of vultures in order to achieve her goal?

As the days rolled towards Christmas, touched-up pictures of she and Evan appeared on front pages of the city's dailies. The text was of their 'cooled' affair, what with Evan in Europe and Klee on another retreat from the world. What Klee didn't know but found out from one of the help she hired, was that her music was becoming as widespread as those outlandish tales. The stories had fueled interest and this was the kind Evan would be pleased over—record sales soared and many places were short of inventory given the Christmas demand.

Without Evan's help, she was unsure how to proceed, so waited for his return and hoped for the best, trying to gather courage to face him and explain that she'd progressed little with original tunes.

During the long days and longer nights, she reminded herself that this latest sensationalism tied in with her wishes, for without her doing much more than she had that day with the reporters, she'd managed to get herself exposed.

The night Evan called to say her story appeared in London's *Mirror*, she barely reacted.

"What is this crap about us, though?" he asked.

"You know how they are, Evan. What was it you told me once? Editorial license?"

His silence betrayed his anger but he quickly moved on to financials and the need for him to organize the re-release of 'Mood.'

"I'll work this from Paris, but don't worry, more records will be on the stands soon."

"Are ye ever coming back?"

"To more gossip? No thanks."

After they hung up, she slumped on the couch, realizing for the first time she would be alone for the holidays.

Until only recently, she'd have found comfort in a book or a walk, or even her latest distraction of cleaning, but tonight and especially after hearing Evan's voice, she needed to get out. To see people if only a sales girl at Macy's. Oddly, something had triggered the desire to be part of the swath of humanity, perhaps her own indulgence that afternoon with reporters, or perhaps her sore heart at missing Evan's companionship. Emerging from within, a force that could, perhaps indefinitely, facilitate her efforts, so she could sing and be applauded without shame, give of herself in other ways than through her voice. This possibility rumbled within, like the echo of the trains along the tracks into O'Connell Station, its feel as distinct as the Galway dawn breaking over the hills.

She felt all new and was only twenty-five.

She thought of Johnny then and, on a dare, rang him at the club.

He was not there. The prior week, Johnny Mear had died in a car crash, drunk and driving out of control. The club was closed to the public until further notice.

# Chapter 32:
# December 25, 1975

THE ENTIRE DAY, a snow storm raged through Glenrock. By nightfall, two feet covered the land. Laurence, who had fallen asleep on the couch with the cat on her lap, didn't hear the knocking at first. Eventually she stirred to the persistent banging at the door.

She checked her watch and asked, "Who is it?"

"Let me in or I'll break in. It's late!"

Laurence raised a hand to her mouth and bit, lying back hard against the couch. "Please, dear God, no."

The windows packed tight with snow, escape was not possible. Crawling on the floor, she made it to the bathroom and locked herself inside. On the floor, she leaned against the toilet, inhaling deeply to keep her head clear. The cat hopped onto the toilet.

The knocking stopped. She had no phone, no way to get help. With no lights on, she figured Régine might leave but too soon voices came from the front walkway, the farmer and his wife.

"No, please don't let her in!" she called.

The door creaked open. Régine let out a disgusted snort and banged snow off her boots.

Laurence let herself out and stood in the narrow hallway leading to the living room and the threesome who stared at her.

"Dear," said the farmer's wife, "in all this wind, you must not have heard your mother knocking."

Her pleading gaze at the landlords went unnoticed as Régine gushed thanks and settled her bags, telling the couple she would be fine and to get along home. Before Laurence knew it she was alone with her mother.

She ran into the bathroom and vomited all over the tiles.

"This place is a holy mess, a hovel and disgrace! I'm surprised those people allow you to stay!" Régine exclaimed. "The storm came at a lousy time. My Bally boots are ruined. Where's my room? Laurence! Come out here!"

Laurence heard her move to the kitchenette and fumble with a box of matches.

"How does this damn stove light anyway? How am I supposed to get a cup of coffee? Get your ass out here!"

The water ran in the sink as Régine cursed while banging cabinets and drawers. The kettle soon agitated and next Laurence heard water being poured into a cup. Tears streamed down her face as she wiped up the floor.

"Quit your God-damn belly-aching and come say hello at least. We have things to discuss then I'll be out of your hair if that's what worries you."

Laurence buried face in hands. The voice alone! She rocked and prayed, rocked and prayed. Régine stepped towards the bathroom and banged hard on the door.

"Go away," Laurence whispered. "Please go away."

The cat cocked its head then leaped to the floor. With arched back and tickling tail, it slid past Laurence then curled at her feet.

"Get out now or I'm coming in!" Régine rattled the door and it eventually flung open. Wrinkling her nose at the stench, she said, "I can see you haven't changed."

She kicked Laurence then moved back towards the kitchen. "Well, I'll wait until you're fully awake. There's no going out in this storm anyway. These hicks won't have the roads plowed until noon tomorrow."

Sometime in the middle of the night, Laurence dozed but came to shortly thereafter. Stepping tenuously into the hallway, she found all the lights on but no Régine. Beyond the closed bedroom door she could hear the regular heavy breathing of her mother. On the couch lay a tiny bundle and when Laurence approached she realized it was a baby. Blinking in disbelief, she stepped closer. Wrapped in blue blanket and sleeping soundly, the newborn had an abundance of black hair, with eyes shut tight in tiny slits. Two pink fists were the only other exposed part of his body and she couldn't help but smile at the peaceful oblivion he exuded.

She fought her own sore, tired body to bend down and lift the child into her arms. He stirred but didn't wake so she settled on the couch with him in her arms, at once enthralled with this petit specimen at the same time on the edge of panic for who was presently residing in her own room.

In time he woke, gurgling and cooing to his new surroundings. He was wet so she found a bag of diapers and changed him. The umbilical cord scab was recent. She struggled to get the material around his squirming body while marveling at his beautiful soft skin and miniscule body parts. When he whimpered she figured he needed milk and that, too, was in the bag so she warmed a bottle and fed him.

Sun broke through fast-moving clouds. The morning progressed. The baby had two more changes and another bottle before Régine woke. Scuffing into the kitchen wearing an expensive silk robe, she fought again with the kettle before addressing her daughter, who watched her warily.

Mug in hand, Régine sipped and padded past on her way back to the bedroom.

"I see you two have met. He eats at 8, 2 and 6. Food jars are in the bag."

# Chapter 33:
# March 1976

EVAN WANTED EVERYTHING TO BE PERFECT. As the chauffeur guided the limo towards the Chandler Pavilion, he phoned his Bel Air home. By now his Parisian chef could report on the five-course meal, a sit-down affair to rival any celebrated after party in Hollywood. Regardless of the outcome of "Silence," Evan planned to take this occasion to hobnob with as many producers and directors as he could. The time had come to make inroads on the West Coast.

Hollywood being what it was, he knew that if "Silence" didn't procure an Oscar, his would be one of the less sought-after names. Nevertheless, it was a chance he'd take. The night was young and if worse came to worse he would celebrate at other parties.

While the chef detailed hors d'oeuvres and main course, he glanced to Elise, his companion for the evening. In navy strapless gown with diamond brooch tucked between the narrow cloth covering her breasts, her blonde hair and green eyes dazzled. One of his up and coming stars, he figured she'd make impressions tonight. Her $15,000 per-show first job was nothing to sniff at either, given she'd only been in Los Angeles several months. She sucked on a joint and gave him her practiced girly smile, all red lips and sexual innuendo. He hung up the phone and planted a kiss.

"So, you prepare for tonight," he said.

"To think I was waiting tables a year ago. You are some sponsor!" After kissing him back, she returned to her smoke, staring out the window as Evan popped the cork on the champagne.

"Ready?"

"As I'll ever be," she said. They clinked glasses. "If I don't show back at your place you'll understand, right?"

"Well, tonight's big for both of us, especially if I accept the award. I'd like you home with me. What were you planning on doing anyway?"

"Nothing," she said, "The jitters I suppose."

He took her in his arms as they lined up with the limos approaching the red carpet.

Klee paced the dressing room. In three minutes she was on stage in front of the entire world. On stage with her song.

Evan suggested she sing a cut from the "Silence" soundtrack. At first she declined, but the Hollywood brass got wind and thought it an innovative move for the stage show.

Jet-lagged from her cross-country flight, she told herself that the dizzy feeling was more to do with fear, to relax and breathe deeply. Without composure, she could not sing.

A woman knocked on the door. "It's time."

She looked in the mirror. The low-cut sleeveless white chiffon dress hugged her body, to her knees where it splayed down her back in a long train. Silver-studded heels sparkled and competed with a ruby ring on her index finger—a good-luck gift from Evan. Curls clipped to one side, her lips and nails vermillion, she could have been right out of a magazine cover and this thought made her giggle. Hiking her dress, she opened the changing room door and followed a woman down the hallway to backstage where, from the sound of things, a TV commercial was in progress. The woman helped her to the dark stage and onto a small platform.

The sea of black in front of her could not block the knowledge that thousands of eyes were upon her. The spirited tango of the orchestra could not diminish the sobering reality she faced, and her own slippery hand on the microphone revealed her bedeviled mood in spite of the applause. As the lights strengthened and the wave of human sound dissipated, she poised for an eternal second and prayed to her gnomes.

"Stay with me, just for the song. I will let you go after, so."

Her introductory notes, deep and sonorous, sufficed to render the hall silent. There wasn't a spectator present, she knew, who didn't want to hear and see her, this her first multi-media show. For months, she'd covered the printed pages but that was chump change to this. As her voice rose and undulated and as she embraced her spirit land, she held to the understanding that opinions formed, whispers carried, and the odds of her ever knowing anonymity were compromised.

Her voice amplified seemingly without assistance, an amalgam of classic structure ruled her every chord as the title track burst from her into the crowd and up to the rafters. The original musical group from Maine played in the orchestra and that brought a level of familiarity to the piece.

When the band worked several chords without her, she searched the bejeweled scene for Evan. Tuxedos and glimmering gowns graced the front row and multi-colored lights shot from all angles. She was on stage, alone, in a room of hundreds.

Later she would muse that moment was curious, for she stared at so many—and millions more through the grace of technology—with no knowledge of who they were. In front and around, people assessed for themselves every little thing about her, impressing her image on their minds. Was the man she sought looking in on her, too?

She concluded by tearing away at the final lyrics, elongating notes of words she had grown so accustomed to, she felt they were her friends. With a sweep of her hand, she ended with a bow. Head bent, eyes closed, the applause took over. She was a thousand miles away, traversing the rocky shores of Kinemmaera, singing her wee sonnets while on the lookout for red hats.

She bowed several more times before she was escorted off-stage by a broad-shouldered, tuxedoed usher. On his arm, she lay the weight of the experience and didn't concern herself when he asked her if she was Okay.

"Hear that crowd out there! You just made the planet your own."

"The planet," she whispered as he released his hold.

She looked into his eyes to thank him but he planted a kiss before she could react.

"I had to," he said. "Tomorrow this will be behind both of us. Enjoy."

He walked away and she lifted a finger to where he kissed her, thinking not of him but of the planet and all its people, every last one.

In front of the TV they rented to watch the Awards, Bea hummed the tune. "Airy that Klee, isn't she? Like a fairy princess."

Laurence patted the baby on her shoulder. "The song is perfect for an underwater film. I can understand why it got nominated."

"That's not all," Bea said, fetching a diaper for Laurence's shoulder. "If you would only let me show it to you, you'd understand."

"I prefer to remember my funky little twenty minute version."

Bea returned to her chair. "Best Documentary" was up. The two stars who received awards the year before joked a bit, then recited the nominations, one of which was "Silence."

"No one pronounces it the way Evan wants," said Bea. "He likes the French accent."

"Silence," Laurence murmured.

"Yes, like that," Bea said, stealing a glance.

"And the winner is... "Silence" by Bea Sage Productions!" the star said.

Bea jumped up. "Hooray! Laurence! We did it!"

Laurence beamed as she toyed with the baby's fingers.

Evan strolled down the aisle with his usual self-confidence and demureness. Bea settled on the edge of her chair.

Flanked by performers congratulating him, in black formal Dior, hair brushed back, and tan speaking to days in the California sun, the Frenchman took the Oscar and cleared his throat. After thanking the Academy and various industry officials, he lowered his voice and looked into the camera.

"And special thanks to Bea of Bea-Sage Productions for releasing this gem from its hiding place and allowing Monsieur Cousteau and me to take it where it belongs.

To the lady on Nantucket who had a dream, I send my ever gratitude. *A la mer, ma chérie, à la mer."*

The head of the slumbering child caught the tear that rolled down Laurence's cheek, her gaze on Evan as he was escorted off stage. She met Bea's stare only after she'd brushed more tears away.

"Always the gentleman Evan," she whispered.

Bea extended hands to the child. "Here I'll put him to bed. You've worked hard enough today. Put your feet up and relax."

She padded to the bedroom while Laurence fixed eyes to the screen and allowed the tears to tumble without concern. In time, she placed head into hands and curled into a ball on the couch.

When Bea returned, she studied Laurence's sleeping form and reminded herself she did well to come to Maine instead of to California. Whatever ran through Laurence's mind was anyone's guess, but Bea sensed Evan wasn't far from her thoughts. She covered Laurence with a blanket, snapped off the lights, and poured herself a Scotch.

What would happen now, seeing as Laurence had decided to keep the child and they got along famously? Would she stay indefinitely in this remote place?

"My poor baby. Now you've a baby of your own," she said.

Right then she made up her mind to secure a copy of "Silence" for Laurence, in case one day she who conceived this idea ever woke from her hell and decided to film again.

In early morning shadows Marcel untangled himself from the woman, lit a cigarette, and went downstairs to the phone. The results of the awards would be known.

Dialing a long-time associate, the man's sleepy voice soon greeted him.

"And?" Marcel asked.

*"Gagné, mon ami, gagné. Monsieur Evan a accepté l'Oscar."*

Marcel pressed lips, hung up and shuffled to his study. The dampness of the morning seeped in, past undulating curtains. The fountains bubbled. In his chair, he contemplated next moves.

As agreed with Evan, if the Oscar came, Marcel would assist two graduates of Polytechnique in the management of de Roche Frères while his nephew stayed on in Hollywood. For as long as it took the students to acclimate to the business, and for however much longer the liquidation of the less healthier divisions took, Marcel would act as corporate head.

The idea had been his for he wished Evan to move forward. Already the talk of Paris and New York, his nephew had garnered a reputation few achieved as the agent of one's dreams. Marcel knew of what he spoke when he emphasized the positive outcome of tonight. The sky was the limit. Now, as Evan prepared to soar, Marcel made good on his promise. Involvement in de Roche affairs had no appeal but, at Giles's funeral, Evan talked of remaining in Paris. There was no way Evan would retrace Marcel's own faulty steps in favor of lesser options. Evan verged on a more rewarding future.

"You must return to the States," he told Evan that night in Paris.

"I can't let the company falter in HER hands," Evan said, referring to Régine.

"She won't get that far," said Marcel. "Go. I promise the company will remain solvent and restructure into financial health."

Following those words, and more drink than Evan had handled in a while, Marcel drove him to the airport and put him on a plane for New York. Even while boarding, he protested.

"C'mon, Marcel, it's too much for you. You're not of that profit and loss ilk."

"I can no longer do what it is you do but I can help you from the sidelines. Nothing would give me more pleasure than sinking the lady Régine."

Evan grew pensive. "She's coming back then."

"She might. She hooked up with some gigolo in Marseille who took her for everything, even the house in Cassis."

"All Papa's money," Evan said.

"Forget her. Your plane is waiting." They embraced goodbye.

As his gaze roved the floor of his study, Marcel told himself that his word was his word. After all, Evan is who he is, the child of Pauline, Marcel's one true friend who had offered her encouragement for so long, never to see the outcome. With her death, they'd not reached goals she and he had dreamed of. She would have been saddened to know Marcel was not much more than an 'also-ran.' He knew now where his duty lay. Evan was poised to grow into what Pauline had envisioned for Marcel, and perhaps even for her son. Helping the process along was the least Marcel could do.

In the coming days, he'd leave Aix behind for Paris. The two Polytechniciens were progressing with company numbers and strategies. Barring economic unknowns, they would soon be running the place. Marcel would stay focused on the undoing of Regine's reign of terror.

At the record player, he dropped the album on the turnstile. "Mood" drove him once again to the frame of mind into which he slipped each time he heard her voice.

The melody carried him to a servile place, to the arms of all the lovers he'd known, to his very heartbeat and its reason for being. Its power gripped his soul and pried open that part of him he thought long ago buried.

As Jean pattered around the kitchen churning coffee beans and readying the bread, Marcel observed from within. The singer rollicked his emotions, from fear of aging to near delirious joy over being alive, a lifting that rose to the ceiling, beyond the windows to the world outside.

He recalled the innumerable women he'd known, illustrated pages in the book of his life, more blot than design, more fading shades than primary glory. As Klee's voice struck him with a thorny pleasure, images sharpened—a pert little nose, that blue regard, movements of a pale hand—her presence that he had dismissed. Her ability to clear his mind and curl around his heart. The sprite who hibernated in him until his heart surged to beg her to appear one more time, if not in person then to some layer of his conscious memory so that he could feel again the ecstasy followed by, he knew only too well, her fading into the folds of his psyche until the next arbitrary, external tease.

Klee's tune ended. A rustling behind him caused him to start. In green silk robe, hair tumbling about her, eyes on him, Régine advanced. Running a hand through his hair, she kneeled at his feet and lay her head on his knees. Tugging his hand she directed him to caress.

He complied, dazed from the music and the memories, yet struggling to focus on his promise to Evan.

He thought, "Whatever it takes. Whatever it takes."

♥ ♥ ♥

In her bedroom, Alice watched the noonday coverage of the Academy Awards. Klee's image flashed on the screen.

"You're on your way now," she whispered, puffing on a cigarette.

Each time she switched channels, she was distracted by footage of famous stars or her daughter. A close up caught Alice's breath. So incredibly arresting was the shot, she touched the screen.

"Lovely," she said, eyes smarting.

She should turn off the set and go about her business. After all, Alice had mastered the knack of dismissal. Connoisseur of flight, she could distance herself from any seducing words as glibly as she painted nails or purchased tea. In this moment, she could have used some of that forcefulness.

But Klee was so pretty, projected from that screen, her presence enhanced by a voice Alice now heard on a daily basis. There she stood, buzz of Hollywood, rave of New York, pride of Ireland. Her own child.

Where Alice had made strides, Klee had leapt to heaven and back. Where Alice's looks faded, Klee's deepened to mature and arresting contours. Where Alice made dents in her circumstances, Klee had bulldozed the old in search of an authentic new.

Therein lay the tale. Looks aside, they could never have had a mother-daughter relationship. Even if Bob Walsh hadn't run Alice out of town, Klee would have outshone, outwitted, outperformed. Klee was never meant to live what so many in Kinemmaera considered a normal life.

"All the years I spent lamenting the poor thing," she said, flicking off the TV.

She arched her back, winced, and returned to bed to light another cigarette. Her aches reminded her of the night before and she grinned at the image of the client. A friend from her Ireland days, Red Corcoran ran into her in London years ago, took her up on her proposal, and had remained loyal and paying ever since. With hair to match his name, he possessed an endearing burliness that Alice cherished. Although he didn't comply with her developed upper-cut standards, she couldn't resist his ruddy cheeks and joviality. He never quibbled about rates and even took her annually to the Scottish Highlands where he conducted business with mining concerns. Whenever Red was in London, he saw about work then saw to Alice. He never let her down.

But last night, as his heaving body bore down, she let things go for too long, experimented too much and today paid the price. Hers was an unglamorous business, unlike that of her American-based youngest child.

Toying with a strand of hair, she recalled Klee singing at Danigan's.

"Old Benny boy, bet you never imagined this for your girl. Then again the likes of you were never meant to claim such a prize."

She tried to sleep but couldn't. Against her better judgment, she swallowed some aspirins and sleeping pills then cancelled her 2:30 client.

Pain aside, the time had come to break with that one. Lou Baxter, alias Roger Petrie, may or may not suspect she was on to him. The day prior, her in-the-know associate informed her that she would be wise to lie low, even change residences. Private detectives snooping around her affairs could prove fatal to her business.

She sighed. He'd been a good lay and even better company. She wondered why he'd not reported her to the police by now. Perhaps he struggled with his gentler, more compliant side—the side she knew all men possessed and which she'd capitalized on not a few times. Then again, hadn't he reveled in their meal at her restaurant, Chez Claude? That early-on probing stare of his had been erased by the time they hit the sack, too. She'd even toyed with the idea he wanted her for more than her body. Chez Claude had that effect on certain types.

She would do well to change name and even her location. Still, she couldn't deny a feeling that he wasn't completely after her for information. What had he learned after all? Not much save her bodily strengths and weaknesses, and her penchant for French dining.

"Odd the few we meet by hazard and who cut a different mold but who leave us perplexed."

Whatever Lou sought, he would have to get from another professional. Alice's ramblings had garnered him no more or less than she gave to clients who didn't bother taking her for a meal. Plus, the one thing that she withheld from the world remained locked inside. And why would Lou even care about something like that?

Though at Chez Claude, they sat at the same table from twenty-five years ago, though they drank the wine and spoke in riddles, she never once uttered the man's name nor did she detail her long-ago soirée. If anything, Lou registered her wistful regard and was curious, but he did not succeed in breaking Alice. No one would, least of all a client.

She felt her muscles giving way to sleep. The better part of the afternoon would pass before the pills' effects drained from her system. Her head would be clearer when she woke up. She would make the appropriate decision, and kick-start her life one more time.

"Maybe a new name. Constance? No, too royal. Clothilde? Too consort-y. Clara? Hmm. That has a ring."

The physical pain dimmed to expose the pounding of her heart. So many culminations at once! The aches, the night before with Lou, this recent wrinkle in her plans, her daughter's achievement. The men that came and went from her bed.

"And the one who never returned," she whispered reaching for a hankie.

All a reminder that she was still human, still capable of love at some level. Like the brine-thick gusts of Galway Bay, salty tears revived imagery of her youth, when she possessed dreams that her youngest child now lived. Tears freed her even as they toyed with her sanity. And once they passed, her routine would offer reprieve. Until the next rise of emotion that—in spite of her crafted exterior—she was helpless to prevent.

Before darkness took over she thought of Klee's father and murmured, "Mix and match in Nature's can, the tinker and the gentleman."

# Part Four
# Morning Glory of the Earth

*To the Woods and Waters Wild*
*Away with us he's going,*
  *The solemn-eyed;*
*He'll hear no more of lowing*
  *Of the calves on the warm hillside.*
*Or the kettle on the hob*
  *Sing peace into his breast;*
*Or see the brown mice bob*
  *Round and round the oatmeal chest.*
*For he comes, the human child,*
*To the woods and waters wild,*
*With a fairy hand in hand,*
*For the world's more full of weeping than he*
*can understand*

'The Stolen Child' by W. B. Yeats

611

# Chapter 1:
# April 1980

SITTING INDIAN-STYLE CENTER STAGE, Klee wears black leather pants and silk shirt. Her hair is dyed black and in a ponytail. She stares at the ceiling, giggling.

"This a new look of yours?" asks the talk show host.

"Mhmmm."

"Well…Klee, we're pleased to have you here today. What do you think of all that applause on your entering?"

She giggles while maintaining her gaze on the rafters. The audience is silent.

"The trade rags buzz about your movies, one you won an Oscar for and the other by your manager. Evan de Roche walked away with Best Director. What's the challenge this time around?"

"Have you ever met tinkers?" she asks, directing her gaze at him.

"As a matter of fact, no. Wanderers they are?"

"Tinkers they are."

"Irish tinkers or can they be Yanks, too?" the host asks to uneasy laughter from the audience.

"They're dirty," she says.

"Ah," he says, looking around.

"They roll by in caravans. They stare. Everyone stares."

"Tell me, Klee, what do you do when you're not making a movie or cutting a record?"

"I think too much."

"About?"

She shakes her head repeatedly, grins and returns to studying the ceiling.

"And now to commercial break!"

# Chapter 2:
# October 1980

"WHY DON'T THEY STOP?" Laurence asked, covering her ears as the buzz saw droned.

Christophe was nowhere to be seen. At five, the child had assumed the habits of one his age, with energy and curiosity that so consumed Laurence, she'd had to quit her day job. To bring in a wage, she freelanced as a copywriter for the local newspaper.

Though she didn't begrudge the child his energies, the extent of her own exertion surprised and confused her. From his baby stage of arrested sleep and frequent colds to the present when he was never long at rest, too often hungry, and requesting games of pretend, she fought urges to scream. Plus, he had an odd habit of pleading with his eyes, silently ordering her presence, garnering her attention, and too often driving her to near distress. In the worst of times, she willed herself to forebear.

In calmer moments, when he snuggled close and she read to him or when he clung to her following a nightmare, she was grateful for her charge and at peace with the unknowns.

She exited the front door. Dirt mounds, cement mixers, and trucks had replaced the rolling fields and blocked her path to the water's edge. A red movement in the distance was Christophe's anorak as the child followed one of the workers organizing building forms. He had befriended the construction crew, and she was grateful that this new playground was at least within eyesight.

"Christophe, come here!" she yelled, advancing towards him. "How many times do I have ask you to stay near the house where I can see you!"

"This is fun!" he exclaimed. "Soon the painting starts, see?" He pointed to deep buckets, long rollers and industrial size brushes.

"These men are busy, Christophe. Come with Mama."

"No!" he screamed. After shooting her a dark look, he scrambled behind a truck.

A jean-clad man approached. "He's not bothering us, Ma'am. Unless you have a problem, he can stay."

She looked over at the house. Its renovation was the talk of the town, and she regretted Bea not having purchased it years before. When the new owner settled in, Glenrock would never be the same.

Around the trucks, she caught sight of Christophe but he was already chatting with workers wearing white pants stained with splashes of color. Finally at his side, she made motions for him to come with her.

"Gonna be a grand old farm for the lady once we get the painting done," a worker said.

Laurence grimaced. The peeling coat of early 1900s gray showed more wood than paint. She tried to envision the carrot orange and bright red trim.

"It'll look like a doll's house," she said.

"Free country, right?" the man asked.

Taking Christophe's arm, they headed home. "Mama, when will the new neighbors move in?"

"Neighbor," she said.

"But when?"

"I don't know, Christophe. Soon."

"Can I go inside and play in the toy room?"

"What toy room?"

"There's a big room that faces the ocean. With a piano. I call it a toy room 'cuz if it were my house, I'd put all my toys there. Even buy lots of new ones."

She ruffled his hair. "Mind your own business, Okay? That house is off limits once the construction is complete."

"Even when she comes? The movie star, Mama?"

"Even more when she comes," she said.

"Her name is Klee. She's a big singer."

Laurence glanced back at the construction and the orange streak taking over one side of the house. "I know."

Before dark and after the workers left, Christophe was securing his bike when a red Toyota advanced along the dirt road. The driver, a woman with wiry black hair, knit brow and wandering gaze got out and leaned against the car.

She called out a few words that he didn't understand. Whatever she said made him smile and he edged towards her.

"You the singer?" he asked when they stood feet apart.

One foot on the ground, she reached into her bag, yawned a few times, then placed sunglasses on.

"You don't need those at night," Christophe said.

"You live nearby?" she asked.

"Next door. I am Christophe."

"I am Klee," she said.

"I know. I knew it all along," he said inching towards her.

"Your name is French," she said.

"I don't like it. Why are you called Klee? That's a funny name."

"You're a curious one now, aren't you?" she asked, reaching for her things in the trunk.

"Can I go into your house?"

"Wee fellow, I don't think you'd take no for an answer."

They walked to the front door and she let him enter ahead of her. He ran through the hallway, laughing as his footfall echoed on gleaming wood floors. She found him sitting Indian style dead center in the main room.

"Can I stay in this toy room?"

The place was coming together, she thought, leaning against the paneled entryway. In the main room, black Aosta marbled flooring and dozens of bay windows were installed along a wall. A baby grand piano, gift on Oscar night, stood to one side of the windows. She stepped to it and ran fingers over the keys, chanting.

"That's not English," Christophe said.

"It's Gaelic. You look like a gnome, Christophe. Are you?"

"Why answer you? You haven't answered me."

"Touché, little man," she said, chuckling.

"Weird laugh."

She squatted next to him. "If I told you I was a gnome would you believe me?"

"Dunno," he said raising fingers to touch her hair. "You gonna put a spell on me?"

"No," she said, closing her hand around his.

"Then you're not a gnome."

She looked to sea, crossed her own legs Indian style. They sat in silence until Laurence called for him.

"Your mother?" she asked. "You'd better go then."

He stood, blinked. "Can I come back to your toy room?"

"It's my music room. You can come back."

He left and she studied the sea before falling asleep.

♥ ♥ ♥

Laurence turned over in bed, rubbing against the bare arm of the sleeping man beside her.

"Babe," he whispered.

Eyes shut, she lay still. He eased a hand to her nightgown-covered arm, then pressed. In time, he fell back to sleep.

She bit her lip and mouthed 'husband,' trying to stir up feelings for this man who was so good to her. Guy was handsome and kind, too, it was shameful to resist his affections.

Since their wedding a year ago, she told herself she did the right thing, and still marveled at how easily the 'I do' slipped from her lips, even more so how fitfully she'd slept on their wedding night. Begun as a friendship when they crossed paths several years before and followed by Guy's eventual move from Quebec to setup an arm of his father's paper processing firm, they grew close. As time went on, Christophe reveled in Guy's visits, and the man was clear from the start about his feelings for Laurence. This created both contentment and conflict for Laurence.

Determined to provide Christophe with the best life possible, she'd be foolish to ignore the stability Guy represented. She reminded herself it was meant to be and only good things could come of their union. An outdoorsman with interests including skiing and biking which Christophe enjoyed too, Guy planned to provide a comfortable life for the three of them.

She'd been frank about her need for solitude, even her inability to reciprocate in bed. She made it clear she primarily sought a father for Christophe. Guy accepted this as he did his parental duty. However deep down, Laurence knew—through gestures and longing regards—that he wanted more. But there would never be sex, if any physical closeness. If Guy half-believed her three years ago, he was beginning to integrate the reality now.

She rolled out of bed and tip-toed to the living room. After insuring that Christophe slept soundly, she settled by the kitchen window to watch the moon.

Though it would be another few days before it was full, its light was strong. Candles flickered next door. Was Klee awake or not? Seemed she had a habit of lights on at all hours. Laurence's irritation at the thought of a neighbor had melted to mild disinterest, since Christophe was completely enthralled by Klee, especially her open door policy. Laurence could hardly complain seeing as Klee had introduced herself and asked permission to have Christophe as guest. What started out as twice weekly visits had turned into hours after school with Klee. Laurence gained free time and Christophe returned home bubbling with stories and energy she could hardly consider detrimental to him.

She went to the cabinet and found the movie Bea had handed her years before: "Silence."

Looking out the window, she whispered, "How silent shall we continue to be, Klee?"

The clock struck 4 AM. She replaced the movie and turned towards the bedroom. Guy stood in the doorway.

"You Okay?" he asked.

Refusing his open arms, she nodded and passed him on her way to bed.

♥ ♥ ♥

Klee woke with a start. Shivering, she shuffled around for more candles then went to the piano.

The moon hung over the water, nearly full, half-smiling, half-drowning the land outside with its light. She played one song then stopped. A cow bellowed, the waves pounded. The monastic feel of the house beckoned her to a place where fame could never roam.

Free of phones and technology, with wood stove for heat and minimal electrical support, she gave credit to the architect for following her grandiose yet austere plans. Too, the house blended with the scenery, from the black marble that enticed winter tree branches inside to the icy white walls that marked her vision of the days to come.

Her bold orange and red exterior gave rise to comments from the curious. So far, the press flew overhead in helicopters rather than chance detection by her surveillance equipment. She'd found her sanctum in Nature.

"My toy room," she murmured, smiling at the thought of her next door friend.

What would it be like to live forever in a toy world, to have cuddly animals as best friends and cushiony chairs for naps and sweet slumber? To have fresh baked goods served by diaphanous kitchen help who knew their place? The seamless pattern of up in the morning, bread and jam, walks on the beach, discovery without the distraction of human interruption?

"My feet brown from the dirt and my jumper gray from wear and tear. Perhaps someone to remind me to brush hair and teeth but who leaves me be? Say your prayers now and sleep well, dear Klee."

She closed her eyes.

"I don't even know what you would have wanted me to call you. Father? Dad? Papa? My school mates used different names, endearments. Father would have been too formal, Daddy too puerile. Papa is the French, would you have liked that?

"I think you're dead, though. I can't imagine it any other way. I wish I could believe differently! You can't have known how many times I held my breath in the presence of an approaching stranger. He was fifty-five, maybe sixty or even seventy. He'd nod at me and my heart would leap thinking he might be you.

"In an odd way, I did have important men in my life—Evan of course, Johnny and Benny. They would have dedicated themselves to me had I asked.

"In Paris—I'll bet you know Paris—there's a park called Montsouris. It's where people amble and children wait for the appearance of Guignol with his unblinking eyes and colorful clothes. I went there to watch the children react to the puppet's antics. Huddling near them, I pretended to be their size, try and fill myself with the same joy as they when Guignol made a joke or caused them to start. Sometimes it worked and I was laughing along with them. But, too soon, my heart would sink to know I would never again be a child and would never again feel that wide-eyed relief that someone had made me laugh. I would never turn to seek out my father's hand guiding me out of the park and along the boulevard to where we'd stop for ice cream before going home.

"How did you envision my life anyway? Did you know your child needed someone to reach towards? Someone touchable?

"None of that matters now. What I never had I'll never know. But the choice to go on is mine, dear Papa, as was the choice to seek you out, as was the choice to take on the world or the choice to leave my wee folk behind such a long time ago.

"They were my single sure thing! They never abandoned me, came to America as readily as they crossed the Adriatic or journeyed through the Alps. They helped me forget and sheltered me. And while sheltered, they coaxed me to sing. And the music carried me for years. I have a great voice. Did you ever hear my song?"

# Chapter 3:
# October 1980

SO KLEE HAD RUN OFF AGAIN with no word, this time to her retreat in Maine. Evan needed her! With all these West Coast bookings to confirm, he couldn't understand this latest antic. Plus, with Los Angeles his home the last five years, it was no longer easy to track her down. He placed a call to Betti, who lived at his New York townhouse, but she had not heard from Klee.

He scolded himself. If he'd known Klee would take off for Maine and actually purchase that run-down farm, he'd have tried to discourage her. But he thought it was a passing thing, that she'd stay in Manhattan where she could loll about with Betti over tea and baking sessions.

Her agent, her manager, her accountant, and since the success of "Mood," owner of her title rights, he thought he knew her. The night he won the Oscar, she attended his party and quickly became the focal point. She graciously gave autographs, and seemed to welcome the flashes of camera shutters. Though she abstained from eating and drinking, she fell into the rhythm expected for a burgeoning career in Hollywood.

She agreed to bookings in Las Vegas, Los Angeles, New York, and with smaller tours in between. Summer festivals in Venezuela and Brazil turned into early autumn shows in Tokyo and Hong Kong and she never stopped for rest or from illness. Magazines put her on the front cover, talk shows booked her, and she had no shortage of guest spots on variety shows. Her renown no longer appeared to preoccupy her and she welcomed the travel, challenging him to engagements so that she had no clue what time zone she was in from week to week.

A few times though, when they were in Europe, she'd fallen into an almost morose frame of mind, insisting on long walks well past midnight during which she confided in him, tales like her mother was a high class hooker, and her stepfather a brute who terrorized the family. But for the sadness in her gaze, he would have dismissed the stories. But her regards bore tears from time to time, and he sensed she grappled with dubious recollections.

He joked to her that she was a 'lonely hunter,' traipsing across the world-wide stage in search of something with specifics that eluded. Pinnacling a remunerative career, she stared at her audiences with the look of a beggar, pleading with orphan eyes as though her very existence depended on some discovery found only out there amongst the masses. She neither agreed with nor disputed his observations.

For her film debut, she fought to keep her locks blonde though the part called for a slick, darker look, as though changing her appearance would interfere with her quest. She insisted her name appear in the brightest of lights with top billing above all her co-stars. At great cost in negotiation fees and countless restless nights, Evan had met her demands.

Thankfully she adapted readily to the acting, inhabiting her roles instantly and complying with directors without histrionics. She manipulated emotions with the swiftness of a chameleon and accepted suggestions for improvement. All this engendered admiration in her audiences and produced even larger turnouts. But the accolades of her fans were received with stone silence. Her main concern was whether anyone had asked to see her.

With a shudder he recalled her talk show encounter, when she'd been replaced by another guest. Pursuant to this event, Evan held her up for a few days in his townhouse to try and understand this behavior. Sitting in his armchair, he asked her point blank what her issue was.

"You can't sit there, Evan," she said, "the wee people use that chair."

"Oh, and I need to ask their permission?" he joked, hoping her mood would switch.

"They won't bother you if you sit on the couch," she replied with a deadpan gaze that chilled him.

And now Maine. Ever since the Mainliners invited her to record her third album on location in Bar Harbor, when she delayed her return to become a no-show to several engagements, Evan realized she slackened her efforts. This caused him untold hours in rebooking, coddling angry agents and finally confronting her with ultimatums.

He drove to Maine, packed her in the car and settled her back in Manhattan. Alone in his place that night, she curled up at the end of the couch as he paced the room, the tension thick.

"I'm going to drop you as client if this continues, do you understand?"

She nodded quietly. "I do."

But her eyes were glassy and it wasn't long before she launched into musings of night walks along rocky shores with the wee people, the moon and how it spoke to her, and how she loved all Maine's deserted islands— coveting their isolation and longing to 'be there all the time.'

"Will you cut it with the wee people, Klee?" he asked. "You should be relocating to Los Angeles. You could fly to Maine any old time when you're not working! You can hire a jet for that matter! But don't LIVE there for God sakes!"

"But there I can give up the fight," she said.

"What fight?"

"You know me but little, old man. You never quite took me seriously when I told you I keep things to myself."

"Look, do your job, Okay? That's all I ask! Is that too much?"

She stared back and, before slumping against pillows, whispered, "If I must. For now."

# Chapter 4

MARCEL PUFFED HIS CIGARETTE. From above, the shower ran to the humming of Régine. The day dawned warmer than expected. The dew had already lifted from the lily beds. Along the walkway, drying lavender bushes rustled. Nearby Jean clipped a hedge, stopped to wipe his brow, and turned to wave.

"No break from the heat today. We eat after ten tonight, heh?"

Marcel nodded, rubbing pearls of dampness from his forearm. The warmth brought him back to the night before, when he and Régine were in bed, she obeying his every command like a wind-up doll.

"Touch me here, 'Gine…Don't move…Like this…and this…Better."

Frenzied pleasure characterized this recent, unlikely coupling and he chuckled at her surprise when he invited her to Aix.

Over the years, the tension between them had never eased. Marcel was well aware she'd always lusted after him. Drawing from the memory of embarrassing public moments, she kept her distance. Many a family gathering had seen her rushing to hide before tears spilled because he'd joked aloud over her fleshy thighs or protruding chin, issues that she herself agonized over.

This drove her wild with resentment laced with wonder at Marcel for knowing her without being close to her. Herself a master at one-upping people, she could never surpass his cunning.

He smiled recalling her near puerile behavior as they made way to the bed. Naked and wanting him, her eyes locked with his in a gaze both anxious and perplexed.

"What is it you want?" she asked, doing her best to act nonchalant.

He didn't bother to answer and pulled her towards him. In a ragdoll's pantomime, she allowed whatever followed. Even with her superficial performance, Marcel sensed her resentment, for a lover's apathy in any form risked the emergence of Régine's self-awareness, and its disturbing notions. For him, their trysts provided time, which was what he was after from the start. They'd been together over two months.

He was glad to be in Aix. Next week, New York, where an important meeting was to transpire, and he would have to be at his best. How life had changed since he took over de Roche Frères. His short-term promise grew into a packed schedule and he couldn't recall the last time he did anything on a whim. Paris became his home, Aix his retreat. He wore tailored suits and ties, purchased from the boutiques on rue du Faubourg St. Honoré. In many ways, little differentiated him from Giles.

The books were finally in order, the financial status rivaled only by Evan's empire overseas, and no longer was de Roche Frères deemed a faltering institution. Technocrats successfully managed all major divisions, cooperative agreements with the big Paris banks gave Marcel exclusive right of return on development projects, and this in turn created demand for several subsidiaries outside France. De Roche Frères was back, better than ever.

As for film, he kept involved by structuring loans and lenient repayment schedules for individuals in whom he saw potential. In addition he supported the few schools that had cropped up. On their behalf he negotiated with American studios and, taking a page from Evan's book, retained the rights to creations he felt had long-term potential.

Though this space in which he moved had no resemblance to the one he'd always dreamed of, nor had it proven the softest cushion for his pain, it was predictable, ready for him each day, holding him occupied until he could no longer keep eyes open. This was as it should be, he told himself.

Life had never been a promised land and, as he wound towards the end, he tracked his pleasures and counted his sorrows and felt himself a largely fortunate man. His road had been his. He'd taken steps and made decisions, in the streets and with the streetwalkers, for himself and for the cinema. He'd done his thing, no more no less.

And all the women who'd come and gone, the night goddesses and sweet tramps, the singers and actresses, stringing themselves along the edges of acceptability and accessibility, they were in his heart. Like white veins in his black marble, each left her mark, and colored his go-forward. He understood this pattern and was grateful, because it made statement to a deeper inclination, one that he was ashamed of but unable—unwilling—to change: he'd never probed his feelings enough to impart them to all those women, even though he gave of himself, and sometimes gave in earnest. The self-trust was never there and so, in the end, the women never really stood a chance.

For the longest time, the only woman of influence had been Pauline. Through her he'd reached his own higher ground, at least professionally. To the degree he could reciprocate platonic love, he'd let her supportive affection rub off. But those lithe bodies, the countless perfumed hands and throats, the hair and eyes that he'd melded with for the night, or for hours. They would never access his inner sanctum, where he controlled without caring, and preserved what he believed to be, freedom.

For years he told himself he never harmed a one. In truth, though, he'd always left before really knowing, before the pleading, or the tears. Temporary was good, he told himself, for a mind that didn't rest tendered a soul that could never renew. Upon this gypsy mentality he built his life, and reveled in an eagerness each night when feasting on another lovely creature—blonde or red or tiny or festive. He took them to cafés and dances and left them behind when the light announced itself.

The one time he lingered, it wasn't for long, and she had also faded with time. Save her words that night, her image had yellowed and curled like an old photo, marred by energies that he himself pressed onto her memory, those forever eyes. That endearing wildflower of his soul who refused to wither completely.

Had he born children or fathered no one? He couldn't agonize over the past that had slipped into a new day as the air dried their sheets and as he stepped to the streets below. Leave he had, to take on his self-indulged role of film man who forged careers, but who kept himself in the wings of backstage. The man who moved in alleyways, stealing fame through the accomplishments of others but disappearing before its claws hooked him. The self-abandon found in the arms of a beautiful woman, or with a drink in an out-of-the-way *bistrot,* or at the delighted smile of a child peering into his camera. All about the moments.

But damn Evan! The one who'd ingratiated him to this place that was so sterile. He had no choice but to seek refuge in his memories, ironically his one way to maintain composure. The nephew, possessed of Pauline's gaze and persistence, had discovered the way to divert Marcel from himself and towards his past, and his past actions.

In an odd way, this state of affairs comforted him. He had his papers and his meetings and his gatherings of investors, he had cold hard reality at all hours. Money accumulated, accounts were rectified, and there was never enough time in the day. He'd moved to the fulltime space he'd always referred to jokingly as respectability. Yet this was precisely where his soul began to whisper to him, of mismanaged intentions, and dangling energies, of where he might have had a chance to feel, and cross the threshold into authentic living.

As the hours ticked by in their methodical, structured way ending here in Aix under the guise of his needing a rest, his whole being had assembled, finally, to witness one thing: that he was never meant to feel good or to feel bad. He was meant only to feel. In this way he was no different from Pauline, or Evan, or his associates or Giles. Even Régine shared this human trait. He was never as unique or as removed as he thought he was, he was only running from the thing that made him like everybody else—the beating of his own heart.

And little by little, with help from the de Longs and from Régine's unconscionable ramblings, he pieced together the story of the angry lady on Cape Cod who, envying her daughter, stood in her way and denied her father, or even a career with Nate in marine biology, or any work that drew them close. There was more to the Régine tale of a miscarriage at the hands of an unqualified doctor, there was more to her trips to the States, there was more to the invisible Laurence. Mémé took the secret to her grave and Georges could only investigate so much. Marcel alone controlled access to

Régine. He'd seen through her trite side to her inner workings and, in so doing, and this was the ache that pulsed within, he'd come to terms with himself.

She appeared in robe and smoking a cigarette. When she tried to run a hand up his arm, he shrugged her away.

"We leave shortly for the States," he said.

"What for? I hate it there," she said.

"Business."

"I don't want to go. It's a damnable place."

"You have no choice. We're already booked. Jean has finalized arrangements."

"But…"

"First class? Champagne, my Régine? Come, where is your spirit of adventure?"

"I'd rather stay in Aix."

He turned and ran his hand down her side. "Come now, ugly thighs, what other man would do all this for you?"

She snorted. "Air France, I hope. And I decide where we stay in New York, understand?"

He drew on his cigarette. "Fine."

"I'm going to rest."

He watched her scurry upstairs, a spider seeking shelter under human scrutiny.

He went to the stereo and lowered "Mood" to the turntable. The tunes drifted from the room to the gardens. He returned to the window and leaned against the edge. Images rose of Klee pictured in magazines and on TV. He wondered about a recent article that said she'd developed eccentric ways and disappeared often. The writer alluded to a nurse in a California mental residence who hinted at having taken care of her.

"We spin webs, Klee," he said, "We entice those creatures and things we think we want in our lives but, when we finally get them, we don't know what to do with them. So we spin some more…"

# Chapter 5:
# Aix

LOU BAXTER STOOD OUTSIDE the Duvivier home. There was no sign of life at 10 AM. He guessed the residents slept and paused to deliberate one more time.

Was he trespassing? Invading a private, sacred space? This thought struck him as odd, given his forty-year career of sneaking around, and extracting guilt-rendering truths and lies from most anyone. But to approach a Duvivier? To Lou it seemed slanderous.

He recalled his uncle's stories of the innovative film man who never accepted accolades, who touched hearts through others' works back when France was for the French and the English were weary of any mention of what transpired on the continent. Duvivier had broken records, laying claim to all those enviable statuses, but never in name and never in person.

When Lou was a young man, he saw "Maria" many times, that sleeper film that rocked many for its stark commentary on the truth behind women of the night. "Stranger," another Duvivier collaborative effort, took a provocative look at the Hungarian gypsy culture, those who meandered across Europe laying claim to temporary spaces and what they could capture from the wind and open roads. Unveiling truth via close-ups, physical touch, and unheralded actors, myriad sensations were suggested, and ultimately encouraged the viewer to analyze and appreciate. Lou never left the theaters emotion-free.

He discarded his cigarette. Seconds from the Duvivier legend, what Lou really wanted to do was sit opposite the man and ask why he never expanded on his talents. How did you do what you did and why oh why did you stop?

Even as Lou asked the question, he edged towards answers this day. His quest to uncover what was at first thought to be a case of abandonment had become the prelude to unfurling a drama powerful enough to please ecstatically or maim horribly.

Detective work would no longer be fun. His life's mission was over after today, this he knew from these final five years. With each uncovered fact, with each look at Klee, with each story she allowed to be written, he knew that the witnessing of the rolling out of Marcel's most demanding production in turn exposed his own, ultimate, detection. That night in London, Alice led Lou to the first part of the answer and, even if she hadn't disappeared, he knew her help was no longer required.

As they sipped wine and she stole glances to that back room, she communicated all he needed to know. Her entire presence took on a gossamer patina. She'd removed herself to the era of her most earnest energies. Each sparse phrase was laden with innuendo and expression. She touched the bottle of *Côte du Rhône* as though it contained her blood. Soon into their dine, Lou already knew he participated in a tale. And for the simple, selfish reason that he'd never known one of this kind, he decided to see the story through.

"Alice, Alice," Lou whispered to himself, staring up at the door knocker in Aix. In spite of Duvivier, he felt envy too.

Lou had focused on digging beyond the surface of others' lives, in part because it brought simplicity to his own life. Distraction in the form of a family or a woman could never be entertained, for that would mean a compromise to the other aspect of himself that he had, in the end, allow to claim him. He disregarded that same message of a Duvivier film, and this made him smile. That which gave life meaning. Simply.

Alice, with her darkly-lit humor, her compliant body, her grip that came and went like some revenant from a disturbing dream, had penetrated his surface. Recall that kept him awake at night, not only because of her complexity, but because of a shocking notion, that of being with her forever. He had fallen. Simply.

Lou sat through the dinner without revealing the fact that he and Claude already knew one another. Lou's father had aided Claude's escape from France to England, and the men worked together in the Resistance. After the war, the two families remained in touch and as a young man Lou had been welcome many times Chez Claude. That night Lou brought Alice home and returned to the restaurant after closing time, when he and Claude talked long into that night.

He shook his head. In the event the results proved unfortunate, he could always say it had been Klee who crossed his path, not the other way around. He dismissed this piece of trivia and knocked on Marcel's door.

# Chapter 6:
# London

THE BUS WOUND TOWARDS HEMPSTEAD. Marcel descended and stared at the grillwork of the restaurant. Everything the same, from the olive green façade to the interior lace curtains. Claude's food was surely the finest still. Inside, candles dripped at a table for two, and bore out the glimmer of a young woman's eyes. Marcel stared at the young clientele.

His woman's laughter had been like no other's, the rainwater scent of a new day, an Irish breeze curling around the bay, a wild bloom arching towards the sun. Her nubile fleshy grip. She was the one, he so often thought, and yet he'd allowed her to become like all the others. Thirty years later, he wouldn't kid himself. She was old now, and gone. But their night lay claim to his psyche. They sat in the corner, drinking wine.

"You're a traveler," she said, chin in palm, gaze on him.

"Wanderer is the better word. Gypsy," he said.

She laughed and shook her head. "Such a story maker! You? A tinker? Never!"

"I didn't say tinker."

"Good, because they're dirty." Another laugh.

"They sing. And travel, no?" he asked.

"They move at will, they do."

"When I travel," he said, "I'm free. On location is when things get rough—the demands, the tempers, the frustrations."

"It's exciting, travel."

"I knew you would understand."

"I don't really. I wish I did." A shadow crossed her face.

"To travel is to engage with life." He reached for her slender fingers. "Pale becomes vibrant, shadows distinct. Alice."

"Are you on location now?"

He looked long. "I hope not."

She threw up her shoulders and grinned, stared to the fish tank and sipped her wine. Those eyes. He thought he'd never again see a woman more beautiful.

"Tell me more about tinkers," he said.

"Nothing to tell."

"Alice," he whispered, blinking back her memory as he neared the same back table, now empty but set as though a couple were to arrive any moment. Had others ordered sole and duck and drank from bottles of *Côte du Rhône*? Had they held hands and revealed themselves with their gazes?

He blinked back the memory as a young man approached and ushered him to Claude's upstairs office. In a dim, wood-paneled room filled with books Claude sat behind a cluttered desk. He stood and extended a weathered hand, maneuvered towards his long-time friend. In spite of a lined face and toothless grin, Claude's at-ease shoulders told Marcel that, save age, not much had changed.

"We meet again, *vieux*," Claude rasped. "The Englishman told you I have something for you."

He went to his top drawer and fiddled with its contents as he rambled. Business was better than ever, his son now ran the place. The youth have tastes of the continent and come in droves on weekends. Reservations only, and the tropical fish are still an attraction.

Gripping a pile of envelopes, he said, "I see the lovers. Their eyes hold so much and I remember my own days of falling in love. Each night, another, prettier than before. We joked over 'one, true' love, eh, Marcel? When the cinema brooded in your eyes? You brought yours here and I cooked. I remember it well."

He extended a yellowed envelope to Marcel.

"She posted it requesting I get it to you. I guess she understood our camaraderie, our shared winks, eh?" He sat, rested his head against the back of his chair and stared out at the rain.

"She never returned?" Marcel asked, gazing at the note, the neat script.

"They never do. The really brazen ones, they hang around for a while, but by the next week they're gone, too. But you know better, Marcel, she was not one of them. She was brazen in a different way.

"Funny. I've studied so many couples over the years, some similar. But never have I come across a pair as you and that Irish girl. We never did learn to opt for what was right in front of us, did we?

"That laissez-faire is preserved in your films, in the lines rippling across your cheeks and brow, in the regret that sneaks from those blue eyes. As for me, I no longer avoid the truth. I have lived through the war, seen black nights descend and never lift. I left France to get away. Yet the London air raids and mangled bodies in the subway found me. One cannot run. I face life now and don't concern myself with the outcome." He looked over. "I'm glad you came. I wondered so long about you, and her."

Claude shrugged. "Perhaps I should have destroyed the letter. You took your time. Whatever it contains is old now, too."

Back on the street, Marcel contemplated the rain. The place where the hotel once stood was converted to a ground-floor artist boutique with rental apartments above. Passing it, he found the nearest bus stop.

She wrote no words, only included the poem on a page torn from a book of 18$^{th}$ century poems.

"The Midnight Court" Bryan Merryman

> Down with marriage! It's out of date;
> It exhausts the stock and cripples the state.
> The priest has failed with whip and blinker,
> Now give a chance to Tom the Tinker,
> And mix and mash in Nature's can
> The tinker and the gentleman!
> Let lovers in every lane extended
> Struggle and strain as God intended
> And locked in frenzy bring to birth
> The morning glory of the earth;
> The starry litter, girl and boy
> Who'll see the world once more with joy.
> Clouds will break and skies will brighten
> Mountains bloom and spirits lighten,
> And men and women praise your might,
> You who restore the old delight.

He fumbled with the paper, stared at the envelope's handwriting, recalling how she'd recited the poem to him, softly into his ear as he lay half asleep by her side. Whispers lingering on her lips.

"The morning glory of the earth…"

Back then, when dawn had come, he readied to leave. She sat in bed, covered by a sheet, her legs snug under

639

her. Against the white linens, she was raven and pale. When he turned to say goodbye he had the instinct to reach for her and never let go.

How they'd met round and round in their bodies. The pauses, the silence after lovemaking, her delicate breathing, being human, together, as it should have been. He would never love again.

He got off the bus and walked, eyes misting. He saw her everywhere, that playful teasing smile, the way she grabbed him, clutching without possessiveness. With his body, she'd discovered the outposts of her own, but did she realize what she'd left for his taking? Perhaps it was really she who took from him, for he'd walked out that door, his feet on the stairs, while her gentle panting rang in his ears. There is once in a life that one loves.

At a shopping area, the sun peeked out and he stopped at a tall iron gate that fronted a luxurious home, a park, trees, dying flowers.

How had he let her die to him?

"And mix and match in Nature's can, the tinker and the gentleman," he said.

When Lou Baxter uttered Alice's name, Marcel hardly blinked. Years before, on returning to Aix and playing the gift album, he'd solved the mystery for himself. His daughter sang to him. Indeed had been singing to him since he first heard her voice in that New York shop, her unworldly plea. "Father, come to me."

There was time. He would come to her. He would make amends. There was certainty, and sorrow, in the void. In the force of his nature. They communicated still.

That night, he dragged Régine to the airport and they boarded a flight to Shannon, Ireland.

♥ ♥ ♥

Lou Baxter watched them board. In the end, Marcel Duvivier followed the dictates of a sonnet and his own gut to produce his finest yet. When Marcel had asked about Alice's whereabouts, Lou had not told him. Up to Duvivier to determine which of his two women to seek out.

But would they be fair to Klee? And would there ever be the retracing of steps? To a family life that would at best be the shadow of what could have been? How could a new mould reconfigure? How could any type of renewal replace the colorful, chagrined, yet ever so determined style of all three? Did mending even matter?

"Mix and match in Nature's can…" he murmured.

He got in his car. Where had Alice gone? And should he tell her now how much he loved her? Before the father of her child did the same?

# Chapter 7

IN THE CENTER OF KINEMMAERA, Marcel rented two rooms at Stacey's Bed and Breakfast. Though compact, the upstairs accommodations shared a rustic bath down the hall, perfect for Marcel but the furthest from Régine's preferences. In black linen blouse and skirt, she whined over the wind and cold at the same time she puffed one cigarette after another. Marcel smirked as he settled in and, when she stopped at his door to continue her ranting, he blew her a kiss. Once organized, he announced that he was taking a walk, then locked her in her room.

Régine screamed such that the owner, Bernie, a spidery woman of seventy, rushed to open the door. After hearing Régine's tale of a recurring case of claustrophobia and her need for frequent outdoor walks, Bernie led her to the bar, prepared a warm whiskey, and scurried in search of walking clothes for her visitor.

In no time, bundled in thick wools and water-proof jacket, her feet protected by Wellington boots, Régine scowled at her lumpy appearance while Bernie suggested paths that followed the sea.

Outside, she covered eyes from the bright sun that hovered at the horizon. Little time remained before dark. She shuffled towards the shops looking for signs of life.

How she hated him, she muttered as her boots pounded the hard dirt surface. The nerve of him shunting her away and thinking he could imprison her! How dare he not include her in whatever clandestine activity he was up to.

A few people glanced her way but no one stopped her. She scowled at their genteel shyness, how they tried to be so unobtrusive in the same maddening style as Cape Codders.

From one end of town to the other, she saw no sign of Marcel. At the Norman keep with gravestones in its yard, she rounded a bend that took her past moored boats and modest blue and pink homes. Back at Stacey's she went inside, furious for wasting time in such clothing.

Bernie prepared a cup of tea which Régine refused in favor of another hot toddy. Farmers began arriving for their daily pints of Guinness. With a glance and nod to the newcomer, they settled at their places, by and large ignoring her as they took in the news on TV. Régine grew garrulous after two more drinks.

"So, Bernie," she asked, "what about this cute little village? Any visiting foreigners other than us?

"Ah, for sure, dear. There's always Germans, they love catching the salmon. And the French come, too, to tent on the outskirts. Yanks of course. They like it here actually. Lots of spirit, the Yanks."

"What's the latest gossip?" Régine asked, thinking back to the habits of those on the Cape and how they reveled in news of any sort.

Oh, we had a few poets come through—of national renown, too! Stayed at the priest's house. Poor man. Died last year. Didn't leave his house to any family— such a darling cottage! Pastor from St. Michael's came the other day talking about using it as a meeting place. Then of course, there was Klee."

Régine gulped. "Oh?"

"The singer, you know. Born here, poor thing. Mind you, many think she's a bit queer but I felt for the child, what with that mother of hers. No wonder…"

"What about her mother?"

With a nod of her head and flick to her long blue-tinted braid, Bernie darted glances to insure no one was listening. Leaning towards Régine, she said, "Took trips to London—men, you know! Oh, it's years ago now. Lord knows the woman left town and all, never to be seen again. I can't help but imagine the desperate life that last child of hers led, no matter her odd looks and bookish ways. Fathered by a one-night stand, they claim. Of course, doesn't matter now, does it? All the money that young thing has. But still, she was a bastard child plain and simple."

Régine swallowed hard. "Tell me more."

An hour later, knowing all she needed to know, Régine bid good evening to take another walk. Before leaving, she snuck upstairs to Marcel's unlocked room and rummaged around, eventually finding what she'd hope she would.

This time, she marched to the church and its gravestones. The winds had calmed and faint moonlight cast shadows in the yard. Not twenty feet from where she stood, Marcel stared down at a gravestone. She hid beside a squat tree. He lingered for a while, occasionally brushing tears. After placing a reverent touch to the stone, he wandered off, whereupon she crept to the stone and confirmed Bernie's observation—that it belonged to that person Romney, Klee's only companion while she lived here.

Back at Stacey's she snuck to her room, closed herself inside, and lit a cigarette using the book of matches she found in Marcel's room, the one that read 'Chez Claude.' Tapping reflectively, she contemplated her next move. Cigarette done, she went downstairs to use the phone, dialing the London number on the matchbook.

The person who took her call confirmed that the restaurant had been around since the war, that the original owner still ran the place.

Back in her room she lay in bed. When Marcel's footsteps finally headed up the staircase, she waited for his door to open. Once the pub closed down and all was silent below, she lit one more cigarette. When it was done, she'd slip into her sheer nightie and confront Marcel.

So, he was trying to bring her down by dragging her to New York or Boston or wherever he had plans to take her so as to ruin her reputation in front of Evan de Roche and hence the entire de Roche organization. Marcel had some gall, given his own story. After all, she'd not had anything to do with the company in ages, it was his baby now. He probably also had plans to find Laurence and expose all that, too, to turn the knife and make her feel guilty, all this in order to protect himself from his own sins! Ah, but he had little real sense of Régine's cunning if that were the case!

Tracing the lines of her silk outfit, she felt the familiar heat of want, the same heat that sustained them in Aix, where she wished dearly they still lolled, oblivious to their pasts, she in his arms, he in hers. In truth, she had found her match in Marcel, and admired his ability to embrace a challenge. Indeed his absence of feeling towards her was the exact formula for endearing her more to him and, she liked to imagine, him to her. They were the same whether he wanted to admit it or not, what with their dreadful secrets, their mistakes of high order, their lack of parenting. When she went in there, she'd seduce him first, for her neediness in that regard was nonnegotiable. Once she exposed him, well, he was hers and then she'd have that body until she tired of him. But, first things first.

Her eyes fell to her fleshy stomach and scaled legs. How worn out her body had become over the years and how she struggled to combat its natural tendencies! With the help of tight bodices and starvation diets, for the most part she'd succeeded. Growing old had compromised her in so many ways. As she sat listening to hot air run through pipes of her room she wondered fleetingly why she couldn't have ended up like Bernie, graying yet amusing, giving and caring, no one to comment on her age or looks because she'd built a life around other, less daunting priorities.

Of course, Marcel wasn't fooled by her attempts to turn back time, but even his posturing endeared her, engendering a feeling of familiarity shared between longtime couples—a camaraderie foreign to her. Even tonight in the graveyard, his sorrow had translated to the closest thing she'd known to identifiable concern, a yearning that, she hesitated to admit, rendered her vulnerable. Yes, her heart desired him too, and though she knew he knew, her battle to feign indifference would be over after tonight, for she'd control him on one level while he controlled her on another and their coupling would be cemented with no turning back.

She squirted on perfume, lit a cigarette and walked to his open door and went in. A book's pages abandoned on his lap, his wanton gaze was so revealing she had trouble keeping silent. Lifting her top over her head, she draped it over his as she snuggled under the covers. He undressed, snapped off the light, and joined her.

His lips were parched and breathe stale as he fondled her. She fought to quell sighs and tried to pretend his motions had no effect but, even though he was miles away, she still verged on climax. Whether she screamed or whether she remained stone still, his body had no intention of cooperating tonight. Though she was aware of this, it did not prevent her from climaxing.

After, as they lay there, she found herself perplexed and hesitant to speak and this surprised her. She thought of Klee, the television face so vividly familiar now with those same blueberry eyes as those of this man, the laissez-faire temperament, too. The softly seductive tunes she sang, chants from a chapel void of ceremony, rippling chords and dissonant themes, a haunting of the purest kind.

She ran fingers through his hair and noted for the first time the slight kink, a trait he passed to his daughter no doubt. But then a vision of Laurence and Nate came to mind, and she shivered to think that the man lying beside her shared a loss the same as Nate's—a daughter among the living with no reference point to father. And who had been the cause for Laurence's pain? And for Klee's? Here they lay, side by side.

Her lips quivered and she touched his cheek. He pushed her hand aside but not before she detected the dampness from tears.

Half dreading, half anxious, she whispered, "Bastard father."

Not a muscle moved until he sat up directly and went to the window. He placed a hand on the ledge, head bent. She covered herself with the sheet and tore at a nail until it broke, then attacked another.

"Marcel. It's time you accept me as yours for I'll never leave you. We are the same and we owe one another. If you go your way, I will follow. If you stay, I'll protect you. We need to be protected, you and I, for the world doesn't look kindly on the likes of us. Your daughter will never take you back. The damage was done that night Chez Claude, mon amour."

"You slut!" he exclaimed.

Narrowing her gaze, she smiled and kept her voice low. "It's tough, I know. I didn't really want to hurt Laurence, but how could one prevent it? When one's own freedom dangles? They're all the same anyway, children, selfish, ego-centric, demanding. Yours found her own place anyway. Trust me, she hates you. Don't bother…"

His fist went through the pane, shattering glass in all directions. She covered her face.

In seconds, shouts rose from below followed by the pattering of feet. He apologized and assured that the damages would be paid for. In time, the house returned to its former quiet.

Régine slipped into a robe and went to the open window. Tracing an edge of cut glass, she drew blood and placed finger to lips. Towards him, she offered the same.

"Taste, mon cher, it's good. It will sustain us. I love you. Always remember, you started this. You, *Monsieur le président de Roche Frères, a tout débouché.*"

"Get out," he said.

In her room, she relaxed against her pillows, comfortable that sleep would soon follow. For sure they'd be returning to Paris in the morning.

❤ ❤ ❤

Yet the next day at Shannon, they boarded a flight to New York. In a scene that would be recalled for years at the ticket counters, Régine threw a tantrum that required the intervention of police and airport officials. Marcel claimed more contacts throughout the world than she, and in time she was forced onto the plane.

In first class, as they flew over the Atlantic, she swore continually and promised revenge. He kept her pumped with champagne and largely ignored her, especially when she mellowed and eased a hand under his shirt or tried to coddle a kiss.

"Go ahead, Duvivier," she finally said after several failed attempts. "You cannot run from the truth that I discovered. You will be suffer, too, once this journey is over. I promise you that, you bastard."

# Chapter 8

AS THE HELICOPTER ROUNDED TOWARDS a landing strip, Barbara Mills studied the Maine coastline. Brown-maroon trees hinted at cooler weather. She hoped her wardrobe would suffice, and contemplated visiting local stores in search of woolen shirts and perhaps boots. Evan fancied a hike and Klee was an outdoor type, too.

Beside her, Evan reviewed papers detailing Klee's engagements. She leaned over to plant a kiss and then returned to view the landscape below.

Her first trip East, she'd jumped at the opportunity. Now that their arrival neared, she grew skittish wondering if Klee would exhibit her tantrums or shun her. The superstar never once gave Barbara the time of day and usually Evan was the one to excuse Klee's antics, but Barbara sensed the animosity anyhow.

Ill-will was foreign to her and, at the age of eighteen, a sheltered upbringing and youth of tame social interactions prevented her from internalizing less than charitable behaviors, even in the Hollywood milieu she now revolved in with Evan.

From their first meeting when she auditioned for a bit part to the whirlwind of activities that followed—dinner clubs, premiers, rehearsals at the big studios—

Evan enlivened her days with his direct, amorous attentions. How fortunate she was to be his girlfriend.

She ignored rumors that he kept many women and that high-maintenance Klee lived a bizarre secret life. She focused instead on his affections and constant surprises of flowers, weekends at the wine country inns of Northern California, and other lavish gifts. She welcomed each day and tried not to dwell on tabloid reporters or gossips who approached her to find out more about their relationship.

He did baffle her at times, though. His hellish pace for days on end worried her regardless of the movie stars, bestselling authors and hit singers to his credit. This darling of the bachelor set seemed to survive on air and business deals, and she wondered was this lifestyle one she could support indefinitely. Plus, when he did take time out for dinners with her or walks on the beach, his distracted regard perplexed her. While most of his attentions targeted major results or confrontations, and his mind rarely departed from work, in the odd moment when he relaxed, his faraway stare bespoke a deeply personal drama. She wondered would she ever really know him. Still, he gave her many things, watched over her, and saw to it that her exposure to the media stayed at a minimum. She hoped they'd one day marry.

"Will Klee be home?" she asked.

"If she's not banging away at the piano, or sleeping, she's on one of her walks."

"You sound tired of her, Evan," she said.

"She's a tiring person, Barbara," he said, holding her hand. "Sometimes I don't know. The old Klee with the Irish temper and bookworm mentality was exasperating but at least I could manage her. This woman is another story entirely."

"That bad?"

"She skipped out on the Palladium show! I had that booked for months and MTV execs were due to sit in. That's the next big music venue and she needed to show her stuff. She didn't even explain herself later." He looked at her. "You're pale. Don't let my stories scare you. She's not going to hurt you."

"So many rumors about her…"

"Companionless, ruthlessly clinging to solitude, a solo act if I ever saw one, so the rumors fly. I could care less. What I want is for her to return to L. A. and complete her contract this year. Otherwise, we're finished, she and I."

"You mean it?"

"I have to take a stand. She's a conduit to my own creativity in so many ways, but a lot of that has run its course. We've found our respective paths. If she doesn't support me advancing her career, she's going to have to find someone else who can put up with her."

"You might be better off…"

"She spends thousands a week on her reading habit, orders the entire contents of book shops to be delivered to this place. Think of that! Even now when she rarely reads! She goes for days without food then flies to New York to binge. If she stops performing, the money dries up and with it, her crazy lifestyle. What happens then?"

The helicopter began its descent. Barbara gripped Evan's hand.

An hour later at Klee's, Barbara sat on the marble floor of the piano room staring at her hostess and trying to quell nervousness. With febrile movement Klee walked in circles around her. Wearing all black, with hair the same, she cackled and chuckled. Would Evan ever finish dressing and come down, Barbara worried?

"What are you doing, Klee?" Barbara finally asked, rising to the sound of Evan making noises in the upstairs hallway.

"Stay where you are!" Klee ordered. "He'll be down so take it easy. I'm…watching you."

"Why be so stalking?"

"I see the new woman in my old man's life. The new woman I see."

Barbara gritted her teeth and straightened her shoulders. "He's wonderful to me."

"He loves only one."

Barbara bit her lower lip. "Klee…"

"Only one!" Klee screamed. "This I know!" She rushed to the piano and banged out chords, pumping the damper pedal with fervor.

"There is only one for Evan. His heart was stolen long ago—like all our hearts—like us all!"

Evan appeared in the doorway and Barbara rushed to him, burying herself in his chest.

"Klee, stop this," Evan said.

He went to the piano and wrestled her hands from the keyboard. "Stop it!"

"Devil boy!"

"What the hell are you on, Klee!"

She leaned back against him, rolled her eyes upwards. "Hee, Evan, little Evan."

"Klee, please." He slowly rocked her head at his chest until she stopped.

Steps were heard in the entryway. A wide-eyed boy stood briefly in the hall then approached Klee.

Klee looked over and her eyes lit up. In French, she said, "Christophe, come. We have our adventure today. I have ideas."

The two went outside. Barbara collapsed on the floor and wept.

"I'm so sorry, Barbara. Please, try and hang in there. We're almost finished here. Go upstairs and rest. I'll be right up."

Once in the bedroom she turned down the covers. Closing the curtains, she noticed Evan standing below. A woman approached him.

Jean-clad and slender, her long dark hair in a braid, she crossed arms in front of a baggy sweatshirt. Even from a distance, Barbara detected her arresting presence and felt discomfort for reasons she did not understand. She pressed her nose to the pane.

The woman stopped some ten feet short of Evan, as if surprised to see him. They stared at one another. Barbara sensed a connection between the two—feelings she dared not label, looks deeper than friendship, emotion-filled former recalls.

Evan spoke in murmurs difficult to hear. The woman nodded, her facial expressions complex, and remained fixed in place until Evan took steps towards her. He extended a hand but she did not take it. He talked. The woman continued to stare, as if Evan's presence conditioned her to a state that only her gaze was capable of communicating. This seemed to be enough for both of them, and their looks were incapable of lies.

She turned away and snapped the curtain closed, but was unable to resist the sight of the two below, and returned to the window. The woman had turned away and was making towards the house next door. Evan watched the woman's every step.

"Only one, only one." Klee's words haunted Barbara that night even as, in the usual way, Evan made love with her and afterwards relaxed into sleep without any mention of the woman next door. Barbara chose not to pry. If he woke during the night, which sometimes he did thinking about business, she was unaware of it.

The next day, he was as attentive and loving as always and thankfully Klee was better behaved, though Evan was unable to extract any promise of sticking to her contract. He didn't waste time after that, and told Barbara he'd done everything he could.

On the first leg of their journey home, he took her hand, kissed it, and said, "Let's get married. I love you."

The following week, they announced their engagement. Evan spent hours with his lawyers, wrapping up ongoing business, closing his offices cross-country, retiring his work force. He called for a meeting in New York to include his team of lawyers, vice-presidents and subsidiary managers. He sent word to Marcel to meet him. He wanted everything settled as quickly as possible.

They made plans to honeymoon in Asia and Australia and then, as Evan put it, "settle down to a low-key California life." He never once mentioned the woman in Glenrock, referred to Klee in the past tense, and drew on Barbara's vitality and strength as if it were his own. As Evan de Roche retired from the world, Barbara became his new, more intimate one.

She fell quickly in to the pattern he desired—candle-lit dinners, walks by the shore, movies for fun only. She easily adapted to this less-distracted man and forgot her past concerns about his divided attentions. Giving him her all, she told herself over and over she was the most fortunate of women. That she was his 'only one.'

# Chapter 9

KLEE WANDERED THE COAST FOR DAYS, most often with Christophe at her side. As they cowered under boulders or scampered across meadows in search of pointy hats and peeping voices, they promised each other they were on the verge of uncovering the fairy hiding places. Klee continually chuckled to herself. Christophe practiced listening to the wind as Klee instructed, and detecting music in the tides and smashing waves.

"There are secrets and eternities in those sounds," she would say.

He begged her to tell him of stardom and her trysts with the rich and famous. Sometimes she conceded a tale or two, and always used accurate names and places so he wouldn't confuse her intentions. She allowed his curiosity for he was pure, disinclined to focus on her odd behavior and looks. She also recognized a fellow dreamer seeking worlds beyond his own horizon.

Though she did not care to mold him in any way, she did explain Romney's influence and what the old woman taught her about vigilance and silence, her songs of simplicity that most ignored in favor of the bustle of 'normalcy.'

"Don't live in cities," she warned, "and listen to your heart. There is much bothersome noise around you so it will be hard, but you have the country and quiet. You have all you need."

"But I want to be famous too," he said. "My friends are jealous of our friendship. The say no one can get near you. But we're good friends, aren't we, Klee?"

Following questions like these, Klee wanted to shake him, spill her sorrowful truth so he could see that the world of glamour was not as he imagined. But he was so young and his were, like most humans, strange distorted requirements.

She conversed often with Romney, her lips moving in silent repartee even in Christophe's presence, who studied her with curiosity and even mimicked her.

They discovered a cave tucked inside cliffs that fell in sharp angles to the sea. There, protected from the salt spray and biting winds, he recited verses she taught him. Correcting his mistakes only rarely, she would nod and continue her odd chuckles, reciting back more lines for him to memorize. He followed her every movement and absorbed her every word. Had she not been beyond emotion, she might have cried at this devotion.

They discussed death but he wanted to live. Live, make money, travel, like Klee. When she scoffed at him, he told her she had no right for she had done all that and more. Her eyes glazed over and she mentally removed herself from him for a time. He was never bothered by this, even when they sat at length in silence. If Laurence called, he left Klee, and often she would spend the night in the darkened space, waking the next day to make for her large, empty house.

For years a story had developed in her mind. Romney helped her correct mistakes and lay out dramas and together they'd laugh over this tale. When she got stuck, Klee would ask Romney to help her but the old woman never would. With a finger to her lips, her sign that it was time to listen for the wee people, Romney ordered Klee to keep to her own thoughts, for that was where she'd access her strength and from where she'd hear from the fairies. She stole moments, then hours, and whole mornings and days as her body went neglected and she sat in the cave working on her story.

She summoned strength to tell Evan she didn't give a fuck about what he did with all her money, that she was already dead so it didn't matter. When Even flew in a medical professional, she hid in the cave until the man left.

Anonymity, the book would have been called, had she the strength.

One day, it was sunny and almost warm. She'd promised Christophe that the next calm day, she'd take him overnight to the cave to watch stars until dawn. So, that afternoon, she rang at Laurence's door.

"I would like to take Christophe camping overnight in the cave."

At the front door, Laurence signaled for Klee to enter. They moved to the kitchen and sat at a heavy wood table where tomatoes and peppers were arranged for canning. After preparing a cup of tea for Klee, Laurence continued with her work.

Klee studied her. The lack of resemblance to Christophe and empty mischief-free regard evinced, as did the sorrow in her eyes, the weariness in her gait, and the determination in certain gestures, as if straying from her straightforward, menial tasks was to be avoided at all cost.

"He enjoys playing with you," she finally said. "But I don't want him overdoing it. His father worries."

"Do you?" Klee asked.

She shrugged. "Christophe can take care of himself, even at his age."

Gradually, Klee realized in whose presence she sat. This was the woman from the film "Silence," the sea-swept hair and big brown eyes, but minus the joy and effervescence. Nonetheless, it was her.

"Why didn't you work with Evan on "Silence?""

Laurence shot Klee a look then regained her composure. "I handed over the rights years ago. It was not what I wished to do."

"Did you ever see the finished product? You were the reason for that Oscar," Klee said. When Laurence didn't respond, she added, "I have four projectors in that house, viewing screens too. There's a copy of your film somewhere. If you ever want to watch, my door's open to you."

Laurence continued chopping.

Klee persisted. "You thrived in those waters. It was more fulfilling than this silly life."

"Why do you call it silly? It has become your life as well."

"For you there is still time."

"I have what I need."

The sounds of jar tops being arranged and her knife rapping the chopping board filled the room. When Laurence finished, Klee helped her carry jars to the pantry. They heard Guy's truck rolling towards the house.

"I'll be gone," Klee said.

Laurence walked her to the door. "Christophe can go with you to the cave, but only for one night."

After Klee left, Guy questioned Laurence's decision, expressing his concern for the boy with such an odd woman for a whole overnight.

"She's lonely, Guy," Laurence said. "Christophe gives her joy."

"How could such a mega-star be lonely? You're ignorant of what the rich are capable of, Laurence.

People like her aren't as sensitive to what it takes to care for a small child."

"Guy, please don't argue. Christophe will be fine."

Guy prattled a while longer but gave in eventually.

♥ ♥ ♥

After Christophe was off with Klee, Laurence busied about the house until Guy left for a two-day trip to the upstate woods. At noon, a telegram arrived. After reading it, she sat at the kitchen table for a long time, then went to the cupboard to fetch the reel of film Bea placed there years before. Next door, she borrowed Klee's projector, and returned to watch the film.

Evan was nowhere to be seen but his mark was invasive, even in the sections dedicated to her diving; he must have instructed that they remain intact. She watched the film several times until shadows crossed the screen and the afternoon turned to dusk. She rewound the tape, closed curtains to block light, and watched the film—her film—again, then again.

Though time had erased their union, she would have traces of Evan yet in this film, and would cherish one of the many reasons why he still loved her and she him.

Now this latest news. Would she develop a personality like her neighbor? Would events force her from her shell? Or would she succumb to these new demands? And what of Christophe and her marriage to Guy?

She carefully packed up the projector then cleared away her day's work from the table. Peering beyond the curtains, she noted how the skies had darkened. The wind, too, howled from a direction that made the bay churn with whitecaps. She turned on the radio for the weather.

# Chapter 10

THE FAX LAY ON THE TABLE. To David Marcu, there was no doubt this scrawl was Klee's handwriting. So, she wished to change the status of her financial holdings. He bit his lower lip then let out a slow whistle. This much money changing hands at this juncture.

As Evan's and Klee's lawyer, he was used to their quirky requests and odd-hour demands. Had it not been for Evan's easy-going style and logical mind, he'd have quit working with them long ago, for Klee had been the opposite. At the same time, he knew he'd never have reached his renown and wealth but for these two key clients.

His meeting with Evan and Marcel an hour away, this glitch was sure to slow things down. Collecting his thoughts, he phoned around unsuccessfully for Evan. He did confirm however that Marcel checked in to the Ritz and awaited word for the meeting.

David already lined up his team of lawyers, clerks, and Wall Street gurus and all were prepared for today's news and how it would likely affect markets and business. Until this morning, he thought he had everything covered.

Why his client was leaving the post as helmsman of the largest holding company on three continents baffled him. At their meeting the week before, he watched closely as Evan announced he was retiring and that David would be in charge of all re-structuring and financial adjustments.

When David asked about Klee, Evan was nonplussed.

"Her money is my money, it's always been that way. It stays lumped together. She hasn't straightened up her act so we're through as far as her celebrity goes, but she still needs someone to manage her holdings. Let it be de Roche USA for the time being."

"Evan, you're talking over a billion for her alone. We need to divest, just in case…"

"Do what you must but keep it as simple as possible."

David nodded. "Anything else I should know?"

"Yes. After Barbara and I are married, I never want to hear from you again. I want you to manage the money, do as Marcel asks but never call, write, or otherwise contact me."

"I assume Marcel makes the decisions on inheritance?"

"You two can work that out."

"And Klee would get her portion."

"Whatever. I step down effective immediately."

"Evan," David said, "this is highly irregular."

"Oh, and take your ten percent as usual. And give Marcel power of attorney."

"I already have your power of attorney."

"Good," Evan said, extending a hand. "David, it's been a pleasure."

David went home that night, told his wife Merle what happened and announced that they were now independently wealthy. He suggested she start hunting for that 19th century manor in the Cevennes they'd dreamed of.

Though Evan was not beyond such a move, David did not seriously entertain the idea that Evan would absent himself like this. Some childish sense of camaraderie kept him from believing his billionaire client would never again want to attend to his affairs by himself. Evan would never really let everything go, would he?"

David brushed back his hair, mulling over the last few weeks and how there was the touch of the profane in it all. Merle would no longer have to work if she didn't want to, he'd only need to show up periodically to approve money transfers and sign paperwork. Would this be how his days would proceed? Long intervals of leisure time at his chateau or exclusive resort? Was that really what he'd worked himself blind for all these years? Would it all be fun as in the past?

His secretary buzzed. "Marcel Duvivier is here."

"I'll meet him in the suite," David said, reaching for his jacket. "We'll need about thirty minutes before the others join us.

# Chapter 11

"HE PROMISED DINNER TONIGHT," Marcel said to David. *"Nom de Dieu,* my young nephew and his games." In navy blue Cartier suit that complimented his eyes, Marcel studied the city below David's high rise windows.

"Important now is the inheritance. You did speak about that?" David asked.

"I am informed of what is to be done."

"You've made your decision, I presume?"

Marcel continued to study traffic below. Turning, he broke into a grin, and reached into his pocket. "Piece of cake, as you say here."

"Pardon?" David asked, accepting a slip of paper from Marcel.

As he read the name, David's face paled.

Régine nodded elegantly at the grey and navy suits filing past her to their seats in the conference room, their owners wearing stern regards. She flashed a wide smile to the random attentive lawyer. In crimson suit, black silk blouse and diamond brooch on her lapel, she crossed ankles and poised her solid gold pen on her blank note pad, where everyone could see her red lacquered nails. Across from her, Marcel reviewed numbers with the handsome lawyer she recognized as Evan's. Others drew folders from briefcases amidst a refined hum and the clink of water glasses. Two secretaries carted in fax machines and arranged paperwork while technicians checked connections to phones and visual aids. From the corridor, a reporter was shooed away. Thirty-eight present, her final count. An impressive lot for this business deal of the decade.

Whatever the reason for her inclusion, she was content to be part of this day. Toying with a strand of hair, she wondered when Evan would arrive and thought how splendid it would be that Marcel was taking over the company in the wake of Evan's stepping down. Given his change of heart about running de Roche Frères US over the last months, his taking of a wife made sense, too. Finally he was giving up on Laurence, something he should have done years ago.

She caught Marcel's stare and returned a sweet smile but to no avail. In his look, no hint of what he was thinking. Those eyes, though mesmerizing, possessed that same controlled yet fevered omniscience as that of his nephew, a trait she envied and fell victim to, in spite of herself.

The doors closed and the meeting began.

In no time, the tension clung to sweaty palms and dampening shirts and ties. A few older men wiped their brows. The breakup of the conglomerate into smaller chunks a given, this absurd new twist was proving harder to swallow. To these men accustomed to drawn-out legal and political battles for turf and dollars, this straightforward final request rendered even the most garrulous among them mute with curiosity if not downright confusion.

Center stage sat Régine, sputtering, cursing, and even moaning in desperate attempts to control what she realized she could no longer, ever, manage. The five-year-old boy currently residing in Glenrock would be the legal inheritor of the entire de Roche empire. Until the child reached the age of majority, Marcel would manage the re-organization and day-to-day affairs on both sides of the Atlantic, a fortune that influenced the very heartbeat of numerous industries and political bases.

"This is absurd!" Régine screamed. "Careless Evan is not in his right mind! Don't you see?"

"I agree," one lawyer finally said. "Highly irregular. We have written contracts for our services over the long term. Have those been worked through?"

Others joined in until the room was a Tower of Babel. Tolerating this interlude of emotion, Marcel sat in his chair, hand in pocket, fondling the fax from his daughter and her mother's poem. His daughter would have her way and, when he finally set eyes on her, he would begin with the news of what transpired in this room.

The energy settled to nervous anticipation when the members realized Marcel was not bending or otherwise open to negotiation. Most of them wore resigned expressions, aware of their redundancy under the emerging corporate structure and likely assessing their financial circumstances in the light of a future without de Roche Frères. Having already made their fortunes, older men wore relaxed expressions, as if their freedom from the corporate world couldn't come soon enough.

Her fears on par with the younger clan, Régine fidgeted and fussed with hair and nails, all the while throwing lascivious regards toward Marcel and muttering under her breath her lack of surprise that Evan had passed on this circus.

"I assume," said Marcel to Régine, "that you understand what has been said and have no further comment."

"This is absurd and you know it," she hissed.

"I'm afraid I do not, Régine. Pray tell."

She stood. Gripping with her claws one chair's back and then the next, she prowled. "Don't do this to me. Don't you dare."

"It's as the parties wish," Marcel said.

She scurried around the table until she was inches from him. "You! You knew all along about this, didn't you! You fucking bastard father you!"

He grabbed her hand and shoved it hard against the table, pressing his fingers against her. Lowering his voice so only she heard, he said, "Leave now, Régine. It's over and there's nothing you can do."

"I most certainly can…"

He pressed his hand hard once again and she winced. "There is nothing you can do."

He stood and, gripping her arm, he led her to the conference door, where he handed her over to two waiting security guards. Her swears could be heard all the way down to the elevators.

After, word spilled to the streets below, into offices and trading rooms, on Wall Street, and to boardrooms worldwide. Newspaper editors scrambled to replace headlines in order to move this story of financial drama to the fore. The singer and her manager of singular origins and habits fronted a corporate change of hands not unlike royal rule centuries before, when underage princes took the control of large countries the fortunes of which they were barely aware.

667

# Chapter 12

"YOU DON'T INTEND TO DRIVE all the way to Maine," Régine said. "There's a storm coming. Look! My outfit is already spoiled by the damp from your dragging me to the street! I will return any time to Paris, so turn this little vehicle around and we'll be off for the airport. Pretend all this never happened."

She bit fingernails and rubbed perspiration from her forehead. "Too many pills." Her supply of uppers and downers exhausted, she had no means of replacing them. Perhaps it was time to cut them out anyway, once this was over with.

Looking in the car mirror, she adjusted disheveled hair. "Ha! You think you can imprison me in a hotel room and that I'd sit quiet and not search your possessions?"

He looked at her quickly. She laughed and stared out at the rain. The maid would find her stamped addressed envelope stashed under the pillow. Since Marcel checked out with no forwarding address, the hotel would be compelled to post it. In a few days, Marcel's photo would be paired with Klee's all over the place. He'd cower and plead for a renegotiation of all this financial mess, beg her to deny the story. Though he was also capable of hurting her, he couldn't mentally torture her

668

any more than he already had. And, should Régine choose the lawsuit and abuse route, any lawyer would come after him like a bull to its target.

Looking back, she should have figured this Klee connection for herself. After all those nights in Provence when he'd be high on whiskey and low in spirit, watching the television mechanically, mulling for long stretches and not sharing his thoughts. When he did deign to address her, his regard was full of contempt, as though he knew every detail of her past deeds. He could imagine such things, given he was capable of the same. But behind his glares, a sorrow so deep she could only attribute it to that which he felt from the bottom of his own vulnerable heart, emotions encircling a child or a lover. Since he was man to no woman, it must be a child that held sway over this man who, all his life, resisted genuine feelings.

Soon all this would be over. He'd pay her to shut up and, for the right price, she would. She'd return to France with enough means to live out her days and this time she'd seek the companionship of no one. Men had always been means to an end, tools. Plus, she'd overstayed her welcome with this one.

Why had she stayed, she wondered? His magic touch? The feel of his body? That horrifically satisfying hold he maintained no matter how hard she tried to feign nonchalance? All these aspects touched her nerves and, for a while, even teased at her own vulnerabilities.

"So, *mon cher*," she whispered, "what do you expect from this reunion? That I will lay myself at my daughter's feet and beg forgiveness? That she will relinquish responsibility for the child? That she and I will kiss and make up? Do you think we will make a cute mother-daughter pair? Do you think I should have a family portrait taken right away? Or once we return to Paris *en famille*?

"You needn't bother. Allow me a portion of the wealth and we're done. She can have the child, and the rest of the money, too. Laurence detests me anyhow. That was the problem all along, but you don't look closely to see that side, do you? She never cared for me, only that father of hers. All the while I was trying so hard to be a good wife and mother, the two of them were carrying on right under my nose. Bet you didn't know that, did you?

"You drive without comment. You watch these dull roads and hills and plot my demise. You say, 'Régine will get her due' but you understand little. How could you? You haven't lived through what I have! You never saw Laurence at work. You know I am the mother of that boy. I have my rights. I can protest and take you to court and the courts will give me my child back. Then you won't have any control over his future. I will!

"You think that once she sees me Laurence will let you past her front door? Ha! You're not thinking carefully enough then! You cannot control everything like you control de Roche Frères. I was the one in control at all times. Why don't you see THAT and use it to your advantage. You and Evan and your cozy relationship. You and he—asses! Stop the car! I need pills. Where's the nearest pharmacy. Stop, I say!

"Hours to go yet. What are you planning? To barge in there and wake them all? You'll never get beyond the foolish dogs, pigs, and cows. They're all close and protective up there. Then again, you cannot comprehend what those qualities really mean."

She pulled out her bottle of Chanel No. 5 perfume, splashed it to her chest, hiked her skirt, and turned knees towards him.

"Don't ignore me. Please. I need you. Why do you think I've stayed with you all these months? For a tryst like your other lovers? Don't think I didn't learn about you while we were together. All over Paris they talk about you as this enigma, but I know better. You're no different than any of us. You're not the mystery you wish people to consider you. You're no more a humble reticent type than I am!"

She touched him and he shrugged her away. Oncoming headlights from a double container truck approached and the vehicle veered too quickly past them. She wept but that did no good. Marcel kept on driving. She fought hunger pangs and the lust coming from her loins. If only she had a drink, or drugs. She opened the bottle of perfume again and splashed lavishly, filling the car with its thick flowery scent. She rolled down the window and laughed continually until her face and hair were soaked. Nothing affected Marcel.

"Do you want me, Marcel? I want you. I want your fingers tracing my body. I want to give you a massage like before. How about it? Don't drive and drive like this. Stop for the night somewhere. We need a break. I've always wanted you. I love you. I do.

"Love. Ha! We talk so, don't we! Quite a pair we are. We make love and don't even discuss love. Who's kidding who? Here, smell me, my lovely perfume. You don't really mean to leave me up there with those hicks, do you? Please let me share your thoughts. PLEASE! I cannot be alone.

"Understand, please. I can't step back. It's over. Just like your past. You and I must move away from our pasts, not revisit them. My daughter has a life. She does not want me in it, I promise you. You're only tearing at scabs. I will not cooperate. Never. She and Nate left me alone years ago. I cannot face her. It hurts too much."

Choking, she clutched her sweater.

"Please let me share with you. We're not so different at all. Please?"

She tugged at his sleeve.

"Care for me, that's all I ask. I will never hurt you. I won't even bother you if that's what you want. We can live under one roof but separate. People do it all the time."

"Why are you following the coast? This journey will take forever this way. Stay on the highway! Oh, I get it. You were listening. We're stopping for the night. Good!

"And in the morning, when she sees me, she will stare at me with those eyes. If you only knew what those eyes front. Even as a baby, she'd give her father that stupid wide-eye look, seducing even then. Was I to pretend I didn't see? God-damn, Marcel, answer me!"

She dug the heel of her foot into his and the car accelerated, veering too far to the left and near an embankment. He shoved her to one side, kneaded his fist into her shoulder, and steadied the car.

"You're mad," she said in a menacing voice. "You've gone over the edge. You think if you do this to me it will end your misery but you will only compound sorrow for yourself! You'll see, old man!"

She watched for a reaction. When he kept on driving, she touched his shoulder with a nail, digging into his jacket, laughing louder and louder. She spat at him and ran nails down the glass of the car windows. She smashed the bottle of perfume against the glass, breaking the window and allowing a rush of damp air in.

"Come on, Papa Evil, give me the wheel and let me take us away from here. Please? Daddy Evil?"

She grabbed the wheel and the car swerved.

In an instant, when he glared at her and before he re-took the wheel, she met his glance and whispered, "Klee. Your daughter. I know."

He righted the car again.

"I know all about you. You'd better turn this car around now! See I am the one in control."

She grabbed the wheel again and again he struggled. She dug heels and spat continually, blinding him to the road ahead, her hands covering his eyes. She screamed and splashed perfume into his eyes.

"Take that Daddy Klee!"

The car spun around to face an approaching truck that sounded its horn in a long continuous bellow before they collided. Then all was dark.

From a distance, Marcel kneeled and watched flames devour the car. His ears had blocked, noise was muffled. Suddenly, with a warning thud, an explosion ripped the car into pieces.

Blood covered his face. He tried to stand. and winced from the deep impression left from her heel.

He hobbled to the truck. The driver's body contorted with what looked to be a broken neck. Flames from the rental car licked black skies and bent to the direction of the strong winds. Inside, Régine's remains were already cinders.

Five miles remained. Rain clouds displaced rapidly and the whip from the downpour hurt his skin, but neither doused the fire. A vicious storm was about to have its way. Using a stick as crutch, he ambled from the scene, the smell of Chanel No. 5 rising above the odors of gas and burning flesh.

# Chapter 13

KLEE PEERED FROM THE CAVE. In the blur of the clouds and rain, a man's form advanced, clinging for seconds to a rocky protrusion here, a supportive branch there. Some one hundred feet from her, he called. In that instant, the world became even smaller, a pinprick dissembling into an uplifting, mesmerizing dream. Movement was both urged and sustained. Advancing into his line of vision was a feat no longer physical in nature. He knew, she knew. What of the connection, here along this cliffside?

She crawled through the narrow opening of the cave, steadied herself at the precarious angle where their lines of vision would meet, gazed for as long as the gale-forces permitted, then relinquished herself to powers that long before held her, for a time in check, and to which she beckoned this man, this presence, who, as he enshrouded her about him, gripped at the instant she faltered, took hold, and succumbed.

9 781951 985325